In memory of Shirley Sackin MacPherson—
much loved, always missed.

Julie Ellis

COMMITMENT

KENSINGTON BOOKS

KENSINGTON BOOKS are published by

Kensington Publishing Corp.
475 Park Avenue South
New York, NY 10016

Kensington Books and the K logo are trademarks of Kensington Publishing Corp.

Library of Congress Catalog Card Number: 93-080087
ISBN 0-8217-4422-4

First Printing: January, 1994

Printed in the United States of America

ACKNOWLEDGMENTS

I would like to thank the staffs of the New York Public Library, the Mid-Manhattan and Lincoln Center branches, the library staff of the New York Historical Society, the Microfilm Library of New York University, the library staff at Harvard University's School of Design for their courteous and helpful assistance in my research.

I would like, also, to express my gratitude to my dear friends, Seymour and Gloria Shubin, for taking myriad snapshots of the Sorbonne during their recent trip to Paris—which did much to refresh my memory. My gratitude, too, to fine young architect Howard Roman for guiding me in my choice of research books in his chosen fields.

My thanks, again, to Claudia and Brad Dickinson of Claudia's Carriage House in Montauk for generously lending me their extensive personal library on the history of Montauk. And, as always, my thanks to my daughter Susan for diligent research assistance and word processing services—and to my son Richard of Sentinel Copy, Inc., for so imaginatively handling the myriad copying and binding that lent order to my research material.

COMMITMENT

Chapter One

In the smaller bedroom of the Simons' suite at the elegant Hotel Savoy in London, nine-year-old Carol sat huddled on the floor of the closet, the door closed tightly against the explosive conversation in the Louis XVI sitting room. She sat with burnished gold hair tumbling over her tense shoulders, slender little legs drawn up to her chest, astonishingly blue eyes overbright as she listened to her mother and father in another of their battles. Mama fought, Carol reasoned. Papa—usually gentle and sweet—defended himself. Always when Mama and Papa fought, she ran to hide in an alarm she didn't truly understand.

"Why can't we go to Paris for three or four days?" Edie Simon screamed. "We may never be so close again! I want to go, Joseph!" Carol knew Mama never called Papa "Joseph" unless she was mad at him. Most times he was "Joe." When she was feeling real good it was "Joey." "Why are you so mean to me?"

"We have reservations on the *Aquitania* for day after tomorrow." Papa sounded so tired, Carol thought in sympathy.

"We can change the reservations." Carol recognized her mother's ominous tone. That meant she was going to get her way or go into a screaming fit about how she never should have married him. "Most tourists have already gone back home. We'll get new reservations." In this summer of 1929, Papa said, it seemed that half of America had rushed to see Europe.

"It's the middle of September. Carol's already missed almost two weeks of school."

"She's smart," her mother dismissed this. "She can afford to miss school."

"Edie, I have to get back to New York," Carol heard Papa insist. "I have to keep an eye on my business. I don't like what I'm hearing about the market," he said worriedly.

"You act like a nervous old man!" Edie lashed back. "You said yourself—after every drop in prices, they go up again and even higher than before. There's no reason for us not to spend three or four days in Paris. We're young, Joe. This is our time to live!"

"We've never lived so well, Edie. But it scares me the way we spend. How do I know that the market won't fall apart? I've always listened to my hunches—that's how we moved from Jefferson Street to Bensonhurst and then to West End Avenue." Carol knew how proud Mama was that Papa had bought the small apartment house where they lived. "But my hunches warn me this bubble will burst. We have to start cutting back—"

"Again, you're talking like a scared old man." In the closet Carol flinched at the venom in her mother's voice. "You start thinking like that, and we'll be back on Jefferson Street."

"Sometimes I think that was when we were happiest," he said softly. She didn't remember Jefferson Street, Carol told herself, nor Bensonhurst.

"I would rather die than go back to Jefferson Street." Horror deepened Edie's voice. "Living like animals in a fifth-floor, two-room, cold water flat. Freezing in the winter, roasting in the summer. *I'd rather die.*"

Edie Simon boarded the *Aquitania* with her small family on schedule. Carol was embarrassed when her mother carried on loudly again about not seeing Paris. She was sure folks in the adjoining cabin could hear. Carol knew her father would have liked to remain longer in London. Papa loved London, she thought tenderly. He hated all the gangsters and the shooting back home. He said that in London not even the police carried guns.

Carol was glad to be back in school, though she felt self-conscious at missing so many days. She loved school. It was like having a big family. Mama and Papa had no surviving relatives to their knowledge—except maybe distant cousins in the Old Country.

She knew how Papa had come over from Germany with his much

older married brother when he was only seven. Papa said that after his parents died, he'd lost touch with the others in Germany. His brother and sister-in-law died before *she* was born—during the awful 'flu epidemic right after the war.

Mama was proud that she—as well as her parents—had been born in this country, though she hated the tiny town where she was born and grew up. She was proud, too, that her grandfather had been mayor of Hamptonville for three terms—*"even though we were the only Jewish family in town."* She'd met Papa when he was a traveling salesman and calling on a store in Hamptonville.

Now life settled down into its regular routine, though at unexpected moments she thought about the London sights that had particularly pleased Papa and her. St. Paul's Cathedral, which Papa said had been designed centuries ago by a famous architect named Christopher Wren. Westminster Abbey and Marlborough House. And the fine English synagogues with their lofty ceilings, their stained-glass windows.

Papa especially liked the Great Synagogue at Duke's Place, at the edge of the East End. It was an elegant brick building in what Papa said was the most simple and beautiful of Grecian architecture, its roof supported by huge stone pillars.

"If I could start my life over again, I'd want to build beautiful houses." She remembered his words when they stood there before the Great Synagogue.

Maybe some day, Carol dreamt, she'd work for an architect. This was her latest daydream. Mama said girls grew up to be wives and mothers. They didn't work except maybe for a little while before they got married.

Carol was aware that Papa seemed anxious when he came home each night from his broker's office. He distrusted the prosperity in the United States. He worried about conditions in other countries. Tonight he was talking about that.

"Great Britain keeps hoping for an upturn in business, but it isn't happening. Germany is in an economic crisis. It's unnatural for people in this country to be living so high when Europe is hit by inflation and unemployment." Papa was so smart, Carol thought adoringly, even if he didn't go beyond the seventh grade.

"Joe, you wouldn't be happy if you couldn't worry," his wife complained. "I was down at Macy's this afternoon," she said, derailing the earlier conversation. "Looking at furniture. We don't have to buy there, of course—we'll go downtown where we can buy on the installment plan and—"

"Edie, we're not buying," he interrupted.

"We've been living in this house for over a year; my God, we *own* the building—and it's barely half furnished."

"We don't need nine rooms of furniture. We're doing well with the five we've furnished."

"Why are you so stubborn?" her mother screeched, and Carol hurried into her bedroom. She hated it when Mama carried on like that.

Carol sat at the supper table and tried to figure out why Papa seemed especially upset tonight. She knew it had something to do with what had been happening today at his broker's office.

"But I listened to the radio." Edie brushed aside her husband's dire reports of tumbling stocks this Thursday in late October. "They said Mr. Whitney led a real buying spree—for all the dropping in prices. They said there had been a real recovery," she concluded triumphantly.

"A lot of people were ruined today. The 'speaks' were mobbed when the Exchange closed. I'm covered, but it took every cent I could raise. I don't want to think about another drop in prices." He was so pale, Carol thought. He looked frightened.

"Joe, half a dozen times in the last year and a half you've been crying, 'we're going to lose everything'," Edie scolded, impatient now. "The market always bounces back."

After supper Carol was allowed to listen to the radio for half an hour, then shipped off to do her homework for school. Tonight it was hard to think about homework. It scared her to see Papa so upset.

The weekend sped past. She went to school on Monday morning convinced that Papa was in a better mood. On Tuesday Papa left the house before she did. Most days he didn't leave for his broker's office until nine o'clock. Last night—after she'd gone to bed and was supposed to be asleep—she'd heard Mama yelling at Papa for making terrible predictions. Monday had been a bad day on Wall Street. All the best stocks were falling, Papa kept saying. He had to get out of the market before prices dropped any lower, even though it meant taking a big loss.

After school on Tuesday she hurried home, eager to show her

mother a test that her teacher had just given back. She'd gotten a 100 again. She'd show it to Papa at supper, and he'd glow.

Rushing down the hall from the elevator she heard her mother screaming. Not "angry" screaming, she realized in alarm. *Mama was scared.*

"Joey, no! Oh God, no!"

Almost simultaneously Carol heard a gunshot. Terrified she reached for the door; it was unlocked. Subconsciously she remembered Papa always warned Mama that in New York people locked doors.

From the hall Carol saw her mother standing at the entrance to the living room—crying uncontrollably yet immobile.

"Mama?" She was ice-cold.

Her mother darted toward her, pulled her into her arms. "Oh, my baby, my baby! What'll happen to us now?"

Before her mother could shield her from the view inside the living room, Carol saw her father lying on the floor. His head in a pool of blood. His eyes closed. A gun lay nearby.

Chapter Two

To Carol the family's next door neighbor—middle-aged, grossly overweight, practical-minded but warm, Sally O'Brien—seemed a protective angel in the ensuing forty-eight hours. Mrs. O'Brien took charge of their lives. With her traveling salesman husband on the road she brought Edie and Carol into her own apartment to remove them from the traumatic scene of Joe Simon's death, and propelled them through the trauma of arranging for the funeral.

Edie moved about in a daze, with one of Carol's small hands held constantly in her own. With her mother Carol went with Sally O'Brien to the funeral parlor. Her mother stared aghast at the funeral director—his voice hypnotic as he plotted a huge commission for himself.

"Mrs. Simon, you don't want a plain pine casket as your late husband's last resting place. Mahogany, with a velvet lining would be—"

"Enough of that," Sally O'Brien interrupted. "He'll have to rough it."

In accordance with the teachings of the Jewish faith, Joe Simon was buried on Thursday morning. Only a handful of people attended. There were no relatives on either Joe's or Edie's side to be notified, and Edie had lost touch with their few friends in Bensonhurst. Standing between her mother and Mrs. O'Brien, Carol was haunted by one question: *Where did Papa get a gun?*

After the funeral Mrs. O'Brien herded Edie and Carol back to her apartment—knowing they dreaded return to the site of the tragedy. But their solicitous neighbor had a practical question in her mind, also. In the last few days the country—the world—had been assaulted by a financial crisis. Many others besides Joe Simon had taken their lives in desperation over the stock market crash.

"Edie, you have to figure out about the future," Mrs. O'Brien began gently.

"There's nothing left," Edie broke in, white-faced. Her eyes were glazed with panic.

"There's something left," Mrs. O'Brien said firmly.

"Joe said we'd lost everything," Edie insisted. "This house, the car, the furniture. How can I meet the mortgage payments on the house when the rents don't cover them? Joe figured on bringing down the mortgage in a few months. Then the house would pay for itself. Now the bank will take it. They'll take the car, even the furniture."

"Your mink coat," Mrs. O'Brien pursued. Her eyes settled on Edie's engagement ring. "That's a big rock. Paid for?"

"The coat and the ring have been paid off," Edie recalled. Carol saw a flicker of relief in her mother's eyes. "We owe for clothes, for the refrigerator—"

"The clothes." Mrs. O'Brien shrugged. "So let them try to catch you. Joe wore beautiful clothes," she said thoughtfully. "My old man used to say, 'Joe Simon looks like an ad for Brooks Brothers.' I'll go with you to the pawnshop on Ninth Avenue. Together we'll argue with the thieves. And tomorrow the rents are due. I'll go with you to collect. First thing in the morning."

"Sally, how many people pay on the first of the month?"

"You'll cry. A few will pay. You'll have a small nest egg. Write out receipts for the rents you collect, then get out of the house before the vultures from the bank find out Joe's passed away."

That same afternoon the three of them invaded a pawnshop on Ninth Avenue. It was clear the pawnshops were doing a thriving take-in business at this critical period in the city. Carol listened in astonishment as her mother seemed to find her voice and argued with the pawnbroker.

"No. That's too little." She shook her head in disgust. "For Brooks Brothers suits and overcoats? Sally, let's go."

"Wait," the pawnbroker urged, and the bargaining began.

After supper at Mrs. O'Brien's apartment Carol was sent off to sleep in the guest bedroom—once the domain of Mrs. O'Brien's now married sons. Later, she knew her mother would slide into the bed beside her. Sleepless, she listened to the soft drone of the two women's voices as they talked in the living room.

Mama was worried because they couldn't sit *shivah* for Papa. She felt an inchoate guilt that she and Mama must disappear from the apartment house tomorrow—after Mama had collected what rents she could pry from their tenants.

In the morning Carol was left at the dining table with a cup of hot chocolate while the two women went off to try to collect rents. She and Mama would live in Borough Park, in Brooklyn. Mama said it was a nice place with mostly one- and two-family houses. Some of the houses rented out cheap furnished apartments up in the attics.

By noon she and her mother were stashing luggage in a locker at Grand Central.

"We'll take this little one with us," Edie said nervously. "It has our night clothes and fresh underwear for tomorrow. In the morning we'll come back for the two suitcases." Though the day was autumnal Edie wore her mink coat, not trusting it to a locker.

As they walked down the long flight of stairs from the Elevated at the 50th Street station in Borough Park, Carol wondered if they would find a place to live today. If they didn't, would they have to go back to sleep at Mrs. O'Brien's apartment? Mama said it was best just to walk away and not go back to the apartment house. They'd leave the car parked on the street. The furniture store would come to repossess the furniture. They'd taken as much of their clothes as they could carry.

How could Papa have done this to them? she asked herself in

sudden anger. They needed him. Couldn't he understand that? But anger was swiftly replaced by grief.

Within twenty minutes they were being shown a furnished attic apartment in a sprawling one-family house that had been converted to two-family plus attic apartments. Carol was shocked at the tiny quarters. Just one fair-sized room and an alcove kitchenette. The bathroom was shared with a tenant in the front apartment. *This was where they had to live?*

Carol settled down into their new life once she was back in school. While she hated the tiny, ugly attic apartment, Carol admired the array of one- and two-family houses that comprised much of the neighborhood, each house with its own small patch of greenery. Here and there was a large house with the sprawling grounds that Papa would have loved.

She loved Papa so much, she told herself defensively, but why had he left Mama and her alone this way? *They needed him.* Why hadn't he thought of them?

On the first anniversary of her husband's death, Edie sold her mink. She had worn it—triumphantly—only once a month during the past winter. Keeping it nice, she confided to Carol, so that it would bring in a solid chunk of money.

"I'm a good manager," she boasted to Carol at regular intervals. "I know how to stretch a dollar."

Edie treasured the beautiful dresses and fine cloth coat from Saks that she had taken with her, but Carol's delicate cottons and wools—from Saks and Best's—were soon outgrown. Edie took her now to Klein's basement to buy school wear.

Times had not got better after the crash. They only got worse, Mama told her. By the summer of 1931 the country was mired in a painful Depression. The number of unemployed soared daily. Carol knew her mother was anxious that their money was dropping so low. Now they went to the movies every other Saturday instead of every Saturday. Admission was twenty-five cents for Edie, ten cents for Carol. *"That thirty-five cents will buy a dozen eggs and a loaf of bread,"* her mother pointed out.

On the first day of Carol's summer vacation from school her mother announced that the two of them were going into New York.

"It's shameful what that pawnshop here offered me for my mother's garnet brooch and ring," Edie said, her voice sharp with tension. "We'll go into the city. Afterward," she said with a faint air of defiance, "we'll walk over to Fifth Avenue and window-shop."

Carol watched in alarm while her mother argued with the pawn-shop owner on Ninth Avenue. His initial offer was lower than that in Borough Park. Finally, Edie brought the price up to match the other. She was clearly shaken at having to accept this.

"Are we going to Fifth Avenue now?" Carol asked eagerly when they emerged from the pawnshop. She loved looking in the windows of the elegant stores.

"We're going home," Edie said, her eyes anxious. "I have a lot of thinking to do."

Back in Borough Park Edie went to visit Mrs. Goodman next door while Carol went to the neighborhood library. Not until after they'd had supper and Carol had done the dishes did Edie announce the results of her thinking.

"We're almost broke, Carol. You'll have to get a job." Carol gaped at her mother in disbelief. "Who's going to hire a forty-year-old woman?" She wouldn't be forty for another year and a half, but Carol was too stunned to mention this.

"Mama, I have to go to school!" Her eyes were dilated in shock.

"We have to eat and pay the rent," Edie said harshly. "Do you want to see us on relief?" Carol remembered that just last night Mama had said that here in New York—the richest city in the country—a welfare family had to live on $2.39 a week.

"But what could I do?" Carol stammered. "I'm eleven years old!"

"In a few months you'll be twelve. You'll say you're fifteen," Edie ordered. "Already you're beginning to develop." A situation Carol found simultaneously embarrassing and enthralling. "You can be a stock girl at Klein's—or maybe at A & S in Brooklyn."

"Mama, why would anybody want to hire me?"

"Mrs. Goodman next door tells me her son works at Klein's. I'll talk to her. She likes to brag about what a *gansa macher*—a big shot—he is. Let her prove it by helping you get a job there."

A week later Carol was a stock girl at Klein's—a major achievement in this harrowing Depression era. But it wasn't going to be the end of education, she vowed. She'd go to night school—like Papa would expect of her. She wasn't a child anymore. If she was old enough to work, then she was old enough to decide what to do with her life.

Despite her mother's startled objections—*"I'm alone all day, and now you want to leave me alone all evening?"*—Carol searched and found night classes she could attend even during the summer. She left the house each morning with a brown paper bag holding the peanut butter and jelly sandwich her mother made for her lunch plus two graham crackers to nibble on her way from work to school. When she at last returned home, she sat down to the spaghetti or rice dish her mother had prepared for their supper.

She loathed the trip from Borough Park to Manhattan six days a week. On lucky days she rushed to a seat, where she could bury herself in a book until it was time to prepare for the painful disgorgement of passengers at her subway stop. But on most days she stood clinging to a strap or pole as the elevated slithered underground—passengers shoving determinedly into the cars at each stop.

She was repelled by the pressure of other human bodies that made it impossible for anyone to fall. She was shocked and outraged by the covert lewdness of male passengers—with only an occasional girl or woman daring to protest vocally. She hated the mixtures of aromas—food, sweat, overly heavy cologne—that permeated the cars.

She early understood that many passengers were desperate job-seekers, struggling to conceal the worn state of their attire, their newspaper-lined shoes that were long in need of resoling. Yet at the same time she realized that not everybody suffered from the agonies of the Depression. There were people who lived their lives as before the stock crash. *"Civil service people,"* her mother declaimed in agitation at regular intervals. *"They're not hurting."*

Carol was sickened by the sights she saw in the city. Men and women poking through garbage cans, trying to salvage discarded newspapers or plainly searching for food. Some were stealthy, as though ashamed to be observed in this act. Others were too distraught to care about pride.

On an unseasonably cold October morning she pushed her way through the cheerless hordes at the BMT station and began the walk east to Union Square. She paused at the sight of an inadequately clad little girl—perhaps six or seven—scavenging through the trash can. She was riveted to this tableau. What seemed to her to personify the fears of so many people. Then with compulsive haste she reached into her brown paper bag and pulled out the waxed-paper-wrapped peanut butter and jelly sandwich. In silence she walked to the still foraging little girl.

"Take this," she whispered, extending the sandwich.

The tiny face looked up warily. The haunted eyes lighted. Small hands reached for the sandwich and the little girl darted away. As though immobilized, Carol stood and watched as the famished child bit into one triangle of the sandwich, then paused and folded the waxed paper over the second triangle. Now she ran, eating one half and perhaps taking the second half home to her family.

Tears filled Carol's eyes. What was happening to the world? Would things ever be right again?

Conditions in the country were not improving. Unemployment figures continued to soar. Men waited all night outside employment offices when jobs were advertised—to be first in line next morning. The lines at the soup kitchens that sprouted across the country were growing.

The years blended one into another, but Carol survived because of the evenings at night school and the encouragement of a pair of dedicated teachers who urged her to go on beyond high school to college.

"You'll be somebody one day, Carol," Miss Silberman predicted with satisfaction. "It's written all over you. Don't let anything stop you. When you finish high school, go on to college."

"I will," Carol promised solemnly. These were Papa's sentiments.

Carol was pleased when her mother acquired a friend after all this time of living in Borough Park. The Goodmans had lost their two-family house to the bank. A woman twenty years older than Edie had moved into the first floor—the owner's floor. With astonishing speed Edie and Mrs. Goldberg became close friends.

"Dora Goldberg's son bought the house for her," Edie reported with a kind of inner excitement. "He's Dora's baby—only twenty-five and already doing well."

Carol was dismayed when her mother insisted a week later that they go to supper with Mrs. Goldberg on the following Friday night.

"Every Friday night like clockwork Marty comes to supper with his mother. Most of the time his two sisters are too busy with their families to come, but Marty's always there."

"I go to school on Fridays," Carol pointed out, reading her mother's mind.

"So you'll miss school this Friday." Her mother shrugged. Her eyes were opaque.

"No," Carol said. "I can't miss school. I have a test on Friday."

"Carol, I want you to meet Marty. Who knows what can come of it? How many young men do you meet?"

"I don't want to meet them." She was sixteen. She wasn't interested in getting married. "School's more important."

"School won't pay the rent and buy food and clothes." Edie's voice was shrill now. "Marty even owns a car."

"I don't want to meet him."

"That's the trouble with this generation!" Edie was trembling now. "No respect for the parents!"

"I'm going to school Friday night," Carol repeated with shaky defiance. "I have a French test."

Chapter Three

Carol knew her mother was scheming to have her meet Marty. She promised herself this would never happen. She hadn't counted on Mrs. Goldberg's collaboration. On a sticky June night that threatened to erupt into a summer storm, she walked down from the Elevated to find her mother and Mrs. Goldberg waiting to meet her.

"It's so hot in the house," Edie complained, "so Dora and I decided to walk. You always come home just at the same time—we decided to meet you."

"And this is your precious baby," Mrs. Goldberg crooned admiringly. "What a beautiful girl! And smart, to be going to night school. Why don't we stop off on Thirteenth Avenue for an egg cream? My treat."

When they returned to their block—the storm still in abeyance—Mrs. Goldberg called out loudly to somebody lounging against the fender of a shiny black Packard.

"Marty, you been waiting long?" she asked. "My son," she said to Carol with pride. "The only one of my children who never forgets he has a mother."

Carol was polite when Mrs. Goldberg introduced her and Marty, even while she vowed her mother wasn't going to push her into going out with him. Marty would have been good-looking, she conceded, if he wasn't so cocky. His clothes were flashy, but expensive. He wore a diamond pinkie ring.

"Hey, this neighborhood is improvin'," he said brashly, his eyes sweeping over Carol's small, curvaceous figure. "Mama, you're gonna see a lotta me from now on."

"Better me than some of those bleached blond *shiksas* you've been running around with," Mrs. Goldberg said with a satisfied smile while her eyes communicated with Edie's.

Marty suggested taking them all for a drive.

"It's a lousy hot night. We can drive along Shore Road, look at all those fancy houses over there."

"I have to work tomorrow," Carol told him. "Mama, you go with them," she encouraged. But she wasn't surprised when the drive was dismissed.

Now life became a struggle to avoid Marty Goldberg. Probably because she didn't want to go out with him he was fighting to take her out, Carol surmised. He couldn't imagine any girl turning down a fellow with his own Packard.

Her mother harangued regularly about the opportunities she was throwing aside by rejecting Marty's invitations. Carol refused to capitulate. She didn't like Marty. She didn't like the way he looked at her—as though he could see right through her dress. She detested the way he bragged about how great he was doing when most people were having such a hard time just to survive.

Then her whole cardboard world fell apart. Stockgirls were being laid off at the store. In mid-August she was given notice. That day was the first time she'd missed a class. She went straight home from work. How was she to tell Mama she'd been laid off?

As she'd feared, her mother was hysterical to learn that this would be her last week of earning a pay envelope.

"What will we do?" Edie wailed. "Who can find work these days? We'll have to go on relief! Papa would turn over in his grave!"

"I'll find another job," Carol insisted, fighting against fear. "I'll start looking right away." She'd take *anything*.

Each morning her mother gave her two nickels for the subway, and Carol went into the city to look for a job—trying to believe there was something out there. She answered every possible ad in the *New York Times,* joined the milling destitute hordes in the employment agencies. The rent would be due in a few days, her mind taunted. They were eating noodle pudding for supper every night.

On the first of the month her mother admitted Mrs. Goldberg had lent her enough to make the rent payment.

"You took money from Mrs. Goldberg?" Carol was ashen.

"You want us to go on relief?" The cardinal shame to her mother. Then Edie smiled knowingly. "Marty's coming over for supper tomorrow night. Dora wants us both to come, too." Her eyes were bright. "Carol, don't be a fool—Marty's mad about you. His mother says that for the first time he's serious about a girl."

"I don't like him," Carol stammered. *She didn't want to think about getting married.* She'd never even gone out with a boy.

"You'll go to supper with me," Edie said grimly. "You'll meet Marty. That doesn't mean you're already planning the honeymoon. But remember, it'll be security for us for the rest of our lives. You won't have to work; you'll stay home and be a lady."

"I don't have a class tomorrow night," Carol said finally. "If you borrowed money from Mrs. Goldberg, I guess it wouldn't be polite not to go to supper." How would they pay Mrs. Goldberg back? What about next month's rent? Would she find a job soon? Her mind was a kaleidoscope of terrifying images—bread lines, soup kitchens, the shanty towns along Riverside Drive and in Central Park.

When Carol came home from the city the next afternoon—again, a futile effort to find work—she discovered her mother had ironed her one nice dress, bought at a synagogue rummage sale before she was laid off.

"You have time to wash your hair," Edie bubbled. "I want you to look your best."

"Mama, we're just going downstairs for supper," Carol protested. But she understood. She'd have to marry Marty, or they'd be on relief.

Mrs. Goldberg lived alone in the five-room plus "sun porch" lower floor of the stucco house next door. Occasionally Marty slept over. His sisters and their families came only on holidays such as Passover and Rosh Hashanah, Edie reported with reproach.

The furniture in the Goldberg apartment was overlarge, oppressively dark. Walking into the living room, Carol felt as though she was entering a prison. No doubt in her mind that her mother would propel her into marriage with Marty.

Marty conducted a frenzied but decorous courtship on the nights Carol didn't go to school. He took her to dinner at Ben Marden's Riviera in New Jersey, to Billy Rose's Diamond Horseshoe on West 46th Street, to movies at the Roxy and the Capitol and the Paramount. Not until he'd taken her—after a three-week pursuit—to Manhattan Beach for the day, along with the two mothers—did he venture to kiss her good night. A chaste schoolboy kiss that hardly damaged her Tangee lipstick.

Carol had been anxious about how she was to act on dates with Marty. But almost from the first date she realized that little was required of her other than to listen. She'd been nervous about her lack of clothes, but her mother had mysteriously acquired money to take her shopping. Not at Klein's basement but at Lerner's. She attributed her mother's sudden minor affluence to money siphoned from Marty to his mother, and then to her own mother.

Marty boasted at compulsive intervals about how well he was doing in business, about the value of his pinkie ring, and how much he spent on his fancy suits and shirts.

"You're a classy babe, Carol," he told her with a fatuous smile. "You oughta be wearin' a mink coat and diamonds."

At the end of four weeks Marty proposed. In her devious way Edie had contrived to get the message across to Marty that if he expected Carol to marry him, his proposal should be accompanied by a diamond engagement ring. The proposal took place in his car, pulled off the new double-laned Henry Hudson Parkway on a steamy, early September night.

Carol's heart pounded while she listened to Marty's awkward proposal. Simultaneously he pulled the velvet box that contained the engagement ring from his pocket.

"It's a perfect stone," he bragged. "I got it from this ritzy guy who needed cash real quick. I had it appraised first," he added virtuously. "Nobody puts nothin' over on Marty Goldberg."

"It's beautiful," Carol managed and held out her finger. Even Mama would be impressed.

Marty took Carol home to his mother. Her own mother was there. It was obvious both women knew this was the night Marty would propose. Dora immediately took charge. The wedding would take place in two weeks. Marty said they'd rent an apartment on Riverside Drive.

"Hey, that's the place to live," Marty drawled. "Everybody who comes to New York wants to live on Riverside Drive." Carol refrained from mentioning that even a cashier at Klein's lived on Riverside Drive—in a fifth floor walk-up hall bedroom. But to most people Riverside Drive was a symbol of wealth.

"Marty, you're sure?" Dora was hesitant at such daring.

"I gotta place already in mind. This guy I know—he had to leave town unexpectedly. He's willin' to rent it out all furnished. All I have to do is say the word. We'll move in straight from the honeymoon."

"You'll go to Lakewood for your honeymoon," his mother plotted, and Marty winced.

"Atlantic City," he corrected. "It's still warm enough for the beach." Now he dropped an arm possessively about Carol. "I'll take off four nights. If I take off more time, my guys will rob me blind."

"Marty, Atlantic City?" His mother seemed dubious about this choice. "That's where all the gangsters go."

"And honeymooners," he added with a self-conscious grin.

Carol sat in silent rebellion. It was as though the others forgot that she had thoughts and feelings. Nobody consulted her about *her* life. She listened while Dora Goldberg and her mother planned her wedding dress, the wedding dinner, the ceremony. The guests would include only Marty's sisters and their families. And after the wedding Mama would move in with Dora Goldberg.

"Don't waste money on a white satin wedding dress," Dora ordered happily, her eyes moving from one to the other, to settle on Carol. "Soon enough, *bubula,* you'll be popping out to here." She gestured with tender exaggeration, and Carol blushed. She prayed they wouldn't have a baby. She remembered what the girls had talked about at the store. *"Only dumb broads get pregnant before they want to. You make sure the guy uses protection."*

"We'll spend our wedding night at the Waldorf," Marty said, startling the others. "Nothin's too good for my wife. After breakfast we'll drive to Atlantic City. I'll make reservations at the classiest hotel in town."

Carol wasn't sure just what Marty's business was, though he and his mother talked about how he had to run all over Brooklyn on his "collections" and how his hours were long and irregular. Because of this Carol had found the courage to exact a promise from him that she could attend school two nights a week until she had her high school diploma. Later, she vowed in a corner of her mind, she would go to college at night. City College accepted women in their evening sessions, she remembered.

Carol braced herself for her wedding night. She wasn't ignorant of the subject. The girls at the store—several of those she knew were married—had on occasion offered raunchy details about their wedding nights. Her mother had been vague but self-consciously reassuring. *"So men have certain desires—marriage can't always be a picnic. So you put up with them. A big deal. A few minutes and it's all over."*

She walked through the traditional wedding ceremony—presided over by a rabbi in Dora Goldberg's living room—without actually feeling part of it. *If Papa hadn't left them that way, she wouldn't have to marry Marty. Why hadn't Papa thought about what he was doing to Mama and her?*

After the sumptuous wedding spread prepared by Dora with some assistance from Edie, Marty's sisters and their families left for their own destinations. Carol and Marty prepared to leave for their room at the Waldorf. Their newly bought luggage contained the black chiffon nightgown handmade by Dora Goldberg—from memory of such attire worn by movie siren Jean Harlow.

Carol and Marty arrived at the sumptuous new Waldorf-Astoria, its tower rising 47 stories above Park Avenue.

"You know what it cost to build this joint?" Even Marty seemed slightly intimidated by the splendor of the hotel. "Forty million bucks. Hey, you'll remember forever that you spent your weddin' night at the Waldorf," he gloated.

Inside the ornate lobby—while a bellboy carried their luggage toward the bank of elevators—Carol waited while Marty registered for them. She felt an intruder amidst such luxury, slightly embarrassed by Marty's flashy clothes, his arrogant yet defensive air.

Inside the elevator she was conscious of the lush carpeting beneath her feet, the wise glint in the bellhop's eyes. He knew they were spending their wedding night here, she guessed, and felt her face grow hot. She should have taken off the corsage of rosebuds her mother had pinned to the shoulder of her dress.

She tried to appear casual as the bellhop opened the door and gestured them inside their room. Instinct told her it was probably one of their most modest, yet involuntarily she admired the furnishings. For an anguished moment her mind darted back through the years to their beautiful suite at the Savoy in London.

"Thank you, sir," the bellhop said warmly to Marty, and she assumed his tip had been lavish.

Now panic spiraled in her, as it had on so many occasions during these past two weeks. Muriel—a special friend when she'd been working at Klein's—had married her boyfriend of only six weeks, but Muriel admitted they were "madly in love with each other." Marty was a stranger to her.

"Hey, baby, you're in the Waldorf-Astoria!" Marty reached for her with a gloating smile. "When you travel with Marty Goldberg, you travel in style."

Marty kissed her. It wasn't like those other times, she thought in shock. She felt his hand slide within the sweetheart neckline of her dress to fondle the high rise of one breast. In the high heels that her mother insisted were a necessary part of bridal attire, she was almost as tall as Marty. She tensed at the hardening mass that pressed invasively between her thighs.

Unexpectedly he released her.

"Take off your clothes," he ordered and crossed to the bed, a hand already unbuckling his belt.

"My nightgown's in my valise," she stammered.

"Baby, you don't need no nightgown," he crooned, pushing his trousers to his feet. He sat on the edge of the bed to remove his shoes. He looked up with a frown when she stood immobile, her eyes mirroring her terror. "Come on, Carol, let's get this show on the road."

"With the lights on?" She reached uncertainly for the zipper at the back of her dress.

"When a guy's got classy merchandise, he wants to see it," Marty told her.

Stripped to skin, his eyes overheated, he moved toward her in soaring impatience and began to help her off with her clothes. He shoved her dress to her waist and ripped aside the lacy brassiere to reach with opening mouth for one taut nipple. Carol clenched her teeth and shut her eyes while he simultaneously prodded her dress to the floor. Then her pink satin panties followed the same path. He stared in soaring excitement as she stood before him in only silk stockings and garter belt. In one swoop he picked her up and dropped her on the bed. Now he reached into a pocket of his trousers, lying at their feet. She watched while he withdrew a tiny packet.

"We don't wanna getcha pregnant," he said, grinning. "We're too young for that crap."

She was a receptacle for his passion. Unsharing. Yet this seemed not to disturb him as he grunted his way to satisfaction.

Carol stared into the darkness—the lamps switched off now—as Marty fell into heavy sleep. Her life would not always be like this, she promised herself rebelliously. There'd be a time when she could walk away. *She had to believe that.*

Chapter Four

As Carol had expected, Marty had chosen one of Atlantic City's most garish hotels for their honeymoon. Still, she was impressed by the magnificent view of the Atlantic Ocean from their room. She was embarrassed by Marty's arrogant attitude to all who served them, though his excessive tipping seemed to elicit warm responses.

Each day Marty escorted her to a dizzying number of tourist spots. He decreed that every one of the resort's six amusement piers—which extended into the ocean—must be explored. They strolled along the sixty-foot-wide, four-mile-long boardwalk—pausing at intervals to ride in the popular rolling chairs.

They visited the shops to buy souvenirs, ate a sickening amount of hot dogs and hamburgers and Atlantic City's famous saltwater taffy. They saw science exhibits, a vaudeville show, a deep-sea diving horse, a chamber of horrors. They played bingo in the evening. And each night Carol steeled herself to endure Marty's frenzied groping and thrusting beneath the light blanket mandated by the night ocean air.

Then the day of departure arrived. Marty stored their luggage in the car, and they headed for New York.

"We'll stop somewhere on the way to eat lunch," he promised grandly.

At twilight Carol and Marty arrived at the greystone townhouse on Riverside Drive where he had rented an apartment. She realized in heart-wrenching recall that it was only two city blocks from the apartment she had shared with her parents. Marty parked the car at the curb, pulled their luggage from the Packard, and swaggered toward the entrance.

On sight Carol loathed the heavy, excessively ornamented Victorian furniture that filled every corner of the two-bedroom apartment. But the view of the Hudson River from the living room was magnificent. Tonight a parade of battleships was silhouetted against the darkening sky. She saw the crisscrossing beams of the ships' searchlights that filled the sky with a weird, shifting brilliance.

"Mama was here," Marty called out in approval. "She did just what I told her. The beds are made, we've got plenty of linens—and I'll bet she stocked the kitchen. Go out there and see what you can throw together for dinner."

In the week before the wedding her mother-in-law had given Carol a crash course in cooking to Marty's taste. *"Give him porterhouse steak or roast beef and he'll be happy."*

"All right, Marty." She went out to the kitchen, opened up the refrigerator, and found a porterhouse steak. *"Just throw it in a frying pan, Carol,"* she remembered Marty's mother saying. *"Cut up a lot of onions and fry 'em in another pan."* There was a bowl of mashed potatoes to be heated in the oven and homemade apple pie.

While they ate supper, Marty listened—with noisy comments—to the rebroadcast of a World Series baseball game. He never listened to the news, Carol thought impatiently, though election day was breathing down their necks and most of the newspapers were frank in opposing Roosevelt for another term. Carol worshipped Eleanor Roosevelt. Here was a woman who wasn't afraid to speak her mind.

Carol settled down into a routine within days. Marty slept till 10 o'clock every morning, then had his breakfast and went out on his "collections," often not returning until 8 or 9 o'clock or even later. On Saturday nights he took her out to a nightclub. On Sundays he slept till early afternoon, spent the rest of the day reading the *Sunday News* and the *Journal*. She contrived to arrange night school classes to mesh with Marty's hours.

She was astonished by the sizable amount of money Marty gave her for groceries. He wanted only the best—and it upset her to see the amount of food that went into the garbage can each night. *When people were starving.* But Marty insisted on seeing a table piled high with food.

At intervals he tossed a handful of bills at her with orders to "buy yourself something pretty." Right away she understood that meant see-through nightgowns and negligées, but she managed to acquire several smart dresses, a beautifully tailored suit. Between grocery money and the "loot for sexy duds"—as Marty referred to these contributions—Carol was able to give her mother money every Friday night when she and Marty went to his mother's house for supper and to hide a few dollars in her lingerie drawer.

Accustomed for four years to hand over her pay envelope to her mother, Carol was oddly excited at having money in her own hands. Marty was forever boasting that "hey, baby, money is power—don'tcha ever forget it." With the bank closings now an ugly memory, she opened a bank account—hiding the passbook from Marty's eyes.

When Marty had ordered her to shop in Saks—"I like to see them Saks boxes lyin' around the house"—she'd saved Saks boxes to hold the bargains she ferreted out in Klein's better departments or at Hearn's on 14th Street. It was exhilarating to see the figures in her passbook grow.

But almost every night—with the lights blazing—Marty indulged his appetite for sex. He expected nothing from her other than to be available. Each time she gritted her teeth and submitted. Like Mama said, she kept telling herself, it was over in ten minutes. And he always made sure, she remembered with relief, to wear a condom.

With the approach of Hanukkah Marty decided to have some friends over to the apartment for supper.

"Just these two guys who work for me," he said with a lordly wave of his pinkie-ringed hand. "And their old ladies. Make steaks for everybody," he ordered. "The best."

Carol swept and dusted and polished furniture for much of the day of their small party. The afternoon was devoted to cooking.

She'd never met any of Marty's friends. She was curious about them now.

She checked the table to make sure everything was in its proper place. She'd bought flowers this morning, rearranged them half a dozen times before she was satisfied. She was uncomfortable in the low-cut dress that Marty had picked out for her on their only joint shopping expedition. He said the red taffeta dress was just like the one Jean Harlow had worn in a movie he liked.

At the sound of the doorbell, she tensed, took a final glance at herself in the mirror, and headed for the foyer in a surge of self-consciousness. Marty was already there, pulling the door open.

"Hey, Lou, you're right on time!" Marty was in high spirits. "I taught you right, hunh?"

Lou and his wife Muriel were at least fifteen years older than Marty, Carol judged while she took Muriel's jacket. Meanwhile, Marty was prodding Lou to take off his jacket.

"We're like family, Lou. Get yourself comfortable."

Carol froze in shock when she spied the holstered gun Lou removed along with his jacket. All at once she was seeing her father lying in a pool of blood—a gun at his side. *Why was Lou carrying a gun?*

Moments later the second couple arrived. They, too, were at least fifteen years Marty's senior. Carol's eyes moved compulsively to the second of Marty's associates. Again, she saw a holstered gun. She tried to focus on the two women, both of whom seemed ill at ease with her. Because their husbands worked for a much younger man, she suspected.

At the dinner table there was an effort among the others to create a festive atmosphere, but Carol was haunted by the knowledge that two guns hung in holsters in the foyer closet. The other two women didn't seem disturbed by the guns. Carol was impatient for the evening to be over so she could question Marty. She was relieved when at last their guests left.

As soon as she had cleared away the table—while Marty kicked off his shoes and sprawled on the sofa with a complacent grin— Carol approached him.

"Marty, why do Lou and Tony carry guns?" she asked tentatively.

He looked up with a scowl.

"You want them to go out to collect in bad neighborhoods with no protection?" His eyes were belligerent. "What kind of a boss would I be?"

"What are they collecting?" Marty had never discussed his business. She didn't know how he made such a good living.

"The rents for the apartment houses I manage. In shitty neighborhoods."

Carol hesitated.

"Do you ever carry a gun?"

All at once his face brightened.

"Hey, baby, you're worried about your old man! Sometimes I carry a gun—when I figure I need it. But don't you worry that gorgeous little head about Marty Goldberg. I know how to take care of myself."

All at once she saw arousal in his eyes. He was on his feet and reaching for her.

"I'd better go clean up the kitchen—"

"To hell with that. You know what Lou said about you?" He fondled her rump as he moved insinuatingly against her slender body. "He said, 'Marty, your wife looks like a movie star!'."

Carol closed her eyes, gearing herself for her husband's clumsy lovemaking. Nothing like what some of the girls at Klein's had said it could be. Not all of them, she conceded in silent candor. Some of them hated it. But none of them hated it the way she did.

Early in February Marty came home around eight o'clock with a brown paper bag loaded with delicatessen.

"Don't put supper on the table," he ordered. "Go over and have somethin' for yourself at the cafeteria. I'm having a private conference with the guys. Come back in about an hour."

Walking up the stairs to the apartment an hour later, Carol hoped the men were all gone by now. Marty had told her to come back in an hour. It was an hour and ten minutes since she'd left the apartment. Approaching the door she heard no sounds other than the radio. She reached for her key, unlocked the door, and walked inside.

Every light in the living room was on. The radio blared at the loud pitch Marty preferred. He wasn't in the living room. Then she heard his voice, coming from the guest room—which he liked to call his office, though he never seemed to use it.

"Look, you handle this the way I tell you. Those bastards won't even know we've taken over their territory until it's too late for them to deal. We're gonna be so rich you won't believe it!"

Without understanding what Marty meant by territory, Carol was unnerved. Heart pounding, she hurried down the foyer to the door on soundless feet, let herself out, closed the door. Now she rang the bell and waited. Whatever Marty was planning, she thought, there was trouble involved. She remembered the holstered guns Lou and Tony carried, and was suddenly cold and trembling.

She waited for Marty to open the door.

"Hi, baby." He pulled her inside and smacked her affectionately on the rump. "The guys are just leavin'."

Carol was convinced now that Marty was involved in some shady action. Was it gambling? she asked herself with anguished regularity. Was that why Lou and Tony—and probably the others who worked for Marty—carried guns? The newspapers reported lurid stories about the gangster operations.

When they went to Borough Park for Friday night supper, she managed a few minutes alone with her mother. She confided her fears about Marty's occupation—suspecting now why his sisters and their husbands were so cold to him. Edie was startled.

"Carol, you're dreaming this up," her mother said impatiently. "Put it out of your mind. Dora told me. Marty manages real estate. You know how hard up people are—he has a terrible time collecting."

But in her alarm Carol became more observant. She eavesdropped on Marty's nightly phone calls. She watched him make notes against long lists in the notebooks he always carried. And all at once she understood. Marty was in what people called "the numbers racket."

Early in April Marty came home one night with a large box under one arm. He was in a jubilant mood.

"Open it up, baby!" he ordered. "It's a present for you. I got a great buy from a wholesaler."

Carol opened the box, pushed aside the enveloping tissue paper, and lifted out the contents. A luxurious full length mink coat.

"The furrier swore it'd fit you. I told him you were about five feet two and weighed under a hundred pounds soakin' wet. If it needs alterations, just say the word and he'll take care of it."

"It's beautiful," she stammered, remembering how Mama had loved her mink.

"Put it on!" Marty reached for the coat, held it for her. "Yeah, the old guy was right," he said complacently, inspecting her with approval. "It fits like it was made for you. Tomorrow night I'm takin' you to the Diamond Horseshoe. You'll wear the red taffeta dress and your mink coat. Every guy will wish he was me—and every broad will die of jealousy. Like Lou said, you look just like a movie star."

The following evening Carol was dressed and waiting when Marty arrived at the apartment. The lush mink coat—cut with a blatant disregard for costs—lay across the foot of their bed.

"Okay, let's get this show on the road," he said high-spiritedly. "We're celebratin' tonight."

"What are we celebrating?" Carol's eyes were wary.

"A big step forward in my career. You know what I'm buyin' you next? A diamond bracelet to go with that sparkler on your weddin' finger. Nothin's too good for my old lady."

The black Packard sat at the curb. Now Carol understood why Marty—whose tastes ran to flamboyant colors—chose to drive a black car. She waited in the tiny vestibule while Marty locked the downstairs door. Then together they emerged onto the greystone stoop, flanked on each side by a potted evergreen.

Carol was vaguely aware of a car pulling up past the Packard and slowing to a crawl. Her mouth dropped in horror as she saw a machine gun thrust its way past the front window—too late for her to cry out.

Marty uttered an outraged groan as the night quiet was splintered by gunfire. In a daze Carol saw him double up, and fall to the steps.

"Marty—" An instant later she was conscious of a searing pain in her left shoulder. As she collapsed to the stairs beside Marty, she saw the car speed away, was vaguely aware of outcries from people on the street—then oblivion.

Chapter Five

Carol emerged into consciousness with a realization of a numb pain. Then suddenly she was hit by an avalanche of harrowing recall.

"Oh my God—" Her voice was an anguished whisper.

"You're going to be all right—" She recognized her mother's voice. Slightly strident. "Don't worry, Carol. You'll be all right."

She opened her eyes. Her mother hovered beside her. She was in a hospital bed. *She'd been shot.*

"It's just a shoulder wound." Edie was struggling to sound matter-of-fact. "Don't try to talk. I've rung for the nurse, like she told me to do when you woke up. You're not to worry," she reiterated. "You'll be out of here in a few days."

"Mrs. Goldberg, I'm Detective Hawkins." Only now did Carol become aware of an unfamiliar, middle-aged man sitting in a chair on the other side of the bed. "I'd like to ask you a few questions if you're up to it."

"Let the nurse decide," Edie ordered majestically. "If she says it's all right, then you talk to my daughter."

Carol struggled to clear her head.

"Marty?" she asked.

"Don't think about him now," Edie soothed. "Just rest up and get well."

Carol's eyes clung to her mother's. She understood. Marty was dead.

A nurse and an intern came into the room. Edie and the detective were banished.

"You'll be going home in a few days," the young intern promised. "You were lucky. A few inches lower, and the bullet would have lodged in your heart." Carol read the questions in his eyes. What was she doing in a situation like this?

"Thank you." She managed a wisp of a smile.

After a few minutes the intern and the nurse left. Edie and the detective returned. The other bed, she realized now, was unoccupied.

"I'd like to ask you a few questions," the detective repeated, almost apologetically.

"Sure." She turned to her mother. "It's all right, Mama. Why don't you have a cup of coffee and then come back?" She sensed the detective wished to speak to her alone.

"How old are you?" Detective Hawkins asked curiously when they were alone.

"Seventeen," she told him.

"My daughter was seventeen yesterday. She graduates high school this summer." Again, Carol felt a surge of sympathy from the detective. She didn't fit the public vision of a gangster's moll, she thought with an unexpected flicker of wry humor. That was how strangers would see her, wasn't it?

"I go to night school," she said, astonishing him with this admission. "I told Marty he had to let me get my high school diploma, or I wouldn't marry him." She hesitated. "He's dead, isn't he?"

Hawkins nodded. He seemed to sense that while Marty's death upset her, she'd felt no love for him.

"He told me he collected rents for apartments he managed. I didn't know he—he was—"

"He was in the numbers' racket and moving too fast," Hawkins said. "Most of the wives don't know."

Now he prodded her into recreating those few terrifying moments on the stoop of the townhouse where they'd lived. Seeking more information than she was able to give.

"If you remember anything else, call me at this number." He reached into a jacket pocket and produced a card. "Anything at all."

"Yes, sir," she promised.

Then her mother was walking into the room again with a defiant smile that said she would not be dismissed.

"I have to protect my daughter's interests," she told the detective. "My son-in-law was wearing an expensive diamond ring. It belongs to my daughter now, and—"

"Mama!" Carol was shocked.

Edie held up a hand and continued.

"The ring belongs to my daughter," she repeated. "I'm asking that you make sure she receives it. Already her two brothers-in-law have taken over Marty's car. Like vultures," she said with contempt. "They shouldn't take the ring; it belongs to his widow."

Mama figured payments were due on the car. They were not. Marty had paid cash for the car, as he had for the ring.

"My personal things are here?" Carol asked shakily. All at once she was aware that her engagement and wedding rings were missing from her finger.

"Everything is being held until you're released," Hawkins reassured her. "There'll be no problem."

It was becoming an effort to stay awake now. The injection the nurse had given her, Carol thought sleepily.

"I'll stay a little longer," she heard her mother say. "I'll be back in the morning and—" But she heard nothing more.

Carol was secretly relieved that she was unable to attend Marty's funeral. She was afraid newspaper reporters might be there. Her mother had told her about the lurid headlines on the front page of the *Daily News* and the story about Marty and his "moll." She was his *wife*.

Edie assumed that—as Carol's mother—she would be expected to be at the services at the funeral parlor and at the cemetery. She was outraged when Marty's sisters told her at the funeral parlor that she wasn't welcome.

" 'Marty's dead because of *her*', his older sister screamed at me," Edie reported indignantly. " 'He did those things to give her diamonds and furs!' Dora told me I have to move out of the apartment right away. Her daughters don't want me there. Thank God, you gave me a key to your apartment. That's where I slept last night."

"The detective isn't coming back again, is he?" Carol recoiled from the prospect.

"No," Edie soothed. "And don't worry about the newspapers. Every day there's another killing. You'll put this behind you." She paused. "But Marty's pinkie ring will be turned over to you. As soon as they're sure there's no claim against it. I made sure about that."

"Marty has a paid bill," Carol remembered. "He was forever bragging about how he always paid for everything in cash—and got receipts. He keeps them all in a manila envelope."

"Tell me where to find it," Edie ordered. "I'll show it to Detective Hawkins."

On Carol's third day in the hospital a huge floral arrangement arrived. She was perplexed by the card that accompanied it.

"It's from somebody named Gussie Corelli," she told her mother when Edie arrived at the hospital for her daily visit. "I don't understand. She says she's sorry about Marty's death, and I can stay in the apartment another month rent-free. After that she has another tenant moving in."

"I remember reading about her in the *News*." Edie seemed shaken. "She owns the apartment. Her husband is in Sing Sing for attempted murder." Marty said he'd had to leave town unexpectedly, Carol recalled.

Four days later the doctors told Carol that she would be released from the hospital the following morning. When her mother arrived, she asked her to bring a dress from the apartment. "I'll never wear that red taffeta again." She shuddered in recall.

"What about a coat?" Edie asked. "It's cold outside."

"A nurse brought up the coat I was wearing when I came here—from wherever they keep things. It's hanging in the closet."

Only when she heard her mother's startled exclamation did she remember that her mother didn't know that Marty's last gift—on the evening he was gunned down—was a mink coat.

"Carol, you never told me," Edie scolded, fondling the luxuriant mink.

"Marty had just given it to me that night," Carol began and paused at her mother's noisy gasp.

"There's a hole in it! At the shoulder!"

"That's where the bullet went in," Carol pointed out, and winced at the sight of dried blood on the lining as her mother folded back the fur.

"We'll take it to a good furrier, and he'll fix it," Edie decided. "You'll get a good chunk of money for it."

"We have to move out of the apartment the end of next month," Carol reminded. Again, their lives had been thrown upside down. Again, by gunfire. *She hated guns.*

"Your engagement ring and Marty's pinkie ring—and the mink coat—will be a comfortable nest egg. You have the receipts Marty got—we won't have any trouble at the pawnshops. We don't take the first offer," Edie plotted. "We'll shop around. But first, you have to rest for a couple of weeks. The doctor said you lost a lot of blood."

"I'm missing school," Carol said in sudden alarm, then shivered. How could she face the others after what happened?

"Now you think about school?" Edie gaped at her in disbelief.

"I want my high school diploma," she said defensively.

"Mama—" She hesitated. "There wasn't a picture of me in the newspapers?" At school she was still Carol Simon, she remembered in relief. Maybe nobody would know she was the girl with Marty when he was killed.

"Some reporter got a copy of the wedding picture," Edie confessed. "They came to me and I said 'no pictures!' But the photographer Dora brought in at the wedding gave it to that creepy reporter. It hardly looked like you at all," Edie comforted. "And it's all blurry. Nobody will recognize you."

Carol and her mother left the hospital and took a cab up to the Riverside Drive apartment. *"You're too shaky to handle all those subway stairs,"* Edie insisted. Carol tensed as the taxi approached the town house. She felt sick in recall.

Carol refused to be put to bed but allowed her mother to settle her with her feet up on the sofa.

"I'll make you a cup of tea, and then you'll nap," Edie told her, gazing about the apartment. "It's real nice here. And it was nice of that Mrs. Corelli to let you stay another month rent-free."

For the next three days Carol allowed her mother to fuss over her, force her to eat when she had no appetite. Recoiling from sleeping in the bed she'd shared with Marty, she spent her nights on the sofa. Her mother slept on the single bed in the second bedroom, that Marty had lordly designated "my office."

When Marty's brothers-in-law appeared at the apartment door on the third night to demand access to Marty's personal things, Edie ordered them out of her sight.

"Get away from my daughter's apartment or I'll call the cops," she warned stridently. "You're trespassing!"

Now, Edie decided, it was time to take Marty's flashy suits into the pawnshops. For that she wouldn't need receipts.

"We're almost out of cash," Edie said, facing reality. "Unless Marty kept money around the house—?" She lifted her eyebrows in question.

"I don't think so," Carol stammered. Now she remembered the passbook to her secret bank account. That was *hers*, she told herself. Mama would sell the rings and the mink coat. The bank account was hers. "Look through the desk in Marty's office," she suggested, diverting her mother from the bedroom she'd shared with Marty. "Even the pockets of his suits—" These hung in the office closet. Marty had left their bedroom closet for her use. He'd liked to open the door and stare at the sexy negligees—"like Jean Harlow wore in the movies"—that hung there. Once, she remembered now, he'd tried to persuade her to bleach her hair platinum blond, but she'd made it clear this would never happen.

"I'll look." Edie's face was etched with determination as she strode toward Marty's "office."

Pushing down a wave of guilt, Carol left the sofa, hurried into the bedroom and to the dresser drawer that held her schoolbooks and the neatly piled up test papers. Beneath the test papers was the slim passbook.

She wasn't holding out on Mama, she soothed her guilt. Mama had the rings and the mink coat. The bank book was the road to her high school diploma and—some day—a college degree. She knew that City College accepted women for evening classes. She wasn't sure just yet what was immediately ahead of her—but a college degree was her destination. Papa always said, "With education you can do whatever you want with your life."

For now Carol concealed the slim bank book inside her bra and returned to the sofa—her heart pounding at this first subterfuge. But *this* belonged to her.

A few moments later her mother hurried into the living room.

"I found almost fifty dollars in the jackets of Marty's suits!" She was triumphant at this discovery. "We've got to plan for the future, Carol." Edie sat on the sofa beside her now. "I've been giving this a lot of thought. I went over to that newsstand at Times Square and bought a copy of the Saratoga newspaper. That's where Papa used to buy them for me every now and then." Saratoga, Carol remembered, was the city nearest to Hamptonville. "I read the real estate section—and Carol, they're just about giving away houses there. When we sell the rings, I'm sure we'll have enough money to buy a nice little house in Hamptonville."

"Mama, you hate Hamptonville!" Carol stared in shock at her mother.

"But it'll be different now." Edie's face exuded satisfaction. "When you own property in Hamptonville, you're somebody. We'll buy a house and rent out a couple of rooms. We'll—"

"How can we leave New York?" Carol's throat was tightening in alarm. Here in New York she could get her education. Not in Hamptonville, which she'd never even seen.

"It's easy to leave New York," Edie said in rare high spirits. "You get on a train and you go."

"I don't want to move to Hamptonville." Carol's mind was charging ahead. Her heart pounded. She *knew* what she wanted. "You take the money and buy a house up there, like you said," she said quickly. "I'll stay here and look for a job. I'll—"

"Where will you find a job in these times?" Edie scoffed at such talk. "You got the job at Klein's because Mrs. Goodman wanted to show off how important her son was."

"I'll look," she compromised. "I'll give myself three months. I still have my wedding ring to pawn; that'll bring enough for three months." Mama had some strange idea that she'd want to keep her wedding ring.

"A month at the most," Edie dismissed this. "Just diamond chips."

"So I'll try for a month," Carol said. *She wasn't going to Hamptonville.* And tomorrow night she'd go back to night school. She could make up for the time she'd lost.

"You're too young," Edie sputtered. "How can I leave you alone in New York?"

"I worked for four years, Mama. I've been married and widowed. I've been shot—and survived. I can handle my own life."

"If you don't find a job—if you have any problems—you promise to come to Hamptonville?" Edie pressed.

"I promise."

Two weeks later Carol joined her mother on a day trip to Hamptonville. With a sense of wonder Carol stared out the window of the train as it pulled into the tiny white clapboard railroad station. She admired the array of blossoming trees, the masses of golden forsythia that surrounded the station.

"Your great-grandfather was mayor of this town," Edie said with a burst of pride. "Your grandfather ran the only dry goods store. Of course, he let it run down to nothing because he was always giving credit to deadbeats. But it's different now. I'm buying a house. I'm paying cash for it. People will look up to Edie Simon."

Edie was happy to discover that Hamptonville Realty was owned by a man with whom she'd gone to high school. Carol saw the respect in his eyes when Edie explained she wouldn't need a mortgage to pay for the house. Carol watched in amazement when her mother began to bargain for the third house they'd seen—modest but pleasant. She'd worried that her mother would be too demanding.

"It has possibilities," Edie said grudgingly. "But there's a lot of room for improvement."

"The owners are very anxious to sell," the broker said. "You can get immediate occupancy."

Carol listened while the other two bargained. At last, the figure mentioned was a hundred dollars below what her mother had said she would be able to pay. Carol waited for her to close the deal.

"Let me think about it," Edie hedged. "I really didn't want to spend quite that much. Not in these times."

Minutes later the broker was on the phone with the owner. The price dropped another hundred. Before Carol and Edie boarded the train back to New York, the owner had a deposit and a local lawyer—recommended by the broker—had been hired to handle the closing.

"The house is to be in both our names," Edie told the lawyer with an indulgent smile for Carol. "It'll belong to my daughter and myself."

With much fretting on the part of her mother Carol rented a tiny furnished hall bedroom on West 71st Street for four dollars a week.

"I don't like seeing you live like that," Edie complained as they left the brownstone and headed back to Riverside Drive. "It's no bigger than a walk-in closet. And the bathroom is all the way down the hall."

"I like the maple furniture." Carol refused to be ruffled by her mother's grunt of contempt. The maple furniture consisted of a lounge chair, a tiny end table, and a minute chest of drawers. A single bed pretended to be a studio couch. "And I won't be there much. I'll be at work or at school." *She'd be free.* For the first time in her life she could make her own decisions.

"You won't get a job," Edie warned. "Not when times are so bad."

"The newspapers keep saying things are getting better." She ignored her mother's whine of skepticism. "I'll find a job," she insisted with determined optimism. That optimism was bolstered by the knowledge that the money in the bank—with careful budgeting—would carry her for at least seven or eight months. By then she would have a job.

There was no way, she vowed, that she would go to Hamptonville to live with her mother. She was on her own now. *Free*. She
remembered the poem by William Ernest Henley that they'd read
in English class earlier this year. Even the title—*Invictus*—had enthralled her. The poem's sentiments were hers.

"... I am the master of my fate:
I am the captain of my soul."

Chapter Six

Carol walked through the cavernous Grand Central Station to
Forty-Second Street—the late spring twilight a delicate background for the montage of brilliantly lighted office towers that rose
into the sky. A few hours earlier she had sat in the office of the real
estate broker in Hamptonville while the neat little house on Elm
Street was sold to her mother. With no mortgage involved the
transaction had been swift.

She understood, Carol told herself, that the house was Mama's.
In some distant future she would inherit it, Mama kept telling her.
It seemed to her that for the first time in her memory Mama was
content with life. The house was *security*. The need for security had
replaced her mother's earlier passion for more and greater luxuries.

On the New York-bound train she had explored her fears that
her mother would feel bereft at being alone. No need to be afraid,
she realized. Mama needed no one. The core of Mama's world was
Edie Simon.

Carol paused on the sidewalk and debated about taking the shut-
tle across to the West Side. She'd walk to Times Square, she decided, relishing the brisk air after hours on the stuffy train. Excitement lent a buoyancy to her steps as she made her way through the
bustling pedestrian horde. She felt, she thought, as though she had
been reborn.

* * *

Each morning Carol joined the anxious throngs that filled the offices of the employment agencies. She fretted that she could neither type nor take shorthand and vowed to sign up for a typing course in the fall—though nothing must interfere with her evening high school classes. She registered for summer school, with the anticipation of receiving her high school diploma the following February.

Once a week she wrote to her mother, who promptly replied with pages of trivia. At the end of four weeks—with no job in sight—she wrote her mother that she was working. She would *not* go to Hamptonville to live.

"The money is very low, but I can manage," she fabricated. She was nervous about dipping into her savings to pay rent and buy food, but she didn't panic. She could handle the situation, she told herself.

On a steamy summer morning she began her usual rounds with the realization that a pretty, dark-haired girl she'd encountered at several agencies in the past was here yet again. She offered a tentative smile as the other girl gazed at her in recognition.

"Isn't this the pits?" the other girl asked breezily, and Carol nodded. "Do you type or take shorthand?"

"No," Carol admitted. "Neither."

"That's all they're looking for here today. My name's Sharon Ross—and I don't take shorthand or type." Sharon exuded an endearing friendliness.

"I'm Carol Simon." Goldberg had been dumped along with her marriage.

"We're wasting time here." Sharon was rummaging in her purse now. "I've got a tip about a fund-raising job—they're looking for a few girls." She pulled out a scrap of paper. "Here it is. It's commission. It could be lousy. Want to give it a try?"

"Sure." Carol's face lighted. Only now did she recognize the depth of her loneliness. She felt better, just standing here talking to Sharon. "Where's the place? What will we have to do if they hire us?"

"Just stand on an assigned street with a can that says 'Save the babies' and ask for contributions. We get ten percent of whatever we collect. And we get it the same night," she emphasized, blue eyes bright with approval.

"All right," Carol said after a moment, though the prospect of approaching strangers on a sidewalk for contributions was unnerving. But she couldn't afford to be choosy. "I don't know how good I'll be at it, but we can try it if they take us."

"It's commission. They'll take us," Sharon surmised. "And if we get the right spot, from what I hear—like in front of Lindy's or Jack Dempsey's or Gallagher's—we can make some real money."

"Why there?" Carol asked. She'd liked the good-humored, voluptuously built Sharon on sight.

"Honey, the guys are easier than women with the loose change," she explained, "and that's where you find a lot of guys eating." Sharon sighed. "I don't exactly look forward to standing out there on the sidewalk and jiggling a can, but it's better than nothing." She inspected Carol's smart suit—worn to impress employment agency personnel—with candid approval. "You've got the right look. You know," she drawled, "the beautiful young debutante out to do her bit for the needy children or whatever the cans advertise. Come on. Let's go."

Carol and Sharon sought out the office where they were to apply. It was in a drab, rundown building off Eighth Avenue. The elevator wasn't working. They walked up the three flights.

"That's it." Sharon pointed to a door at the head of the stairs.

They walked inside to see several girls standing at a counter and filling out application forms. Carol and Sharon reached for forms and did the same. There were no chairs. They stood and waited to be interviewed. Carol reminded herself the job paid only commissions. That could be almost nothing. She'd try it a few days, see how it worked out.

A woman emerged from an inside office, inspected the applicants with bored but appraising eyes.

"You and you and you," she said, indicating Carol, Sharon, and a young blonde. "Go inside and I'll give you the lowdown. The rest of you, leave your applications on the counter there."

The three chosen for interviewing went into the inner office. Carol immediately realized that they were being hired. Without inviting the girls to sit, the woman launched into an explanation of what was required of them.

"If you're smart—if you know how to hustle your bustle—you can pick up three or four dollars a day. You gotta look like you're doing this because you want to help raise money for abandoned babies. You smile a lot at the guys." The woman reached for a can that read: "Save the Babies—They Need You." She demonstrated, then gave them final instructions. "Okay, that's it. Pick up the cans at ten A.M.—stay on your corner until around six P.M., then come back here. Remember, you waste time on your lunch and you're losing money. That's it. See you in the morning."

Carol knew from the first five minutes on the spot assigned to her—the coveted Lindy's—that she would loathe this job. The moment someone stared hard at her she was convinced she'd been recognized from the photograph in the *Daily News*. But she would stay because Sharon was working three blocks south on Broadway, and she was eager to have Sharon as a friend.

At the end of the first day—her feet aching from the long hours of standing—she returned to the office to discover she'd earned $1.65. Sharon's commission was $1.80.

"Look, it's money we wouldn't have if we just made the employment office rounds. Our chances of finding a decent job are like finding a thousand dollar bill on the street. What do you say we celebrate our first day by eating at the Automat? I'm starving."

They made their way to the nearest Automat. Here they settled for individual beef pies and what Sharon pronounced the best cup of coffee in the city, for a total expenditure of twenty cents. Sharon told Carol she was working for the summer and planned to start college in September.

"It's a real sacrifice for my family," she said with candor. By now Carol knew that Sharon's family consisted of her mother, her father, her maternal grandfather, and a married sister and her husband and toddler son, all of whom were crowded into a small Bronx apartment. "But Mom figures she and Dad will see me through Hunter, and then I can go for my master's in social work in evening classes at Columbia. With luck." She held up two crossed fingers. "I don't think Beverly—that's my sister—was exactly enthralled when Mom decided to move us from our nice apartment in the West Bronx to one in the East Bronx, but the rent's lower. That makes up for me not bringing in money."

Carol haltingly talked about herself—knowing, even then, that Sharon would forever be part of her life. She told Sharon about her father's death and how her mother and she had struggled to survive. She stumbled over talk about her brief marriage.

"I had to marry Marty. My mother made that clear. And then

he—he had this accident and he died." She couldn't bring herself to tell Sharon how Marty died, though she told herself she would one day.

Reluctantly they parted company at an IRT subway entrance. Carol watched Sharon start down the stairs, then headed north on Broadway. With Sharon as her friend the city suddenly seemed a warmer, more friendly place.

Though Carol hated this new job, she soon became better at it. By the end of their third week she was having days when her commission amounted to almost three dollars. On Sundays Sharon came down from the Bronx to spend the day with her. They'd go for walks along the Hudson River, to the Metropolitan or the Museum of Natural History. They'd treat themselves to coffee and cheese Danish at a Broadway cafeteria and later make spaghetti or franks on a hot plate in Carol's hall bedroom.

She showed Sharon the apartment house on West End Avenue where she'd lived with her parents. She talked about the trip to London.

"You know my most secret wish?" Sharon asked ebulliently. "To go to Paris someday. I can't talk about that at home," she said, laughing. "To my family a trip to Boston or Washington would be a major event. But one of these days I want to see Paris. Maybe we'll do it together."

On a sweltering August afternoon Carol stood at her usual site in front of Lindy's and tried to tabulate mentally how many coins had been dropped in the can she jiggled appealingly at passersby. She glanced up with a welcoming—though puzzled—smile when she saw Sharon charging toward her.

"It's too hot to walk that fast," she began, but Sharon interrupted.

"Put the can in your purse and keep walking," she ordered. "Do it," she hissed when Carol seemed bewildered.

Carol obeyed, falling into step beside Sharon. Her heart was pounding. *What was wrong?*

"Sharon, what is it?" she whispered.

"Let's go into the Fifty-fourth Street Automat for coffee, and I'll tell you," Sharon said grimly with a furtive glance over one shoulder.

When they were seated at a corner table in the lightly populated Automat, fragrant cups of coffee before them, Sharon explained.

"Look, I don't know just what the problem is, but I took a break to go to the ladies room in the Automat down below, and I saw these two cops pull Anita—you know, the girl who was hired the same day as us—into a police car. It's something to do with the cans." Carol gazed at her in bewilderment. "Honey, the fund-raising is not for abandoned babies," she explained grimly. "Those creeps we work for take the money home for themselves. I think there'll be something in tomorrow's *News*. There was a *Daily News* car there, and a photographer taking pictures."

"Oh, my God!" Carol's voice was an anguished gasp.

"Don't look so scared," Sharon comforted. "We know now—we won't go back on the job."

"We could go to jail," Carol whispered, all at once visualizing the newspaper spreads on the shooting of Marty and herself.

"Carol, you're shaking," Sharon said solicitously. "We're okay. We'll go in and hand over the cans and say we're through. If we see any police hanging around, we won't go in. I guess we should have realized it was something like that," she said wryly. "When neither one of us recognized the fund they talked about."

"Is it safe to go to the office?" Carol's mind was in chaos. The police would find out she was Marty's widow. They wouldn't believe she didn't know the fund-raising was phony.

"Look, they don't know us," Sharon comforted. "Like I said, if we see cops around, we'll walk away from it. Carol, stop looking so scared," she pleaded.

Now Carol blurted out her horror at discovering Marty was a gangster, the nightmare of being shot down along with him, of seeing herself labeled a "gangster's moll."

"It happened back in April," she concluded, fighting tears. "Didn't you read about it in the newspapers?"

"Honey, there's some gangster being shot down every day in this city," Sharon said sympathetically. "Unless it's somebody notorious, like 'Pretty Boy' Floyd, or John Dillinger or 'Bonnie and Clyde'—nobody remembers. But you poor kid—no wonder you were so scared."

"I suppose we have to go back to the office," Carol said reluctantly. "Unless the police are there—"

"Let's do it now and get it over with—" Sharon drained her cup and managed an optimistic smile. "It wasn't that great a job, anyway."

Sharon had only planned on finishing out this week, Carol remembered as they left the Automat and headed for the so-called fund-raisers' office. Sharon had to enroll at Hunter next week and start classes right after that. Carol dreaded the prospect of making the agency rounds again.

Arriving at their destination, they discovered the office was dark. A notice pasted to the door explained that the organization was out of business.

"Okay." Sharon grinned insouciantly. "That means whatever we collected belongs to us." Carol gaped at her in consternation. "We can't go out on the street and give it back." She thought a moment. "Why don't we go up to your room, cut the cans and share the loot? It's an unexpected bonus."

In the privacy of Carol's room—with summer sunlight pouring through the single window—Carol produced a knife and Sharon proceeded to cut open the two cans. They divided the coins into dollar piles that were growing into an awesome amount.

"Over forty bucks!" Sharon crowed. "Hey, that's a good day's take!"

"I feel so guilty." Carol's eyes sought reassurance.

"We can't do anything else." Sharon was realistic. "Let's go over to the cafeteria and have ourselves a celebration dinner. And afterward we'll walk down to Columbus Circle and listen to the speakers." Sharon knew Carol's evening classes had just wound up for the summer.

"What speakers?" Carol asked curiously.

"You live right here in Manhattan, and you don't know about the circus every night down at the Circle?"

"I remember once I drove past the Circle with Marty, and there was a crowd of people listening to speakers standing on boxes," Carol recalled. "Marty cursed because the traffic was so heavy around there."

"That's the heart of the West Side," Sharon said with messianic fervor. "Whatever you want to hear—though mostly it's about politics," she conceded, "somebody's discussing it. It's exciting. Maybe because so many of the people there are students—you know, like us."

They had an early, highly appreciated dinner at a Broadway cafeteria famous for its generous portions, then walked south on Broadway toward Columbus Circle. Carol relished the comradeship she shared with Sharon, whom she considered awesomely sophisticated though only one year her senior. Sharon, in turn, was enthralled by Carol's having lived what she considered such a colorful life in such a short span of time.

"We should have sat longer in the cafeteria," Sharon said, brushing perspiration from her forehead with a wisp of a handkerchief. "At least, we had air-conditioning there."

"We could cut over and sit in the park for a while." Carol tugged at the back of her white cotton peasant blouse, which clung damply between her shoulder blades. "There might be a breeze there."

For a while they sprawled on a grassy knoll in Central Park—seeking with myriad others some relief from the August heat wave. Then—as dusk fell over the city—they left the Park and strolled over to Columbus Circle. The huge electric signs on nearby buildings lent a splash of color to the 77-foot granite columns that supported a marble statue of Columbus. Already clusters of people surrounded speakers. Leaflets were being circulated.

Carol and Sharon moved from one speaker to another in silent agreement—savoring without exploring the impassioned message of each. Both had some vague awareness that in October of 1935 Mussolini's troops had invaded and taken over Ethiopia, that Japan had just launched a full-scale attack on central China and had captured the country's major cities—and that Adolf Hitler had sent his troops into the demilitarized Rhineland.

They knew that German Jews were coming into the United States, in flight from Hitler's oppressive edicts—the Nuremberg Laws set in motion two years ago, that deprived Jews in Germany of their citizenship, barred them from public office and the professions. They were shocked by Hitler's decrees, yet Germany seemed another world from their own. America was determined to stay out of the aggression in Europe and Asia. Its people had troubles enough of their own.

"Isn't he good-looking?" Sharon whispered to Carol while they hovered at the fringe of a crowd surrounding a young student who echoed the sentiments of many college students.

"Let President Roosevelt and Congress understand!" he shouted. "We will not fight unless this country itself is invaded. It's time for another nationwide Student Strike for Peace!"

Students from rich families could afford to take time out for strikes, Carol thought with hard-earned wisdom. The poor struggled to survive. Still, half a million undergraduates, she'd read somewhere, had signed a pledge not to fight even if Congress declared war. They'd demonstrated at Columbia, and Berkeley, Harvard, Johns Hopkins, and CCNY.

"Sharon!" a young masculine voice called out high-spiritedly from a few feet away. "What the hell are you doing down here?"

Sharon swung about to face him, and Carol followed suit.

"Where the hell have you been?" Sharon challenged. "I love the way you just float in and out of my life. Oh, Carol, this is Jerry Kline," she flipped. "He's going to be the next Clifford Odets."

"Sharon, no," he scolded. He was slight, with sardonic brown eyes and sandy hair. Inspecting him with interest—because it was obvious Sharon had more than a passing interest in Jerry Kline— Carol decided he looked like a young Leslie Howard. The same lean, sensitive face. Older than Sharon and herself, she guessed, probably twenty-two or twenty-three.

"What do you mean, no?" Sharon scoffed. "You're not the theater's next white hope?"

"Odets isn't my style," he drawled, smiling sidewise at Carol. "I'm tired of the poverty-stricken and oppressed. My plays are written for laughs."

"Where've you been?" Sharon asked. "I haven't seen you since we went to that concert at the Metropolitan last spring."

"Managing." He shrugged, his smile lopsided.

"You could afford a nickel for a phone call, you know." Sharon's eyes seemed to be carrying on another silent conversation with Jerry.

"You didn't call me," he pointed out.

"Nobody ever answers that hall phone in your building." Sharon made no objection to his drawing her so close that color stained Carol's high cheekbones.

"You working?" Sharon asked, while the three of them edged away from the tight circle around the speaker.

"I have a shit job for now. Another messenger deal." His eyes darkened in distaste. "Let's get out of here and cool off in the park. You can bring me up to date on what I've missed all these months."

"Maybe I'll just go on home now," Carol said self-consciously. Instinct told her Jerry was eager to be alone with Sharon.

"It's too hot to stay in your room until it's time to go to bed," Sharon told her. "Let's go to the park."

Carol was content to listen while Sharon and Jerry exchanged barbs. They left the Circle and strolled to the park—settling on a knoll that faced Central Park South. Sharon told Jerry about their near-brush with the law. She made it sound now like an hilarious adventure, Carol thought.

"Careful. I can't afford to bail you out." Jerry slid an arm about Sharon's waist, pulled her to him as they lounged on the still-hot grass. Perhaps a dozen feet away a girl with her arms entwined about an obviously amorous young man was singing—in a voice close to professional—an aria from *Lohengrin*.

"I wish she'd settle for something by George Gershwin," Sharon giggled.

"I hate Wagner," Jerry said with low-keyed disdain. "He was so damn anti-Semitic. That's what broke up his friendship with Nietzsche."

"Don't you start with all that talk about the philosophers," Sharon ordered and turned to Carol. "Jerry's so intellectual sometimes. Always sneaking in some weird course at night school."

"Who was Nietzsche?" Carol asked.

"Not another one," Sharon sighed. "I don't want any heavy conversation tonight. I'll be stuck with the books soon enough."

"Wouldn't it be exciting to live up there?" Carol's eyes focused on the brilliantly lighted top floors of a tall building rising high over Central Park South. "Can you imagine the views?" Her voice was hushed.

"Look at the penthouses," Jerry said with sardonic humor, "but don't expect to live in them. They're not for the likes of us."

"Why not?" Carol challenged. "Because things are bad now doesn't mean they'll always be that way."

"Hey, you're talking to a girl who's been to London," Sharon teased gently.

"I was only nine," Carol said, self-conscious now. "And we were just there for two weeks."

"Once a bloody capitalist," Jerry joshed, "you never give up." Unexpectedly he withdrew his arms from around Sharon and pulled himself to his feet. "I have to meet a friend downtown. Why don't you two come to dinner tomorrow? You'll meet my new roommate."

"Male?" Sharon asked.

"Male," Jerry said. "I need somebody to help me pay the rent."

"Where're you living now?" Sharon remained sprawled on the grass. Carol was aware of a provocative glint in her eyes.

"Same place down on Christopher Street. You remember it, don't you?"

"Oh, I remember." Sharon's eyes were reminiscent now. "What time?"

"Seven okay?"

"Seven's fine," Sharon replied shrugging. "All right with you, Carol?"

"Yes." Carol's face was bright with anticipation. She reveled at being included in this invitation.

"See you two tomorrow—" Jerry strode off, subway bound.

"Have you known Jerry a long time?" Carol asked as Sharon's gaze followed him.

"About a year. He's got this crazy way of popping in and out of my life. I met him at the Greenwich Village art fair last summer. I was there with a girl from school—you know, killing Saturday afternoon. Jerry picked us up." She paused. "He's had a weird life. His mother died when he was four, and his father dumped him on some cousins. His old man showed up once or twice a year until the cousins said they couldn't keep Jerry any longer. Then his father put him in an orphanage. He was eleven."

"How awful," Carol said, instantly sympathetic.

"Jerry never saw him again until four years ago. He was on a subway and turned around and there's his father. They talked a few minutes—Jerry was crying—and then the old bastard got off at the next stop with some crack about 'see you around some time.' So if Jerry seems to have a chip on his shoulder he's got a reason."

"Is he serious about writing plays?"

"Oh sure, he's serious about that. And I think he's good. I read a couple of one-act plays he wrote. A theater group he works with down in the Village did one of them. He took me down to see it. I was impressed."

"But he doesn't believe he'll ever be famous," Carol concluded. "You know, what he said about never living in penthouses."

"Maybe he's scared to dream. But at our age we shouldn't be so skeptical about life." For a moment defiance colored Sharon's voice. "Anyhow, tomorrow night we'll go down to his place. We'll probably have franks and beans and soda, then walk over to Washington

Square to cool off. Sometimes Jerry's fun. Other times I want to hit him over the head." She glanced at her watch—her parents' high school graduation present. "Hey, it's getting late. I've got that trip uptown. I'll walk you up Broadway to the Seventy-second Street station."

"What about tomorrow? You're not going to bother job-hunting when school's opening so soon, are you?"

"I'll need a part-time job," Sharon told her, then giggled. "Let's play hooky tomorrow. Remember, we had a sensational payoff today. I'll pick you up at your place around nine. We'll go out and spend the day at Coney Island. We'll pretend it's the Riviera!"

Chapter Seven

Carol awoke to a sultry, gray morning. Clouds gathered in murky clusters in the sky. Did this mean she and Sharon wouldn't go to Coney Island? she asked herself. The possibility was disappointing.

She glanced at the clock atop the much-scratched small chest of drawers. It was past eight already. Sharon would be here, soon, she realized. Oh, let them go to Coney Island! She loved the ocean.

Her mind raced back in time to the summers when her father had driven the family to Manhattan Beach for outings. She remembered the week they'd spent there in a rented house—the summer before they went to London. No apartment buildings were allowed at Manhattan Beach, she remembered with fresh awe—just private houses. It had been so beautiful.

Carol rose from the narrow bed, reached for the seersucker robe that lay across the room's one chair. Robe tied about her waist, she hurried with towel and soap in hand to the bathroom down the hall to shower. She wondered nervously if Sharon expected her to have a bathing suit. She didn't own one.

She hadn't been in the water since Papa took Mama and her to

Brighton on that trip to England. He'd told them that the Brighton Beach next to Coney Island had been named for the famous resort. Even if she couldn't go in the water today, it would be fun just to walk along the edge of the ocean.

Feeling refreshed from her shower, Carol returned to her room—knowing she'd be hot and uncomfortable again within ten minutes. It would be nice to have a fan in her room, she thought wistfully—though Papa used to say fans just pushed around the hot air.

She opened the door to her small closet, inspected its contents. In deference to the weather she chose an off-the-shoulder blouse and cotton skirt. She dressed quickly, reached for a hairbrush, ran it over her burnished-gold page boy. A smile lit her face at the sound of a brisk knock on the door. Sharon was here. With a glow of welcome she rushed to respond.

"I think your landlady is sore at having to answer the door this early in the morning." Sharon giggled infectiously. "But as Jerry would say, 'screw the capitalists!'." Sharon inspected her flowered skirt and white peasant blouse with approval. "You're not wearing a bathing suit under that," she added with surprise. "Or did you just drop the straps?"

"I don't own a bathing suit," Carol confessed.

"That's okay. I brought along the one I bought two summers ago—when I was skinny from pneumonia. I know I'll never be skinny enough to wear it again." She reached into the shopping bag she carried, pulled out a bright red jersey one-piece suit with very little back. "It'll look terrific on you. You may be thin, but you've got plenty fore and aft—where it counts."

"What do the bathhouses cost?" Carol asked, timorous at spending their unexpected cache.

"Honey, that's for tourists and people who don't worry about money," Sharon chortled. "Put the bathing suit on under your clothes. With a skirt and blouse it's simple. Once at the beach you take them off. Everybody does it. Oh, I brought along a thermos of iced tea, cookies, and towels. We'll splurge on franks at Nathan's."

"But we're going to Jerry's apartment for dinner," Carol said uncertainly. "In bathing suits?"

"So we have our bathing suits under our skirts and blouses." Sharon shrugged this aside. "Change and let's head for the subway. It's roasting here." She tugged at her blouse. "It may rain by the time we reach Stillwell Avenue, but at least we'll have a breeze from the ocean."

Self-conscious at stripping to skin, Carol changed. Nothing bothered Sharon, she thought with admiration. *She* might have been married and all, but Sharon knew so much more about life than she did. She was glad she'd met Sharon. They'd be friends forever.

They hurried to the subway at 72nd and Broadway, waited for the Express to Times Square, where they'd change for the BMT to Coney Island. The rush hour was past, Carol noted gratefully, and with the threat of rain few riders seemed bound for the beach.

"I can't believe you've lived in New York all your life, and you've never been to Coney Island," Sharon effervesced.

"Maybe when I was very little," Carol conceded. "I just don't remember."

"That's right," she drawled. "You were a lousy capitalist, who went to Manhattan Beach."

As they anticipated, they arrived at the Stillwell Avenue subway stop to discover a faint drizzle falling outdoors. Still, they were not alone in pursuing a day at the beach.

"So we'll get wet," Sharon said ebulliently. "In this heat we'll dry out before it's time to go back to the city."

Despite the early hour and the light turnout the air was already oppressive with the mingled aromas of grilling franks, popcorn, cotton candy, and *knishes*. Now Sharon played tour guide. She pointed out the bathhouses, which ranged from elaborate establishments with swimming pools and restaurants to tiny backyard dressing rooms. She showed Carol Steeplechase Park and Luna Park and Dreamland Park. They debated about going on the Ferris wheel, then decided they were already hungry and doubled back to Nathan's for franks.

With franks in tow they walked along the lightly populated boardwalk, paused to inspect the impressive fourteen-story, Spanish-style Half Moon Hotel.

"That's for honeymooners and people with money," Sharon explained. "Like the fancy restaurants."

Now they climbed down steps that led to the beach—the turgid water of the ocean seeming endless, devoid of swimmers this morning. The drizzle had stopped, but the sun hid behind huge clumps of clouds. They stepped out of skirts, pulled off blouses, kicked off shoes, in the way of others who had arrived for a day at what Sharon said was known as "the empire of the nickel"—the cost of the subway ride to Coney Island.

They sprawled on the sand and sipped iced tea poured from the thermos into paper cups and nibbled cookies. They talked with the candor of two young people who'd known each other all their lives rather than three weeks.

By 6 P.M. they were back in Manhattan and strolling about Washington Square. The conversation focused now on school.

"I know I'm going on to college," Carol said somberly. Despite her high grades, she worried that she would not be admitted to the evening sessions at Hunter, where the demands were high and the competition keen. "But I don't know what I want to be."

"You don't have to declare your major the first year," Sharon consoled. "You'll have plenty of time to think about it."

"I know what I don't want to be," Carol acknowledged. "I don't want to be a teacher or a librarian or a nurse. Why do so many people think that's all a woman can be?" She squinted in thought. "I'd like to work in an architect's office, but not as a secretary. I want to do something that's part of building houses."

"You'll talk to your freshman advisor," Sharon said. "You'll be pointed in the right direction."

"You *know* what you want to be," Carol reminded wistfully.

"The realistic side of me knows," Sharon said slowly. "The other me would love to be involved in music. A pop singer—or a pianist. I loved piano lessons, but I had to stop when I was eleven and Dad lost his job. I probably could never have made it as a pianist," she conceded after a moment. "And I know I don't have a really good voice—okay for a small town glee club, maybe. Still, I dream sometimes." Carol heard the hint of defiance in her voice. "Two glasses of wine at a party, and I'm singing 'The Man I Love', with my legs crossed and my skirt hoisted up to heaven."

Fifteen minutes before seven Sharon decided it was time to head for Jerry's apartment.

"So we'll be a few minutes early. I don't feel like window-shopping on Eighth Street when I can't go in and buy anything."

Carol liked the neighborhood where Jerry lived—the low buildings and the narrow, winding streets. Jerry had a basement apartment, Sharon told her, leading her down three steps below street level. Carol admired the window box bright with red geraniums.

"Jerry's apartment is in the back." Sharon giggled. "If he had a flower box, he'd never remember to water it. All he thinks about is writing plays—and fooling around. He's the first fellow I ever slept with." She smiled at Carol's involuntary start. "Okay, he's the only one. I know he's got too many problems to think about getting married. He's only twenty-two. But he gets all worked up so fast—and it's contagious. You've been married—you understand."

"I hated it," Carol whispered, her face flushed in recall. "I—"

"Jerry's coming to the door," Sharon said. "I hope he bought soda. I'm dying for something cold to drink."

Like Carol's furnished room, Jerry's apartment was little larger than a pair of walk-in closets, plus a pullman kitchenette and what she presumed was a similar sized bath. But he had his own bathroom, she thought wistfully, just as that door swung open and Jerry's new roommate emerged.

"Wow, that shower felt great after shoving around cartons of produce all day," he greeted them exuberantly, his eyes friendly and approving as they moved from Sharon to Carol. "I'm Greg," he announced. He was a slim five feet five or six, with handsome features, unruly sandy hair, and expressive blue eyes. "This *klutz* has no social graces."

"Greg drives a truck for his brother," Jerry explained. "By day. At night he's an actor with NVP."

"That's New Village Players," Greg interpreted. "Hey, we open three new one-act plays right after Labor Day. What about you two helping out as usherettes?"

"I'll be going to school nights," Carol said, but the prospect was oddly enticing.

"They only play over weekends," Sharon told her. "Yeah, why not?"

Carol was astonished by her enjoyment in this casual evening. They weren't double-dating, she reassured herself. They were two girls and two guys having fun. Though Sharon and Jerry were uninhibited enough to exchange passionate kisses, Greg was satisfied just to talk with fervor about his ambitions to be a serious actor.

"I don't want to be some dumb movie star who plays the love interest." For an instant he appeared self-conscious, and Carol guessed it was because he wasn't the conventional six-foot leading man type. "I want to do the kind of things Paul Muni does. You know, meaty parts. Did you see him in *The Good Earth?*"

"Yes." Carol's face was reverent. "And in *The Life of Emile Zola.* He's wonderful!"

Greg launched into a scene from *The Good Earth*—portraying Muni's part with a skill that mesmerized the other three. Greg *was* Muni, Carol thought in soaring admiration. When he finished, spreading his hands in a gesture of finality, she automatically applauded.

When Sharon decided it was time she and Carol headed for home, Jerry brought up their coming down to New Village Players to work as backstage staff as well as ushering when weekend performances began.

"What'll we do?" Sharon asked. Carol knew she loved the theater, though Broadway theater was out of their reach except when 25-cent second balcony seats might be obtainable.

"You'll work," Jerry promised. "Holding the script or handing out props or building sets—or sweeping floors," he conceded with a grin. "Nobody just sits around Leo."

"Who's Leo?" Carol asked.

"Leo Delaney. He's the producer/director/coach of NVP," Greg explained, his eyes almost reverent. "He's dedicated to finding new theater talent—playwrights and actors. He bullies us, holds our hands, and tells us we'll make it in theater if he has to knock our brains out."

"Sometimes it's a revolving door," Jerry said. "Leo makes heavy demands. If you're not serious, you get out fast. But for a few of us—like Greg and me—he's the brass ring on the merry-go-round."

"Leo holds classes, directs the plays. Acting members pay fifty cents a week to belong. Except for me. I'm his reliable character actor." Greg mugged appealingly. "The other actors are either students or kids who work at daytime jobs and spend evenings and weekends at the playhouse. And every week Leo groans about whether he'll be thrown out for not paying the rent."

"Leo only does original plays," Jerry picked up with an air of triumph. "He's vowing to find the new Broadway playwrights and the next major actors and actresses. He's got the kind of enthusiasm that even stirs up cynics like me. And a harem of 'ladies of a certain age' who help him keep the landlord at bay."

"None of us sit around at the Astor soda fount and talk about 'making rounds'," Greg said. "We're not out there trying for theater jobs because we can't afford to give up whatever jobs we have. But after hours and weekends we work at what we want to do—and we hope somebody might see us and say, 'wow, has that guy got talent!' Of course," he added mockingly, "we know that the chances are one in a million. But it's our ticket for the Irish Sweepstakes."

On the uptown subway Sharon reported what Jerry had told her about Greg.

"He's been working for his older brother since he finished high school two years ago but taking night acting classes and appearing with amateur theater groups, too. He could have gone out with a summer theater group this year, but his mother and brother threw fits. He has to give money at home; his mother is a widow. They threw another fit when they found out he was moving in with Jerry. But half his salary goes home to his mother."

"He's so good," Carol said with respect.

"He's got a problem—at least in his mind—about not being taller. Now he's fighting with his mother about changing his name."

"That's right. He said something about calling himself Gregory Fields instead of Gregory Feinstein." Carol looked for the sign as the train pulled into the subway station. Still several stops to go. Sharon would stay on the "local" with her until West 72nd Street. "He says it'd look better on a marquee." Greg would make it as an actor, she decided with the confidence of the young.

"That's not the main reason," Sharon said. "His brother—nineteen years older—is Chuck Fein. You know, the big-time gangster that was shot down by another mob three years ago and nearly died. It was all over the newspapers. Anyhow, Chuck was smart enough to get out after that and got into a legitimate business, but the newspapers keep bringing up the old stuff about his being a mobster and the murders he's supposed to have ordered. Jerry said Greg dies a little every time he reads about his brother in the newspapers."

"I know how he feels," Carol whispered. Maybe that was one reason why she went back to being Carol Simon. "He shouldn't have to suffer for what his brother did." Chuck Fein was big-time, as Sharon said. Marty had been a small-time hoodlum, but still she was nervous if anybody looked hard at her.

"It'll be fun to go down to Jerry and Greg's theater group," Sharon said. "I won't be meeting any guys at Hunter—and Jerry's scared to death of being tied down." Her eyes were curious now. "How do you like Greg?"

"He's nice. But don't get any romantic notions about us," Carol warned. "I don't want to get romantic about anybody."

"You'll change your mind," Sharon predicted, "when the right guy comes along. You'll forget how you hated sleeping with Marty and all his craziness."

"I don't know if I ever will," Carol told her with a shiver of revulsion. Even now, it made her sick to remember Marty reaching for her under the blankets. "I just don't know."

It amazed Carol that her life over weekends became so totally involved with NVP—as members and hangers-on referred to the Village theater group. During the third week of night school she landed a job as cashier at a West Side cafeteria through another night school student. The money was low, but so were her expenses.

Midweek her life consisted of a treadmill of work, night classes, and dogged studying. She worked half a day on Saturdays, but Friday and Saturday evenings and much of Sundays were what Sharon labeled "playtime." Still, over weekends Carol managed to sandwich in hours of studying, earnest hours at the 42nd Street library where she alternated between researching for school papers—compulsively seeking top grades—and devouring as much as she could about architects and architecture.

Both she and Sharon relished the closeness that developed among the group, the air of contagious optimism that permeated the company. For Carol it was as though she'd suddenly become part of a warm, loving family.

Jerry made it clear to Carol and Sharon that there was much camaraderie among all the members of NVP, but they had made their way into the "inner circle." When they went out for coffee after rehearsals, Leo welcomed whoever wished to come along—but the "inner circle" always accompanied Leo, flanked him at the tables they pulled together to accommodate the current group.

Jerry and Greg were Leo's two prime protégés—the ones always faithful to his ideals. Others came and went, Jerry said.

"You two," he told Carol and Sharon, "are Leo's sounding board. His unbiased audience."

Carol was aware that the burly, magnetically charming Irishman would often turn to her when he was introducing a new bit of business at a rehearsal. Greg teased her about being Leo's assistant director. "Your face shows every emotion. If you don't like something, he changes it." Usually Leo ordered her to hold the script at rehearsals, to prompt whoever forgot a line.

Carol was ecstatic when she made an impulsive suggestion about the stage set for Jerry's one-act play in rehearsal and Leo pounced on her with approval. She and Sharon were asked to repaint the flimsy flats to incorporate her idea.

"You'll get program credit as scenic designer," Leo promised exuberantly.

When the company offered their performances, Carol and Sharon ushered, then sat in the minuscule audience to enhance its size. Leo was constantly fighting to pay the rent, low as it was. It was a precarious way of life, but it was very precious to Carol and to the others.

At the approach to Thanksgiving Carol wrote her mother about coming up to spend the day in Hamptonville. She wouldn't be working. All at once it was important to be with Mama. But her mother urged her not to come.

"Better you should save the money, Carol. Who knows how long you'll have that job?"

Carol tried to hide her disappointment. Not that Mama had ever bothered to make a turkey on Thanksgiving—not even when Papa was alive, she remembered. The closest thing she'd known to a real Thanksgiving was when—in the first grade—their teacher made cranberry sauce in their classroom on the day before the holiday. But the prospect of being alone in the city on a special holiday was, somehow, unnerving. Maybe she'd go to the Automat for a chicken pie. She wasn't the only person who'd be alone on Thanksgiving.

Then on the Monday before the holiday Sharon insisted that she go home with her to the Bronx on Wednesday evening.

"You'll sleep over and have Thanksgiving dinner with us."

The night before, the two girls shared Sharon's bed in her tiny bedroom, talked in whispers until sleep finally overcame them. They awoke late in the morning, then hurried to help Sharon's mother in the kitchen.

It was a cherished experience for Carol, who'd never experienced the warmth of a large family. She sensed that Sharon's sister Beverly was slightly defensive because Sharon was in college and she'd left high school late in her junior year to get married. Sharon's grandfather was a wise, old Talmudic student who spilled over a potent charm, and her toddler nephew Joshua was ingratiating. She was touched by Mr. Ross's obvious embarrassment at being unemployed except for occasional odd jobs when his wife worked as a cutter in the garment industry.

"Pop makes the best noodle *kuchel*," Sharon said affectionately. "Even Mom can't beat it." Carol knew that for the past four years her father was the family housekeeper.

"I wonder where Jerry was yesterday," Sharon said while they clung to subway straps en route to Manhattan on Friday morning. Hunter was closed for the long weekend, but she'd decided to research an assignment in the 42nd Street library until it was time to go to her part-time job. "I invited him to come out with us, but he made some crack about family dinners being depressing. I know Greg invited him to go home with him, too, but it was no deal. He makes me so furious sometimes."

On Christmas Eve—after a party at the makeshift playhouse—Carol went up to the Bronx with Sharon again. The party had been different from earlier such occasions. Carol had been shaken when Greg—bolstered by three rum Cokes—had pulled her into his arms for a heated kiss. She'd been shaken to realize she had reacted with pleasure. But an instant later she pretended that they'd just exchanged a Christmas Eve kiss.

"Merry Christmas," she said shakily. "And a belated Happy Hanukkah."

Of their inner circle, only Leo wasn't Jewish. She didn't know about Seth Walden, the latest addition to NVP and fast infiltrating their "inner circle." Not that it mattered to her if they went to synagogue or church or mosque, she considered. She didn't choose her friends because of their religion.

Seth—who came from Georgia—was what Leo called the typical "young leading man," with clean-cut features and a trim, athletic body. His sandy hair usually rumpled, his brown eyes warm and appealing. He was a freshman up at Columbia and wanted to write plays. If the bankroll held out, Leo said, he'd do the curtain-raiser Seth brought down when he joined NVP. Leo thought Seth had a lot of talent.

When Carol had talked with Leo about the set for the next group of plays, he'd told her she ought to think about studying set designing. *"Honey, you've got a real talent for it."* That was fun for now; it wasn't what she wanted to do with her life. She wanted to work at something that was exciting, that made her feel good inside. It must be awful to spend most of your life at something you didn't like, she thought, remembering her job at Klein's, her current job at the cafeteria. So boring!

She'd often told herself she'd love to work in an architect's office—but not as a secretary, she always stipulated. What could she do in an architect's office? It had been a vague image in her mind. For the first time she seriously explored this. She could learn drafting, she pinpointed. Then all at once she felt a surge of heady defiance. She didn't have to settle for drafting. She'd do what Papa had yearned to do. *She would become an architect.*

Chapter Eight

Carol was upset when her mother objected to her coming up to Hamptonville for New Year's Eve and New Year's Day.

"You'll come up for a weekend during Passover," her mother decreed. "Providing you're still working and have the train fare saved up."

They still exchanged weekly letters, but these said little. She and Mama had become strangers, she thought with a sense of loss. Mainly, Mama complained about the physical labor involved in keeping the house clean.

"Sometimes I feel like I'm no better than a maid," her mother wrote repeatedly. "But I manage to get by as long as I watch what I spend for the table. I go to the library every week and get out my books. That doesn't cost me anything. I'm on the list for *Gone With The Wind.* It seems as though half the people in town still haven't read it."

Yet despite the complaints Carol sensed a new complacency in her mother. In truth, she accepted her life. All right, Carol told herself, she'd see Mama during Passover week.

Leo threw a party at the playhouse on New Year's Eve. Carol

enjoyed it immensely—though she'd dreaded this first New Year's Eve on her own. Afterward Sharon went home with her rather than making the long trek to the Bronx. Huddled on the narrow bed under a blanket topped with their coats—because there was never heat after 11 P.M.—they talked in high-spirited whispers until dawn crept into the room.

It seemed to Carol that her life had sped backward and she was *young* again. She hadn't felt young since she'd had to leave school to go to work, she thought as she hurried from her Friday evening class to the playhouse early in the new year. It was a wonderful feeling.

In three weeks she'd receive her high school diploma. But that was just the beginning. She had to earn her bachelor's degree at Hunter evening sessions. It would take her longer than Sharon, of course. But that wouldn't stop her, she vowed with recurrent enthusiasm.

When she talked to her advisor about becoming an architect, she'd been warned about the fearful hurdles. In all of the United States there were only a few hundred women architects. But why shouldn't a woman be an architect? How she would accomplish this remained vague in her mind, but *it could happen.*

When she arrived at the playhouse—in time to play usher while Sharon sat at the improvised box office to collect admission—Carol learned that a current crisis had just been averted. Leo had persuaded one of the older women among his camp-followers to play patron to the group. The rent would be paid. Two of Jerry's one-act plays plus Seth's curtain-raiser would be presented early in the spring. Seth was euphoric. Jerry was mildly pleased.

After the performance Leo gathered his "inner circle" and prodded them off to the neighborhood Automat. The conversation roamed from theater to politics. Seth talked wistfully about wanting to quit school to go to fight in Spain.

"You won't go." Jerry's smile was cynical.

"I don't see you going," Leo shot back.

"I'm using my head." Jerry lifted an eyebrow in good-humored mockery. "What chance have the Loyalists got to win? The Germans and Italians have been shooting in troops like crazy to support Franco. Even the Pope is on Franco's side."

"I'm giving some time to this group on campus that's trying to raise funds for the Abraham Lincoln Brigade," Seth said apologetically.

"That's important." Carol rushed to Seth's defense.

"We need some help tomorrow to get out a mailing." Seth glanced about the table with a pleading air. "Who's willing?"

"I can help," Carol said. "I don't work this Saturday afternoon."

"As long as it's not before noon, I can make it," Sharon said. "It's almost two A.M. now. I've got to get *some* sleep."

They broke up with an air of candid reluctance. Jerry was making a covert effort to persuade Sharon to stay over at his place. She'd done that last week—the night Greg went up to the Bronx and slept over at his mother's apartment. Sharon wouldn't stay if Greg was there.

Carol, Sharon, and Seth headed for the uptown IRT. Carol was aware that Greg was annoyed that Seth took the same subway as she and Sharon. She sensed a covert competition between the two of them for her attention. But she'd made it clear to both, she told herself guiltily, that they were all just very good friends.

Settled in seats at a deserted end of their subway car, the two girls and Seth focused for a few minutes on school talk. Carol had confided in no one except Sharon about her determination to become an architect. She was outspoken, though, about starting college next month.

"I'll go for a master's in social work after Hunter," Sharon said. "The slow way. At night."

"My parents figure I'll eventually get into teaching at the college level." Seth was somber. "They go along with my English major and all my talk about 'getting a job in publishing'—but they figure that's all daydreaming. They're sure I'll settle down to get a master's in Atlanta—close to home—and end up teaching at Emory. My brother Harvey—he's eight years younger than me—is going to be a lawyer and go into politics. Mom has it all worked out in her mind."

"What do your folks do down in Georgia?" Sharon asked. To her a small Georgia town seemed exotic.

"My father owns a pawnshop. It was rough for a while, but he says it's getting better now."

"It must be if you can afford to go to Columbia," Sharon said ebulliently. Columbia was expensive Ivy League.

"I wouldn't be at Columbia except for my grandmother. She has this nest egg she's been sitting on since my grandfather died four years ago. He'd told her to save it to send me up to Columbia for a year or two—however long the money holds out. He knew I was dying to come up here to school." Seth's smile was whimsical. "He didn't realize I wanted to be here in the heart of theater."

"My father always said that college was the key to whatever you wanted in life," Carol said tenderly.

"Thanks for helping out with the mailing tomorrow," Seth told the two girls. "It's important."

Carol left the subway at the West 72nd Street station, and Sharon changed there for an express to the Bronx. Seth would go on up to the 116th Street stop and his dorm on the Columbia campus.

Tonight Carol was glad she lived close to the subway. The weather was bitter cold. Everybody walked swiftly with shoulders hunched. Nobody lingered in conversation. At this hour, she guessed in distaste, her room would be like an iceberg.

Rather than hang her coat in the closet Carol draped it over the washed-thin blanket provided by her landlady. Within a few minutes she was in bed, the alarm clock set so as to make sure she wouldn't oversleep in the morning. She was glad Seth had asked them to help out with the mailing. It was important to help fight Fascism.

Despite the dank cold of her tiny room, Carol felt an unexpected surge of well-being. How lucky she was to have met Sharon that way—to have found such special friends. It seemed as though they'd known each other forever. Seth and Jerry and Greg were so talented; sometimes she felt almost humble in their presence. Of all those who came in and out of New Village Players, she thought sleepily, these were the three she knew would make it one day. And she recognized in them the ambition she nurtured within herself. This was a precious bond between them—and a strong tie to Leo, whom they all almost worshipped.

Early in February Carol received her high school diploma. It was the first miracle in her new life, she thought exultantly as she sat with Sharon and Seth over coffee and pumpkin pie in the Automat after the exercises. It was the anticipation of this day that had helped her survive the years as a stock girl in Klein's, even her marriage to Marty.

"So, do you feel any different?" Seth joshed, but his eyes were sympathetic.

"Tomorrow night I'll be a college student." Carol's smile was brilliant. "I'm on my way. Of course, you two will have your degrees ages before me."

"Knowing you, I suspect it won't be too long," Sharon said affectionately. "I never knew anybody who was in such a rush."

"I think I'll be able to come back for my sophomore year at Columbia." All at once Seth was serious. "But after that it's back to Bellevue and commuting to a college in Atlanta. I'll miss New York."

Carol understood why he wanted to stay in New York. For a quarter—when seats were available in the second balcony—they saw the finest plays on Broadway. And where in Bellevue, Georgia, could Seth watch a play of his own come to life on a stage?

On the Saturday morning of the Passover weekend Carol waited in line to buy her ticket to Hamptonville. She noted the headline on the *Daily News* held by the man ahead of her. "Mobster gunned down." Her eyes focused on the date. It was a year ago today that she and Marty were shot. It seemed a million years ago.

She'd written her mother about beginning her first college courses. The letter that came back suggested she'd be wiser to take a course in typing and shorthand. *"Then you might get a job as a secretary. Maybe even a civil service job."*

Alighting from the train in Hamptonville Carol felt a flicker of panic. *Where was Mama?* Then she spied her mother walking toward the tiny white clapboard depot.

"Your train must have been early," Edie greeted her effusively. "I thought I'd be here way ahead of time."

Carol exchanged an awkward embrace with her mother, fell into step beside her as Edie began to chatter about the latest inconvenience of being a landlady. To Mama it was as though they had seen each other just yesterday, Carol thought. *It was almost a year.*

The weekend sped past, with Edie introducing Carol to several neighbors as "my little girl, who's down in New York at school." Carol was relieved to be on the train bound for the city again. Her mother had erected a wall between them, she decided, troubled by this.

They lived in different worlds now, she forced herself to accept. This was what Mama wanted for herself. Mama didn't need her anymore. She didn't need anybody. She'd found security.

As prearranged, Sharon was waiting for her at Grand Central Station.

"Men are bastards," Sharon greeted her. "Did I ever tell you that?"

"What particular man?" Carol asked as they headed through the early Sunday eve crowd toward 42nd Street.

"Jerry, of course." Sharon's flippancy was edged with youthful hurt and bitterness now. "He took off. For parts unknown," she drawled. "Third time since I've known him. You'd think I was after him with a shotgun. All I said Saturday morning—when we woke up in his bed—" She giggled at Carol's uplifted eyebrows. "I told Mom I was sleeping over at your place. Actually, Greg went up to the Bronx for the night. Anyhow, I said, 'God, wouldn't it be sensational to wake up every morning like this?' There he was—rarin' to go, even before breakfast! And he gave me this sickly grin. I made breakfast for us, then headed for the Bronx and work." Sharon sold tickets at a Bronx RKO on Saturdays until six o'clock. "When I showed up at the playhouse last night, Greg told me Jerry had taken off. Not a word to me."

"What about the apartment?"

"He promised Greg he'd send his share of the rent. But he wasn't sure when he'd be back."

"What about his two one-act plays? They're supposed to open next weekend."

"More delays," Sharon explained. "Two people left the cast. Leo has to replace them. Greg says Jerry's decided it's nuts to write one-act plays. He wants to try for a full-length play."

"He's going to do this riding the rails?" Carol was skeptical. On earlier occasions, Jerry said he'd crossed the country in boxcars. "Why doesn't he try for a job on the Federal Writers' Project?"

"Jerry can't stand waiting in lines and filling out applications. Besides, he says he hasn't got a chance. Too many writers with real backgrounds are hungry for jobs. But let's forget about Jerry. I'm putting that maniac out of my mind," Sharon said defiantly. "Why can't I fall for a normal guy?"

They stopped at Nedick's for hot dogs and coffee, then headed for the playhouse. Sundays were just casual get-togethers for who-ever wandered in unless the company was giving performances. When Carol and Sharon arrived, they found Leo and Seth in a loud but good-humored argument about the Social Security Law, passed by Congress two years ago.

"What do you mean, Leo? How can something so far-thinking and new be a conservative law?" Seth demanded. He was proud of his liberal thinking.

"It's a conservative law," Leo drawled in the teasing vein the others knew but which was escaping Seth at this moment. "Every country in Europe has social security laws. Governments over there consider it their duty to their citizens. Here we're making workers finance their own security."

"But it's never happened here before," Carol said earnestly. "That's what is important."

Greg arrived, full of euphoria after seeing a matinee performance of Robert Sherwood's *Abe Lincoln in Illinois*. As always after going to see a play, he launched into a mini-performance of scenes that particularly impressed him. Greg was so good, Carol thought again. Why wasn't he working in theater?

But she knew the answer to this. Greg couldn't even try for a job. Half his salary had to go home to his mother. He scrimped to pay his rent and eat.

"Let's run over to Childs for pancakes and coffee," Leo said with a grandiose gesture. "My treat. One of my old flames was feeling generous last night."

Falling into step along with the others—en route to the nearest Childs—Carol told herself that these were the most important years of her life. The friendships of these years would endure forever. It was a warm and beautiful conviction.

Chapter Nine

The months were surging past. In June Seth left for home—where he'd work for the summer in his father's pawnshop. Three weeks later Jerry returned, restless that he had not progressed beyond a rough draft of his first full-length play. He said nothing about where he'd been. It seemed, Carol thought while she watched him resume his on-and-off affair with Sharon, as though he'd never been away. She worried that Sharon allowed this to happen.

Greg talked hungrily about using his two-week August vacation to make theater rounds. Casting was active for the new theater season. Still, the others were astonished when he actually did this.

Right after the Labor Day weekend Greg arrived at a reading of the one-act play Seth had written while in Bellevue to announce that he'd landed a bit part in a new Broadway play.

"I can't believe it," he chortled. Though Seth was surely pleased for Greg, Carol sensed his disappointment that Greg wouldn't be available for his new play. "I went out for two weeks of making rounds—but I figured the odds were a million to one that I'd land something. Not only do I have three lines," he said jubilantly, "but they're letting me understudy the lead!"

"When do you open?" Leo asked. The atmosphere was convivial. Here was proof that talent would win out.

"Oh, not until early November. We're going right into rehearsal next week, then out on the road. God, it's really happening!"

At regular intervals Greg reported on the production's progress. There was much rewriting—most of it on the insistence of the fading Hollywood star in the leading role. The company was in silent rebellion about their star's temperamental outbursts. At the Boston opening he suddenly developed laryngitis. The director wanted to send Greg on in his place. The producers decided they'd had enough; they closed the play.

Carol sympathized with Greg's anguish. He was frank about the ugly scenes at home because he'd walked out on his job with his brother's firm. At his mother's insistence his brother rehired him. Outwardly he appeared chastened. But the inner circle at NVP knew his ambitions had only gone underground.

At the approach of Christmas Jerry took off yet again. This time he made no promise of meeting his share of the rent.

"I've got to get a new roommate by January first," Greg said gloomily at a late Saturday coffee session at the Automat. "Or move back home. I can't handle the rent alone."

"Put up a card in some of the Village hangouts," Leo told him.

"The rent's low. People down here are always coming and going. You might find somebody."

"I don't suppose one of you would be interested?" Greg turned to Carol and Sharon with a beguiling smile. "I'll sleep in the living room; my roommate gets the bedroom."

"You won't get any takers from those two," Leo said with a chuckle. Carol remembered that he'd made tentative plays for both of them. Sharon said he did that automatically whenever a new girl came into his orbit. "Put up signs."

On the Friday following New Year's—when Greg was fighting against panic—Leo announced he'd found someone looking to share a cheap apartment.

"He's a guy I knew when I was out in California. We'll talk about it after rehearsal." Leo turned to Carol. "What are you doing about the set for Seth's new play?"

"I've been working on it," Carol said. The play meant so much to Seth that she was eager to come up with something truly good—on a shoestring, of course, she reminded herself. Seth had gone home for the winter school break. She was amazed at how much she missed him.

"I tell you, Carol, you ought to take some courses in set designing." Leo scrutinized her with respect.

"I can't afford to take courses." She shrugged this aside. When she could, they wouldn't be courses in set designing.

"This guy Matt Harris—who wants to move in with Greg—might help with building sets," Leo said and whistled to Sharon to come sit beside him with the script. "Okay, let's get this show on the road."

Close to eleven—when Leo was calling an end to rehearsal—Carol saw a strange man stroll into the playhouse. Younger than Leo but older than Greg and Seth, she judged. Probably about 26 or 27. He had an arresting air of authority about him that held her attention—and he was awfully good-looking, she thought. Unruly dark hair, magnetic brown eyes.

As though feeling the weight of the newcomer's gaze, Leo turned around.

"Come on down, Matt. We're breaking for the night."

Leo exchanged some brief discussion with the cast onstage, dismissed them, and turned to Matt.

"A few of us always go out for coffee after weekend rehearsals," he explained. "You can talk with Greg about the apartment then."

Tonight only Greg, Carol, and Sharon joined Leo and Matt on the trek to the Automat. Without seeing the apartment Matt offered to move in the following morning.

"I can't hold down a job and go to school and keep on traveling out to Queens to sleep," Matt said, clearly delighted at the new living arrangements. "Even though my apartment is a steal."

"When did you go back to school?" Leo asked. "When I left California, you'd just dropped out and were looking for a job."

"I couldn't survive on the part-time jobs I was picking up, though some had their good points." Matt grinned reminiscently. "Cat-sitting for the likes of Cary Grant and Bruce Cabot. And I did some house-sitting. But I figured I had a better chance back here in New York."

"Where do you go to school?" Sharon asked.

"At Cooper Union. I'm taking a long time with the education because I don't stay with it. But now I'm set."

"What are you studying at Cooper Union?" All at once Carol was impatient to know. You had to be bright to get into Cooper Union; tuition was free but you had to take competitive exams, she remembered. She'd never have the nerve for that. Thousands of students took the tests every year.

"I'm going to be an architect," he said, his voice almost reverent. "It took me a long time, but now I know what I want to do with the rest of my life."

"When will you graduate?" Greg asked.

"Not for at least another two years, the way I'm going." Matt chuckled. "I'm taking as light a course load as I can; I have a full-time job. You won't see much of me around the apartment," he told Greg. "I'll be asleep or cracking the books."

Carol was enthralled that Matt Harris was studying architecture. Since he'd be sharing Greg's apartment, they'd be sure to see a lot of him, she thought with soaring anticipation. And from the way Leo was talking, she suspected he'd rope Matt in to help with the sets—despite his classes at Cooper Union and his job.

Harris wasn't his real name, Matt had told them. He'd changed his name, he said, to put emotional distance between himself and his family. His father was Italian and his mother Jewish. His father "drank a lot" and pushed his mother around. *"But afterward they always had this passionate reunion. They had no room in their lives for my sister and me."*

His sister Lisa—five years his senior—had run away from home at 19 to get married. He hadn't seen her since then. He hadn't seen his parents for almost seven years. *"They were always moving around the country. They wandered out of touch with me."*

Carol told herself it was crazy to be so excited because she knew an architectural student, yet she felt as though she'd taken one step closer to invading that field herself. In the weeks ahead—as Matt became part of their inner circle—Carol began to weave blissful dreams of one day working for Matt when he went into practice. He didn't want to work for a large firm, he said. He meant to be his own boss. She'd be an apprentice architect.

Without revealing her own dreams Carol was learning aspects of the architectural world from Matt, who relished talking about his studies. Already he knew so much, Carol marveled while she and the others listened to him expound on the requirements of an architect at an after-rehearsal get together. Recently Leo had discovered a small Village coffee shop where their table could be extended to handle as many as followed in Leo's tracks.

"Look, architecture is an art, just like acting and writing," Matt said with a messianic glow. "It's like Ruskin said—'A great architect must be a great sculptor or painter. If he is not a sculptor or painter, he can only be a builder.' "

"We don't hear about great architects," Seth said seriously.

"The average American doesn't," Matt pinpointed. "We're such isolationists in this country. After the war we cut ourselves off not only from European politics but from European art. What does the name Le Corbusier mean to any of you?" he challenged.

"He's a Swiss architect who works in France," Carol said, then paused, disconcerted by her instinctive response.

"Right." Matt inspected her with a new interest. Up till now, she surmised, he'd thought of her as just another of Leo's court—playing at set designing. "How do you know that?"

"I read about him in a magazine," she said. "In *Architectural Record*, I think. I love to look at pictures of beautiful buildings."

Matt broke into ironic laughter. "I doubt that Le Corbusier would approve of your calling his buildings beautiful. He referred to a house as a 'machine to live in.' His major concern was their being functional."

"I love the houses that Frank Lloyd Wright designs." Carol pushed aside a feeling of rebuff. "I've seen pictures in several magazines." All at once she was defensive.

"Ah, Frank Lloyd Wright," Matt said reminiscently. "Probably the most influential architect in this country today. I'm fascinated by his concept of organic architecture—the way he insists that exterior and interior aspects have to be integrated."

"I like his long, low, one-floored houses with the long stretches of windows," Carol said shyly. "And the wide overhanging eaves."

"You should see Wright's Imperial Hotel in Tokyo—finished back in 1922. Other architects screamed that his principles of the floating cantilever was structurally unsound; but when a major earthquake hit Tokyo in 1923, the Imperial was one of the few undamaged buildings in the city."

"Have you seen it?" Carol asked eagerly. She read everything she could find about Frank Lloyd Wright.

"Only photographs," Matt conceded. "But one of these days, I've promised myself, I'll stay at the Imperial."

"What is a cantilever?" Greg asked curiously.

"It's a structural beam that's supported at one end and free at the other," Matt began to explain.

"Greg, don't encourage him," Leo interrupted. "He'll go on forever."

"It's an ancient structural principle that works," Matt picked up, unperturbed. "Leo, you're like so many Americans who don't know the difference between a builder and an architect. Expand your horizons."

"We may be expanding our horizons." All at once Leo was grim. "If nobody stops that bastard Hitler—and Mussolini," he added, "we could all be fighting a war in Europe."

"We won't get involved," Matt derided. "Americans want no part of war."

"Then why did Roosevelt send a special message to Congress back in January to recommend a $535 million defense program for the next two years?" Matt challenged.

"Hey, no war talk allowed," Sharon broke in. "This is my night to play."

Carol was conscious of Matt's furtive glances in her direction as the conversation acquired a lighter tone. When the group left the café, he fell into step beside her—the others moving slightly ahead through the Friday evening Village throngs.

"What are you doing next Saturday afternoon?" Matt asked casually.

"I work until one," she said, her heart all at once pounding.

"Okay, I'll pick you up at one." His hand closed in at her elbow. "Do you know the Museum of Modern Art?"

"No," she admitted. She and Sharon visited the Metropolitan, the Frick, the Whitney—where admission was free on most or all days. The Museum of Modern Art cost 25 cents, was free only on Mondays.

"When the Museum of Modern Art opened back in 1929, it brought something new and important to this city," Matt said with infinite respect. "It goes beyond painting and sculpture to include reproductions of architectural designs. The museum presented a controversial exhibit of modern architecture that introduced the style developed by Walter Gropius, Mies van der Rohe, and Le Corbusier—"

"I didn't know that." Carol was simultaneously awed and excited.

"They've presented exhibits of Louis Sullivan and Frank Lloyd Wright, as well. Did you know that Wright always refers to Sullivan as 'Dear Master'? But of course, you don't," Matt continued before she could reply. He chuckled indulgently. "Still it's great to talk to somebody who's heard of Le Corbusier and Frank Lloyd Wright. You make me feel a little less alone." His eyes inspected her small oval face with a disconcerting warmth. "Even if you are such a kid," he teased.

"I'm almost nineteen," she told him, her own eyes demanding respect. "I was supporting myself when I was twelve. I've been married and widowed." That surprised him. He didn't know about Marty. "I'm not a kid."

"I'll remember that," he promised. "My beautiful little friend, who admires Le Corbusier and Wright."

"I don't know much about Le Corbusier," she said. "Tell me about him—"

He thought she was beautiful. She was astonished and awed by this. He called her "my beautiful little friend." Something new and wonderful had come into her life with Matt, she told herself in gratitude. Something to be cherished.

Chapter Ten

Carol waited eagerly outside the cafeteria for Matt to appear. The first hints of spring were in the air. The sun provided a deliciously warm embrace as she waited. At impatient intervals her eyes sought out the wall clock inside the cafeteria. It was almost a quarter past, she noted with simmering anxiety.

Was she mistaken about the time Matt was to pick her up? Had he gone to another cafeteria—to the one two blocks down? At twenty past one she told herself Matt had forgotten about their meeting. It wasn't a *date*. She'd wait another five minutes, she decided. If he wasn't here by then, forget it.

Then she spied him striding toward her. He exuded an air of optimism and ambition that she cherished. Matt had no doubts about where his life was headed.

"Sorry I'm late," he said casually, his smile ingratiating. "I got all involved in a project I was working on; I didn't realize what time it was."

"That's okay." Her face was bright with welcome. It didn't matter—he was here. "I was enjoying the sunshine."

"Let's head down to the museum. You up to walking?" It was a good-humored challenge.

"Yes. I love to walk." She was conscious of his protective hand at her elbow.

"We'll take a roundabout route," he said. "Pick up some architectural highlights. Do you know the Dakota Apartments?"

"No," she confessed, caught up in a spiraling sense of adventure.

"What about the Ansonia Hotel?"

"On Broadway between Seventy-third and Seventy-fourth," she pinpointed. "It has all sorts of gorgeous detail."

"Late Beaux-Arts style," he identified. "We'll cross over to the Dakota, then head down to the Ansonia. Then later—after we've been to the Museum of Modern Art—I want to show you some of the fabulous mansions around Manhattan." His voice deepened in anticipation. "Most of all, that's what I want to do—design magnificent private homes."

At Rockefeller Plaza they strolled slowly about the area. Matt pointed out various aspects of its construction.

"Look at the way the architecture is integrated with the sculpture, the murals, the wood veneering, the woodwork—and the site planning is like nothing ever seen before in any American city!"

They left Rockefeller Plaza to walk west, then south along Broadway. Matt paused with her before the Paramount Building, between 43rd and 44th streets.

"It's both Mayan and Art Deco," he said and Carol felt his words being etched on her brain. "When it was built back in the twenties, the architects created an image that would allow more light into the street than is usual—yet it was to rise higher than any other building at the time. Thirty floors, Carol."

"And now the Empire State Building climbs one hundred and two floors into the sky," Carol said softly. "When I first saw it, I thought, 'how does it keep from toppling over!' " She laughed at her own naiveté.

Matt showed her the elegant J.P. Morgan Jr. house on Madison Avenue at 37th Street, then walked with her farther downtown, to the Gramercy Park area. They stood together before the beautiful National Arts Club, then before the Players Club—remodeled into its present splendor by Stanford White—which sat right next door.

The day sped past. All at once the city was bathed in twilight. For Carol this was always a magical time in Manhattan—when it became a glittering masterpiece. But she remembered now that she must be at the playhouse to usher tonight. On Saturdays Leo made an effort to paper the house—handing out free tickets around the neighborhood. He always said performances improved when there were "live bodies" out front.

"Let's go on down to the playhouse." Matt seemed to read her mind. "We'll pick up whoever's hanging around and take them over to the apartment for dinner. Greg's making a shitload of spaghetti—and the biggest salad you've ever seen, courtesy of his brother's produce company." He chuckled reminiscently. "God, do we eat salad these days."

"Leo said you're prompting this weekend," Carol recalled.

"Yeah. Leo doesn't let anybody off the hook."

Greg served dinner for six. While everyone was conscious of the need to watch the time, table conversation was lively. Tonight there was much talk about New York's World Fair, scheduled to open in a few days.

"Look, the economy is turning around," Leo began exuberantly, "and with the Fair opening—"

"For some people it's turning around," Seth interrupted. "Try explaining that to people who can't find jobs."

"More and more are finding jobs," Leo pounced. "Look at the way the defense plants are hiring. More plants are starting up every day."

"Doesn't it make you sick to think that jobs are coming up in this country because of the hell breaking loose across the ocean?" Matt asked with distaste.

"With the World's Fair opening up we'll see lots of money pouring into the city." Leo refused to abandon his air of optimism. "All those tourist dollars! And remember the jobs the fair created. Roads, bridges, the fair building that had to be built."

Conversation focused now on the splendor of the fair. Not that any of them were apt to be visiting the fair, Carol thought wistfully. It wasn't just the 75-cent admission. Once inside, people would have to spend money as though it grew on trees. From what they read, admission was just a tiny part of attending the World's Fair.

Then Leo broke into the lively conversation.

"Hey, it's time to leave for the playhouse."

In the course of the evening Carol was conscious that Seth was unfamiliarly taciturn. Not until he was on the subway with Sharon and herself did she learn the reason for this.

"I've had to apply for a transfer to Emory," he told them as they clung to a pole on the uptown IRT. "There's no way I can afford a third year at Columbia."

"Oh Seth, we'll miss you." Carol was shaken at the prospect of Seth's not being part of their lives after this semester at Columbia. They were all so close.

"What about getting a job and finishing up at evening classes?" Sharon said.

"My parents would have a fit. Besides, I couldn't even afford night classes at Columbia. I suppose I could get a job and go to evening classes at City College," he conceded. "But that's all so insecure. I can live at home and go to Emory—my parents can handle that. And I'll finish up in two years instead of having to hang around for all that extra time night school would take. The faster I finish college, the sooner I can get back to New York and theater."

"We'll miss you," Sharon said sympathetically. "You write us, Seth."

Last summer Seth had gone home, but they knew he was coming back. It was as though part of their family was breaking away, Carol thought with a towering sense of loss. Oh yes, they'd miss Seth.

Late in May—at the end of the school year—Seth prepared to leave for Georgia. He'd work at his father's pawnshop during the summer, commute to Emory when the new school year opened in September. There was a party for him at Greg and Matt's apartment the Saturday evening before he was to leave.

This was going to be a weird summer, Carol thought as the apartment filled with playhouse members. She and Sharon—along with Matt—were the only ones without theatrical aspirations. Leo had given up trying to persuade her to study set designing. But for the first time since she and Sharon had been part of Leo's world, he was closing down for the summer. The playhouse was rented out to a children's theater company.

Leo himself had a job as acting teacher and director of its theater company at a small college upstate. Greg was bitter at not being able to try for a summer theater job. After the fiasco of his anticipated Broadway debut, his mother and brother rejected any such effort. He had to help support his mother. Matt was not taking summer classes; he said he was drained from the combination of work and a heavy school schedule.

"The summer's for recuperation. I'll work and sleep. No classes. Or maybe I'll get a job as a waiter at some hotel in the Catskills. The city's a hellhole in the summer, and I hear the tips at the end of the season up there in the borscht belt are sensational."

The party didn't break up until after 4 A.M. Sharon was sleeping over with Carol. The following day they'd see Seth off for Georgia. Despite her tiredness Carol found it difficult to fall asleep. The coming summer seemed disturbingly desolate. Leo would be teaching at that college upstate. Seth was going home to Georgia—and not coming back in the fall. Nobody knew where Jerry was these days—Sharon had two postcards, with no return address. And now Matt talked about quitting his job to work as a waiter at some hotel in the Catskills.

*   *   *

As planned, Seth met Carol and Sharon at their favorite Broadway cafeteria for a late breakfast. Neither of the girls was working today. The three managed to create a festive atmosphere, though Carol knew that Seth was unhappy about leaving New York.

"God, I can't wait to get my degree and head back here!" At last Seth's anguish broke through his shaky convivial facade. "There's no theater down there. I'll make sure I have time to write, and I'll send whatever I do up to Leo. But it'll be like living in a desert!"

"You said Emory's a good school," Sharon consoled. "And you've been accepted."

"I think maybe Jerry's right about there being no future for us in writing one-act plays," he said somberly.

"Noel Coward has done all right with one-act plays," Carol said cajolingly. When would Seth have time to write a three-act play when he was going to school full-time?

"Leo wouldn't offer a three-act play unless he was convinced it had a real chance. He figures the odds are on his side when he does a curtain-raiser and two one-acts. The audience has to like one of them. But wouldn't it be sensational if I could come up with a full-length play that Leo was willing to gamble on!" Seth's expressive brown eyes glowed.

"You will one day," Carol said. "You'll make time to write down there in Georgia—we know you."

"You're only nineteen, Seth," Sharon scolded. "Give yourself a break."

Then it was time to leave the cafeteria and head for Penn Station. The three of them tried to act as though Seth was just going home for summer vacation, but it wasn't coming off, Carol thought. They didn't know when they'd see him again. Maybe not until he had his degree from Emory.

Carol and Sharon left Penn Station with a shared sense of desolation.

"Let's live dangerously and have an early dinner at the Automat," Sharon suggested restlessly. "Then we can get in at the movies before the prices go up."

"Dinner *and* a movie?" Carol tried for an air of flippancy. "That is living dangerously." But she understood—Sharon was depressed.

When they were seated at a table in the Automat with their pot pies and coffee—and both watchful of the time because they had no intention of paying the night prices at the Loew's—Sharon confessed to ambivalence about continuing day classes at Hunter.

"I haven't said a word to anybody at home, but I'm thinking—maybe it's time to go out and get a full-time job and go to Hunter evening classes. Don't look at me with such horror," she said as Carol gaped in shock. "You're doing it, aren't you?"

"I have to," Carol said. "Your folks are willing to see you through to graduation."

"It doesn't make sense." Sharon was somber. "Some people are going out and getting decent jobs now. I'm so damn sick of not having any money. And now Beverly is pregnant again. That means the new baby will sleep in her and Dan's room—and Josh will have to share my closet of a bedroom. Five grown-ups and two kids in that little apartment are too much. If I get a job, you and I could share an apartment right here in town. I wouldn't be chasing to and from the Bronx all the time. I'd have some money in my hands. And I can still go to college at night."

"It would be terrific if we could share an apartment!"

"What about a studio in your building?" Sharon's smile was dazzling. "Like the one down the hall from you—with two studio couches and a tiny kitchenette and its own bath. Wouldn't that be great? How much is the rent on that?"

"Ten dollars a week. Sharon, together we could afford it."

"I won't say anything at home, but I'm going to start looking for a job. When I have something, then I'll break the news. Mom will carry on about how I'm messing up my education, but I think she'll really be relieved. You know how tight money is—not to mention how much easier it'll be in the morning when everybody's rushing to use the bathroom at the same time. Now there'll be one less."

"Sharon, do you think you'll find a job?" Carol asked prayerfully. "I know the newspapers keep saying economic conditions are improving—"

"Baby, if it's humanly possible I'll find a job," Sharon vowed. "I've got two years of college behind me, and I can type. And I've got *chutzpah*. I'll talk my way into something that'll pay enough for me to get by on."

All at once, Carol thought, the world seemed slightly less desolate.

* * *

Seth was relieved when he emerged from his lower berth to discover that the incessantly garrulous woman and her little girl who shared the upper berth were preparing to leave the train. He'd offered to switch berths so they could have the lower, but the little girl insisted on their sleeping in the upper berth.

"You have a good trip home, you hear," the woman urged him effervescently. "And you tell your mama she raised a real polite young man."

By the time Seth returned from the dining car—he'd decided on toast and coffee for breakfast when he saw the prices on the menu—the porter had made up the berths. He settled himself by the window and tried to read, but he found it impossible to concentrate. Nor had he slept well last night. He couldn't erase from his mind the memory of Carol's lovely face—a hint of tears in her eyes—when she kissed him goodbye at the train gate at Penn Station.

He always reminded himself how Carol had gone through a bad few months of marriage, that she hadn't put that behind her yet. He'd kept himself from giving her even a hint of how he felt about her. Sure, they were both too young to talk seriously, but he knew he wanted to spend the rest of his life with her.

Then Matt came along—and Carol followed him around like a little puppy. She was enthralled by all his talk about becoming an architect. Matt was too old, too wise about the world for her. Carol still had stars in her eyes.

She liked *him* a lot. He was sure of that. Sometimes he had to walk away from her because he was dying to tell her how he felt about her, but he knew the timing was wrong. They could be sensational together. When he was with her, he just wanted to tell her that together they could get everything they wanted from this world.

But sometimes he was sure she just saw him as a kid brother. Actually he was several months older than she. If he came back to New York with a terrific play in his hands, she'd feel differently, he told himself in a sudden burst of optimism.

Through the remainder of the long, stifling hot hours to the Bellevue depot, Seth's thoughts roamed between images of himself and Carol and fantasies about his future career in the New York theater. When he was with Carol, he just wanted to hold her in his arms. And he wanted to lay a successful career as a Broadway playwright at her feet.

Then the train was chugging into the small, neat, turn-of-the-century depot. As soon as he stepped down from the train, he saw his mother—small, slender, still youthfully pretty at forty-two—waiting for him. Her smile was warm and eager as she inspected disembarking passengers.

"Eli, there he is!" Her melodic Southern voice reached him. Only then did he see his father. Dad had taken time off from the pawnshop to meet him. He was touched by this.

Then he was enveloped in loving embraces, flanked by his parents as they headed toward the ancient family car. As usual Mom and Dad talked over one another in their rush to tell him all that had been happening in his absence. Grandma had won a radio at a synagogue raffle. Harvey—his younger brother by eight years—had skipped a grade at school. A refugee family from Berlin had taken up residence in town.

"Business is picking up," his father said proudly. "I need you, Seth. With you in the shop, I don't have to worry about the help stealing me blind."

He'd just be in the shop for the summer, Seth told himself, suddenly tense. He could deal with that. But could he deal with two more years of college? At Emory in Atlanta—nine hundred miles from New York City. Nine hundred miles from Carol and the world he loved.

He didn't want to work in the pawnshop, even during school vacation. He had no intention of becoming an English teacher, he admitted in silent, anguished defiance. Why couldn't he come right out and tell Mom and Dad?

All he asked of life was a chance to write plays and to be with Carol. What were the odds that it could happen that way? He didn't want to think about that. . . .

Chapter Eleven

Carol was pleasantly astonished when she came home from work four days later to find Sharon waiting in her room—to which she'd long had a key—with news that she would be starting a full-time job the following Monday.

"Let's go out to dinner at the cafeteria to celebrate," Sharon bubbled. "My treat."

"What's the job?" Carol asked. "What's the salary?" What wonderful timing, she thought joyously. Just this morning she'd learned that the studio apartment on her floor would be available next week. "Do your parents know yet?"

"Slow down," Sharon said, laughing. "I'll be a receptionist at an advertising agency. The two years at college—and the English major—did it. It pays fifteen a week. And Mom and Dad don't know yet. They thought I was just looking for a full-time summer job— and not holding out much hope I'd find it."

"The studio down the hall will be available next week! I'll tell Mrs. Mahoney we want to take it. Let's stop off on the way to the cafeteria and make sure we get it."

"When you sign up for evening classes, I'll sign up with you," Sharon decided, pausing at the mirror over Carol's wash basin to run a comb over her dark page boy. "I won't take a heavy schedule like you. At least, not this first term. Oh God, Carol! I'm really breaking out on my own! I'll have to budget." She was suddenly serious. "But you do it. Why can't I?"

For the next few days they were caught up in the euphoria of sharing an apartment, which washed away their depression about the coming summer. Sharon went through the trauma of telling her parents that she was transferring to night school and moving into the city.

"Only because Mom likes you so much, she didn't carry on about how no decent girl leaves home at nineteen to live in Manhattan." Sharon giggled. "She considers you'll be a good influence on me. And I think she was impressed that I got a job so fast."

Leo offered a final Saturday performance at the playhouse—to an audience of five. The night was unseasonably humid, with the playhouse fans providing meager relief.

"Let's all head over to the cafeteria for coffee and Danish," Leo said when the minuscule audience had trudged out into equally humid outdoor air. "On me. Tomorrow I clean up the place—we'll let everything sit for tonight."

They were emerging from the playhouse—everyone caught up in nostalgia—when Sharon spied Jerry approaching from the corner.

"I don't believe it," she drawled. "Look what the hot night swept in."

"Hey, Jerry!" Greg grinned broadly. "You figure you'd find a place to flop at the old stand," he surmised. Carol knew he was worried that Matt might renege on his promise to handle his share of the apartment rent. Matt was leaving in the morning for the Catskills and a job as resort hotel waiter. Now Jerry could take over.

Matt made it clear he would expect Jerry to move out after Labor Day.

"When I hit town again, you're history," he warned good-humoredly.

"Where were you this time?" Sharon asked Jerry while they moved en masse toward the cafeteria. Carol heard the undercurrent of reproach in her voice. Sharon wasn't going to start up with Jerry again, was she?

"There was this old broad who wanted somebody to share the driving out to Chicago." Jerry dropped an arm about Sharon's shoulders. "She said when we got out there, she'd make her brother give me a job. I worked a while, saved a few bucks, and hitchhiked back to the city. That's the story." He hesitated, leaned forward to corral Greg's attention. "I've got my gear stashed in a locker at Penn Station but nowhere to spend tonight." It had been arranged that he'd move into Greg's apartment the following day. "What about sleeping on your sofa?"

"If you promise me a major role in your first Broadway play," Greg joshed.

"It's a deal. I'll write in a part just for you."

With Seth down in Georgia and both Matt and Leo gone from the city, Carol and Sharon settled down to a world that consisted of work, summer school, and weekend dinners either at Greg and Jerry's apartment or theirs. After dinner the four of them sought relief from the Manhattan heat in an air-conditioned movie house or on long walks along the Hudson. Sharon made it clear that Jerry was far off base in hoping that Greg and Carol would spend weekend nights at one apartment and the two of them in the other. Greg would have been willing. Carol avoided any romantic attachment.

She tried to tell herself she wasn't harboring special feelings for Matt. She was just intent on learning everything she could about architecture from him, she rationalized. And like Seth and Greg and Leo, he was a very close friend.

She refrained from labeling Jerry as the same; she was fearful Sharon would be hurt by him. Yet there were nights when she lay sleepless, wondering how Matt was doing at that hotel in the borscht belt. Neither he nor Leo wrote more than an occasional postcard. Seth wrote regularly—about his dislike for his usual summer job, about his sense of isolation. *"I can't get down to any serious work here. It's like I can't concentrate away from New York. And I miss you all—"*

In mid-August Carol went up to Hamptonville for a Sunday. Her mother said she'd rented out the other bedroom—there was no place for her to stay for the weekend. Carol refrained from mentioning that she could share her mother's bed for a night. Mama had built a whole new life for herself—there was no room for *her.*

Arriving at the Hamptonville house, Carol immediately understood why Edie didn't want her to stay overnight. Though not a word to that effect was uttered, she interpreted the situation. Her mother was amorously involved with her new young roomer. A daughter who was almost twenty destroyed the image Edie had created for herself. She looked years younger, Carol thought, very pretty and newly vivacious. A stranger.

On the Sunday evening before the Labor Day weekend Carol and Sharon were broiling franks and heating beans while Greg was opening a soda bottle and Jerry setting the table when a familiar code was signaled on the doorbell.

"That's Leo!" Greg recognized and went to buzz the door open for him. "His college deal must be finished for the year."

Leo arrived with a bakery box of chocolate eclairs and in jubilant spirits.

"I'm off the hook," he announced after kissing Carol and Sharon and exchanging warm embraces with Greg and Jerry.

"When do you reopen the playhouse?" Greg asked Leo. "I need to work." Greg was always saying that playwrights could work whenever they wanted—they just had to sit at the typewriter—but an actor couldn't work without a playhouse and a crew.

"Feed me and I'll tell you," Leo promised. "Add another place at the table."

While they ate, Leo elaborated on his plans for the new season. The children's company would be out by Labor Day. He'd take over the playhouse again the following day.

"I need plays," he told Jerry.

"I'm polishing up a long one-act script," Jerry said after a moment. "I haven't got around yet to that full-length masterpiece that's going to astound Broadway."

"We'll get an avalanche of shit as soon as I'm settled in," Leo predicted. "Anybody hear from Seth?"

"He said he'd be sending up a curtain-raiser," Carol reported. "He's having a rough time writing down there."

"Oh, a bulletin." Leo reached for a second frankfurter. "This old bag I know is lending me her house out at Rockaway for the Labor Day weekend—along with her jalopy. How would you kids like to go out there with me? The house is right near the beach. We can have a ball."

"I'm off the whole weekend." Sharon's face was bright with anticipation. "So's Carol."

"I don't work on Saturdays during the summer," Greg said. "I'm available."

"I'm at the old messenger deal," Jerry told Leo. "I can take off Saturday."

"We'll drive out Friday night. Half of New York will be running out of town, too," Leo warned, "so maybe we ought to leave late and avoid some of the traffic. Suppose we all meet here, put on the feed bag, bitch about the heat, and pile into the jalopy around eight or nine." He glanced about for confirmation. The others nodded in avid approval. "Okay, it's all set."

Carol awoke Friday morning with an instant awareness that tonight she and Sharon—still sleeping soundly on the other studio couch—would be en route for a long weekend at Rockaway Beach.

She'd never been to Rockaway, she mused; it would be like taking a trip out of town. She pulled herself into a semi-sitting position and contemplated the day. Even this early in the morning the humidity was oppressive. Oh wow, it would be wonderful to spend three days and nights away from the hot city!

She was startled by the raucous intrusion of the alarm clock. Sharon groaned in protest, reached out to grope for the alarm without opening her eyes.

"We'd better rise and shine," Carol said softly, though Sharon had more time than she before having to head for the office.

"You rise and I'll shine," Sharon said, kicking aside the sheet. "I'll put up coffee in five minutes."

Not until she was brushing her hair and Sharon—on cooking duty this morning—was bringing breakfast to the tiny table did she switch on the small Emerson radio they'd chipped in to buy when Sharon moved in with her.

But the familiar music that usually invaded the room was replaced this morning by a news bulletin being reported by a male voice in a rush of shock and disbelief.

". . . and at this moment the German army is attacking Poland on three fronts. War began at daybreak this morning . . ."

Frozen in shock Carol and Sharon listened to the newscaster. The Nazis had begun an offensive with extreme violence. Several Polish cities were being bombed by Nazi planes. In England plans were underfoot to evacuate British children from the cities.

"I don't believe this," Sharon whispered, pale and shaken.

"Seth said it would happen if nobody stopped Hitler," Carol remembered. "He said Poland would be next."

But for most Americans what had been happening in Europe and Asia during these Depression years was something they read about in the newspapers, she thought. Something that was overshadowed by the devastating situations at home. From Seth and Matt and Leo she had learned to be concerned about what was happening around the world. Still, even before they were brought into awareness, Carol told herself in a tidal wave of guilt, she and Sharon had worried about the Spanish civil war.

This morning Carol hurried to work with a sense of urgency. Taking her place behind the cash register at the cafeteria, she was conscious of anxious faces here and there as diners heatedly discussed the morning news. The atmosphere was electric. She saw the

headlines splashed across a copy of the morning's *New York Times:*
GERMAN ARMY ATTACKS POLAND; CITIES BOMBED; PORT BLOCKADED;
DANZIG ACCEPTED INTO REICH.

What had happened was not a surprise to some far-thinking
Americans, she thought. Would there be another world war? Would
the United States be involved? It was a terrifying prospect. Her
heart began to pound as she imagined the men in their tight little
clique being sent to fight. Perhaps to die.

Charles Lindbergh talked on the radio about the United States
not becoming involved in foreign problems. He said that whatever
happened across the ocean was "no threat to our security." Senator
Vandenberg swore he'd never agree to sending American boys to
war. FDR seemed dedicated to the Neutrality Act. But could this
country remain neutral in the face of what was happening in
Europe?

By noon hordes of New Yorkers—weary of the enervating summer—were pouring out of the city. Cars clogged the city streets.
But this would not be the restful weekend she'd anticipated, Carol
surmised. Knowing Leo, she was sure the radio would pour out incessant news of the fighting in Poland.

Each hour of the day seemed endless, until at last she left work
to hurry home for her valise. Sharon was going directly from her
Madison Avenue office. Soon Carol was pushing her way into the
Village-bound subway. The air was pungent with the scents of
sweat, cheap cologne, here and there a whiff of expensive perfume
blending with the aroma of garlic.

Walking into Greg's apartment, she was astonished—and euphoric—to discover that Matt had appeared four days ahead of his
scheduled return. Though he was unaware of this, Matt was her life-
line to a career in architecture. She told herself incessantly that
through Matt she would learn what paths to take.

Subconsciously she was aware that she was the last to arrive and
that Greg was making one of his huge salads in preparation for dinner while Sharon was flipping over hamburgers in a skillet. Across
the small living room Leo and Jerry were arguing about the pros-
pects of the United States's involvement in the fighting in Poland.

"Oh baby, it's great to see you!" Matt reached to pull her close,
kissed her with a fervor that was far from brotherly. "All I've been
looking at all summer are fat cows. It wasn't enough I had to sling
hash every day—I was supposed to dance with the women guests at

night! Except on weekends," he conceded with a chuckle, "when the husbands arrived en masse."

"How'd you manage to get away before the big weekend?" Sharon left the minuscule kitchenette to join them.

"I had a row with the owner. A real bastard." Matt shrugged, but Carol saw a glint of triumph in his eyes. "Still, when I cried on the shoulders of the cows at my table, they all came across with *mucho* sympathy and good tips. I can't complain. And now I get a weekend at Rockaway to celebrate."

"Some celebration," Leo scolded. "When all hell's breaking loose in Europe."

All through dinner Leo kept switching stations on the radio in search of fresh news about the war. He derided the efforts of the English and French, who had issued a 48-hour warning to Hitler to pull his forces out of Poland.

"Hitler's laughing his guts out," Leo guessed. "He's had his way all along. He moved into the Rhineland, invaded and annexed Austria, took over Czechoslovakia, occupied Memel. The invasion of Poland was the natural next step."

At shortly past nine they climbed into Leo's borrowed old-model Packard. Carol and Sharon were seated in front with Leo, the other three in the rear. Even this far into the evening the roads were heavily traveled. To while away the time they sang.

But the group singing could not erase from Carol's mind the terrible reality of Nazi violence in Poland. She recoiled from images of soldiers advancing with guns in hand—dealing death to everyone in their path. She remembered walking into the apartment on West End Avenue to find Papa lying in a pool of blood—a gun beside him. She remembered the horror of being shot down in the street with Marty. *"Oh God, I hate guns!"*

Chapter Twelve

This had been such a crazy year so far, Carol thought, troubled as she recalled the parade of shockers perpetrated by Hitler. Then the Spanish civil war ended in March when Madrid surrendered to Franco. In April Italy invaded Albania. She'd known even before *Kristallnacht* that terrible things were being done to the Jews in Germany, though until she'd met Sharon and Jerry—and then the others—she'd lived in a kind of cocoon that separated her from the rest of the world. Nobody could live in a cocoon now.

As they approached Rockaway—known only to Greg in addition to himself—Leo talked about the narrow windswept strip of land that late in the last century had been a retreat for society leaders, before they discovered the Hampton dunes.

"The boardwalk is five miles long," Leo boasted. "There are more than a hundred hotels in the Rockaways. It's a slightly classier Coney Island. On weekends like this close to a million people walk along the boardwalk and lie on the gorgeous white beach."

"Don't forget Playland," Greg said ebulliently. "We have to go on the rides one night. A few are sensational. Just don't eat before we go!"

They discovered a holiday atmosphere when they arrived at their destination—a block off the boardwalk. A comforting breeze came in from the ocean. The house was a modest two-family frame structure. Leo's friend lived on the lower floor, rented out the upstairs apartment.

"Why don't we go for a walk on the beach?" Greg suggested exuberantly. "Everybody grab a sweater and let's take off." At this moment, Carol thought, the fighting in Poland seemed far away.

In the morning Carol awoke to the drone of the radio somewhere in the house. The aromas of perking coffee and bacon sizzling in a skillet drifted into the tiny bedroom she shared with Sharon. Moments later Sharon was awake. The two girls changed into bathing suits and headed for the kitchen.

"What's happening?" Carol asked. Leo and Matt were listening to a newscast.

"Warsaw's calling on the Allies for help," Matt reported. "The Nazis have bombed more than twenty cities—Warsaw was bombed all night. France is mobilizing. They've got eight million men on call."

"Oh God," Carol shuddered.

"The bacon's ready," Sharon announced from the gas range. "Wake up the others. I'll make the eggs."

"The Netherlands have declared a state of war," Leo continued while Matt sauntered off to wake up Greg and Jerry. "Denmark declares neutrality. The Swiss are mobilizing. Latvia announced 'strict neutrality.'"

The day was an odd mixture of somber recognition of reality and lighthearted cavorting on the beach—where Sharon at regular intervals warned everybody against severe sunburns. Not until dinner time—when they collapsed on the floor of the living room to devour franks and cole slaw and quarts of soda from paper plates and paper cups—did the outside world intrude.

Radio-reported war news trickled relentlessly into the room. There had been traffic jams all day at Times Square as crowds scanned the latest bulletins that flashed around the Times Building. London had sent a final demand to Hitler to stop the attacks in Poland. Warsaw reported that "the Poles hold fast." But many Polish civilians—including women and children—had been killed or wounded.

"Enough of this!" Greg declared, beginning to collect paper plates and cups. "Let's go to Playland. I'll pay until I run out of dough," he promised.

With a mutual determination to find some pleasure in this unexpected weekend at Rockaway, they trooped off to Playland. On one of the rides Carol was shaken when Matt kissed her with unexpected passion. She was startled that she had responded. She was relieved, though, that Matt seemed to regard it as a casual moment of fun.

On Sunday morning Sharon and Jerry went off to buy the *New York Times*. Considering the length of time they were gone, Carol assumed they'd discovered a private nook for some degree of lovemaking.

After breakfast they all sprawled around the living room floor and read the *Times* to a background of radio news. They were not surprised to learn that Hitler disregarded England and France's demands for a cease-fire in Poland. Immediately after London church services Chamberlain spoke to the British people on radio from 10 Downing Street. He announced that a state of war now existed between Great Britain and Germany. Almost immediately after the broadcast air-raid sirens screeched throughout the city. Unidentified planes were flying over London. Seventeen minutes later the "all clear" was heard.

Warsaw reported that 21 women and children were killed when Nazi bombs hit their apartments. The families of American diplomats stationed in Germany were standing by to leave. The *Ile de France* had sailed from Le Havre with more than 900 Americans aboard.

"We'll never be hit by Nazi bombs," Jerry said with a smug smile. "You can count on that."

"Life will go on the same as before over here," Matt predicted somberly. "Probably much better because you know how many jobs are going to open up with England and France moving into the war. We'll see a real boost in the economy."

"Oh, Matt," Carol protested. "That sounds so awful."

"It'll be up to us to provide what they need over there," Leo pointed out. "That means millions of jobs. But let's hope," he added softly, "that all we have to do is supply goods. Not fighting men."

After an afternoon at the beach they returned to the house for a hastily assembled dinner. As people all over the nation were doing, they were preparing to listen to FDR's evening "Fireside Chat." At the appointed time they gathered about the living room radio. Leo and Sharon brought in cups and a percolator of coffee. It was weird, Carol thought, how people clutched at a cup of coffee in moments of crisis.

Then FDR's eloquent voice filled the room. The atmosphere was charged with the realization that this was a time that would go down in history. Roosevelt told his nationwide audience that "the peace of all countries everywhere is in danger." He said yet again that he was determined "to use every effort" to keep America out of the war.

There was a brief silence in the room when the "Fireside Chat" was over.

"The isolationists will start screaming that Roosevelt's leading us right into the war," Matt broke the silence. "But if England and France are in danger, how long can we keep out of it?"

"FDR will manage for a while," Jerry said dryly, "then we'll be sucked in." He glanced about the room. "And we're the ones who'll have to fight this war."

"Knock off the gloom," Leo ordered. "I've been thinking. If we leave here by noon tomorrow, we'll have a strong chance of missing the mad rush back into the city. If we leave in the evening it will be a bitch. We'll sit in traffic for five hours. Let's have a late breakfast, then hit the road."

On Monday morning Sharon and Jerry took off for a last dip in the ocean while the others clustered around the radio to hear the latest on the war. The faint breeze from the Atlantic slightly alleviated the torpid heat. The city must be like a furnace, Carol thought.

Then the war news was interrupted by a report on the torpedoing and sinking of the British liner *Athenia* off the Hebrides.

"Where's that?" Carol asked.

"They're a group of islands off the coast of Scotland," Matt said. "Norsemen invaded the Hebrides in the 800s, then in 1266 it became a Scottish possession. The people still live the way they did centuries ago. Most of them still speak Gaelic. They—"

"Listen to the news," Leo interrupted tersely.

The British liner had been attacked yesterday by a Nazi U–boat. A yacht had rushed to reply to its SOS. With much difficulty around 400 passengers had been saved. It was believed that 30 Americans were among those who had drowned.

"One lifeboat overturned when almost within range of rescue," the newscaster reported. "There was no way to save those aboard."

"How are we going to stay out after this?" Matt demanded. "American lives have been lost!"

"The government will cling to isolationism," Jerry said. "Americans will be told not to travel abroad. Look, we're two wide oceans away from the fighting. The Japs are after China—they're not coming to our shores. And do you honestly see Nazi planes or subs crossing the Atlantic to take us on?"

"But remember what FDR said on the radio," Greg—who normally shied away from the FDR "fireside chats"—picked up. " 'This nation will remain neutral, but I cannot ask every American to remain neutral in thought.'" Ever the actor, Greg mimicked the Roosevelt speech to perfection. "What the hell does that mean?"

"It means," Matt said grimly, "that unless this country is physically attacked, we'll stay on the sidelines."

"But nothing can be the same when so many countries are at war," Carol said shakily. "We have to be affected here at home."

It seemed obscene to Carol that here in America people went on with their daily lives as though nothing horrible was happening in Europe. A letter from Seth said that down in Georgia—as in New York—grocery stores were selling sugar and flour in fifty-pound lots, canned goods by the case. But that was just in the first two or three weeks, Carol acknowledged, when many were scared that the war in Europe would bring about scarcities here at home.

"I've started school," Seth wrote, "and between school and working Saturdays with Dad, I don't get a chance to sit down to tinker with the play that's floating around in my head. It's hard, too, to think about writing when so much is happening in the world. I met a guy at school who fought with the Abraham Lincoln Brigade. A million people died in Spain, he said—and he came home disillusioned about the whole civil war. He said one side was as bad as the other."

An air of prosperity was invading the country as orders for goods swamped American manufacturers and suppliers. There were heated battles between those Americans who believed firmly in isolationism and others who felt the United States couldn't just stand by and do nothing. Yet, in truth, since Hitler's destruction of Poland the war seemed to be at a standstill. Senator Borah called it "the phony war."

Their lives hadn't changed because of the fighting in Europe, Carol analyzed while she and Sharon waited in line to see Bette Davis in *Dark Victory*. Two women ahead of them were talking avidly about the coming premiere of *Gone With The Wind* in Atlanta— as though, Carol thought, this was the most exciting event in the world. Three boys about the age of Sharon and herself were boasting about the fat paychecks they anticipated from their new jobs at a factory now running around the clock.

"Sharon, maybe it's time for us to look around for better jobs," Carol said thoughtfully, then felt herself grow hot with guilt. "I don't mean we ought to profit from the war—but if so many new jobs are coming up, shouldn't we take advantage?" She squinted in thought. "I'm going to learn to type."

"When?" Sharon challenged as the line moved slowly toward the box office.

"I'll make time," Carol vowed. "I might even land a job as a typist in an architectural firm." Her face was luminous. "That would be one foot in the door."

"Let's start reading the 'Help Wanted' ads," Sharon said, clearly enjoying the challenge. "Hey, we might even earn enough to pay for a one-bedroom apartment."

"But Jerry doesn't get rights to sleep in the living room," Carol warned. At the moment Jerry was sleeping on whatever living room sofa he could wangle. "I know. You think you're crazy about him— when he's around. He's trouble," Carol said softly. "Don't think about him on a long-term basis."

"Carol, he's had such a rough life," Sharon reproached. "And he's so talented."

"A lot of people have rough lives," Carol shot back. "They don't all run roughshod over other people. Jerry's all wrapped up in Jerry. He comes back to you when it's comfortable for him."

"Okay, Mommie," Sharon jibed. "I'll remember. Jerry's just for occasional fun."

But Sharon didn't truly believe that, did she?

Chapter Thirteen

On this Friday afternoon, December 15th, Seth abandoned his original plan to stop by the library on his way home from school. He'd promised his mother and grandmother he'd drive them into Atlanta to see all the excitement surrounding the world premiere of *Gone With The Wind* at the Loew's Grand. Mom hated driving in the city, and Dad kept the pawnshop open late on Fridays.

The day was chilly. Carol wrote in her last letter that they'd had snow in the city. He loved tramping through the New York streets in the midst of a snowstorm. It was, somehow, exciting and challenging. He'd known how much he'd miss the city. He hadn't suspected how much he'd miss Carol.

His face softened as he remembered how Carol and Sharon had seen him off at Penn Station. Carol wrote that she was learning to type in what spare time she could manage. Maybe some day she'd type his plays for him, he thought whimsically. He'd never got beyond the two-finger stage of typing.

He envisioned a life where he'd spend hours closed off in a small, private room while he brought together the plots and thoughts that swarmed through his mind, then emerging to find Carol waiting with warm words of encouragement and love.

Why couldn't he find the time to write? he asked himself in recurrent frustration. Here was this play jogging around in his mind, that ought to be on paper. He'd been outraged when Russian troops invaded peaceful little Finland last month—despite a nonaggression pact. He longed to put that anger into a play. *When could he write?* He had the commute to and from school, classes, the long hours of studying. On Saturdays he put in a twelve-hour day at the pawnshop. *When could he write?*

He drove into Bellevue with a sense of entrapment. His body was here but his heart and soul were in New York. He'd write Carol and Sharon about the premiere of *Gone With The Wind* tonight. Of course, he'd be on the outside—with thousands of others—but the whole country seemed to be focusing on Atlanta since Wednesday, when the movie stars began to arrive in town.

When Sharon finally got her reserved copy from the public library, he recalled, she said she'd read straight through the night, called in sick the next day, then went on reading. Carol said she had no time to read anything except books required for school. Seth had never known anybody who worked as hard as Carol, he thought tenderly.

He pulled into the driveway before the pleasant two-story white frame house and felt a loving possessiveness. It wasn't one of those fine colonial mansions along Maple Avenue, but there was a lot of love in that house. He'd lived here ever since he could remember—when Mom and Dad moved in, along with Harvey and himself, after Grandpa became too crippled with arthritis to go into the pawnshop every day. Grandma had stayed home to take care of Grandpa and the house while Mom and Dad took over the business.

They were all disappointed that he didn't want to be the third generation in the shop. They'd have forgotten that if he'd decided to go to medical school or law school. Sometimes he thought Dad suspected he wanted to write, though he never talked about that at home. Only those in Leo's group—and a few at Columbia—knew his real dream. To the family he just talked about "being an English major and going into publishing." They figured he'd get over that and settle for teaching. They'd never understand his wanting to be a playwright. To them that was fantasy land.

As he emerged from the car, he saw his mother thrust open the front door of the house.

"Oh, thank goodness, you're here," she bubbled, short dark hair blowing in the wind. "I left the shop at one o'clock to have plenty of time to wash my hair and get dressed. Grandma has a very early dinner waiting for us."

"You're sure we can take time to eat?" Seth teased, striding up to the veranda. It was weird to see his genteel, tradition-oriented mother so excited about a movie premiere.

"We'll eat." She nodded vigorously, her soft brown eyes—so like his own—sparkling in anticipation of a memorable evening. "There's no telling how long we'll be standing there in front of the Grand. And you change into your good suit," she ordered.

"Why?" he chuckled, walking into the house with her. "We're not going into the theater."

"You always try to look your best when you're out with people," his mother exhorted. "Every one of the two thousand seats in the Grand have been sold, and the newspapers predict tens of thousands will be outside. Mayor Hartsfield announced that the governors of Tennessee, Alabama, South Carolina, and Florida as well as our Governor Rivers are in Atlanta for the premiere."

"There're a million people in Atlanta today," Seth said humorously. "Seven hundred thousand more than normal—and the traffic in town is wild!"

"Hannah?" Leah Walden's vibrant voice filtered from the kitchen into the long hallway. "Did I hear Seth drive up?"

"Seth's here, Mama. We'll eat and be out of here in plenty of time to be at the theater by six."

The potbellied stove in the kitchen created a cozy atmosphere as

the two women and Seth settled themselves at the table at one corner of the kitchen to eat. The Walden house had been built before
steam heat became popular in Bellevue.

"You told Eli his dinner would be in the oven?" Leah asked her
daughter-in-law solicitously.

"He knows," Hannah assured her. "And I told him not to worry
if we're late in getting home. I don't know when there was an occasion in Atlanta that caused so much excitement!"

"Not since Sherman and his troops marched into Atlanta," Seth
said with a wry smile, and his mother gasped in shock.

"Seth, don't be sacrilegious," she scolded. "You just remember,
your great-great uncle on my side fought with General Hood in Atlanta."

Seth was inclined on occasion to tease his mother about her pride
at being fifth-generation Georgia born, but tonight he was enjoying
her pleasure in the Atlanta festivities. He knew how hard the family
had struggled during the last ten years. Mom was proud they'd
managed to stay off relief, to hold on to the pawnshop and the house.

Mom would like Carol, he thought involuntarily. She was probably the only Jewish woman in Bellevue who worked for a living.
Southern ladies didn't go out to work—and Mom was the personifi-
cation of the refined Southern lady. But when her family's well
being was at stake, Mom worked and was proud of doing so. Yet she
was embarrassed because Grandma still had a touch of German accent in her otherwise Southern speech.

Earlier than anticipated, they climbed into the car. Mom and
Grandma sat in the back. A nervous driver herself, Mom considered
it necessary to avoid distracting whoever was behind the wheel.

"Did you read about the ball last night in this morning's *Constitution?*" Hannah asked her mother-in-law as they headed toward
the road to Atlanta.

"Oh, it was something!" Leah said. "Folks will be talking about it
ten years from now."

"I understand the Atlanta Junior League really did themselves
proud." There was a wistful note in Hannah's voice. Seth knew that
his mother yearned to be "Old Society," even while she knew that
local Jews—no matter how wealthy or how far back their roots
went—would never attain that status. No Jew belonged to the
Bellevue Country Club, nor to the Piedmont Driving Club or the
Capital City Club in Atlanta. "I hear the auditorium was so colorful

and the stage presentation fabulous. Margaret Mitchell wasn't there, though. She said she was saving her strength for tonight. Oh, I would have loved to have been there."

"You heard the NBC broadcast, Mom," Seth tossed over his shoulder. "The whole country heard it."

"I laughed myself silly," Leah confessed, "when I read how Clark Gable was introduced as 'Mr. Carole Lombard.' That's the Junior League way," she explained to Seth.

Seth parked as close to the Grand as was possible. Then he walked with his mother and grandmother to the theater, where already a huge crowd—clearly in a festive mood—was assembled. The area had been closed to traffic, renamed "Celebrity Square" for the night.

They were astonished to find a number of spectators garbed in antebellum costumes. Hoopskirts seeming five feet in diameter vied for space among the crowd.

"Mom, why didn't you dig some of those old costumes out of the attic for you and Grandma?" Seth joshed, keeping a protective arm about each of the women.

"Oh Seth, I think that's so tacky," his mother scoffed.

"Inconsiderate," his grandmother snapped. "What gives them the right to take up so much space?"

"Did you ever see such strong lights?" Hannah gazed about in awed disbelief. "I read somewhere—I think in the *Constitution*— that this is the greatest known peacetime concentration of lights."

Five 800-million candlepower army searchlights played across the front of the theater. The facade had been transformed to appear to be a stately, columned, colonial mansion. A huge cameo of "Scarlett" and "Rhett" hung above the improvised mansion.

At intervals Seth turned to his mother and grandmother in fear that the interminable standing was tiring for them. They seemed unaware of the passing time, as did others in the enormous crowd.

As tension mounted among the spectators—anxious for the arrival of the Hollywood contingent, Seth slipped a hand into his jacket pocket and brought out a tiny box.

"Nunnally's anyone?" he asked flippantly, holding up the candy box, first before his grandmother's eyes and then his mother's.

"Seth, you angel," his mother crooned. "You know how we adore Nunnally chocolates!"

Cars had been arriving for a while now. Drivers were required to show admittance tickets at designated points. National guardsmen held back the spectators. There were bursts of applause as arrivals were recognized. Now the stars began to arrive, each announced by loudspeaker and on radio and welcomed with applause from the onlookers. Gable was the last to arrive. The applause was deafening—the greatest accorded the parade of stars.

At last Seth's mother and grandmother conceded it was time to leave. They pushed their way through the throngs to the waiting car blocks away—both women content to review the evening in blissful silence thus far. Not until they were seated in the car and Seth was struggling to manipulate through the sea of humanity was the silence broken.

"After the premiere there's going to be a *Gone With The Wind* breakfast at the Piedmont Driving Club," Leah recalled. A 'true Southern breakfast' for five hundred guests. Even the Hollywood people will be impressed."

"But how will they explain to the club's membership," Hannah began with deceptive sweetness, "that they're bringing a Jew—the producer of *Gone With The Wind*, Mr. David O. Selznick—into the sacred confines of the Piedmont Driving Club?"

"And why weren't Prissy and Mammy—Butterfly McQueen and Hattie McDaniel—there tonight?" Leah said plaintively, then stopped dead in sudden comprehension. "I guess the Atlanta Committee couldn't expect them to sit in the peanut gallery."

Later—lying sleepless in his bedroom while Harvey snored in the adjoining twin bed—Seth battled a deepening urge to drop out of school, to go back to New York, find a job, and concentrate on writing. Why must he have a college degree when he already knew what he wanted to do with his life? And he needed to be close to Carol.

Carol and Sharon arrived at the playhouse early on New Year's Eve to decorate the stage area with masses of colorful balloons. Leo was giving a party. Moments later Jerry appeared, banished Sharon from the ladder, and began to arrange clusters of balloons in strategic spots, as ordered by Carol and Sharon.

The company was in rehearsal for a new production of three one-act plays, but rehearsals had been called off for tonight. Leo wasn't happy with any of the three plays—none of which had been written by Seth or Jerry.

A group from the current cast—always a changing scene—hurried down the aisle with brown paper parcels containing delicatessen for the buffet spread Leo was providing. With an air of festivity they approved of the decorations, then concentrated on setting up a buffet. Leo had warned them he'd be late. He had to go to a cocktail party being given by a sometimes contributor to the group's coffers.

One of the cast found the small radio that Leo kept backstage and brought it out to initiate the party. The resonant voice of a male newscaster filtered into the area. He'd obviously been rehashing the major news events of the past year and was now predicting that Prime Minister Chamberlain would probably win the Nobel Peace Prize for his efforts at Munich. At the end of September, Chamberlain had met with Hitler, Mussolini, and French Premier Edouard Daladier and signed the pact that gave Sudetenland to Germany.

"For Chrissake, we don't want that on New Year's Eve!" A newly arrived actor leaned forward to switch to a music program.

"If Chamberlain wins the Nobel Peace Prize, history will laugh like hell at this generation," Jerry said with a cynical grin. "Do people really believe he has stopped the world from facing war?"

"I read somewhere that the British press is saying he might be knighted for it—even though he's still in office. That has happened only twice before in British history," Carol contributed.

"This one's a walking encyclopedia," Sharon joshed. "She couldn't find time to read *Gone With The Wind*, but stuff like this she knows."

"Sure," Jerry drawled. "She doesn't listen to "Lux Radio Theater" or "Lucky Strike Hit Parade." She only listens to Ed Murrow, William Shirer, and H.V. Kaltenborn."

"A lot of people follow the news," Carol said defensively. "Look at the way the networks are providing news on a 24-hour basis now."

"She picked up the habit from Leo and Seth," Sharon told Jerry.

"You two hear from Seth?" Jerry asked. The relationship between Jerry and Seth was strange, Carol thought. On the surface they appeared close friends, though there had been no correspondence between them to her knowledge. She suspected that underneath Jerry's show of friendship there was a strain of bitter competition with Seth. Jerry was so hungry for success—because of his desolate childhood, she told herself compassionately.

"We had a letter from Seth a few days ago," Sharon told Jerry. "He's dying to get back to New York and theater."

"If you can call this crap theater." Jerry's smile was disparaging. "How much lower can we get? Leo's at the bottom of the barrel."

"Nobody else produces your plays." Carol was angry.

"Nobody's going from here to Broadway," Jerry shot back. "I know," he anticipated Carol's retort. "Two of the kids who've worked with him have walk-ons in Broadway shows. What does that mean?"

"It means," Carol pursued, "that with Leo they gained the confidence to go out and make rounds." Which Greg should be doing, she thought—if his family would back him up.

"Hey, look who just blew in!" Sharon's voice was electric. She waved in frantic welcome.

"Seth!" Carol's face was luminous. It was wonderful to see him, but had he quit school as he'd threatened to do? Oh, that would be an awful mistake!

Clutching a briefcase, Seth bolted up the steps, kissed Carol and Sharon, exchanged a warm handshake with Jerry, waved to cast members he knew. Carol cherished the show of affection among the friends she'd made here at the playhouse. Her father had been demonstrative, she remembered wistfully. Her mother might bestow a kiss on birthdays.

"When did you get in town?" Sharon asked, and Carol reminded herself this was school vacation time.

"About an hour ago. I caught a ride with a man from back home who was driving up on business. I couldn't resist coming up for a few days." Then he hadn't quit school, Carol thought in relief. "Hey, Jerry, you got a place for me to sleep until I head back home?"

"If you want to sleep on the floor," Jerry said. "I've got a hall bedroom that's the size of a walk-in closet, but it only costs three bucks a week. I can give you a pillow and a blanket—you get to pick your chunk of the floor."

"Talk to Greg and Matt when they get here," Carol said quickly. "Their sofa will be better than the floor. For a few days they won't mind, I bet."

Within minutes of each other Matt and Leo arrived, then a cluster of former members of the playhouse. Greg was the last to appear. He strode onto the stage with an air of triumph and brandishing a magnum of champagne.

"I snitched this from the party my brother's giving for his employees," he told them. "We need champagne to welcome in 1940!"

The atmosphere was convivial. Bottles of cheap wine were opened. Somebody fiddled with the radio dials until the rollicking strains of "Beer Barrel Polka" filled the air. Immediately several couples began to dance.

At one side of the stage Carol and Sharon focused on conversation with Seth. He explained that he was scheduled to go back home on January 4th.

"No free ride home. My grandmother slipped me the money for a Greyhound bus ticket." He paused. "Unless I decide to chuck college and stay here—"

"Drop out of school?" Carol asked accusingly.

"I haven't written a line since I left New York." His eyes pleaded for understanding.

"You went to college here and you managed to write," Carol reminded. "Why can't you do it down there? You know Leo's dying to have a play from you."

"It's different back home." He seemed to be searching for words. "It's not like living in a dorm. I get caught up in family when I'm not studying. On Saturdays I work at the pawnshop—" He gestured his frustration. "I don't know what happens—I just don't find time to write."

"Make time," Carol said earnestly. "Even if it takes you a whole year to write a one-act play, you'll be writing. But don't give up on school."

"Why not?" Seth challenged. "Not every playwright has a college degree."

"You have a chance to have one," Carol said passionately. "Don't let it slip away. I'm not saying it'll teach you to write—you know that already. But it'll give you so much as a human being. Nobody succeeds right off the bat. With a college degree, you'll have an easier time finding a job. You can support yourself while you write plays at night or in the mornings or whenever. Seth, don't throw away your education."

"Listen to her." Seth tried for a jocular tone, yet she knew she had reached through to him. "Doesn't she sound like a college recruiter?"

"Seth, you're such a good writer," Carol said softly. "Someday you'll be a great writer."

"Isn't she terrific for the morale?" Matt joined them, dropped an arm about each of the two girls. "When you're depressed and discouraged, all you need to feel better is five minutes with Carol Simon. We could make a fortune if we could bottle that kind of enthusiasm."

The gaiety of the evening escalated to fever pitch as the final hour of the year was ebbing away. Then Leo was summoning them to listen to the radio countdown to midnight and the arrival of 1940. With paper cups in hand they waited for him to pour from the magnum of champagne Greg had brought.

"Happy New Year!" the radio announcer yelled jubilantly at last, and the mighty surge of voices in the background—from the celebrating hordes in Times Square—echoed over the radio.

"It's not just a new year," Seth said softly when he'd kissed Carol with a restraint that was painful, "it's a whole new decade."

"I wonder what the world will be like when we see it in 1950." Carol felt little nostalgia for 1939. It was the future that fascinated her. "What will we have accomplished by then?"

"I want to see 1950 in with you," Seth said. As their eyes clung, Carol felt suffused by disconcerting, unfamiliar emotions. "I mean," Seth continued, "I hope we'll all see it in together. You and I and Sharon and Greg and the others—"

But at intervals through the evening Carol was aware that Seth's eyes lingered on her with eloquent intensity. She was disturbed by the emotions this evoked in her. She and Seth were very close friends. She'd missed him these months he'd been away. But she wasn't ready for anything else. Maybe she'd never be ready. . . .

Around 2 A.M. Leo and his "inner circle" closed up the playhouse and headed for an all-night cafeteria for scrambled eggs and coffee. Seth was relieved that he could sleep on the sofa at Greg and Matt's apartment for the four nights he'd be in town. He had little cash beyond the cost of his bus ticket home.

"Seth, get off your butt and do some writing." Leo fell into step beside him as the group strode through the cold night air. "Jerry's doing nothing, either. I feel deserted."

"Maybe I'll start something when I get back home. I have a few ideas floating around in my head." He'd forgotten how tough it was to share a room with a kid brother. Harvey was only eleven and always dragging home friends. In what little free time he could manage, how could he work with those little kids whooping it up in the same room?

"It's getting tougher to keep the playhouse going," Leo admitted. "All of a sudden jobs are opening up. Night shift jobs," he emphasized. "If this keeps up, we'll have a hell of a time getting casts together—not to mention decent plays."

"Hey, did I tell you guys?" Matt called from behind them. He was walking with an arm protectively around Carol and Sharon because in these first hours of the new year the narrow Village streets were crowded. "I heard you talking about the new prosperity that's showing itself. I just latched on to a new job—and the money is terrific. Of course, with the long hours I'll have to cut back on courses at school next semester."

"Oh, Matt—" Carol seemed upset, Seth thought. "That means you won't graduate on schedule."

"I'll make a new schedule." He shrugged this off. "Carol, don't look like that," he said in mock dismay. "I'll be an architect soon enough."

"By the time you're thirty, I hope?" Sharon jibed good-humoredly.

"I'll probably just squeeze through," Matt surmised and turned to Carol. "Remember, baby, we're going to that party at the Hotel Chelsea this afternoon. Don't you oversleep."

"Matt's not interested in the party. He just wants to get inside and architecturally dissect the building," Sharon twitted.

Carol's going with Matt. The realization unnerved Seth. Couldn't she see how wrong Matt was for her? Seth felt a tightening in his stomach, a painful sense of desolation. To Carol he was just a kid, he taunted himself. Matt was a man. Matt had been all over the country, had done all kinds of crazy things. Why should Carol care about *him?*

Chapter Fourteen

Despite her heavy course load at school and a 45-hour work week, Carol managed time to become a voracious newspaper reader. She felt an overwhelming sympathy for the British, who early in the year began to experience rationing. This far, the rationing was limited to bacon, butter, and sugar, but additional rationing was expected.

Carol continued to be shocked that the Soviets were waging war against Finland—what FDR condemned as "this dreadful rape." In March a peace treaty was signed between Finland and the Soviets, with Finland losing considerable territory. In April Seth wrote to ask if any of their group had seen Robert Sherwood's new play, *There Shall Be No Night.*

"I read a couple of reviews," Seth wrote, "and it sounds just terrific. The kind of play I wish to hell I had written. It's about the Finnish situation, you know. At moments like this I'm furious at being stuck down here in Georgia—away from the Broadway theater. I keep reminding myself that in a little more than a year I'll have my degree from Emory and be heading back to New York."

Carol and Sharon were both eager to improve their monetary situation with better jobs, but despite the improving economy they were having little success. Millions of people were still out of work.

"Look, we're at the bottom of the totem pole," Sharon rationalized. "There are all those women out there with years of experience behind them. And most of the new jobs are in factories. What do we know about that? Of course, Matt's making more money than he even expected when he took that job in the defense plant, what with all the overtime."

"And at the end of this semester he's dropping out of school so he can put in more hours and make more money." Carol was troubled. "He ought to concentrate on getting his degree. He keeps saying architecture means more to him than anything—but money is coming first now."

"Lots of people are putting school behind them," Sharon reminded. "I mean, most of us have been broke so long—" She gestured with an eloquent spread of her hands.

"School comes first," Carol insisted stubbornly. "Nothing would make me drop out." Her eyes held Sharon's. "We're getting our degrees."

"I don't know what I'm going to do with mine," Sharon admitted. "What do you do when you have a Bachelor of Arts with an English major? I know," she added before Carol could reply. "I can get a few education courses and teach—or get a job in publishing. No money in either job," she said with a sigh.

"I don't know how it's going to happen," Carol said quietly, "but I mean to go on somehow to pick up a degree in architecture. That's why I need a better job," she said in frustration. "To be able to pay Columbia tuition. Maybe," she added in reckless abandon, "to go to do postgraduate work at the Sorbonne in Paris. Let's take plenty of French courses!"

"If you go to Paris, I'm tagging along," Sharon said exuberantly. "The minute we land better jobs, I'll start saving. To hell with a larger apartment and gorgeous clothes. I want a bank account that'll take me to Paris."

This same month the Nazis invaded Denmark and Norway. Denmark surrendered almost immediately. Britain sent 25,000 men to fight beside the Norwegians, but despite the fierce defense they were forced into retreat. Early in May Nazi planes swooped down on Belgium, Holland, and Luxembourg. Infantry and Panzer units swarmed over the borders. Paratroopers dropped from the skies. In England Chamberlain resigned and Winston Churchill became prime minister. And on May 17th the Nazis invaded France.

Matt talked over Saturday night dinner at his apartment with Greg and Carol and Sharon about a Canadian in one of his classes who spoke about quitting school to return to Canada.

"Remember, Canada declared war on Germany last September. Cliff says he'll probably go home next month and sign up for air training. He's trying to persuade me to go with him."

"That's nuts," Greg protested. "You're not Canadian."

"We're going to get into it sooner or later," Matt said. "I'd like to see it over with fast, so we can settle down to our lives."

"FDR keeps saying he's going 'to use every effort' to keep us out of the war," Greg said somberly. "You don't believe that?"

"I don't think circumstances will allow it," Matt countered.

"You're not serious about going with Cliff?" Carol asked anxiously. Matt talked a lot about Cliff, though none of his playhouse friends had met his new buddy. "Are you?"

"I'm thinking about it," Matt conceded. "A lot."

Later that night, sitting around their small studio apartment and dividing up the Sunday *Times*—available on Saturday evening on Manhattan's West Side—Carol and Sharon discussed the prospect of war shattering their close group.

"I don't want to think about any of the fellows going off to fight in a war." Carol frowned in rejection. "It's awful enough to hear what's happening in Europe to people we don't even know."

"Jerry's worried about a possible draft. He says there's a lot of talk in Washington about that. But he says they'll have to catch him first," Sharon said with an effort at flippancy.

"I thought Jerry and Leo would be over for dinner tonight. What happened?" Carol was curious. Still, she was relieved that Sharon wasn't spending this Saturday night with Jerry in his closet of a room down on East 22nd Street. Jerry would disappear again, and Sharon would mope for weeks.

"They're holed up over at the playhouse." There'd been no performances for the last four weekends. Instead, Leo was rehearsing a new trio of one-act plays. "Leo wants Jerry to cut ten minutes out of his new one-act. He says the pace is too slow."

"Jerry's fighting it," Carol surmised. "And he's worried that the cast can't handle the parts." She'd read the new play. It was *good.* She and Matt were doing the set—on a budget that required great restraint. She didn't like seeing Sharon so hung up on Jerry, but she had great respect for his talent. "He'll come into rehearsal next week," she guessed, "and try to get across to the cast how it should be played." Jerry was frustrated that most of the acting talent, Greg excluded, that came in and out of the playhouse was poor.

"I don't know why Jerry and Leo think they have to sit up all night with the project," Sharon said impatiently, then giggled. "I'm real horny tonight."

"Sharon—" Carol shook her head in indulgent dismay.

"You kill me," Sharon said affectionately. "You're such a gorgeous-looking kid, and you're letting all the fun pass you by. Wash Marty out of your mind—he was an animal. I'll bet Matt's hot as a pistol."

"Sharon, you know." Carol was somber. "I can't think about fellows the way you do." She felt very close to Matt—he was always teaching her something about architecture—and that made him terribly important in her life. It was exciting to run around the city with him to see and talk about buildings he admired—or hated. Yet sometimes she thought about Seth in a way she hadn't believed possible. Like how nice it would be to have him hold her close. Just that—nothing more. But guys thought that was teasing. "Maybe some day—" Her voice trailed off into silence.

"There's no physical pleasure in the world that can compare to *that* moment," Sharon said softly. "That moment when both of you come together inside *you*. Not with somebody you dislike—not like with Marty," she emphasized, "but with a fellow who knows how to make you feel like a woman."

"Do you suppose we might get cheap seats for a Saturday matinee for *There Shall Be No Night?*" Carol clutched at the drama section in a determination to derail this conversational track. "Seth would be so excited if we wrote and told him we'd seen it and how we felt about it."

"Now Seth," Sharon picked up triumphantly. "I'll bet you two could start a bonfire together."

"Get your mind out of bed," Carol ordered, hot color flooding her face. "Let's check on the 'Help Wanted' this week."

It was far in the future, Carol acknowledged, but she needed to save up money to take her into architectural school. Nothing so dominated her mind as her determination to become a full-fledged architect. There were women who accomplished this with little formal training, she reminded herself, but these were modern times. She had to offer more than a course in drafting. She *must* have a degree in architecture.

Between May 27th and June 3rd—like most of the civilized world—Carol and Sharon were glued to their radio at every possible moment. With the surrender of Belgium almost 400,000 British and French troops were trapped by Nazi forces. They managed to retreat to Dunkirk, a port on the French Coast. From there British naval vessels plus a flotilla of small craft manned by amateur sailors driven to heroic efforts evacuated 338,000 British, French, and Belgian troops.

Again, Leo was closing up the playhouse for the summer to teach and direct at an upstate college. Jerry had taken off a month ago on a house-sitting job near Boston—with high hopes that this would provide him with time to write a three-act play. Sharon was furious that there'd been no word from him except for a postcard on his arrival there. *"So he's trying to write a play! He could manage a letter once a week!"* Matt was putting in long hours on his defense job.

"College comes later," Matt said somberly at a small farewell dinner at Greg and his apartment the night before Leo's departure. "Right now I'm piling up cash."

Table conversation turned to FDR's run for an unprecedented third term.

"Hell, with what's happening in the world today, how can we change horses in midstream?" Leo demanded. "FDR is an easy winner for a third term."

"That's history-making," Carol said and exchanged a wry smile with Sharon. Neither of them would be old enough to vote in the coming election.

"Let's hear what's happening with the war." Glancing at his watch Matt shoved back his chair and crossed to the radio. It was time for a news program. The others left the littered dinner table to settle close to the radio.

Nine days ago the Nazis had launched a new and strong offensive in France—their destination Paris. Immediately wealthy Parisian socialites had fled to Biarritz. For the past seventy-two hours the roads out of Paris had been clogged with cars, bicycles, desperate people on foot. The world knew it was a matter of time before Paris fell. There was something especially tragic about the Nazis taking Paris, Carol thought.

All at once—as Matt found the station he sought—the sonorous voice of the newscaster invaded the room. The atmosphere was suddenly tense. Carol's throat tightened as ugly reality penetrated her consciousness.

". . . and the streets of Paris were near deserted as Nazi troops marched up the Champs-Elysées today."

Gripped in somber silence they listened to the newscast. Then Matt strode again to the radio and switched off the sound. Carol suspected that the fighting in France reminded him that four days ago Italy had declared war on France and Britain. He was upset about that. He knew that on his father's side he had an aunt and uncle, several cousins in Italy. He was fearful of a day when Italian–Americans might be fighting native-born Italians. No doubt in his mind that the United States would be drawn into the war.

"Oh God, I'll never see Paris now," Sharon moaned. "Ever since my French teacher in high school carried on about her 'summer in Paris', I knew it was the one city in the world I most wanted to see."

"All those French movies at the Apollo helped," Carol said.

"Don't worry, Sharon, you'll see Paris," Leo comforted. "You may have to wait a few years, but it won't be forever in German hands."

"I thought a couple of years ago about trying to get over on one of those cheap tours the shipping companies kept advertising about. If I'm going to be an architect, shouldn't I see Paris?" Matt challenged. "The Eiffel Tower, the Cathedral of Notre Dame, the Arc de Triomphe, Le Corbusier's houses—"

Carol's mind hurtled back through the years to that day in 1929—in a suite at the Hotel Savoy in London. Even now she could hear her mother screaming: *"Why can't we go to Paris for three or four days? We may never be so close again! I want to go, Joseph!"* But in just a little while their whole world changed.

Mama didn't think about Paris anymore, Carol was convinced. She'd traded in that dream for another life. Once every few weeks her mother wrote a brief letter, mostly reporting on the weather or the latest novel she'd read. Though it was clear there was no room in that secretive new life for her, Carol hoped that her mother had at last found contentment.

"Look, I've got to pack and be on the early morning train," Leo said briskly. "Let me get out of here."

There was a flurry of farewells, then Leo was gone and a gloom hung over the four he'd left behind. It was as though their close group was slowly disintegrating, Carol thought. Seth was down in Georgia—Jerry in Massachusetts—Leo headed for upstate New York.

"Hell, I'm pissed!" Greg punctured the silence that weighed them down. "I could be working in summer stock if I could break away from the job—"

"Summer stock was all cast weeks ago," Matt pointed out. "You could say you'll be around for the early casting that starts in August."

"I won't even make rounds," Greg said bitterly. "Not after what happened with my great supposed Broadway debut."

"That was almost two years ago," Sharon said. "When are you going to get off the hook?"

"I have to give money home every week," he reminded. "My brother has a wife and three kids and a business he's trying to keep afloat. He gives what he can, but it's not enough. My only way out is to land a long-term Hollywood contract. But I'm not the Hollywood type—"

"Neither is Paul Muni," Carol pointed out, "but look how great he's done in pictures."

"Muni went to Hollywood from the theater," Greg said. "And I don't mean the crappy theater I've done."

"Don't let Leo hear you call it that," Sharon said, laughing.

"I read somewhere that Paul Muni was thirty-three before he made a film," Carol said reverently. She never missed seeing a Muni film. "You're twenty-two."

"Last night the girl in the apartment upstairs got me in to see *Time Of Your Life*. She's an usher in the theater," Greg said. "It was great. It won both the Pulitzer Prize and the New York Drama Critics' Circle award. That's never happened until now."

For a moment the small living room was the stage set of the Saroyan play as Greg became first one character and then another. But Matt seemed restless tonight, she observed. He hated his job at the defense plant, but he was determined to stash away as much money as he could.

"Hey, this party needs some livening up," Matt said when Greg finished his vignettes from *Time Of Your Life*. "Where's the nearest liquor store?"

"Let's go find it." Greg's face brightened. "You gals throw the dishes in the sink."

"That's right," Sharon scolded good-humoredly. "Leave the dirty work to the women."

Together Carol and Sharon cleared the table, washed and dried the dishes. Sharon, too, seemed restless tonight, Carol decided. Even before Sharon admitted it, she suspected this was caused by Jerry's cavalier attitude.

"I thought Jerry was becoming a human being." Sharon collapsed into a corner of the faded green sofa that had served on occasions as Jerry's bed. "Lately he seemed to be more responsible. He's been so determined to knock out a really commercial three-act play.

No more arty crap, he said," she drawled. "So he takes off to house-sit and I get one postcard in over a month."

"Sharon, you're not going to change Jerry. He's only concerned with himself and his writing." Seth wasn't like that, Carol thought involuntarily. Nobody could be more dedicated to writing than Seth, yet he had room in his life for compassion and friendship. She was wary of Jerry's friendship. He used them for his own convenience.

"Jerry knows how to make me feel so great," Sharon said. "I can forgive a lot for that."

"When he's around," Carol said with unfamiliar brusqueness. "You'll find somebody else—who isn't always running off without a word until it suits him to wander back into the fold."

"The guys are back." Sharon rose from the sofa with an air of defiance. "I'll get the wineglasses. To hell with Jerry."

In moments the atmosphere in the living room had erupted into conviviality. Matt was swearing at the difficulty in uncorking a bot-tle of port. Carol masked her distaste for the wine and sipped from her glass, which Matt filled to the brim. Greg fiddled with the radio until he'd found a disk jockey program that featured swing.

Greg reached for Sharon and began to dance to the hard-driving beat of Artie Shaw and his band. Carol was relieved that Matt was satisfied to sprawl on the sofa with the bottle of port close by. Sharon had taught her to dance, but she still felt self-conscious and insecure.

"You know what I'd like to do when things settle down in Europe?" Matt said and continued before Carol could reply. "I'd like to finish up and get my degree in architecture here, then run over to Paris and take some classes at the Sorbonne. Wow, wouldn't that be something?"

"Terrific," Carol agreed, her face luminous as she envisioned Matt as another Le Corbusier or a Frank Lloyd Wright.

She listened contentedly while Matt expounded on his own theo-ries about the houses of the future. He was so bright and so elo-quent, she thought. He could do anything he wanted to do. She was enveloped in a hazy sense of well-being—warm and relaxed from the sweet port wine.

Subconsciously she was aware that the radio music had switched from Artie Shaw to Duke Ellington. Sharon and Greg were dancing with a new fervor to what Ellington called his "jungle music." She was disconcerted by the sensuous thrusts of their bodies, seeming to blend into one. Sharon's eyes were closed, her mouth faintly parted. Greg radiated a kind of ecstasy that made Carol feel herself a voyeur.

"It's getting late," she said self-consciously. "Sharon, we ought to be going home."

"Carol, relax." Sharon frowned at this intrusion. "We're both off tomorrow. What's the rush?"

"You tell her, baby," Greg murmured in sultry approval.

Matt reached for the bottle of wine, refilled his glass and Carol's. Without relinquishing their hold on each other, Sharon and Greg paused, pantomimed to Matt to refill their empty glasses, standing on a nearby end table. In a communal spirit the four lifted their glasses in a silent toast, then drank.

Now the music changed again. The haunting strains of "Deep Purple" drifted into the room.

"That's my kind of music," Matt said, singing along with the vocalist. "Come on, Carol—" In a burst of exuberance he rose to his feet, pulled her along with him.

"I'm not very good," she said uneasily, setting down her wineglass beside Matt's. She didn't want anything to derail this lovely, cozy feeling.

"Anything you do, I'm sure you do well," he murmured, drawing her into his arms.

To her astonishment Carol realized it was easy to follow Matt. He pulled her closer as he began again to sing along with the vocalist. This felt so good, she thought. Dancing with Matt, feeling loved and protected. She offered no resistance when Matt pulled her in so close that she was conscious of every angle of his body. She was caught up in emotions she had long denied. In a corner of her mind she realized this was not the way it had been with Marty.

A few moments later she saw the whispered conversation between Sharon and Greg. Then—hand in hand—Sharon's head on Greg's shoulder they walked into the tiny bedroom. While they paused in a passionate embrace, Greg reached to kick the door closed behind them.

The poignant lyrics and music of "Over The Rainbow" drifted into the living room. Matt took Carol's face between his hands and lowered his mouth to hers. He kissed her gently at first, allowing her time to accept and respond. Then he kissed her with an intensity that for a moment unnerved her. Her arms tightened about his shoulders as the urgency in her soared to match his own. She'd never felt this way before.

Her heart was pounding when Matt's mouth at last released hers. Holding her close, he managed to lean forward and switch off the lamp beside the sofa.

"The other lamp, too," she whispered.

His arm about her, Matt propelled her toward the lamp beside the lounge chair. He reached for the switch. Now the room was in total darkness. From inside the bedroom came muffled sounds of heated lovemaking.

"I want to make love to you so much," Matt murmured, his mouth at her ear while one hand found its way beneath her blouse. "I've waited a long time—"

"I've been afraid for so long," she said, light-headed from the wine. "But not anymore."

She closed her eyes and whimpered in startled pleasure as his hand fondled a breast. His pelvis pressed impatiently against her own, and she was suddenly impatient to welcome him within her. Remembering what Sharon had said about moments like this— *"There's no physical pleasure in the world that can compare to that moment. That moment when both of you come together inside you."*

She waited while his hands fumbled beneath her floral printed skirt. She felt the scrap of pink rayon jersey being coaxed over her hips, down long, slender thighs and legs. He swept her off her feet, and moments later she felt the wide, broad sofa beneath her.

"I waited a long time for you," he murmured heatedly.

But he wasn't waiting anymore. Oh yes, she thought in soaring exhilaration. Sharon was right. Nothing ever like this.

Later Matt crossed to a closet, pulled down a pillow, found a sheet. He lifted her head and slid the pillow beneath. Then he joined her on the sofa and pulled the sheet over them.

"Comfortable?" he asked, tossing a leg across her thighs.

"Yes," she whispered, inching against the back of the sofa to allow him more room.

She felt his warm breath against her cheek. She remembered what Sharon had said when she insisted she didn't want to get romantic about anybody: *"You'll change your mind when the right man comes along."* Oh yes, that was true.

Chapter Fifteen

Carol had always dreaded the oppressive, torpid heat of New York summers. But this summer was different. Not that the days and nights weren't miserably hot. She and Sharon still lay sleepless on sweltering nights, with the small oscillating fan above the chest of drawers doing little to ease their discomfort. Or they abandoned their cauldron of an apartment to seek relief along Riverside Drive. But on much of each weekend they were with Matt and Greg.

Sometimes the four of them went into an air-conditioned movie or to an air-conditioned cafeteria for dinner—mainly to cool off. Afterward they retreated to the corner of Eden they found in the Village apartment. On Saturday nights the two girls slept over.

Returning home to their own apartment on a sweltering Sunday evening in mid-August Sharon was candid about her relationship with Greg.

"Look, Greg and I know we're not in love—but we can have terrific sex together. That'll do until something better comes along."

"I never thought I could feel this way about any man," Carol confided with an air of recurrent astonishment. "It's like believing in fairy tales again."

"Matt's a real sexy guy," Sharon conceded. "Half the girls who come into the playhouse are dying to go out with him. But I wonder how much of it for you is because he's so wrapped up in architecture."

"Sharon, no!" Carol was startled. "He's—he's made me come fully alive."

"Have you ever told him about wanting to get a degree in architecture yourself someday?"

"That's way in the future," Carol hedged. "No, I haven't come right out and said it—but he must suspect."

"Men are dense," Sharon warned. "And Matt's all wrapped up in his own ambitions. I'll bet you he'd fall flat on his rump in shock if you told him."

"I'll tell him at the right moment," Carol said. "Maybe I'll start out being an apprentice in Matt's office." She felt euphoric at the prospect. "Did you know that Frank Lloyd Wright dropped out of college after two years? He worked as a draftsman in Louis Sullivan's office for several years, then started out on his own."

"That's why you've been asking about drafting courses," Sharon pounced. "Carol, you're not dropping out of school!"

"Of course not." Carol was shocked that Sharon could even think that she might. "But a course in drafting would be something to have for the future." Like Sharon and Seth she was an English major, though she felt defensive that she harbored no thoughts of pursuing a career that would utilize it. College, she'd always thought, should lead to a profession. Still, Papa always talked about getting a "good, rounded liberal arts education"—and that was what she was doing.

The following Thursday Carol left work to find Matt waiting outside the cafeteria for her.

"Hi!" Her face lit up at the sight of him. "You know I have classes tonight," she reminded.

"I figured we'd go over to that Chinese place and have a cheap, fast dinner before your first class." He reached to take her books from her, linked his other arm through hers.

"Is something wrong?" All at once she was anxious. It was rare for Matt to be off from work this early. He was putting in a lot of overtime.

"No, baby," he soothed. "It's just that I had a call from Leo late last night." Greg and Matt were smug about having a telephone of their own. Carol and Sharon depended upon the hall phone in their brownstone. "He wants us to come up for a weekend at the college and help him with the set for the last play of the season. He'd like to make a real splash. He says his crew of students can't ever come up with anything like we've done at the playhouse."

"Matt, how can we go up for the weekend?" Carol was bewildered. Even the train fare was a lot of money on her salary.

"Leo says the college will pay for our transportation. They'll put you up in the girls' dorm, and I'll stay with Leo. And they'll feed us," he said with a grin. "Hell, the college board figures they're getting a pair of professionals cheap. After all, we're set designers for Leo's playhouse in New York. You're not working next Saturday," he reminded. "We can take a train up Friday night, a train back on Sunday evening. And you don't have classes the following week so there's no sweat about homework. We'll work our tails off, but it'll be fun to spend a weekend out of the city with Leo."

Over their Chinese dinner they discussed the project. Matt was happy for a chance to leave the hot city behind them for a weekend. Carol was troubled by the realization that the college was barely forty miles west of Hamptonville. Still, she knew she'd make no effort to see her mother. She suspected that her mother deliberately stretched out the time between their letters.

When was the last time she'd heard from Mama? Almost two months ago. Mama took a long time answering because she herself wrote as soon as she received a letter. Mama wanted to put the old life behind her, Carol taunted herself. No room in the new one for a daughter. Still, she knew that next weekend she would be ever conscious that her mother was only an hour's drive away.

As Matt had promised, the weekend upstate was a joy.

"God, it was a pleasure to see a chunk of greenery beside Central Park or Riverside Drive," he told Leo while the two men and Carol waited for the train to pull into the tiny railway station.

"Wait till the cast shows up tomorrow morning and sees that set," Leo chortled. "They'll think they've died and gone to heaven. You two did a sensational job."

"Next week Broadway." Matt dropped an arm about Carol's shoulders. "This kid's got one great imagination. Who else could make a gorgeous bar out of a hunk of tin and a can of gold paint?"

Carol was pleased that they found seats in a half-empty car. She was tired yet happy—until Matt began to talk about the rumors from Washington regarding an expected announcement of a military draft.

"You heard Roosevelt's speech back on June tenth," Matt reminded. "He made it damn clear that this country would have 'the equipment and training equal to the task of every emergency defense.' That means compulsory military training. A draft."

"Matt, it seems so awful." Carol recoiled from the prospect. But she knew a draft bill had been brought before Congress last month, though thus far it had been highly controversial.

"Look, this country, Canada, and Cuba—plus a few South American countries—are the only ones without compulsory military training. Carol, our army ranks seventeenth among the armies of the world—we don't have the capacity of the Polish army when Hitler's troops marched in. If we're to have sufficient defense, we must increase our military forces. Believe me, I don't want to be drafted," he added ruefully. "And I suspect that only a chunk of us will be drafted—unless the situation in Europe gets worse."

"The Gallup poll said the public was fifty-fifty for conscription," Carol remembered, reluctant to concede this much.

"That was on June first," Matt said. "Those in favor rose to sixty-seven percent after France fell. A military draft is the first thing Congress will take up when it reconvenes next month."

"I don't want to think about it." Carol shivered despite the sultry August heat. War meant guns. "Why didn't somebody stop Hitler before he got this far?"

"I'm not a philosopher," Matt said somberly. "I don't have the answers." He slid an arm about her shoulders, pulled her close. "Do you have to go home tonight? I can kick Greg out of the bedroom."

"I have to go home." She managed a wistful smile. "I have to wash my hair and do my nails—to be ready for work tomorrow. I always do that on Sunday nights."

"Must you be a creature of habit?" he joshed.

"We'll make up for this Saturday night. I have no school all next week." Her eyes glowed with promise. She missed their night together, too, she thought with nostalgia. But she felt uncomfortable at the prospect of going home with Matt and throwing Greg out of the bedroom. It was different, somehow, on Saturdays—when Greg and Sharon disappeared into the bedroom and the living room belonged to Matt and herself.

"I'll try to hang on," he said tenderly. "I wait all week for Saturday night."

While Carol sat on the edge of her bed and towel-dried her hair, Sharon reported on her weekend.

"I had to go in to work yesterday, you remember. There was this special meeting with an important new client who wants to move into radio. At last, it looks as though I'm making some headway." She radiated triumph. "The big boy's secretary called in sick; he said she'd probably taken off for Fire Island. So they brought me in to retype the revised report. And I found a glaring error his secretary missed. So, guess who's up for a promotion—in their new radio department? All at once they discovered the receptionist has a brain."

"Sharon, that's wonderful! When will you know?"

"Some time next week. Great, huh?"

The following evening Carol went straight to classes from work. Sharon had no class on Monday evenings. While Carol unlocked the apartment door on her return from school, she heard Sharon's joyous burst of news.

"I got the new job, Carol! I'm now a special assistant to the old boy—in the agency's just formed radio department. I'm getting a seven-dollar-a-week raise!"

"Oh Sharon, that's wonderful!" Carol's smile was dazzling as she closed the door behind her.

"And that's not all," Sharon said. "I've got an interview for you for the receptionist's job. It's for ten A.M. tomorrow morning."

"How can I go? I'll be at work, Sharon—"

"I'll call in sick for you. You've got a sore throat," Sharon improvised. "But you'll have a lot of hot tea and honey, then come in around noon. So somebody will fill in for you for three and a half hours."

"Do I dare?" She was torn between eager hope and guilt.

"You dare." Sharon was firm. "It's a raise plus you can squeeze in study time during the day when things are slow. I do."

"I'll bank the extra money." Carol glowed. "I could start saving for architectural school." They'd both agreed that—though their studio apartment was tiny even for one—they'd hang on to a low rent even if raises came their way.

Well before 10 A.M. Carol sat tense and apprehensive as she waited to be interviewed. Yet ten minutes after she was seated in the personnel office she was hired. The agency understood that she had to give two weeks' notice to the cafeteria, she realized with relief. She walked out of the office in an aura of joyous disbelief. All at once her dream of going to architectural school was more than a fairy tale. She'd open a savings account. It couldn't happen right away, she conceded—but her dream would become a reality.

Carol was happy when Leo reopened the playhouse a week later. While she repeatedly made it clear to Leo and the others that she harbored no passionate desire to become a stage set designer, she was eager for weekends revolving around the playhouse activities.

"I tell you, I was impressed when we opened the last play of the season and the set got a hand when the curtain went up," Leo said ebulliently while the group from the playhouse gathered around the shoved-together tables in a nearby cafeteria. Tonight Sharon wasn't

with them. She'd gone to a family affair on this Saturday evening
and would be sleeping over at her parents' apartment. "It was awesome," Leo pursued. "The curtain went up. Nobody's on stage. And
there's this burst of applause! For the set."

"Wow!" A new would-be actress in the company turned to Carol
with wide-eyed admiration. "I'll bet you were thrilled."

"I wasn't there," Carol told her and exchanged a smile with
Matt. "We just went up to do the set."

Now the conversation turned to the new plays in rehearsal—a
curtain-raiser by Seth and two one-acts by newcomers. Leo was enthralled by the curtain-raiser, less enthusiastic about the two one-
actors.

"I wish Seth would settle down and write something that runs
more than ten minutes," Leo said in frustration. "And where the
hell is Jerry?"

"Probably still house-sitting in Boston," Carol surmised. "Nobody's heard a word."

It was almost 3 A.M. when they left the cafeteria to go their separate way. Carol intercepted a whispered exchange between Matt
and Greg. She guessed Matt had told Greg he was taking her home
and would probably stay over. They'd never spent a night together
without Sharon and Greg in the next room, she remembered. It
would be special.

Matt took her hand protectively in his as they pushed past a
rowdy cluster at the approach to the IRT.

"We'll pick up the Sunday *Times* at the other end," he told Carol.

The subway train was crowded, even at this hour. Young people
winding up a Saturday night on the town, defense plant workers
homeward bound after extended night shifts. Matt kept a protective arm around her waist as they clung to a pole until the train
pulled into the West 72nd Street station.

Matt bought the Sunday *Times*, and hand in hand they sauntered south to 71st Street and the brownstone where Carol lived.
This felt so right, she thought, coming home with Matt. He'd told
her that he'd brought along his toothbrush and shaving gear. In-
stinctively she knew this was not the first such occasion for Matt,
yet she refused to be upset by the knowledge.

"You've got coffee?" he asked while he unlocked the downstairs
door. "I can't read the Sunday *Times* without coffee."

But they spent little time with the newspaper once they were in the small studio. Matt drank half a cup of coffee, skimmed the first section of the newspaper, then silently reached for Carol.

"This feels so good," he murmured, echoing her own thoughts. "Just the two of us, and the whole night is ours."

After swaying with her for a few moments, his mouth buried against her throat, Matt left her to switch off the lamps, shoved the two windows open to their fullest, and returned. Somewhere across the court—from an all-night disk jockey program—came the plaintive strains of "Careless," a current hit song.

In the darkness Matt undressed her in the slow, seductive manner she relished, then himself. They lay together on one narrow bed and made love, dozed, then made love again. To Carol it was ever a miracle that they could find such pleasure in each other. Then, arms and legs entwined despite the heat of this September night, they slept.

Carol awoke with the instant realization that Matt was awake and showering. All at once self-conscious she reached to pull up the sheet to cover her nakedness. Suppose she hadn't met Sharon that day in the employment agency? None of this would have happened. How your whole life could hinge on one tiny incident like that!

"You snored," Matt kidded as he stepped out of the minuscule shower. "Do you know it's almost noon?" He was rubbing himself dry with one of the threadbare towels supplied by their landlord.

"I don't snore," she protested.

"No," he conceded. "You look so beautiful, lying there like that—" His eyes mentally stripped away the sheet.

"I'll shower and put up coffee." Yet she saw his arousal, that matched her own.

"Later," he said, dropping the towel. "This is a treat I can't resist."

Matt opened the refrigerator door and inspected its contents while Carol dressed.

"You've got eggs and milk. Put up the coffee while I run up to Zabar's for bagels and lox." He grinned. "I feel rich after this week's paycheck."

"Me, too," Carol said, enveloped in happiness. "At least, I will when I see my first paycheck from the ad agency."

"Leo's right, you know." All at once he was serious. "You've got a real talent for set designing. You ought to take some courses."

"That's not what I want—" She felt exhilarated by this sudden admission.

"What do you want?" His eyes were gently teasing.

"I want to get a degree in architecture." Her heart was pounding, but she managed a smile.

"You've got to be kidding?" He stared at her in disbelief. "Architecture is a man's field."

"Why?" she challenged. "Why must professions be divided—some for men, others for women?"

"It's always been that way. Do you know how few women architects there are in this country?"

"I know there *are* women architects." She was shaken by his reaction. "I've read about them in *Architectural Record.*"

"How many women?" Matt challenged. "A few hundred in the whole country. The odds against them are insane."

"Architectural schools are open to women, Matt. They wouldn't be if there were no women architects." She refused to retreat, though she was trembling. *Why couldn't Matt understand?*

"Some architectural schools are open to women because they need the fancy tuition fees," he said bluntly. "Honey—" He reached to pull her close with an indulgent smile. "I'll build the houses, and you'll decorate them. We'll be a team. We'll set up our own business. You know I want no part of a big firm—I want to be my own boss. We'll be Harris and Simon. How does that sound?"

"Great—" But only if it was Harris & Simon, Architects, she told herself in silent defiance.

"By then, it'll be Harris and Harris," he corrected himself. His smile was brilliant. Carol felt a rush of joyous comprehension. "We've got a while to go," he conceded tenderly, "but we're young. We can wait." Now he slapped her on the rump. "Put up the coffee. I have a rendezvous with Zabar's."

Carol went to the tiny kitchen alcove to put up the coffee—hearing Matt's voice echoing in her mind. *"By then it'll be Harris and Harris."* But not Harris & Harris, Architect and Decorator. Harris & Harris, Architects. Why couldn't she be Matt's wife and an architect?

Was she asking too much of life? Must she make a choice?

Chapter Sixteen

Carol walked beside Sharon along the Hudson River promenade that parallels Riverside Drive. The faint breeze from the river was pleasant on this late Sunday afternoon. Matt had left earlier to spend some time with his Canadian buddy, who was finally heading home—"one step ahead of the draft." Carol had just told Sharon about Matt's oblique proposal.

"He didn't ask you if you went along with this?" Sharon was indignant.

"Matt knows how I feel about him," Carol said defensively.

"But he should have asked," Sharon said.

"We can't get married for a long time. We're not even officially engaged." She paused for a moment, recalling her engagement to Marty—of two weeks' duration. But this was as different as night and day. She adored Matt. "You know Matt—he's not the conventional type. I didn't expect him to fall to his knees and hold out an engagement ring."

"What kind of a guy takes it for granted the girl wants to marry him?" Sharon flared.

"A guy who knows the girl loves him."

"But he thinks it's nutty for you to talk about going to architectural school!" Sharon's eyes were accusing. "Because you're a woman. How are you going to handle that?"

"I don't know. Anyhow, I don't have to deal with it yet." The prospect of losing Matt was unbearable.

"When I see a wedding ring on your finger and a marriage license in your purse, then I'll believe," Sharon said with candor. "I can't imagine you giving up on architecture. Not the way you feel about it. Why the hell do men think they can decide what jobs are open to women and which are not? We can be nurses, teachers, salesclerks, secretaries, beauticians—but not much else."

"I just have to make Matt understand how important it is to me." Carol struggled for confidence. "I can be an architect. *I know I can.*"

* * *

On September 16th the first United States peacetime draft became law. Carol and Sharon sprawled morosely across their narrow beds and listened to the late news on the radio—dominated tonight by the reaction of the American public to the landmark act of Congress.

"It's only for one year," Sharon said, switching off the radio.

"Come on, Sharon, you don't believe that," Carol reproached. "Not the way the war's going in Europe. Matt, Seth, Greg, Jerry—even Leo—will have to register." They might have to fight, she thought in soaring alarm.

"My brother-in-law won't have to worry," Sharon said. "Though Bev called me at the office this morning, and she was panicky. I finally convinced her that husbands and fathers would be exempt." She paused. "At least, for now."

It seemed to Carol that there was a new urgency in every waking moment. Each day the front pages of the newspapers carried new photos of the devastation wrought on London by Nazi bombers. Across the United States draft boards were being set up with haste. On October 16th more than 16 million American young men registered for the draft.

On October 29th the first numbers were drawn. Meeting Carol for coffee when she emerged from night school, Matt tried to be encouraging.

"Remember, baby, over sixteen million guys registered. How many draftees will be picked out of that number? The odds are in my favor."

"You work in a defense plant." Carol struggled to appear casual. "They won't draft defense workers—" They wouldn't draft married men, either, she thought subconsciously. Everybody knew how the Marriage License Bureau had been deluged since the draft bill was passed. But pride kept her from mentioning this.

Later that evening—while they prepared for bed—Carol and Sharon talked about the draft. She sensed a certain hostility in Sharon now toward Matt because of his high-handed attitude about women in unconventional careers. She herself tried not to be hurt. She rationalized that Matt thought he was right—that she'd be butting her head against a stone wall. Now she struggled to make Sharon understand Matt's thinking.

"Sure, Matt's a great guy," Sharon acknowledged. "And he's very sexy. Almost every girl who comes into the playhouse gives him those dreamy looks. But men are nuts!" she said explosively. "They don't want to understand that women can do a lot of things that *they've* decided we can't do."

"It's so crazy." Carol sighed. "And frustrating—"

"God, you'd think we were threatening their manhood. And there're a lot of things that men can do that they think is beneath them. Take my brother-in-law." Sharon clucked in derision. "Do you think he'd ever change a diaper or take the kid out in his stroller? That's women's work."

"Men don't feel like that in England," Carol said. "Women are working in the defense factories. They're driving ambulances. They're even part of the Royal Navy."

"I wonder where Jerry is." Sharon was somber. "I thought he'd be back once the summer was over."

"Forget Jerry," Carol said, but her eyes were sympathetic. "I thought he'd been replaced by Greg."

"Greg's fun, I like him an awful lot. But Jerry's something else. You know, my first love—" She turned down the sheet and climbed into bed. "Oh, enough about men. Let's go to sleep."

On November 5th American voters went to the polls and reelected Franklin Roosevelt for an unprecedented third term. Industry was mobilizing for war, though the Gallup Poll showed—in December of 1940—that 40 percent of Americans wanted the country to stay out of the war. Despite all the jobs coming up, over 9 million men were without work. Carol complained that published figures always referred to "unemployed men"—though in the last ten years, statistics indicated, the number of working women had increased by half a million. And some of these were married women. She was outraged by the popular conception that married women spent their time in the kitchen or listening to "Vic and Sade" and other popular soap operas.

Seth had hoped to come up to New York during the winter break at Emory, but as the time approached he wrote Carol that this was impossible. His father had lost two clerks to the war plants—capable of paying higher salaries. He couldn't take off even four or five days at this point.

"At least, I know I'll graduate in May. God, I can't wait to get back to New York. I feel as though I've been in exile for a year and a half."

Carol was upset that she couldn't bring about a change in Matt's attitude about women architects. She didn't care about statistics. Women—admittedly very few—were working as architects. She could do it, too.

Each time she ventured to bring this up again, he made a ribald crack. Like last night:

"Face it, Carol. The only way a woman goes up the ladder in an architectural office is by climbing between the sheets with the boss."

Seth wouldn't feel that way, Carol told herself—nursing her hurt—and sat down to write him. She received a reply by return mail.

"I can't say I'm really surprised that you want to go on for an architectural degree. I suspected it. You kept saying you didn't want to be a set designer, but you were always lapping up everything Matt said about building houses—and there was never a time we all were together that he didn't talk about that. I think it's great that you know what you want to do with your life. Most people don't know. And you'll make it—I'm sure of that, Carol."

Tears of gratitude flooded her eyes when she read Seth's letter. She read it again and again—cherishing his understanding. It didn't matter to him that she would be a woman in a field that had long been dominated by men. Seth thought she had a place there. She'd tried so hard to convince herself that Matt was worried she'd waste years of her life in studying for a profession that had no place for her—but his attitude was upsetting.

As always she shared Seth's letter with Sharon. She sat on a corner of her bed—feet tucked beneath her—and watched while Sharon read Seth's latest letter.

"That's Seth," Sharon said gently, returning the letter to Carol. "But remember, he's our own age. He thinks like us. Matt's older."

"Eight years?" Carol challenged.

"Matt's been through a lot in those eight years." Sharon's smile was wry. "He's lived all over the country, known so many people. He's set in his thinking."

"Does he have to think like the last century?" Carol asked defiantly. "Why can't women design houses? They have a much better feeling for that than men. They can bring something special to architecture."

"What's this going to do to you and Matt?" Sharon asked after a moment.

"I can't fight him. I just can't. But I can't give up my life."

"You're obsessed with Matt. It'll wear off—but not what you feel for architecture. Anyhow, you've got years of school ahead of you."

On New Year's Eve, 1941, Leo gave his traditional party at the playhouse. But this year both Seth and Jerry were absent.

"I don't know how much longer Leo can keep the playhouse going," Greg said quietly to Carol and Sharon as the three of them stood aside from the others at one corner of the stage. "The cast turnover is getting lousy."

"Swing shift defense jobs or the draft." Sharon sighed. "It's not going to get better."

"Leo looks harried," Carol sympathized. "He says if he's drafted, he'll ask to get into Special Services—but that means he'll have to start all over again once he's served his year."

"That business of one year is a crock," Greg said, reiterating Carol's own thought. "Once we're drafted, we'll be in for the duration—and God knows how long that'll be."

"Just keep your fingers crossed that you're not drafted—nor Leo." Carol gazed across the stage to where two couples had begun to lindy to a Tommy Dorsey record. The two girls were playing at theater, she guessed, both from some rich Connecticut suburb. Neither realized the two boys preferred each other to themselves. Leo said they were 4-F—"*I don't have to worry about losing those two to the draft.*"

"What happened to Matt?" Greg asked. "He never misses a party."

"He's working late," Carol told him. "He said he'd be here well before midnight, though." If Matt had stayed in school, she thought in frustration, he'd have been sure of a draft deferment.

"God, he's piling up cash." Greg chuckled. "When I threatened to go into a defense plant, my brother gave me a raise. He wasn't happy about it—but he needs me." He reached into a pocket and pulled out a cigarette.

"Hey, stop with the cigarettes," Sharon ordered. "You read that article Carol ripped out of an old *New York Times* she found in the prop room. About how this guy—over a year ago—told some Cancer Congress that he'd produced cancer in mice by painting them with tobacco tars."

"Bullshit," Greg dismissed this and dropped an arm around Sharon. "I like you better when you're not playing the Intellectual."

Seth sprawled on his twin bed in the room he shared with Harvey and listened to the convivial sounds that drifted up to the second-floor bedroom. He was grateful that Harvey was sleeping over at a friend's house on this New Year's Eve. He wouldn't have to listen to Harvey's constant yakking.

He knew Mom was upset that he insisted on remaining in his room while she welcomed a few friends over to celebrate. She didn't believe him when he said he was dying to finish reading the new Hemingway—*For Whom The Bells Toll*—which he'd got from the library but hadn't as yet even opened. She couldn't understand why he wanted to be alone tonight.

His mind was crowded with memories of last New Year's Eve. God, he'd blown his chances with Carol that night. He felt a surge of heat as he remembered those moments—relived endless times in memory—when he'd said, *"I want to see 1950 in with you."* Her eyes had told him she shared his feelings—and then he'd stupidly added, "I mean, I hope we'll all see it in together—"

Why had he spoiled those moments? So scared he might lose her friendship—that she wasn't ready, after her awful marriage, for that kind of closeness. And then he'd jumped to the conclusion—just because Matt was taking her to some party—that there was something going between Matt and her. *That was dumb.*

A tender smile lifted the corners of his mouth as he remembered her last letter. How many other people knew she wanted to be an architect? She must have told Matt—he practically wore a sign around his neck that said *"I'm* going to be an architect." What was Matt's reaction? Instinct told him Matt wasn't impressed—his male ego would be hurt because Carol was trying to do what he meant to do.

Seth heard the doorbell downstairs, the sounds of new arrivals. From the heavy German accents he surmised they were Mr. and Mrs. Kahn and their sixteen-year-old daughter Clara—Bellevue's one refugee family—who'd arrived early last year. Mr. Kahn had been a prominent German lawyer until Hitler came into power. Then he was forbidden to practice law, and Clara was dismissed from her school. Now he worked as a salesman in a secondhand store. Clara was struggling to cope with classes conducted in a new language. Grandma—who'd left Berlin as a little girl—was working with the local Jewish community to raise funds to help other refugee families.

"Sophie, don't worry about that ugly business with the Ku Klux Klan!" His mother's voice rose eloquently from below. "This isn't Hitler's Germany."

"It's not good," Seth heard his father say. "It's always a small band of ugly people who get all the attention. Most Atlantans—and those in surrounding towns like ours—were horrified when that colored barber was flogged to death."

"The KKK hate Negroes, Jews, and Catholics," Mr. Kahn said somberly. "How can we not be concerned?"

"Otto, this isn't Germany," Seth's grandmother said firmly. "You'll never see a *Kristallnacht* in this country."

"But I read in the newspapers that the Ku Klux Klan are having their convention right in Atlanta in June," Otto began. "Who knows what—"

"Papa, you make Mama nervous when you talk like that," Clara broke in. "Mrs. Walden, the flowers there on the mantel are beautiful. However do you have roses this late in the year?"

He'd never thought much about being Jewish, Seth pondered. Of course, he'd grown up hearing about the lynching of Leo Frank— who was supposed to have killed a young Christian girl in Atlanta. Many people were convinced he was innocent—even the governor had tried to save him. But that had been another time. History.

His friends here in Bellevue had occasionally been Jewish—he never chose by religious faith. He stayed out of school on Rosh Hashanah and Yom Kippur. He'd had his bar mitzvah because that was expected of him, and Harvey would have his bar mitzvah this coming year. But even at the playhouse—where most of those close to him were Jewish—he hadn't thought about it. But now—reading the insanity in Germany, hearing the Kahns talk about what happened to them in Berlin—he was very aware of it.

At intervals Mom tried to bring Clara Kahn and him together. He liked Clara—she was pretty, bright, and eager to be friends. But no girl except Carol could ever be special for him. After graduation he'd go back to New York. He'd tell Carol how he felt about her. Hope lifted his spirits. Let him be with Carol on next New Year's Eve.

* * *

Early in the new year—with Leo running into monumental problems to keep the playhouse going—Greg announced at a get-together in the apartment he shared with Matt that he was going to take off one day a week to make theater rounds.

"What does your brother say?" Sharon asked.

"I arranged to have Wednesdays off because he needs me to work on the weekends." Greg grinned in triumph. "He doesn't know how I mean to spend it."

"And with business the way it is," Carol comprehended, "even if he fires you, you can always pick up another job." It was unbelievable, she thought, how suddenly jobs were out there for the taking.

"Right on the head," Greg concurred. "I have enough stashed away to give money home during a rehearsal period. If the play runs, I'll be making more than Chuck pays me—even at Equity minimum. It's now or never for me."

"Do it," Leo encouraged. "I don't know how long I'll be able to keep the playhouse running." He chuckled. "And who knows when I'll be drafted?"

Three weeks later—after an aborted rehearsal, with two cast members not showing up—Greg announced that he'd snared a part in a new Broadway production. The atmosphere in the playhouse was electric.

"Quiet," Greg ordered exuberantly when the others burst into a flood of questions. "It's not a big part. I'll be onstage barely five minutes. But oh, is it showy! Of course, they told me they have to read a few more guys who have appointments set up by their agents—but the part is mine! Sorry, Leo, you'll have to replace me—"

"Hey, it's about time you had a break!" Sharon leaned forward to kiss him. "Nobody deserves it more than you."

Four evenings later—with Greg scheduled to start rehearsals in two weeks—Greg arrived at the playhouse with a grim expression that warned of trouble. Had he been dropped from the play? Carol asked herself anxiously. Was there somebody with pull that had pushed him out?

"I'm drafted," Greg announced. His eyes betrayed his anguish. "You haven't been home to get the mail yet," he told Matt, "or you would have seen it."

"Oh hell!" Sharon exchanged a glance with Carol.

"Can you get an extension?" Carol asked. "I mean, because of the play—"

"Are you kidding?" Greg's smile was derisive. " 'Greeting.' it begins. 'Having submitted yourself to a local board blah-blah-blah', and then it tells you to inform your employer of this notice. So he can replace you if you're accepted. No danger I won't be accepted," he said bitterly, "but isn't this a bitch of a time for it to arrive?"

"The timing is awful." Carol remembered how Seth had longed to go to Spain three years ago to fight against fascism. He wouldn't do something crazy like enlisting, would he? "But being drafted doesn't mean it's the end of the road for you, Greg. So you'll have to spend a year in uniform." She was struggling against the terror that spiraled in her, at the devastating image of Greg—or Seth and the others—with a gun in hand. "You'll pick up again where you left off. You'll—"

"It's eighteen months now," Matt broke in. "That's what it says in small print. But it's a matter of time before this country gets suckered into the war." Carol felt his rebellion at the prospect of having his life interrupted. "In six months every man in the right age group could be in uniform and waiting to be shipped overseas to fight."

"Of course, you could play the fairy bit and be rejected," Sharon said lightly. "Or maybe the psycho scene—"

But they all knew Greg would not do this. The war had reached out to touch them personally, Carol thought in anguish. Her eyes moved from Greg, to Matt, to Leo. She thought about Seth, down in Georgia, and Jerry—maybe still house-sitting near Boston. How soon before they were all in uniform? How soon before they'd be over in Europe—fighting the Nazis?

Chapter Seventeen

Carol wasn't surprised that Matt was making no effort to find another roommate. With his bulging pay envelope he felt he could afford the luxury of keeping the apartment for himself. He'd warily suggested that Carol move in with him but had backtracked at her shocked reproach.

"Doesn't he understand that all he has to do is make that short trip to City Hall with you, and you'll move in with him?" Sharon challenged on a balmy April night while they'd walked across Central Park from night classes at Hunter.

"He doesn't want to tie himself down until he has his degree," Carol said self-consciously.

"Which will be when? He isn't even taking classes now. He could be drafted any day." Sharon was skeptical about Matt's intentions.

"I can't push him, Sharon." She couldn't conceive of life without Matt. She couldn't afford to push him—and perhaps lose him.

"You are obsessed by Matt." Sharon was often blunt, but Carol understood she was sympathetic. "And he's still throwing that crap about you taking classes in set design when you have enough money in the bank. Or maybe becoming an interior decorator. He nearly fell on his face when I told him Bev had just landed a job in an aircraft plant—a woman doing a man's work. Thank God for Mom—she'll take care of the kid."

"I wonder when we'll hear from Greg again." Carol deliberately rechanneled the conversation. He was in boot camp in Texas.

"They don't give them much time to write," Sharon drawled. "But he sure bitched about his GI haircut."

Carol found a letter from Seth waiting on the hall table at their brownstone.

"Open it," Sharon ordered exuberantly. "With graduation only a few weeks off maybe he's set to come back."

"Who can read in these dim lights? Wait till we get upstairs." But she was always delighted to receive a letter from Seth.

In their apartment Carol dropped to the edge of one of the pair of simulated studio couches and began to read Seth's letter aloud while Sharon put up water for tea.

"I'm working myself up to tell my folks that I'm going back to New York," Seth had written. *"Mom's still pushing me to take some education courses this summer and then apply for a teaching job here in Bellevue, since male teachers might be drafted. I've tried to explain that I'm registered for the draft, too. The Board of Ed won't be hiring men teachers. Anyhow, that's the last job I want. Of course, I'll take anything in New York. Just so I can have evenings and weekends to write. God, plenty of other playwrights have gone that route!"*

"He won't have any trouble getting a job," Sharon predicted. "He's young, bright, and he'll soon be clutching his college degree. Maybe he can move in with Matt."

"I don't think Matt wants a roommate anymore." Carol felt strangely uncomfortable at the prospect of Seth moving into Matt's apartment. She'd always felt a little self-conscious at being with Matt while Greg and Sharon were in the next room—but without understanding why, she recoiled from staying over with Matt while Seth would be relegated to the living room sofa. "He says he's too old for roommates."

"Unless her name is Carol," Sharon derided good-humoredly.

Semi-awake on this humid early May Sunday, Seth turned over on his stomach and tried to block out the sound of the phone ringing in the living room. He pried his eyes open reluctantly to view the clock. It was past 1 P.M. Wow, he'd slept late! Now his eyes rested on the other bed. It was in disarray. Harvey was off to play baseball.

The phone had stopped ringing. Grandma had picked it up, Seth assumed. Mom and Dad had gone to the Feinberg kid's bar mitzvah, he remembered. He'd begged off; he'd had finals all week and worked at the shop for twelve hours yesterday.

"Oh my God!" His grandmother's voice was agitated. "How are they?" Seth was suddenly fully awake, his heart pounding. He thrust aside the perspiration-dampened sheet and rushed into the hall. "Yes, we'll be there right away!"

"Grandma?" Seth was hurrying down the stairs. "What's happened?"

"They're going to be all right." She tried to sound convincing. "But some drunken driver slammed into the car. Mom and Dad are in the hospital. How will we get over there?" All at once she was panicky. "The bus will take forever."

"Call a taxi, Grandma," Seth said with enforced calm. "No, I'll go next door and ask the Martins if I can borrow their car. They'll understand."

"What was a drunken driver doing on the road at this hour on a Sunday?" his grandmother demanded indignantly. "That's crazy."

"I'll be dressed in five minutes," Seth said, bolting for the stairs again. "Grandma, you call the Martins. They know I'm a good driver; they won't mind lending us the car."

In fifteen minutes Seth was pulling into the parking area behind Memorial Hospital. His grandmother was pale and shaken but refusing to admit to alarm. That was Grandma, he thought tenderly as they walked hand in hand to the hospital entrance. Everybody expected her to be strong.

They were sent up to the third floor reception room—washed in sunlight—to wait for word.

"We'll sit here." Leah Walden settled herself at a corner of the chintz-covered sofa and gestured to Seth to join her. Only her pallor betrayed her inner turmoil. "They're going to be all right," she said with a show of conviction.

"Sure, Grandma." Seth managed a smile. The whole world lived a second away from tragedy, he thought in pain.

One moment Mom and Dad must have been talking about the bar mitzvah—and the next moment a drunken idiot had plowed into them, causing what havoc? *Let them be all right.* All at once he felt guilty at having stalled on telling them about going back to New York.

"Seth, there's Mom!" Leah was on her feet as a nurse and an orderly appeared pushing a gurney and heading down the hallway flanked by patients' rooms.

Seth and his grandmother hurried across the reception area.

"We're her family," Leah said breathlessly, her eyes clinging to her daughter-in-law's face. "We—"

"She's doing fine," the nurse said gently. "You can see her in a few minutes. She's sedated, but she's suffered only minor cuts and bruises. I'll call you."

"My son?" Leah asked. "Eli Walden—"

"The doctors are with him. They'll talk with you in a while." The nurse smiled reassuringly and indicated to the orderly to proceed with the gurney.

"Just a few cuts and bruises." Seth knew his grandmother meant to reassure him. "She'll be home in a couple of days. Thank God, it wasn't serious." But her eyes told him her anxiety about his father was soaring.

"Sit down, Grandma," Seth urged, prodding her toward the sofa. "It'll take them a while to get Mom settled in her room." *What about Dad?*

In a few minutes the nurse appeared at the head of the hall and gestured to them.

"We can see Mom now—" Seth leapt to his feet. His grandmother was instantly beside him.

They walked into the hospital room assigned to Seth's mother. She lay in the bed by the window—the other bed was empty.

"Hannah—" Leah leaned solicitously over her daughter-in-law. "They told us you have only minor cuts and bruises."

Hannah's face lighted as her eyes rested on her visitors.

"It was so frightening," she whispered. "The car was on the wrong side of the road, coming toward us. Dad couldn't do anything—"

"A drunken driver," Seth said. He felt shaken at the sight of his mother, her forehead and one jaw bandaged, a bruise at her throat.

"How's Dad?" his mother asked in sudden agitation. "What about Eli?" she demanded of her mother-in-law.

"He'll be all right." His grandmother contrived the calm that had comforted the family in every crisis in their lives. "They're doing some tests or X-rays to make sure. In a few days you'll forget all about this."

"I want to know about Eli," Hannah said forcefully, though Seth sensed that she had to struggle against sedation.

"Seth, go out in the reception room and see what you can find out," his grandmother ordered. "I'll stay here with Mom—"

From his grandmother's pantomime he understood she expected his mother to drift off to sleep. Already, he noted, her eyelids were drooping. All right, he'd go out and wait for word from the doctors.

Much later Seth and his grandmother spoke with one of the hospital doctors. His father was suffering from a fractured hip, along with some cuts and bruises.

"It was a clean fracture—we don't foresee any complications," the doctor told them. "All he requires now is bed rest while that hip heals. It'll be a long-term recovery," he warned with a compassionate smile, "but he'll be as good as new."

He couldn't leave for New York after graduation, Seth realized with shock. He'd have to take over running the shop until Dad was on his feet again. It was hard as hell to get good help these days. Mom couldn't run the shop alone.

How long would it be? A fractured hip—that meant months of recuperation and therapy. No way he could go to New York until Dad was back behind the counter at the shop. *If they hadn't gone to that damn bar mitzvah, this wouldn't have happened.* And immediately he felt guilty that he could think about himself at a moment such as this.

This summer Leo was not going up to the college in upstate New York. The course he'd given for the past two summers had been canceled. There would be no summer theater on campus. Now he focused on holding on to the playhouse.

Early in July—when Leo was frenziedly trying to bring together a children's play, scheduled to open the following weekend—Jerry sauntered into the playhouse as though he'd been away for a few days. Startled—and with an anxious glance at Sharon, who was prompting—Carol gestured for silence. When Leo was directing, nobody talked. Matt waved a hand in greeting.

When Leo had dismissed the cast, Jerry announced with triumph that he'd finally finished a three-act play.

"Let's go out to an air-conditioned place for coffee, and you'll tell us about it," Leo said. "Is it good?"

"I think it's damned commercial," Jerry said confidently.

"Meaning a comedy?" Sharon asked. Carol knew she was determined to appear casual.

"A comedy mystery," Jerry drawled. "Audiences don't want to see heavy drama these days. Leo, what about a tryout at the college?"

"You notice I'm still in town," Leo pointed out dryly. "No college job this summer."

"When did you get back?" Matt asked Jerry while Leo closed up the rear and flipped out the lights.

"About three hours ago. My gear is checked at Penn Station."

He gazed reflectively at Matt. "Can I bunk at your place for the night?"

"For the night," Matt said.

"What's with Greg and Seth?" Jerry asked as the five of them headed toward the air-conditioned cafeteria they favored these days.

"Greg's in the army," Sharon told him. "He's stationed down in Texas. Seth graduated from Emory. He couldn't come up to New York as he'd planned because his father was in a car accident and fractured a hip. He can't leave for a while."

"That's a bum rap," Jerry sympathized. "Is he writing?"

"No time," Carol said. "Nothing since that last curtain-raiser."

Over coffee and Danish Jerry talked exuberantly about his play.

"Hell, there's a great part in it for Greg." Jerry sighed. "I wrote it for him."

"I don't know how much longer I can hang on to the playhouse," Leo told Jerry. "It's getting harder by the day to get actors. They're pouring into the defense plants—working long, crazy hours. Or they're getting drafted."

"None of us here at this table—except you two gals," Matt said with a grin, "knows when he'll be sucked into the draft. We can't plan one day ahead."

"Like FDR said on the radio, we're living in an unlimited national emergency." Jerry shrugged. "What else could it be with the Nazi armies mowing down everything in their paths?"

Isolationists were running into much opposition. This had been intensified when the Nazis invaded the USSR. on June 22nd. Winston Churchill offered Russia full British support. He said, *"I have only one purpose: the destruction of Hitler."* And word had just come through that American troops were to relieve the British in Iceland, which meant American destroyers would be escorting convoys as far as Iceland, where the British navy would take over. And if attacked, the American destroyers would surely have to defend themselves, Carol thought uneasily.

Carol was surprised when—before the evening was over—Matt agreed to share the apartment with Jerry.

"Why not?" he told Carol on a late Saturday afternoon when they were shopping for dinner at the apartment. Leo was off to Long Beach with one of his "ladies of a certain age"—in hopes of acquiring the July rent for the playhouse, which was still unpaid.

Matt and Carol, Jerry and Sharon would have dinner, go to a 42nd Street movie, and then come back to the apartment. "Jerry's no problem, and I can stash away more money. I want to be able to finish off school without having to hang on to a job at the same time."

"That sounds great." Only to Sharon—who shared the situation—did Carol ever confess that at moments she was drained by the effort to keep up a heavy night school program along with a full-time job. "Do you figure you can handle that soon?" Matt bragged about the way he was banking chunks of his earnings every week.

"Honey, in the middle of a war?" he clucked. "You know I could be drafted tomorrow."

"Matt, don't say that." Her heart was suddenly pounding as she visualized Matt in uniform. Most thinking people said it was a matter of time before this country would be fighting, too. But in truth, Carol told herself in a rare moment of cynicism, most people—except those affected by the draft—didn't seem to think about the war at all. Most were concerned with personal problems. Could they buy one of the new cars pouring out of Detroit like spaghetti? Over 5,000,000 last year and this year should be as good. They were piling up overtime on the job, running to the movies every Saturday night, spending money—Carol thought—as though it was picked from a window box every morning.

"Baby, nothing's going to happen to me." Matt broke into her introspection. "I have a date with destiny. In years the architectural world will be calling me 'the new Frank Lloyd Wright.' "

"Right now," she reminded, "we have a date with a gas range. It's our turn to cook dinner."

Later—sitting in the Saturday-night-mobbed Apollo and watching the last Jean Gabin movie to come out of France—Carol thought about the uncertainty of their lives. Jerry crowed about being both very nearsighted and flatfooted. He was sure it was unlikely he'd be drafted. Matt figured he was safe from the draft because of his job, but she was conscious of a new restlessness in him. For the first time in so many years people were not worried about money—but there was this new, unsettling specter that hung over them. *Would American men have to fight in Europe?*

With Matt's arm about her as they watched the film, she thought about her mother—up in Hamptonville. It was weird the way she heard from Mama four or five times a year—plus a birthday card on each birthday. Mama had made it clear her presence would not be appreciated in Hamptonville. She wanted to cut her only child out of her life. There was no way not to recognize that.

In the coming months Americans were assaulted by the outcries of the isolationists. Many were shocked by the impassioned speeches of Charles Lindbergh.

"I can't believe this!" Carol whispered in dismay on a September evening while she and Matt listened to a radio report of a Lindbergh speech in Des Moines.

"Sssh," Matt ordered and reached for her hand.

"Lindbergh has said that 'the three most important groups who have been pressing this country toward war are the British, the Jewish, and the Roosevelt administration,'" the newscaster said. "He went on to blame American Jews, saying 'The greatest danger to this country lies in their large ownership and influence in our motion pictures, our press, our radio, and our government.'"

"The anti-Semitic bastard!" Matt exploded now. "He sounds like a bloody Nazi!"

Though estranged from his parents, Matt was ever conscious of his Jewish and Italian ancestry. He hated Hitler with a passion matched by his contempt for Mussolini—and his fears that he himself might one day be fighting Italian cousins.

Late in September—prodded by Jerry—Leo made an effort to cast a company to present Jerry's three-act play. In two weeks Leo conceded this was impossible in the current climate. Now he was urging Jerry to put in more work on the play rather than to sit back and wait for performances to make revisions.

"Damn it, Jerry, you're always in such a rush. Get down to business and polish this. Its potential is terrific."

With the landlord breathing down his neck for the October rent, Leo finally capitulated and gave up the playhouse. He went to work at the same plant as Matt. On weekends, he promised Jerry, he'd put in time reading rewrites of the play. Like Seth, Jerry had enormous respect for Leo's advice.

On October 17th the U.S. destroyer *Kearny* was torpedoed by a German submarine off the coast of Iceland. Two weeks later the U.S. destroyer *Reuben James* was sunk by German sub—with 100 lives lost. Carol could not understand why this was not considered as "war."

On Thanksgiving day Carol went to the Bronx with Sharon for

an early afternoon Thanksgiving dinner. Then the two rushed down to Matt's Village apartment for a late evening dinner with him, Jerry, and Leo. It wasn't a typical Thanksgiving dinner. Steaks were substituted for the traditional turkey. Leo had bought a strawberry shortcake rather than pumpkin pie.

"Enjoy," he ordered the others when they sat down at the dinner table. "This may be the last peacetime Thanksgiving dinner for a long time."

"Leo, you're such a damn pessimist," Sharon scolded.

"I'm a realist," he said and chuckled. "Okay, on occasion I'm a realist. We're going to get hemmed in on two sides. Across the Atlantic we've got the Axis. Across the Pacific we've got the Japanese."

"Come on, Leo." Jerry's smile was skeptical. "The Japs aren't coming all across the Pacific to attack us."

"Yeah, they've got troubles of their own," Matt agreed. For years now the Japanese had been savagely fighting the Chinese—with the United States refusing to declare an arms embargo and regularly shipping arms to the Chinese in vast quantities. "And now Roosevelt has ordered an embargo on scrap iron and gasoline shipments to them—plus freezing their assets in this country."

"Did anybody hear if Greg is home for Thanksgiving?" Jerry asked. "Hell, he should be due for a pass."

"He's out in California now," Sharon said. "That's too far away to come home on even a four-day pass."

Sharon wrote regularly to Greg, while Carol added a few lines to her letter. Carol wrote to Seth, with Sharon adding a bit at the end. Now Carol gazed somberly about the table and wondered how soon it would be before the others were drafted. How soon before Sharon and herself would be the only ones of their tight little group who weren't in military uniform?

If she and Matt were married, there was a chance he wouldn't be drafted.

Leo had seldom talked about his family, though the others knew he had a pair of married sisters living in Boston. They were surprised when he decided to pull up stakes and move up there for what he referred to as "the duration."

"If I'm going to get stuck in a rotten job, I might as well be up there and have some of the comforts of home. The kind of job I have here I can find up there. The old girls will feed me well, lend me their cars, and try to marry me off. They won't have any luck—but we'll all have fun in the trying."

On the first Saturday in December Carol and Sharon saw Leo off for Boston. Both Matt and Jerry were working. The two girls rejoiced in not having to work on Saturdays now except in emergencies. Both were pleased with their jobs at the ad agency. Carol because—as Sharon had predicted—she found slow periods when she could surreptitiously study. Sharon found a certain excitement in her boss's role of radio producer.

Though wistful about Leo's departure, Carol and Sharon were in high spirits on this Saturday afternoon. Tonight they were going with Matt and Jerry to see the Lillian Hellman play, *Watch on the Rhine*. Matt was treating.

"Seth's dying to see it," Carol remembered. "He figures his father will be back in the shop any day now. And then he'll break the news that he's leaving."

"Tell him not to worry—the play'll be running for months yet. The reviews were terrific."

"He says if he has to starve for a week, he wants to see it."

"Look, I feel rich. I'll take us out to dinner tonight. If we're going to the theater, I don't feel like messing with the kitchen." Sharon giggled. "Somewhere cheap—Chinese or Italian."

They had dinner at a new Italian restaurant in the Village, then headed for the uptown subway. Emerging at Times Square, they joined the Saturday night throngs. At the theater Carol relished the festive atmosphere. And tonight they weren't sitting in a second balcony. Matt had managed fairly good seats. Involuntarily—as the house lights dimmed and the curtain rose—Carol thought about Seth. How he would have loved being here with them!

After the theater they went to the Automat for cake and coffee. The patrons were in a convivial mood—despite the sprinkling of military uniforms that bore witness to the state of the world. Tonight it seemed, Carol thought, like the Robert Browning poem. "God's in his heaven—/All's right with the world."

Later lying in Matt's arms on the wide sofa that substituted as a bed, Carol was aware of the first faint grayness of dawn seeping through the drapes. Matt was asleep already. She felt a beautiful serenity, a sense of time standing still. The warmth of Matt's body plus the flimsy much-washed blanket warded off the dank chill that invaded the apartment. They'd sleep till noon, she guessed while her eyelids fluttered closed.

She came awake slowly. The room lay in shadows, with the curtains drawn tight. No morning light seeping in from outdoors. The aroma of fresh coffee elicited an appreciative smile from her. Funny, how something like that could provide such a warm, mellow feeling, she mused—reluctant to abandon these moments.

"You planning on sleeping all day?" Matt's voice intruded good-humoredly.

"Not with coffee perking on the stove." She lifted her face for his light kiss. "What about a cup to persuade me to get up?"

"Such service these women demand," Matt drawled and headed for the percolator.

"What time is it?"

"Almost two-thirty—in the afternoon." With coffee mug in hand he sauntered back to the sofa, gave the mug to Carol, sat on the edge of the sofa.

"It looks cold and gray outside," Carol said, though in the best of days little sunshine penetrated the basement apartment.

"We don't have to go anywhere." He took the mug from Carol, sipped, returned it to her.

From the depths of her mind Carol dredged out her mother's constant exhortation—*"You don't drink after anybody, Carol. You don't know what you'll pick up."* Her whole life had been turned around in these years since she was on her own, she thought in gratitude.

"No sounds from the bedroom," Carol said. "Sharon and Jerry must be still asleep."

"Let's get a little music into this scene." Matt rose and crossed to switch on the radio.

". . . but we don't have much more to report at this moment." The announcer's voice was agitated. Carol and Matt were instantly alert. "We know only that Japanese planes have bombed Pearl Harbor."

"Oh, my God!" Matt charged to the bedroom and flung the door wide. "Hey, get your butts out here!" he yelled, drowning out the voice of the announcer. "Pearl Harbor—in Hawaii—was bombed by Jap planes!"

* * *

In Bellevue, Georgia, Seth sprawled across his bed and reread for the dozenth time his last letter from Carol. In this letter—more than any of the others, though he taunted himself that he'd tried to block the truth from his mind—the message came through loud and clear: Carol and Matt were seriously involved.

He'd kept telling himself he'd be heading back for New York by the end of the month—Dad was in the shop part-time now—and he'd make Carol understand how he felt about her. He'd convinced himself he hadn't been wrong in sensing she felt something special for him. Write that off as a lost dream.

He heard the front door open and close downstairs. Mom and Dad and Grandma were back from the benefit luncheon at the synagogue. The luncheon was to raise funds for Jewish refugees.

"I can't believe it! I still can't believe it!" His mother's voice was unnaturally strident.

"Hannah, we knew it was going to happen," Eli said. "We just didn't know where or when—"

"If Aaron Gilman didn't have one of those new car radios that he turned on in the parking area, we still wouldn't know, Eli," his mother said with an air of stunned disbelief.

What wouldn't they have known, Seth asked himself, and leapt to his feet and out to the hall.

"Mom—" he called and charged down the stairs. "What's going on?"

"We're in the war, Seth—" Her voice broke. "Wasn't it enough that we've lived through one world war?"

The family settled in the kitchen while Leah offered her perennial panacea for each crisis in life. She put up a pot of tea and brought out the canister where she kept her current supply of homemade cookies. Seth switched on the kitchen radio so they could hear the latest word on what was happening at Pearl Harbor.

"You wanted to rush home to hear the rest of the football game at the Polo Grounds," Hannah reminded Eli with anguish. "We live in such an insane world. From one day to the next we don't know what new horror is going to invade out lives."

Seth sat in silence. His mind in chaos. No doubt in his mind that he'd be drafted within weeks. Why wait? Dad was okay—he was back in the shop. What did he have waiting for him in New York? Tomorrow, Seth decided, he'd go over to the recruitment office and enlist.

Chapter Eighteen

While she and Sharon climbed the dimly lighted stairs to their apartment, Carol shifted the mail she'd picked up from the console table in the entrance hall downstairs.

"There's a letter from Seth," Carol announced with a lilt in her voice as Sharon unlocked the door and pushed it open. "Maybe he'll be up for New Year's."

"Read it to me while I start dinner," Sharon said. It was her night to cook.

They threw off their coats and settled into their midweek routine.

"Hamburgers or franks?" Sharon asked, peering into their minute refrigerator.

"Hamburger," Carol said. "We have to use it up." She dropped the rest of the mail at one corner of the studio couch where she sat, ripped open the envelope from Seth, and scanned the first few sentences.

"Oh, my God!"

"What's the matter?" Sharon spun around to face Carol.

"Seth's enlisted." Her heart was pounding. "He said he saw no point in waiting to be drafted—"

"Where is he?" Sharon asked. "What's the postmark on the envelope?"

"Bellevue," Carol said after a quick glance. "He hasn't been sent to boot camp yet. Don't they give them three days or something before they report?"

"What else does he say?" Sharon reached for a skillet, deposited it on a burner. Her voice betrayed her own anxiety.

"He said he couldn't believe what happened at Pearl Harbor— and that this country has to fight now." Carol paused, her eyes rushing ahead, reading aloud now. " 'Don't worry if you don't hear from me. I don't imagine I'll have much time for writing in boot camp— and what comes after. Let's hope this damn war is over in a hurry— though I doubt it'll be that way. We'll get together after the craziness is over and catch up on what's happened in-between.' *He's not even going to write us?"* Carol was shocked.

"That's what he says now. We'll hear from him," Sharon surmised. "You know Seth and his one-track mind. He's going off to fight a war; for a while he won't be thinking of anything else."

"But we're all so close," Carol protested. It was unnerving to know that Seth had enlisted, that he'd be fighting in a war. Couldn't he understand it was more important for them to hear from him? Greg wrote. "How can Seth not write us?"

"I think he wanted more than friendship for you and him," Sharon said gently after a moment. "There've been times when I was sure you felt the same way."

"Sharon, how can you say that?" Carol stared at her in disbelief. "Seth is one of our closest friends—like Greg." She paused, all at once remembering the heated lovemaking on occasion between Greg and Sharon. "You know about Matt and me." But Seth didn't know—he'd been away over two years.

"Seth saw you follow Matt around like an adoring puppy, and it didn't make him happy. Maybe he's decided it's time to cut loose from you. But I don't think you're in love with Matt," Sharon said bluntly. "You're obsessed by him and that aura of the 'next great architect' that he wears like a halo."

Carol ignored this. It wasn't the first time Sharon had challenged her feelings for Matt.

"It's going to feel so strange not to be hearing from Seth regularly," Carol said, struggling to adjust to this. "But he's still one of our closest friends—"

As usual on Saturday evening Carol and Sharon headed downtown for Matt's apartment. A tie-up on the southbound subway delayed them almost half an hour. They found Jerry waiting at the door.

"Matt must be working late," Jerry said. "And I forgot my key. Let's go around the corner for coffee. He'll be along soon." They'd all become accustomed to Matt's often elongated working hours, and Jerry had a penchant for forgetting his keys.

Over coffee Carol told Jerry about Seth's enlistment.

"The dumb schmuck." Jerry shook his head in disapproval. "Why couldn't he wait? The war could be over before he's called up."

"You don't believe that," Sharon shot back. But Carol knew she worried about Jerry's being drafted, despite his extreme nearsight-edness.

They lingered at the coffee shop for twenty minutes, then walked in the crisp night air back to the apartment. Matt had just arrived. Immediately they were engulfed in somber talk about the war. Now two of their close group were in uniform. How long, Carol asked herself, before Matt and Leo and Jerry would join them? It was their generation that must do the fighting.

Like all Americans Carol knew what the British had been endur-ing since September 1939. Since December 7th the war seemed alarmingly close to their own West Coast. The newspapers warned them that Japanese war planes were far more effective than any-thing in the American air force. And Carol had read that the Japa-nese considered it a glory to die for their emperor.

By New Year's Day, 1942, Japanese troops were in the Philip-pines, on Wake Island and Guam. German submarines—traveling in wolf packs—were exacting an alarming toll in the Atlantic. Mer-chants ships were being torpedoed and sunk, within sight of the American coastline.

In February Leo wrote that he was tired of waiting around. He was enlisting in the Marines. Two weeks later Matt enlisted in the infantry.

"I'm sick of wondering when that letter will arrive," he told Carol. "Let's fight this damn war and get it over with. I want to be back in school. With a lot of luck I'll come home and get into Har-vard." Carol knew he'd been saving for this. "Walter Gropius is head of the department of architecture—you know, the guy who set up the German Bauhaus school. God, could I learn from a man like that!"

Only Jerry remained out of uniform. Both Leo and Matt were holed up in basic training. They wrote brief, pithy letters about their new lives. Then Greg wrote that he was being transferred to a camp in North Carolina.

"Can you believe it, kids? I'm becoming a machine gun instruc-tor! After we did an amateur show here, I had a chance at Special Services—but hell, we have a war to fight."

At regular intervals Carol worried about Seth. It never ceased to disturb her that he had broken off from his New York friends. *Where was he?*

* * *

Late in July Matt received a 24-hour pass. He phoned Carol at work to say that he wasn't sure what train he'd make from Virginia.

"I'll come straight to your apartment from Penn Station," he told her. Jerry had two roommates in Matt's old apartment. "Baby, I can't wait to see you!"

On hearing the news Sharon immediately said she'd go up to the Bronx and sleep over. She'd hang around just long enough to see Matt, then head for the subway. Both worried that Matt's company might be on alert—heading soon either for the Pacific or London.

At shortly before 9 P.M. Matt arrived. Sharon exchanged an exuberant kiss, hugged him warmly.

"Take care of yourself, you big lug." With a jaunty wave she left the apartment.

"Are you on alert?" Carol asked anxiously.

"No," he said, reaching for her. "This is just a plain twenty-four-hour pass. And let's don't waste a minute of it—"

American forces were fighting a torturous campaign to regain the Pacific Islands. Eight months after Pearl Harbor American marines landed at Guadalcanal and began a tenacious drive against the Japanese. American troops were arriving in London in force and impatient for action. The British RAF was conducting massive air raids over Germany—350 planes a night went out to bomb Berlin, Cologne, other major German cities.

At Seth's camp in Virginia rumors were circulating frantically. The word was that American forces would soon open another front—and *they* would be part of it. Nobody could figure out where this would be. Then late in November 1942, Seth's company was put on alert. Not until they were aboard their blacked-out troopship did they learn they were heading for North Africa.

"Hey, what do you know about North Africa?" a fellow soldier asked Seth curiously when—after days at sea—they were told they were less than an hour from their destination. Oran, in Algeria.

"I don't know much," Seth conceded. "Just that the slaves in America had been brought over from Africa."

"How do you think Africans are going to feel about us? I mean, all that stuff about our keeping slaves before the Civil War?"

"I don't think North Africa is inhabited just by colored tribes,"

Seth said humorously. "The French took over much of it over a century ago. Oran's a modern city."

Ever since his two years in New York he had been troubled by
the South's sentiments toward its colored population. He was troubled by a segregated army and navy. Now he smiled, remembering
conversations about this with his grandmother.

*"Seth, I'll never understand why the color of somebody's skin de-
cides where they'll live and where their children will go to school.
Your grandfather and I used to talk about it—by ourselves.
Grandpa said maybe if we'd been born here in the South, we'd understand."*

Once he'd spent a whole Saturday in Low Library up at Columbia—just reading books on Negro history. He'd been astonished
to learn that hundred of years ago highly developed kingdoms existed in some areas of Africa. Negro kings lived in splendor. Between 1200 and 1600 a Negro–Arabic university existed at Tim-
buktu in West Africa and was famous not only in all of Africa but in
the Middle East and Spain.

He'd discovered that slavery had long been practiced in Africa,
though only kings owned more than a few. Arab slave traders captured Negroes, sold them in North Africa or the Middle East. With
the discovery of America the slave trade became a highly profitable
business. African kings fought one another to capture slaves to sell
or barter for guns, cloth, rum, and other coveted items.

"Anyhow, we won't have to worry about snowstorms in North
Africa—" Seth's companion intruded on his thoughts. "Isn't Algeria
on the Mediterranean Sea? We'll stretch out on the sand and wallow
in the sun."

Carol and Sharon dreaded the approach of New Year's Eve. Of
their close circle only Jerry was home to share the holiday with
them. Their office party began at noon. There was a frenzied effort
to create an air of gaiety, though the young men all appeared self-
conscious at not being in uniform.

"Hell, we're in better shape than last New Year's Eve," Sharon's
fiftyish boss—Victor Blair—said with forced conviviality. "Then we
were still numb from the attack on Pearl Harbor. This year we see
our guys pushing the Japs back in the Pacific. We've got our forces
fighting alongside the British and driving the Germans out of North

Africa." But Carol flinched as she remembered the costs of these actions.

As soon as it was polite to do so, Carol and Sharon escaped the party. They walked in the cold afternoon air, all the way from the office to their apartment. En route they stopped to shop groceries. Jerry was coming up to have dinner with them. They'd decided to splurge on a Broadway movie afterward. They'd hoped to see a play, but all the low-priced seats were sold out when they'd checked last night.

"Greg said he was dying to see Paul Muni in *Counselor-At-Law*," Sharon remembered.

"And the Lunts in *The Pirate* and Tallullah Bankhead and Frederic March in *The Skin of Our Teeth*," Carol added. "Can't you just see Greg doing a scene from each of the plays?" But Greg was down in North Carolina, with no chance of getting a leave. He'd got a 24-hour pass when his mother was down with pneumonia three weeks ago. No time to see a play then. He'd just managed to meet them for a quick Chinese dinner.

"Greg's so talented he's awesome," Sharon said. "He'll make it big when this lousy war is over."

"Jerry's got commercial this last year or so," Carol reminded her. "No more serious theater. He says with the war on theatergoers want to laugh. I hate the cracks he makes about Seth and Greg being mesmerized by 'serious theater.'"

"Look, he's impatient for success. That's not so awful."

At the apartment they threw themselves into cleaning, then began the preparations for their more elaborate than usual dinner. What would New Year's Eve be like for Matt? Carol asked herself. And Greg and Leo? And Seth, wherever he was—

Jerry arrived at six with a bottle of port.

"God, you're smelling up the whole house," he said appreciatively, sniffing at the range. "If I'd known you were cooking up a storm, I would have skipped lunch."

They managed a festive mood over dinner, though Carol jumped to run to the door every time she heard the hall phone ring. She'd hoped Matt might call her. But he said that on important holidays the lines waiting at the phones were too long for anybody as impatient as he was.

"Let's do the dishes and get to the movies," Sharon said. "Every place will be mobbed tonight."

Carol sat in the darkened movie house—with not an empty seat on this New Year's Eve—and saw little of the film. For all people talked about how the Allies were winning the war, she thought, it was far from over. Matt said troops were being shipped out so fast it made his head swim. *"They need every man they can beat into fighting shape in Europe and the Pacific. This war is like a bloody see-saw."*

By the time they emerged from the movie house Times Square was jammed all the way up past Duffy Square. Horns blared. Cowbells clanked. Jerry stationed himself between Carol and Sharon, an arm about each.

"We'll never get down to the Times Building in this," Sharon predicted. "How many people do you think are here?"

"Close to half a million," Jerry guessed as they inched their way south. The night was crisply cold, the sky splashed with stars.

This wasn't like other New Year's Eves, Carol mused. There was a strange, weird quality tonight. It wasn't just the dimness, she decided. The laughter—the gaiety—all sounded forced. So many people moved like zombies. Most of them were young—like Sharon and herself. A lot of teenagers. Couples, groups of girls alone. Here and there servicemen in the uniforms of the Allies.

"It's getting close to midnight," Jerry said exuberantly. "We're not going to get down to see that ball drop from the flagstaff on top of the New York Times tower."

"We can't even move," Sharon effervesced.

Mounted police, foot patrol, civilian defense auxiliaries tried futilely to keep open a lane for emergency vehicles. There were no private cars because of gas rationing, but taxis were arriving at the perimeters of the area—bursting with passengers from every borough.

"We can't even buy a horn!" a teenager shrieked in outrage. "We shoulda brought them from Brooklyn!"

Carol saw the lineup of police cars, ambulances, fire trucks—standing by for any emergency that might arise. A large silver WNYC sound truck was parked at Duffy square. A tall young woman with an anguished face and holding a folded-back copy of the day's *New York Times* stood beside Carol. When a flashlight in the crowd fell across the newspaper, Carol saw that it was folded back to the day's list of war casualties.

A coldness shot through Carol. She knew what was so strange

about this New Year's Eve celebration. The ghosts of those who had died in the awful war hovered above them. How dare they celebrate the arrival of a new year that was sure to bring more death and destruction!

"It's midnight," a man behind them complained. "What's going on?"

Then all at once wide bands of light played about the sky. Lights from the plane spotter stations around the city, someone identified these. Then slowly the waiting horde realized this was the welcome to January 1st, 1943. Now the noise of horns and bells was deafening.

Though the mobs closer to the Times Building were unaware as yet, an announcer from the WNYC sound truck was calling for ten seconds of silence—in respect for American servicemen overseas. Quickly the men removed their hats. Tears welled in many eyes. Sharon reached across Jerry for Carol's hand. Her eyes blurred, Carol managed a shaky smile.

Then the voice of Lucy Monroe filled the square, bringing silence to the area. Moments later the crowd joined her in singing "The Star-Spangled Banner."

What would the next New Year's Eve bring? Please God, Carol silently prayed, let it bring peace.

On New Year's Day Carol and Sharon slept until past noon. They'd sat around with Jerry over endless cups of coffee last night and talked about other New Year's Eves they'd shared. What were Matt and Greg and Leo doing this New Year's Eve? And where was Seth?

Shivering in the dank cold of the apartment, Carol reach for the bathrobe at the foot of her bed and pulled it about her. Put up coffee, turn on the other three gas burners, she ordered herself—for what meager heat they might provide.

A moment later Sharon opened her eyes, grunted in distaste.

"Oh God, it's 1943! We've been at war for over a year."

"I'm putting up coffee. You'll feel better in a few minutes," Carol soothed.

"Was I awful in sending Jerry home at five A.M.?" Sharon asked, huddling under a blanket topped by her winter coat.

"He was nuts to think we'd let him sleep on the floor."

"He wouldn't have been on the floor long." Sharon giggled. "It's the first time I can remember when I said 'no' to him."

"I like Jerry," Carol said. "Part of him I like. Not the way he hangs around you when it suits him. You never know when he's going to take off."

"He's staying put these days. Of course, he says we're all living one day at a time now. But he's working like a dog on his play," Sharon said.

"He loves this 'one day at a time' routine." Carol was impatient that he ran away from any commitment to Sharon. Except for that she liked him, she conceded. He was bright and talented—and she felt such compassion for his frequent bouts of depression.

"I wish to hell we were both through with school. That should be behind us now." With an air of reluctance Sharon abandoned her bed, thrust her feet into slippers and reached for her robe. "What am I going to do with a B.A. in English Lit?"

"Find a job in publishing," Carol said. They'd been through this so many times, with Sharon threatening to drop out of Hunter. "That's what Seth always throws at his parents."

"I don't know what I want to do with my life." Sharon sighed. "Except get married."

"Don't look at Jerry," Carol warned. "He just wants to play." She hesitated, her mind on a familiar track now. "I've been thinking, Sharon—"

"That's dangerous." Sharon laughed, but she was attentive.

"I should be saving money toward architectural school—"

"Honey, you are saving. You're better at it than I am," Sharon admitted ruefully.

"Do you think I should take a course in typing? I might move into a better-paying job at the agency."

"When are you going to find time for that?" Sharon challenged.

"I'll find it," Carol said. "Maybe Jerry will let me practice on his typewriter."

"Oh, he'll love that." Sharon moved closer to the gas range, hands outstretched for the warmth it offered. "You can type in his apartment, and we can play up here."

In the early months of the new year Carol and Sharon were shaken when—within weeks of one another—Greg, Matt, and Leo were shipped out. Leo went into the fierce, bloody fighting in the Pacific. Greg was in North Africa—where the Allies were in seesaw

battle with Axis forces. Matt was jubilant about being in England—
"Close enough to London to get in some fine old times there. And I
can't wait to see their old landmarks—designed by architects like
Christopher Wren and Inigo Jones."

Carol and Sharon blessed the tiny but swift V-mails that had
been available since June of last year. Letters arrived regularly
from Matt and Greg and Leo, and they conscientiously replied immediately. But when seven weeks went past without word from
Leo, they were anxious.

"Leo's probably found himself some action with a gorgeous army
nurse or a Red Cross gal," Sharon decided. "He's got no time now
for the likes of us." But she and Carol worried.

Then late in September they received a letter from one of Leo's
sisters. He had given them the addresses of close friends.

"Leo wanted you to know if something happened to him out
there in the Pacific. It breaks my heart to tell you. Leo died a hero—
at Attu, in the Aleutian Islands."

At first Carol and Sharon were too numb to cry. Leo dead? They
had known it could happen—but now that it had happened, they
found it unbelievable. Dying in battle happened to strangers. *Not
vibrant, mesmerizing Leo.* In the midst of the ferocious fighting in
the Pacific—as his marine unit laboriously moved from one island to
another—Leo had written about his grandiose plans for the future.

*"When this shitty war is over and we're all back home again, I
mean to show New York some real plays. Maybe even see a Pulitzer
prize for Seth and Jerry."*

But Leo would never argue again with Seth and Jerry about re-
writing a scene in a play, Carol thought in anguish. He'd never tear
into a cast in an effort to elicit every possible drop of talent his current crop of actors might possess. He would never again yell at her
to "take some damn courses in set designing." For Leo it was all
over.

More than ever Carol and Sharon worried about Matt—somewhere in England and churning for action. They worried about
Greg—in Sicily now. And where was Seth? Carol constantly asked
herself. *Was he all right?*

Chapter Nineteen

Late in March Matt was jubilant at catching a ride into an airfield near London on a U.S. Air Force bomber—and triumphant at having acquired a 24-hour pass. The army wouldn't approve of his "fraternization" with one of their nurses—*Lieutenant* Iris Grady, when he was a lowly sergeant—but he knew Iris had pulled strings to arrange this rendezvous.

That one had *chutzpah,* he thought with satisfaction as the bomber came in for a landing. He knew that the first time they met—on New Year's Day. And hot as a pistol, he remembered, feeling a surge of passion.

They'd bumped into each other in the blackout. He'd asked if she knew a place where he could get a decent meal, and she'd taken him to a small restaurant she knew. He was in London on a special assignment. She was on a 24-hour pass.

Halfway through dinner the bombs began to drop. They'd gone down into the restaurant cellar with other patrons. In a private corner they'd exchanged a hot, experimental kiss.

"Let's get the hell out of here," she'd whispered. "I have the key to a flat just around the corner."

For tonight she had managed to acquire reservations at a small hotel near Hyde Park. He glanced at his watch. She was waiting for him there. God, he wanted to have her flat on her back this minute! Remembering their last time together in a borrowed suite at the swanky Dorchester—when they'd ignored the air raid sirens to make love—he impatiently sought a ride into town.

In barely three months they'd managed time together on four occasions—usually for no longer than four or five hours. It took a lot of conniving, but it was worth it. Now they'd both managed a 24-hour pass.

Matt stiffened to attention at the side of an approaching army jeep. His hand went out in the familiar signal. The jeep pulled to a stop beside him.

"Where are ya headed?" a freckle-faced corporal asked.

"London," Matt told him.

"Hop in," the corporal said breezily.

They exchanged earthy conversation on the drive into London. He didn't mention his ultimate destination, but Matt was sure the corporal guessed.

"Happy nooky!" The corporal winked in approval as he pulled to a stop before what once had been a luxurious private home but was now converted to a hotel.

He hadn't heard that word since the last time he saw his old man. Did Pop and the old lady ever wonder where he was? Matt asked himself. Did they give a shit?

He strode across the tiny lobby—ignoring the desk clerk—and headed up the stairs. Fourth floor, he remembered—room 17.

Iris opened the door at his knock.

"You made good time," she approved. "I just got here."

"Is there a bath?" he drawled, inspecting the lissome length of her. God, she was sexy! Even in that stupid uniform.

"Would I accept less?" She moved toward him, her mouth parting as it reached for his.

"That was good," he said huskily when his mouth released hers. "Run me a bath, and we'll share it."

"Sweetie, you haven't seen this tub! You'll have to soap just to get in."

"To hell with the bath," he said in sudden impatience. "That'll come later."

Throwing off his jacket, he saw the V-mail that fell from a pocket to the floor. Carol sure kept the mail coming: he'd told her how much mail call meant to everybody over here. Iris hadn't seen it—she was rushing to strip to skin, he thought and kicked the V-mail under the bed.

For an instant he felt a surge of guilt, then dismissed this. Ten to one Carol was climbing under the sheets with somebody else, too. Hell, they hadn't been together in over a year! That had been a whole other life.

Magnificent spring sunlight poured into the tiny studio apartment this morning as Carol sealed her current letter to Matt. She glanced at the clock on the dresser. It was time to leave to meet Sharon at the cafeteria. Every Saturday they treated themselves to breakfast there. Last night Sharon had gone home for dinner and to sleep over—to pacify her parents. After all this time they were still not adjusted to an unmarried daughter's living away from home.

Carol reached for her suit jacket, pulled it on over her sweater. The morning was warm, she thought with a surge of pleasure—no need for a winter coat. Geared to utilizing every free moment for study, she reached for the textbook on architecture she'd bought at a bookstore across from the Columbia campus. If Sharon was late, she'd read.

En route to the door she paused for a glance at herself in the mirror. She was acquiring such a passion for beautiful clothes—a passion that must be ignored. Every possible dollar went into the bank for classes after Hunter.

She hurried down the dark, dank stairs. The morning's mail was already on the downstairs hall table. She picked up the one letter addressed to her; nothing from Matt today. She recognized her mother's tiny scrawl on the envelope. Her mother wrote no more than four times a year now—always little more than a note with mild complaints about her daily life.

She thrust the letter into her purse to read later and headed toward Broadway. She paused at West End Avenue to drop her letter to Matt in a mailbox. Her face grew tender as the envelope slid from view. It was wonderful the way he wrote so often. Scraps of those letters were etched on her brain. *"Baby, I can't wait to get home to you." "Carol, we'll make up for these lousy years apart." "All I think about is holding you in my arms again."*

Matt had decided that once she graduated she ought to take some courses in drafting. He'd washed from his mind her talk about being an architect. *"Then you can work for me in my office."* He was impatient that the war was dragging on this way—he wanted to be back in school and working for his degree. Thus far she had avoided mentioning that she'd have her B.A. from Hunter in June.

She and Sharon were both excited about graduation. Already she was exploring the college scene for her next move. With her new job in the agency's radio department she'd acquired a ten-dollar raise in salary, which was impressive. Of course, she remembered ruefully, their paychecks were missing the 5 percent being withheld as the new Victory tax.

She was praying to be accepted for classes at the Columbia School of Architecture, though she was horrified when she learned the cost of tuition. Hunter had been free. She devoured every issue of *Architectural Record.* She kept all of Matt's letters, both V-mails and the long airmails—not just out of sentiment but because he wrote her in glorious detail about British architecture. She was convinced the day would come when the names on their office door would read: HARRIS & HARRIS, ARCHITECTS.

Pushing her way through the cafeteria's revolving door, she spied Sharon at their usual table. Sharon lifted a hand in greeting, hurried to join her at the counter. Then—clutching their trays—they headed for the table Sharon had staked out for them.

"God, what a gorgeous day!" Sharon said as they threaded their way through the morning crowd. "Let's walk downtown and see if we can pick up some chocolate bars." Regularly they stopped at the newspaper and candy stores along Broadway in hopes of acquiring a stockpile to send to Matt and Greg.

"I had a letter from my mother," Carol said while she reached for her coffee cup. Mornings like this, she mused guiltily, she could almost forget the war.

"What did the old bat have to say this time?"

"I haven't read it yet," Carol admitted.

"Right. Enjoy your breakfast," Sharon drawled.

"How are things at home?" Carol asked. She was fond of Sharon's family—Sharon's mother so different from her own.

"Hectic as always." Sharon smiled indulgently. "Mom was shocked, I hear, when she found out Bev's secret vice is reading confession magazines. She'd been reading them since she was fifteen. She used to hide them under her mattress. Mom wanted her to be an intellectual. That just doesn't run in the family."

Not until she'd finished her pancakes and had drained her cup of the last drops of coffee did Carol open her mother's letter. With each letter she felt a renewed sense of loss. Her eyes scanned the first sentence and widened with shock.

"She's moving to Florida," Carol told Sharon. "She's left already!"

"What about the house?" Sharon asked. "You paid for that."

"She doesn't say." It was ridiculous, Carol scolded herself, to feel as though she was being abandoned. "Anyhow, she's always considered the house as hers."

"Are you going to let her get away with it?"

"Yeah—" Carol managed a shaky smile. "Besides, I don't even know where she'll be living. She just said not to worry if I don't hear, that she'll be busy settling down in a new place." Mama never meant to write again, Carol thought in a burst of prescience. Mama wanted the old life behind her forever.

"Let's walk all the way down to Fifth Avenue. We'll just look in the windows," Sharon soothed, "and think about the gorgeous clothes we'll buy when we're rich."

"Is Jerry coming up for dinner tonight?" Carol asked.

"He'll be up Sunday. He's bartending somewhere tonight. Why don't we go to a movie? Early, before the prices change."

A few minutes before 6 P.M. they were seated in a neighborhood movie theater. The newsreel was just beginning—always a somber moment in this time of war. The coverage dealt with American troops in Italy. The commentator's mellow voice was reporting on their painful progress over the mountainous Italian terrain when all at once Carol cried out as a jeep rolled into view.

"There's Seth!" Her voice was joyous.

"He's in Italy!" Sharon reached out to clutch her arm. "Oh, wow!"

"We'll stay over to see the newsreel again," Carol said. Already the newsreel had moved to another area.

Carol watched the remainder of the newsreel and then the film, but she churned with impatience to see the newsreel again. *Seth was in Italy. He was all right.* So far he was all right. Would he ever run into Greg, who was probably not far behind him—somewhere in Southern Italy.

Rumors filled every crevice of the minds of restless GIs. They knew they were about to embark on a major campaign. The weather was vile—the storm over the English Channel the worst in many years. General Eisenhower—the Allies' supreme commander—decreed that the invasion of France must wait yet another day.

Shortly after noon on June 6th Carol looked up from her typewriter to see Sharon approaching with a glint in her eyes that appeared both triumphant and fearful.

"Mom just called me," Sharon said. "She was listening to "The Romance of Helen Trent," and an announcer broke in to say that Allied forces are landing on the northern coast of France!"

"Matt'll be there," Carol said shakily.

"Can you go out to lunch now?"

"Let's go!" Carol reached into her desk drawer for her purse, then signaled to a coworker that she was going out to lunch.

They hurried to a nearby coffee shop, waited in line for a table. A radio was blaring out the news. Almost 4,000 ships were scheduled to carry troops to their destination. There were another 800 warships and 11,000 planes. On this first day 176,000 men would be arriving on the Normandy coast. It was expected that over 4,000,000 Allied troops would land in the coming days.

Everyone knew the fighting would be bitter, the losses increasing as the Allied armies neared the Rhine. Still, victory seemed within the grasp of the Allies. Nobody dared to think at what cost.

On August 26th—the day after its liberation—Matt arrived in Paris with three other GIs. Their jeep—like others—inched through the streets as crowds danced and sang. Jubilant girls hung onto the jeeps, reaching to kiss the liberating soldiers. Everywhere the sound of the "Marseillaise."

Matt was astonished that the city appeared untouched by war. Nothing like London. The girls and women were smartly dressed.

"Hey, where's this dump you want?" the driver asked Matt. He knew that Matt was meeting an army nurse at a hotel in the heart of the city.

"It's not a dump," Matt told him with a grin. "Stop and let me ask directions. I'm staying at the Ritz for the next twenty-four hours!"

The three in the jeep were amused by the insistence of a Frenchman to lead them to the Ritz on foot. He pushed his way through the crowd, boisterously beckoning the jeep driver to follow.

"Don't be AWOL," one of Matt's companions warned. "And don't let 'em find out you're screwing a fancy officer," he added in a mock whisper. "They're not for enlisted men!"

Then the jeep—strewn with flowers bestowed by joyous French girls—drew to a stop on the Place Vendôme, before the four-arched entrance to the Hotel Ritz.

"It's little," one of Matt's companions said in astonishment. "It looks like a fancy town house."

"It used to be," Matt said, hurrying from the jeep. "But inside—" He gestured eloquently. "Ooh-la-la!"

"All you'll see is the bedroom ceiling," the GI at the wheel joshed. "Remember, you're on the loose for just twenty-four hours. We're still fighting a war."

How the hell did Iris always manage to find a room for them? Matt asked himself exuberantly as he approached the *concierge*. He was pleased to learn that she had already arrived. If the *concierge* had any suspicions that he was not the lieutenant's "husband," he masked this well. But right now in Paris every American army sergeant was regarded as a general.

Churning with excitement, his mouth dry in anticipation, Matt knocked on the door. It was opened instantly.

"Sorry I couldn't manage a suite," Iris drawled, standing before him in a black chiffon nightgown. Matt's eyes swept from the huge dark nipples on blatant display over the voluptuous length of her.

"Where did you find that?" he asked, reaching for her.

"A romantic old lady opened her shop for me," Iris said. "Though she knew I wouldn't be wearing it for long—"

"I don't suppose there's any hot water?"

"I have a hot tub waiting for you—" She contrived to keep some distance between herself and his mud-splattered uniform. "Probably the only hot water in Paris."

While he soaked with sensuous delight in several inches of hot, perfumed water, Iris brought two glasses of champagne into the bathroom.

"Hurry up or I'll go out in the street and grab myself another guy," she warned. "Do you know how long it's been since I saw you?"

"Five weeks and four days," he told her.

"Finish your champagne and get out of there," she ordered.

When he rose, glistening and sweet-smelling from the tub, Iris closed in about him with an oversized bath towel. Moments later—despite her protests that he was still wet—they were rolling together on the bed. Wow, this was a hot one, he thought in triumph while they moved in soaring heat.

"Don't leave," she whispered when he lay immobile above her. "Again, in a few minutes—" Already her hands were evoking fresh heat in him.

Later—after they'd had dinner and more champagne—they returned to their room for the night.

"You're strangely pensive all at once," Matt said curiously. "Running out of steam?"

"I'm asking myself, 'what's the best way to tell him?' "

"Tell me what?" He sat at the edge of the bed and took off his shoes—suddenly wary. Had she found another guy?

"You remember all those jokes about how a good WAC—or nurse—never gets PWOP?" Pregnant without permission. "Well, I'm guilty." Her smile was defiant yet provocative.

"My kid?" he asked, suddenly wary.

"Who else's?" she flared.

"There's a big army out there," he shot back.

"You bastard!" she blazed. "You know I haven't been with anybody else!"

"Why the hell did you let that happen?" He was shaken, yet at the same time oddly fascinated by the prospect of being a father. "You're a nurse—you ought to know how to take care of yourself."

"When was there time?" she countered. "We're fighting a war."

"How far along?" he asked after a moment, trying to deal with this unexpected situation.

"At least two months—maybe more." Her eyes were bright with questions.

"How soon before they'll send you home?" *His* kid. He'd be a better father than his old man ever was—if he got the chance.

"As soon as I show. Maybe five or six weeks—"

"We'll figure out a way to get married before you're sent home," he decided. "Somewhere in this crazy town." He hadn't seen Carol in two years; they were living in two different worlds. They were different people now. "Hey, we're going to have one great kid," he boasted in a surge of anticipation and pride.

They'd be a family—something he'd never had. Carol was a kid. She'd get over him fast enough. When the war was over—and it had to be soon—he and Iris would settle in some college town, where he could go to school part-time to finish up earning his degree. Iris could have the kid, then go into private nursing to help him through school. Maybe he'd even go for a master's. Who needed New York and that crazy rat race?

Chapter Twenty

Carol waited impatiently for letters from Matt after the liberation of Paris. She knew he'd been in France since D-Day. Had he been in Paris? Oh, how he would love that!

She'd received a batch of V-mails from France, plus one long airmail with an appalling amount cut by the censors. For the past three weeks she'd received no mail from him.

Tonight—standing at the kitchenette range while perspiration seemed to exude from every pore—she recalled that it had been even longer since they'd heard from Greg.

She glanced up with a smile as Sharon came into the apartment.

"Wouldn't you know Mr. Blair would keep me late on the hottest Friday in September?" Sharon shook her head in annoyance, kicked off her pumps, and headed for the closet. "You don't mind if I shower before we eat? Even my leg makeup is running in this heat!" Stockings had long since given way to leg makeup, to be laboriously applied each morning from toenail to midthigh.

"Go ahead," Carol encouraged. "The onions are just right. I'll throw in the hamburgers. I've already made the salad. But shower fast."

"No mail, I gather?" Sharon pulled a five-year-old peasant skirt—bought before government regulations banned such lavish use of material—from the closet, reached for a peasant blouse that would have been lavishly ruffled except for those regulations. "Matt or Greg?"

"Nothing," Carol said, her smile rueful. "I worry when we run into these delays. But go shower and cool off."

"Maybe we'll go to a movie later. God bless air-conditioning—" Sharon disappeared into the minuscule bathroom.

She ought to stay home and study, Carol thought. She was excited at taking the first course that would eventually lead to a degree in architecture. With recurrent frustration she railed at her inability to go to school full-time. She hadn't written to Matt yet about signing up for this course at Columbia. She hadn't even mentioned that she and Sharon had their degrees from Hunter. That would be mean—when he wanted so much to get on with his schooling.

She'd brought the hamburgers to the table and was at the refrigerator reaching in for the salad when Sharon emerged from the shower.

"That little fan on the dresser doesn't do a damn thing," Sharon complained, dropping into a chair and sniffing appreciatively at the mound of onions atop her hamburger. "It'll even be hot sitting on the Drive tonight. Let's escape to a movie," she said again.

"I should study—"

"Study tomorrow. It's supposed to rain all day—that should cool things off." Sharon paused. "You know, I'm beginning to worry about Greg."

"There've been waits between letters before," Carol comforted, but she, too, worried.

"Not this long. Of course, everything's going crazy in Europe. Even Hitler must realize he's lost the war!" The Allies had broken the Siegfried Line, were inside Germany.

"Maybe we could call Greg's mother," Carol said when Sharon had stacked the few dishes in the sink and brought the pitcher of lemonade to the table. "No," she rejected, recoiling from conversation with Mrs. Fein. "We'll call his brother." They just wanted some reassurance, she told herself guiltily. Greg's brother shouldn't mind their calling.

En route to the neighborhood movie, they stopped at the downstairs hall phone. Sharon called information, asked for the phone number, then dialed the number for Chuck Fein's apartment. Carol gathered a woman had answered. Probably Greg's sister-in-law.

"We just wanted to check on Greg," Sharon said with an effort at casualness. "We're close friends of his from the theater group and—"

In the dim light of the hallway Carol could see the color drain from Sharon's face.

"We didn't know," she whispered. "We had letters regularly, then nothing—" Sharon closed her eyes as she listened to the voice at the other end, reached out a hand to Carol. "Yes, it's awful—"

Sharon hung up the phone and turned to Carol.

"Greg died in the bombing of a post office in Florence, Italy," she managed to say. "Carol, I don't want to believe it—"

* * *

Now Carol came home each night with a prayer there would be a letter from Matt. Everybody kept saying the war was almost over, but soldiers were still dying. *Greg was dead.*

The presence of gold stars in the windows of so many apartments and houses told of the anguish behind those windows. What kind of a world did they live in, Carol asked herself, when some of its best and brightest died so young? So violently! First Leo, now Greg. Both were gone from their own small circle—almost their *family.* All that talent in Greg and Leo lost to the world. And she lived with constant terror because Matt was somewhere in France—and where was Seth?

Early in October Carol walked into the hallway of their brownstone to see a familiar scrawl on the letter at the top of the pile. From Matt, she thought joyously. She didn't bother to check through the other letters; Sharon would do that when she came in. She just wanted to be upstairs and reading Matt's letter. Not one of those tiny V-mails, she thought tenderly—one of his long airmail letters.

She darted up the dark stairs—almost falling in her eagerness to reach the apartment. She unlocked the door, went inside, slammed it closed behind her. Her face radiant with anticipation, she flipped on the overhead light, dropped into a chair to read Matt's long-awaited letter—relief surging through her that it had arrived.

"Dear Carol, there's no easy way to tell you this. It's been a long time since we've seen each other. It seems like another lifetime. I'm marrying an army nurse I met over here. I wish you all the best. Matt."

Carol sat immobile, struggling to absorb the contents of the brief letter. This happened to other girls, she thought in shock. Not to her. What about all those letters he wrote, all the things he said? All his plans for their future?

He didn't marry an army nurse he'd known only a few days, she tormented herself. He'd been seeing her, sleeping with her, while he wrote those letters about how impatient he was for the war to be over so he could come home to *her.*

She knew she was not alone in finding her world suddenly shattered by a letter from an overseas serviceman. How did those others survive? How would she survive?

She felt herself incapable of leaving her chair, starting dinner. She was assaulted by myriad emotions—shock, disbelief, rage, anguish. As though it were somewhere in the distance, she heard a key in the door.

"That dumb jerk who said there was butter in the stores was out of her stupid mind," Sharon began, then stopped dead. "Carol?"

"This just came from Matt—" She handed the brief letter to Sharon.

Sharon's eyes raced over the few sentences.

"The rotten son of a bitch!"

"Why did he lie to me all this time?" Carol's voice was shrill with pain. "He didn't just spend a weekend with her, then decide to marry her. Why did he keep writing all those letters?" *This couldn't be happening—not to Matt and her.*

"I never had much faith in Matt's intentions." Sharon was grim. "I felt about him the way you feel about Jerry. For a while they were terrific fun—but for the long haul? No way!"

"Remember how Matt talked about how we'd open up an office when he had his degree? He'd design houses, and I would decorate them—"

"With Matt you'd never have a chance to be an architect," Sharon said bluntly. "That would wreck his male ego. You don't need Matt. You know what you want to do with your life. And along the way you'll find somebody who fits your bed just as well as Matt."

"I feel so stupid—" Carol's voice broke. "Like some dumb little kid."

"You're not going to let this throw you," Sharon insisted. "Take me, I know Jerry will play just as long as it's fun for him. I know he'll take off again—the way he always does. But I can have a life without him. Hell, we may even get to Paris one day," she said with shaky humor. "We're in charge of our lives, Carol. Don't you ever forget that."

At the agency Christmas party Carol met Denise Williams, an attractive, fortyish brunette who'd just worked out a deal with Victor Blair to package an experimental television series for the agency's new TV department. She was astonished when—in a moment when they were alone together—Denise offered her a job in her newly established office.

"I can pay you what you're getting here at the agency—and it won't be the deadly boring job you have now," Denise told her with contagious high spirits. "And there'll be raises as I become established. Vic says you're bright and efficient and that you'll learn fast."

"He won't be upset if I leave?" Carol was startled by this offer, yet intrigued by its potential. No more money, Denise Williams said, but raises to come. And yes, she *was* bored with this job.

"Vic would like you to come with me," Denise emphasized. "My office will really be an extension of the agency's television department. Suppose you start on the first of the year? That's okay with Vic."

Carol contrived to leave the party at the earliest moment. She was impatient to share her news with Sharon. Mr. Blair had actually set it up, she understood. Instinct warned her that this would be a more chaotic job, with little opportunity for studying during business hours. Still, Denise Williams—and clearly she was expected to call her new boss by her given name—talked about raises.

While she and Sharon headed for the uptown subway, Carol told her about the job.

"It's wild," she continued, ambivalent now.

"I caught a whiff of it when Denise was talking to Mr. Blair this morning," Sharon said. "They've got more than a business deal going between them—" She smiled knowingly.

"But Mr. Blair's married." Carol remembered the photograph of his wife and three teenaged children on his desk.

"Sweetie, don't be naive. I'll take any bet that he and Denise have something going. How else did she land this great deal with the agency?"

"That was naive of me," Carol conceded. People did things these days they wouldn't have dreamt of doing five years ago. Like Sharon and herself. The war had put everybody on a roller coaster. "It was weird how Denise just took it for granted I'd want to work for her. I don't know anything about television. I've never even seen it."

"At this point nobody does," Sharon said, giggling. "But Mr. Blair's sure that once the war is over, television will take off like crazy. He wants the agency to be in on the ground floor."

Carol knew immediately that working for Denise Williams would be far more interesting than her job at the agency. Denise's office was under siege by would-be radio actors and those with a shaky foothold. And at heady intervals Denise was involved with movie and stage stars who were willing to listen to her ambitious efforts to package programs.

Up until now, Carol understood, Denise had been a radio talent agent. Now she was what she called "a packager." Also, in addition to working in radio and the new television medium, Denise was interested in agenting plays for the Broadway theater, wooing would-be investors.

"What about Jerry's play?" Sharon demanded avidly when Carol reported on this latest aspect of Denise's activities.

"She's working with some big agent," Carol explained. "This woman sends her plays, and she tries to interest her own contacts in a Broadway production. Let me settle into the job, then I'll try to get her to read Jerry's play."

At the end of most business days Vic Blair appeared at Denise's office. Their major concern at this point, Carol realized, was getting together the experimental television drama series for one of Blair's accounts. Sharon was right, she understood, about Denise and Blair having an affair. But that was none of her business, Carol told herself. Still, it bothered her that he was cheating on his wife.

Late in January Denise expressed her total dissatisfaction with the one-act plays—usually licensed for amateur productions—that had been submitted for the series.

"God, the garbage," Denise complained. "I know television is new, but it's important to present entertaining plays."

"What about some of the one-act plays that have been shown down in the Village?" Carol grasped at this opportunity. "A lot are awful, but there've been some good ones."

"Take a couple of these home with you tonight." Denise reached for two of the printed booklets on her desk. "Tell me what you think of them."

After dinner—guilty that she was taking time off from studying—Carol settled down to read one of the plays, tossed the other at Sharon.

"Denise says she thinks they're lousy. But she wants my opinion."

"Are you thinking what I think you're thinking?" Sharon's voice was electric.

"You bet! I'll read these two, of course—and then tomorrow I'll walk in with some of Jerry's one-act plays. The ones with small casts," she pinpointed. "That's important for the budget."

"Do you have them here?" Sharon asked in sudden alarm.

"I will in about two hours. I left a message for Jerry at his office."

As Carol had suspected, the one-act plays were designed for high school amateur groups. In the morning she went in to the office with three of Jerry's plays. Denise listened to her report, then agreed to read Jerry's plays.

"There are more by this playwright, but the casts are too large," Carol explained. She took a deep breath, then rushed ahead as rehearsed. "Of course, you could probably hire him to write more for the series. You know, along your guidelines." Why couldn't she lay her hands on some of Seth's plays? she asked herself in frustration. He'd be so excited at the possibility of seeing them on television.

"I'll read these tonight," Denise promised. "Vic wants to move ahead fast. While the client's still in the mood."

With dizzying swiftness Denise made an offer for three of Jerry's plays and added that she'd be willing to buy another five if he could turn them out in her time slot.

"Subject to Vic's approval, of course," Denise added. "Talk to your friend. If he wants to go along, we'll have dinner and set up the deal. I'm tied up the rest of this week, but dinner on Monday?"

"Could it be Tuesday?" Carol asked. She had a class on Monday evenings.

"I'll clear Tuesday," Denise said. "But make him understand he'll have to write fast."

When Carol arrived home after work, she found Sharon and Jerry already there.

"We're having canned soup and deli," Sharon announced. "Nobody's in the mood to cook tonight!"

While Sharon brought the soup and a plate of cold cuts to the table, Carol reported on Denise's offer for the plays Leo had produced.

"She's packaging the series for the agency," Carol explained. "She'll handle everything, including the money."

"Which stinks!" Sharon said disgustedly. "Five dollars a play?"

"That's just for one performance. That's what the other scripts would cost. And Jerry still owns the play."

"I'm not turning it down!" Jerry glowed in anticipation. "Hell, I'll have a play on television. It's getting in on the ground floor."

"And she's interested in another five if you can turn them out to fit her schedule. She said she can squeeze the agency budget to pay you twenty dollars for each one of those."

"It's not like radio money—but I'll take it, I'll take it!"

Greg had been in each of Jerry's plays, Carol remembered painfully. *He'd been so good.* Denise would have a hard time finding someone with his talents and available for the kind of money she could pay. Greg belonged on Broadway in major roles—but he'd died in a bombing in Sicily.

Chapter Twenty-one

Carol, Sharon, and Jerry were totally involved in this new project. Carol and Jerry had an expense-account dinner with Denise to discuss the additional plays and how fast he could bring them in. He figured he could do one a week, writing nights and weekends.

If the series continued, Carol thought with soaring enthusiasm, she must write to Seth's parents and explain that her boss might be able to sell his plays for him. *Where was Seth?* First, of course, she had to go along with the eight-week series that Jerry was to write.

Denise handled the casting for the plays. Carol was amazed when Denise instructed her to take on initial interviews and weed out those she thought were unlikely candidates. At unwary moments Carol felt guilty that—in the midst of the war—she was so enthralled with her activities.

On February 7th American troops entered Manila. On February 23rd the American flag was raised on Mount Suribachi, Iwo Jima. In Europe a tidal wave of Russian troops were pushing back the Nazi armies. In the West the Americans crossed the Rhine at Remagen—the first time since Napoleon that invading forces had crossed the Rhine, heading toward the heart of Germany.

Jerry was delivering manuscripts on schedule. While this was a modest experimental program, Denise hinted that there was a chance that the series might be extended. Prodded by Sharon and with the way paved by Carol, Jerry talked to Denise about his play. Denise told him to bring it in. She would read it as soon as she had some free time.

This was the play Leo had hoped to produce after the war in whatever Village playhouse he could acquire, Carol remembered with fresh anguish. This was the play that was to propel Greg onto the Broadway scene. But Leo and Greg were dead.

Then on April 12th the world was shaken to hear of the death of FDR in Warm Springs, Georgia. The country was in mourning. Vice-President Harry Truman took over the presidency. Twenty-five days later—mid-morning of May 7th—a woman from the office next to Denise's burst in with the news.

"The war in Europe is over!" she shrieked joyously. "The Germans have surrendered unconditionally. My son will be coming home!"

New York erupted into joyous celebration—as in towns and cities throughout the country. Peace had come to Europe. But the war continued in the Pacific, the serious-minded remembered.

"I don't have to worry anymore about being drafted," Jerry surmised. "How much longer can the fighting keep on in the Pacific?"

"Too long," Carol said somberly. "Every minute is too long."

Matt would be coming home with his army nurse bride, she tormented herself. But she could survive without him. That was a part of her life that was forever closed. Yet there were nights when sleep eluded her, when she remembered lost dreams.

Greg wouldn't be coming home—and when the war in the Pacific was at last over, as it surely must be soon, Leo wouldn't be among the returning GIs. At frightened intervals she wondered about Seth.

Denise announced that she would be going away on Memorial Day morning and remain at her beach house out on Fire Island until Sunday. Carol would be in charge of the office. Late that day Carol learned that Vic Blair would be away from the agency for the same time slot.

On Friday Carol had just walked into the office when the phone began to ring. She hurried to answer.

"Denise Williams Associates," she said brightly.

"Carol, it's me. I need some figures on the budget for the television series. Look in the file in my middle desk drawer," Denise ordered. "Just check on the first page of the budget sheet. What's the figure I've allotted for actors for the proposed new series? It'll be at the end of the page."

"I'll get it." Carol put down the phone, pulled out the file. "Okay, I have it," she told Denise after a moment and quoted the figure.

"All right, I'll take care of the readjustment when I get back into town. Oh, you might as well close up at noon today. Everybody will be taking off early—there won't be any calls."

"Thanks, Denise. And have a great weekend." Actually Denise would be away five days, Carol thought wistfully.

She reached to put the file back in the desk drawer. It slipped from her hands as she visualized the long Memorial Day weekend that the lucky ones would be enjoying.

"Damn!"

She bent to retrieve the papers that had fallen to the floor. Putting the pages together, she spied one marked "Manuscript Budget." She gaped in disbelief at the figures quoted there. That was for the projected new series, she realized, then glanced at the following page, which broke down the costs on the series now in work.

Her eyes clung to the figures quoted for the plays bought from Jerry—one hundred dollars each for the first three, one thousand for the next five. Denise had paid Jerry five dollars each for the first three and twenty dollars each for the next five. *How could Denise do that to Jerry?*

Churning with rage she phoned Sharon to tell her what she'd just discovered.

"I'm not as surprised as you are," Sharon admitted. "Denise and Vic are in this together. They'll squeeze every cent they can get out of this deal for themselves."

"We can't tell Jerry," Carol acknowledged, "but we can hint that he should ask more for the next round."

"If the series is renewed," Sharon said. "I have a hunch the client will settle just for radio after this deal. Still, it was good experience for Jerry. He can say he's written an eight-week television series."

"I'm going to push Denise to read Jerry's play." Carol fumed at the injustice of the situation, yet longed to help Jerry's career. "She won't be able to mess around like that if she finds a producer for the play. All she can collect is her commission."

"Don't stew, baby," Sharon ordered. "The world's full of sharks like Denise and Vic."

"As soon as Denise comes back from the cottage, I'm going to start talking about Jerry's play," Carol resolved.

As Sharon had warned, Vic Blair wasn't able to sell a continuation of the television series. The client backtracked into radio. But Carol prodded Denise into reading Jerry's play.

"I think it's terrific," Denise reported enthusiastically. "The cast is small. The budget will be low. And it's damned commercial. I'll start sending it around immediately. Of course, warn Jerry that these things can take an awful long time to develop. Maybe even a year. But I mean to push it hard. I won't let it sit around in a producer's desk drawer for six months."

Carol reported to Jerry and Sharon that Denise was sending out six copies of *A Diamond In The Rough.* The three of them were euphoric—briefly. Within one month—with Denise making calls to find out if the play had been read—five copies came back.

"So five producers turned it down—" Sharon tried to shrug this off, though Jerry was depressed. "All you need is one."

Then the sixth producer phoned to discuss the play with Denise. He was interested in going into production by the first of the new year, provided Jerry would do some rewrites, Denise reported at a hastily called meeting in her office.

"I'll do them." Jerry was elated. "Just let me sit down and talk with the guy."

"There's no guarantee he'll operate on schedule," Denise cautioned, but she was obviously optimistic. "Do the rewrites, then he'll start chasing down the financing."

"Has he done any plays on Broadway?" Carol asked cautiously.

"He hasn't got program credit," Denise acknowledged, "but he did most of the work, even raised a chunk of the money for two plays last year. One had a decent run. And he's very enthusiastic about your play, Jerry."

Jerry revised for David Larson, his would-be producer, then revised for a backer who wanted a small but juicy part for "a niece." The weeks were racing past. The newspapers were full of reports of the troops returning from Europe.

At regular intervals Carol remembered that Matt would be among them—but he wasn't coming home to her. Where was Seth? Had he come through all right? She wouldn't allow herself to wonder if he had been wounded in action—or if he'd shared Leo and Greg's fate.

Seth and a pair of fellow soldiers sat at a table and drank cheap French wine. They were all impatient for word to come through about when they were to board their homebound troopship. They'd probably be packed together like the proverbial sardines in a can, Seth thought, but no blackouts this time—no questions in their minds about who among them wouldn't make it home.

He hadn't written a line since he'd enlisted, he berated himself, but half a dozen ideas for plays were charging around in his mind— plays against the war. He remembered *Bury the Dead*, the terrific one-act antiwar play by Irwin Shaw written before the war. Would people want to see an antiwar play now?

"Hey, Seth," one of the other two soldiers interrupted his musing, "do you agree with Chuck? Do you think we'll be shipped out to the Pacific when we get home?"

"Hey, the war may be over here in Europe, but they're still fighting in the Pacific," Chuck reinforced his conviction.

"At least we'll get a furlough first," Seth guessed. "Maybe a month or six weeks. With any luck at all the fighting there will be over before we can be shipped out."

"Christ, I can't wait to see my kid. She's two-and-a-half and she's never seen her old man!" Chuck's face was incandescent as he envisioned their meeting.

"What's the first thing you'll do when you get home?" the other soldier asked with a grin. A popular question these last weeks of waiting. "Me, I want to eat a two-inch-thick steak, a plateful of French fries, and wash it down with real coffee."

"I want to hump my wife for twenty-four hours straight—after I've seen my kid," Chuck said softly. "I've been dreaming about that."

Most guys were going home to wives and girlfriends, Seth thought in rebellion. He wished he was going home to Carol.

On August 14th—after atomic bombs were dropped first on Hiroshima, then Nagasaki—the Japanese surrendered. The war was over. Those on the victorious side celebrated for two days.

Already the American government was taking steps to ease the lives of returning servicemen. There would be government loans for veterans wishing to start up their own businesses. Tuition and a living allowance were available for every veteran who wanted to go to college.

The summer in Bellevue seemed particularly hot and humid to Seth, though in the two weeks he'd been back home he'd done little besides eat and sleep. He sprawled on the porch glider in the uncomfortable late afternoon, pungent with the scent of roses and honeysuckle. A copy of the latest Sunday *New York Times* available in Bellevue lay beside him. There were so many plays he was dying to see. O'Neill's *The Iceman Cometh,* Hellman's *Another Part of the Forest,* Maxwell Anderson's *Joan of Lorraine.*

He'd been discharged in Fort Dix. Why hadn't he gone the short distance to New York for a few days? he asked himself impatiently. But he knew the answer to that. He couldn't go to New York without seeing Carol—and he couldn't bear seeing her married to Matt. They must be married by now.

He straightened up with a welcoming smile as his mother appeared. She always left the shop an hour before Dad to come home and prepare dinner. Grandma's arthritis had grown worse through the years. Cooking was a difficult task.

"What an awful day," his mother complained. "We may have dinner a little late. I can't start in the kitchen before I have a cool bath."

"Why don't we go out for dinner tonight?" Seth encouraged. Business was good. They could afford this small luxury.

"Not right now, darling," Hannah said tenderly. "We're saving every cent in case Dad decides to buy out Mister Jackson's store." Elderly Mr. Jackson ran a menswear shop next to his father's pawnshop.

"Hasn't Dad got enough to handle right now?" Seth said uneasily. He knew his parents were waiting for him to say that he'd go into the pawnshop in his father's place. *Couldn't they understand he'd hate that?*

"It's such a wonderful opportunity." Hannah smiled, but her eyes were somber. "You know how well Dad gets along with the colored community." Jackson's store dealt mainly with the colored trade, with an occasional farm family coming in. "Dad treats them with respect—and they appreciate that."

"Miz Hannah, would you and Mist' Seth like a glass of lemonade?" Della smiled at them behind the screened door.

"Della, that would be nice. And then you run along home," Hannah said. "I'll start dinner in a little bit."

Now his mother reported on the latest happenings in the community. His face appeared attentive. His mind wandered. Della was polite and friendly, but at intervals he saw a glint in her eyes that he recognized.

Nobody here at home seemed to understand that the end of the war hadn't come without questions in the minds of their colored folks. He remembered a conversation with a colored sergeant in Italy.

"We're over here fighting for democracy in Europe," the sergeant had said in frustration, "but coloreds back home don't live with democracy. That's for you white folks."

Overseas, colored soldiers had been treated the same as whites. The ugliness had come from white American soldiers, who on occasion had beat up colored soldiers because they'd dared to go out with white girls.

People in the South—most of them—didn't understand that the world was changing. Mom kept saying, "We've always been good to our coloreds." But that wasn't enough. Southerners had to open their eyes and *see*. The Constitution provided rights that American Negroes were not enjoying.

He must get out of this town, he told himself with a mixture of guilt and exhilaration. The GI Bill gave him a chance to focus on what he wanted to do with his life. He'd given three and a half years to the war. Now it was his turn.

Along with Jerry, Carol, and Sharon were wrapped up in David Larson's pursuit of financing for the play. Denise set up backers' auditions, with Carol and Sharon as her enthusiastic behind-the-scenes crew. Then David promoted serious interest in a very wealthy semi-retired building contractor who was seeking diversion. David was sure he could convince him that being a theatrical backer would provide much entertainment.

For Carol and Sharon as well as Jerry this was a traumatic period. After the pain of Leo and Greg's deaths the possibility of Jerry's getting a Broadway production was incredibly sweet. Still, Carol worried that Sharon might find herself on the outside if Jerry became a successful playwright. Right now he made it clear that if the play was a Broadway hit there would be no obstacle to his marrying Sharon. Skepticism simmered in Carol, though she ordered herself to be silent.

Weeks sped past while David Larson wooed his prospective backer.

Late in October Sharon arrived home only minutes after Carol.

"I don't know what's up," she said. "Jerry showed up in Vic's office just before closing. I didn't get a chance to talk to him—"

"Maybe the agency is setting up another television deal," Carol surmised. "And they want Jerry to do the scripts."

"I don't know about that." They both started at a sharp knock on the door. "Jerry," Sharon said and rushed to admit him.

"You two characters free this weekend?" he asked nonchalantly.

"No, I'm flying to Paris to have dinner at Maxim's," Sharon drawled. "What's up?"

"Vic just asked me if I'd drive out to the Island and close up his beach house. He figured I'd enjoy a weekend away from the city." Jerry grinned in approval. "He's lending me his wife's beat-up car. I'll pick it up first thing in the morning. We can drive out tomorrow night, stay until Sunday, then drive in."

"It'll be cold—" Sharon stared doubtfully at Carol.

"It'll be great. Nobody on the beach but us," Carol said in joyous anticipation. The crowds on the beach always detracted from the pleasure in being there. "Oh Sharon, I'm dying to get away from the city for a couple of days!"

"Where is it on the Island?" Sharon asked curiously.

"Way out," Jerry said, "in a little village called Wainscott. It goes back to the mid-1600s, Vic said. It's still very rural. There's a tiny Main Street, and a general store—but not much else."

"I'll love it," Carol predicted.

On Friday evening the three of them headed over the Queensborough Bridge en route to Wainscott. Carol settled herself on the back seat, vowing to sleep all the way out. Sharon sat up front with Jerry—one thigh pressed ardently against his. Before Carol drifted off to sleep, she was conscious that at intervals Jerry allowed his right hand to leave the wheel and disappear into the darkness of the car.

Sharon woke her when they had pulled up before the cottage.

"We're here, Sleeping Beauty!" Sharon chirped. "The cottage is right on the water—"

She'd never seen Sharon in such high spirits, Carol thought as they hurried through the foggy night into the tiny two-story cottage. Jerry, too, seemed less cynical, almost tender toward Sharon. Perhaps she was wrong about Jerry, Carol chided herself. Sharon teased her sometimes about becoming such a skeptic.

"God, it's cold in here." Sharon shivered as she glanced about the small rustic living room that led into an equally small kitchen.

"It won't be soon," Jerry promised, pulling her close. "We'll have some coffee and go up to bed."

"What about the fireplace?" Carol asked hopefully.

"No wood," Jerry pointed out. "But Vic said the kerosene stove will warm up the downstairs."

"You light the stove, and Sharon and I will get coffee and Danish on the table," Carol said. They'd brought coffee makings and Danish from the city, along with supplies for breakfast. Tomorrow they'd look for the local grocery store.

Soon the small stove was radiating heat—along with the aroma of kerosene that blended incongruously with the salt-scented night air. They ate swiftly and went up to the bedrooms. With complacent grins Sharon and Jerry disappeared into one bedroom. Carol went into the other, noting with approval that there were a pair of comforters on the double bed. It was colder here by the ocean than it had been in the city.

Shoulders hunched against the cold, Carol changed into a flannel nightgown, pulled on her bathrobe. She hesitated a moment, then crossed to gaze out the window. Fog hung low over the water. The beach was barely visible. Yet there was an aura of serenity that reached out to embrace Carol. It was though, she thought whimsically, they were cut adrift from the rest of the world. As though, for a little while, time was standing still.

The two hours of sleep in the car made it difficult to drift off again, she soon realized. Traitorously—as faint sounds emerged from behind the door of the other bedroom—memories of nights with Matt assaulted her. But she didn't need a man in her life, she told herself defiantly. She had a lot of learning to do and a career to build. That was something that would forever belong to her. Nobody could take that away.

She awoke early as sunlight filtered through the curtains into her bedroom. Last night's fog had disappeared. The only sounds to disturb the morning quiet was the cawing of a pair of seagulls perched on a windowsill and the beating of the surf against the sand. She was aware of an unfamiliar but exhilarating stillness.

She tossed back the comforters and reached for her bathrobe— shoulders hunched against the cold that infiltrated the uninsulated cottage. She dressed quickly beneath the meager comfort of her robe. In warm slacks and a heavy sweater—her jacket about her shoulders—she left the bedroom and headed downstairs. The embracing aromas of fresh coffee greeted her.

"Hi—" Sharon turned to her with a brilliant smile. "I'm taking coffee upstairs for Jerry and me. We're in no rush for breakfast. All right with you?"

"Go play," Carol said indulgently. "I'll have coffee and go for a walk on the beach."

She poured coffee for herself, stood at a window that faced the Atlantic. This wasn't Coney Island or Atlantic City, she thought with a rush of pleasure. The sunlight bathed a deserted stretch of beach before her. All at once she was impatient to be walking along the water. She gulped down the rest of the coffee, checked to see that gloves were in a pocket of her jacket, and hurried outside.

Later they'd explore the village. Now she was content to walk alone on the white sandy beach, washed with early morning sunlight. Just ahead she spied driftwood, decided in a burst of exuberance to collect this so that they might use the fireplace tonight. Maybe they would roast franks for dinner.

Unwarily her mind darted back to an October Sunday before the war—when she and Sharon had gone with Matt and Greg to Coney Island. There'd been only a few people on the beach. Matt had stopped to talk with a couple who'd built a fire and were roasting franks. *"Next time we'll have to do that,"* he'd said. But then came Pearl Harbor, and there were no more October Sundays for Matt and her. She'd been so young and so stupid, she rebuked herself.

The whole world had changed since that October of '39, she thought painfully. Why did Greg and Leo have to die? Why had so many of the young and talented been killed off? Why did it have to be?

Again, she wondered about Seth. Had he come home from Italy? Was he all right? She and Sharon ought to write him. They still had his address down in Bellevue. Yet, somehow, she couldn't bring herself to do this. If Seth wanted to be in touch with them again, he knew where to write. People didn't move these days—it was too hard to find apartments. And if he, too, was gone, she didn't want to know it.

Some economists were fearful that returning GIs would find themselves jobless. It soon became clear this was not to be, though the "52–20 Club"—52 weeks of $20 a week for every unemployed veteran—and the other aspects of the GI Bill had been brought into being to help thwart such a situation. Women war workers were leaving the labor force in startling numbers. Their menfolks were coming home; they were eager to raise families. And salaries had almost doubled since Pearl Harbor.

With the approach of New Year's Eve—1946 right over the horizon—Carol and Sharon tried to ease Jerry's impatience about David Larson's plans for *A Diamond In The Rough*. Larson admitted that his major potential backer was slow in coming through with a final "yes," though he himself was thoroughly enthusiastic about the play.

"It's right for the times," Carol heard him say to Denise. "It's got suspense and comedy. That's what people want now."

The following morning David Larson phoned Denise. Listening to Denise's responses, Carol understood that something had gone wrong with the plans for Jerry's play. Her heart pounding, she waited for Denise to call her into the inner office.

"Carol—" Denise's voice was sharp with irritation.

Carol hurried inside.

"That was David?" she asked, trying to hide her anxiety.

"He said the production's off," Denise said flatly. "His great backer is putting his money into some company that's producing jelly without sugar. The old man's sure he'll make another fortune."

"But David will look for other backers, won't he?" Carol tried to be hopeful.

"He's dumping that on my shoulders. If I can come up with somebody, he'll consider it. I've been through all my contacts." Denise avoided meeting her eyes. "And I don't have time to spend on a wild-goose chase. We have to start casting Vic's new radio series any week now."

"What about Jerry's play?" Carol pushed. Just like that, it was all over?

"He should try some agent." Denise was shuffling papers on her desk. "I'll give you a couple of names. Explain the situation to him,

Carol. And I'll jot down the names of the producers who've turned it down. Any agent he picks up will want to know that."

Carol dreaded the encounter with Jerry tonight. He was coming over for dinner with Sharon, she remembered. She'd grab a sandwich at a soda fountain near the campus before class. She'd see Jerry when she got home.

She debated about calling Sharon. Better warn her. It was going to be an awful shock. Call now while Denise was out on appointments.

"Oh God, Carol—" Sharon was shaken. "Jerry's going to blow a fuse!"

"I'll tell him when I come home from class," Carol said. "Denise dumped it off on me." Oh, did she dread this!

"She's not going to try to make any other deal?" Sharon asked.

"Both she and Larson are bailing out. She gave me the name of two play agents and the names of the producers who've seen the manuscript."

"Jerry was so excited," Sharon wailed. "It's going to be awful."

"Sharon, I have to go. My other phone's ringing," Carol broke off. "Talk to you later."

For the rest of the day and all through her evening class, Carol cringed at the prospect of telling Jerry that the production was off. *Everybody had been so sure it was going through.* So the old man backed out, she thought in frustration. Why couldn't David and Denise try for another investor? *They both loved the play.* But then, her respect for Denise had dropped to zero since she'd discovered the way they'd cheated Jerry on the TV scripts—billing the agency for so much and giving him so little.

The minute she walked into the apartment, Carol knew that Sharon had hinted at a problem with the production. Both Sharon and Jerry looked tense and uneasy.

"What's the scoop?" Jerry demanded while Carol slid out of her coat.

"Mister Moneybags pulled out," Carol said, mentally flinching at this devastating message. "David says he has nobody else interested in putting up money." She hesitated. "And Denise says she's run out of contacts."

"Damn it!" Jerry leapt to his feet. "They made it seem like it was a surefire deal! All that crap about a two-year run, a London company. Now they're throwing me away like a piece of garbage."

"Denise gave me the names of two agents she thought you ought to try." Carol reached for her purse. Poor Jerry, she thought—what an awful letdown.

"Oh sure, start that routine," Jerry sneered. "A play can sit in an agent's office for a year and then get thrown back in your face."

"Jerry, David likes it a lot. There'll be others who'll like it." Sharon tried for an air of optimism.

"This was my one chance at the brass ring," Jerry said bitterly. "That penthouse on Central Park South, a Cadillac, a summer house at Southampton. Remember how you talked about that, Sharon? We've got 'loser' written all over us!"

"That's a rotten attitude to take," Sharon flared. "One setback and you're ready to throw in the towel?"

"Tell Denise I said 'thanks for nothing.'" He reached for his jacket, pulled it on. "What an ass I was to think something good could happen to me."

"Jerry, you're behaving like a two-year-old who just busted his favorite toy," Sharon scolded. "Why don't you just—"

"I don't want to talk about it anymore." He reached for the door, opened it, and charged out into the hall, slamming the door behind him.

"We won't see him again for six months," Sharon predicted. "And damn it, I won't care!"

Chapter Twenty-two

As Carol and Sharon expected, Jerry disappeared again from their lives. He walked out of his apartment, leaving nothing behind, no word for Sharon.

Sharon was alternately angry and depressed at the lack of a social life now.

"You can handle it," Sharon told Carol on a blustery Friday

night in January when they were standing in line for cheap seats for *Anna Lucasta,* now in its second year on Broadway. "You're so damned dedicated to becoming an architect you can put up with anything."

"It won't always be this way," Carol comforted. For months shiploads of GIs had been returning from Europe and the Pacific. All of them, Sharon swore bitterly, had girlfriends waiting for them—or foreign brides waiting to be brought to American shores. "This is a time when people are trying to pick up their lives."

"I'm not picking up Jerry and you're not picking up Matt," Sharon said grimly. "No loss—they're a pair of bastards. But damn, I want something more than working and going to a Saturday movie. Or the big deal, like tonight, when we treat ourselves to a Broadway play."

"Sign up for an evening class next term," Carol encouraged. "They'll be loaded with guys."

"They go to day classes. With the government paying, why shouldn't they?"

"Some will be going to night classes. Not every veteran wants to live on twenty dollars a week."

"I heard a guy on the subway last week," Sharon recalled. "He said, 'If I land a job, it'll be a big twenty-five bucks a week. After taxes, carfare, and lunch money, I'll have less than a twenty a week.' I gather he figures staying in the '52—20' club for the whole year."

"That's some," Carol conceded, "but most of them want to get their lives on track again. They want to move up the ladder. Go to a night class," Carol pushed.

"Maybe a French course," Sharon decided after a moment. Her grin was shaky. "You know me, the perennial Francophile."

Sharon signed up for an evening class in French, became an avid reader—struggling to accept the lack of a man in her life. She was mildly pleased at a job promotion at the agency and a substantial increase in salary.

"Let's save up for a trip to Paris," she told Carol in a burst of restlessness. "Nobody's rushing me to the Marriage License Bureau—"

"Maybe you'll meet an ex-GI studying in Paris," Carol joshed. A stream of American veterans were making a return trip to Europe to study. "If they're still there when we can afford a trip."

"It's not so farfetched," Sharon said. "I hear some of the prewar liners that became troop ships are being reconverted as passenger liners. So we'll go steerage," she said in rising good humor. "For a week in Paris I'll skip lunch for the next two years."

Though they could afford a less claustrophobic apartment, they remained in their tiny, cheap studio—pleased by their growing bank accounts. With shiploads of GIs returning home, apartments were in frenzied demand. But both Carol and Sharon felt themselves in limbo. Life had to offer more.

Carol was impatient at the slow progress of her schooling. She ached to be free to study full time. Then late in the spring she read an article in an architectural magazine about a woman with no formal training who'd opened up her own practice.

"If she doesn't have a degree in architecture," Sharon challenged as Carol talked about this while they strolled along the river's edge on a balmy Sunday, "how can she have a practice?"

"She went to work in an architect's office right out of high school." Carol was enthralled at such a daring route. "She learned on the job. Then just before the war, she opened up her own office."

"How long did she work for this architect?" Sharon demanded. "Twenty years?"

"No!" Carol was defiant. "Okay, for a long time," she conceded. "But if I could land a job in an architect's office while I'm taking classes, maybe I could work my way up to taking on assignments even before I earn my degree. It just seems so long, the way I'm going."

"I'll bet she had a rough time getting the first commission on her own," Sharon warned.

"With enough drafting courses behind me, I should be able to find a job with an architectural firm," Carol said with growing conviction. "I'll work cheap—"

"You're a woman," Sharon said cynically. "That's expected. And you said yourself, there're not many women in the field."

"That has to change." Carol refused to consider otherwise. "This summer I'll start looking for a job with some large architectural firm. I don't care what I have to do—at least, I'll be in the field. I'll learn."

Denise closed the office for a week in early June. This was Carol's week of paid vacation. She spent each day in an effort to find a job—any job—in an architectural office. Reluctantly she conceded that the only job she'd been offered was as a receptionist—at considerably less than she was earning.

"If it was a job on the inside, I'd have grabbed it," she told Sharon. "But I'd just sit outside at the reception desk. And do you know," she said in a burst of frustration, "I haven't seen one office where they have a woman even working at drafting?"

"They figure a woman won't be able to deal with contractors and workmen," Sharon surmised. "They—"

"In this day and age?" Carol interrupted. "Look at the jobs women had during the war!" She felt a fresh surge of indignation. "Women can handle any job that a man can do—if they have the proper training."

"All right. You're getting training. You'll look around some more. But what the hell am I going to do with my life?" Sharon sighed in disgust. "I've gone as far as I can at the agency. Mom's starting again with 'Why don't you try for a civil service job? You're sure of a pension when you work for the government.' She's talking about a pension when I've just started living. I'm twenty-six years old—who's thinking about pensions?"

"What about going for a master's in English?" Carol said after a moment. "You're always reading. You might enjoy working in publishing."

"That's what Seth used to tell his parents he was going to do," Sharon recalled. "Not that he meant it. I wonder where the hell he is?"

"Back with his father in the pawnshop—or we'd have heard from him," Carol decided. She couldn't bring herself to say, "If he survived the war."

"I couldn't face the thought of working for a master's," Sharon admitted. "But maybe I'll take some courses in that direction. I am so bloody bored with my life," she burst out yet again. "I feel in such a rut."

Denise decided to close the office on Fridays during the months of July and August, which allowed for long weekends at Vic's Wainscott cottage. Carol seized this opportunity to explore the job field again. She was frustrated by her continual failure to latch on to something practical.

Sitting in an employment agency on a steamy Friday afternoon in July she began a conversation with a vivacious blonde.

"Of course, I only want to work about three or four months," the blonde confided to Carol. "My boyfriend's going to school under the GI Bill. In Italy," she said triumphantly. "As soon as I have enough to pay for passage and a little more, I'm going over to be with him. We'll get married there."

"Do you speak Italian?" Carol asked curiously.

"Not a word," she admitted. "Oh, I won't worry about landing a job. Ted and I can live on his GI allowance. Everything's so cheap over there you wouldn't believe it! That's why so many Americans are going over."

Carol said nothing to Sharon about what was fomenting in her mind. Was it really that cheap to live in Paris? Now she haunted the library to ferret out reports on this situation via magazine articles. She was astonished to learn that in France GI allowances were translated into 26,000 to 42,000 francs a month, so favorable was the exchange. Most French workers earned 20,000 francs a month. Many of the professors who were teaching ex-GIs were earning less than their students received for going on for higher education.

Like most Americans Carol and Sharon saved slavishly during the war years—and they hadn't changed this pattern since the war ended. On what they'd saved, she calculated with towering excitement, they could live in Paris for a year and still have money to see them through till they found jobs again in New York.

Instinct told her that if she approached an architectural firm for a job and talked about having "taken courses in architecture at the Sorbonne," she'd be considered far more seriously than she was now. She was too impatient to wait until she had a degree to work in her chosen field.

At last mentally committed to the venturous step of spending time in Paris, Carol presented this prospect to Sharon as they headed on a Saturday evening for a neighborhood movie.

Sharon stopped dead in astonishment.

"Go to Paris to live?" She gaped at Carol in disbelief.

"Just for a year." Carol's face was radiant as she considered this. "I figured it out. With the dollar exchange we can afford it. We won't be living at the Ritz, but we'll manage." Still Sharon seemed unable to digest this. "You always talk about how you're dying to see Paris—"

"My mother will have a fit—"

"You'll write your folks every week. You'll phone on special holidays. Even overseas phone calls are cheap for Americans."

"Do we dare?" Sharon was torn between joyous agreement and fear of such a revolutionary move.

"We dare." Carol was emphatic.

"Oh God, I can't believe it!" Sharon reached to hug Carol in quick acquiescence. "Notre Dame, the Champs-Elysées, Montmartre. Carol, do you really think we can pull it off?"

"Let's forget the movie. We'll go home, and I'll show you figures. I've even checked on the cost for passage."

"How soon will we go? I have to give the agency two weeks' notice—"

"We won't leave that fast." Carol laughed in relief. She'd sold Sharon on this. "Maybe August." It would have to be by then if she was to enroll for a course or two at the Sorbonne. Only one, she decided realistically. It wouldn't be easy to take classes in French. "We'll have to get passports," she continued. "I'll need school transcripts. We have to make ship reservations and—"

"Let's go on the *Queen Elizabeth*," Sharon said exuberantly. "The big boss at the agency went over on it last spring, when it became a commercial ship again. He said it was wonderful. So-o luxurious." During the war years the *Queen Elizabeth* had been a troopship.

"It goes to England," Carol pointed out.

"So let's treat ourselves to three days in London, then go to Paris." Sharon was euphoric. "We deserve it."

"Yes," Carol said softly, her mind shooting back through the years to that long ago trip to London with her parents. "We'll treat ourselves."

Carol and Sharon were absorbed in every detail relating to their plotted adventure. They would sail on the *Queen Elizabeth*—tourist class, of course, they agreed. Tourist class was $165 a crossing compared to $365 for first-class. Together they coaxed Sharon's parents into acceptance, though Carol suspected they didn't believe she and Sharon would actually remain away for a year.

Their passports acquired, Carol and Sharon booked passage for mid-August. The *Queen Elizabeth* would take them to Southampton, England. From there they would travel to London for a three-day stay. "In a bed-and-breakfast," Carol decreed. They couldn't afford a suite at the Hotel Savoy, as her father had provided on that London stay when she was nine. Again—as she did at irregular intervals—Carol wondered where in Florida her mother was living these days. She'd never received even a postcard.

On the appointed day—both suffering sudden misgivings at this revolutionary step in their lives—Carol and Sharon were accompanied to Pier 90 by Sharon's parents. Determined not to reveal her own alarm, Sharon's mother had brought them a bottle of domestic champagne, along with a parcel of canned meats, a salami, and chocolates because food was in short supply in Europe.

"Write me what you need," Mrs. Ross instructed. "I'll send packages."

As they stood on the pier examining the totally reconditioned *Queen Elizabeth,* Sharon's father briefed them on what he had learned about the world's biggest liner.

"Did you know she carried more than half a million soldiers to England during the war?" He gazed with admiration at the 1,031 foot ship, resplendent in a new coat of white, red, and black paint. "I read in *Time* that twenty-one thousand pieces of furniture and ten miles of carpeting went into refurbishing her."

Then in a last-minute flurry of excitement Carol and Sharon exchanged warm farewells with Mr. and Mrs. Ross and hurried aboard the ship, scheduled to dock at Southampton in roughly 4 days, 16 hours, and 19 minutes—not a spectacular speed, considering that commercial planes were covering the same crossing in around 16 hours. But the flight to London cost $375 one way.

Though this was close to off-season for trips abroad, the *Queen Elizabeth* was heavily booked. Americans were intrigued by the low cost of living across the Atlantic in the early postwar period. Despite the chilly weather Carol and Sharon spent much time on deck—vowing not to be caught up in the buying craze that affected many passengers. The charming shipboard shops were filled with enticing merchandise.

"Can you imagine Leo if he was here with us? Limitless Haig and Haig at fifty cents a drink!" Leo had always kept a bottle in his desk—for special occasions, he claimed. "Even now, Carol, I can't fully accept that he and Greg are dead."

"I know—" That tight little clique of theirs was nonexistent now. They'd all—except for Jerry—had this crazy conviction they'd go through life together. Now Greg and Leo were gone forever, Matt was married to some army nurse, and Jerry off on another of his wild excursions. Nobody knew where Seth was.

For Carol their brief stay in London was a blend of pleasure and pain. She remembered the trip here with her parents. Dad had loved London. Mom had made him so miserable with her carrying-on because he refused to go on to Paris before they returned home. Even then he'd been worried about the stock market—so soon to crash.

Amid a frenzy of sightseeing—because Sharon was determined to see as much as possible within three days—Carol was unnerved when they stood before London landmarks that Matt had written about in awesome detail. Matt had walked these same streets, admired the same sights. Was it here in London that Matt met his army nurse? But that didn't matter anymore—she'd washed him out of her memory. Almost.

She and Sharon were upset by the bombed-out buildings they encountered on every side. How many civilians had died when those bombs hit? How many Allied soldiers?

In a burst of guilty yet joyous extravagance Carol and Sharon decided to fly from London to Paris. They tried to appear sophisticated—as though this was not the first time they'd been aboard a plane. Since only months after the end of the war Americans had been eager to resume European travel. In January of 1945—with the war not yet over—Pan Am had rushed to set up transatlantic schedules—making the crossing in a miraculous 15 hours and 50 minutes. American Airlines carried its first passengers to Scandinavia in October 1945. The race was on.

Carol and Sharon had been awed to learn—at London's new Heathrow Airport—that it was possible to buy a round-the-world plane ticket from Pan Am. The world was becoming so small, Carol thought.

"I can't believe that we'll be in Paris in less than three hours," Sharon whispered when they were settled in their seats.

Arriving in the city on the bus from Orly Airport, they were astonished to discover many of the small shops were closed, restaurants dark.

"Is it a holiday?" Sharon asked Carol as their taxi pulled up before the inexpensive *pension* they'd chosen for their first night or two in Paris. Immediately they must find a cheap apartment near the Sorbonne—located on the Boulevard St. Michel, on the left bank.

"It's August." Carol's smile was dazzling. She was enthralled at being here. "Parisians are taking off for their first real vacations since before the war. Remember that article about it in a London paper? The one that talked about the Peace Conference—"

"Right." Sharon nodded. "Maybe that's one of the reasons we were able to get reservations at this *pension*." It had been recommended by Sharon's French professor.

They were amazed, too, that Paris—in such contrast to London—seemed untouched by the war. No signs of bombings, the bridges intact—though the city showed no physical hardships, Carol thought compassionately that wasn't true of the people. She was especially touched by the thinness of the children.

Their room had an air of shabby gentility. The maid who had brought them up explained that because of the many shortages the owner had not been able to bring the *pension* up to its prewar standards.

"Why don't we finish unpacking later?" Carol said, eager to explore the Left Bank.

"You can't wait to see the Sorbonne," Sharon interpreted indulgently. "Okay, let's go."

Carol knew from research that the Sorbonne had been the heart of the University of Paris since the 13th century. She knew, too, that—like Hunter—the Sorbonne had no campus. They asked directions, headed for the buildings that dominated the Left Bank.

"The 'New Sorbonne' was completed in 1627," Carol told Sharon as they walked along the ancient, twisting streets to their destination—past musty old bookstores, sidewalk cafés, crowded bistros. "Richelieu is buried in the chapel."

They were conscious of the aromas of cooking that floated from the bistros into the streets, of the unfamiliar languages spoken by the hordes of young people that were everywhere—not only the languages of Europe but of China, Africa, the Middle East. The Sorbonne—with its all but free tuition—attracted students from every corner of the world.

Then they arrived at the sprawl of centuries-aged buildings and walked with awe from one impressive structure to another.

"This was a thriving university before Columbus discovered America," Carol said with awe. "A seat of learning before the first rural schoolhouse went up back home." Her eyes devoured the architectural details of the finest university buildings of the world. "Oh Sharon, I'm so glad we've come here!"

In the evening they chatted with an elderly American woman living in the *pension* about their need to find a cheap apartment.

"We were told to try the Left Bank," Carol began.

"Oh, my young friends, are you in luck!" The American expatriate glowed. "I know of a sublet that's coming up. It'll cost you more than the present tenant pays—but no more than thirty a month in American dollars. It's very modest," she warned, "but then you young ones don't care about such things. It's a cellar—and the young woman there now says the heat and hot water are not what you'd find on the Right Bank. Perhaps no heat at all," she surmised. "And little hot water—"

"We'll manage," Sharon rushed to reassure her.

"The present tenant is a little *midinette* who's going on to better things." The American woman smiled sentimentally. "She's marrying an American soldier who's come back here to open up a business because she was reluctant to leave Paris. Even in these hard times."

Carol's smile was all at once forced. She didn't want to hear about foreign brides of American GIs.

"Have you lived here long?" Sharon rushed to change the subject.

"Almost thirty years. I came here because the dollar goes much further. I rushed back to the States days before the Nazis invaded the city, then came back as soon as this was possible."

In the morning their new friend made a phone call, arranged for them to see the apartment on one of the narrow, winding streets of the Left Bank. By dusk they were settled into the paint-hungry, sparsely furnished cellar apartment that consisted of a small living room, minuscule bedroom, a makeshift kitchen, and ancient bath.

"But we have windows," Sharon pointed out in an effort at cheerfulness.

"Right." Carol giggled, inspecting their view of feet and ankles of passersby. "We'll paint—when paint's available—and put up curtains, with maybe some plants for the windows."

"Ones that don't need much sun," Sharon said. "Oh, I can't believe it! We're actually living in Paris!"

They quickly became aware that living in postwar Paris was fraught with problems they hadn't faced in postwar New York. Hot water was nonexistent, and they suspected there'd be no heat when winter arrived. They stood in line for bread, produce, meat. Except for the wealthy—willing to deal with the black market, food was scarce and expensive. Eggs and chocolates were nonexistent. A meal in a good restaurant cost more than the average Frenchman earned in three or four days. In line in a butcher shop, they listened to the conversation between two housewives, buying half a pound of ground meat as a treat for their families.

"I have to tell the children it's beef," one woman confided. "How can I tell them—when they all love horses—that they're eating horsemeat?"

"That does it," Carol said philosophically. "We've just become vegetarians."

But for all the discomforts they encountered, they reveled at being in Paris. Carol was entranced with the one class she could afford to take. Early in September Sharon was delighted when she was able to find occasional days of typing at an American office.

They roamed the Boulevard St.-Michel—known to the hordes of young people who occupied the area as "Boul Mich"—and the Boulevard St.-Germain. The weather was still sufficiently warm for the outdoor cafés to sprawl on the sidewalks beneath endless stretches of plane trees without their winter enclosures.

They explored all of Paris in the coming weeks, with the streets now miraculously free of tourists. Carol read avidly in the university library, occasionally allowing herself the luxury of a special book—at bargain rates—discovered at one of the stream of bookstores on the Left Bank.

They heard much English spoken in the Latin Quarter, along with American-accented French in varying degrees of fluency. This was the turf of the 1,500 or more American ex-GIs studying in Paris. The Americans mixed with the French as though no language barrier existed. The French and the American young sat at tables in the Café de Flore, the Deux Magots, the Dupont and argued about art and literature and politics—and about anti-fascism and communism. There was an air of freedom here that Carol and Sharon relished.

Occasionally in the evenings—because they were ever watchful of their funds—Carol and Sharon went to the new Café Le Tabou, a long, narrow, smoky room below street level. Here there was much talk about Jean-Paul Sartre and Albert Camus, the celebrated French writers. Camus, they learned, was only thirty and already being talked about as a candidate for the Nobel Prize in literature.

Sartre also taught at the university, though Carol had never encountered him at that massive institution.

"Carol, that's Sartre over there," Sharon whispered excitedly on
a late October evening. "A guy at the next table says he comes here
often to listen to the jazz trumpeter."

"Didn't he write a play that's supposed to be marvelous?" Carol
squinted in thought. "I think it's called *Les Morts Sans
Sepulture*—"

"The Unburied Dead," Sharon translated. "It's about the French
Resistance." She smiled faintly. "Seth would love it. Jerry would
say 'damned noncommercial.' "

Then quite suddenly it was winter—cold and gray and dismal.
For weeks there was not a glimmer of sunlight. An air of melancholy
hung over the city. The sidewalk cafés were encased in glass. Residents complained of cold or grippe.

With the approach of the new year, Carol and Sharon suffered
the first pangs of homesickness—caught up in the memories of earlier New Year's Eves. They'd made many casual acquaintances
since their arrival in Paris—but no real friends. Had they made a
mistake in coming to Paris? Carol asked herself with painful fre-
quency now. It was *her* fault that they had come, she admitted guiltily.

"Let's splurge on New Year's Eve," she said defiantly to Sharon,
three days before the holiday. "We'll go to the Saint-Germain on
Rue Saint-Benoit—eat, drink, and listen to jazz."

Had they made a mistake in coming here? Should they admit it
and go back home while they still had a fair amount of money left?
This time of year they'd have no problem in booking passage.

Chapter Twenty-three

Seth stood at a window in his garret room that looked down on pewter-tinted slate roofs broken at intervals by dingy, twisted chimney pots. Through a broken pane in one window came the faint scent of the Seine. On this final day of December twilight had arrived early. Now the lights of Paris glowed with an air of optimism that failed to ignite a matching feeling in himself. His tiny apartment—like much of Paris—was devoid of heat. All over Europe there was a shortage of coal. Electricity was rationed. And the weather was unusually harsh.

Why had he told Jack and George he'd go to the theater with them tonight? This time of month—when they were all waiting for their next Veteran Administration checks—money was tight. Still, he was impatient to see the two Sartre plays at the Theater Antoine. How could a French Existentialist write about the American South? he asked himself with recurrent amazement.

People who'd seen *La Putain Respectuese*—"The Respectful Prostitute"—said Sartre had contrived to make the lynching of a Negro in the Deep South both farcical and melodramatic. One of the critics had called it a satire on America's Deep South.

Sartre had recently gone on a lecture tour of the United States, Seth remembered. Had his vision, perhaps, been clearer than that of native-born Americans?

Postwar Paris was entertaining a surprising number of American Negro expatriates. They tasted a freedom here that was denied them at home, Seth admitted with painful candor. Not only in the South did they face discrimination, he remembered. It was just less obvious in other parts of the country.

Engrossed in thought, Seth started at the pounding on his door.

"It's open," he called. That would be George and Jack.

The two ex-GIs charged into the room.

"Come on, this is a night to party!" Jack said exuberantly and looked around. "You got a bottle of decent wine tucked away somewhere?"

"This close to payday?" George scoffed before Seth could answer. "We'll be lucky to be able to pay the dinner check. First, the theater, then we eat."

"And drink," Seth added with an effort at conviviality "Okay, let's go over to the Antoine."

"You making any New Year's Resolutions?" Jack asked as the three of them made their way down the narrow, twisting stairs.

"I am," George said, all at once solemn. "No more cutting classes. And I'm going to dig into the books. There's a life after college. I need that degree."

"Yeah." Seth's smile was wry. "Sometimes I think a lot of us are spending more time at the Café Flore than in the classrooms. When this is supposed to become the best educated generation in history!"

"Aw, shut up," Jack drawled. "The trouble with you, Seth— you're so serious about life. Loosen up! It's New Year's Eve."

Knowing the shops were closed and they wouldn't make some rash purchase they couldn't afford, Carol and Sharon strolled along the Rue du Faubourg-St.-Honoré—the most fashionable street in France—and gazed at awesomely expensive merchandise in the shop windows. This was the part of Paris that was inhabited by the wealthy American colony—those who lived near the Bois de Boulogne or in mansions beyond the city gates, who didn't stand in line beside the French for the often limited rations available but sent their servants to deal with this. They were the ones who bought expensive imports at the American commissaries.

"Just once before we leave Paris," Sharon said wistfully, "I want to have dinner—or I'll settle for lunch—in a fancy restaurant in the Bois de Boulogne."

"Sharon, are you sorry we came over?" Carol asked.

"Oh no!" Sharon said, overly emphatic. "Okay, at Thanksgiving I was homesick—and now again. It's only natural," she said defensively. "Each New Year's Eve brings back memories of all the others behind us. We kind of compare and go for some 'moaning of the bar'. But then comes New Year's Day, and nostalgia bites the dust."

But instinct told her that Sharon was grandstanding. The first two months in Paris were enthralling for both of them. Now Sharon was at loose ends, Carol thought. Occasional typing jobs helped with money, but their social lives were uneventful. And they were past the avid tourist stage. Paris wasn't working out the way they'd anticipated.

"Let's take the Metro home," Carol said, "then head for the Saint-Germain."

By the time they arrived at the cellar club, the room was crowded, noisy, hazy with smoke. Still, there was a welcome air of conviviality here. As she and Sharon settled at one of the few unoccupied tables Carol heard the impassioned conversation between a young French woman and an American art student at an adjoining table. They were discussing the Negro writer Richard Wright, who'd been in Paris since May. Carol recalled hearing Seth and Jerry talk about Wright. One of his novels had become a Broadway play.

"Carol, you haven't heard a word I've been saying," Sharon scolded.

Carol was saved from a reply by the sudden rush of jazz into the room. Along with the others she listened with rapt attention, though in truth she was not an avid jazz fan. She was restless, trying to deal with the approach of another year. She'd be twenty-seven—and so far from a degree in architecture, she thought fretfully.

Had Matt gone back to school under the GI Bill, as so many veterans were doing? She didn't care what Matt did, she thought in sudden startled realization. The career was what mattered now.

"Isn't this a great group?" Sharon whispered.

Carol's eyes roamed aboutd the room. Most of the patrons were about their age, she thought—or younger. Most sat in silence—absorbed by the music. Then her eyes fell on a bearded young man across the room. Her heart began to pound. She was unnerved by his resemblance to Seth. That was how Seth would look with a beard.

"Sharon—" Her voice was taut. Her throat tight. "I'd like to leave."

"Are you all right?" Sharon asked solicitously.

"Let's just go." She pushed back her chair and rose to her feet.

"Okay—"

Carol realized that the man who so resembled Seth was gazing at her. He must have noticed her staring and thought she was trying to pick him up. Color flooded her face.

"Who were you looking at so intently?" Sharon glanced over her shoulder for a moment before following Carol to the entrance.

"It's nothing," Carol said. "Let's just get out of here."

Across the room Seth ignored the whispered discussion between Jack and George about *le jazz hot*. Except that she wore her hair differently—in a kind of pompadour, the girl who was just leaving was startlingly like Carol. Everybody had a double, he thought—and then froze. Her companion had turned her head to look in his direction. *Sharon. Carol and Sharon were here in Paris.*

"I've have to go," he mumbled, leaping to his feet and pulling francs from his pocket. "Talk to you later—" He tossed his share of their bill on the table.

"What's with you?" Jack demanded, but Seth was already pushing his way through the crowded room.

Rushing out into the cold, dank air, Seth gazed first in one direction, then the other. They couldn't have disappeared so fast! And he wasn't wrong—*Carol and Sharon were in Paris.* In anguished frustration he strode toward the left. His eyes searched for sight of them. Had they gone the other way? he asked himself apprehensively.

Then as the crowd ahead weaved, jockeyed for new positions, he spied them.

"Carol!" he yelled above the lively street noises. "Sharon!"

They swung around in unison—their faces reflecting their astonishment and joy as they recognized him.

"I thought I saw you in the club," Carol called to him as she and Sharon pushed through the hordes to join him. "Then I told myself it was some French student who resembled you. The beard threw me off—"

They exchanged warm, excited embraces, then Seth placed himself between the two young women, an arm about each as they moved ahead because it was impossible to stand in place in this New Year's Eve crowd.

"For a moment I couldn't believe what I was seeing," Seth told them. "Then you turned around, Sharon—and I knew it was the two of you."

"Oh God, we've got so much to catch up on!" Sharon said exuberantly.

"My apartment—my room," Seth corrected himself with a grin, "is just a few blocks away. Let's go up there—if you can handle five creaky flights of stairs."

"We're just as close and in the cellar," Sharon told him. "Let's go there."

"How long have you been here?" Carol asked Seth—enraptured by their encounter.

"A year this month," Seth said. She wasn't here with Matt, he guessed. She and Sharon were on their own. "I'm studying at the university. I couldn't handle Bellevue after the war. What are you two doing here at this time of year?" Americans were straggling over for two-week vacations—but in the summer.

"Don't you remember me and my long love affair with Paris?" Sharon chided good-humoredly. "Then when Carol talked about how good it would look on her résumé if she could mention 'classes at the Sorbonne,' we decided to live dangerously and come. Of course, we knew about all the ex-GIs living here on practically nothing. We figured we could manage for a year."

They walked swiftly toward their destination—the three of them caught up in the miracle of having met after months of living in the same area. Not until they were in the dubious warmth of the cellar apartment—the windowsills stuffed with paper in an effort to keep out the cold—did Seth ask about the others in their once tight circle.

"I lost track of Leo and Greg after I was shipped out," he began and paused for a moment as he saw their pained expressions. "The word isn't good," he guessed.

"Greg died in a post-office bombing in Italy," Carol told him. "Leo in the Pacific."

"Oh God, I was so sure they'd make it through." Seth was cold with shock. *Why* had he been so sure? Because they were both so talented and with great futures ahead of them? That was no insurance in time of war.

"It was a long time before we could really believe it," Carol whispered.

"And Jerry—did he ever get dragged in? He used to brag about being blind as a bat and flatfooted." Seth hesitated. "What about Matt?"

"Jerry never got drafted," Sharon told him. "Though if the war had lasted another six months, he expected to be sucked in. Matt was in England and France. As far as we know, he came through in fine shape." *Then he and Carol had broken up, Seth pinpointed with a surge of excitement.* "The last we heard, his company had arrived in Paris, and he was marrying some army nurse."

Involuntarily Seth turned to Carol. Again, she'd been badly hurt, he guessed. First, there had been her disastrous marriage—and now Matt had married somebody else. Here was a second chance for *him.* But he must be careful. Don't rush her. Don't muff this chance. But oh God, he'd never stopped loving her.

"You haven't changed a bit," he told Carol. "Either of you," he turned to include Sharon. "I can't believe I haven't seen you in years!" Nothing had changed for him. More than anything in this world, he wanted Carol to be a permanent part of his life.

Carol and Sharon sat with Seth over endless cups of coffee, interrupting one another at frequent intervals to explore memories of prewar days and nights in New York. The three of them loathe to part as the old year segued into the new.

They talked about Seth's graduate studies at the Sorbonne.

"I admit I've been sparring for time," he said seriously. "All these classes in European literature. But I think it's helped me with my writing. I figure on going back home when classes are over. I mean, USA home—not Bellevue. Maybe I'll take a crack at television. That's going to be the big new scene."

"Sometimes I'm jealous of you two," Sharon said whimsically. "You know what you want to do with your lives. Me—I'm like most people. Just riding with the tide."

Dawn crept over the Paris rooftops, and still they talked. Seth listened avidly to their reports of Jerry's brush with Broadway.

"Hell, he knows it's a rough racket," Seth said, and Carol knew he was prepared to face disappointments. "Theater's a crazy business. But maybe when television takes off, it'll be a better picture. Jerry must have gotten a terrific kick out of seeing the plays on television." He chuckled for a moment. "And pissed when he found out how he'd been screwed on the money."

"We didn't tell him," Carol hurried to explain. "We figured that would just hurt him again."

"Carol was going to try to sell her boss on your plays if the series was renewed," Sharon said. "But the agency decided to go back to radio."

"I can't believe we're sitting together here this way," Seth said gently, his eyes moving from Carol to Sharon. "It's like a dream."

"A dream with shitty coffee." Sharon sighed, then smiled. "Remember the terrific coffee back at the Automat?"

Now it became a pattern for the three of them to spend much of their free time together—in this coldest winter since 1870, with Paris often buried in snow. At intervals Seth's buddies—Jack and George—joined them. Carol understood that George—from Boston and with two years at Boston University behind him—was settling down to serious study. Jack came from a farm family in Nebraska. He was, Seth explained indulgently, having himself a "high old time" before he went back home to a small agricultural college.

Carol relished Seth's enthusiasm for her career plans. He agreed that having studied at the Sorbonne would carry weight on her résumé. He understood that not every girl was panting to settle down in a pretty little house, to be a housewife and mother. Matt could never understand that some girls meant to have careers, she remembered. Seth could.

Then all at once it was spring in Paris. The cold, gray, horrendous winter was behind them. The seemingly endless days and nights when rain pelted the city were now in eclipse. Iris, daffodils, and jonquils were in bloom. Pink and white chestnut blossoms drifted in the air. It seemed to Carol that all of Paris's 295,000 trees were sending forth their leaves.

On the Rue de Rivoli shops along the arcades were being given a fresh coat of paint. Sidewalks around the city were being newly paved. The display windows on the Faubourg-St.-Honoré offered dresses and gloves and shoes that said joyously, "Spring is here!"

"Oh, it's great to be warm again," Carol gloated as she walked with Sharon and Seth along the Rue St.-Honoré on a glorious Saturday afternoon.

"Look at the grocery windows," Seth chortled. "Real live strawberries and asparagus." Both strangely bedded in cotton wool. "Do you know how long it's been since I've had strawberries and cream?" He reached into his pocket to pull out his wallet. "Come on, I'm buying strawberries and asparagus. We'll eat like rich Americans tonight."

On the way to Seth's apartment they stopped to buy fish fresh out of the Seine, by the Point Neuf. Sharon was going to cook while Carol read Seth's latest one-act play—which he talked with contagious enthusiasm about transforming into a television playlet.

These last weeks had been wonderful, Carol thought. She cherished the hours she and Sharon spent with Seth.

A few times lately Sharon had gone out with Jack.

"Oh, I know there's no future with Jack," Sharon had admitted, "but we're having fun. So he'll go back to Nebraska, and I'll go back to New York—but oh, wow, will I have memories!"

There were moments, Carol told herself, when she felt a kind of electricity between Seth and herself. But he never said anything—never even tried to kiss her. He didn't want any commitments, she decided. He knew writing was a tough career to tackle.

Before she and Sharon left Seth's apartment, he asked her if she'd like to do some off-beat sightseeing the next morning—when neither of them had a class. They both knew that Sharon and Jack were going to bicycle into the countryside tomorrow.

"I promised my grandmother I'd give her a firsthand report on some of the Jewish highlights here," he explained. "She's a great lady."

"I'd love it," Carol said. "This weather is so gorgeous I want to be outdoors as much as I can."

"I'll pick you up tomorrow around ten," he told her. "Wear comfortable walking shoes."

"Not French shoes," Sharon said with a groan, sliding into her first pair of these—that had been kicked off the moment they'd reached Seth's apartment. "French feet and American feet don't match."

The next morning Carol was waiting when Seth arrived. They hurried out into the magnificent April sunlight. Seth had their itinerary all mapped out.

"We'll see Heinrich Heine's grave in Montmartre Cemetery, and then the house where he wrote his 'Hebrew Melodies,' " he began. "Did you know that Jews lived in France as far back as the fourth century?"

"I read somewhere that there were Rothschilds in France in 1811," Carol recalled. "But the fourth century?" She was awed by this.

"Actually some historians say there were Jews here in Roman times. But we know that by the sixth century the Church councils were already putting restrictions on French Jews. Still, they continued to prosper. My grandmother is fascinated by Jewish history—she's tracked down every book that might add to what she already knew about Jews all over Europe." He chuckled reminiscently. "My kid brother Harvey just brushes her off, but I'm a willing audience. In the eighth and ninth centuries—under Charlemagne and his successors, Jews did well. Charlemagne's physician was Jewish. Of course, it seems the Jews were alternately expelled and recalled to France during the next few centuries."

Their first stop was Heine's grave—where thousands visit every year. In the course of the spring-kissed day they visited the graves of Alfred Dreyfus, poet Gustave Kahn, Sara Bernhardt, Rachel. They saw Sir Jacob Epstein's controversial monument at the grave of Oscar Wilde and the statue of Baroness Clara de Hirsch in the rear of the Bon Marché department store on Square Boucicaut.

"We've got to see the houses where Marcel Proust lived," Seth said with infinite respect. "I took a week out of my life to read Proust."

At intervals they stopped at sidewalk cafés—tiny iron tables and awnings set up now to welcome the warm weather. It was the first time she'd been alone with Seth, Carol realized. She mustn't allow herself to romanticize this occasion, even though she suspected Seth felt more for her than friendship. Sharon was right. What she'd felt for Matt was obsession. What she felt for Seth was new and wonderful—and frightening. There could be nothing more for them. They were two people dedicated to their careers—no room in their lives for other distractions.

At last—tired but exhilarated—they returned to the cellar apartment. They'd have dinner with Sharon and Jack.

"Sharon got some real coffee yesterday," Carol told Seth. "She succumbed to the black market." Her heart was pounding because Seth's eyes—following her about the room—told her what he refused to put into words. "Let's have some while we wait for Sharon and Jack to show up."

She went to the stove to put up coffee, but before she could accomplish this, she felt Seth's hands at her shoulders.

"Carol, I don't want to rush you," he said softly, "but I want you to know I've loved you since almost the first time we met—"

"Seth—" She swung about to face him. Her eyes searched his. "I thought you wanted to be just a friend. A dear and close friend. I thought there was no room in your life for more."

"I was afraid of losing you," he whispered. "But today was so wonderful. I didn't want it to end."

"I love you, Seth. I think I always have—"

She lifted her mouth to his in glorious welcome. She'd known two other men in her life. Two mistakes, she told herself. This was real.

They parted reluctantly at the sound of Sharon's voice outside the door. But Carol's eyes were shining and one hand clung to Seth's. She remembered the poem by Elizabeth Barrett Browning:

"How do I love thee?
Let me count the ways—"

That was how she loved Seth. This was for always.

Chapter Twenty-four

In serious discussion about their future, Carol and Seth agreed to finish out the school year, then return home. Sharon was delighted when Carol reported this.

"I know," she said, "that it's crazy to wonder what's doing with Jerry. But all the other times he came back home to roost, I was there for him. He was devastated when the production of his play fell through. He had to go away and lick his wounds."

"Do you plan to be there every time Jerry comes back for comfort?" Carol challenged. She worried about Sharon's future. "I'm telling you what you used to tell me about Matt. You're obsessed by the guy."

"You got over Matt. I'm not over Jerry," Sharon said bluntly. "I know it's nuts, but that's the way it is."

Though they didn't plan to head for home until mid-June, they immediately made ship reservations. Seth pointed out that he and Carol would have to go to Bellevue to be married.

"The family would be upset if we aren't married there," Seth said. "But we'll head right back for New York," he promised. "We both need to be there." For her schooling, Carol understood, and for Seth's determination to break into television.

Carol knew that Seth was bewildered by her refusal to sleep with him. Sharon, too, was frankly puzzled.

"I don't get it, Carol," she began, then giggled. "I'm getting it, but you're not. Sure, I mope now and then over Jerry—but Jack's sensational in the sack."

"I can wait." Carol's color was high.

"Why do you have to wait?" Sharon demanded. "All that pleasure—and it costs you nothing!"

Carol admitted to herself that she was being absurd. She wasn't some wide-eyed little virgin. But she couldn't sleep with Seth *here*. Paris was a reminder of the agonizing time when she'd felt herself abandoned by Matt. She and Seth made love—up to a point, she thought defensively. They'd waited this long. They could wait another few weeks.

On a night when they were alone in the beautiful solitude of his garret apartment, Seth again made a hopeful overture to ignore their usual guideline.

"Seth, I can't," she whispered. "Not here. I love Paris—for the school and because this is where we found each other again. But on another level Paris is tainted for me." Her eyes pleaded with him to understand. He knew about Matt, about the letter that had been sent from Paris right after its liberation.

"We'll work around that," he said gaily. *He did understand.* "We'll take off for London next weekend. I've been dying to go there ever since I came over to Paris."

"Over a weekend?" Carol was skeptical.

"We'll fly," Seth said and chuckled. "London is a suburb of Paris these days."

"It'll be so expensive, Seth—" Yet the prospect was enticing. "How can we afford it?"

"I told you Grandma sent me a birthday check last week. A big one. She'll be paying for our honeymoon-in-advance. I think she'd like that."

On Saturday morning Carol and Seth left for London. Three hours after boarding the plane they were at the new Heathrow Airport in London. Their immediate destination was the small, modest hotel near Russell Square that George—who'd spent time in London during the war—had recommended.

Their room was small, with its one window allowing for meager sunlight. The walls were paint-hungry, the bedspread washed thin, the blanket at the foot of the bed faded and patched.

"At least, we have our own bathroom," Seth said with good humor and crossed to lock the door to their room. "A demand of the crazy Americans."

"It's ours," Carol said softly as she gazed about the space—knowing that she would forever remember this cubicle where she and Seth first consummated their love.

"Next time the Claridge," he promised, reaching for her hand. "It may take a while, of course. After my first Broadway hit—or television series."

"I suppose we should unpack—" She glanced at their two week-enders.

"Later." He pulled her into his arms. "I've waited so long for this."

"I love you, Seth," she whispered. "So very much."

"I'd like a demonstration," he said as his lips joined hers.

It was glorious, she thought, that there would be no stopping this time. The knowledge lent a special depth to their passion.

Carol was lovingly amused by Seth's determination to see as many of the sites he'd listed on their itinerary as possible.

"London is special for writers," he told her, an arm about her waist as they walked briskly from the house on Tedworth Square where Mark Twain had lived for the four years he was in London to the three-storied brick house on Tite Street where Oscar Wilde had moved with his bride. They had already visited the elegant, iron-fenced house on Doughty Street, where Charles Dickens had written the last of *Pickwick Papers* and *Oliver Twist*, and the house on Fitzroy Square where Bernard Shaw wrote five of his plays.

"All of Shaw's plays were rejected for up to ten years," Seth had said reverently. "And Jerry blows his stack because his first effort at Broadway fell through. Shaw was over forty before he received any real recognition as a playwright."

Exhausted but enthralled with what they had seen, Carol and Seth stopped at a small restaurant for an early dinner. Their knees brushing under the small table, they focused briefly on ordering from the somewhat limited menu—a reminder that England, like France, still suffered from a shortage of food.

"One more stop and then we'll go home," he said, his eyes full of promise. "Dad's always been a great admirer of Disraeli. I won't dare go back to Bellevue if I can't say I've seen Disraeli's last home. Though I admit it wasn't Disraeli's seven novels that impressed Dad."

"He was Queen Victoria's famous prime minister," Carol recalled. "Her Jewish prime minister."

"Disraeli bought the Suez Canal for Victoria. He made her Empress of India. And in turn she made him Earl of Beaconsfield. I read somewhere that when Disraeli was dying—at the house we'll see on Curzon Street—local authorities ordered straw to be laid on the road outside the house so that the noise of carriage wheels wouldn't disturb him."

From Disraeli's house they returned to their small hotel—to make love with exhilarating abandon. It was as though, Carol thought, they'd removed themselves from time. They made love and talked about the future they were determined to form for themselves—and then made love again.

They awoke in the morning far later than they had planned—almost simultaneously.

"Even in the morning you're beautiful," Seth told her, drawing her close beneath the flimsy blanket. "I wish we could stay here forever like this."

"No, Seth," she said with mock reproach. "How would you write here? What would your life be like without a typewriter?"

"I thought of smuggling one in my luggage," he teased. "But I settled for a notebook." He flung one leg across hers. "Enjoying your honeymoon, Mrs. Walden?"

"Oh, so much." For a reluctant moment she remembered the nightmarish days in Atlantic City with Marty. But that seemed a thousand years ago.

"We'll go out for breakfast and more conventional sightseeing in a little while," he promised. "This time you'll be the guide."

She closed her eyes as Seth's mouth sought hers and a hand caressed her breast.

*   *   *

They arrived at the cellar apartment at nine in the evening. Sharon had left a note that she'd gone with Jack to the theater to see the new Genet play.

"I hate to go back to my lonely garret," Seth said, his smile wistful. "I don't suppose you'd come with me—leave a note for Sharon?"

"No," Carol said after a moment, but her eyes were apologetic. "I know I'm being ridiculous, but except for our weekend in London I want to pretend we're an engaged couple who'll spend our nights together *after* we're married." She managed a shaky laugh. "Isn't everyone allowed one idiotic conviction? Mine is that if we play the conventional couple, then everything will go well for us. I've struck out twice. This will be forever."

Four evenings later over dinner in his garrett—contrived to allow Sharon and Jack the privacy of the cellar apartment—Seth told Carol he'd been making inquiries about how they could be married in Paris. Questions in his eyes because he knew her odd feelings about this city.

"I thought you wanted to get married in Bellevue," she reminded.

"I hate the empty nights without you. Why deny ourselves? We'll be married by a rabbi. That way my family will forgive us. I want a rabbi to marry us," he emphasized. "Not some impersonal ceremony by whoever performs civil marriages."

"What must we do?" What formalities must they follow? Would it be terribly involved? But all the while her heart sang; very soon she and Seth would be married!

His smile was dazzling.

"I'll handle all the details. Buy yourself a gorgeous dress." He reached into a pocket for his wallet. "Courtesy of Grandma." His face was tender. "We'll take a rash of snapshots to send home. They'll all declare you the most beautiful bride they've ever seen."

"Will they like me?" Carol asked uncertainly. "Will they be upset that I was married before? That I have no family—except my mother, wherever she may be."

"My family will be your family," he said gently. "There's love there to go around."

A week later they were married by the rabbi of a Montparnasse synagogue. Carol wore a yellow taffeta, with a full skirt that billowed beneath a stemlike waist. The dress designed in the style of

Christian Dior's exciting "New Look" had been made for her in haste by a young seamstress in their building.

Carol and Sharon had early discovered that in Paris—except for the very rich, who were dressed by the likes of Chanel and Schiaparelli and the newly famous Dior—French women sought out "clever little dressmakers" who by devious means copied the couture clothes. Paris women didn't have the access to ready-mades available in American department stores.

Standing under the *chupah* with Seth, Carol felt as though she had been reborn. She washed from her memory the time beneath the *chupah* with Marty—and her mother and Marty's mother hovering, she thought, like a pair of smug witches.

Radiant and approving, Sharon stood by, clutching the bridal bouquet during the ceremony. Jack and George were unfamiliarly solemn. The two men had pooled their resources to provide a wedding dinner. George had confided before the ceremony that he, too, was returning home at the end of the school year.

The day after the wedding Seth sat down to write his parents that he was married. Carol watched him anxiously while he struggled with the letter.

"They're going to be unhappy that you married somebody they don't even know," she predicted.

"I've hinted to Grandma that there was a special girl in my life," he said. "I'm sure she passed the word along. Besides," he said reassuringly, "they'll know you soon enough."

In addition to telling his parents he was married, Seth knew he must explain that they would live in New York. And now—for the first time in his life—he was open about his ambitions to write. In the past he'd talked vaguely about "going into publishing." Now he wrote with enthusiasm about becoming a television writer.

"Why did you never tell your family about your writing?" Carol asked. They didn't even know about the one-act plays he'd written at Columbia and that Leo had produced.

"It was crazy, I know. It just sounded pretentious—" He was trying to sort out the reasons. "Maybe because I knew Dad had wanted so much to be a journalist before he settled down to work in the pawnshop. And I grew up in the Depression—it was drummed into my head that I had to have a profession to make a living. To Mom that meant teaching—or becoming a lawyer or a doctor." His grin was rueful. "So here I am in Paris and trying like hell—via the postal system—to get a job in New York as a French teacher."

"That'll give you time to write." Carol repeated Seth's own rationale for teaching. "There'll be all those school holidays and summer vacations."

"We'll make it, Carol," he vowed. "Both of us."

They planned to go down to Bellevue for a week's stay. While they were visiting Seth's parents, Sharon would be looking for apartments for herself and for them. The three of them would be looking for what Carol called "bread and butter jobs."

"You're going to write every moment possible," Carol told Seth with mock sternness, "and I'm squeezing in as many courses toward an architectural degree that I can handle."

Seth suggested that he and Carol take a side trip to Marseille before going home, so that she might see for herself the beginning of Le Corbusier's modern village, but she was nervous now about their spending a cent more than necessary. Still, she was fascinated by all that she heard about the internationally famous architect—the man who coined such phrases as "A house is a machine for living" and "Communize the common services; free your wife of domestic slavery."

Early in June—with the tourist season just beginning and passage to New York easy to obtain—Carol, Seth, and Sharon boarded the *America* at Cherbourg. The three shared a feeling of gladness at going home, along with a certain sadness at leaving Paris behind. Paris had been so good to them, Carol thought while she stood at the railing with Seth and watched French soil disappear from view. Paris had been a dream come to life; now they were going back to reality.

In New York Sharon went home to the Bronx until she could find an apartment for herself and—hopefully—one for Carol and Seth. The day after their ship docked, Carol and Seth boarded a train at Penn Station for the trip to Bellevue. Ever conscious of their limited funds, Carol insisted they travel by day coach.

At night they dozed against the pillows supplied by the train porters, though neither slept for more than brief spurts. The coach was hot and dusty. Three rows ahead of them a toddler—uncomfortable in the oppressive heat—cried incessantly. Carol watched the passing scenery with an enthusiasm strained by the physical discomfort of the train.

"You see those fields there?" Seth pointed out the window. "That's cotton. Dad's always saying the Southern farmers have to wake up and realize there're other things to plant besides cotton."

"We're south of the Mason-Dixon now," Carol said in sudden realization.

"Oh yes." Seth's smile was wry. "You won't see any colored passengers in the 'white' cars now, and when we get off in Bellevue," he warned, "you'll see waiting rooms and water fountains that are marked 'Whites' and 'Colored.' "

"I've never seen anything like that." Carol recoiled from the image.

"When Gold Star mothers were brought to Europe to see the graves of their sons, white mothers traveled on one ship and colored mothers on another. Most people in the South don't want to face it— but changes must be made."

"I feel guilty that we're not telling your parents that I was married before," Carol said softly.

"We'll tell them in time." Seth dropped an arm about her shoulders. "It just seemed easier not to bring that up right now. It wasn't a real marriage. Your mother threw you into it. And it lasted only a few months. Relax, sugar. They're going to love you."

Chapter Twenty-five

Hannah Walden hurried into the house. Glancing into the dining room en route to the kitchen, she noted with relief that Della—bless her—had set the table before she left for home. The good damask cloth that was used for special occasions, she approved.

"Mama, what are you doing?" she scolded her mother-in-law, standing at the gas range and laboriously turning over the huge pot roast. "You could scald yourself." Mama had such trouble with her hands this last year, but she hated to admit her arthritis was slowing her down.

"The roast needed to be turned," Leah said with good-humored apology. "Della peeled the potatoes and carrots and I shelled the peas. That I can still do."

"I'm glad I got up early to make the cake." Seth's favorite Sachertorte, which Mama had taught her to make. "It would be awful in the house with the oven on now." She was rattling on this way from nerves, Hannah thought. Seth was coming home a married man—his wife a total stranger. God knows, she wanted him to marry. She looked forward to grandchildren. He was twenty-seven—time he settled down.

"What time are they due?" Leah asked.

"I checked with the depot. They should be arriving at seven-fifteen P.M. I still can't believe Seth's married." Hannah's voice was unnaturally strident. "To some girl we've never even seen!" She busied herself at the stove. By the time she and Eli brought Seth and his wife home from the depot the pot roast would be ready.

"You've seen their wedding snapshots. She's very pretty. And Seth's known her for several years," Leah reminded. "He knew her when he was at Columbia."

"What do we know about her?" Hannah broke in. "Just that she's a New Yorker, and Seth knew her when he was up at Columbia."

"You know that she's Jewish and that Seth loves her," his grandmother said. *"Genug."* Enough.

"Why couldn't he have married Clara? Such a sweet, lovely girl—"

"Hannah, you wanted him to marry Clara because you figured he would stay in Bellevue."

"And what's wrong about that?" Hannah asked defensively. "Is it wrong for me to want my son to live close by?" It unnerved her sometimes, the way her mother-in-law could read her mind. "This girl he married in Paris—she's a New Yorker. That's why he says they'll live in New York."

"He needs to be in New York if he's to work in television. He—"

"And what's this craziness about television?" Hannah interrupted again. "How many people do we know who own television sets?"

"Hannah, relax," Leah coaxed affectionately. "You're not losing

Seth because he thinks he wants to live in New York. Give him room—let him stretch his legs—"

"He stretched them when he went to Paris," Hannah said dryly. "Wasn't it enough to spend three and a half years in the army?" Her face softened now. "Thank God, he came home in one piece."

"You're hot and tired," Leah sympathized. "Everything's under control in the kitchen. Take a lukewarm tub, then come sit out on the porch and have a nice glass of iced tea. Seth won't be arriving for over an hour."

Carol fought against panic as the train approached the small depot at Bellevue. Seth's family must be all upset that he'd married some girl from New York, she warned herself. They'd been hurt that he'd dashed off to Paris after the war. And now he had told them he was going to live in New York.

"Carol, relax—" Seth smiled encouragingly. He always understood her mood; she didn't have to say a word, she thought with a burst of love. "They're all going to adore you. Harvey'll be jealous that I snared such a beautiful wife." Harvey, Carol remembered, was nineteen and going to into his junior year at Emory.

"The flowers are just beautiful," Carol said, gazing at the lush display of rose bushes, hydrangeas, beds of petunias and pansies that flanked the small, white brick depot.

"Bellevue's a beautiful town." Seth was on his feet now, bringing down their luggage from its rack. "But remember," he joshed, "we're going back to New York. That's beautiful in other ways."

The moment they had stepped down from the train—a porter contriving to manipulate their four valises—Carol heard a melodic feminine voice calling to Seth. Trailing behind him, she recognized his parents from the photographs he'd shown her.

"Oh darling, it's so wonderful to see you. It's been too long," his mother effervesced as Seth embraced first her and then his father. "And this is Carol." Hannah exuded traditional Southern graciousness. "Seth, she's lovely."

Seth's mother leaned forward to kiss her. Almost shyly his father extended a hand in welcome, then leaned forward to kiss her, also.

"Welcome home," Eli Walden said gently.

How like Seth he was, Carol thought. And Seth's mother was charming. She began to relax as they settled themselves in the prewar Chevy—Seth in the front with his father, his mother in the back with her. Hannah was full of questions about their trip from Cherbourg to New York.

"Before the war a trip to Europe always seemed something for rich people to do. Now everybody wants to see Europe. Did you run into a lot of American tourists on the ship?"

"This early in the season they were all headed for Europe rather than returning," Carol explained.

"I always used to think how exciting it would be to travel to Europe on the *Ile de France.*" Hannah's voice was wistful. "I've never been farther from Bellevue than New Orleans."

"The last we heard of the *Ile de France,*" Carol said, her smile rueful, "she was carrying French troops to fight in Indo-China."

"But the war is over—" Hannah was bewildered.

"The French are fighting Communist rebels in their colony there," Seth explained, his face somber. "Let's hope they come to terms soon."

"Oh Carol, that's one of the oldest houses in Bellevue—" Hannah pointed to a white multicolumned Greek Revival house on their right.

"It's beautiful," Carol said. "And these lawns—" She gestured in admiration at the wide sweep of verdant grass—broken by narrow sidewalks—that seemed endless.

Within minutes they were turning into the pebbled driveway of the modest Walden house.

"There's Grandma!" Seth leaned forward to wave to the small, round woman who sat in one of the half-dozen rockers that lined the front porch. He rushed from the car as it came to a stop, vaulted up the steps to greet his grandmother. Now he reached out a hand to Carol as she approached. "Grandma, this is Carol."

"She's even prettier than her pictures." Leah drew Carol into her arms with endearing warmth. "I don't know where the years go. It seems such a little while ago that Seth's father brought his bride to me. I loved her right away, too."

"Seth told me so much about you," Carol said shyly. "All wonderful," she added.

It was his grandmother, Carol remembered, who had paid for Seth's two years at Columbia. If not for that, they might never have met.

Seth had written his family that her father died when she was nine and that her mother lived in Florida, Carol remembered. He'd explained that Mama was eccentric—that she'd gone to Florida with no word about where she'd be living. Did they wonder about that? Carol worried. Did they ask themselves what kind of daughter was she that her mother would behave that way?

"I'll go out to the kitchen and start bringing in dinner," Hannah told the others. "Eli, help the children take their luggage up to their room."

"Where's Harvey?" Leah frowned. "I told him to be here no later than seven."

"You know Harvey." Hannah's smile was apologetic. "He gets all involved and forgets the time. He'll be here soon," she told Carol.

"I'll help you, Hannah." Leah followed her daughter-in-law down the hall to the kitchen.

For a moment—while Seth and his father went to the car for the luggage—Carol stood alone in the hall. It was a house where family was important, she thought. She inspected the groupings of framed photographs that hung on the walls, the family portraits on the console table. Oh, that was Seth when he was about five!

Seth and his father came into the hallway—both perspiring in the sultry heat. His father shook his head in good-humored rejection when Carol reached to take one valise from him.

"You and Seth will be in his old bedroom," Eli said, leading the way up the stairs. "Harvey will sleep in the guest room."

Seth chuckled.

"I'll bet he's bitching about that. The guest room—really Grandma's sewing room—is about half the size of my room in Paris," he told Carol, "and you know how tiny that was."

"He'll survive," Eli said, shrugging. "All he does is sleep here."

The two men carried the luggage inside. Carol followed them.

"Oh, this is huge!" Carol gazed with admiration about the neat, light-filled bedroom. The wallpaper was a delicate floral pattern, the furniture inexpensive maple. The twin beds replaced now by a double. The bedspread and drapes were tasteful. "In New York—and in Paris—rooms are so small."

"Unless you're rich," Seth reminded. He hesitated. "Dad, is Mom upset that we're not staying in Bellevue?"

"She'll get over it." His father was matter-of-fact. "You two have to live your own lives."

Not until they were halfway through dinner did Harvey arrive.

"Hey, I'm sorry to be late," he said, striding into the dining room. He didn't resemble Seth at all, Carol decided, though he was quite good-looking.

"Some nerve!" Seth leapt to his feet, embraced his brother. "I expected you to be out front with a brass band!"

"I'll get your dinner." Hannah pushed back her chair—her eyes telling Carol that her younger son held a special place in her heart. The son, Carol remembered, who was going to be a lawyer.

"Harvey, this is my wife—" Seth pulled his brother to her side. "May you be as lucky."

At dinner Carol was content to listen to the lively conversation among the others. The three men were arguing now about local politics, along with happenings in nearby Atlanta.

"It's frightening the way crime has increased in Atlanta this last year," Eli said. "And it's mostly teenagers. Some as young as twelve. And it's not the young hoodlums you'd expect. Many of them are kids from good families. Affluent white families."

"Something is wrong in their homes." Leah nodded with conviction. "I blame the parents."

"Mayor Hartsfield is playing politics." Harvey appeared ambivalent. "You have to respect him for being sharp to what's happening in Atlanta, but he may be going too far."

"What are you talking about?" Seth asked. Carol recalled Seth's saying that Harvey already harbored thoughts about going into politics one day.

"You know how when he came into office he talked about becoming 'mayor to all the people'—but he didn't do much about that. He didn't take down the 'White' and 'Colored' signs at the rest rooms and water fountains at the airport—he just made them so small you could hardly see them. But when the United States Supreme Court handed down the decision against white primaries last year, he knew he had a new situation on his hands."

"He went to the Butler Street YMCA and spoke to the colored leaders," Eli picked up. Carol remembered that Seth was proud of his father's warm relationship with the colored community. "He told them that once they got out there and registered to vote, the whole picture would change."

"That's what I mean," Harvey pounced. "He's politicking for the time when the colored vote could be important. But I think he's damned wrong to try to push things ahead so fast."

"All the talk about the coloreds going out to vote is just talk," Hannah said nervously. "Northern agitators make it sound as though we do terrible things to our colored folks. We all get along well."

"Seth, I was thinking how nice it would be if you two could stay down here an extra day." Leah was making a deliberate effort to change the conversation into less volatile channels. "Then you'd be here for your father's birthday."

"Dad, I should have remembered." Seth was contrite. "It's just that so much has been happening—"

"Can't we stay another day, Seth?" Carol asked. "It would just mean changing our train reservations."

"Sure. We wouldn't want to miss your birthday, Dad." His eyes were bright with affection. Here was such a warm, loving family, Carol thought. She was glad to be part of it. "I'll go over to the depot in the morning and change our reservations."

Eli and Hannah arranged to leave the family car at the house during Seth and Carol's stay. Both were eager, Carol realized, for Seth to show her around the town—hoping, she suspected, that they might just change their minds and remain here.

Carol was enthralled by the physical beauty of Bellevue. The lovely houses, the spreading lawns, the masses of summer flowers on every side, the elegant magnolias and pines and live oaks. She admired its small business section—Main Street was divided by islands of grass and trees and flowers—but she was repelled by her firsthand view of Southern segregation.

"It's one thing to read about it, but another to see it." She struggled to explain her feelings to Seth. They'd just left the depot after changing their reservations and she'd seen the benches reserved for "Coloreds," the rest rooms and the water fountain similarly designated. "I know everything isn't perfect up north. But here—" She gestured in frustration. "It's wherever you look."

"For Mom and Dad—and almost everybody else down here—it's a way of life. Dad admits changes have to come. Mom's scared of change. She pretends not to understand what's happening today. But a lot of colored men—and colored women—left home to fight in the war. They've come home to ask a lot of questions. Take Della. Her brother was with the army in Burma. He came back home after V–E Day, but he left in four months."

Carol was intrigued to learn—through a chance encounter in town with a woman lawyer who had gone through public school with Seth—that Georgia women were fighting for women's rights.

"Oh, we're going to make it this time," Seth's former classmate told them joyously. "The General Assembly will *have* to pass laws that permit women to serve on juries. We have that Supreme Court decision from last December to back us up. The court ruled that the Constitution requires a jury to represent a cross-section of the community."

Two evenings before Carol and Seth were to return to New York, she received a phone call from Sharon.

"You won't believe how tough it is to find an apartment these days," Sharon wailed. "We knew it was bad before we went to Paris, but we weren't out there looking. People want key money, or to sell you junky furniture for a fortune. And people are waiting in line for that! But through a friend of Bev's—she just got married and is buying a house out on Long Island—I've found a place on West Eighty-fourth Street. You and Seth can stay with me while you look."

"What about rents?" Carol asked anxiously.

"High," Sharon admitted. "Anyhow, Bev's friend is leaving the furniture, so I don't have to worry about that. There's a decent double bed in the bedroom." She giggled. "Not much room for anything else in it, but you and Seth can manage. I'll sleep on the studio couch in the living room. You going stir-crazy down there yet?"

"It's beautiful, Sharon. I doubt if we could survive on a full-time basis, but it's like a vacation for us right now."

"I'll be back at the old agency starting next Monday—working for Vic. I gather he and Denise have split. She's out in California now. And I'm moving into the apartment tonight. Mom's giving me linens and towels and such. Come right there from Penn Station. Oh, and guess what?" she effervesced. "I'm inheriting a phone!"

The apartment was in the West Eighties. Carol had feared it might be in the Bronx or Brooklyn. The only problem, Sharon warned good-humoredly, was that it was next door to a day nursery.

"The kids—from three to five years old—pour out into the yard behind the nursery before eight A.M., and *nobody* sleeps any later than that."

"How's the job situation?" Carol was anxious about this.

"There seem to be plenty to go around. You know, all those gals leaving the work force to cook, clean, and wax floors. The economy in this country is booming. It's a whole different scene from Europe. But let me get off the line—this call is probably costing Mom a fortune."

Carol was happy that she and Seth had agreed to remain an extra day. She realized how much it meant to the family that they were there for her father-in-law's 53rd birthday. This was the kind of family life she'd never known but had always yearned to share.

At intervals she was aware—despite their efforts at creating a convivial mood—that Seth's parents and his grandmother were silently grieving that he meant to make New York his home. Harvey didn't care, she surmised. He was only concerned about himself. She'd never known anybody so totally spoiled. He was Mom's precious baby, who was going to be a lawyer. She loved Seth, of course—but Harvey was special.

The following day Carol and Seth left for New York. This time they traveled in a Pullman section, at Leah's insistence.

"Humor an old lady," she'd said forcefully. "So I'll leave a few dollars less when I die."

Chapter Twenty-six

Carol and Seth were unnerved by the rental situation in New York. Reluctantly they considered moving away from their beloved Manhattan, but then Sharon discovered—in conversation with a neighbor—that a vacancy would be available the first of the month in her building. Another newly married couple was moving out to Long Island.

"They can buy a house out in Levittown under the GI Bill with almost nothing down," Seth pointed out. "Couples are just waiting for the houses to go up."

They grabbed at the apartment, though they flinched at slipping the super a hundred dollars for the right to move in. And the rent was shockingly high. Still, it was in Manhattan, they told themselves. With both of them working, they'd manage. It was slightly larger than Sharon's minuscule apartment, two floors above—and it, too, had a phone installed. The previous tenants left some of their furniture behind. A few pieces—enough to make the tiny apartment livable—were worth keeping. Sharon's mother contributed a card table to hold Seth's portable typewriter. Seth was focusing his attention on writing for television. He was convinced it would be a great market for writers who could adapt to its needs.

"In the theater if you try to use more than one set, the budget goes zooming upward. In television it's a minor deal. The writer has so much more freedom."

At last, Seth received word that the job he'd been trying to nail had come through. When classes began in September, he'd teach French in a private school a fifteen-minute walk from the apartment. For the remainder of the summer he'd work at a Times Square soda fountain.

Carol was trying for a job—any job—in an architectural firm. She was coming face to face with reality. In architectural offices women were secretaries or receptionists. Not even her courses in drafting, or her classes at the Sorbonne helped to combat this.

"Carol, go to school full-time," Seth ordered on a hot evening when—like so many others—they sought refuge on Riverside Drive. "Concentrate on finding a part-time job. With that and what I'm earning we'll manage."

"Seth, do you know how expensive tuition is?" *How could he suggest such a thing?* But the prospect was enticing.

"If I show my school contract to a bank, I can swing a personal loan. If the bank turns me down, I'll go to a finance company."

"We'll never be able to meet the payments," Carol protested.

"We can do it," Seth insisted. "Have you got a pencil or pen in your purse? I'll show you."

"How do I know I'll be accepted as a matriculated student?" she wavered.

"You'll be accepted," Seth said gently. "Why do you always have such doubts about what you can do?"

In these last months of 1947 Americans complained about how prices kept climbing—for food, clothing, many necessities of life.

President Truman called the housing shortage "the foremost of the many problems facing the nation." The government had promised 2.7 million new houses by 1948, but that was clearly not to be.

Some Americans worried that ex-GIs were exploiting the GI Bill, that they'd never return to work. But jobs were out there for the taking, and wages were rising. The Depression days—still a painful time only ten years ago—were history, though industries were afflicted by a succession of strikes.

To Carol and Seth life had never seemed so good. Though Seth was hardly fond of teaching, he felt a stability in their lives that he relished. Except for Carol's tuition, they were keeping their overhead low. She was ecstatic at being in school full-time. Her Saturday job paid much of the monthly payments to the bank. Seth was absorbed in adapting his writing style to fit in with the new television medium. It was predicted that one million sets would be sold next year. Already plans to show the 1948 presidential election on television were being discussed.

Shortly before New Year's Eve Sharon phoned Carol on arriving home from the office.

"Carol, you won't believe what happened today!"

"I'll believe. Tell me."

"I went over for a grilled cheese and coffee at that soda fount across from the agency, and"—Sharon paused dramatically—"guess who came over to take my order?"

"Jerry?" Carol asked after an instant. *Damn him for popping into Sharon's life again.*

"Just as casual as though we had seen each other last week. He asked about you."

"Seth's tied up in a meeting at the school. He phoned to say he'd be late. Why don't you run up and eat with me? I'll feed him whenever he gets home."

"I'm on my way."

Over a hastily thrown-together spaghetti dinner Carol and Sharon discussed Jerry's sudden appearance again.

"The last time we saw him was just before New Year's two years ago," Carol reminded. "And now he's all ready to play house with you again?"

"I told him he could come over for dinner tomorrow night." Sharon giggled self-consciously. "He wanted to make it tonight."

"Jerry's no good for you," Carol exploded. "When are you going to realize that?"

"So who else is beating a path to my door?" Sharon said defensively. "I'm three months from twenty-eight, a little over two years from thirty. I take what fun comes along. Now shut up about Jerry and tell me you're enjoying your winter intercession."

"I'm studying," Carol chuckled. "What else would I be doing?"

"Why don't you and Seth come down to my place for dinner tomorrow?" Sharon said. "Jerry and Seth will have a lot to talk about. Jerry's looking around for a downtown group that might be interested in doing his play—and dying to get into television. I told him to forget about Denise and Vic," she added flatly. "Vic is backing away from television; he says clients are wary about it. And Denise, of course, has disappeared into the Hollywood scene."

The following evening Carol and Seth went down to Sharon's apartment for dinner with her and Jerry. Meat loaf and potatoes were in the oven, Sharon announced blithely when she opened the door to them—and Carol suspected she and Jerry were fresh out of bed. She recognized Sharon's warm glow, the relaxed, sleepy-eyed glint.

"Your timing is perfect," Sharon approved, her grin confirming what Carol had suspected.

Almost immediately Jerry and Seth were deep in discussion about theater and television.

"With both you have to know the right people," Jerry said, the old bitterness surfacing. "Without the right contacts you're shit out of luck." Over coffee Jerry shifted the conversation into politics. He talked about a recent Gallup Poll that said Truman was sure to lose if he ran for the presidency.

"I don't think so," Seth rejected this. "Truman's done a lot for various groups in the country. The farmers, labor, the Jews because he's in favor of Zionism, the colored people because he ordered that Negro officers be commissioned in the armed forces. He's fought for housing on a massive scale."

"That's crap," Jerry broke in with a cynical smile. "Politicians are all alike. All they want to know is how much they can get out of a deal. They don't care about people like us."

"According to you, Jerry, we all ought to dig a hole in the ground and bury ourselves," Carol flared contemptuously.

"We'd save ourselves a lot of grief," Jerry said, "but we're too scared to do it. Take Seth and me. We'll spend the rest of our lives beating our brains out trying to make it as writers. What are the odds?"

"Nothing's ever easy." Carol's color was high. She hated Jerry's pessimism. "You have to go out there and fight for what you want."

"Enough of this," Sharon ordered. "What do you say we throw a New Year's Eve bash? I'll invite a couple of people from the office. Seth, ask some people from the school. It's been so damn long since we had a real party."

Carol spent much of the winter intercession in study. Seth was wrestling with a script he wanted to submit for television. Sharon was constantly with Jerry, though Carol knew they were having heated disagreements because Sharon refused to allow Jerry to move into her apartment.

"I told him not without a marriage license," Sharon reported. "What's so special about him that he can't take on the responsibility of being a husband?"

Early in February Jerry told Sharon he was moving in with a girl from the office where he was now a file clerk.

"He said I wouldn't let him in so he had to look elsewhere," Sharon reported in rage. "I told him to give his new girlfriend my condolences. What do you bet she throws him out in three months?" She considered this a moment. "Six months," she amended. "He's great in bed."

Carol and Seth settled into a comfortable pattern. She relished going to school full-time. At last she was developing self-confidence. *This* was what she was going to do with her life.

She refused to be upset by the knowledge of how few women were enrolled in her classes, and that there were less than a thousand women architects in the whole country. It was enough for her to know that architectural schools—even Harvard now—accepted women students. She knew, also, that in architecture—as in other fields—women were paid much less than men.

One of her special pleasures was to sit at a Broadway coffee shop with fellow students and argue about individual approaches to architecture.

"It's not how a building looks on the outside," she reiterated regularly. "It's how it serves the people who use it—whether it's a house or an office building or a library. Are those people comfortable inside?"

Seth finished his script, submitted it, and started on another—though he admitted his teaching was more demanding of his time than he'd expected. Sharon was spending longer hours than normal at the agency because of a high-pressured campaign to bring an account into radio.

"I suppose I hang around longer than I absolutely have to," Sharon admitted to Carol on a spring night when Seth was involved in a school meeting and they were treating themselves to dinner at Tip Toe Inn. "But there's this new junior exec—Gil Randall." Her face spoke eloquently. "He's good-looking—and so intense about everything, in a good way. Very different from Jerry. I keep waiting for him to ask me out. I think he's nervous about dating somebody from the office."

"What did he do during the war?" Carol asked.

"He said he sat out most of the war as an instructor down in Fort Benning, Georgia. But he did see a year of action in Europe."

"That's near Bellevue!" Carol pinpointed. "Sharon, ask him to dinner at our place. Tell him your best friend's husband comes from Bellevue, Georgia. They'll have lots to talk about."

On Saturday evening Sharon brought Gil Randall to dinner. She and Carol were delighted that he and Seth clearly enjoyed meeting each other. Then midway through dinner Sharon talked about the battle at the agency over the future of television.

"I can't understand their being so shortsighted," Gil said with an air of frustration. "Radio has peaked. There's already a drop in the ratings and in advertising sales. Some radio stars are already moving into television."

Carol and Sharon basked in the excitement generated by the two men—both intrigued by the prospect of getting in on the ground floor of a fascinating new medium. Gil admitted he was eager to move into the production end of television.

"Not right away," he conceded, "but once I've proven to an agency that I know the field. If something doesn't break soon at McKinley and Jackson, I'll look around for another spot."

Gil would be a terrific contact for Seth, Carol thought. Not right away, she cautioned herself, but once he had a foothold in production. Meanwhile, Seth was trying to tailor his scripts to fit the current television shows. His first script had been rejected, but the editor was interested in seeing further material.

The two couples began to spend much time together. Gil had no family in New York. His mother had died when he was four. His father—a Cleveland surgeon—had remarried a year later. The others gathered Gil's relationship with his stepmother had never been warm. At intervals Carol worried about the reaction of Sharon's family to her growing closeness to a man who wasn't Jewish.

In early June Carol and Seth went to Bellevue for a week. Despite the exchange of letters and a phone call each month, Seth confessed he longed to spend some time with his family. He had wangled a summer teaching job. Carol had signed up for summer courses. This was the perfect time.

"It'll be a free vacation," he joshed. "All it'll cost us is train fare."

Bellevue was already steamy hot. Still, Carol enjoyed the lazy days and evenings, the warmth of Seth's parents and grandmother. While pleased that Seth was teaching, his mother hinted regularly that he'd have no problem finding a teaching job either in Bellevue or Atlanta.

Carol listened absorbedly to her father-in-law's report on the stringent new building safety law expected to be enacted by the Georgia General Assembly brought on by the tragic Winecoff Hotel fire of two years ago, when 127 people died and nearly 100 were injured in America's worst hotel fire.

"The Assembly is working on methods to enforce national safety standards in all public buildings," Eli said with pride.

"You have to see the gorgeous new Store for Homes at Rich's," Hannah broke in. "You'll be interested in that, Carol. There's a glass-enclosed bridge at the fifth-floor level that connects it with the main store."

"I think it's fine the way you're keeping up with your studies," Leah told Carol. "Maybe some day you'll build houses or a school or a hospital right here in Bellevue. And won't we be proud of you!"

"Bellevue's acquired a few new families since last year," Eli picked up. "But in Atlanta!" He whistled eloquently. "The suburbs are just exploding."

"It's like that up in New York, too," Carol said. Already Sharon and Gil were talking about buying a house out on Long Island or up in Westchester if business went well for him. As an ex-GI he didn't have to worry about getting a mortgage. "They're putting up houses as fast as they can—and people are always waiting to buy."

When Carol and Seth returned to New York, they learned that Sharon and Gil were making wedding plans.

"We'll get married the Sunday before Thanksgiving. Nothing fancy," Sharon told Carol. "I warned Mom not to start talking to caterers. We'll be married in the living room at home." Meaning the Bronx, Carol understood. "With just family—and of course, that includes you and Seth. And we'll take off that week for the honeymoon. Gil knows he's not getting a virgin," she said, laughing. "He found that out a while ago," she reminded good-humoredly. "We'll be married by a rabbi," she added. "Gil offered to convert."

Sharon and Gil were married early on the Sunday afternoon before Thanksgiving. How sad, Carol thought, that Gil's father and stepmother couldn't be here. His father had written that he had to attend a medical convention. Sharon suspected he was angry because Gil had converted to Judaism. Involuntarily Carol remembered that her mother had not been present when she married Seth—nor his family. But Seth's family was warm and caring. She was ever grateful for that.

Sharon and Gil prepared to leave by taxi after cutting the wedding cake. They had to rush to Idlewild to catch a plane to Miami. Sharon was awed by the prospect of being in Miami a little more than four hours after boarding the plane.

"It takes twenty-four hours on the train," she bubbled. "And if you go by car it's four or five days!"

Sentimental tears filled Carol's eyes when she kissed Sharon goodbye. Nobody could ever be closer to her than Sharon. They had been through so much together. Nothing could break the tie between them.

Life was being good to them, Carol told herself as she and Seth took the subway from the Bronx to the West 86th Street station. The car was crowded. Seth kept an arm protectively about her waist as they clung to a pole.

"Gil said he's either going to see the agency into television, or he's moving on," Seth told her. "Wherever he'll be, I'll have a friend in court." He smiled whimsically. "I'm beginning to sound like Jerry."

One month after Gil and Sharon returned from their honeymoon, he left McKinley & Jackson—but he had another job waiting in the wings.

"They're gung-ho at Adams and Bentley about television," Gil said with satisfaction at their customary Saturday night dinner together. "I'll move up fast there."

"I'll probably have to leave the agency, too," Sharon said uneasily.

"Why?" Gil asked, startled by this assumption.

"Vic's going to be mad as hell that you're leaving. That's going to color his feelings about me. But it's okay," she soothed. "I'm not worried about finding another job."

"If things go right for me, you'll be leaving anyway," he said, leaning forward to exchange a tender kiss with Sharon.

Carol knew they were both eager to start a family, though Sharon insisted they should wait until they had a larger apartment—or maybe a little house in suburbia.

Each weekday morning when the hordes of kids charged into the nursery school's outdoor play area next door—except the one morning when she had early classes—Carol felt a twinge of wistfulness that she and Seth were careful that *she* not get pregnant. First she must finish school, and Seth had to break into television writing.

As Sharon had predicted, Vic Blair was furious at Gil for leaving the agency. His rage reached out to include her. He contrived to have her appear to be responsible for the agency's losing a client. In an ugly confrontation he fired her. She stalked out of the agency and hurried home. Gil was still at his office. She hurried upstairs to tell Carol what had happened.

"I'll never get a decent reference out of him." Sharon was still trembling from the encounter. "My name will be mud in the ad agency field."

"Gil's doing well," Carol comforted. "You don't have to worry."

"Carol, I'll go stir-crazy if I'm not working. How the hell do I explain about references when I look for another job?"

"Say you've been in Paris. Studying," she pinpointed. "Try for a job on a magazine. You're an English major—that's supposed to carry weight."

"I'll give it a whirl," Sharon promised.

After a brief round of employment agencies, she landed a job as an editorial assistant at what she labeled a "schlock" confession magazine.

"They were impressed by the Paris scene. I told them I'd been studying at the Sorbonne, but I got homesick. I don't know if it was that—or the creepy publisher liked the look of my legs—but I'm hired. I start work Monday." She broke into laughter. "Carol, you wouldn't believe this cruddy place if you saw it! But the money—they told me at the agency—is much more than I'd get at one of those fancy magazines like *Glamour* and *Mademoiselle.* You need a private trust fund to work for one of them."

Seth was struggling to finish another script for submission to the television stations.

"You can't stop at one rejection," he said earnestly. "You have to have a few scripts circulating—that's the routine."

Carol was worried that Seth was trying too hard to fit his writing into the prescribed groove. He wasn't writing for himself. But he insisted that would come later. With her architectural degree little more than a year away, Carol looked for—and found—a part-time drafting job to replace her Saturday deal. Though she was aware that the men in the office considered it amusing to have a draftswoman in the firm, she fought to prove her ability.

Almost from his first month at the new agency Gil knew he'd found his niche. By the following spring he was promoted to head of the small but increasingly important television department. He hired Seth to write an audition script for a prospective series based on an agency idea. He was delighted with what Seth brought in, but the prospective sponsor had a daughter with some slight writing experience.

Finally Gil admitted defeat.

"The old boy insists his daughter be hired to do the series," he apologized.

"Is she a television writer?" Carol demanded.

"She writes fiction for the women's magazines," Gil said tiredly. "Now she wants to move into television. Her father's paying the bills. What can we do?"

"If the show is lousy, you'll lose him as an account," Sharon warned.

"Everybody at the agency loved Seth's script. Maybe the old boy will change his mind when he sees what his daughter brings in. I'll keep my eyes open. If he shows signs of caving in, then you'll be the next choice, Seth."

"Jerry wasn't entirely wrong," Seth said with rare cynicism. "It pays to have great connections."

Early in the summer Sharon realized she was pregnant. She and Gil were both ecstatic. Right away Gil bought a new Dodge.

"We have to get a house," he said jubilantly. "The city's no place to raise kids."

On the following Sunday morning the two couples drove out to Long Island to look at a housing development. Carol was repelled by what she saw when they arrived at their destination. An endless procession of small frame houses, all seeming identical at first glance, though they were designed in three basic styles. An architect's nightmare, Carol thought.

"You know that joke you keep hearing?" she said in distaste. "About how if you've had too many martinis you could walk into the wrong house? How could a builder put up such an ugly development?" But there was a line of young couples eager to buy.

Saturday night Gil went down and bought the Sunday *New York Times*. They searched through the "Houses for Sale" section, focusing on Westchester County.

"Oh, I almost forgot," Seth announced while Sharon checked off several houses advertised in the *Times*. "A guy at the school told me about a house he knows that's for sale up in Westchester—in Dobbs Ferry. The couple are splitting up and want to sell fast." Divorce, Carol thought, had never been so popular as in these first postwar years. "He figured you ought to get a great break on the price."

"How do we see it?" Sharon asked, immediately intrigued.

"It's with brokers but not exclusively. He said to go to the house next door and ask for the key. If you like it, the neighbor will give you the guy's phone number. He's living here in the city now."

"I don't know much about Westchester. Where's Dobbs Ferry?" Gil asked. "Is it a long commute?"

"About thirty-five minutes by car, I understand. Unless you're caught in rush-hour traffic. You can't do much better than that."

The following Saturday the two couples drove up to Dobbs Ferry to see the house Seth had mentioned. From there, Gil said, they'd go to a real estate broker in town. But Carol knew from the glow on Sharon's face when they drove up before the house that this was the one she and Gil would buy. Gil went to ask for the key while the others admired the miniature white colonial from the outside, then walked to the small, columned veranda.

Gil returned with the key. "Okay, let's go inside." He unlocked the door and pushed it open. Sunlight flooded the empty rooms. The scent of roses drifted in from a garden that had been years in the making.

"What a beautiful staircase," Carol admired. She hadn't expected it in a house that appeared small.

"It just leads to the upstairs attic," Gil began.

"You can put in dormers later, probably add two large bedrooms." Carol's eyes were appraising the space.

"That's your department, Carol," Sharon said. "You tell us if we should buy it. If we can afford it," she added uncertainly.

"They're anxious to sell," Seth reminded. "To reach a divorce settlement."

After a week of negotiations Sharon and Gil arranged to buy the house. With the contract signed and closing scheduled for sixty days later, the two couples drove out on a Saturday morning for another look about the house.

"We can't go in for expansion yet," Gil said in high good humor as they walked up to the house, "but when that time comes, you're the architect, Carol."

After they'd had a picnic lunch on the dining-room floor, they left the house in an air of euphoria. Glancing over her shoulder for a final look at the charming little house before climbing into the car, Carol all at once visualized Seth and herself living in a house such as this one—with a couple of kids and a puppy.

Were she and Seth wrong in focusing on careers? They were twenty-nine years old. Were they cheating themselves of the important things in life to chase after elusive dreams?

Chapter Twenty-seven

On a humid Saturday morning Seth and Gil sat in the Dodge and talked about the vast strides in television while Carol and Sharon inspected furniture in White Plains stores. Fast delivery was urgent. Sharon and Gil were closing on the house in three weeks.

"We have to settle for just the absolute minimum," Sharon said, simultaneously self-conscious and proud that she was already having trouble with zippers and buttons. "I know Gil is doing well, but our expenses are going wild. A bed and a dresser for our bedroom, a table and four chairs for the dining room, a sofa—and that's it for the living room for now. Mom and Dad are buying us a crib and carriage, and Bev and Dan are giving us a bassinet and a comforter for the crib."

"Remember, we're giving the layette," Carol said. "But you pick what you want."

After an hour of debating and making decisions Sharon declared she was exhausted.

"I keep telling Gil that being tired is part of the early months, but he's insisting I give my notice next week. I could work for another six weeks. I'd commute with Gil—he'll be driving into the city. But he says, 'no.'"

"I think it's sweet, the way he's so protective," Carol said gently. Seth would be that way, too. And again, she felt a wistfulness that she and Seth must put off having a baby.

"How's the job?" Sharon asked. "The same old shit?" Only to Sharon had Carol admitted she was frustrated that she was doing so little drafting, that much too often one of the architects would thrust typing assignments at her. She never mentioned her dissatisfaction with the job to Seth. She didn't want to distract him from his writing.

"Clients who come in figure I'm the typist or the secretary. With all the jobs women took on during the war, wouldn't you think men would understand that we can do anything they can do?" Carol sighed. "I get so angry sometimes—but I'm learning, I keep re-

minding myself. By next year this time I'll be a full-fledged architect."

Carol and Seth went down to Bellevue for the last week in August, when both were free from school commitments. As always
Carol enjoyed the slow-paced life, the genuine warmth of Seth's
family. Now she was comfortable calling them "Mom" and "Dad"
and "Grandma". At intervals Seth's mother dropped blatant hints
about their settling down in Bellevue, starting a family.

"He could teach French down here just as well as up in New
York," Hannah told her regularly. To Seth's mother his writing was
little more than a hobby.

Much talk in the family this week revolved around Harvey's beginning his law studies. He was still an insufferably spoiled brat,
Carol thought. He made such demands of his family. Seth seemed
unaware of this—but Grandma knew, Carol thought tenderly. What
really bugged her, she told herself with recurrent frustration, was
the way her mother-in-law looked down on Seth's writing. It was
great to be a lawyer—a writer was a nobody.

Along with people all over the country—though for Georgians
there was a special pain, the family had been shaken by the tragic
death of author Margaret Mitchell on August 16th. Five days earlier
she'd been hit by a speeding car with a drunken, off-duty taxi driver
at the wheel.

"That man had twenty-four traffic violations before he struck
down Margaret Mitchell," Eli told Carol and Seth. "Maybe now we'll
get some stringent laws that'll screen people holding taxi permits. I
tell you, people around here are furious about the way she was cut
down. You should have seen all the people—from Atlanta and other
towns—who lined the curbs as the funeral cortege moved through
the streets to Oakland Cemetery."

"Why does something awful have to happen before action is
taken to avoid a catastrophe?" Seth asked intensely.

His grandmother turned the conversation to the fine new Standard Club clubhouse at Brookhaven—nearing completion now.
Carol recalled that the Standard Club—a social club with special interests in music and art—had been founded in 1905 by an enterpris-
ing Jewish group who were denied membership in such elite Atlanta institutions as the Piedmont Driving Club and the Capital
City Club.

"And there's the new million-dollar Jewish Community Center

in Atlanta that's something to be proud of," Leah continued. "It even has a fully equipped nursery school," she added archly.

Carol knew how eager the family was to see her and Seth with children. But they had so much to do before they could afford that. Yet she felt an errant wistfulness when she gazed out the windows of their apartment to the nursery school children playing in the yard next door. Everything in life had its time, she told herself. This was not the time for her to become pregnant.

Despite her advanced pregnancy Sharon was determined to have her family—and Carol and Seth—at the Dobbs Ferry house for Thanksgiving. Carol and Seth arrived Wednesday evening. Gil picked them up with the car at the train station.

"Sharon wanted to come with me," Gil told them. "I made her lie down. I know we'll be up till all hours tonight. You haven't seen her in two weeks—she's as big as a house." He was bursting with a combination of pride and fear, Carol sympathized.

"She'll be bigger," Seth kidded gently. "There's another six or seven weeks to go."

"She's dying of impatience." Gil chuckled. "We both are. And I guess I'm scared, too. Hey, I've never been a father before."

For Carol this was the best of all Thanksgivings. With the four-day school weekend she and Seth were free to remain in Dobbs Ferry until Sunday evening. Gil had to go into the office on Friday, but for the four of them it was to be an especially joyous time.

On Thanksgiving day the small, sun-filled house ricocheted with the family warmth Carol so appreciated. The crowning touch, she thought whimsically as she and Sharon brought two pumpkin pies to the leaves-extended dining room table, were the red roses that were making a final burst from a decade-old bush outside one dining room window.

"Can you believe those roses on Thanksgiving day?" Sharon's mother read her mind. "It's because the bushes get the morning sun—"

"This is a long way from East Tremont," Sharon's grandfather said with pleasure—his voice still colored by the accents of his native Russia. "My granddaughter with a beautiful house in Westchester County."

"So what's wrong with my house on Long Island?" Beverly asked.

"No class," Dan said dryly before his grandfather-in-law could reply. "But we like it. For the kids it's great. For them I can survive the long commute five days a week."

"When I was a little boy living in a village near Kiev, would I ever have believed I'd have two granddaughters with beautiful houses of their own?" Grandpa was trying to be the diplomat, Carol thought affectionately. He wanted to reassure Beverly that he respected her house out on Long Island. *How could developers put up such monstrosities? Had they even bothered to hire an architect?* "In our house in Russia we didn't even have a floor—dirt, that was our floor."

Around seven Gil drove his in-laws to the railroad station for the trip back into the city. Carol ordered Sharon to stretch out on the living-room sofa while she and Seth tackled the masses of dishes piled high in the sink.

"We'll throw together supper from the leftovers and have it in the living room around eight," Carol decided as she washed and Seth dried. "We'll eat and watch television." Two months ago Gil splurged and bought a Magnovox television set for the house. He referred to it as a business investment.

Later they abandoned television for conversation and more coffee. The two women listened while Gil and Seth somberly discussed what had recently been labeled "the cold war" with Russia. Americans had thought that the end of WWII had brought them into world leadership—a triumph for democracy, but now they worried about the way the Soviet Union had ignored the wartime agreements with the Allies and were gobbling up half of Europe.

The newspapers were full of talk about the strength of the Russian army—with almost three times as many combat planes as the United States, four times the number of troops, many more tank divisions. Americans had clung to the belief that their country alone had the know-how to produce an atomic bomb, but late this past summer the world learned that the Soviet Union had exploded its first atomic bomb.

"There's only one thing worse than one nation having the atomic bomb—that's two nations having it," Nobel Prize-winning chemist Harold Urey told reporters, and that feeling was shared with millions of Americans.

Almost fearfully Carol introduced the subject of the House Un-

American Activities Committee—something that concerned the two couples.

"It's kind of scary," Carol said, "the way they're trying to label anybody with liberal beliefs as Communists."

"The Hollywood situation is scary." Seth was somber. "It's Un-American to blacklist writers. It's turning the clock back hundreds of years."

"They're not blacklisting just Hollywood writers," Gil shot back. "That extends to actors and directors, too. *Anybody* the damned committee points a finger at. And sooner or later, it's going to reach out and smear radio and television. I don't want to think about what could happen!"

After breakfast on Saturday morning Seth and Gil drove off to buy wood for the fireplace. The two women lounged on the sofa with coffee cups in easy reach—Sharon at frequent intervals shifting her awkward bulk in search of a comfortable position.

"Do you miss the city?" Carol asked. Sometimes she wondered if Sharon's restlessness was due to her advanced pregnancy or to boredom.

Sharon hesitated. "Look, don't say a word to Gil about it—but it'll take a while for me to get used to living out here. Once the baby's born and I'm busy with it, everything will be different. I won't have time to mope." Sharon's smile was forced. "I keep telling myself how lucky I am to have this house—and Gil and the baby. Not to have to go chasing to a job every day. I just need to be kept busier. I love the house." She paused. "Gil's so proud that he's able to provide for us this way."

"It'll be different once you're busy with the baby," Carol agreed. "Remember, Gil's to call us the moment you go into labor."

"Carol, I don't want you rushing up here in the middle of the night," Sharon warned. She was scheduled to deliver at a White Plains hospital. "You know babies pick the damnest hours to be born. But Gil will call you when I go to the hospital, and he'll update you until the squirt arrives."

"Next Thanksgiving," Carol said softly, "you'll have four generations at the dinner table. That's beautiful."

"When you and Seth have a baby, you'll have four generations on his side, too," Sharon reminded.

"That'll be awhile."

"I have this sentimental dream that I'll have a boy and then you'll have a girl, and they'll grow up to fall in love."

"Sharon, that from you?" Carol broke into laughter. Then suddenly laughter froze. All at once her mind focused on dates. "Oh, my God—"

"What is it?"

"Sharon, I'm almost ten days late! I didn't realize it till this minute. But that happens." She ordered herself to be realistic.

"Not to you," Sharon pinpointed. "I'm the one who was forever a week or two weeks late. For me that was normal. Not for you." Sharon's eyes were bright with tenderness. "Oh Carol, I think it's wonderful."

"It's probably just that I'm overtired." She nodded with conviction. "This last year of school—and the job." She gestured eloquently. *This wasn't the time—with graduation only months away.* "I've been working my butt off. That throws you off-cycle sometimes."

"You're pregnant," Sharon said and struggled to lean forward to hug her. "Oh Lord, I can't wait to be flat again." She laughed. "I'll save all my maternity tops for you, and the baby clothes. Carol, it'll be wonderful!"

"I don't know for sure." Carol was assaulted by myriad emotions. Awe, anticipation, fear of what this would do to their tightly orchestrated lives. She'd watched Sharon's advancing pregnancy with secret envy. "I'll probably wake up tomorrow morning with cramps—and that'll be it." She tried to sound amused at her own suspicions.

"Go for a pregnancy test," Sharon ordered. "I can't wait to know for sure. And tell Seth."

"How can I tell him when I don't know myself?" Carol countered. Would he feel trapped? If she was pregnant, he'd have to hang on to the teaching job. At least for now, she amended.

"Tell him," Sharon insisted. "In all the years I've known you, you've never been a day late. I used to envy you for that," she remembered, giggling.

"I'll tell him if the test is positive," Carol promised. "And don't you say a word. The father is supposed to be the first to know."

She hadn't meant to tell Seth about her suspicions. What was the point, she rationalized, when she didn't truly know? But lying in his arms that night in the darkness of the guest room, she whispered what had occupied her thoughts ever since this morning.

"I'm not sure," she warned him. "I could be wrong—"

"You're not wrong." He shared Sharon's conviction. "Oh honey, what a wonderful surprise."

"You're not angry? I know we hadn't planned on a baby—not for years."

"It's a precious gift." He pulled the slender length of her closer to him. "You're not to worry. We'll manage."

"I can stay in school." Now her mind was crystal clear. Seth wasn't upset—he was *happy*. "We timed this just right." She laughed shakily. "The baby won't be born until late July, the way I figure. I'll graduate! If I'm pregnant," she added.

"We were careless a couple of times last month," Seth reminded. "It was so damn cold in the apartment. First I didn't want to get out of bed, then you didn't want to. Wait till Mom hears! She and Dad—and Grandma—will be so excited!"

It seemed to Carol that she and Seth had opened the door to a new room in their lives. At the same time a mass of new, unexpected problems arose. Would the school object to her continuing classes when she became obviously pregnant? Would they be able to manage financially? Thank God, she thought, Seth's school provided them with Blue Cross health insurance. But even so there would be doctor bills. The bedroom was too small to accommodate a crib; it would have to go into the living room.

Their lives narrowed, the focus being on the baby. At the moment Carol grappled with the reality that architecture must—for now—take a back seat. But she would have her degree—nothing would prevent that. The baby was an expansion of their dreams, she told herself, suffused with love as she moved from deftly utilizing safety pins where zippers refused to meet into maternity tops and skirts.

By the beginning of her fourth month Seth was urging her to give up her job. She was eager to bank as much as possible because they were still paying off her college loans. The decision was taken from her hands. Her boss fired her.

"The nerve of that creep!" Carol blazed to Sharon on one of their extended phone calls. Gil teased—with no real complaint—that he was subsidizing New York Telephone. "So I'm showing—are any of their clients going to complain about that?"

Often on Saturdays now Gil drove into the city for a few hours work at the office, and Carol and Seth drove up to Dobbs Ferry with him, to sleep over Saturday nights and drive back into Manhattan Monday mornings with Gil.

Early in February Sharon gave birth to a seven-pound three-ounce daughter, to be named Michelle Jeanne Randall.

"She's gorgeous," Carol said lovingly as she stood beside Sharon's bed that evening—after a visit to the nursery.

"Okay, so she'll fall in love and marry a slightly younger man," Sharon said blithely. "Just don't carry that little guy longer than nine months."

Carol was touched when Hannah wrote that she would come to New York to "help out with the baby your first week home." Here was incontrovertible proof that Seth's family was her family, too. She felt cherished and loved.

She knew, too, that Seth's family was pleased that the baby would be named Jonathan if a boy and Janet if a girl. She and Seth were going along with the family's assumption that the baby was being named for Seth's paternal grandfather—Leah's late husband—because they knew what happiness this provided Grandma. In truth, Carol reminded herself, the name would be for Papa, too. Both men had been named Joseph. In Jewish tradition a name beginning with the same letter as the person being honored was acceptable.

At dark moments doubts flooded Carol's mind. They'd told themselves Seth would work at teaching until she was through architectural school. Then—once she was working in her chosen field—they could afford to gamble on his being a full-time writer. He was trapped, she taunted herself—as his father, yearning to be a journalist, had been trapped. Yet she knew how deeply he already loved the baby.

At other moments they were caught up in the excitement of Seth's possibly breaking into television via Gil's position as head of his agency's new television department.

"Damn it," Seth finally said in frustration, "every account that Gil deals with sells a product directed to women buyers. They all want women scriptwriters!"

"Seth, try for one of the evening drama programs," Carol urged. "Finish up a script and go after an agent."

"What agent will bother with me?" Seth challenged in recurrent despair. "They want clients with a sales record."

"Try," Carol persisted. "You're good. Some agent has to recognize that."

With Carol prodding him Seth focused on an hour-long script tailored for a major evening show. By early May he had a final draft. With a lead provided by Gil he tracked down an agent who read the script and liked it.

"He'll sell it," Carol predicted, enveloped in euphoria. "We've made a turn in the road. Everything's working out right for us."

"It'll probably take months," Seth warned, but she sensed his elation. "Grandma always says good things come in bunches. You'll graduate in two weeks, the baby's due in July, and—God willing—Hank'll sell the script this summer. Don't say anything to the family until we know Hank's made a sale," he cautioned and grinned. "Dad will probably go out and buy a television set now."

"My husband the television playwright," Carol murmured. "The family will be bursting with pride."

"Not as much as if I'd brought home a law degree." Seth chuckled but his eyes were somber. *Harvey* was bringing home the law degree.

Carol didn't attend her graduation exercises. She was self-conscious now in the final months of her pregnancy, relieved that she'd been able to complete the school year. But Seth rushed out to have her degree framed and hung it in the bedroom, where they would see it each morning when they awoke.

"One of us has made a major accomplishment," Seth told Carol. "You worked your little butt off for years—but you're an architect." All at once his face was somber. "I used to promise myself I'd have a play on Broadway by the time I was thirty."

"So you'll have a play on television at thirty," Carol said. *She* was thirty, she thought with a twinge of rare cynicism, and what had she accomplished? So she had her degree in architecture—when would she be able to utilize it? And instantly she was flooded with guilt. Soon she'd have the baby. Career could wait. "Can you imagine how many people will see the telecast?" she pursued. "Didn't you tell me manufacturers expect to have three million sets sold by the end of this year? And figure how many people will watch each set."

"Carol, Hank hasn't sold the script yet," Seth warned.

"He will," she insisted. "It's our time."

Late in June Seth's agent—Hank Morris—phoned to tell Seth he'd sold the script. Hanging over Seth's shoulder when she realized who was on the phone, Carol heard the magic words.

"Somebody didn't deliver on schedule," Hank reported. "I was able to get a quick reading. They're buying it."

"I told you your time would come!" Carol clutched joyously at Seth when he was off the phone. "I know you're good. Leo always knew that."

"I can't give up the teaching yet," Seth pointed out, but Carol sensed his elation. "It's a beginning, though. And that check will cover the bills for the baby. We won't have to worry about another bank loan."

On the eve of the July 4th weekend Gil drove into Manhattan to bring Carol and Seth out to the Dobbs Ferry house. As Carol had expected, much of the talk focused on the outbreak of hostilities in Korea. On the 25th of June troops of Communist-ruled North Korea had crossed the 38th parallel to invade South Korea. It threatened to be a bloody war.

"Look, we'll have to send in American troops," Gil rationalized. "So will other member nations of the UN."

"I've seen enough dead soldiers," Seth said somberly. "I thought war would never break out again in our lifetime."

"Still, communism has to be stopped before it sucks in the rest of the globe. There ought to be another way—" Gil shook his head with an air of frustration.

"I don't want to see this country mired down in a war in Asia. I think we ought to focus on the Soviet Union," Seth pinpointed. "The Russians need to understand they can't rule the world."

On the second weekend in July Carol went into labor. Sharon left Michelle with Gil and rushed into Manhattan to be with her. Twelve hours after arriving at the hospital Carol held her son in her arms.

"Look at all that hair!" Seth marveled with paternal pride.

"He's got a great set of lungs, too," Carol added, her eyes bright with happy tears. "You should have heard his first squall."

"He looks like you," Seth decided, nodding in pleasure.

"Like my father," Carol said. How proud Papa would be if he was here now. Their son would never know his maternal grandmother, she thought in a surge of pain. Wherever she was. Still, he'd have a lot of love from Seth's side of the family.

Seth took the day off from summer school classes to bring Carol and Jonathan home from the hospital. Then he hurried down to Penn Station to meet his mother and bring her to the apartment. He knew she was enthralled at the prospect of seeing New York, but clearly at the moment her sole thought was to see her grandson.

Carol stood with Hannah beside the crib—at one corner of the living room—and basked in her mother-in-law's pleasure.

"You two have given me the greatest gift possible," she whispered, one hand caressing a tiny fist. "And he's the image of Seth at this age."

Carol suppressed a smile. Jonnie looked exactly like Papa, she thought—as she herself did, people used to say when she was little.

"Mom, he looks just like—" Seth began and paused at Carol's pantomimed reproach. "Just like my baby pictures," he finished.

"Grandma's so angry with herself that she can't sew or crochet much these days—because of her arthritis. But she sent up three sacques and two beautiful little caps she managed to do. And you should hear your brother, Seth. Harvey's so excited at being an uncle."

Carol doubted that Harvey felt anything about the newest addition to the family. The family—except Grandma—was blind when it came to him, she thought impatiently.

"I'll fix lunch, Mom," Carol said. "You must be starving by now."

"*I* will fix lunch," Hannah insisted. "I came up here to be helpful. And to see my precious Jonathan," she crooned.

"You'll make dinner," Seth said. "I bought cold cuts before I went to the hospital. I'll put up coffee, then bring lunch to the table. It's kind of a small apartment," he said apologetically. "There's not a real dining room—just the little alcove for the dining table."

"But we're buying a television set," Carol said, her smile brilliant. "So we'll be able to see Seth's play when it's telecast next month."

"Everybody's so excited about it." Hannah's face was tender. "We thought we'd go over to the Morgansterns to watch—they have a beautiful new set—but now Dad says it's time we joined the new decade. He's driving over to Rich's to buy a set while I'm up here."

"Then business is good," Seth decided. He and Carol knew that his parents were conservative in their spending.

"It's very good." Hannah smiled. "Everybody in Bellevue seems to be doing well." Now her smile lost its spontaneity. "Of course, we all worry about the Communists and what they're trying to do to this country."

"Mom, we're not going to be attacked by the Soviet Union," Seth said quietly.

"Maybe not," she conceded. "But they're talking already in Bellevue about reactivating civil defense units. I don't want Harvey dragged into a war," Hannah said tensely. "Wasn't it enough that you had to serve?"

"The business with the Hollywood Ten was atrocious." Seth seemed uneasy about pursuing this conversation, yet drawn into it. "And that new paperback some nuts just brought out—it's called *Red Channels*—is going to wreck careers and lives if something isn't done to stop it. A friend of ours in advertising told us they're gunning for Philip Loeb. You know, Mom, he plays Papa in 'The Goldbergs.' "

"*He's* a Communist?" Hannah was shocked. "I don't believe it!"

"These fanatics label anybody a Communist who's ever had liberal leanings. I could be earmarked," Seth said contemptuously. "And Carol. Back in my Columbia days Carol and I did some volunteer work for the Abraham Lincoln Brigade. That's all it takes to be smeared by these creeps!"

Jonathan's wail punctured the conversation.

"It's time for his bottle." Carol reached to scoop up her son.

"I'll heat it." Seth headed for the refrigerator. "We'll have lunch in a few minutes, Mom."

"I'll put up the coffee and bring out the cold cuts," Hannah said. "You two take care of my grandson. It's so nice to see a father who's handy. But that's happening these days." She beamed in approval. "Fathers give bottles, change diapers, even push a baby carriage."

With Jonathan asleep again in his crib the three adults settled down for second cups of coffee and more conversation.

"Dad worried about buying the television set without my being along," Hannah reported with an indulgent smile, "but I told him just to pick out the best buy he could find. Even with times so good," she confessed, "I still watch every dollar." She hesitated. "I know how exciting it is to have sold your first television script, Seth—but you won't do something foolish like quitting your teaching job?"

"No, Mom, I wouldn't dream of quitting my job." Seth managed a smile. "At this point I don't have any security in writing."

Why had Mom said that? Carol railed in silence. It was as though she considered Seth's writing to be no more than a hobby. Couldn't she understand how important his writing was to him? Didn't she know how he longed for her respect?

Chapter Twenty-eight

Carol and Seth's world revolved around Jonnie. Despite Carol's insistence that he needed his sleep, Seth was awake and on his feet when Jonnie demanded his 2 A.M. feeding and a diaper change was inevitable.

"We're a team," he reiterated regularly.

On the September night when Seth's television play was to be telecast, he and Carol entertained Sharon and Gil for dinner. After dinner they'd watched the program together.

"Let me see my precious," Sharon ordered moments after she arrived with Gil. "Did you tell him you have him fixed up with this gorgeous little brunette?"

"He knows," Carol said ebulliently. "He can't wait to meet her."

Over dinner Sharon reported that she and Gil were considering selling their house to buy another in the same area.

"Our next door neighbor—he's head of a local bank—told us about this great deal coming up," Gil explained.

"It's going to be wild." Sharon seemed simultaneously alarmed and thrilled. "We'll be sitting with two houses to pay for until we sell the first one."

"We'll manage," Gil reassured her. "I'm betting we make a big profit on the first house. Real estate prices are going up."

After dinner they gathered around the television set to wait for Seth's program to begin. Carol sat with one hand in Seth's while they watched the telecast.

"I wish to hell Leo was here to see it," Seth said somberly. "And wouldn't Greg have been terrific as the male lead? This guy is good, but Greg would have lighted up the screen."

In the midst of a burst of congratulations when the program was over, Seth rushed to answer the phone before it might wake Jonnie. The call was from Bellevue. Seth spoke first with his mother, then his father and grandmother. For a moment Carol—ever conscious of the Bellevue phone bill—spoke with each.

"Oh, it was wonderful!" Carol agreed. Off in the distance she heard a ribald remark from Harvey. After all, what did a network television program mean in comparison to his progress at law school? she asked herself derisively.

Late the following month—when Gil was in California on business—Carol and Seth and Jonnie went to spend a week with Sharon and Michelle. Seth commuted to the school. Carol relished the week at the Dobbs Ferry house. There were still flowers in bloom, but at the same time the first burst of autumnal color was on display. Autumn was her favorite season—full of promise after the sultry New York summers.

This was a very special time for Sharon and her, she thought while they sat at dinner in a blissfully quiet house—Michelle and Jonnie both asleep. Seth was in New York for a special Friday evening event at the school.

"Gil's so excited about the new house," Sharon said. "He says we'll close in three weeks."

"You're still not mad about the suburban scene," Carol guessed.

"I'm bored." Sharon was candid. "I don't fit in. The women I know talk about babies, waxing floors, and what they're making for dinner. The big adventure is Saturday at the supermarket."

"Have you considered moving back to the city?"

"Gil wouldn't hear of it. He figures this is the best of all worlds for Michelle. I think he's fighting to show his father he can be a success, too. And his father couldn't care less," Sharon said bluntly.

"You won't feel so tied down when you have the second car." Gil had decided Sharon must learn to drive. He took their present car into New York; they'd need a second one for her.

"That'll help. I'll even be able to come into New York with Michelle once I'm driving."

"Does Gil like commuting?" Carol asked curiously. He'd made a few cryptic remarks.

"He hates it," Sharon said, "but that doesn't count because he's giving his daughter the perfect life. I think most of the men out here loathe the commute. They do it 'for the kids.' " She pushed back her chair. "Let me get our coffee."

Carol had just given Jonnie his 10 o'clock bottle and put him to bed when she heard the car pull into the driveway. She hurried eagerly to the door to greet Seth. She understood how Sharon felt trapped out here, with Gil working late most evenings.

It was incredible, Carol thought in the following weeks, how much time was involved in caring for Jonnie and their small apartment. Yet she was ever conscious of a void in her life. For so many years school had been part of each day. Now there was no school.

She fought against a recurrent frustration that architecture played no role in her daily activities. When Sharon and Gil moved into the new house, she would restructure the kitchen and one of the baths. That would be something to do.

Seth kept telling her that when Jonnie was a little older she'd be able to look around for some part-time work. It wasn't going to be easy, she told herself—but what had ever been easy for her?

Three days after Christmas Sharon and Gil moved into the new house. Immediately Carol set about replanning the kitchen and the guest bathroom. It was her first professional opportunity—simultaneously exhilarating and intimidating.

With the plans drawn up—and Seth watching over Jonnie—she approached a local contractor. She ignored his surprise at having to deal with a woman architect. When would men learn to accept women in the field? She dealt—politely but firmly—with his countersuggestions.

"It's important to keep step-saving in mind in a kitchen," she pointed out. "And the addition of the bay window will bring much needed sunlight into the kitchen."

"It'll take more time," he grumbled.

"My client is aware of that," Carol said crisply. *He wouldn't argue this way with a male architect.* "These are the changes she wishes."

Still, Carol breathed a deep sigh of relief when the changes she'd designed were completed. Nothing terrible had happened. Sharon was ecstatic about the results.

"Carol, I love the kitchen now—and the bathroom. Sunlight just pours into the kitchen—I can't wait to put a half-circle of plants in the bay window. And the bathroom looks so luxurious!"

"Yeah, everything came out good," the contractor agreed with reluctant respect.

"Take photos," Gil urged Carol. "You can show them to prospective clients."

For so long she'd waited to prove herself, Carol thought—tears of pleasure filling her eyes. Now she could call herself an architect.

Carol knew that Seth was elated when his agent sold another television script, yet she sensed his frustration that he couldn't salvage more time for writing. He made up endless work schedules, but inevitably conflicts arose—problems at school, nights of walking the floor with Jonnie amidst painful teething, Jonnie's terrifying bout of croup.

One of Sharon's new neighbors saw her redesigned kitchen and guest bathroom and immediately asked about the architect. Carol was hired to add a master bedroom suite to the neighbor's house. She felt guilty that she had to leave Jonnie in Seth's care the post-school afternoons she took trains up to Dobbs Ferry to consult with the new client. *Time when Seth should be writing.*

The assignment to add the new master bedroom suite was followed late in the spring by a request from the client's married daughter for a consultation on a three-bedroom beach house, to be built on the dunes facing the Atlantic, close to Montauk Point.

"You're launched," Seth said with approval. "And you were so nervous about having to fight your way into a major architectural firm. You're doing it on your own!"

Fall blended into winter with no new assignment in sight. Knowing her restlessness, Seth urged her to try for a job in an architectural firm. She had credentials now—satisfied clients.

"You'll hire somebody responsible to look after Jonnie during working hours," he said. "Even if you earn just enough to cover her salary, you'll be getting a foothold professionally."

Carol wasn't genuinely surprised when she found no job offerings listed in the *New York Times*. She sat down and typed up a batch of letters to architectural firms in the city, waited with aching impatience for a response. She received not one reply.

"There's got to be an opening in some firm," she fumed to Sharon in one of their long phone calls. "I'll bet if my name was Carl instead of Carol I'd get some response."

On a bitterly cold December Saturday night Seth went down as usual to pick up the Sunday *Times*. While Seth pored over the theater section, Carol combed the "Help Wanted" columns—including those for men. She discovered two ads for "recent architectural school graduates."

She studied the requirements. One firm asked for a letter, to be addressed to a box number. The other instructed prospective applicants to appear on Monday morning at the firm's office. She'd ask Mrs. Reynolds, who lived with her grown daughter in the apartment above them and who was eager for baby-sitting jobs if she would sit with Jonnie Monday morning.

At 9 A.M. sharp Carol walked into the reception room of Pearson & Campbell, Architects. She carried a briefcase containing snapshots of her past assignments. She gave no indication of her nervousness as she approached the receptionist—just settling herself at her desk.

"I'm here in response to the ad in yesterday's *Times*," Carol began.

"Oh, it's not for a secretary," the receptionist told her with mild reproach.

"I'm an architect," Carol said briskly, her heart pounding.

"Oh." The receptionist was clearly startled. "Well, fill this out." She handed Carol a mimeographed form. "Mr. Campbell will be interviewing. He's not in yet."

While Carol filled out the application form, three young men arrived, presented themselves to the receptionist, then sat down to fill out application forms. Carol was aware of furtive glances in her direction. None of the three considered her competition, she thought wryly. They probably thought she was here for a secretarial or file clerk job. From the brief conversation between two of the applicants she understood there were several associates in addition to the partners. This was a large, successful firm.

At 9:15 A.M. the door opened and a dignified, expensively suited man in his mid-fifties strode into the reception room. From the receptionist's smile, even before she said an effusive "Good morning, Mr. Campbell", Carol knew this was one of the partners.

She was irked when one of the three young men was ushered in first. One by one the male applicants were interviewed. The expression of each on leaving Mr. Campbell's office was guarded. She waited to be summoned for her interview. Why was she the last? Had the receptionist not told Mr. Campbell the order of their arrival?

Her smile was faintly strained when the receptionist—after word from Campbell's inner sanctum—instructed her to go inside.

"We have a letter from you on file," he said brusquely as she approached. So her letter had been noticed, she thought with a flurry of satisfaction. "It's not our practice to hire women architects. It causes problems with contractors and laborers." But he was indicating that she was to sit down.

"I've worked with contractors and laborers," Carol said calmly. "Most recently on a beach house on the eastern end of Long Island. I ran into no problems. I understood the situation, and I handled it." As she talked, she opened her briefcase, pulled out her plans for the beach house, photographs-in-progress, and a photograph of the finished house. "My experience isn't wide, but my clients have all been pleased."

She struggled to remain poised as Campbell shot a series of questions at her. She sensed he was impressed by her college records—her studies at the Sorbonne. Yet his disapproval—distrust because she was a woman trying to break into a man's field—reached out to turn her cold.

She tried not to show her astonishment when he abruptly told her the job was hers if she could start within two weeks.

She flinched inwardly when he mentioned the salary she would receive. It was half of what he would have paid a man, she thought in rage. Greed got her this job.

She was impatient to be home and talking with Sharon. She wouldn't be able to tell Seth she had the job until lunch time—when he'd call her. Inside the apartment, she charged to the phone. She noted mentally that Mrs. Reynolds had taken Jonnie to the Drive.

"Because I'm a woman he expects me to work for nothing!" Carol blazed after bringing Sharon up to date on her interview. "But I was afraid to argue."

"It's a start," Sharon comforted. "You'll learn a lot there—and you'll move up. This insane attitude toward women architects and lawyers and doctors and anything besides the traditional women's jobs has to change!"

"When women have been out there doing men's jobs—like during the war, some of them don't want to go back into the kitchen," Carol said emphatically.

"I know—most of them figure career goes out the window once they get married. *But why should it?*"

"You're not letting it stop you," Sharon said softly. "Seth wouldn't ask that of you. But Gil would be shocked if he thought I even considered going back to work."

"I'd better get off the phone," Carol said. "In case Seth's trying to reach me."

"I think it's wonderful that you landed the job. So they're screwing you on the salary—you're getting what you want out of it for now. You're on your way, Carol!"

Chapter Twenty-nine

The weeks ahead were fraught with traps. Carol quickly realized that because she was a woman she was expected to be better than any of the young male associates. The partners watched for any indication of disapproval from clients, though as she had anticipated, the assignments handed over to her were those looked down upon by the other associates. She was silently enraged when several prospective clients assumed she was one of the firm's secretaries.

She kept her private life to herself. No one at Pearson & Campbell knew she was married, knew that she had a son. She was grateful that she'd acquired—through a neighbor's cleaning woman—a warm, motherly nursemaid to care for Jonnie. Without responsible domestic help she would not be able to pursue her career.

Jewel lived up to her name, Carol said repeatedly to Sharon.

And like most young fathers of the era, Seth enjoyed sharing the responsibilities of caring for Jonnie in the hours when Jewel was not there. She would have been so happy, Carol thought, if only there was more time for Seth to write.

On the strength of the money brought in by Seth's television sales, they discarded the old furniture left by the previous tenant, shopped with a new abandon for replacements. Seth decided they should buy a secondhand car. That would be their escape from the city.

"If we can afford to pay cash," Carol decreed. Loans unnerved her.

"Okay," Seth agreed indulgently. "We'll pay cash."

Carol knew Seth was becoming obsessed with the thought of doing a play—for the theater—that would lay bare the horror of the flagrant blacklisting that was spreading across the country. On a March weekend at the Dobbs Ferry house the subject came up yet again after both children had been put to bed for the night and the four adults were at dinner.

"I know it's suicide even to attempt to do something so controversial," Seth said seriously. "But it's eating away at me. Gil, you see it every day. The way innocent people are having their lives wrecked because of the people behind *Red Channels* and *Counterattack*. We hear about people like John Garfield and Philip Loeb and Canada Lee—how they can't find work in movies, television, or theater. The list seems endless! But there are so many others, too. Ordinary people like us!" A pulse pounded in his forehead. "I know a teacher at NYU—he spent three years fighting in the Pacific—who quit his job last week and ran when he was mentioned in one of those rags. He quit before he could be fired and have it on his record that he was a subversive! It's not happening just in advertising and television and the movies. It's a plague that's infecting this whole country."

"It'll run its course soon," Gil predicted uneasily. "But for God's sake, Seth, don't stick your nose out in these crazy times."

Gil had said that before, Carol thought. He was right, of course. But Seth would seethe until he'd put his feelings into words.

"Gil, tell him," Sharon said urgently.

"Tell me what?" Seth's gaze shot from Sharon to Gil.

"I didn't want to say anything until the deal's settled. You know how wild things are in this business. One day you think you have a client sewed up, and the next minute the whole thing collapses."

"Gil, what are you talking about?" Seth demanded.

"It may come to nothing," Gil warned. "I'm working to move a client from radio into television. Paul Bartlett of Bartlett Foods. If it goes through, it'll be a half-hour dramatic series. I've already mentioned you as the prospective writer. But remember, it could be months before we have any real decision—and it could blow up into nothing."

"What kind of a series?" Carol asked, exchanging an excited glance with Seth.

"A family comedy deal," Gil said. "That's Bartlett's idea. He feels a family show ties in with his products and—"

"Gil, I don't write comedy." Seth's air of anticipation evaporated.

"Seth, of course you do," Carol protested. "The last one-act you did for Leo was a wonderful little comedy. And the second TV script was full of tender laughter."

"Seth, we're not talking about one-liners," Gil said. "A warm family series. Bartlett has some ideas about the story line—once he's convinced television is the way to go."

"Does he want to see an audition script?" Already, Carol thought, Seth's mind was working. "Would he give me something to work from?"

"I don't want you to dig in until he's committed himself," Gil explained. "I've talked about you," he said again. "I told him you have network credits as well as stage background. That you're one of the new young writers who are the future of television. We'll have to play it by ear. But I have a gut feeling that this is going to be terrific for both of us."

"Gil didn't say anything before," Sharon said gently, "because he didn't want to build you up to something great, then have to tell you it fell through."

"It's going to work!" Carol was radiant with conviction. "It's time for Seth's talents to be recognized in a serious way. And yours, too, Gil," she added softly. She knew he was churning to move into production.

"From your mouth to God's ear," Sharon said, reaching for Gil's hand. "Things are going so well these days I get scared sometimes."

* * *

Carol felt compelled to bring work home two or three evenings each week. She was ever conscious of the pressure of the job. On a balmy April Saturday she had to go in to confer with a client. She felt guilty that Seth would have to watch over Jonnie.

"Honey, don't worry," he comforted. "We'll go over to the Drive and have ourselves a ball. It's a gorgeous day."

"You should be working on a new script," she said worriedly. They didn't know if Gil's project would come through—but there were the other one-shot markets.

He hesitated. "I'm not sure I should be working on this one—"

"The stage script?" she asked, trying to hide her anxiety.

"Yeah. I know it's crazy. I should be working on something to offer the networks. But these scenes keep chasing about in my mind. I could offer it under another name," he said hopefully. "Maybe to one of the new groups that are popping up downtown." She remembered how he kept reading in *Show Business* about them. "I just want to write it and see it on a stage. If Leo was alive, he'd do it."

"Let's talk about it later," she hedged. "I have to run now."

On the subway Carol thought about Seth's obsession to write this new play. He worked hard at his teaching job—he deserved to work on a script that gave him real personal satisfaction. But there was this series with Gil's agency hanging fire. He mustn't do anything to put that in jeopardy.

Once in the office—focusing on plans for the new client's suburban residence—she was able to push this problem into a corner of her mind. Not until she returned to the apartment four hours later and discovered Jonnie blissfully napping on their bed after his outing on the Drive and Seth hunched over the typewriter in the living room—so immersed in what he was writing that he didn't hear her come in—did she recall their parting conversation.

"Hi!" Seth was suddenly aware that she was in the kitchen and putting up coffee. "Perfect timing—I'm dying for coffee."

But they didn't discuss what Seth had been working on in her absence. Instead, he wanted to know about the client with whom she'd been meeting. A demanding woman who refused to understand that plans couldn't be capriciously changed in the midst of construction.

Then Jonnie awoke and exuberantly demanded their attention. He was so sweet and bright, Carol thought lovingly. He'd been unexpected, but now it was impossible to imagine their lives without him.

"Hey, when are you going to be toilet trained?" Seth scolded but with good humor when Jonnie reached a hand down to indicate he needed a diaper change. "Your girlfriend goes on a potty."

"Sharon says girls are always toilet trained earlier," Carol said in mock despair.

"All right, old boy, let's get you dry." He reached to gather up Jonnie and take him into the bathroom.

They began the nighttime ritual. Jonnie had his dinner, his hands and face washed, then changed into his pajamas. Jewel gave him his bath every morning. Now he was allowed to watch "Kukla, Fran and Ollie."

Amid the usual protests Carol carried Jonnie off to bed, a pair of straight chairs serving as guard rails. Later he'd be transferred into the crib, which sat in a corner of the living room. Carol wished wistfully that they had either a bedroom larger than an oversized closet or a second bedroom. It was a miracle, she thought with gratitude, that Seth could type without awakening Jonnie.

She and Seth had dinner, sprawled on the sofa to watch television. She knew his afternoon's work had gone well because it was clear he was in an amorous mood. One followed the other, she thought tenderly as he dropped an arm about her shoulder.

"Do you want to watch this crap?" he asked.

"Not really," she said.

"Let me close the bedroom door." He rose to his feet.

Normally they never made love unless Jonnie was in his crib rather than sleeping on their bed—when he was "a captive," Seth labeled this. They shared a common fear of being caught by Jonnie in the act of making love.

"It felt so good this afternoon," he told Carol when he returned to the sofa to draw her into his arms. "Writing what I *want* to write. I had this marvelous feeling of euphoria. Something like being slightly drunk on fine champagne."

"There'll be a time when you'll write only what moves you," Carol said earnestly. She knew that—as much as he relished selling for television—he sometimes rebelled at fitting his work into a formula. "Once you're established you'll have more freedom."

"You know my worst nightmare," he whispered, reaching for the buttons down the front of her blouse. "It's waking up to find I've been dreaming all this. How would I ever survive without you and Jonnie?"

Finally they lay limp and content on the limited width of the sofa, yet loathe to break the spell of these moments.

"I suppose I should—" Carol began.

"Wait," Seth said with sudden urgency. "Jonnie's fast asleep. Let's live dangerously."

Normally Seth went down to the newsstand on Broadway around this time on Saturday night to pick up the Sunday *Times*.

"Suppose I wait till morning to pick up the paper," he suggested. "I'll bring up the *Times* and bagels and lox from Zabar's." He chuckled. "That's something we never had in Bellevue. You wanted lox, you had to drive into Atlanta."

"Don't bother going down for the *Times*," Carol approved. "But what about pancakes and coffee now?"

"You're cooking?" He grinned and slapped her across the rump.

"I'm cooking." She rose from the sofa and headed for the kitchen. Life had been good to them, she thought—still relaxed and happy from making love. It had been a long route to Seth—but she'd made it.

Seth awoke to sunlight streaming into their tiny bedroom. His eyes swept to the clock. Jonnie was sleeping amazingly late this morning, he thought—and in sudden alarm hurried from the bed into the living room. Jonnie was standing up in his crib and staring avidly out the window.

"Hi there, old boy." He crossed to hug his small son. "What are you watching out the window?"

"Doggies!" Jonnie's smile was beatific. "Look, Daddy!" He pointed to the young German shepherd romping in the yard below with what appeared to be an English setter but who—they knew— carried Dalmatian spots beneath her setter fur.

"You'll get a chance to play with him later," Seth promised. The dogs belonged to the couple in the basement apartment, and they adored Jonnie.

"Seth?" Carol's voice carried an element of astonishment. "How did we sleep so late?"

"Because Jonnie decreed that," he called back. "You hungry, Jonnie?"

"No," Jonnie said with conviction. "I wanna watch the doggies."

"I'll start the coffee, then go down to Zabar's and pick up the *Times*," he told Carol as she appeared in the doorway. "Did I ever tell you that you look beautiful in the morning?"

"A few times," she conceded. "But keep it up. I love it. I'll grab a quick shower, then bathe Jonnie. How are you, baby?" she crooned, walking to the crib to hug him.

"I'm not a baby," he said. "I'm a boy."

With a cherished sense of well-being Seth brought out the coffee beans and their coffee grinder, part of their Sunday morning routine. While Carol showered, he transferred the ground coffee into the percolator. Belatedly—his grin apologetic—he remembered to change Jonnie. He waited until Carol emerged from the bathroom to leave the house.

"Okay, I'm running," he said. "Need anything downstairs besides bagels and lox for breakfast?"

"Not a thing. I'll give you a head start, then put a light under the coffee."

Out in the morning air Seth wished he'd worn a warmer sweater under his light jacket. The temperature had dropped fifteen degrees since last night. Still, there were blatant signs of spring—buds on the trees, an audacious bunch of daffodils growing in a patch of earth before a brownstone.

He sighed philosophically when he saw the long line in Zabar's. Over the shoulder of the man ahead of him he scanned the front page of the *Times* theater section while he waited. Behind him two women were discussing the coming presidential election. Last month President Truman had announced he wouldn't seek reelection.

"I don't care if a Democrat or a Republican gets in," one woman said emphatically. "I just want somebody who'll stop this wild inflation."

"I'm dying to see Adlai Stevenson elected," the other woman said. "Now there's a statesman for you."

"If the Republicans nominate Eisenhower, forget it," a man behind her chimed in. "Who can beat Ike? Hell, even the Democrats wanted him."

Finally Seth emerged from Zabar's with his bagels and lox in tow. He quickened his pace against the cold wind that had come up while he waited in the store. Head down, impatient to be in the comfortable warmth of the apartment, he didn't see the man swinging around the corner until they'd collided.

"I'm sorry," he said automatically and then gaped in astonishment at the face so close to his own. "Jerry!"

"Seth!" Jerry grinned, pleased at this encounter. "I can't believe it! I haven't seen you in—hell, it must be four years!"

"Are you living around here?" Seth asked.

"On Eighty-fourth between West End and the Drive. I've been in California for the last three years." Jerry grimaced. "Couldn't take any more of that climate."

"Look, why don't you come up to the apartment with me for breakfast and a reunion?" Seth said impulsively. "We've got a lot to catch up on. And I know Carol would love to see you. That is, if you don't have to get home."

"I'm not married or otherwise attached." Jerry shrugged with an air of cynicism. "Sure, I'd love to come up."

"I'll just pick up the *Times*." And give Carol a quick buzz, Seth decided guiltily. Let her know he was bringing up Jerry. "I was too lazy to go down last night for it."

He stopped at a corner phone booth to call Carol.

"It's okay to bring him up, isn't it?" He'd detected an unexpected wariness in Carol's voice.

"Sure," she said quickly. "I was just surprised that you'd bumped into him that way."

He rejoined Jerry, paused at the corner newsstand to pick up the *Times*, laughed at Jerry's amazement when he reported that he was a father now.

"Jonnie will be two in July," Seth said, his voice rich with pride and affection. "He's the greatest."

Jerry turned the talk to writing. He had done little on the Coast, he admitted, though he'd tried to break into screenwriting.

"It's the same old story out there. It's who you know that counts. I had a few close deals, but not one ever came through. I thought you'd hang in there with theater." Jerry sound almost reproachful, Seth thought. "You were so gung-ho about making it to Broadway." Jerry had a short memory, Seth thought—he'd been enthusiastic about television the last time Jerry popped into their lives. "But I suppose it's different when you're married and have responsibilities." Seth sensed a tinge of smugness in his voice.

"I got hooked on television," Seth told him. "I'm still writing—

it's just that my directions have changed." Almost self-conscious-ly—because he suspected Jerry had encountered little in the way of professional success—he talked about his sales to television.

"When you get down to reality," Jerry said, "neither flicks nor TV compare to live theater. That's what the two of us need, Seth."

Carol had the table set when the two men walked into the apart-ment. The aromas of freshly perked coffee and frying onions per-meated the room. For a few moments the three adults were caught up in exuberant conversation, until Jonnie tugged at his father's leg in an imperious bid for attention.

"You never know who you're going to run into on the street," Jerry derided good-humoredly while Seth picked up his small son. He seemed wary about Jonnie, Carol noted. Jerry wasn't used to kids. "Particularly on the Upper West Side."

"Let's have breakfast," Carol said, reaching for the bag from Zabar's.

"Mommie, I wanna bagel." Jonnie held out a hand.

"All right, you'll have one," she soothed and reached into the bag Seth had deposited on the dining table. "Oh, they're still warm."

Over breakfast the conversation roamed from the prewar years to somber reminiscences about Leo and Greg. Nobody knew about Matt's whereabouts. They'd heard nothing since right after the lib-eration of Paris.

"I figured Matt would survive," Jerry said. "He's the type. What about Sharon? What's she doing with herself these days?"

"Sharon's married." It wasn't going to upset her that Jerry had popped back into their lives, was it? No, Carol reassured herself. Sharon loved Gil—they had something great going for them. "She has a daughter a few months older than Jonnie."

"It'd be fun to see her." Carol saw a quizzical glint in Jerry's eyes. "Her husband doing okay?"

"Very well." She wouldn't mention that Gil was in television. Jerry would be climbing over their backs if he knew.

"Gil's head of television in an ad agency," Seth said and Carol frowned in silent reproach.

"Is that how you got into TV?" Jerry asked Seth.

"No. I got myself an agent who seems to have good contacts." Seth smiled. "I'm not exactly making a living out of television," he acknowledged, "but Hank Morris is pushing hard for me. I'll stay with the teaching for a while, though."

"Everything's a matter of contacts," Jerry reiterated with a touch of the familiar bitterness. "I got my feet wet in television early on, but I'm really excited about what's happening in theater. Not on Broadway," he pinpointed. "Downtown. I think we're going to see a real renaissance of theater away from Broadway. Which, of course—every playwright hopes—will lead to Broadway. Too bad Leo isn't around. He was ahead of his time."

"You pushing a new play?" Seth asked. Carol sensed a wistfulness in him.

"I took apart the one I thought was headed for Broadway. Remember, Carol?" His voice was almost accusing. Because *she* had introduced him to Denise Williams? Carol asked herself. "That was *so* close."

"It was a tough break," she conceded.

"Anyhow, I remembered what Leo said, that I was always working too fast. I've spent a lot of time reworking the play, and I know it's commercial now." There was a messianic intensity in his eyes. "I met this woman at a Village party—a bored society broad who's dying for a fling as a producer. Not Broadway just yet, I gather. Her husband wouldn't go for that kind of money. Anyhow, she's looking around for a playhouse downtown that she can rent cheap—or a place that she can convert into a playhouse without too big an investment. Something small—maybe to hold seventy-five or a hundred. If she latches on to a play with real commercial potential, she's sure she can rope her husband and some of his rich buddies to back a Broadway production."

"So you gave her your script," Seth interpreted.

"She's reading it now. She'd down in Bermuda for three weeks. We'll talk when she gets back." Jerry's smile was casual, but his eyes hinted at pent-up excitement.

Carol took Jonnie into the bedroom to read to him in lieu of time on the Drive this morning. Reading to him, she could eavesdrop on the conversation in the living room. She knew that talking theater with Jerry would be exhilarating for Seth. She knew, also, that it would enhance his frustration at not writing the play that gnawed at him.

Why did she feel so uneasy about Jerry's popping up this way? It was absurd to think that he could endanger Sharon's marriage. Why did she have this weird feeling that with Jerry's appearance something evil had come into their lives.

Chapter Thirty

Inevitably Carol called Sharon to invite her and Gil to come into the city the following Saturday for dinner and a reunion with Jerry.

"If you'd rather not, Sharon, I can make excuses to Jerry," she added. "I'll tell—"

"Honey, I'm over Jerry," Sharon interrupted. "That's like another lifetime. And don't worry about Gil. He knows he wasn't the first man I slept with—and it doesn't bother him. We have that kind of relationship." She paused for a moment. "I won't tell him that Jerry was one of the guys," she admitted. "But even if Jerry makes it obvious, I know Gil can handle it. That's the wonderful part of our marriage—we both know what we have is forever."

Carol had always felt a concealed hostility toward Jerry—always feared that Jerry would hurt Sharon. But the era when that could happen was dead, she told herself in relief as the five of them sat down to dinner.

The two women were content to listen while the men argued over the future of television as opposed to theater. Now the talk veered to the makeshift playhouses that were making an appearance on the Lower East Side—some just a playing area surrounded on three sides by seats.

"We're not talking about Delancey and Rivington streets," Jerry explained. "Off Second Avenue, way down. I talked to Sheila last night from Bermuda—" He grinned at Seth's lifted eyebrow. "She sees herself as the patron of the down-at-the-heel young playwright. Okay, not so young now—but to her fifty plus, I'm still young." His eyes strayed to Sharon for an instant. "And great in the hay," he boasted. "I gather she's not getting what she wants at home."

"She likes the play?" Seth pursued.

"She's mad about it. I've got orders to start looking around right away for a playhouse. She wants me to run an ad in *Show Business* for a director. Only the director gets paid," Jerry conceded. "She's planning on a non-Equity cast, where the kids work their butts off for a chance to be seen onstage. Of course, half the kids who'll come down to read have Equity cards. They'll just work under another name. The big deal is to have a showcase, a place to have agents come down and see you work."

"I've kind of lost track about what's happening in theater," Seth admitted. Again Carol felt a wistfulness in him. "I know what's doing on Broadway because I read the *New York Times*."

"By early September I'll have the play in rehearsal," Jerry predicted. "I figure six weeks for rehearsal since we'll be limited to evenings and weekends. Most kids trying to crash theater hold temp jobs to keep eating and to pay the rent."

"We'll come down for opening night," Gil said enthusiastically. "We'll throw a party afterward. Sardi's," he promised.

Carol and Seth listened regularly to Jerry's progress reports. By early summer he'd nailed down a prospective playhouse that Sheila felt could be put into shape at minor expense. She signed a year's lease before taking off for Southampton. A contractor was hired to do the required work and an architect friend would supervise and handle their acquiring a license.

"It's a bitch to get a license." Jerry's enthusiasm was tempered by anxiety now. "They put up all kinds of crazy roadblocks."

"You'll get it," Seth encouraged. "You're on a roll, Jerry."

"This has got to be *it*," Jerry said tensely. "I'm thirty-six. If I don't make it now, I never will."

"I'm not far behind," Seth reminded. "I'm thirty-two."

"That's not staring at forty," Jerry shot back. "Anything Sheila wants, Sheila gets," he said bluntly. "And right now she wants me." But underneath his air of braggadocio Carol sensed his terror.

She remembered the poem by Marvell that Jerry liked to quote . . . "At my back I always hear/Time's winged chariot hurrying near . . ." There were moments, too, when she felt that way. Why was it so difficult for the world to accept women architects? Why couldn't people understand that women brought something special to the field?

On a Wednesday late in June Sharon phoned Carol to invite her and Seth—and Jonnie—to come up to the house for the approaching weekend.

"Bring Jerry along, too," she said. "He's always such a loner.

And the heat has been so bitchy this week. Gil says the city has been an inferno."

"If you're sure." Carol was ambivalent. "I mean, we kind of focus on the kids—"

"It'll be good for Jerry. But don't think he means anything to me," Sharon said firmly. "Being around Jerry makes me feel how far I've come since the old days. Kind of smug," she conceded and giggled. "I hope this play comes off for him. He seems so desperate for it to work."

"I hope so," Carol agreed.

Part of her mind dwelt on Seth's confession last night that he had almost finished the rough draft of his play about the current witch-hunting. He *knew* he couldn't try for a production. Gil was working so hard to push his major account into television—and that meant a real break for Seth. They couldn't afford to do something controversial.

The situation in television wasn't getting any better. She and Seth felt sick over what was happening. Jean Muir had been thrown off "The Aldrich Family," beloved Philip Loeb removed from "The Goldberg's"—the list was long.

Just recently John Garfield and Canada Lee had died within a few days of each other. They'd been killed, Seth declared, by *Red Channels*. As with thousands of others—both known and unknown—they'd fought desperately to revive careers that had been wrecked. Three weeks ago a woman teacher at Seth's school had been fired when it was reported that she had signed a petition at Yankee Stadium urging that Negroes be admitted to major league baseball.

Jerry was delighted to go out to Dobbs Ferry for the steamy weekend. On the brief train ride Carol devoted herself to entertaining Jonnie. It was inevitable, she thought, that Seth and Jerry would talk theater. Yet she was disturbed by the glow in Seth's eyes when he told Jerry that—despite his interest in TV—he'd just finished the rough draft of a play.

Gil met them at the station. Sharon had stayed at the house to prepare lunch. Gil reported that he and Sharon were going out to Southampton the following weekend.

"Sharon's parents and grandfather are coming out to stay with Michelle." Gil chuckled. "She'll probably be spoiled rotten by the time we get back. But the client invited, and I wasn't about to say 'no.' "

"Television is interesting," Jerry said, almost condescendingly, "but it'll never have the class of theater."

Carol's initial concern that Jerry might not fit into the picture soon evaporated. He clearly relished the affluent suburban life-style. The three men lounged on chaises on the terrace behind the house while Carol and Sharon transferred lunch from kitchen to terrace and Michelle and Jonnie played happily in the backyard sand-box.

"All right, to the table everybody," Sharon ordered. "Michelle, you let Jonnie have the ball! You can play with it together."

Carol was pleased that Seth seemed to be relaxing today. He enjoyed shoptalk with Gil and Jerry. She was touched by Jerry's admiring yet oddly shy glances at the children. She knew that he had grown up in a series of foster homes. She remembered his emotional encounter with his father on a subway some years ago—and how his father had walked away after brief conversation, as though they were slight acquaintances. The hungry glow in Jerry's eyes evoked deep compassion in her.

Later—lying in bed with Seth in a guest room—she talked about this in whispers.

"I forget sometimes that Jerry's cynical act is just a front. He was hurt so badly as a child."

"Jerry craves success because for him that'll mean acceptance and love," Seth told her. "Success will give him a family. Those audiences out front every night will give him love."

"I hope the play comes through for him."

"Yeah," Seth agreed. "He's kind of derisive at moments about the way Gil and I are clinging to the prospect of a television series, but deep inside he's envious. He's aching for audience approval, but also he wants the high living that goes with success. You know all the cracks he used to make about people who live in expensive penthouses and drive fancy cars. That's part of the picture he wants for himself."

"If Sheila takes the play uptown, he just might get it," Carol said gently. "Jerry's good."

Sunday—again—was a relaxing day. On the train that took them back into Manhattan, Carol felt a pleasant sense of peace. Tired from a long day in the sun, Jonnie slept with his head in her lap. On the seat across the aisle Seth and Jerry were talking about the season's crop of Broadway plays and how production costs were escalating. They'd all fall asleep the minute they hit the pillows tonight, she thought.

The following weekend Carol was unnerved by suspicions that she was pregnant again. She was impatient for Sharon to be back from Southampton so they could discuss this. She could be late, she tried to calm herself. She'd say nothing to Seth until she was sure. Seth adored Jonnie—but how would be feel about another child at this point? *They hadn't planned on it.*

If the television series came through, they'd be in great shape financially. But Gil warned it might be months before they knew. How long could she work if she was pregnant? Instinct warned her that the firm would fire her the instant they knew. So much depended on the television series coming through, she thought anxiously. Gil was optimistic—but things could misfire.

Maybe—when the firm fired her—she could find some freelance assignments on her own. She had *some* contacts now. The clients she worked with were always the difficult ones—but she handled them well and they'd been satisfied.

Five days later—when the unmistakable signs appeared—she told Seth she was pregnant again. The words tumbled out in a rush as they prepared for bed. She watched with trepidation for his reaction.

"Carol, that's beautiful," he said reaching to draw her close. His voice hushed with pleasure.

"As soon as they know at the office that I'm pregnant, I'll be fired," she warned. "It's so crazy; I could work right up to the last couple of weeks if they'd let me."

"Sssh," he said lovingly, "we'll manage all right. We have money in the bank—and Gil's so sure the series will come through. And if it doesn't, I'm still teaching. I have a salary every week."

"I was afraid you'd be upset." *He didn't want to teach. He wanted to write.*

"How could I be upset? It'll be great for Jonnie to have a little sister or brother. I feel so rich—" He chuckled tenderly. "Mom and Dad and Grandma will be out of their minds!"

* * *

Carol worried that she was beginning to "show." It infuriated her to know that her days at the office were running out. Why did the world expect a woman to quit her job—or to be fired—once she was obviously pregnant? She wasn't surprised when Mr. Campbell called her to his office. She knew what was about to happen.

He glanced up from his desk when she appeared in his doorway.

"This will be your last day," he told her, his face set in anger. "Your final check will be mailed to you."

Carol met his stony gaze with contempt. No need for further conversation. She wouldn't demean herself by making a retort. She turned away in silence and strode down the hall to her own working space. Her face was hot; furious tears stung her eyes. The time would come when a pregnant woman would not be a pariah in an office. Not for her, perhaps—but for her daughter, if she should be so blessed.

Seth was matter-of-fact when she told him.

"Okay, so you expected to push through another three or four weeks. Don't worry—we'll be all right."

"I'll give Jewel two weeks' notice," she said, feeling a sense of loss. Jewel was a treasure. "And I'll write her the most glowing reference."

"She'll find another family. We'll spread the word around. Jewel will have a job in no time."

"I'll tell Sharon to let it be known that I'm available for assignments," Carol said with a show of bravado. "Maybe something will come up."

"Perhaps we should hang on to Jewel for now. We've got a cushion in the bank," he reminded. "Something might come up for you."

"It's not likely." She sighed. "Visibly pregnant architects will not be in demand."

In the following weeks Carol clung to the knowledge that they had a comfortable bank account from Seth's previous television sales. And now Gil had asked Seth to sit in on a conference with his client to work out the format for the proposed television series to be packaged by the agency. She warned herself not to be jubilant about this. Nothing was sure until a contract was signed.

She knew she'd miss the office assignments, yet she had not expected to feel such an intense sense of loss. Now she rather than Jewel took Jonnie to the park twice each day. She met the mothers and nurses of the toddlers who had become Jonnie's playmates. It was a kind of club, she thought in whimsical moments.

She met Laura, a fortyish mother of Jonnie's special friend, and was intrigued to learn that this mother was making an effort to continue her career even while at home with her son.

"God, I'd go out of my mind if I couldn't do something beside cook, clean, do laundry, and bring Normie to the park every day. I'm working up a line of costume jewelry. I've already picked up some orders from Bloomingdale's and Altman's. And the money helps, too," Laura said candidly.

The second small boy with whom Jonnie played was watched by his mother and grandmother. They'd known Jewel and—Carol suspected—were disapproving of a working mother. When she talked with joyful anticipation about giving Jonnie a younger brother or sister, the two women grunted cynically.

"It's easy for you," this other mother scoffed. "Maids will raise your kids."

Carol forced herself to hide her rage. Jewel hadn't been raising Jonnie. He knew he had a mother. She was there for many hours of the day and night, she reminded herself defensively. She was there to comfort him when he was sick, to walk the floor with him when he was cutting teeth. And most days Seth was home from school shortly after three. They were both with Jonnie constantly on weekends. It wasn't wrong for a mother to have a career.

As Jerry had predicted, his play was scheduled for a fall production. He and Sheila had hired a Hollywood director—originally a stage director—for a minuscule salary.

"Roger Jackson is terrific, but he was blacklisted in Hollywood—so of course, he can't get a job in television or radio, either. He was glad to pick up any assignment," Jerry reported.

Carol had never seen Jerry in such cheerful spirits. Not all the cast was good, he reported, but he was rhapsodic about the girl who played the lead. He predicted they'd get terrific reviews. *"Enough to send us to Broadway!"*

The play was about to go into its final week of rehearsal when Jerry called up on a Sunday in a state of alarming agitation.

"Can I come up and talk?" he asked. "All hell's about to bust loose!"

"Come right up," Carol said, immediately anxious. "We're about to have breakfast. Why don't you—"

"Just coffee for me," he interrupted tersely. "I'll be there in fifteen minutes."

Carol and Seth were having coffee when Jerry arrived. He looked exhausted, she thought—his face drawn, eyes bloodshot.

"Sheila's husband is on the warpath," Jerry said without preliminaries. "He's had some private investigator snooping. Oh, I'm not her first 'protégé,' " he said contemptuously. "We all know that. But all of a sudden the old man's pissed. Either she drops the whole theater *shtick*, or he's divorcing her."

"Oh, Jerry." Carol was pale with shock. "When you're so close to opening?"

"She's already called Roger." Jerry reached for the cup Carol placed before him, gulped as though seeking strength to continue. "She's dumped him. He'll whistle for the rest of his money. I have to go down to the playhouse at two o'clock—when Roger called rehearsal—and tell them Sheila's padlocking the place. It's over—*kaput*."

"Is there some way you can salvage the opening, at least?" Carol asked, struggling to be realistic. "The rent must have been paid for the month. The cast and crew are working without pay. Couldn't you—"

"No," Jerry broke in impatiently. "Sheila's husband wants to shut down the whole deal. If we could find another playhouse quick, we might be able to do it as a sort of co-op venture." But he seemed dubious, Carol thought. *What an awful letdown for Jerry.*

"Maybe you could run the play for a week," Seth picked up. "At least, give the cast a chance to be seen. And you might be able to bring down an agent to take a look at the play." He'd talked to Hank about representing Jerry, Carol recalled, but Hank was only interested in TV.

"No, that won't work. These kids have no money to throw in for a week's rent," Jerry scoffed. "Any more than I have!"

Carol and Seth exchanged a swift, compassionate glance.

"If you can get into a place for a week, Carol and I will lend you the rent. It can't be much for one lousy week." Seth managed a smile, but his eyes were somber. More than anybody, Carol realized, Seth understood what this meant to Jerry.

"I'll tell the kids to hang on," Jerry said after a moment. "I'll chase around to see what I can come up with. Thanks for trying to bail me out."

For the few days Jerry spent every free moment trying to track down space. Carol made endless phone calls. By the time a possible playhouse was spotted, Jerry reported the cast was thinning out, chasing after other parts.

"It's useless," he said. "It's a big joke on old Jerry again."

Chapter Thirty-one

As usual when he was in a dark mood, Jerry disappeared from their lives. He had no phone, but Seth twice left notes under the door of his furnished room. He never responded. Carol admitted to Sharon that she worried about him. Sharon refused to be emotionally involved.

"He'll go away and lick his wounds, then find some woman to console him. Jerry always picks himself up and moves on," Sharon said on a balmy autumn day when she had driven into the city to spend a few hours with Carol. Later Gil would come over to join them for dinner. "What about you?" she probed. "How're you feeling?"

"Fine," Carol said. "Except that I'm going stir-crazy at not being able to work."

"I love the way Fannie Hurst wrote about how American girls 'are retrogressing into . . . that thing known as The Home.' Not all of us are happy about it," Sharon said bluntly.

"I read everything I can lay my hands on about building. And I fume," Carol said with distaste, "at the way developers are throwing up those crackerbox houses for all those ex-GIs dying to buy with GI mortgages."

"They're cheap," Sharon pointed out. "That's how Bev and Dan were able to buy. They're thrilled to be homeowners—something our parents were never able to do."

"But why can't developers build with a little imagination? Even cheap houses. Why can't they give some thought to the needs of the people who're going to live in them? Because they've been planned by men," Carol pointed out triumphantly. "A woman architect would know what to include."

"One of these days you'll design a house for Gil and me," Sharon promised with an effervescent smile. "A gorgeous house that'll be the talk of Westchester County. Or maybe," she said, her smile devious now, "Gil will buy us a townhouse in Manhattan, and you'll gut it and redesign it and it'll appear in *House Beautiful* or *House and Garden*."

At shortly before 4 P.M. Seth arrived home from school. The two children were napping in the bedroom. Seth shooed Carol and Sharon out of the apartment.

"Go somewhere and have coffee and a Danish," he ordered good-humoredly. "Pretend you're two carefree girls with nothing to do but gossip."

"I have to start dinner soon," Carol protested, but the prospect of running out with Sharon was appealing.

"So we'll eat a little later," he said, shrugging. "A hundred to one Gil won't show up when you expect him anyway," he guessed with a chuckle. Gil's working hours were notoriously long.

Over coffee and Danish at Schrafft's Carol and Sharon exchanged confidences about their respective husbands. Sharon was concerned that Gil was so obsessive about winning promotions in the agency. Carol worried that Seth was unhappy in switching his interests from theater to television.

"I know how enthusiastic he talks about television, how anxious he is for Gil to sell the series. But then he talks about the play, and his face lights up like a Hollywood premiere. He's put his whole heart and soul into that play!"

"The TV series will get him out of the classroom. It'll give you some financial security. He's building an important career for himself, Carol. You know how rough it is to break into the theater as a playwright."

"But I worry that the theater is where he truly wants to be." Seth loved theater the way she loved architecture. "It's writing, yes," she agreed. "It'll free him from teaching. But how will he feel ten or twenty years from now? Will he feel cheated?"

"The three of you—soon to be the four of you—could starve to death on what he might earn in theater. And for God's sake, Carol, you know he can't get involved in a play like that these days! That's asking for trouble!"

"Even Seth admits that." Carol's smile was wry. "But I see him hurting, and I worry."

When they returned to the apartment, they found Jonnie and Michelle awake and playing under Seth's guidance. Carol went into the kitchenette to put up dinner. A few minutes later Sharon joined her to prepare dinner for the children.

"Gil didn't call, did he?" Sharon asked Seth belatedly.

"No," Seth told her.

"Then maybe he'll be on time for dinner," she concluded.

Jonnie and Michelle were fed, washed, and changed into night clothes, then settled before the television set to watch "Kukla, Fran and Ollie." Moments after the program ended—with Michelle and Jonnie fighting to remain awake until Gil arrived—the doorbell rang.

"Daddy, Daddy!" Michelle chirped in triumph.

"Uncle Gil!" Jonnie chimed in.

Gil greeted both children in the exuberant manner they relished, pausing first to hand over a parcel that was obviously a bottle of wine or something similar.

"All right, off to bed with both of you!" He reached down to sweep Michelle and Jonnie into his arms and moved toward the bedroom.

A few minutes later Gil emerged from the bedroom. Sharon swung open the refrigerator door to show the bottle of champagne chilling inside.

"My, we're getting ritzy," Sharon drawled. "Dom Pérignon!"

"Hey, this is an occasion." He paused dramatically. "I've just come from an important session with Paul Bartlett. Seth, he's given the okay to commission you to write an audition script. The money's shitty for this script," he warned, "but if Bartlett signs for the series, it goes way up. The three of us are having dinner together tomorrow night to set the story line. Tell Hank Morris to call me tomorrow so we can work out terms for the audition script."

"Oh Gil, that's wonderful!" Carol glowed, but involuntarily her eyes swung to Seth. Was he happy about this—or did he feel trapped?

"That's great, Gil!" Seth's smile was electric.

"There's no guarantee," Gil reminded, but he was smiling. "Still,

every indication is positive. I'm heading for the Coast next week."
He turned to Sharon with an apologetic grin. "I have to talk to a
couple of Hollywood names about starring in the series. That's an
important factor in selling the old boy. He figures a movie name will
draw a big audience."

"I'll start on the script as soon as we're set on a story line," Seth
promised.

Carol sensed his enthusiasm was sincere. He *was* excited about
the future of television. But she knew that part of him wanted to do
the witch-hunting play more strongly than anything else.

Carol plotted to provide Seth with as much uncluttered time as
possible so that he could focus on the script. When he came home
from school each day, he played briefly with Jonnie. Then Carol took
Jonnie to Riverside Drive. On weekends Carol contrived to keep
Jonnie outdoors as much as possible so Seth could work without interruptions.

Early in December Gil flew out to the Coast again. He was fighting zealously to persuade Hollywood star Nadine Ascot—considerably past her prime—to gamble on playing a mother role in a television series. He returned to New York with her acceptance. She'd
agreed that television was gaining in stature.

"It's just a matter now of negotiating terms with Nadine's agent.
But we've got our star," he reassured Carol and Seth over a "victory dinner" at Toots Shor's while Sharon glowed. "How's the script
going?" he asked Seth.

"I'm polishing now. Another week and it's yours."

"That's great. I'll give it to Bartlett, then he'll have his wife read
it." He grinned as Seth winced. "Don't worry about Ellen Bartlett.
She's shrewd—she'll recognize talent."

"What's the next step?" Carol asked.

"Well, Paul and his wife have to okay the script, then I submit it
to Nadine Ascot. We may have a minor problem making her understand that this is a family series—that other characters have to
have strong scenes, too. And she wants it stressed in the script that
she was very young when the first kid was born. But nobody's beating a path to her door with movie roles right now. She may stall us a
bit, but she'll play ball."

"She has script approval," Seth guessed uneasily.

"This is going to work." Gil refused to be anxious. "Oh, you don't have to rush with the script. Bartlett's taking a three-week swing about the country—visiting the company's various plants. But the minute he comes back, he'll sit down and read the script."

"Gil, you're definitely set as producer, aren't you?" This had been worked out earlier, but Sharon needed reassurance.

"I'm the producer," Gil confirmed. "It's an agency package. Bartlett's planning on premiering the series in April. I'm going to start talking time slots next week."

"The baby will be here in time to watch the opening program," Carol said tenderly. "Though I doubt she'll understand."

"Oh, you're sure it's a girl," Gil joshed.

"Carol is," Seth said, chuckling. "All we have is a name for a girl."

Right after the first of the year Seth was called into the agency for meetings with Bartlett and Nadine Ascot. Gil had prewarned him about the Hollywood temperament he might encounter—and he was prepared to cope. To keep the peace he did some minor re-writing.

Then Nadine rejected the original schedule. She insisted on an eight-week summer series. If audience reaction was good, she'd agree to continue.

"But what about her contract?" Carol asked in disbelief when Seth announced Nadine's latest demand. "Will the agency let her get away with this?"

"They can't drag her onto the set." Seth was disappointed at the delay but realistic. "They can sue, but what will that gain them? Gil says she insists on the summer deal because she couldn't line up a summer stock package. This way she'll talk about being too tied up with TV to go out for the summer."

"That'll give you a chance to get ahead on the scripts," Carol comforted.

"No deal. Paul wants us to be only one week ahead at the opening. In case he decides on changes in the format. Maybe it's just as well. When you come home with the baby, we'll be busy for a while."

They'd talked much about looking for a larger apartment, had chosen instead to turn the bedroom into a nursery for Jonnie and his little sister or brother and to move their bed into the living room as an oversized studio couch. But once Seth's checks for the series came in on a regular basis, they'd look like mad for a larger apartment. Not an easy task, Carol warned Seth—finding an apartment these days was still a major campaign.

At the end of January—two weeks earlier than anticipated—Carol went into labor. Sharon and Gil rushed into Manhattan. Gil would stay at the apartment with the two children while Sharon held Seth's hand at the hospital. In remarkably short time Karen Laurie Walden arrived in the world. A tiny replica of Carol.

Seth insisted that there was no need for his mother to rush up to help with the baby. Carol had made arrangements for Jewel's sister to come in for Karen's first two weeks home. Carol was pleased at the family's joy in Karen's arrival. A little girl, Leah admitted, was especially welcome.

Though Seth was enthralled at the prospect of the series—and the awesomely large checks that would appear each week, he was restless at the delay. He'd finished the witch-hunting play. He couldn't proceed on future scripts for the series until Paul Bartlett gave the agency the go-ahead. He was unaccustomed to having open time on his hands.

Her first night home from the hospital Carol read the final draft of the witch-hunting play—thus far, untitled.

"I love it," she said earnestly. "Oh Seth, it needs to be seen! What a shame that you can't take the gamble."

"Everybody's so damned scared!" He shook his head in frustration. "And with good reason."

"You might try for a downtown production under another name," she said slowly, knowing how desperately Seth needed to see this play come to life. "You said some writers in Hollywood are doing that now. Nobody would have to know you'd written it."

"Carol, the subject matter is too controversial. Nobody will produce it, no matter how much they like it."

"Seth—" Carol hesitated. Was she being foolish even to suggest this? But this was the perfect time—before Seth was all involved in the TV series. She plunged ahead. "You produce it," she said. "Under another name. Just a week of performances." They'd have to guarantee a week to keep a cast together. A one-night stand wouldn't hold them. "That would mean so much to you, wouldn't it?"

"Oh God, yes!"

"We have money put away. It won't be expensive with a non-Equity cast. You remember what Jerry said about—"

"Carol, do we dare?" Seth broke in, his face luminous.

"Under a fictitious name, yes. Nobody will know if we're careful. Make up one name as producer, another as writer. We can afford it," she emphasized. "The money will be pouring in when the series begins. Give yourself this pleasure. Rent a playhouse for one week. You won't need it for rehearsals—a studio, even an empty store, will be all right. Figure out when you'll be ready to play and—"

"If we could find the director that was doing Jerry's play," Seth picked up. "Roger Jackson. He's good, and he's hungry for work."

"Run a notice in *Show Business* that you'll start casting in three weeks," Carol plotted. "Have actors mail photos and résumés to a box number. Mention that you're interested in directors, also. What do you want to bet that he'll reply?"

"We may be crazy, but I have to do it," Seth said urgently. "For my own private satisfaction."

Seth found a makeshift playhouse that he could rent for a week at an affordable price. With the playhouse dark, the owner agreed to its use as rehearsal space for a low rental. Now Seth sent in a casting notice to *Show Business*, also a call for a director. He was deluged with résumés and photos—and among others Roger Jackson replied to the call for a director.

"I'm meeting him at the playhouse tomorrow night," Seth reported exuberantly while Carol gave Jonnie his dinner. Jewel's sister had completed her two-week stint. "We couldn't ask for a better director." Some of his exuberance ebbed away. "But I get a little scared when I think what we're spending—between Roger and the rents and a couple of ads in the *New York Post* when we open." In a corner of his mind, Carol knew, he was hoping they'd be able to extend the run—though without heavy advertising this was doubtful.

"Let's take it one day at a time," Carol urged. "You've got the playhouse and rehearsal space. Roger's sure to come in as director. You start casting, go into rehearsal, and open on schedule."

"I wouldn't have the nerve to do this without you—you know that, Carol," he said softly.

"I can't wait to see the first performance." Carol was suffused with pleasure. "I'll be like old times. When Leo was alive—"

"I keep seeing Greg in the male lead," Seth said. "Wars rob us of such talent. I never thought when I came home after World War II that we'd be fighting in Korea a few years later."

Carol gazed at Jonnie, and fear encased her. She didn't want to believe there'd be a time when Jonnie might have to go off to fight in a war. Why couldn't the world learn to live in peace?

Seth told Carol that he felt as though he was living a triple life. He was Seth Walden, teacher—but he was also Jonathan Harvey, playwright, and Seth Stevens, producer. Only with Roger was he candid about his identity. Roger, of course, understood.

Carol knew Seth was anxious about all the delay between the agency and Hank Morris in ironing out details of the contract. Not until the contract was signed—on both sides—would he feel that this was a definite deal. The play would be a diversion, Carol told herself. Seth would have less time to fret.

Seth came home from the first night of the play rehearsal in a haze of euphoria.

"Roger loves the script," he said in a blend of wonder and satisfaction. "He thinks we have *chutzpah* to do it," he added, chuckling, "but he says it's an important play."

"I agree." Oh, she was glad Seth was to have this production!

Two nights later Seth came home to report that two of the sixteen members were withdrawing.

"They were frank," he said, his eyes troubled. "They're scared to death of the subject matter, worried about being blacklisted."

"You'll replace them." Carol masked the anxiety this evoked in her. "You'll be able to open on schedule." Not to open would cost them additional rent.

"I'm sure of it." Seth forced a smile. "We have a lot of names on file. These kids want to be seen. Some of them don't even know about blacklisting—all they read are *Show Business* and *Variety*."

The following morning Hank called the apartment.

"Have Seth come up to the office when he gets home from school. The contract's ready to sign! I've got everything I wanted for Seth."

"Oh, that's marvelous," Carol said in relief. There'd been the contract—and check—for the audition script, but this contract covered the whole series plus an option for an extension.

Thank God, it had finally come through.

Chapter Thirty-two

Three nights later Seth came home from rehearsal to report that Jerry had shown up at the playhouse.

"He's kept in touch with Roger. When Roger started to describe the play he was doing, he was sure it was mine."

"Jerry knows to keep quiet about your real name?" Carol asked in sudden alarm.

"Oh sure. I clued him in right away. He sat in on the rehearsal for about an hour, then took off. He's at loose ends. He offered to come and do lighting for us."

"We all did lighting for Leo," Carol remembered nostalgically. She understood, too, that Jerry needed to be around theater.

Carol was grateful that at six weeks tiny Karen began to sleep through from eleven at night until five the next morning. At the first cry she hurried to pick up Karen so that Seth could sleep until seven. He was working so hard, she thought repeatedly. The hours at school, lesson plans in late afternoon, then the evening rehearsals. And he was on standby for the beginning of the TV series.

At intervals Nadine grew terrified of the approaching television performances. Seth, Gil, and Paul Bartlett took turns building her ego. There were lunches and dinners at Toots Shor's and Sardi's. Promotion for the series began to appear in *Variety* and the new *TV Guide*. Seth was mentioned as the writer, interviewed by the *Times*. Carol cut out the clippings and started a scrapbook.

Seth had signed his contract with the agency. Why was it taking Bartlett so long to sign his contract with Seth? Until that happened Seth was out on a limb. Hank said it was normal—but she wouldn't relax until the sponsor had signed.

Seth and Roger decided that they would utilize the first three nights of the theater rental period as dress rehearsals and offer performances Thursday through Sunday. The cast was given passes—to make sure there were what Seth humorously called "live bodies" out front on performance nights. Carol phoned and arranged for free admission for members of the armed forces that appeared at

USO offices, left word at strategic places—as she had learned from Leo all those years ago—that free admissions were available.

Gil's secretary at the agency mimeographed programs. With Jonnie and Karen in tow Carol had gone to a neighborhood printer to have posters made. Seth distributed them to shops along Second Avenue—where proprietors were becoming aware of the crop of small-time theater entrepreneurs invading their area.

In an aching need to be part of the happenings, Carol gave in to Seth's urging—despite her concern about additional expenses—and hired Jewel's sister to baby-sit with the children for the week of dress rehearsals and performances. On performance nights she would sit at the improvised box office.

On Monday evening Seth and Carol met with Roger and Jerry for dinner at Ratner's on Second Avenue. Seth was exhausted but exhilarated that he'd brought the company this far.

"We've got some good people," he said when the gregarious waiter had taken their orders and left the table. "A few are not so good," he admitted.

"The performances will have a strong impact," Roger predicted. "Don't worry."

"Even Leo would have been climbing walls to have to deal with a cast as large as ours," Jerry said, his eyes nostalgic. "God, we were so fucking young then!"

"We're not ancient now." Carol comprehended the frustration she felt in Jerry. He was conscious that she and Seth had moved ahead while he had stood still through the years. Twice he'd been close to seeing a dream become reality, only to lose it.

"Seth's written a play that's so powerful it's almost actor-proof," Roger told the others. "Of course, I had to boot a couple of people in the ass to make them understand they weren't giving a weather report."

"What's with the television series?" Jerry asked Seth.

"The first program goes on a week from tonight," Seth said. "The cast is in rehearsal. I told you, Jerry—"

"Yeah." His eyes were enigmatic. He was hurting, Carol thought with a surge of sympathy. Here Seth had the play opening Thursday, then next Monday the premiere of the TV series. Jerry kept striking out. Talent wasn't enough—luck was part of the deal.

The atmosphere in the tiny playhouse on dress rehearsal night was electric. Every one of the sixteen cast members clutched at the hope that an agent would come down on a performance night and be entranced by his or her performance.

Though this was a dress rehearsal, Roger stopped the cast at intervals to hammer a point. They all knew his professional background. They knew he was getting the best possible performance from each of them. Carol could feel their respect.

After the run-through the company headed for the Second Avenue coffee shop that remained open until midnight. Though most of the cast had to be at jobs the following morning, no one wished to miss this get-together.

The cast was impatient to meet the playwright. They knew Seth as Seth Stevens, the producer. He improvised a story about the playwright being a recluse who lived on a farm in Duchess County—close enough to be available for the rewrites that were introduced at intervals. They found it strange that he wouldn't even come down for the opening.

"What kind of ego has this guy got?" one actor demanded curiously. "Doesn't he want to see his own play onstage?" In truth, there was no stage in the usual sense. A playing area was marked off with seats surrounding it on three sides. The "backstage" was a room to the rear—with two doorways that were effectively used for entrances and exits—that was utilized as a communal dressing room.

"You'll all go on Thursday night and be great," Roger said with calculated enthusiasm. "I see that in my crystal ball."

"Do you think we'll get any reviews?" an ambitious young actress—whose major experience to date was in one TV commercial—asked hopefully.

"We've invited the critics, but there's no guarantee any will show up," Seth told her. It was extremely rare for a non-Equity company to be reviewed.

He was honest. He had been from the beginning, Carol thought defensively. If it was known that the writer of Nadine Ascot's new, highly publicized television series was the playwright, they might have gotten coverage, Carol considered; but that would be inviting catastrophe. Reviewers might have come down out of curiosity if Roger was using his own name. But Roger was hoping to land another directing job Off-Broadway—and that meant using a pseudonym.

She and Seth knew this production was born of his compulsion to see the play in action. He'd seen nothing produced since before the war, when Leo had always been ready to do whatever play he wrote.

Seth needed to stem a deep hunger—but in the back of both of their minds lingered some quiet, unrealistic hope that the play would take off. A few writers contrived to work under false names in Hollywood—though for a fraction of their normal money—but most blacklisted writers found all doors closed to them.

On opening night Carol was caught in the exhilarating air of excitement that permeated the playhouse. Every seat was occupied, though most of the audience was on passes. Their tiny ad in the *New York Post* had brought down a few of those who were intrigued by the struggling movement downtown to provide theater at prices closer to those of a movie.

At a signal from Seth, Carol closed up the improvised box office and went inside. Earlier Sharon had served as usher. Now she and Carol joined Seth and Gil in seats at the rear. Jerry was backstage to handle the lighting. The house was dark now except for the playing area.

From the first moments, Carol sensed, the audience was caught up in the play. She reached for Seth's hand when applause broke out in critical scenes. *The audience liked it.* There'd be no reviews—she knew that—but this was the kind of approval Seth had needed.

At the end of the third act there was a moment of silence before the audience erupted into thunderous applause. Gil leaned across Sharon to whisper to Seth.

"They like what's being said. They know it's important."

Seth was touched when three graduate students asked to come backstage to congratulate the playwright. He explained the situation—glorying in their admiration for the message the play delivered. He promised to give the playwright their compliments.

Afterward Gil treated the entire company to a late supper at Ratner's. There were murmurs of disappointment that no critics had been out front. Two among the cast were triumphant that they had persuaded agents to come down. The others appeared hopeful—plotting to visit the two agents the following day.

"It's important to be seen," a talented young character actress said with quiet intensity. "Is there any chance of a longer run?"

"Oh, I couldn't stay after this week," the romantic male lead said with undisguised arrogance. "I'm reading for another play that's

Equity." The actors' union was beginning to make deals with the new small companies that could afford to hire two or three Equity members at scaled-down salaries.

When they left Ratner's and began to disperse, Gil offered to drive Carol and Seth, Jerry, and Roger to their apartments. Roger lived in the Village, was dropped off first. When Gil spied a parking spot in front of Carol and Seth's building, he suggested that the five of them go up for coffee and more conversation.

"Great!" Seth approved. He was drunk with pleasure tonight, Carol thought tenderly.

The baby-sitter left after reporting an uneventful evening.

"They've been so good," she said. "I gave Karen her bottle at ten, and she went right back to sleep."

Again, the others rehashed with relish the events of the evening.

"Television can't compare to the high you got tonight," Jerry twitted Seth. "Sure, the money's terrific—but you don't have the audience communication you find even in a half-assed production like tonight's."

Jerry was finding a vicarious pleasure in tonight's performance, Carol interpreted. It had been a long time since he'd seen something he'd written performed on a stage. He'd had a smell of success when Denise and Vic propelled him into early TV—where payment had been a joke. But for Jerry, she thought sympathetically, theater was the real god. Even a small house appreciated what they saw. And Jerry was good—he deserved a break.

They talked in soft tones so as not to disturb Jonnie and Karen. Soon Gil reluctantly decided he and Sharon should head for home.

"We've got another thirty-minute drive ahead of us," he remembered. "Come on, old lady, let's get rolling. Seth, it was a great evening. I'm glad you went ahead and did the play, though I admit I was nervous at first."

"Hey, the playwright's a guy named Jonathan Harvey. I'm home free," Seth said exuberantly.

Jerry declined a ride home. He was four blocks from his furnished studio. He was too revved up to go to sleep—he'd go into the all-night cafeteria and have yet another cup of coffee, he decided. If he overslept in the morning, he'd just call in sick when he woke up. They weren't going to fire him.

Did Seth know how damn lucky he was? Latching on to Gil that way was the best deal he ever made. All *he* ever had were bad breaks. God, with Sheila he'd been so close to a Broadway production he could taste it! *Nothing ever worked out for him.* Not since the day he was born.

His mind focused on Seth and Carol's kids. He'd never had one moment in his life like those kids had every day. Maybe it would have been different if his mother had lived. He didn't even have any memory of her—just of those lousy years of being shifted around among cousins and then the orphanage. And a father who didn't give a shit about him.

Seth was so smug about everything working out right for him. He took it for granted that the TV series would be a smash. He'd be rolling in dough. Jerry felt a tightening in his throat, a futile inner rage. He was as good a writer as Seth. Why did nothing ever go right for him?

"Hey, Jerry!" a masculine voice called to him as he walked into the cafeteria and took a ticket from the dispenser at the entrance. "Over here!"

His eyes followed the track of the somewhat familiar voice. He grinned and pantomimed that he'd go to the service counter for coffee, then join his neighbor. What was his name? Chuck, he recalled now. Chuck was a part-time actor who'd kept his furnished room while he was out on tour with a children's theater company. When he wasn't acting, he was a soda jerk in Times Square. Chuck had been away three or four months.

"When did you land in town?" Jerry asked, sliding into the chair across from Chuck.

"Two days ago. The company manager ran out of funds. You know, another of those non-Equity disasters." Chuck shrugged. "At least, we were out long enough for me to go on unemployment insurance.." He chuckled smugly. "I wonder if the state government realizes how many theatrical careers they're subsidizing?"

"I was never so lucky," Jerry said. Chuck knew he had some theater background. Mostly, Chuck had been impressed by his early foray into television.

"What're you doing these days?" Chuck asked.

"The usual shit. Working to eat and pay the rent. Oh, I'm involved in some crappy Off-Broadway deal for a few performances."

"Your play?" Chuck was instantly alert, hopeful of a part.

"No, this is a friend's deal. I'm helping out with the lighting.

They're closing Sunday." He saw the eager light in Chuck's eyes ebb away.

"You game for some partying tonight?" Chuck asked.

"This late?" Jerry lifted an eyebrow.

"So what? There's this old broad with a fancy apartment over on Central Park West. She goes to the theater two nights a week, and afterward she throws these brawls. She doesn't get anybody important," Chuck admitted, "but it's free food and free booze. When I'm in town I always go over. Every now and then I pick up a lead."

"You've been out of town for a while. You're sure she's still on the same track?"

"I called a few minutes ago. She was home from the theater. She said to come arunnin'."

"So let's go," Jerry agreed.

Carol emerged from the bedroom after a final check on the children before joining Seth in bed. Tomorrow would be a tough day for him, she thought. They were both too keyed up to fall asleep for hours—and Seth left for the school at 8:15 in the morning. Karen would be awake before 6 A.M.

She reached quickly to pick up the phone before it might awake the children.

"Hi, we just got home five minutes ago," Sharon said ebulliently. "Is Seth floating on air?"

"Sort of. It was so sweet of Gil and you to take everybody out after the performance." Carol settled herself at the edge of the bed and reached a hand for Seth's.

"I felt as though the clock had moved back a dozen years." Sharon's voice was nostalgic. "You know, standing there ushering people down to their seats. I almost expected to see Leo going out to check the box office—and Greg wowing the audience with a terrific performance."

"Yeah—" Those were times that were forever etched in their memories. "Jerry said something like that, too. I think he enjoyed tonight."

"Jerry was dying of jealousy," Sharon said bluntly.

"Oh, Sharon, you're such a skeptic," Carol scolded.

"I know Jerry. He was eaten up alive from the minute he walked into the playhouse. But he's masochistic—he couldn't stay away." Sharon paused. "I told Gil about Jerry and me—in those wacky young years," she added with a chuckle. "He'd already figured it out. But I had to be honest with him. And nothing's changed for us," she emphasized. "What we have is real—for always."

Jerry was impressed by the huge, elegantly furnished living room of Amanda Ridgeway's apartment. There must be almost two dozen guests scattered about the room, he guessed—most of them young. All of them figured a rich broad like Amanda Ridgeway had terrific contacts. Those were the magic words—especially in the entertainment world. Who knew that better than he?

He and Chuck strolled over to the bar, manned by a white-jacketed bartender. The buffet still offered choice tidbits.

"Look, does she mind crashers?" All at once Jerry was nervous.

"Are you kidding?" Chuck derided. "As long as you've been involved in theater, Amanda loves you. You'll meet her later."

"How does she feel about television?" Jerry sipped at his Scotch on the rocks.

"Oh, she's big on that. She's always writing letters to Ed Sullivan and to the TV networks."

A pretty blonde approached them.

"How're you doin'?" Chuck asked blithely, then introduced her to Jerry. "Three years ago we were out on a borscht belt tour with the same company. Boy, the meals they served us in those kosher hotels were something! Who could act after all that food?"

"We could never have milk or cream with our coffee," the blonde complained.

"That's part of the kosher thing," Jerry explained, at the same time watching Amanda move from one group of guests to another.

Amanda Ridgeway was a small, pudgy, middle-aged woman who managed to convey an impression of power, he thought. Not just because of her money. She oozed self-confidence—and a determination to make her will felt. What was her *schtick?* he wondered curiously.

Then she was walking toward Chuck and himself as the blonde edged away to talk to a male model.

"I haven't seen you for a while, sweetie," Amanda said, her smile ingratiating. A hundred to one, Jerry thought with amusement, she didn't remember Chuck's name.

"I've been out on tour," Chuck said casually. The inference was that the tour was an Equity company. "I just got back two days ago."

"And all set to make TV rounds." She laughed. "Everybody I meet these days is dying to score big on television." She turned to Jerry. "What about you?" she challenged.

"I'm not an actor," he explained. "I'm a playwright. Only theater interests me." Seth, the dumb *schmuck*, was panting to sell out to television. For one self-conscious moment he remembered his own eagerness to wallow in the television scene.

"I worry about television," Amanda said, her smile wistful. "It has such marvelous potential—but it frightens me because of its power. We all know that the wrong people have a way of infiltrating and getting their dangerous messages across to so many millions. It's even worse than Hollywood because it comes right into American homes." She paused, seeming to be appraising Jerry. "Still, it's the medium of the future. I know you love theater, but if you should consider writing for television, I have some contacts."

Jerry suppressed a smile. Another horny, middle-aged broad, he labeled her. He'd been down this road before.

"I have a friend who's writing the Nadine Ascot series," he told Amanda, and saw Chuck's eyes brighten. "But he's also producing his own play in one of those Off-Broadway dives downtown—off Second Avenue. Just for this week—" Seth was greedy. He wanted it *all*. TV and the theater. Everything came so easy to Seth. "Not my kind of play." He smiled arrogantly.

"What's your kind?" Amanda pressed. Her smile said she was interested in pursuing this. She signaled the bartender to freshen Jerry and Chuck's drinks.

"Commercial theater. I think it's a playwright's job to provide entertainment. If you have a message," he pulled out the old cliché, "use Western Union." Chuck nodded vigorously, eager for Amanda's approval.

"Your friend has a message?" All at once the atmosphere was electric.

"Oh yes," Jerry drawled. He felt a dizzying sense of power. This wasn't just some rich bitch out to fill her bed. She was part of some organization out to rid America of commie infiltration. She knew a lot of important people. "He's all up in arms against the McCarthy scene." He saw her eyes move to the pair of two older men across the room in a kind of silent communication. "In the play he rips the commie hunt to shreds."

"And now he's going to infiltrate the Nadine Ascot program," she said with righteous indignation. "How awful!"

"He's always been on that side of the road." A rush of triumph flooded him. "I remember before the war, when we were both involved with the same theater group—he was fighting to enlist help in getting petitions signed that favored the Abraham Lincoln Brigade in Spain."

Amanda would clip Seth's wings, he told himself with savage satisfaction—the Scotch on the rocks making him lightheaded. He didn't have to give her Seth's name. She knew Seth was writing Nadine Ascot's series. She'd find out in a minute that he was also Jonathan Harvey, playwright. Those two goons across the room would be down at the playhouse tomorrow to check for themselves. It didn't take the FBI to figure out which play was Seth's. There weren't that many plays running this week downtown off Second Avenue.

Chapter Thirty-three

Carol had given Karen her bottle, deposited her in the playpen, and was preparing Jonnie's cereal when the phone rang on Monday morning.

"Seth?" she called, and heard the water pounding in the tub. He was in the shower. She turned off the gas under the cereal and hurried to pick up the phone. Probably a wrong number at this hour, she guessed. Their number was one digit removed from that of the nearest police precinct. It seemed as though half the cops who called in sick reached them instead on the first try. "Hello—"

"Carol, let me talk to Seth—" It was Gil, his voice strained, almost hoarse.

"He's in the shower," she began instantly anxious.

"Tell him to call in sick and meet me at the office in about half an hour. I'm driving in as soon as I hang up."

"Gil, what's going on?" Carol asked, but he was already off the phone. Was there trouble about tonight's premiere? *Had something happened to Nadine Ascot?* Her throat tightening in alarm she hurried into the bathroom. "Seth!" she yelled above the sound of the shower. "Seth!"

The water stopped.

"Yeah?"

"Gil just phoned. He wants you to meet him at the office in half an hour."

Seth pushed back the shower curtain.

"What's up?"

"I don't know, but it sounds bad. He said for you to call in sick."

"What could have gone wrong?" He stepped out of the tub and took the towel Carol extended. "Nadine couldn't be asking for revisions at this late date."

While Seth rushed to dress, Carol poured him a cup of coffee, brought it to him. Tonight was the premiere of the series. What could be bringing Gil into the office at 7:30 A.M.?

"I'll call Sharon," she decided while Seth gulped down his coffee.

Sharon said that she knew nothing about what was happening. The phone rang at the house as Gil had sat down to breakfast.

"Paul Bartlett's a nut about getting an early start," Sharon reminded. "He likes to be at his desk no later than 7 A.M.. I heard him yelling into the phone. Gil hung up and then called Seth. He rushed out of the house without telling me a thing."

"I'll talk to you later. Jonnie's sounding off for breakfast."

Probably Nadine was having another attack of nerves, Carol reasoned. She needed hand-holding. But why put the others through this? she asked herself impatiently.

Still searching his brain for Gil's reason for summoning him into the office at this hour, Seth waited impatiently for the single elevator in operation to descend. Had Nadine been in an accident? Was she throwing another temper tantrum about the script not revolving totally around her? Was she in a panic about her first appearance on television?

The elevator glided to a stop. Seth stalked inside.

"Twenty-two," he said. This was not an operator he knew. Not at this time of morning.

The elevator shot upward, stopped at his floor. Seth hurried out into the before-hours empty reception area, headed down the circuitous path to Gil's office. He wasn't there. Okay, he must be in the conference room.

Approaching he heard voices in agitated conversation. Gil and Paul's voices.

"What's the matter with that stupid prick?" Paul was yelling as he walked into the office. "Are his brains in his ass?"

"What's going on?" Seth asked quietly, gearing himself for trouble. *Were they talking about him?*

"That's what's going on!" Paul said grimly, pointing to a pile of perhaps seventy letters and postcards on the corner of the huge conference table. "I came into my office this morning, went into the mail room, and had these dumped in my lap. Every one of them threatening to boycott Bartlett Foods if we go on with you as the writer of Nadine Ascot's program!"

"Why?" Seth was pale with disbelief. It couldn't be because of the play—nobody knew he wrote it.

"You signed petitions for the Abraham Lincoln Brigade," Paul said with acid contempt. "You worked to raise funds for that commie outfit. And that wasn't enough! You write a play that dares to question the behavior of patriotic Americans, then produce it under a phony name. How did you expect to keep it secret?"

"Paul, you've got a few letters," Gil began warily. "You know how—"

"Seventy letters." Paul's eyes swung to Seth. "For that many letters to come in over the weekend means hundreds of thousands of others are up in arms."

"Who knows me?" Seth countered. His mind in chaos. "I've had a handful of plays broadcast on television. I'm not a big name."

"You've been mentioned in all the publicity about the program," Paul reminded. "You were interviewed about the series. The word's out now. You're a goddamn Red! *They* are spreading the word."

Who were "they," Seth asked himself—but he knew. The hysterical clusters out there in the shadows, the publications—*Counterattack* and *Red Channels*—that were selling their putrid publications and misslanted reports for what was becoming major money.

"This will all die down," Gil said, straining for calm. His face was drained of color. "We can't let—"

"We can't let Bartlett Foods be tainted by a commie writer." Paul's eyes narrowed. "I went through the contract. There's a morals clause. You're fired, Seth." He turned to Gil. "You have scripts for the first two weeks. Dig up a replacement writer—or writers—fast." His hostility expanded to include Gil. "You're the producer, Gil—didn't you check on his background?"

"Gil didn't know about the play," Seth broke in quickly and saw the relief that washed over Gil's face. "We just have a professional relationship. But I was an eighteen-year-old kid when I worked for the Abraham Lincoln Brigade. We were all fighting fascism!"

"I don't give a shit what you did when you were eighteen," Paul told him. "But how dumb can you be in these times, to write and produce a play that backs up the Reds!"

"It doesn't back up the Reds!" Seth refuted. "It tries to tell Americans what witch-hunting is doing to this country!"

"Get out of my sight," Paul seethed. "Gil, we'll have to put out a letter of apology—from the agency and Bartlett Foods. Line up the best public relations people you can find. Viewers have to know that Bartlett Foods has no truck with dirty commies!"

Seth walked out of the conference room, down the long, circuitous hall to the bank of elevators. His head pounded as he tried to assimilate what had happened. He was off the show. He was blacklisted.

Chapter Thirty-four

Carol put Karen in her crib and hurried to answer the phone. She was relieved that this morning Jonnie was visiting a little friend in an apartment in the next building. He'd be there until after lunch.

"Hello—" She was breathless from anxiety.

"Have you heard from Seth?" Sharon asked.

"Not a word." She'd hoped this was Seth. "I know he'll call as soon as he can."

"Gil hasn't called, either. We're all probably worrying for nothing." Sharon was making an effort to sound optimistic.

She heard a key in the door. "Sharon, I think Seth's here. Hold on."

The door swung open. Seth walked inside. He was pale, haggard. Carol's heart began to pound.

"Sharon, I'll call you back," she said and hung up. "Seth—"

"It's not good." As though drained of every ounce of strength, he dropped onto a corner of the sofa.

"Nadine's walking out?" Anger tightened her throat. Nadine had a reputation for walking off movie sets in a temperamental outburst. But this wasn't a movie set. She had to be there for a live performance—it couldn't be filmed later. "Is she out of her mind?" Carol hovered before him in disbelief.

"There's no easy way to tell you." Seth lifted his eyes to hers. She felt a surge of alarm at what she saw there. "They know about the play, Carol. They even know about the Abraham Lincoln Brigade bit. I was so sure we'd covered ourselves." He shook his head in frustration. "I'm off the show. I'm blacklisted."

"How could they know?" *This was a nightmare. It wasn't real.* "Seth, tell me exactly what happened."

"You know how Paul is at his office every morning at seven A.M. Well, this morning he walked in and found Saturday's mail piled on his desk. Almost seventy letters from outraged consumers. You know the *schtick*. They all said the same thing: 'Throw the commie off the show, or watch us boycott Bartlett Foods.' Every sponsor goes into panic when those bastards start up. And Gil can't do anything—the agency will be hit, too. It's the familiar story—the agency has to go along with the client's demands or lose the account. I'm out of the show. Out of television." He flinched in anguish. "I could be out of the school."

"I shouldn't have encouraged you to produce the play," Carol tormented herself. "It's my fault!"

"No, Carol," he rejected firmly. "But who started this hate campaign against me? You know how they operate. Somebody drops the word, and they go into their letter-writing campaign. No questions asked. Who did this, Carol?"

"Nobody knew." Carol fought for control. "Only Roger." She paused, searching her mind for answers. "Roger doesn't drink, does he?"

"Not even coffee," Seth told her. "He didn't get drunk and say the wrong thing."

"Is Gil in trouble over this?" *Why had she pushed Seth into doing the play? She knew it was dangerous.*

"I tried to cover for him. I told Paul that Gil knew nothing about the play. That we only saw each other professionally."

"I'd better call Sharon." Fighting against panic, Carol rose to her feet. "She's terribly anxious."

"Tell her Gil's in the clear," Seth said. "I'm sure Paul believed me." But he was anxious, Carol guessed. "Where's Jonnie?"

"Spending the morning with his friend next door. Karen's asleep." She reached for the phone—her mind in chaos.

Sharon was at first shaken, then outraged. "You know who did this, don't you?"

"No." Carol was bewildered. "We were so careful—"

"It was Jerry," Sharon said with conviction. "He's such a jealous bastard. He couldn't stand Seth's success!"

"Sharon, I can't believe—"

"You'd better believe," Sharon interrupted. "Only three people other than you and I and Seth knew about the play. Gil, Roger, and Jerry. And only Jerry knew about the brief fling Seth had with the Abraham Lincoln Brigade, and that you and I pitched in, too. I never mentioned it to Gil—it happened so long ago. *But Jerry knew.* I remember he made cracks at the time."

"Oh my God," Carol whispered. Seth lifted his eyebrows in inquiry. "It was Jerry," she told him.

"I wonder if mentioned me, too." Sharon was caught up in fresh anxiety. "That would cost Gil his job! He'd be considered a fellow traveler—married to me. Nobody has to prove anything. The label just has to be slapped on you."

They talked a few moments longer, then Carol was off the phone.

"It's not the end of the world, Seth." Carol struggled for calm. "This insanity can't go on forever. It has to stop soon. I'll take any bet that most people are disgusted with this witch-hunting."

"But the others are noisy and destructive," Seth jumped in. "They're determined to arouse groundless fears. They create havoc." A vein pounded in his forehead. "I don't know what's going to happen with the school if they find out. If I'm fired from teaching, what the hell do I do? Try for a job in a department store at forty dollars a week? We can't live on that."

Early in the afternoon Gil called.

"Seth's asleep," Carol explained. "He's exhausted."

"I didn't want to phone from the office," Gil confessed. "I suppose I'm getting paranoid. Paul's on the warpath. He received almost a thousand letters more in today's mail. We got almost as many at the agency. I've pointed out to Paul that bunches of the letters come from the same post office. It's an assembly-line routine—a plotted campaign by a few rabble-rousers."

"Are you okay?" Carol asked solicitously.

"I believe so." Yet doubt infiltrated his voice. "Of course, if Jerry implicated Sharon, I'll be finished at the agency. How's Seth?"

"He wanted to track down Jerry and make mincemeat out of him. I pointed out that wasn't going to help. He's scared to death that word of this will reach the school."

Carol had put the children to bed and she and Seth were sitting down to dinner when the phone rang. Seth went to pick up the receiver.

"Hello."

"Seth, I have to talk to you." It was the dean of his school—clearly agitated.

"Yes?" Seth was noncommittal. One hand over the receiver, he identified the caller for Carol. She rushed to stand beside Seth and listen in.

"Your classes this final week will be taken over by a substitute," the dean said tersely. "Your contract will not be renewed. We've had four phone calls today from parents. The school can't afford a Red smear—"

"I'm not a Red," Seth interrupted in a surge of fury. "Not now or ever!"

"I don't know whether you are or not," the dean told him. "I just know that we can't have anyone on our faculty who is under suspicion. Your last check will be mailed to you shortly. Don't come into the school again."

"Word gets around fast." Seth closed his eyes for a moment. "I can't believe this is happening."

At her insistence Carol and Seth sat down to dinner. They made a pretense of eating. On what should have been one of the most exciting evenings of their lives, she thought, they were encased in anguish—terrified for the future.

Earlier it had been arranged that Carol and Sharon would watch the premiere of the show in an office at the network. Seth and Gil would be in the control room. Afterward they were all to attend Paul Bartlett's party at "21."

Sharon refused to come into the city tonight; she'd canceled the baby-sitter. She was too distraught to be part of the occasion, she'd confided to Carol in one of several phone calls in the course of the day. "I can't go down there and pretend nothing's happened. Gil will make some excuse for me."

When the dinner table was cleared and the dishes washed and dried, Carol and Seth settled themselves before the television set with a mixture of pain and pleasure. At intervals while they waited for the program to begin, Seth went to the bedroom door to look in on Jonnie and Karen. Carol knew his troubled thoughts: how was he to provide for his family in the face of the blacklist?

When the program began, Seth reached for Carol's hand. They watched, absorbed by the performance. Despite all her hysteria—all the battles because she resented every laugh line that went to another cast member—Nadine was superb. At the first commercial Carol went to the refrigerator to bring out a pitcher of iced coffee. The day had been abnormally hot and humid for early June. Evening had brought no relief.

"It'll be a hit. It'll run for years," Seth predicted, his agony at what he'd lost mirrored in his eyes.

"My fault," Carol said for the dozenth time. "I *know* what's going on in this country. Why did I push you to do the play?"

"I won't have you blame yourself. It was that bastard Jerry. It's so damn hard for me to believe he'd do this to us. I've never felt such violence toward anybody. Not even during the war when our lives were on the line. I hope he pays for what he did to us!" One eyelid quivered as his mind dwelt on Jerry's betrayal.

"Seth, don't be eaten up by rage," Carol pleaded. "People who do terrible things pay for them in time. We'll come out of this. We're strong."

The commercial was over. The program resumed. Seth was right, Carol thought. The agency and Bartlett Foods had a hit on their hands. But Seth would gain nothing from it. He'd take a thin story line and built it into a solid production. In truth, he had made the show. But his name was left off the credits, despite the advance publicity.

The show was only seconds off the air when Sharon called from Dobbs Ferry. If Gil stayed clear of the Red-smearing, he was in for a tremendous career boost, Sharon admitted—but she was anxious.

"I don't know how much Jerry talked," Sharon reminded. "If he mentioned me—and I'm linked to Gil—we're in hot water, with a mortgage up to our necks and car loan payments."

Only a few minutes after Sharon got off the phone, another call came in. Seth's mother reported that the family had watched the show and loved it. Carol hovered close enough to hear while she and Seth talked.

"Dad said you wouldn't be home—you'd probably be at the studio. But I just had to try to reach you. Seth, we're so proud of you!"

Then his father and grandmother spoke with him for a few moments.

"Wait," Leah cautioned. "Don't get off yet. Harvey wants to talk to you." But Carol guessed she was commanding Harvey to come to the phone.

"Hey, Seth, you're a celebrity," he drawled. "But why didn't they mention your name on the credits?"

"An oversight," Seth lied. Later he would tell the family what happened, Carol understood. He didn't want to destroy their pleasure yet.

Carol knew that neither she nor Seth would sleep much tonight. At intervals he left the bed to pace about the apartment—in bare feet so as not to disturb her or the kids, she thought tenderly. She'd never seen him so furious as when he realized Jerry had betrayed them.

As usual Jonnie and Karen awoke a little past six. Carol hurried into the bedroom to quiet them down. Seth was at last asleep.

Carol went through the morning routine with the children, then left the apartment to take them to the Drive. For the rest of the world nothing had changed since yesterday—but their lives had been turned upside down. As it had for many others in the last few years.

When she returned to the apartment, Carol heard water pounding in the tub. Seth was showering. She put Jonnie down with one of his favorite puzzles, deposited Karen in the playpen. When Seth emerged from the shower, they breakfasted together. For a little while they'd pretend this was just another holiday morning—when Seth wouldn't have to go in to the school.

"How could Jerry do this?" Seth harangued throughout the morning. "We were all so close. Why did he want to ruin us?"

"We'll cope," Carol repeatedly insisted. "We've got money in the bank. This insanity has to stop soon." But it had been building up for years. Would it ever stop?

In midafternoon Seth went out to pick up the papers. He hardly thought that he was important enough to be mentioned, but had an obsessive need to read what the television critics had said about last night's premiere of the "Nadine Ascot Show." While the children napped, Seth and Carol searched through the newspapers.

"Seth, they loved the show. It's a hit!" For a moment her face was radiant.

"Read Westbrook Pegler," Seth said grimly, handing over the folded-back newspaper. "He tells the world that I'm another lousy commie out to infiltrate network television. That's just the beginning. You know the routine."

They told themselves they would be realistic. They would sit down and work out how they were to handle themselves. But they kept running into dead-ends. No, he couldn't change his name, Seth pointed out. When he applied for a job, they'd ask for his Social Security number. He might hang on for a few weeks—but when quarterly returns went in, Social Security would write back that name and number didn't match.

"There's no point in trying another teaching slot," Seth said tiredly. "I'm washed up in that field. Forget television and radio, of course—I'm on all the lists now. I'll try for a selling job," he said with distaste. "I'll have to make up some lies about where I worked and why I left." He frowned in thought.

"Say you've just come up from Bellevue," Carol improvised. "Give them a line about managing a store for your father down there. He'll back you up."

"I can't keep stalling with Mom and Dad." He sighed. "The family will have to know what's happened." But he continued to stall.

Each morning Seth went out to file job applications. He and Carol tried to convince themselves that outside of the entertainment field employment offices wouldn't be concerned about his blacklisting—they wouldn't remember that he'd been mentioned by Pegler and George Sokolsky and others in the witch-hunt. Carol was shaken when she discovered that she, too, was listed with Seth in *Red Channels* as a "subversive."

Jerry had disappeared from their lives, yet at recurrent intervals Carol envisioned herself running into him on the street, castigating him for what he had done. She would never understand such betrayal.

At the end of June Seth was hired as a sales clerk in a men's clothing store in Times Square. Their savings would subsidize his salary, which would cover little more than their rent. Now he had to call home and tell the family what had happened—in case the store checked his employment record.

Seth spoke first to his father, who'd picked up the phone, then to his mother. They were aghast at what had happened, quick to offer sympathy. Both urged Seth to return to Bellevue.

"We've got so much room now," his mother said lovingly. "I told you we were adding an addition downstairs for Grandma. The stairs were getting too much for her with her arthritis. We added another bedroom and bath. Harvey's off in his own apartment now." The only apartment house in Bellevue. "So upstairs there's a bedroom for you and Carol and another for the children. Darling, it would make us so happy to have you all here."

Seth's father pulled the phone away to talk to him again.

"There's a job in the store for you any time you want it. We've expanded, and I'm always short of help. You know how I worry about having trustworthy help. Wait," Eli said now. "Mom wants to talk to you again."

"Seth, you could probably get a job in a school down here or in Atlanta. They don't have to know what happened in New York. You're a local boy who decided to come back home."

"We'll work things out," Seth hedged. "But I had to tell you what's happening." He paused. "Tell Dad to write that letter to the store here in New York."

"He'll do it tonight," Hannah promised. "I'll mail it at the post office in the morning."

"Mom—" Seth hesitated. "Tell Dad to say I'm a distant cousin. It'll look better that way."

The summer dragged on, a recurrent nightmare as each Monday night Carol and Seth sat down to watch the program. Each Monday vowing they wouldn't watch, yet obsessively drawn to do so. *Vari-*

ety was predicting the series would be renewed, would attract a huge audience.

On a sultry August afternoon—just days after an armistice was signed in Korea—Carol returned from an outing on the Drive with the children to hear the phone ringing as she unlocked the door. Rushing inside—expecting the caller to be Sharon—she deposited Karen in the playpen and reached for the phone.

"Hello—"

"Is this Carol Walden?" a brisk male voice inquired.

"Yes—" With her free hand she reached for a puzzle and gave it to Jonnie. He settled on the floor with an eager smile.

"Mrs. Walden, this is Doctor Gardiner at Bellevue Psychiatric. We have a patient here—Jerry Kline. He was brought in last night after a suicide attempt."

"Oh, my God!" Carol was dizzy with shock.

"He's asked to see you. I think it's important that you come in."

"I—I have two small children," she stammered, her mind assaulted by visions of Jerry in some violent attempt to die. "I can't come down till my husband returns home. That won't be till after six this evening." How could he ask to see *her*, after what he had done to them?

"You can see him at any time. I'll be here until eight P.M. Stop by my office first. We'll talk."

"How—" Carol forced herself to continue. "How did he attempt suicide?" All at once she remembered her father, lying in a pool of blood—the gun beside him, heard her mother's screams.

"He was in a neighbor's apartment, he told us. When the neighbor took a phone call, he went into the bathroom, broke a glass and slashed his wrists. Physically he'll be all right," Dr. Gardiner told her. "He's undergoing therapy now." Dr. Gardiner paused. "Often suicide is a plea for help. Jerry wanted to die."

"I'll be there," Carol whispered. "Probably around seven."

A few minutes after 7 P.M. Carol sat in a chair in Dr. Gardiner's office and listened to a full report of Jerry's suicide attempt.

"If his neighbor had not spent time as a hospital aide and hadn't known what to do, he would have bled to death." Dr. Gardiner's eyes were compassionate. "It's very important for him to talk to you. He'll be here for at least two or three weeks—until we're convinced he's no longer suicidal—but he insists he must talk to you. I'm glad you were able to come down so quickly."

Dr. Gardiner wrote out a pass, instructed her on where she was to go. Her heart pounding, her feelings ambivalent, she followed directions. At the floor where Jerry was being held, she waited—in an aura of unreality—while first one pair and then another pair of heavy metal doors were opened to admit her. A male nurse escorted her through the open ward to a row of small, private rooms.

"He's in here." The orderly pointed to a doorway, devoid of a door.

Jerry lay with his bandaged wrist resting across his chest. For a moment he was unaware of her presence. She saw the anguish in his eyes. *What had made him betray Seth that way? Didn't he know what he was doing to them?*

"Jerry—" She tried to steady her voice. Why had she come? To give him absolution? Yet even as fresh rage threatened to choke her, she felt his pain.

"Carol, I have to talk to you—" He was weak from loss of blood, she realized—too weak to lift his head as he tried to do. "You don't know—"

"I know," she told him and saw him wince. "Jerry, why?"

"I went crazy for a little while. Seth had everything—I had nothing. It's always been that way for me. You've known me a long time—" For a moment he closed his eyes.

"You have a real talent, Jerry. You know that without my telling you. Your time will come." *How can I stand here and talk this way—knowing what he's done to Seth and me?*

"I wish I could believe that." His eyes clung compulsively to hers. The doctor said he'd wanted to die, Carol remembered—but in a peculiar way he was begging her to give him hope.

"Recognition seldom comes early. Aren't you the one who told me that Shaw was over forty before he was accepted as a playwright?" It had been Seth, she recalled belatedly—that wonderful weekend in London.

"I wish I'd succeeded with this—" His gaze focused on his bandaged wrist. "I can't do anything right." His familiar bitterness erupted yet again. "But I want you to know that you and Seth won't have to worry about running into me around the neighborhood. As soon as they let me out of here, I'm heading for California again. No more lousy New York winters for me." He paused, shook his head as though struggling to cast aside private demons. "It was a rotten thing to do. I'm sorry, Carol."

"I'm sorry, too," she said quietly. "I hope you find what you're looking for in California."

She turned and walked slowly from the room, through the ward to the steel doors where a guard waited to allow her to leave. Had Dr. Gardiner expected her to say to Jerry, "It's all right—what you did to us. We forgive you?" She couldn't say that. It was wrong—terribly wrong.

Now she remembered her anger—after the initial heart-stopping shock—when her father killed himself. She'd been angry and hurt that he had left her mother and herself alone in a terrifying world. But tonight—after seeing the agony in Jerry's eyes—she understood. Papa's pain had been more than he could bear.

Chapter Thirty-five

Seth loathed his job. He was trampled by despair over their future. Carol tried—futilely—to acquire a free-lance assignment. Seth's mother wrote regularly to remind him that there was always a job for him in their business and plenty of room in the house.

Each week—no matter how hard they scrimped—they were forced to draw money from the bank. Regularly unexpected emergencies arose. The car—which had seemed a real buy and provided them with cherished weekends with Sharon and Gil—suddenly needed a ring job. They cringed at the cost but couldn't bring themselves to give up the car.

In October they came face to face with the result of having lost their health insurance when Seth was fired by the school. Carol sat on a playground bench and watched while Jonnie and Karen played with three other children in the sandbox. All at once Jonnie and another boy were climbing out of the sandbox. The other little boy shoved Jonnie exuberantly. He went down striking his forehead on the harsh pavement.

Instantly Carol realized the cut on Jonnie's forehead would require stitches. Frightened, struggling to calm Jonnie, she left Karen's stroller with another mother and rushed by cab with the two children to the Roosevelt Hospital emergency room.

The cut wasn't serious.

"He might have a slight scar," the doctor said, "but it'll fade as he grows."

Carol was aghast when she was presented with the bill. *How could a tiny cut cost so much?* She was grateful that Jonnie was all right—in four days the stitches would be removed and he'd be none the worse, she comforted herself—but now she'd live in terror of another medical emergency.

With the approach of the new year Carol and Seth came to grips with reality. Their savings account was dangerously low. They couldn't possibly live on Seth's salary and remain in their apartment. Both recoiled from the prospect of moving into a tenement flat somewhere, fighting to survive. If it were just the two of them, they conceded, they'd try to sit out the hard times—but they wanted more for Jonnie and Karen.

"This doesn't mean we'll stay forever in Bellevue," Seth said defensively. "The situation has to change here."

But Joe McCarthy was still riding high, Carol thought—the House Un-American Committee still wreaking its havoc. Hysteria continued to rule.

Seth was right, she told herself—for now they must move to Bellevue. It would be good for the children to know Seth's family. Putting such distance between themselves and Sharon and Gil and their children would be rough. *They* were her family.

Carol and Seth tried to make the move to Bellevue seem a major adventure. Karen was too young to understand. Jonnie was intrigued by the prospect of driving so far.

"I just hope the car holds up," Seth said grimly the night before they were to leave. Their furniture was being bought by the new tenants. Most of their personal belongings had been shipped ahead by Railway Express. Everything else would be piled into the car in the morning.

"It'll hold up," Carol predicted, determined to be optimistic.

They left Manhattan at seven in the morning. The sky was gray and grim, matching her mood, Carol thought. But this wasn't forever. They'd come back to New York in time.

It was difficult to imagine living away from the city. Would they have to live with Seth's parents—or would they be able to afford a house of their own? They were a family. It would be difficult to fit into another family—even Seth's.

Carol sat on the back seat with Karen on her lap and Jonnie beside her. She'd brought along a supply of storybooks to read to them plus several puzzles for Jonnie and stuffed animals for Karen. Seth had a road map spread on the seat beside him.

At regular intervals they stopped to leave the car and allow Jonnie and Karen—triumphant at walking now—to play for a little while. They had breakfast and lunch and snacks from the cooler in the car trunk. In the evening they stopped for a hot dinner, then checked into a motel for the night.

Carol was grateful that they were not running into snow. She vowed that once they were in Bellevue, she would learn to drive. There had just never been time in New York. And Seth had pointed out that domestic help came cheap in the South. Once he was drawing a salary, they could hire a nursemaid for the kids—and she could look around for an architectural assignment.

Oh, she wanted so much to get back to work, she thought. It wasn't that she didn't love Jonnie and Karen—the familiar guilt tugged at her again—but there was this need in her to put her training to use. It was an exhilarating satisfaction to see something she had designed come to life.

In a small town in North Carolina, Carol came to the realization that they were south of the Mason–Dixon line. Jonnie had announced that he needed to go to the bathroom. Seeing the local Greyhound bus station ahead, Seth pulled into the parking area.

"All right, Jonnie, let's go," Carol said with a cajoling smile, while Seth reached to hoist Karen onto the front seat with him.

Inside the sparsely occupied waiting room, Jonnie broke away and darted toward a water fountain. She noted the step placed there so children could reach it on their own. And then all at once she spied the sign above the water fountain: COLORED.

"Jonnie, not that one," she called, her voice strident.

"Jonnie!"

She moved forward to pull him away, prodded him toward the water fountain with a sign that read: WHITES.

"Mommie, why can't I drink there?" Jonnie scolded.

"This one's colder," she improvised, her heart pounding. She was unnerved at suddenly coming face to face with Southern segregation. While Jonnie slurped at the stream of water, she glanced about apprehensively—as though fearing hostile eyes. She was conscious now, too, of the segregated benches in the small waiting room.

She settled in the car again with a sigh of relief. Why had she been so unnerved? This wasn't her first visit to the South.

"Problems?" Seth asked quietly when they were back on the road. It always amazed her how sensitive Seth was to her moods.

"I nearly walked right up to a water fountain that said 'Colored.' I had to pull Jonnie away." Her smile was strained. Jonnie wasn't listening, she noted—he was showing a picture book to Karen. "It was kind of startling."

"Honey, you've been in Bellevue," he reproached, but his eyes were compassionate. "We have segregation there, too."

"It was different then." She tried to rationalize the situation. "We got off the train, and your parents were there to meet us. We all just walked through the station. Most of the time in Bellevue, we were in the house or sightseeing from the car. It didn't smack me in the face the way seeing those water fountains did." They were visitors then, her mind taunted. Now this was to be their world.

"It'll have to change in time." He mustered a smile. "Even fifth-generation Southerners like Mom know that in their hearts."

When they passed buses on the highway, Carol involuntarily glanced at the colored passengers standing in the rear when there were empty seats in the "whites only" section. In farm territory in South Carolina her eyes clung to the rows of seedy shacks that were home to colored farm laborers. When at last they were approaching Bellevue, Seth pointed out the new one-room colored school that had been erected since they'd last been there.

"It's pretty in the spring, Mom said, with all the flowers in bloom." Seth paused. "But there's no electricity and no running water."

They arrived at the pleasant Walden house in Bellevue at dusk. They were barely out of the car when Hannah came rushing toward them. Despite the arthritis that slowed her down, Leah was a few feet behind her. Becoming aware of their arrival, Della—who had been with the family for years—appeared in the doorway to offer help with the children. The spontaneity, the warmth of their welcome brought grateful tears to Carol's eyes.

"They're tired, and they're hungry," Della crooned, picking up Karen and then offering a hand to Jonnie. "I'll take them out to the kitchen and give them some supper."

With no reluctance Jonnie and Karen accepted Della as a new friend. Carol and Seth went upstairs with his mother and grandmother. Later he'd bring up their luggage. Harvey's old room had been transformed into a nursery. There was a new crib for Karen and a youth bed for Jonnie, each graced by a pair of stuffed animals. Carol basked in the love she felt surrounding her.

Seth's parents insisted he take a week off before he came into the store. They rejected Seth's proposal that he contribute to the household expenses.

"Seth, this is your home." His mother was shocked at such a suggestion. "Yours and Carol's and the kids."

"We feel enriched by your presence," Eli said softly. "It's a treat for us to have you here. Do you realize that I've never seen my two grandchildren until now?"

"We're four generations under the same roof," Leah said with pride. "That makes me feel my life has been worth living."

On this first evening in Bellevue Carol was touched by her father-in-law's eagerness to make her feel at home. He was anxious for her to love the town as he did.

"Oh, we've had some changes in the past few years," Eli acknowledged. "The cotton mill is unionized now. A lot of new houses are going up because—whether we like it or not—Bellevue's growing. There's talk now of a shoe factory moving here—because wages are so much lower than in the Northeast."

"And it's hard to find domestic help," Hannah contributed. "We're lucky to have Della. Of course, we're good to her, too," she added conscientiously.

"Sometimes the changes here in the South are so subtle they pass unnoticed," Leah said. "Other times they smack you right in the face. But that's progress—and we have to live with it."

Carol rearranged their bedroom to provide a comfortable corner where Seth could write. He *would* write, she promised herself. This was an interim period in their lives—and Seth would continue to write.

Each morning Seth, his father, and his mother set off together for the store—much enlarged through the years. They didn't return until well past six. Della cooked dinner, served it, then left for the night. Carol insisted on clearing the table and doing the dishes after dinner.

She waited for Seth to embark on some new writing venture— play or television script. They'd talked about his trying to sell to television under another name. But his typewriter remained untouched. He was exhausted from their struggle in New York, she commiserated. He came home tired each night from a job he disliked.

Once a week Sharon phoned. Finally she and Gil were convinced Jerry had not implicated them. Though the ratings for the "Nadine Ascot Show" were high, morale was low among the company.

"Nadine's a terror," Sharon reported. "And Gil works so hard. The only time I really see him is on weekends. He's just drained when he comes home each night."

"You feel any better about suburbia?" Carol asked.

"I'm climbing the walls. You know I love Michelle—but I need something more in my life than taking care of her and the house and waiting for Gil to come home. *I feel trapped.*"

"Gil would have a fit if you talked about going back to work," Carol guessed.

"Honey, Gil considers it his responsibility to provide for his family. He'll never understand that it's not the money that makes me want to go back to work. Hell, I'd be thrilled right now just to be working again at that *schlock* confession magazine factory."

Seth and Leah urged Carol to hire Della's teenaged niece— eager for after-school work—to watch the children on weekday afternoons. With Della's niece Bonnie looking after the kids, she could look around for a part-time job—though she knew this wouldn't be easy to find. She was shocked to discover there was not one architectural firm in Bellevue.

"Learn to drive," Seth urged. "We'll go out every Sunday. Once you have a license, you can drive to Atlanta. It's a big city—you'll have a chance there."

"Your mother will be horrified if I go to work and leave the kids all day," Carol said. "I know she was in the store when you were young, but Grandma was home."

"Grandma is still home to supervise—and you'll find a good

nursemaid," Seth said forcefully. "You're an architect, Carol. That part of your life isn't over because we're living in Bellevue."

Most evenings the family gathered before the television set to watch favorite programs. On Friday evenings Harvey came for dinner—leaving at the earliest possible moment. Carol was silently infuriated by his air of superiority toward Seth. Harvey basked in self-importance—the successful young lawyer with political ambitions.

Hannah fretted that Carol was not getting out to meet local people.

"I don't do much gallivanting, what with the hours I spend in the store," she apologized, "but you and Seth should be meeting other young couples. And with Bonnie looking after Jonnie and Karen every afternoon, you should start joining things."

"Mom, let her unwind," Seth scolded good-humoredly. "We've been through a rough time."

As on their earlier visits to Bellevue, Carol was amazed at the relaxed way of life, the aura of calm that pervaded the small town. Nobody ever seemed to rush, she marveled—everybody was so friendly. They even spoke slowly, she thought, though that didn't extend to Seth.

Leah chuckled when Carol tried to express her feelings about this one afternoon.

"Sugar, don't you let all that Southern charm fool you. Folks here are like anywhere else—they just have that nice way about them. You go to a party, and everybody's pouring out the compliments. 'Oh, darling, that's such a sensational dress—wherever did you buy it?' Then the lady with the sensational dress goes out of the room, and she says 'Doesn't she *know* that color makes her look ten years older?' "

"I'll remember." Carol smiled in conspiratorial amusement.

On Tuesday evenings the family inevitably watched Edward R. Murrow's "See It Now." Carol and Seth were excited when—on his March 9th program—Murrow went after Joseph McCarthy. They could almost feel the end of what Harry Truman had labeled "McCarthyism."

In mid-April Carol read that an Atlanta woman—the first in Fulton County and only the second in the state—was serving on a jury.

"It's about time," Leah said with satisfaction when Carol reported this. "Women could be part of the armed forces during the war—but they couldn't serve on a jury."

"I don't understand any woman wanting to serve on a jury," Hannah confessed. "I mean—it's so unfeminine."

"From you, Hannah, that's strange." Leah chuckled. "For years you've worked as hard as any man in the store. You don't stay home and bake cookies and run to volunteer luncheons and garden parties. By God, you're a modern woman. Don't you think you deserve rights?"

"I vote. Every election," Hannah said conscientiously. "But to serve on a jury? To have to sit there and hear the awful things that are said in the courtrooms?" She flinched distastefully. "I'm satisfied to let the men handle that."

On April 22nd the galvanizing Army–McCarthy hearings began.

"Thank God, Senator Lyndon Johnson from Texas demanded the hearings be televised," Seth said with satisfaction.

Carol and Seth—along with the rest of the family—were mesmerized by the melodrama of the Army–McCarthy hearings. The newspapers reported that at times as many as 20 million Americans were watching the televised hearings. Carol and Seth watched with the conviction that this was the beginning of the end of the blacklisting. Once this was accomplished they could resume their normal lives. They could return to New York.

Seth had made inquiries about a possible teaching job in the Bellevue high school the following school year, though he was nervous about having to admit he'd been fired from his assignment in New York. But the admission was unnecessary. There would be no openings.

"Anyhow, I'm pulling down more money here than I would as a teacher," he told Carol.

"This is temporary," Carol reminded, determinedly to be optimistic. "Once the hearings are over, we'll see a whole turnaround. You'll sell to TV again." But Seth wasn't writing—and that disturbed her.

Carol was impatient with her slowness in learning to drive. Seth was in the store six days a week—only on Sundays was he free to take her out in the car. She was terrified the first time he drove her to Atlanta and put her behind the wheel. In Bellevue there was little traffic. Atlanta was a city. But her finding a job depended upon being able to commute to Atlanta. She clenched her teeth and vowed she wouldn't be daunted.

Then—with the impact of a tornado—Bellevue was hit with the news that on the final day of its session the United States Supreme Court had handed down a decision in the case of Brown vs. Board of Education. *Segregation in the public schools was ruled unconstitutional.* It was illegal. This was the major topic of conversation in every home in Bellevue that evening of May 17, 1954.

"It's about time," Eli said gently when Harvey burst into the house at dinner to report on the monumental decision.

"Harvey, sit down and have dinner with us," his mother urged with a strained smile. "I'll get you a plate and silverware."

"It's the second Emancipation Proclamation," Seth said. "And it'll cause almost as much upheaval."

"Folks in the South aren't going to take this," Harvey warned.

"Three of the justices on the Supreme Court are Southerners," Seth reminded. "That tells you something, doesn't it?"

"Well, I hear there's talk already of passing a constitutional amendment in this state that'll turn our public schools into private schools," Harvey said, a glint of triumph in his eyes.

"They can't do that!" Seth lashed back.

"You want to bet?" Harvey asked smugly.

"I don't understand this—" Hannah came back into the dining room. "How can the Supreme Court tell us how to run our lives down here?"

"Georgia happens to be part of the United States, Hannah." Leah was impatient. "What goes for New York and California goes for Georgia, too."

"But it isn't natural." Hannah was troubled. "We've always had our schools, and the colored folks have theirs."

"For fifty-eight years the South had rolled along on the Plessy–Ferguson decision." Seth was somber. "That was the ruling that required colored students to be provided equal but separate schools," he explained to Carol.

"Damn it, why isn't that good enough?" Harvey challenged.

"Because the colored schools have never been equal. We all know that. What Plessy–Ferguson did was to create a caste system," Eli picked up. "This has been coming for a long time."

"We've always had such good relations with our coloreds," Hannah said defensively. "Why, in Atlanta there's a colored man on the

Board of Education. This business with the Supreme Court is Northerners trying to create trouble." Her face was flushed.

"Mom, it's long past due," Seth told her. Carol remembered how—when they first met—Seth had worried about what his father had just called a caste system.

"It'll have to go slow and easy." Eli was somber. "But keep in mind that Southerners have always been proud of their sense of fairness. They'll come to realize we can't have two societies in the South—one white, one black."

"We've had one way of life here in the South since this country was founded. Now the Courts are telling us this is wrong?" Hannah lifted her head in defiance.

"It's not going to happen overnight," Eli soothed. "We've got some tough years ahead, but we'll come around to seeing what has to be done."

"It mustn't go too slow," Leah warned. "The coloreds in the South have been waiting a long time."

"But it's wrong," Hannah sputtered. "We've all always got along so well."

"We've been engrained since birth by wrong logic." Seth seemed caught up in painful recall. "Dad, do you remember that time you took me with you when you drove over to Tuskegee College to help somebody get into the school?"

His father nodded.

"You were about twelve."

"We met Booker T. Washington's son on the campus," Seth continued. "You shook hands with him—and I was shocked. *Because you shook hands with a colored man.* You talked to him as though he was an equal. And that's when I started to examine my soul."

"It was your going to school up in New York." Hannah was upset. "That's where you picked up those crazy ideas. Even then I knew it was a mistake."

"Mom, we've got to join the human race," Seth said gently.

"Bullshit." Harvey ignored his mother's reproachful gasp. "Of course, this ruling will be a factor in the voting in the state," he conceded. "The colored vote is becoming important. But I'm still betting we get through an amendment that converts our public schools into a private system. And there goes Brown verses Board of Education."

* * *

On the surface, Carol thought, the momentous Brown vs. Board of Education decision seemed to make little difference in Bellevue. In the weeks ahead she saw no indication that the ruling would change the local school situation. Yet there were menacing undercurrents, rash remarks. *"First it's the schools, then it'll be everything else."*

Carol suspected that most Southerners deliberately ignored the Supreme Court ruling on school segregation. The Army–McCarthy hearings—seeming to drag on endlessly—captured far more attention. They continued through May and into mid-June, finally winding up on June 17th. Carol was convinced that the voice of army counsel Joseph Welch would linger forever in her memory with his agonizing question to Joseph McCarthy: *"Have you no sense of decency, sir?"*

The McCarthy spell was broken, Carol rejoiced. But in talking with Sharon on the phone she felt some of her optimism ebbing away. Sharon reported that Gil saw no changes in the situation at the New York ad agencies and the television networks.

"But it's just a matter of time," she told Gil defiantly when he took the phone from Sharon to talk with her. "A few months?"

"Maybe, but don't count on a changeover that fast," Gil warned. "It's coming—but it'll take time."

Each Friday when Harvey came to dinner, he hinted at devious plots that would lead to court battles and circumvention of the Supreme Court's decision on school desegregation. But on this sultry Friday in late June Carol was unnerved when he mentioned rumors of a revival of the Ku Klux Klan.

"A lot of people in this state are upset at what the Supreme Court's trying to do to us. I heard there was a meeting last night to discuss a Klan chapter right here in Bellevue. I don't like it," Harvey said, yet Carol was suspicious of his true feelings. "Still, I can understand what's happening."

"Only a bunch of rabble-rousing rednecks would try to bring back the Klan!" Eli said angrily.

"By the way," Harvey said with devious casualness. "I've been offered a new job. More money, some real political opportunities." Carol intercepted his triumphant glance in Seth's direction. "This year's governor's race is going to be a zinger—and I mean to be in the middle of it."

"Harvey, I thought you were so pleased to be working for Judge McGee." Hannah seemed uneasy.

Harvey shrugged. "I've gone as far as I can with him. It's time to move on."

"Don't you get yourself mixed up with the Klan business," Leah said tartly. "You just remember. They don't just dislike the colored people. They feel the same way about Jews and Catholics."

"Grandma, relax," Harvey soothed. "The South has to protect its interests—but we're not going to see Klan parades and cross-burnings. Smart legal minds will be handling the issue. I'll take any bets—Georgia schools won't be integrated."

In another year Jonnie would be old enough for kindergarten. What would schools in Bellevue be like then? But with any luck at all, Carol told herself—jolted by this thinking—she and Seth and the kids would be back in New York. The family knew—their being here was an interim thing. An emergency. The whole insane McCarthy period was on its way out. Gil said it might take a while, but they could deal with that.

Seth would move back into television again.

Chapter Thirty-six

Bellevue residents were struggling to survive in a record-breaking heat wave. On every street could be heard the drone of fans, though Leah warned Carol that the fans did little more than circulate hot air. Twice a day the neighborhood children—including Jonnie and Karen—romped beneath the spray of garden hoses. On some sultry nights Carol tiptoed into the children's room to brush their perspiring faces with cold water-dampened washcloths.

The lawns that lined the residential avenues were dying, burnt by the relentless sun. Farmers were fearful of what threatened to be a serious drought. Crops were withering in the fields. Wells were drying up.

Despite the sultry days and matching nights Carol was impatient to be working again. And she was ever conscious, too, of what the additional money could accomplish. Seth's parents were wonderful—but she and Seth needed a house of their own.

Gil kept warning them it'd be at least a year before the ad agencies and the networks weren't terrified anymore of the blacklisting. The only time she and Seth were alone was when they went up to sleep. She suspected, too, that in the privacy of his own home, Seth would settle down to write.

In the precious parcel of time when they prepared for bed each night, he talked to her with an increasing intensity about the play he wanted to write about integration. *When did he have time to write?* Living in their own house, she would ration time for him to be alone at the typewriter. The way she had in New York.

If she was working, too, they could afford their own house. It wasn't wrong for them to want this. They'd see much of Seth's family. But they'd have time for themselves.

Once she was working—even with the added expense of their own house—they'd start saving. They couldn't just pile into the car and drive back to New York once the witch-hunting was behind them. They had Jonnie and Karen now. They'd need a backlog of money to get settled in an apartment, to live on until they were both working.

Living in New York was expensive—it wasn't like down here. She'd need full-time domestic help if she was working—and in the city that wasn't like hiring a nice colored girl in Bellevue for a few dollars a week.

She felt a surge of excitement when she acquired her driver's license. She admitted only to Sharon—in one of their cherished phone calls—that she was terrified the first time she drove into Atlanta alone. But Atlanta was the source of jobs. Business was booming. An immense amount of construction was going on there.

Each morning—now that Bonnie was coming in full-time—Carol drove into Atlanta to make the rounds of architectural offices. As in New York, she encountered strong prejudice against women architects. She was offered a job as receptionist in one office, a secretarial post in another—*"if you know shorthand."*

She was relieved that her mother-in-law had not tried to persuade her against resuming her career.

"Mom's too smart for that," Seth said when she'd brought up the subject. "She knows you're strong-minded—and she's not going to do anything to antagonize Jonnie and Karen's Mommie. You've made her a grandmother, and she won't ever forget it."

On her third week of job-hunting—with possibilities all but exhausted—Carol was hired as a draftsman in the large architectural firm of Arthur Gilbert and Son. She knew she was hired because she'd work for far less than the salary that would be paid to a man. It was the same old story, she thought grimly while she listened to her new boss outline the work requirements. Still, it was a job. She was determined to keep it.

Gradually Carol relaxed in the job. She made it clear at diplomatic intervals that she was a full-fledged architect with a degree from Columbia. She promised herself the time would come when an architectural assignment would be thrown her way.

Early in the fall she persuaded Seth that they should rent a house on a one-year lease.

"Grandma says the attic is loaded with discarded furniture—we won't have to buy anything. Seth, it's important for us."

Now Seth explained to the family that it was time he and Carol moved into a place of their own. Carol knew Hannah was hurt. Leah was ingratiatingly supportive.

They quickly found a cottage only four blocks from the Walden house. Hannah provided them with linens and dishes. On the Sunday before they moved in, Seth and his father painted the small five rooms. Carol was euphoric.

Sharon sent exquisite glassware as a housewarming gift because she remembered Carol's love for this.

"Hang on to the cartons," she told Carol over the phone. "So you won't have a problem packing them when you come back."

"Oh, that can't be soon enough. I miss you all so much. I miss the city."

Carol was annoyed that one of the men in the office always called her "Sugar"—never Carol or Mrs. Walden. He was inclined to drop an arm affectionately about her at moments when they were unobserved by the others. And on occasion he asked her to type up memos for him. The other men behaved as though she wasn't there.

She was determined to hang on to her job. Now that they were not living with Seth's family, their expenses soared. She'd hoped to put money away each week, but unexpected expenditures kept arising.

Despite his constant talk about the play he wanted to write, Seth was finding little time for this. Six mornings a week he left the house a few minutes past eight. He didn't return until well past six. On Sundays he slept till noon, spent most of the day with the children and her. Once or twice a week he salvaged an hour at the typewriter.

"I'll start getting up at five A.M.," he vowed as the new year approached. "I'll work from five to seven. I'm coasting—I hate it!"

Though Carol felt recurrent guilt that Bonnie was working for them full-time in lieu of returning to school, she was grateful that Bonnie wanted this arrangement brought about by Della.

Jonnie and Karen adored Bonnie—and she loved them. Carol left the house each morning with the knowledge that the children were in capable hands—and their great-grandmother only four blocks away in the event of any emergency. Each afternoon Bonnie took them over to spend an hour with Leah, the dispenser of special goodies.

On New Year's Eve Carol and Seth went to his parents' house for a family party.

"You'll sleep over, of course," Hannah had said when the subject first arose. "So the children can be here with us, too."

It was an evening awash with candid sentiment. Carol was touched by the warmth that permeated the household. Harvey remained for dinner, then dashed off.

"I think he's seeing some girl," Leah whispered to Carol when he'd left. "I met two of the ladies from the synagogue for lunch last week—it was a birthday for one of them—and I saw Harvey across the room with a very pretty blonde. I believe she's one of the Eldridge sisters. She and Harvey looked all wrapped up in each other."

"The family that owns half the state?" Carol exchanged a knowing glance with Leah.

"Hannah won't be happy if Harvey married out of his faith." Leah's eyes were troubled. "She keeps trying to push one of the girls from the synagogue crowd on him."

"He may not be serious." How like Harvey to chase after a wife who could further his career. His major conversation these days was politics—and the importance of "knowing the right people."

As the first moments of 1955 approached, Carol saw Eli reach for Hannah's hand. After all the years of their marriage, she thought tenderly, Eli and Hannah were still in love. The way she and Seth would be, she told herself.

"Happy 1955," Seth murmured as outside sounds joyously welcomed the new year. "Great times are coming."

It was the first New Year's Eve since she was sixteen that she hadn't spent with Sharon, Carol thought as the family toasted the New Year with the peach brandy that Eli made each year for this occasion. She'd talked earlier with Sharon rather than trying to call her at midnight.

"We've got to go to some deadly party in the city that a client is giving," Sharon had told her. "Our lives revolve around Gil's job."

Carol and Seth had hoped that with the censure of McCarthy by the Senate, this new year would see blacklisting in eclipse. But this was not happening. Sharon wrote that AFTRA—the American Federation of Television and Radio Actors—was doing little to help its blacklisted membership. She said that fine actors such as Sidney Poitier, Lee Grant, and Ruby Dee were fighting to save their careers.

"The situation has to change soon," Carol insisted.

"When?" Seth challenged with recurrent despair. "When you and I are grandparents?"

Carol and Seth were uneasy when President Eisenhower announced in March that atomic weapons would be used in the event of war. They were cynical when in the same month the House of Representatives raised Congressional salaries by 50 percent.

"I know the economy is going great guns, but isn't that kind of ridiculous?" Seth scoffed.

Ninety days later over a million federal employees were given a 7.5 percent raise.

"People are spending like crazy—everybody getting raises." Seth was somber. "But what does that mean to me? I'm trapped in the store."

"It's temporary," Carol said—for the thousandth time. "And you're using this time to advantage." Three mornings each week Seth rose at 5 A.M. to work on the new play.

"I don't know what I'll do with the play when I finish it," Seth admitted, "but I have to write it."

Late in August Harvey came over on a Sunday evening for dinner and to drop a bomb. When the women had cleared the table and brought out another pitcher of iced tea, he announced that he was eloping the following day with Elaine Eldridge.

His mother was pale with shock. "Harvey, she's not of your faith."

"Mom, we're not concerned about that." Harvey was casual. "But her family will throw a fit—that's why we're eloping. She has this uncle up on a plantation near Charleston—he's a judge. He'll marry us." Unexpectedly Harvey chuckled. "He and Elaine's mother are mortal enemies. I think he's enjoying this."

"You never gave us a hint," Hannah sputtered. "Not a word about this!"

"Because I knew you'd be upset." His eyes moved about the dinner table. "I've been seeing Elaine for almost a year. We think alike. We'll have a great life together. Sure, her family will carry on at first, but they'll come around," he said complacently.

"Where will you live?" Hannah asked, struggling for calm. "Have you made plans?"

"We'll live in my apartment. For now—" His eyes were eloquent. "Elaine's parents will probably come across with a house before too long. How would it look for them if they didn't help out their youngest daughter?"

"How do they feel about their daughter marrying a Jew?" Hannah asked bluntly.

"They'll have to accept it. She'll tell them after we're married," he pointed out. "Elaine's always been her father's favorite." He glanced at Seth, and Carol remembered that Harvey had always accused their father of favoring Seth over himself. Wasn't it enough, she thought, that Hannah spoiled him rotten? "The old man'll relent soon enough."

"I'd looked forward to your wedding," Hannah said wistfully. "I wanted to be there to walk with you down the aisle to the *chupah*."

"You can give a small dinner when we come back home and announce we're married," Harvey said cajolingly. He'd worked out all the details, Carol thought. "Just our family and Elaine's and a few close friends."

"Not at the country club." Leah's smile was ironic. "The groom and his family don't meet their requirements." The bride's family had been among the founders.

"It doesn't have to be at the country club," Harvey said impatiently. "That new restaurant that just opened up on the River Road—The Rendezvous. I hear it's terrific."

"So are the prices," Leah clucked.

"We can afford it," Hannah said quickly. "I'm glad you told us before the ceremony, Harvey." She was straining to accept what Carol knew must be a painful blow. "But I wouldn't want to be there when Elaine tells her parents."

A few days later Sharon called from New York.

"Do you have a place for me to bunk for four days?" she asked ebulliently. "Nothing fancy—the living-room sofa will do."

"You're coming down?" Carol was joyous.

"Gil has to fly out to the Coast for several days. Dad'll be on vacation at the same time. He and Mom are coming out to stay in the house and take care of Michelle. I'll fly down next Wednesday and fly back Sunday."

"Sharon, I can't wait to see you! Tell me what time to pick you up at the airport." Oh, it would be wonderful to see Sharon!

"Can you get off from the office? If not, there must be some taxi service."

"I haven't had my vacation days yet. I'll take them that week," she decided recklessly. She wouldn't be fired—not when they paid her so poorly. And who at the office worked as hard as she?

Everybody talked about the importance of flying these days, Carol remembered as she waited at the airport for Sharon. Seth said there were about 175 flights in and out of the Atlanta airport every day. There was talk, too, about building a huge new airport to accommodate all the business travelers coming into Atlanta or changing flights there. Somehow, New York seemed less distant when she realized that by plane it was less than three hours away.

Driving away from the airport with Sharon beside her, Carol felt a delicious abandon—as though the whole world had suddenly acquired magnificent new hues.

"There's a gorgeous new restaurant at the edge of town," she told Sharon. The Rendezvous—where Hannah and Eli were arranging the dinner for Harvey and Elaine when they returned from their Bermuda honeymoon. "Let's live dangerously and have lunch there."

The charming, softly illuminated restaurant was already becoming crowded. Still, despite a lack of reservations, Carol and Sharon were escorted to a table.

"This is a long way from the Automat," Sharon said with a smile when they'd ordered and the waiter had left their table. "We used to fantasize about eating in places like this."

"Do you have any new snaps of Michelle?" Carol asked.

"Oh, she's growing like mad! Do you realize she'll be starting kindergarten in ten days? I'm losing my baby."

"Have you thought about having another?" Carol asked tenderly.

"We've been avoiding it," Sharon admitted. "Gil's doing so well, but we never seem to be able to save. And we had such a scare when Jerry pulled that crap. It could have hit Gil and me, too."

"What's the latest on the blacklisting?" Carol's eyes searched Sharon's.

"Gil says the networks and the agencies are still scared. Carol, it can't go on much longer."

"What's going to stop it?" she asked in a rush of bitterness. "I thought the Army–McCarthy hearings would be the beginning of the end. Seth and I are thirty-five years old. It's time we moved ahead."

"Nothing new on your job?" Sharon asked compassionately.

"It's the same old routine. I'm working—doing little more than drafting."

"I tried to talk to Gil about my going back to work. Michelle'll be in school full-time in another year. I ran into my old boss in New York the other day. He offered me a job right off the bat. I told him there was nothing I'd like better than to get back to work but that my husband won't hear of it." She shook her head in a gesture of frustration.

"Seth is one of the few husbands who understand. I was so restless until I got back to work."

"You know how much I love Gil and Michelle, but I'm suffocating in suburbia. I've gained about nine pounds in the last four months— I'm on Metracal now to get it off. I listen to these women up in Westchester who're all trying to be the perfect corporate wife—and I feel like saying, 'Fuck it. I want to be *me.*' The one good thing about Gil's job is that we don't have to worry about being transferred. When real estate brokers show houses up there, they don't say 'the So-and So's live here!' They say, 'That's AT&T and that's Coca-Cola—' "

"Seth's working on a play," Carol began and Sharon's face brightened. "It's not commercial," she warned, "but you know Seth when he has his mind set on something. And, at least, it gives him some personal satisfaction to see it moving along. Slowly—oh, so slowly."

"Gil's sure television will be back to normal in another year. Seth's such a good writer. He'll find his way again."

"That's what we're living for," Carol said softly.

The four days of Sharon's visit sped past, yet Carol felt revitalized by her presence. After Sharon left, she went in to the office with fresh enthusiasm, a determination to create a breakthrough for herself. She loathed the attitudes she encountered from the men in the firm—ranging from indulgence to contempt. She was a competent, creative architect. It was time this was recognized.

Eight days after Sharon's departure—with her pleasure and encouragement from that visit still in high gear—Carol returned from lunch with an instant awareness of a heated argument in one of the private offices at the far end of their floor. She recognized the voices. Jason Gilbert was fighting with Clark Kennedy, the architect slated to become a partner in the firm.

"Look, life's too short to put up with a bitch like Mrs. Wallace!" Kennedy interrupted Gilbert's tirade. "Keep your partnership—if you ever meant to go through with it," he added scathingly. It wasn't just Mrs. Wallace that brought out his anger, Carol surmised. He was tired of Gilbert's nastiness. "I've got other leads in this town."

Carol stood before her drafting table and made a pretense at work, but her mind was exploring sudden new possibilities. The others, too, tried to appear to be unaware of what had happened. She'd heard Mrs. Wallace's complaints. They were justified. The Wallace house—if it was built—would be one of the most expensive in fashionable Buckhead. Mrs. Wallace was a client Jason Gilbert didn't want to lose. And to be able to say that *she*—Carol Walden—had designed the Wallace house in Buckhead would look great on her résumé.

Her heart pounding Carol left her drafting table to walk back to Jason Gilbert's office. She knew that what she was about to suggest was daring—but it could prove the giant step she needed at Arthur Gilbert and Son. Though the door to Gilbert's office was open, she knocked—a deference he considered his due.

Scowling, he looked up at her.

"What do you want?"

"We couldn't help but hear the argument you had with Mr. Kennedy," she began, struggling for poise.

"So?" Gilbert stared belligerently.

"I know Mrs. Wallace is a valued client. And some of her complaints were legitimate. I doubt that Mr. Kennedy understood what she expects in a house. Another woman would understand."

"And you do?"

She ignored his sarcasm. "Mr. Kennedy understands office buildings and shopping centers. He doesn't know what a woman like Mrs. Wallace demands of a house." In a corner of her mind she remembered hearing Gilbert chastise Kennedy and another architect for considering themselves too important to design houses. "Private homes may seem small change compared to office buildings—but with all the talk of expansion in the outlying areas, they can add up to big fees."

"You have experience designing expensive houses?" His eyes dared her to confirm this. He didn't ask her to sit down.

"When I was in New York, I designed two of the finest houses in a Westchester community and a beach house at Southampton, Long Island," she lied calmly. "For clients who were satisfied. Even laudatory." If need be, Sharon would get letters for her. "I came to Georgia and found women architects are denied their due." Not just Georgia—all over the country, but no need to mention that. "I can handle Mrs. Wallace." She refused to relinquish her air of supreme self-confidence.

Kennedy inspected her with reluctant respect. He hadn't expected to be challenged this way, Carol surmised.

"And just how would you approach the situation? She won't take well to having her architect walk out on her." He was concerned about losing Mrs. Wallace as a client. She could bring him other wealthy clients.

"I'll call her, explain that as head of the firm you came to the conclusion that a woman architect would have more insight—and that you've assigned me to design her house. You sympathize with her complaints about Kennedy," Carol emphasized diplomatically. "I'll ask her to have lunch with me." She took a deep breath—Gilbert was known to scream at the sight of luncheon tabs. "At The

Rendezvous. If I don't return with Mrs. Wallace as our client, I'll pay for the lunch."

"If you don't come back with Mrs. Wallace happy at having you as her architect, you're out of this firm," he said coldly. "Keep that in mind."

Chapter Thirty-seven

The moment she mentioned The Rendezvous to Mrs. Wallace, Carol sensed they were *simpatico*. They arranged to have lunch on Friday. Carol was relieved that she would have time to plan her approach.

She went to the Atlanta Public Library to skim through the society pages of the Atlanta newspapers—searching to build up a profile of Diane Wallace. It was important to know Mrs. Wallace's lifestyle before she presented her suggestions for the house. She learned that Mrs. Wallace had lived in Atlanta only two years. She had moved here with her husband when he had relocated the national headquarters of his corporation in the city.

Remembering that late last year the Margaret Mitchell Memorial Room had opened at the library—and that Sharon was fascinated by anything to do with the author of *Gone With The Wind*—she detoured from research to visit the room where glass display cases held Mitchell's Pulitzer Prize, her honorary degree from Smith College, her personal library of Civil War books, along with copies of *Gone With The Wind* in a stream of foreign languages. Sharon would love hearing about it.

At lunch with Diane Wallace, Carol was delighted that she'd visited the Mitchell Memorial Room. Mrs. Wallace was intrigued by the Margaret Mitchell legend. Carol's instincts told her that the slightly plump but stylish Diane Wallace—still a romanticist in her early fifties—would enjoy living in a mansion that evoked the movie version of Margaret Mitchell's Tara, yet was designed to provide the conveniences and luxuries of the present. Before they chose dessert—both settling for The Rendezvous's very special pecan pie, heaped with whipped cream—Carol sensed this was the beginning of a new era in her career as an architect. Her status had taken a giant step upward.

As work on the house progressed, Carol confided to Seth that she was happier than at any time since their arrival in Bellevue. She was doing what she had so arduously trained to do—and Seth was moving ahead on his play. The economy in Georgia had never been better. The war plants had given it a tremendous boost. It no longer depended on cotton and tobacco. Lockheed Aircraft alone siphoned into Atlanta around two-thirds as much money as Georgia saw from its entire cotton crop.

The problem of integration continued to plague the South. Carol and Seth worried that—despite a request filed by the Atlanta branch of the NAACP—not even a token nine Negro children were allowed to register when school opened for the 1955–56 year. Bellevue prided itself on regarding Atlanta as its mentor. No colored students would be admitted to the Bellevue public schools.

Back in July the Georgia Board of Education had voted to revoke the license of any teacher expressing approval of integrated schools, but in November the Atlanta golf courses were desegregated without incident. That same month—despite Governor Griffin's angry protests—the Board of Regents voted 14–1 to allow Georgia Tech to play in the Sugar Bowl against the University of Pittsburgh, although the Pennsylvania school had a Negro substitute fullback.

"We're seeing some breakthrough," Seth told Carol with mild satisfaction. "It's a beginning."

As Harvey had predicted, his in-laws were now accepting him as part of the family, though it was clear there'd be no socializing with the other Waldens. With Diane Wallace's house near completion early in the new year, Carol hoped that she'd be awarded the assignment to design the house that Mr. and Mrs. Eldridge planned to build for their daughter and Harvey. The Wallace house—which Diane adored—was attracting much attention in Atlanta circles. Carol's boss was contriving to take credit for its design.

Carol drove home from the office on a bleak January evening to find Leah waiting at the door to greet her.

"I am so furious!" Leah handed Carol the evening *Bellevue En-quirer*. "The Eldridges gave the job for Harvey and Elaine's house to some architect down in Columbus! Couldn't Harvey have said he'd like you to design it?"

"I don't know that he has that much influence with his in-laws." Carol tried to push down her disappointment.

"All Harvey cares about is Harvey," Leah said bluntly. "All his life Hannah's spoiled that boy!"

She'd survive without Harvey's house, Carol told herself. When she and Seth were back in New York, she'd have the job in Atlanta to offer as references. She was building up a background—that was important for her career.

On Michelle's birthday in February Sharon called to report on the party she'd given that afternoon.

"It was wild," Sharon said exuberantly. "It started out to be a party for six little girls, and it ended up with fourteen—boys and girls. Plus assorted nursemaids and mothers. Thank God, I took your advice and hired a clown to come in to entertain them. Michelle loved it!"

"She'll be in first grade in September," Carol said, "and Jonnie, too. Where are the years going?"

"It's scary, you know?" Sharon sighed. "We're almost on the wrong side of thirty-five. Remember when we thought forty was *old?*"

"Any new word about the blacklisting?" Carol asked, somber now.

"Still nothing positive. Now Gil's predicting it'll be at least another eighteen months." She hesitated. "Maybe Seth should try submitting to some of the free-lance markets under a pseudonym."

"He'd be coming in cold—with no credits to get him readings. You know how tough that is. He feels we just have to sit out the blacklisting."

But when would it end?

Carol stirred, aware of the phone ringing in the living room. She forced her eyes open, squinted at the clock on the night table. It was 2 A.M.

"Seth—" She reached to waken him. She'd always been fearful of phone calls in the middle of the night. Who was calling them at this hour? "Seth, the phone's ringing—"

"Probably a wrong number," he murmured drowsily.

"I'd better answer it before it wakes the kids."

With sudden urgency she slid from beneath the blankets and reached for her robe, lying at the foot of the bed. She hurried—barefoot despite the damp cold of the night—out of the bedroom and down the brief hallway to the living room. She was vaguely conscious that Seth was following her now. Breathless with anxiety she picked up the phone.

"Hello—"

"Carol, Gil's dead—" Sharon sounded dazed, disbelieving.

"What's happened?" Cold and trembling, Carol reached out a hand to Seth. "It's Gil," she whispered, sick with shock. *This wasn't real.*

"He was driving home from a late meeting in the city. He was six miles from home. Some drunken idiot plowed into him—head-on. He didn't have a chance—" Sharon's voice broke. "He was tired. His reflexes must have been dulled—he couldn't swerve out of the way fast enough."

"I'll take a plane up first thing in the morning," Carol told her. "Will you be at the house or at your mother's?"

"It's too expensive for you to fly up," Sharon rejected. "But I just had to talk to you."

"I'll be up in the morning," Carol insisted. "On the first plane out. I'll take a cab from the airport. Will you be at the house?" she asked again.

"Yes. Call me when you know about what time you'll be arriving." Carol sensed Sharon's need for her presence. "I'll meet you at the airport. Dad's taking care of everything. Carol, I can't believe it—"

Carol and Sharon spoke a few minutes longer. Seth silently reached for the phone, and he talked briefly.

"I'll call the airport now to see when the first plane takes off tomorrow—" Carol paused. "This morning—"

"I'll make the call," Seth said gently. "Go out to the kitchen and put up coffee." There'd be no more sleep.

"Seth, the children!" Carol was assaulted by alarm. "How can I leave?"

"Bonnie will be here at seven o'clock," Seth said. "If you have to leave for the airport before then, we'll drop them off with Mom and Grandma and leave a note for Bonnie to pick them up. They'll be with me when Bonnie leaves. Don't feel you have to rush back, Carol. Stay as long as Sharon needs you."

Seth drove Carol to the Atlanta airport in the cold, gray winter morning. On board, she saw him waiting for the plane to take off before driving away. It was so hard to realize that Gil was dead, she thought as the plane finally lifted from the ground. Nobody knew from one minute to the next when tragedy would hit.

They'd lost Greg and Leo to World War II. Now Gil was gone. Why? Why did they have to die so young? Why had she been chosen to survive when she and Marty had been shot down?

She gazed out the window without seeing. What could she possibly say to Sharon that could make her feel better? But at least, let them be together. They'd always be there for each other in awful times. And thank God for Sharon's family. They'd help her see this through.

Poor Michelle, fatherless at six. Poor baby. Her mind darted back through the years to the anguish of losing her own father.

A light snow was falling when Carol arrived at LaGuardia. Sharon—her face etched with pain—was waiting for her.

"I'm so glad you came," Sharon whispered as they clung together.

"How's Michelle?" Carol asked.

"She hasn't grasped what's happened. She just knows that it's something awful." Sharon's voice betrayed her shock and exhaustion. She probably hadn't slept, Carol thought. Neither had she and Seth. They'd sat in the kitchen, talking until daybreak, then gone back upstairs to dress. "I warned Gil that he was working too hard. Why didn't he listen to me?" Unexpectedly Sharon tensed with anger. "This shouldn't have happened."

"Did you call Gil's father?" Carol asked while they walked to the car.

"He's flying in for the funeral tomorrow. I invited him to stay at the house. He said he preferred a hotel in the city. Carol, he was so cold." Sharon flinched in recall.

The snow increased in intensity as they drove toward Dobbs Ferry. By the time they reached the Sawmill River Parkway, the road was white.

"It wasn't even snowing last night," Sharon said tightly. "Gil is—" she paused, caught her breath for a moment. "Gil was a terrific driver. If he hadn't been exhausted, he'd have swerved out of the way of that car."

Sharon's parents, her sister and brother-in-law and their son Josh, had gathered together at the house to provide what comfort they could. Sharon's grandfather had died three years ago.

Carol realized with a start that she hadn't seen Sharon's parents and her sister Bev in six years—the last time was when they'd met at the hospital the day after Michelle was born. She hadn't seen Bev's son Josh since his bar mitzvah seven years ago. Could he actually be a junior at Queens College? Sharon said he'd been spoiled to death—Beverly had lost her second baby in her fifth month and Josh was inundated with love.

"Carol, you look so young," Bev said. "Nobody would guess you have two kids."

"Carol's always looked like a movie star," Mrs. Ross said fondly. "I always said that to Sharon."

The phone rang. Bev went to answer. Immediately they realized a neighbor was calling.

"They don't even know yet," Sharon said tiredly.

The day dragged by. Solicitous neighbors arrived, each bearing some hot dish. Gil's father called and spoke briefly with Sharon.

"He's staying at the Plaza," Sharon told the others. "He wanted to confirm the time and place of the funeral services."

"That's all he has to say?" Mrs. Ross demanded. "He doesn't ask about his only grandchild?"

"I'm not sure he remembers he has a grandchild." Sharon was bitter. "He's never seen her. I think he sent a gift when she was born. I've never seen him—only photographs Gil hung in the den."

In the evening Sharon's brother-in-law drove the family and Carol to the funeral home. Bev stayed at the house with Michelle. Gil would be buried the following morning. When they returned to the house, they found Beverly had prepared a late supper for them.

"Michelle's asleep," she said. "Nobody's eaten much today. Sit down and have some food now."

Far into the night—while the others slept—Carol and Sharon talked.

"I'll have to sell the house," Sharon told Carol. "The monthly payments are huge. It'll be a distress sale—I'll be lucky to come out a few thousand ahead. The cars will have to go, or the bank will just take them over. It looked as though we were doing well financially, but our expenses were so damn high."

"Did Gil have any life insurance?" Carol asked. With inflation running on the way it was, a few thousand from the house wouldn't last long. In a corner of her mind she remembered Seth carried no insurance. It was an expense they were avoiding.

"Gil dropped his GI insurance when he got out of the army. He was always talking about taking out a big policy, but it was one of the things we put off 'for next year.' "

"Will you stay out here until you sell?" It would be agonizing for her, Carol thought.

"Mom wants me to close up the house and move back into the apartment with them, but a lived-in house sells faster than one that's empty." Her voice broke. "Oh God, how can I sit here and talk this way? Gil isn't even buried!"

"Gil would want you to be realistic," Carol said gently. "For Michelle's sake, Sharon."

By early morning the snow had finally stopped, but the day was gray and cold. They could hear snow plows out on the road. Mrs. Ross was in the kitchen before 7 A.M. and making breakfast. Everyone was awake.

Last night Carol and Sharon had debated about whether Michelle should go to the funeral. Neighbors had offered to take care of her. After much debate Sharon had decided Michelle was to go with them.

"The casket will be closed. I told her last night that Daddy has gone to heaven. She can accept that. When her kitten died last year, I explained that Smokey had gone to heaven. Then we buried his body under a birch tree in the yard."

Carol, Sharon, Michelle, and Mrs. Ross drove in Sharon's car, with Mr. Ross at the wheel. Bev, Dan, and Josh followed in their car.

They were the first to arrive at the funeral home. Soon people from Gil's office arrived, followed by long-time friends of Sharon's parents. Sharon stood with a composure that Carol knew was fragile—one of Michelle's hands tightly in hers. Carol was at her other side. Not until the services were about to begin did Gil's father arrive. Carol's eyes had followed Sharon's gaze.

"Gil's father?" she whispered, and Sharon nodded.

Mr. Randall made no effort to communicate with the family. He sat ramrod stiff, his face betraying his grief, his eyes fastened on the casket. He resented that Gil was being buried as a Jew, Carol thought. He was saying good-bye to his son—but he was angry, also. He left without saying a word to anyone.

Later at the Queens cemetery Carol spied him at the edge of the small group that gathered about the burial plot. He was the first to leave. Carol saw him disappear into a chauffeured limousine, no doubt rented for the occasion. She knew that Sharon and Michelle would never see him again.

The family returned to the house, where sympathetic neighbors had prepared a buffet. Today was unreal, Carol thought in a fresh surge of grief. *How could Gil be dead?*

Carol was impatient with the piddling assignments that were thrown her way by Jason Gilbert in the weeks ahead. Why didn't he pursue residential assignments? she fumed. Diane Wallace's house was a wonderful recommendation for the firm. But Jason spent most of his energy on trying to nab big deals—office buildings, a hospital, factories.

Carol was eager to design more beautiful houses, yet in a corner of her mind lurked a wistful wish to be involved in one of the low-income projects being built in Atlanta. Statistics that cropped up regularly bothered her. In prosperous, bustling Atlanta over 100,-000 people were living in some of the country's worst slums. And from these slums came most of the criminals that plagued the city, the juvenile delinquents who committed a sea of petty offenses. But it was unlikely that Jason Gilbert's firm would ever be interested in low-rent urban development.

Though Hannah often questioned her enthusiasm for the long commute to Atlanta, Carol never once considered abandoning this. Even on cold, gray mornings with the threat of snow in the air, she made the long drive into the city. On this unseasonably cold, early April morning—when the air should have been balmy with the arrival of spring—she huddled beneath the blankets in the night-cold master bedroom for a five-minute reprieve.

She reached a hand out to the empty place beside her—still warm from the weight of Seth's body. He'd been up for half an hour and at the typewriter, set up at a corner of the kitchen table where the click of the keys would not awaken Jonnie or Karen. Now she heard the rumblings of heat coming up in the radiators. Seth's first action on arising in the morning was to send up the heat, so that the house would be warm by the time the children awoke.

Carol slid from beneath the blankets, reached for her robe at the foot of the bed while her feet sought the comfortable warmth of fleece-lined slippers on the floor. Six mornings a week she went out to the kitchen to put up coffee for Seth and herself, which they drank in silent communication. She knew he enjoyed her presence, even while his mind focused on the morning's writing.

"Oh, I needed that," he said with relish when she deposited a mug of coffee beside him and sat at the table to drink her coffee.

"How's it going?"

"I'm having a problem," Seth admitted, his eyes troubled. "I feel like such a traitor to Mom in what I'm trying to say in this play. In her heart she knows integration has to come, yet she's so scared of what it'll bring to the South."

"Dad and Grandma understand." But they weren't fifth-generation Old South, Carol thought somberly.

"Every thinking Southerner knows in his heart that things have to change," Seth said with an air of frustration, "yet it's creating some ugly feelings. You know Mom's not a bigot—she just grew up in a certain way and it's hard for her to change."

"Dad keeps pointing out how so many Northerners are coming into Atlanta," Carol reminded. "And some of them are moving into Bellevue. I suspect that'll help change the thinking here."

"They come here because they find the living is so much easier." Seth repeated what his father often said. "Northerners who trained at Fort Benning and the other Southern army bases during World War II and Korea. Some of them married Southern girls. And of course, there're all the Northerners coming from the plants relocating here. Atlanta's becoming very cosmopolitan."

The living *was* easier, Carol thought, disquieted by this concession. The pace was so much more relaxed. But New York was where Seth needed to live if he was to write for television and the theater.

"I'll go and get dressed." Carol pushed back her chair.

"Carol, do you think I'm nuts—breaking my back over the play this way?" Seth asked.

"No, I don't think you're nuts." Her smile was determinedly confident. "One way or another, this play is going to come to life on a stage somewhere."

"I'm slow as hell," he warned. "I write, and then go back and re-write—and rewrite and rewrite."

"So it'll take time to finish. I know it's going to be terrific. We won't let it just gather dust on a shelf," she promised with the conviction he cherished. "We'll find a way to see it produced."

But it would be rough, she thought. Seth would have to be in New York for that to happen. They'd face up to the problems when Seth decided the play was ready to be seen. He wouldn't let her read what he'd written thus far. They talked about it often—Seth said she was his sounding board. But he wanted her to wait to read the finished manuscript.

"That's the only way you'll get the full impact," he told her.

Was she wrong in encouraging him to focus on the play? Without it he'd be drowning in despair. Sharon kept saying he ought to try to make it back into television under a pseudonym—that television was the real action.

"Let Seth make a name for himself in television," Sharon said repeatedly. "He was on the way up before—he can do it again. Once he's established and making real money in television, then he can afford to gamble on the theater. You have to be practical in this world."

Seth hated working in the pawnshop. For his father it had become a way of life. Dad had his steady customers who came in not only to buy but to ask for his help in solving their personal problems, Carol thought. He was important in their daily lives and that gave him great personal satisfaction. Grandma called him "the Mayor of Clinton Street."

How were she and Seth to escape from Bellevue? she asked herself with recurrent frustration. Even after all this time the blacklisting cloud hung over their heads—like the fallout from an atom bomb. Had they landed in a trap with no way out?

Chapter Thirty-eight

The spring—that had brought a lovely warmth, a burst of colorful flowers and blossoming trees—segued into a torpid, enervating summer. This was the time of year Carol longed to be away from Bellevue. Anyone who could sought refuge in air-conditioned movies or swimming pools. Until the threat of yet another drought, children romped two or three times a day beneath the spray of garden hoses. Many a night Carol and Seth sat on the front porch glider—loathe to go into the oven-hot house.

These mornings Seth made no pretense at trying to write. After a long day at the shop in this weather he was too exhausted to rise at 5 A.M.

"I'll get back to the play as soon as this hot spell lets up," Seth said apologetically to Carol late in August. But they seemed to go from one hot spell into another—with only a twenty-four-hour break, Carol thought rebelliously.

"Sharon says its hot as hell up in New York," Carol said in wry comfort.

"Too bad the house was sold in May. She and Michelle would have been a lot more comfortable in Dobbs Ferry."

"Sharon couldn't hang on, with those huge mortgage payments," Carol reminded.

Since the closing on the house, Sharon and Michelle had been living with her parents in the Bronx. Sharon admitted her financial situation was precarious. She'd started to work a few weeks ago, but her salary wouldn't stretch to cover the cost of a Manhattan apartment plus after-school day care for Michelle.

Carol and Sharon spoke less frequently—and at lesser length—these days, out of deference to their phone bills. Sharon hated living in the Bronx again, making the long trek by IRT to her job—at the same magazine where she had worked before Michelle was born.

"My boss is a total nut," she reported. "But you remember from before. Only now it's worse."

At regular intervals Sharon bought a copy of *Show Business* to send down to Seth. She knew how he hungered to be part of theater. Then when the hot weather at last subsided, he began to work on the play again.

He looked so tired from the long grind, Carol thought worriedly—though he blamed this on the Georgia heat. But he was obsessed with the play, determined to finish it. Carol didn't want to consider where he'd go with it once he decided it was ready to be seen.

Shortly before Christmas Carol received a phone call from Diane Wallace. She'd finally persuaded her married daughter and her husband to move to Atlanta.

"They're such jugheads," Diane said indulgently. "They thought Atlanta was some backwoods Southern town. Then they came down and realized what we have going for us here. I promised them a new house if Fred would come to work for my husband. And I want you to design the house for them. Tell Jason Gilbert I'll have nobody but you."

Carol put down the phone and sat motionless for a few moments. Her heart pounded with triumph. Diane Wallace had just lifted her status immeasurably. Striving to appear poised, not to reveal her excitement, Carol approached Jason Gilbert. She knew she held the winning cards—he'd have to give her a substantial raise.

On the long drive home from Atlanta she searched her mind for a way to use this windfall to help Seth get his play produced. With the extra money coming in each week they wouldn't be afraid to withdraw their small savings from the bank because they could replace it. Her hands tightened on the wheel as she considered the possibilities that lay ahead.

New York theater downtown was active. Off-Broadway was attracting much attention now that new Equity rulings made it possible for Equity actors to appear Off-Broadway. A company didn't have to be all Equity—there were regulations that allowed for very small houses to hire only two or three Equity members to be considered an Equity company. And that meant reviews in the New York dailies, she pinpointed exultantly.

If they could handle a short Off-Broadway run—long enough to garner reviews—then Seth's play could well be the catalyst to propel him back into television. They both knew the play was not for the commercial Broadway theater. He'd have to use a pseudonym, of course, she remembered with a surge of fresh bitterness.

Instinct warned her that Seth might be afraid to gamble with their savings. If there were just themselves, yes, but he felt such a strong responsibility toward the children. But this was for Jonnie and Karen as much as for themselves. It was the children's future, too, that was at stake.

She was impatient to be home now, to discuss this new possibility with Seth. As usual, she found dinner on the gas range and ready to be served. Bonnie had given the children their dinner, bathed them, and put them into pajamas.

"Jonnie's been invited to a birthday party next week," Bonnie reported warmly, "and since Karen's such a good little girl, Miz Raymond said she could come, too—even though she's younger than the others. And oh, is she excited!"

This was a special time for Seth and her—when all their attention for the next hour focused on Jonnie and Karen. After each had been read a story and put to bed, Carol and Seth would sit down to dinner. Tonight she was impatient for the time with the children to be over so that she could talk to Seth.

In her mind she'd been tabulating figures. Their last effort Off-Broadway had been non-Equity, but she knew the Equity salary scale. Other costs couldn't have escalated much since then. If they were careful, they could handle a two-week production of *We Hold These Truths*—Seth's integration play. The mechanics were vague in her mind, but her confidence in their ability to handle these was high.

Churning with eagerness, she waited until they'd brought dinner to the table and were seated to offer her first small explosion. She told Seth about the assignment from Diane Wallace and her encounter with Jason.

"Carol, that's wonderful!" Seth glowed. "The old bastard is beginning to appreciate you."

"He was scared I'd walk out and take the Wallace assignment with me." Already she was mentally looking ahead to the time when she could set up her own office. *And it would come.*

Now she brought up the subject of their planning a production of the play on Off-Broadway. She saw his eyes light up as she outlined her thoughts on this.

"We've got enough money in the bank to handle it. Not a fancy Off-Broadway production—one of the very modest ones. You'll have to make a couple of quick trips up to New York, of course—to set everything up, then to approve the casting." From past experience she was familiar with what was entailed. From Leo they'd learned how to cut corners. "We'll have to run an ad in *Show Business* for a director—"

"Coproducer and director," Seth pinpointed. "If he has a chunk of the profits in addition to salary, he'll be more apt to go along with the deal. If there are profits," he added wryly, then flinched. "Carol, how can we do this? The car could fall apart at any time. We should be on the lookout for a replacement. We—"

"This is more important than another car," she interrupted. "I know it'll be rough trying to handle this long-distance, but we'll manage. You haven't taken a vacation since you've been in the shop. You can take a few days off. Fly up to New York to interview a director, look around at playhouses and check prices. There are so many more available than in Leo's day. Oh, we'll need ad rates for the *New York Post* and the *Times*. We—"

"Carol, I want you to read the play tonight," he said urgently. "It's done except for some minor polishing. I want to know you think it has a chance."

"Right after dinner," she promised. "Oh Seth, I'm so excited about this!"

While Seth paced restlessly about the house—looking in at intervals on Jonnie and Karen to make sure they hadn't thrown off their blankets—Carol sat curled up in her favorite chair and read the script. At intervals—without speaking—Seth brought her coffee. Finally, she laid aside the script and lifted her eyes to Seth. They were damp with tears, yet joyous.

"It's the best material you've ever written, Seth."

They focused now on how they were to handle this venture— both aware of the difficulties in the long-distance situation. But they would manage, Carol vowed. Seth's play would be seen. He'd be establishing himself under a new name—safe from the vicious blacklisters who'd driven them to refuge in Bellevue.

They knew they must wait until early in the new year to try to locate a coproducer/director. They'd place three ads in *Show Business* beginning in early January, Seth decided. He was aiming for a late spring production.

Carol was involved in the plans for the house for Diane Wallace's daughter. Unlike her mother, Carol quickly interpreted, the daughter would be happier in a house along the Frank Lloyd Wright lines.

The property Diane had bought presented challenges—but Carol was able to maneuver. Diane was already talking about having one of the national women's magazines do a spread on the house when it was finished. What a terrific career boost for her, Carol thought.

Soon Seth was wrestling with the need to weed out the crackpots who'd answered his ad. Groaning at the size of their next telephone bill, he called New York for long phone interviews with applicants.

"God, I wish Leo was here," he told Carol after a particularly lengthy phone discussion. "But this last guy seems a lot like him. He's had a couple of well-received productions Off-Broadway. Short runs but he got good reviews."

"What did you tell him?" Carol felt a surge of excitement. They were making headway.

"I said I'd be up in New York the early part of next week." Carol relished the electric determination she heard in Seth's voice. "I told him I want him to read the script. If he likes it, we're in business."

"I'll run off copies on that old mimeograph machine your dad keeps at the house," Carol said, then paused. "Seth, we have to tell your parents now."

"Yeah." He sighed. "Mom's going to be upset."

"Seth, we have to do this." To his mother Seth's writing was the enemy, Carol thought defensively. It represented insecurity, his leaving Bellevue.

"It's a gamble," he reminded. "We could lose every cent we've managed to save."

"We can't afford not to gamble," she insisted.

The following Sunday morning Seth boarded a flight for New York. A mixture of eager anticipation and apprehension churned in his mind. He still smarted from the kick in the teeth he received from the blacklisting. Was there a chance he could pull himself above that cloud? If he bombed out on this deal, would there ever be another chance?

He had Carol and the kids—was he being greedy in wanting more? Yet the prospect of spending his life behind the counter of the pawnshop turned him sick. Most people worked at jobs they either loathed or that bored them to death—but they adjusted. Look at Dad. He'd wanted to be a journalist, but he'd made a corner for himself in this town that he could tolerate.

Seth's face softened as he remembered his father's pleasure those three times in his life when a letter he'd written to the *New York Times* had been published, his satisfaction when the local newspapers occasionally printed a "letter to the editor" that he submitted. He felt a touch of poignant pain when he remembered an errant remark his father had made at a Passover seder after drinking more than his usual one glass of wine: *"The world never used my talents well, Seth. Sometimes I'm sure a little talent is a curse."*

Now Seth forced himself to concentrate on what lay ahead. Once in the city he'd check his valise in a locker at Grand Central, then head downtown to meet Clark Conway at Ratner's on Second Avenue. He'd give him a copy of the script. Clark would read it tonight and meet with him for coffee tomorrow morning at the bakery/luncheonette that was becoming a hangout for the Off-Broadway crowd.

After the meeting with Conway he'd take the IRT up to the Bronx. Sharon had insisted he stay at her parents' apartment—and they'd agreed—while he was in the city. She knew how he and Carol were nursing every dollar.

He had suspected that coming into New York would be a nostalgic occasion. He wasn't prepared for the flood of memories that assaulted him as he left the subway at Astor Place and headed south on Second Avenue. Lord, he felt old! He'd been eighteen when he'd first discovered Leo in the Village. They'd all been so close. Now Leo and Greg were dead. God knows where Matt and Jerry were—and the others who had wandered in and out of the playhouse.

Seth tried to brush away nostalgia. It was weird how just walking past people he could feel the air of theater that was taking over here. Even before he and Carol had to run to Bellevue for survival, the roots of Off-Broadway were being planted here. Now it was flourishing; people were calling it the East Village.

Seth found Clark Conway waiting for him at a front table in Ratner's. He recognized him immediately from his description of himself—and from the copy of a Sean O'Casey play collection on the table as planned. He bore a striking resemblance to Leo, Seth thought, and found an odd reassurance in this.

From almost their first exchange Seth liked Clark. Seth gave him the manila envelope containing a copy of the play—now titled *Danger Signal,* and then they launched into avid conversation. Clark knew his way around theater, Seth told himself in relief—he had chosen well. Clark had done some advance research. Tomorrow he'd take Seth to see several available playhouses—their numbers had ballooned through the years Seth had been away. He had a small core of actors he knew who might be available—both Equity and non-Equity.

"I'll read the play tonight," Clark promised. "Tomorrow we'll talk."

Sharon's parents offered a warm welcome, but Seth knew they had no comprehension of what he was undertaking. He and Sharon talked far into the night, though her mother emerged once to remind them gently that Sharon had to be awake before 7 A.M. to go into work.

"Seth, tell me whatever I can do to help," Sharon urged. "It's almost like old times."

The next seventy-two hours raced past. Clark was enthusiastic about the play, accepted the modest financial arrangements. He predicted that they'd be able to go into rehearsal by mid-March. He would choose a cast, then Seth would fly up for a reading and approve or reject the actors. They broke down expenses—Clark's fee, the cost of the playhouse, the Equity bond to cover the two Equity actors, the money to be allotted for three small ads in the *New York Post* and two even smaller ads in the *Times*.

"It's an important play, Seth," Clark said at their final meeting. "It would be terrific if we could get a quote from somebody important."

"I don't know anybody important," Seth said ruefully, "but let me think about it when I get back home."

Carol waited impatiently for Seth's plane to arrive. Jonnie and Karen were delighted that they were staying over tonight with their grandparents and great-grandmother. They'd be spoiled rotten, of course. She'd driven them over to the Walden house, then headed for the airport. It would be sweet to have a night alone with Seth, she thought with guilty pleasure. No worries about the kids wandering into their bedroom at an inopportune moment.

It had felt so strange to sleep alone these last three nights. It had been difficult to fall asleep. She was conscious of fresh sympathy for Sharon. Poor baby, she must be having such a rough time. She and Gil had been so close.

Finally Seth's plane arrived. She and Seth clung together for precious moments before heading for the car. Seth's words tumbled over one another in his eagerness to brief her on what had happened.

"You'd like Clark," he told her while he slid behind the wheel of the car. "He reminds me so much of Leo."

"You're probably famished," she said, her head on his shoulder. "Dinner's waiting."

"I missed you," he said quietly.

"I missed you, too," she told him.

Later—after they'd made love and Seth was sound asleep—Carol thought about Clark Conway's remark that it would be great to get a quote "from somebody important." The play carried an important message. There must be influential people who'd want to see that message spread.

All at once Carol's heart was pounding. She knew who would understand what Seth was saying. Would she dare to write Eleanor Roosevelt? *Where* would she write her? Call Sharon in the morning, she ordered herself. A quote from Eleanor Roosevelt would be tremendous. Say nothing to Seth about this. *But do it.*

At Sharon's instructions Carol wrote Eleanor Roosevelt care of the *World-Telegram*—which carried her "My Say" column. Both agreed not to report this to Seth, lest he receive yet another disappointment. But with astonishing speed Carol received a letter from Mrs. Roosevelt from her New York apartment on East 74th Street. In reply to Carol's impassioned inquiry she wrote that yes, she would be happy to read the play.

Ecstatic yet realizing this was a race against time, Carol ignored their tight budget and sent the script to Mrs. Roosevelt via airmail. If Eleanor Roosevelt should come through with a good quote—and Carol forced herself to concede this might not be so—it would be futile if it arrived two weeks after the play opened. They couldn't afford to run longer than two weeks.

Then Clark phoned Seth to say he had assembled a cast that pleased him and wanted to schedule a reading. Seth flew to New York for a forty-eight-hour stay. He returned to report that the two female leads were terrific—the others adequate.

"The two women can carry the show, and Clark's direction will bring out a lot from the rest of the cast. They go into rehearsal tomorrow." Seth radiated optimism. "I like the way Clark digs into the script. I think we'll get some good reviews."

During the second week of rehearsal Carol came home to find a second letter from Eleanor Roosevelt had arrived. Praying silently she ripped open the envelope, read the brief message.

"Thank you very much for your thought in letting me see a copy of *Danger Signal*. I read it and found it very interesting."

Carol visualized an ad for the play—highlighting a quote: "Very interesting! Eleanor Roosevelt." That would bring people down to see the play.

Carol remembered that this was the night Seth stayed late at the shop. She couldn't bear to wait to tell him! She'd ask Bonnie if she could stay for another half hour.

"Bonnie, I hate to ask this," she apologized, "but I have to talk to Mr. Seth."

"You just go on, Miss Carol," Bonnie said, her smile warm. "I'll stay."

Carol drove to the shop, hurried inside. She saw the initial concern on Seth's face at her unexpected appearance, but her own radiance was reassuring. Haltingly she explained her correspondence with Eleanor Roosevelt, handed him the letter. In euphoric shock he scanned the contents.

"Dad!" he yelled, though his father was involved with a customer. "You've got to come see this! You won't believe what's happened!"

Chapter Thirty-nine

Carol knew that nothing had so impressed her mother-in-law as the letter from Eleanor Roosevelt had done. Seth basked in his mother's excitement. When Harvey and Elaine came for dinner the next evening—as they did twice a month—she talked with towering pride about the Roosevelt letter.

"It's a fine endorsement of Seth's play," Hannah said and Elaine nodded in agreement. Elaine, too, was one of the millions of American women who regarded the First Lady with enormous admiration.

"What's the play about?" Harvey asked. Carol was infuriated by the hint of condescension in his voice.

Seth hesitated. Thus far he'd avoided discussing this. "It deals with the problem of integration in the South." He turned apologetically to his mother. "I've tried to be fair—to show every side of the situation."

"What the hell's the matter with you, Seth? You want to add to the fire?" Harvey demanded contemptuously. "Not that I expect it'll have any real impact. How many people do you suppose will see it?"

"It's an important subject," Carol blazed. "This country has to face it."

"It's the law," Elaine said with deceptive softness. "We have to respect the law."

"Elaine, stop talking like an idiot," Harvey ordered. Carol saw the clash of their eyes. This was not the perfect marriage, she suspected—and not just because of a conflict in political ideas. The family rarely saw Elaine—just those two evenings a month when she and Harvey came to dinner at the Walden house—but to her astonishment Carol liked her sister-in-law.

"Seth, you and Carol must go up to New York for the first night's performance." Leah interrupted the ugly moment. "You can fly up in the morning, fly back the next day. Jonnie and Karen will stay with us."

"Grandma, that's an extravagance we can't afford," Seth rejected this. "We'll find out soon enough if the play is reviewed—which it should be—and what the critics have to say about it. There won't be a lot of reviews," he warned. "With luck the *New York Post* and the *New York Times.*"

Carol intercepted a swift exchange between Seth's parents.

"Seth, your father and I want you to go up for the opening. The plane tickets will be a wedding anniversary present from us," Hannah said.

"Mom, that's an expensive gift," Seth protested, but his face lit up in anticipation.

"And I want to give you a wedding anniversary present, too," Leah said. "Three hundred dollars for newspaper ads."

"It'll be like buying tickets for the Kentucky Derby." Harvey's smile was supercilious—contrived to conceal his anger, Carol thought. "Anyhow, if I decide to run for the City Council next go-round, I know where to go for campaign funds."

Clark was jubilant when Seth called about the quote from Eleanor Roosevelt, which was to be added to their ads now. He reported that rehearsals were going well, though one non-Equity cast member had walked out.

"Nothing to worry about; she's already been replaced."

Seth sent Clark two checks—made out to the small ad agency that handled advertising for Off-Broadway playhouses—to enlarge the ads for *Danger Signal.* He and Carol were impatient for the opening. They'd arrive in New York in the early afternoon of the dress rehearsal day, attend the dress rehearsal and the opening performance and return to New York the following morning. They'd spend the two nights at the apartment Sharon shared with her parents.

The evening before they were to leave, Sharon phoned.

"Something's nutty," she told Carol. "Didn't you tell me there'd be an ad in the *Post* today? I picked up the paper and couldn't find it anywhere."

"Oh God, somebody messed up the schedule," Carol moaned. "Let's just pray they're running it tomorrow."

"Tell Seth to call Clark to get on their necks," Sharon said.

"How could they make a mistake like that?" Carol was distraught. Ads were so important. "It's crazy."

"It happens," Sharon said, then tried for a more optimistic tone. "So you'll have ads after the opening. With any luck at all you can add a quote from a review."

"We'll see you tomorrow. It'll be late," Carol warned. "You know how dress rehearsals drag out."

"Why don't I meet you for dinner over on Second Avenue, then we'll go to the dress rehearsal together?" Sharon asked. "Unless Seth would rather I didn't come—"

"He'd love to have you there with us. What time shall we meet?"

"I'll leave the office at five-thirty—I'll be at Ratner's at six. Okay?"

"Wonderful. Oh Sharon, I'm so excited I can't think straight! Seth's waited so long for this!" But why did the newspaper have to screw up on the ad?

On the flight into New York Carol struggled to appear full of confidence about the play's reception. She knew Seth had slept little last night. He'd tried to call Clark at the playhouse, but the phone there was out of order. He didn't answer his home phone; Seth guessed he was sleeping over at his girlfriend's apartment, which he did once or twice a week. She'd been concerned that the playhouse phone was out of order, but Seth explained that Clark had set up an answering service to take reservations.

"That way you don't have to worry about keeping somebody in the box office," he pointed out.

At last the plane came down at LaGuardia. It was the perfect late April day Carol thought—an omen of what lay ahead? she asked herself in a surge of hope. Probably all their worrying was for nothing.

"Let's find a newsstand," Seth said, his face taut with anxiety.

They charged through the airport until they located a newsstand. Seth reached for a copy of the *Times* and the *Post*. He deposited their valises at his feet, handed the *Post* to Carol, and opened the *Times* to the theater section.

"There's no ad," Carol said in disbelief after a moment. "Seth, what's happening?"

"No ad in the *Times*, either," he told her. "Let's grab a taxi and head straight for the playhouse."

On the long drive into Manhattan Carol and Seth tried to dissect the situation.

"How could the ads be screwed up in both newspapers?" Seth demanded. "One, maybe. Not two."

"They were placed by the same agency," Carol pointed out, fighting against panic. "Somebody could have entered the wrong month—maybe May instead of April. You know, if a typist used numbers instead of names for the month—and hit the wrong key."

"The ads weren't in yesterday. Clark should have checked the paper, made sure the ads were in today's papers. Hell, we're opening tomorrow night!" He paused. "*If* we're opening!"

"Seth, there has to be some explanation for all this." Carol strived for calm. "You made the checks out to the landlord at the playhouse, for the rehearsal space—and to the ad agency. Clark couldn't have walked away with the money."

"Maybe I'm being overly suspicious." Seth reached to clutch her hand in his. "But this means so much to us."

The taxi driver dropped them off before the small playhouse. Carol felt a rush of misgivings as she and Seth stood at the curb and inspected the front of the building. There were no indications that a production was to open the following evening. But this was Off-Broadway at its most modest, Carol reminded herself. Perhaps the posters and cast photographs wouldn't come out until evening.

"The place looks closed up," Seth said grimly. "Clark told me the dress rehearsal was scheduled for seven-thirty. That's less than four hours away."

"The doors are locked," Carol conceded. "So Clark won't open till later."

"But why aren't there any signs posted?" Seth persisted, pale and shaken. "They should have been there since the beginning of rehearsals."

"Try calling Clark," Carol urged. *What was happening?* "There must be a public phone around somewhere."

"Yeah—" Seth was terse. "Let's try Second Avenue."

They hurried over to Second, located a public phone. Seth dialed, frowned as he waited for a reply. Still hanging on, he shook his head to indicate Clark wasn't responding.

"Let's go over to his apartment." Carol's mind was in chaos. They were so sure they'd covered themselves. Seth had joshed about her being overly suspicious of people. "You said he lives on Christopher Street," she remembered. "What's the address?"

"It's in my notebook." He fished in his jacket pocket, pulled out the notebook, flipped through pages until he located Clark's address. "Let's head over there."

They walked west with compulsive haste, finally arrived at the modest brownstone where Clark lived in a basement apartment. Seth rang Clark's bell. Nobody answered. He tried again, and then again.

"I'll ring the super," he said.

In a few moments they were questioning the building superintendent.

"He packed up and cut out two days ago. Left his furniture—such as it is—behind. Owed two months' rent, too," the super said contemptuously.

"I don't suppose he left a forwarding address?" Carol asked, her heart pounding at this unexpected disaster.

"He left in the middle of the night. No forwarding address. Look, I'm kind of busy," the super said.

"Thank you," Seth said. "Sorry to have bothered you."

Carol and Seth walked away from the house—both in shock.

"All I gave Clark personally was his fee," Seth said, bewildered by the situation. "What did he do with the checks for the rent, the Equity bond, the ads—even the printing place?"

"Let's go over to the printer's," Carol said. "That's right near the playhouse. That'll tell us what Clark's pulled."

"We'll take a cab across town," Seth said.

From the printer came the answer they dreaded hearing. Clark had presented himself as Seth Walden, the name on the checks. He'd placed an order, handed over a check, and then canceled the order—after the check had cleared.

"He said he'd lost his backer—the play was off," the owner of the small printing firm explained. "What could I do? I'd deposited the check—I gave him back cash, the way he asked."

Now Carol and Seth understood. Clark had followed this procedure with all the others. There had not been one day's rehearsal on the play. Only the reading that Seth had witnessed when he came up to New York, supposedly to give his approval of the cast.

Slowly they walked back to Second Avenue, eschewing another taxi. Sharon would be meeting them at Ratner's shortly.

"I was out of my mind to think this would work!" Seth lashed at himself. "It was a crazy dream."

"It would have worked if Clark wasn't a crook," Carol said defensively.

"We'll talk to the landlord tomorrow—if we can find him. And go up to Actors Equity about the bond. But it'll be the same story. We've been conned."

Over and over Seth reviled himself as they walked across town in an afternoon that had become gray and cloudy, with a raw chill in the air.

"All that money right down the drain!" He shook his head in pain. "All our savings. The money Mom and Dad gave us—and Grandma."

"We had to take the gamble," Carol said. It wasn't the loss of the money that was hurting Seth so badly—it was the death of a dream. *Where did they go now?* "Seth, it's an awful break, but it isn't the end of the world."

"I'm a born loser," he said tightly. "Everything I touch crumbles to dust. If I don't make it by forty—forget it," he said harshly. "And that's only two and a half years away."

"Shaw didn't have any real success until he was past forty." She quoted what Seth had said to her when they'd spent that precious weekend in London. "I believe in you. In time talent has to be recognized."

"Remember the song from *South Pacific*—where Mary Martin sings about being a 'cockeyed optimist'? That's you, Carol. I had my one little fling in television—that's all there'll ever be for me as a writer. I'm like Dad," he said softly. "Great dreams—that'll go nowhere."

"That's not true," she contradicted. How could she tell him his father was a warm, sweet, special man—but that his father didn't have his talent? "Dad talked about being a journalist, but he never worked at it. You've proven yourself. First at Leo's playhouse, then in television. You'll make it, Seth."

"Have you any idea how many people are out there in the world with my kind of dreams? All so sure we're God's gift to the theater or publishing or art. All dreams, Carol—nothing more."

"You won't stop trying, Seth. You won't stop writing. When you have a talent like yours, you don't rule—*it* does. You're possessed—and that's wonderful." But she saw only despair in him.

"No more." He took a deep breath, exhaled slowly. "I learned something today, Carol. We're not all meant to see our talents come into full bloom. That goes to the chosen few."

"You sound like Jerry now."

"I'm talking reality. Jerry learned that long before I did." He glanced at his watch. Seth was shutting her out, she thought in panic. "Let's get moving. Sharon will be at the restaurant."

Carol felt sick. Across her mind flashed Oscar Wilde's words: "For each man kills the thing he loves . . ." In her bungling eagerness to help Seth, had she destroyed his dream?

Chapter Forty

In the weeks and months ahead Carol fought futilely to penetrate the wall Seth raised between them each time she tried to talk about the debacle in New York. *"It's over. It was a stupid effort."* He exploded in unfamiliar rage when she brought it up again in the summer.

"For God's sake, Carol, will you stop it? It's over! It was a stupid effort! I should have known better!"

She was shaken by the hostility in his eyes. In all the years they'd been married, he'd never yelled at her this way. His anger was always directed at bigotry and inequities he saw in government. But she understood this rage at her was born of his anguish and frustration about his writing.

Saying nothing to Seth—and in cahoots with his grandmother, who would receive the mail at the Walden house—she sent the playscript out to one Broadway producer, then another. She guessed that the letter from Eleanor Roosevelt would guarantee a reading. By the end of the year she had received three turndowns. *"Not commercial." "Too delicate a subject at this time." "Fine writing, but the timing is wrong."*

On New Year's Eve—before they were to go to the Walden house with Jonnie and Karen for the family party—Carol forced herself to confess what she had done. She was afraid Seth would explode at her. Instead, tears filled his eyes and he pulled her into his arms.

"How would I ever survive without you?" he asked tenderly. "You and the kids—the three of you make my life worth living."

"Seth, this last letter," she said, praying for a breakthrough. "You saw what he said—'fine writing, but the timing is wrong.' Put the play aside for now and go on to something else."

"I can't," he confessed after an anguished moment. "I've got this block. When other writers talked about it, I scoffed. I was never at a loss for something to write. But I am now. I think I'm afraid to try again."

"Write *something*," Carol urged. "Maybe a one-act play. Anything to get you moving again. Seth, this is not the end of the road for your writing."

"We'll talk about it another time," he said evasively. "Let's get our act together. Mom'll be expecting us at the house in a little while."

There had not been one word of recrimination from Mom and Dad, nor Grandma, about the lost money, Carol thought in gratitude as they drove up before the house. Only Harvey had made snide remarks.

"Hey, kids, stop fighting," Seth ordered. Jonnie and Karen argued noisily about who would carry in the bottle of champagne he'd bought to celebrate the arrival of the new year.

"She's too little," Jonnie said. "She might drop it."

"I wanna carry it," Karen said plaintively. "Mommie, tell him!"

"You carry the flowers," Carol decided, handing Karen the bunch of tawny chrysanthemums before she could resort to tears. Jonnie was apt to cave in if Karen cried. She didn't want him to feel he had to give in before feminine tears. "Remember, give them to Great-Gran," she said as she pointed to Seth's grandmother.

"I'll remember," Karen promised, her smile angelic.

The atmosphere in the house was festive. In deference to the children, Hannah had arranged to serve dinner early.

"Where are Harvey and Elaine?" Seth asked as they all gathered in the dining room—the dining table expanded to accommodate seven. Yet another leaf would have been needed if his brother and sister-in-law were to be here.

"They're going to some affair at the country club," Hannah said self-consciously. "They wanted to be here, but Harvey thought it would be good for him to meet people at the club. You know, now that he's talking about running for the City Council."

"Sure." Seth sounded defensive, Carol thought. Harvey was moving into politics. He clerked at the shop.

Harvey was the only member of the family who'd ever seen the inside of the Bellevue Country Club, Carol remembered. Not even her mother-in-law's fifth-generation standing could buy them entry. Harvey was accepted because of Elaine's family.

"*Who needs them?*" Leah always scoffed. "*I wouldn't go if somebody invited me.*"

Harvey was ever conscious of his political ambitions. The country club set was important to him. But Carol recalled her mother-in-law's pride that the first child born in Savannah had been Jewish—that the first Jewish governor in the country had been David Emanuel, who took office in Georgia in 1801. Grandma had confided to her that Bellevue Jews had become strongly conscious of their heritage since the Holocaust.

After dinner—despite rigorous protests—Jonnie and Karen were ordered to bed. Tonight Leah—taking deep pleasure in this—read them their bedtime stories. Carol was ever grateful for Seth's family. Without them Jonnie and Karen would have only their parents. Always on special evenings Carol thought about her mother. Did Mama ever wonder if she had grandchildren? Did Mama care?

Carol was pleased with the new assignments that were coming her way at Arthur Gilbert and Son, but she was silently furious in the knowledge that the male associates were drawing salaries considerably larger than her own despite her substantial raise. She continued to be an outsider in the expanding firm, though she knew she was bringing in the most prestigious clients.

She worried constantly about Seth's state of mind. He seemed immobilized by his writer's block. He was afraid to write, she told herself in anguish. He couldn't bear another disappointment.

The situation on integration in the South continued to be explosive. In Atlanta—and Bellevue religiously followed in Atlanta's footsteps—Mayor Hartsfield ever proclaimed the need for peaceful race relations, but Governor Griffin was determined that Georgia schools would remain segregated. In February Reverend Martin Luther King Jr. and Reverend William Holmes Borders launched a campaign to desegregate Atlanta's buses.

"They'll take it into the Federal courts," Seth predicted, "and they'll win."

Carol worried that the Atlanta school system would be destroyed by the governor. She was concerned, too, that Jonnie and Karen—young as they were—might be caught up in the anger of so many Southern parents at the prospect of integrated schools. She was shaken when Jonnie came home from school one day and reported the ugly racist remarks of another child in his class.

"I don't ever want to hear you talk like that!" she blazed and Jonnie stared at her in disbelief. She had never been truly angry at him in her life, she realized.

Now she sat down and talked to Jonnie. She vowed to make him understand the awfulness of bigotry. He listened, his eyes serious, while Carol explained what was happening in the South.

"You love Bonnie, don't you?" she asked.

"Yes," he said with a sudden smile.

"You may not like all colored folks, nor all white folks," she pursued. "But you never say nasty things about anybody—white or colored." She paused. "You know you're Jewish. You've started Sunday school at the temple. There are folks who say bad things about Jews. Like the Ku Klux Klan. Daddy told you about the Klan."

Jonnie nodded solemnly. He was not yet eight, but he had to know what the world around him was like, Carol told herself.

On a Sunday morning in early October Carol and Seth arose to learn that at 3:30 A.M. a tremendous blast had shaken Atlanta. Police cars had cruised the streets without locating the site of the explosion. Then, the TV newscaster reported, the janitor at the Temple of the Hebrew Benevolent Congregation had arrived for work to discover a gaping hole at the entrance to the handsome million-dollar structure on Peachtree Street.

White stone columns that had stood beside the doors were destroyed, stained-glass windows broken, the school and administrative offices damaged. According to the police, thirty or forty sticks of dynamite had been planted at some time during the night, then exploded at 3:30 A.M. It was the first time that a religious structure had ever been deliberately damaged in Atlanta.

"Who could have done that?" Carol was pale and distraught. "There's never been trouble like this in Atlanta."

"Not since the Leo Frank case," Seth agreed. "And that was in 1913."

Atlanta had been dragged into the racial hatred and violence that afflicted other Southern cities. A week ago in Clinton, Tennessee, the integrated Clinton High School had been bombed by terrorists. In Little Rock, Arkansas, Governor Orval Farbus had closed the public school when faced by a Federal order to integrate. Now—in Atlanta—the racial hatred had expanded to include Jews.

Carol and Seth were unaware that Jonnie had left his bedroom and was sitting cross-legged on the floor in his pajamas—his eyes riveted to the television screen as the cameras focused on the destruction of the temple.

"Jonnie, you must be hungry," Carol said gently and exchanged a swift, uneasy glance with Seth. "I'll start breakfast."

"Why did somebody dynamite that temple in Atlanta?" Jonnie asked, troubled that this had happened.

"Jonnie, here's Mayor Hartsfield," Seth said. "Let's listen to what he has to say."

Mayor Hartsfield was outraged by the temple bombing. He offered a $1,000 reward for information that would lead to the conviction of the terrorists.

"Whether they like it or not, every political rabble-rouser is the godfather of these cross-burners and dynamiters who sneak about in the dark and give a bad name to the South," Mayor Hartsfield said.

The three listened intently to all that the mayor said, then Carol rose from her chair and turned off the television. Jonnie seemed so disturbed by what had happened; enough of that for an eight-year-old boy.

"Let's go out to the kitchen," she said determinedly cheerful.

"Will the Jews in Atlanta have to go to Israel now?" Jonnie asked. "Will we have to go to Israel?"

"Jonnie, everything will be all right," Seth reassured him. "A handful of awful people bombed the temple. They'll be caught and sent to jail. You heard how the mayor is offering a reward already for their capture."

"Jonnie, what do you know about Israel?" Carol asked curiously.

"Great-Gran told me about it," Jonnie said and repeated Leah's words with a clarity and understanding that astonished his parents.

Often children understood so much more than parents gave them credit for, Carol thought. She was pleased that Jonnie knew about Israel—an important part of his heritage—yet she worried that he was troubled beyond a young child's concern over what had happened in Atlanta early this morning. You wanted them to know, she rationalized, yet you worried about their anxieties. Several days later Sharon called from New York—a rarity in these days when she was ever conscious of her limited funds. She'd read a report in *Newsweek* about the temple bombing.

"It was just a bunch of creeps," Carol reassured her. "We're not seeing a resurgence of the KKK or anything like that."

They talked with an awareness that each minute was running up the phone bill for Sharon's parents. But Carol was glad Sharon had called. Only with Sharon could she share her concern about Seth's not writing, his dark mood about this. Both of them remembered Jerry's depression when his expected Broadway debut collapsed—they remembered his suicide attempt.

"Have you ever run into Jerry?" Carol asked.

"He's disappeared into the wild blue yonder," Sharon said. "And that suits me fine."

"What's with the damned blacklisting?" Carol asked. Though Sharon didn't work in television or theater or films—those fields most affected—as an editor at a schlock magazine group, she came in contact with writers.

"You can feel a change," Sharon said, "though I hear a lot of writers and actors still aren't working. Are you thinking that it might be time for Seth to try to move back into television?" she asked hopefully. "The air *is* clearing—"

Only now did Carol confide in Sharon about Seth's writer's block. Only with Sharon would she discuss this.

"Look, I know it's not what Seth wants to write—and the money is shitty—but if he'd try some stories for the new magazine the boss just dumped on me, I could probably buy from him. He could knock out one of these sexy men's mag stories in an afternoon. It might help him break through the ice."

"I'll talk to him," Carol said, "then have him call you." But she knew in her heart that this would be a futile effort.

"How's your snotty brother-in-law doing with his political career?" Sharon asked.

"He's planning on running for the City Council in the next election," Carol told her. "Providing his father-in-law comes forth with substantial campaign funds."

"How long has he been married?"

"Over three years," Carol told her. "We don't see much of them, but Elaine is sweet and very pretty and kind of vulnerable. She deserves better."

"They remind me of you and Matt," Sharon said and laughed at Carol's gasp of reproach. "Honey, you were so infatuated with that bastard, and all he cared about was himself."

"Next week Harvey and Elaine are flying to Monaco for ten days. It's been a hot tourist spot since Grace Kelly married Prince Rainier." Carol paused. "Somehow—from the little we see of her—I don't think Elaine's terribly happy with Harvey. But she's so anxious to see him move into politics. I suspect she figures her parents will have more respect for him."

"Tell Harvey to get her pregnant—then Daddy will come across with campaign funds. But I'd better get off before Mom's phone bill looks like the national debt. Kiss the kids for me. And send more snapshots."

Seth was startled—and upset—when his mother self-consciously suggested at a slow moment in the store that when Harvey and Elaine came for dinner tomorrow night they arrange for Bonnie to baby-sit with Jonnie and Karen.

"It's like a going-away party for Harvey and Elaine." She struggled to appear casual. "A grown-up dinner party."

"Are you inviting people besides family?" he asked.

"No, just you and Carol and Harvey and Elaine. But it should be special."

"Mom, are you hiding something from me?" he joshed. "Are they going to announce that Elaine's pregnant?"

"No." His mother's voice was unexpectedly sharp. "And don't you ride them about that. When the time's ripe, they'll start a family."

"I barely exchange a dozen words with Harvey these days." He was the older brother who was stuck in a dull groove. Harvey respected only movers and shakers.

"You always take what he says the wrong way," she scolded. "You know Harvey loves you. You're his big brother—he looks up to you."

"I may be his big brother, but he's never looked up to me. Mom, accept it—Harvey and I have a whole different approach to life." Not entirely true, he derided himself in silence; once his ambition had equaled Harvey's. But Harvey would make it.

Customers came into the store and they were caught up in business. But later—when he told Carol about the Sunday dinner plans—he wondered if his mother worried about the state of Harvey's marriage. Did she know that Harvey was fooling around on the side? Did Elaine know?

"Why are we getting so la-de-da?" Carol asked, a hint of laughter in her voice. "The next thing you know, Harvey'll be suggesting we meet for dinner at the country club."

"He's not a member." Seth picked up her light mood. "He's tolerated for the sake of Elaine and her family. We haven't made the grade yet, sugar."

"I like Elaine." Carol was contemplative. "Marrying Harvey was her big rebellion. It's not an easy situation for her."

"Wait till Harvey brings her into the governor's mansion. Then her family will forgive her for marrying him. After all, New York had a Jewish governor for years."

"But this is Georgia," Carol reminded and stopped short. "We're forgetting what your mother always says—Georgia had a Jewish governor in 1801."

"With Harvey's kind of ambition he just might make it," Seth said. "Ever since he was a little kid he had this monumental drive to get what he wanted."

Was Carol disappointed that he didn't have Harvey's drive? God knows, he wanted to get back into writing again. *But it just wasn't happening.* Maybe he'd had too many disappointments. Maybe because he knew the odds were against him.

Chapter Forty-one

In the evening attire that he knew emphasized his flamboyant good looks, Harvey gazed through a sitting-room window in their luxurious suite in the elegant Hotel de Paris and waited for Elaine to dress for dinner. On this third day in Monaco he was bored. His initial triumph at being here—in this tiny principality that lies between the towering Alps and the Mediterranean—had evaporated. Why couldn't Elaine have listened to him and agreed to divide their stay between Monaco and Antibes? But she was fascinated by the Grace Kelly fairy tale—so they had to come to this creepy country that was half the size of Central Park in New York.

Just thinking about the golden beach at Antibes with its lineup of gorgeous, long-legged girls in skimpy bikinis made him horny.

Here in Monte Carlo all they saw were old people—and most of them British. Why the hell did the British always make him feel clumsy and uncultured?

The lights in the miniature semicircular harbor glowed like a scattering of diamonds against the night sky. Somebody had said last night that the 325-foot yacht at anchor—the largest of several there—belonged to Aristotle Onassis. People said he practically ran Monte Carlo, that he'd set up his offices here because nobody had to pay taxes. God, it must feel great to have his kind of money and power!

Money was power, he thought restlessly. When was Elaine's old man going to stop hedging and back his political career? But he knew the answer to that, he forced himself to acknowledge. The old bastard wanted a grandson.

"Harvey," Elaine called to him from the doorway. To a lot of men she was beautiful—even sexy—but he felt nothing as she stood there before him in a simple but no doubt wildly expensive white satin slip. "Should I wear the white strapless or the black crepe?"

"The white strapless," he told her. The two designer gowns had been lying across their bed for the past hour. "Black is for old women."

"All right," she said softly, almost cajolingly.

She was pissed since she found out for sure that he strayed from their bed. She wouldn't divorce him, he told himself complacently. That would be admitting she made a mistake in marrying him. Why didn't she go off and have an affair? *Get pregnant.* She'd be forever beholden to him for keeping her secret.

What about that young Tyrone Power type—he couldn't be more than twenty-one or twenty—who couldn't take his eyes off her each night in the hotel restaurant, or wherever they met in this musical comedy town? The kid was here with his father, who spent most of *his* time in the casino. They were British. From snatches of conversation they'd overheard, he knew the old boy was trying to convince his son to go to law school.

He'd had this wild hope when Elaine prodded him into coming here with her that—miraculously—she'd drift into a swift affair and get pregnant. She was drinking more than she usually did. She used to nurse one drink all evening. And if she fell into bed with a man, she'd never think of taking care of herself. Neither one of them ever did. She thought it was because he was eager for a family. He *needed* the image of a beautiful wife and perfect child if he was to move ahead in politics.

Elaine was nervous that she hadn't got pregnant yet. It wasn't because she avoided sex. He was astonished to find that she was a hot little bitch in bed. Never mind that glacial, puritanical exterior. She didn't say anything about it, but he knew she was worried because she didn't get pregnant. She didn't know he couldn't give her a baby. Not after having the mumps when he was eleven.

All at once his mind was churning. Wasn't this what she had coyly called her "fertile period?" The time of the month when she was most likely to get pregnant? They hadn't slept together since they arrived—though she'd made wistful overtures. They'd be here just one more week. Could he throw Elaine into the arms—and bed—of that boy? So he was seven or eight years younger—he was panting to give it to her.

What was his name? Harvey focused impatiently on identifying his quarry. The old boy had called him Cliff, he recalled in triumph. Of course, the odds were against any of this happening, he warned himself, but what did he have to lose? His entire future hung in the balance. Give the old bastard a grandson—and he wouldn't have to worry about campaign funds. He was thirty; it was time to get moving.

When Elaine emerged from their bedroom, Harvey admitted that she looked beautiful. Not the type to push him into a cold shower if he couldn't throw her on her back, but he'd seen the way she set some guys' teeth on edge.

"Let's get down to that greasy spoon." His smile was supercilious.

"Harvey, it's one of the great restaurants of the world," Elaine protested.

As soon as they entered the restaurant, Harvey spied Cliff and his father. They'd exchanged small talk earlier. Tonight he made a point of pausing for brief conversation. Cliff's eyes were devouring Elaine. Right after dinner the old man would head next door for the casino. He'd be there, too. Let nature take its course.

Though he inwardly admitted that the meal served them was superb, he complained about each course, made disinterested stabs at everything that was served. While Elaine debated over which sumptuous dessert to order, he threw his napkin on the table and said he was leaving.

"I'll have a steak at the *Bar du Cercle Prive* and then wander over to the roulette table. Sign the tab when you've had your dessert and coffee." Ignoring her stare of dismay, he rose to his feet and stalked away.

Elaine fought back tears as she ordered dessert and coffee. She felt sick with humiliation at being abandoned this way. Women didn't sit alone in a restaurant. It had been a mistake to come here, she reproached herself. But she'd been intrigued by the prospect of seeing the country—actually three villages—where Princess Grace lived in a fairy-tale castle that sat high above the sea.

Was everybody staring at her? Were they wondering why Harvey had walked out on her this way? Involuntarily she allowed her eyes to move about the room. Then all at once she was conscious of the intense gaze of the handsome young Englishman here with his father. But his father—like Harvey—had taken off for the casino.

For a moment their eyes clung. Then she lowered her own in a surge of embarrassment. She was relieved when she saw the waiter approaching with her dessert. She pretended to be absorbed in enjoying her chocolate mousse.

She was startled when the young Englishman rose from his table and approached her own.

"We both seem to have been deserted in favor of the casino," he said with a whimsical smile. "May I join you?" But already he was signaling his waiter to bring his demitasse to her table.

"Why not?" She managed a casual smile.

"I'm Cliff Foley." He sat across from her with an air of pleasure. "You're Elaine Walden," he recalled. "We've exchanged enough informal conversation to consider we've been formally introduced."

"I agree," she said lightly. It was pleasant to sit here with a handsome young man whose eyes told her he found her very attractive. Harvey had looked at her that way before they were married.

It was so easy to talk with Cliff Foley, she marveled. She was sure he was five or six years younger than she, but that was no barrier. He told her that his father—long a widower—was addicted to the casino.

"We come here whenever he forces himself to play the heavy father," Cliff said humorously. "He's trying to convince me that my life won't be complete unless I'm a barrister."

"What would you like to do?" she asked.

"I want to write music," he told her, serious now.

They sat in the restaurant until they realized that the waiters were politely waiting for them to leave. In a blend of confusion and amusement they left, both reluctant to part. Elaine knew that—like last night—Harvey would remain in the casino till dawn. He'd pointed out that it was possible to gamble and manage to lose only small sums. The time of the spectacular gamblers was past.

Cliff delighted her with stories about Monte Carlo. He told her that the local residents were not allowed in the casinos, that Monaco was so small its golf course was outside its boundaries—in France.

"I was surprised that the beach is so rocky," Elaine admitted. "And there's so much noise. The motorcycle and the little Italian motor scooters and the motorized bicycles." She shuddered with mock dismay.

"But it's a beautiful town that mesmerizes most people. All those nineteenth-century houses built on tier after tier, seeming to blend into the mountains. I say," he began and seemed suddenly shy, "would you let me be your tour guide tomorrow morning? There are some beautiful sights you should see."

"I'd love that," she said after a startled moment. Why not? As Cliff surmised, Harvey would sleep till noon, disappear until close to dinnertime. "It sounds like such fun."

As she had expected, Harvey returned to their suite long after she had fallen asleep. He complained that there was no nightlife in Monte Carlo—only the casino. *"They pull in the sidewalks after eleven P.M."* Their first night they'd gone to the one nightclub in town—the Knickerbocker—which Harvey labeled expensive and dull. But nothing seemed to please him here.

In the morning she met Cliff as planned—feeling guilty pleasure in this. It was clear that he loved Monaco, even while he joshed about some of its little eccentricities as they walked along the winding, palm-tree-lined streets of the semitropical village—sun-drenched and fragrant with the scent of flowers.

"I'd forgot to warn you against wearing slacks," he said, his eyes admiring her smart Yves Saint Laurent suit, bought on her brief stayover in New York. "In Monaco women are forbidden to wear what the rule makers consider men's clothes, but it's fine to wear bikinis." Laughter lurked in his eyes.

"I love the way it's possible to walk everywhere," she told Cliff. "Back home we're forever in a car."

It seemed only natural to lunch with Cliff; they both knew they'd be alone until late in the afternoon. Over luncheon in a small restaurant favored by student visitors, Cliff told her—almost shyly—about his love for American music. They shared a passion for the music of Rodgers and Hammerstein and Aaron Copland. Despite his father's tirade's, Cliff was determined to pursue a musical career.

They met casually in the hotel restaurant that evening—giving no inkling that they'd spent hours together during the course of the day. And when Cliff's father and then Harvey took off for the casino, they left the restaurant to walk along the pebbly beach—ignoring its discomfort—and explored their innermost thoughts. Each knew this was a fleeting period in their lives, that after this week they would never meet again. Yet it was a precious period for both.

With Cliff, Elaine felt admired and cherished. Humiliated by Harvey's lack of interest in her feelings, his abdication of his role as husband, she reveled in Cliff's candid determination to spend every possible moment alone with her.

"You must see all of Monaco," he insisted. "You'll keep the memory with you always." His eyes told her that what they shared between them would remain with him forever. "Tomorrow I'll show you La Condamine—between Monte Carlo and the town of Monaco. It's the marketplace. Always crowded and colorful. And the next day you must see the Cathedral of Saint Nicholas—and after that the Oceanographic Museum and—"

"I must bring my camera," Elaine broke in effervescently. "I promised my sister-in-law I'd bring back snapshots of the houses and public buildings. Carol's an architect," she explained.

"I don't think I've ever known a woman architect," Cliff said.

"Oh, Carol's a very special person," she told him. Harvey disliked Carol, she thought involuntarily. He hated women who pursued careers.

"You're a very special woman," he told her softly.

In a dreamlike trance Elaine agreed to spend segments of each afternoon with him in the student-cheap hotel he rented for this purpose. After an hour or two of passionate dalliance in the modest hotel room, they returned to their palatial suites at the Hotel de Paris. No obligations on either side, she told herself—just this ecstatic pleasure of living a secret life that would end too soon.

* * *

For a while Elaine concluded that the trip had been good for Harvey. Regularly on Saturday nights—after spending an evening at the country club—Harvey made love to her. It wasn't the sweetly passionate experience she'd shared with Cliff. Her lovemaking with Harvey was over before she felt it had really begun. She harbored no illusions. To Harvey she was a faceless body to satisfy his physical needs.

Then sudden suspicions tugged at her. Was she at last pregnant? Was it Harvey's child—or Cliff's? *How would she know?* She lay sleepless night after night—haunted by this question. Would Harvey guess what had happened? Would he doubt that he was the father?

Still, she forced herself to tell Harvey she suspected she was pregnant. To her momentary relief he seemed ecstatic. Let the baby look like him, she prayed. Would she ever *know* whose child she carried? Forever, she taunted herself, this question would run punishingly across her mind.

Chapter Forty-two

Early in the new year Sharon vowed to make a change in her lifestyle. She wrote Carol—even before she told her parents—that she was sick of the long commute from the Bronx and figured that with her recent raise and stern budgeting she could move into Manhattan with Michelle.

"It's not just the commute," she admitted. "It's bad for Michelle to be raised this way. She doesn't know who makes the ground rules for her—Mom or me. Mom means well, of course—you know how she loves Michelle—but we're different generations. Our ideas on raising kids clash. And let's face it, I'm going out of my mind living like I was in a convent. I'll never love another guy the way I loved Gil, but you remember—I can settle for sex without love. I wasn't born to live in a convent."

She stalled until after Michelle's birthday in February—on a Sunday afternoon when she was alone in the house with her mother—to announce her plans.

"Sharon, how could you manage?" Her mother was visibly upset. "On your own, yes, but with Michelle?"

"I've thought it all out. I'll put Michelle in a private school that has after-school activities. I'll get an apartment near the school. She's nine years old; she can walk home from school alone. I'll make sure I'm not stuck at the office until all hours. I'll—"

"Private schools costs lots of money," Mrs. Ross said worriedly. "On your salary how can you manage?"

"I'll use Michelle's Social Security." Each month she received a check from the government for Michelle—from Gil's Social Security benefits and which she'd banked regularly against possible emergencies. "I've found a school that costs a little less than her checks." She wouldn't mention that it was a parochial school. Cheaper than posh private schools. Mom would have a fit. "At nineteen I could handle the commute. Not at thirty-nine."

"You'll wait until September?" her mother asked. "When the new school term starts? And what about summer vacations?" she added with fresh anxiety.

"We'll move as soon as I can find an apartment. In the summer—" She paused, pushed ahead. "In the summer there're day camps in the city. Michelle will be fine."

"You're sure you can manage?" Her mother remained uneasy.

"I can manage, Mom." She was staring at forty—she had to get her life back on track.

Not until three weeks later—when Sharon had rented a one-bedroom apartment in the West Eighties that she could afford—did she learn that her parents, too, were leaving the Bronx. Her father was retiring.

"For a long time Bev and Dan have talked about adding on another room, making a little apartment for Dad and me when he decided to retire," her mother explained. "With Dad's pension and Social Security, we can meet the payments for the addition and take care of our needs. It'll be an easy life for us."

"Mom, you and Dad waited to do this because of Michelle and me," Sharon said softly. "Dad could have retired a year ago."

"We wanted to be here for you. It's not easy to raise a child alone."

"I can do it because I have family to support me." Tears glistened in Sharon's eyes. They'd never had a lot of money, but they had one another. That was a special—precious—kind of richness. She thought about Gil's father, who'd come to his funeral and wept for his son—but was blind to the joys of being a grandfather. She remembered Carol's mother, who'd disappeared from Carol's life to live in a family-empty world of her own. Thank God, for *her* family. Thank God for Seth's family, whom Carol loved and who loved her and the kids.

Carol worried at intervals about how Sharon was faring on her own in New York. But it was like coming home, Sharon wrote—she loved living on the Upper West Side again. Michelle liked her new school, had made new friends.

"The job's insane," Sharon wrote, "but it means freedom, so I'm holding on. Also, I'm learning a lot! God, talk about trial and error! But in time I'll be able to move up into something better. Did you ever think back at Hunter that I'd be a real, live editor? We put out shit, of course, but I'm building myself a profession. And tell Seth that any time he wants to write for us, I'm here waiting to buy from him."

Carol knew that Sharon could buy only if Seth wrote something that was right for her magazine. The money was minuscule, but she tried repeatedly to push Seth into taking a stab at writing for Sharon's market. She mustn't hit too hard, she cautioned herself; just let him know that he was still a writing "pro"—that he could sell.

Then one humid Sunday morning in May—the first hot spell of the year—Carol awoke to realize that Seth wasn't in bed. On Sundays he usually slept late—until she sent one of the kids to call him for breakfast.

With a sudden inchoate flurry of alarm she left the perspiration-sodden bed and hurried out of the room and down the hall. Her heart began to pound when she heard the unfamiliar sound of flying typewriter keys. Seth was in the dining room, long ago designated as Seth's office. *He was writing.*

She hesitated, debating about showing herself. But eagerness propelled her across the living room and into the entrance to the dining room. Seth sat hunched over the typewriter. His face tense and absorbed, etched with a kind of ecstasy she identified with his writing efforts.

As though feeling the weight of her gaze, Seth raised his eyes to meet hers. It was unnecessary for them to speak. The long dry spell had been punctured.

"I'll make some coffee," she said softly, her eyes luminous.

Not until Carol returned with a mug of coffee for him and one for herself did Seth abandon the typewriter.

"Maybe I'm nuts," he said, "but I think I can rewrite the play as a novel. Publishing isn't as crazy as the theater or television. At least," he amended with a grin, "I don't think so. Look how many books are published every year."

"It's a wonderful idea." Glowing at this development, Carol sat at the table beside him.

"You might say Sharon's pushed me into this," he said whimsically. "Sharon and you—with all that crap about my writing for that sexy magazine she edits. I can't see myself doing that—I don't think I can," he said with candor. "But I'm almost sure I can take the play and rewrite it as a novel. I like that possibility," he pursued, squinting in thought. "In the theater you're dependent upon actors, a director, a producer. You know the insanity in television. But writing a novel gives me total control. I don't need actors to bring it to life. But it's going to take time."

"I know you can do it." She was conscious of a towering excitement.

Seth chuckled tenderly.

"Sugar, if I said, I think I can go to the moon, you'd agree with me."

Thus began a new and precious period for Carol and Seth. She gloried in his enthusiasm for switching from play to novel. He conceded the transition was difficult, but he welcomed the challenge. The blacklisting was all but dead—an ugly memory. Now she longed to see them move into a larger house—with separate bedrooms for Jonnie and Karen and a real office for Seth.

She was touched when Elaine asked her to redesign a wing of the house that was to be the baby's nursery and an adjoining playroom. Elaine's pregnancy had brought them close together. She was astonished that Hannah was so matter-of-fact about the approaching arrival of a third grandchild. She remembered how her mother-in-law had rushed up to New York to be with her when she came home from the hospital with Jonnie.

Mom never felt truly comfortable with Elaine, she thought, because of the family's wealth and social position and because Elaine was not of their faith. But Elaine was a devoted wife to Harvey. Sometimes she was impatient with Elaine's eagerness to please him.

The construction business in Atlanta was booming. Jason landed a major commercial commission. The entire staff except for Carol was involved in the new structure. Carol was appointed head of the newly setup residential division, a triumph for her. This was the area she found exciting. In six months, she vowed, she'd prove herself so useful that Jason wouldn't dare refuse her request for a substantial raise.

Late in June—at a few minutes past 3 A.M.—Elaine gave birth to a son. In jubilant spirits Harvey awoke Carol and Seth at 5 A.M. to announce the baby's birth. He'd also called his parents, he told them.

"God, I'm going home to get some sleep now," he said, yawning noisily. "I won't go in to the office until afternoon."

Ten minutes later—knowing they'd be awake—Hannah phoned. Carol answered, guessing it would be her mother-in-law.

"They're naming the baby Timothy Lloyd, for Elaine's father," Hannah said without preliminaries, clearly distraught. "Doesn't Harvey know it's bad luck to name a child after a living relative?"

"Mom, that's just a superstition," Carol soothed.

"Jews honor that belief," Hannah told her. "And I can't believe that a grandchild of mine is to be baptized."

"He's still your grandchild. You'll love him just as much as you do Jonnie and Karen."

"Harvey's out of his mind with excitement." Hannah switched tracks. "I've never seen him so elated. He said Elaine's father will be handing out Havana cigars all over town."

Harvey was elated over presenting his father-in-law with a grandson, Carol interpreted. Seth kept saying that was all he needed to get his in-laws behind him with a political campaign chest. Last time they'd had dinner together at Mom and Dad's, Harvey had talked compulsively about the need for "new faces" in local government. An article in *Time* magazine had just proclaimed that Atlanta had the highest crime rate in the country—"and as Atlanta

goes, so goes Bellevue," Harvey declaimed. But Carol found it difficult to view Harvey as a local crusader against crime.

Late in August Carol and Seth took a week's vacation. They
went with Jonnie and Karen to Sea Island, where they stayed at a
cottage that was owned by Elaine's college roommate. Last fall
Elaine and Harvey had arranged for the rental for themselves—
before Elaine became pregnant.

Seth called this their belated honeymoon. They'd arranged for a
motherly colored woman to watch over the children every afternoon. They strolled along the beach, cooled by ocean breezes, or
walked beneath the tall palms, the pines, and the live oaks. And
before the children were brought back to the cottage, they made
love.

"You look about twenty," Seth told her as she lay in the curve of
his arms on this next-to-the-last afternoon at Sea Island. "Nobody
would believe you have two kids."

"This week I feel about twenty," she said, glorying in these cherished hours alone with him.

"Did I tell you that Eugene O'Neill wrote *Ah Wilderness* here?"
Seth revered O'Neill as America's greatest playwright.

"Are you sorry you're turning the play into a novel?" she asked
with sudden trepidation.

"God, no. I feel great about it. Just sorry that I'm taking so long.
But another month or two and I'll be through with the polishing.
Then starts the search for an agent."

Carol's optimism soared when she read the novel. She understood now what Seth meant about switching from play to novel form
in a way that would make the characters come alive.

"Seth, it's all so visual," she told him.

"You work out blueprints, and the house is visual to you," he reminded. "That's why you're so good."

Then began the long process to find an agent to handle Seth's
book. First, a letter of inquiry had to go out—with Sharon suggesting possible agents. Then when an agent expressed interest, a copy
of the manuscript was sent. It was late fall before Seth had the first
interest—and then a fast turndown.

"The writing's fine," the agent wrote. "I'd like to see something
else by you. But this manuscript is just too controversial in these
times. Not commercial."

"It's not controversial—it's timely!" Carol railed. "The Supreme Court handed down a ruling. Segregation is illegal."

"Ask Sharon to recommend another agent." Seth refused to be angry. "I told you it wouldn't be easy."

Carol was waiting for the psychological moment to approach Jason about a raise to go with her new title at the company. No one in the firm was dealing with private residences except her. Repeatedly she told herself that Jason wouldn't dare deny her this raise. Their male architects earned almost double what she was paid.

Then right after New Year's, Jason announced that his nephew would be coming into the business.

"My sister's son," he told the staff he'd gathered together for a meeting. "A hotshot architect with a degree from Harvard School of Design and three years with a major firm out in Los Angeles. He's worked on houses for some of the big stars." He paused and mentioned three Hollywood names. "He'll focus for now on private residences." He ignored Carol's stare of dismay. "He'll start work Monday morning."

On sight Carol disliked Jason's nephew, Dennis Caldwell. He was about thirty, she judged, with sensuous good looks and a determination to charm. But for many women his good looks and charm would be marred by an air of arrogance. He'd expect to win over women clients by sexual appeal rather than talent. There was no doubt in Carol's mind that Dennis Caldwell would have first crack at major assignments in what had been her undisputed realm.

She had learned to cope with the firm's male staff—none of whom approved of a woman in architecture, though she'd earned their reluctant respect in the years she'd been here. But almost immediately she sensed she'd have problems with Dennis Caldwell, though not on a professional basis. He had a habit of dropping an arm about her, of touching, of mentally undressing her on those occasions when they happened to be alone at the office.

Only with Sharon did she discuss this unexpected situation.

"It's maddening that Jason just threw a plum assignment to him that should have been mine," she told Sharon on their monthly phone call in March—after a frustrated discussion about Seth's continued lack of a literary agent. "Of course, he may bomb out with this client—the word is that he's tough. But I didn't expect to have to fight off hands. Dennis must be ten years younger than me."

"You don't look almost forty," Sharon reminded. "You could

knock off a dozen years and people would believe you—if they didn't know about the kids," she added with a chuckle. "Or you could say you were precocious—pregnant at thirteen."

"He thinks he can get away with it. That I won't dare go running to Jason to complain." Carol churned with fresh anger as she remembered an encounter this morning. "He figures the job is important to me. And it is."

"Honey, you won't find a woman in business or the professions who hasn't run into one of those creeps—and they can be anything from twenty to ninety. When Dad was in the hospital last year for his prostate surgery, there was an eighty-three-year-old guy sharing his room. Dad said the character used to grab at the ass or tits of every nurse that came near him. If Dennis gets too rambunctious, kick him where it hurts most."

"I don't need that kind of problem." Carol sighed. "I just wish Seth could find himself an agent—somebody with good contacts. The book is so timely."

"You and Seth both know how slow these things are," Sharon consoled. "You'll find somebody."

Chapter Forty-three

The issue of desegregation was on every Georgian's mind in this first year of the new decade. In Atlanta—despite the outcries of a core of segregationists—local officials, the Chamber of Commerce, the newspapers, the school board and other organizations agreed with the mayor's demand that Atlanta be permitted to desegregate, though the state vowed to prevent this.

In February four Negro college students in Greensboro, North Carolina, began sit-ins at a local lunch counter. On March 9th in Atlanta a group of Negro college students formed a group and announced in local newspapers that they meant "to use every legal and nonviolent means at our disposal to secure full citizenship rights in this great democracy of ours." At the same time the General Assembly had passed a strong trespass law designed to halt sit-ins, and Governor Vandiver denounced the Atlanta students as "left-wingers."

Atlanta already braced itself for trouble when the court-ordered date for school desegregation would arrive in August, 1961. Then suddenly the Federal court ordered the University of Georgia in Athens to admit two Negro students, Charlayne Hunter and Hamilton Holmes—both of Atlanta—at the beginning of the winter quarter in January 1961. Georgians determined to accept the Supreme Court decision feared the efforts of die-hard segregationists when that day arrived.

After violent clashes between Seth and Harvey at family dinners, Hannah ordered that politics not be discussed. Like many Southerners their mother was in tune with Harvey, but desegregation was the law and—again, like many Southerners—she felt she must respect this.

In April Carol and Seth were excited when a New York agent wrote and expressed enthusiasm for Seth's novel. It appalled them that so much time had passed before they arrived at this point. Now the agent was submitting the novel.

"But don't expect a fast response," he warned conscientiously. "We might not hear for months."

Carol was upset that she was having a difficult time in avoiding Dennis Caldwell. Finally she forced herself to tell Jason that his nephew was being obnoxious.

"He's a young whippersnapper," Jason dismissed this indulgently. "These kids are another generation. They make a lot of noise, but they don't mean anything. You're taking what he says the wrong way."

There was only one way to take Dennis Caldwell's innuendos, she thought bitterly. And he just laughed when she told him to keep his hands to himself. Nobody on the staff other than Jason liked him. Everybody figured he'd soon be gone.

Their receptionist had quit after Dennis's first three months on the job. The receptionist hadn't said why she left, but everybody knew. Jason had hired a stern-faced sixtyish woman to replace her.

Where once she used to relish arriving at the office, now she dreaded yet another encounter with Dennis. He was becoming bolder, she reasoned, because he felt she didn't dare put up too much fuss lest she lose the job. But soon she discovered that Dennis was having a problem with his current client. Moments after Jason arrived this morning, he summoned both Dennis and her to discuss the situation.

"This is the kind of showplace that'll bring us important clients," Jason said portentously. "We can't afford to mess it up. I want the two of you to settle down and come up with something that'll please Tom Brooks. I promised the old bastard you'd have something to show him by next Monday. The three of us will meet with him at his office."

"He doesn't know what the hell he wants." Dennis was tense, fighting to conceal his rage. "Whatever we come up with he'll knock down."

"Dennis, I want this deal to go through." Jason turned to Carol. "This guy is one of the richest men in the South. He's getting married for the third time, and he wants to impress his bride with his new house. I told him you'd spent a year in Paris, studying at the Sorbonne." She was surprised that Jason remembered. "Give him something spectacular."

Carol hid her annoyance that she and Dennis were expected to consult on the project tonight. Jason told them to order sandwiches and coffee sent in. He had a dinner meeting with a client.

"We'll sit down tomorrow and discuss what you two have come up with," he said brusquely. "Just remember—nothing can be too expensive if it pleases the son of a bitch."

Carol phoned Bonnie and arranged for her to remain at the house until Seth came home. Then she made a quick call to Seth. If her raise came through—and with this project a success that would be definite—they could afford a larger house. Bonnie would be delighted to sleep in. That would make life easier all around. As usual when she had to work late, she felt guilty at not being at the dinner table with Seth and the children. That was a precious time for her.

At shortly past five Dennis appeared at the door of her small office.

"I'm ordering sandwiches," he said. "Let's get dinner—such as it is—out of the way before we caucus. What do you want?" He seemed self-conscious—almost defensive—at having to work in partnership with her.

"Chicken on rye and black coffee," she told him. She was uneasily aware that the others were beginning to leave for the day. *Wasn't anyone besides themselves working late tonight?* "Meanwhile, I'll go over Brooks's folder."

She forced herself to focus on the Brooks house and his list of complaints about what Dennis had suggested thus far. In her mind she was gradually building a profile of the man. She'd spent her lunch hour at the public library—poring over business and society pages of the *Atlanta Constitution* and the *Atlanta Journal*.

Tom Brooks had come originally from Dallas. He'd been an Atlanta resident for the past twenty years, but business took him out of town on a regular basis. She noted that his social life seemed to be similar to that of Diane Wallace. He was extremely wealthy without being of "old Georgia stock." He was often listed among the guests at Diane's posh parties. Instinct told her he'd want a house that telegraphed his wealth without being ornate or ostentatious. Now the house began to take concrete shape in her mind.

She was so engrossed in her notes that she started when Dennis appeared with the brown paper bag that contained her dinner. In the distance she heard the staccato click of a typewriter. Miss Miller had stayed late to type up a report, she thought with relief. She wasn't here alone with Dennis.

"Come into my office when you've finished eating," Dennis said. "Let's try to get out of here in a couple of hours."

She ate while she made further notes on the prospective Brooks house. Then she headed for Dennis's office. Miss Miller had stopped typing and was dropping the cover over her typewriter. The only lights on the floor now were those in her office, Dennis's office, the hall, and the small reception area.

"Good night," Miss Miller said briskly and reached for her purse.

"Good night, Miss Miller," Carol said, repressing a flurry of unease. *Damn, she didn't want to be here alone with Dennis.*

Dennis sat scowling over a first draft of the lower floor of the Brooks house.

"This is going to be a bitch," he warned Carol without looking up. He was anxious, she thought. That was good. He knew they had to come up with rough plans that would keep Brooks from pulling out. "What have you got so far?"

For over two hours they exchanged ideas, argued, plotted further changes in Dennis's plans.

"I think we've got enough to show Jason in the morning," Dennis at last said smugly. "And it's going to be so-o expensive," he drawled.

"I think Jason *and* Tom Brooks will be pleased." Carol rose from her chair, impatient now to be driving home.

"I'm pleased." All at once his eyes were sweeping over her. The message unmistakable. "What do you say we go somewhere and celebrate?"

"The only place I'm going is home," she said coldly.

"Come on, Carol—be human," he scolded and with one swift movement drew her close. "We're going to make this deal with Brooks work. Jason knows the old boy will take one look at you and melt." One hand fondled her rump.

"Stop it, Dennis!" She made a futile effort to release herself. This was absurd, she thought, fighting panic. "Let me go!"

"You're gorgeous when you're angry," he chortled, thrusting his hips against hers. His other hand made its way down the neckline of her dress. His breath was hot on her. "I've waited a long time for you."

"You'll wait forever!" She reached with one hand to grasp his wrist, with the other slapped him across one cheek.

"You little hot-blooded bitch—" His mouth came down hard on hers as he reached to lift her skirt.

"I left you two to work on a project." Jason's scathing voice broke into the heated atmosphere. "Not to play house."

In shock Dennis released her, gaped at his uncle.

"I realized I'd forgot my briefcase when I left the restaurant," Jason told Dennis.

"I told you what he was like," Carol gasped. "You wouldn't believe me!" she lashed at Jason.

"We've got a great proposal for Brooks." Dennis had recovered from his initial shock. "We were just celebrating."

"If you hadn't come in, he would have raped me," Carol told Jason. *Why did she keep trembling this way? It was over.*

"She led me on," Dennis drawled. "She wanted it as much as me."

"He tried to rape me!" Why did Jason refuse to meet her eyes? "You saw!"

"You led him on," Jason repeated Dennis's accusation. "What did you expect?" He smiled slyly. "Now go on home and forget about it.

We've got a meeting tomorrow morning at nine sharp. I want to see what you two cooked up for Tom Brooks."

"I won't be here." *How could Jason behave this way? He saw what was happening.* "I have too much respect for myself to take this kind of garbage. I'm through with this firm."

"You bet you're through," Jason shot back. "You're through in this town! I promise you—I'll see to that!"

Tears of rage blinding her Carol strode down the hall and out of the office to the elevators. When women went out into the business world, they were prey to monsters like Dennis—with asses like Jason backing them up. *When was that going to change?*

Carol drove through the sultry night—impatient at the distance to be covered before she was with Seth. How was she to explain her quitting? Seth would be furious if she told him the truth. Never a violent man, he might be provoked by this.

She had no recourse to file a complaint with the police; thanks to Jason's arrival she hadn't been raped. And who would have believed her if it had happened? Jason would have used his important connections to protect Dennis. It would have been her word against Dennis's.

She'd tell Seth that she was being unbearably humiliated by both Jason and Dennis, that they had only contempt for a woman architect. Now she sought for words to explain the situation to Seth. It wasn't the end of the world; she'd made some good contacts in Atlanta. Jason Gilbert couldn't stop her.

She'd open up her own office, she thought in sudden exhilaration. On a very small scale, of course—but she had credentials now. Already her mind churned with possible angles for success on her own. Was Diane Wallace still in town or had she left for the summer? Let Diane be in Atlanta, she prayed.

Carol Walden, Architect—she visualized the lettering on the door of an admittedly small office. She'd have to snare a client fast, she warned herself. For a moment she was intimidated by the expenses that lay ahead—with no salary at the end of each week. She was *good*, she reminded herself. To find a job as an architect a man had only to be good. A woman had to be outstanding.

When she arrived home, she found Seth reading in the living room. He glanced up with a warm smile when she appeared.

"I have a pitcher of lemonade out in the kitchen," he told her as he rose to his feet. "I wish this damn heat wave would let up."

"Shall we have it out on the porch?" she asked. They'd splurged on an air conditioner for each of the two bedrooms, but the rest of the house was like a cauldron.

"Sit on the porch and get bitten up by mosquitos?" he asked with a wry laugh. "Let's have it in our room."

While Seth went out to the kitchen, she changed swiftly into a short cotton nightie. She'd never wear this dress again, she promised herself in a surge of distaste. She'd thought she had gained control of her emotions in the long commute home, but the memory refused to be pushed aside. She shuddered in recall as she felt the ugly insistence of Dennis's mouth on hers and his hands—hot and perspiring—moving down the neckline of her dress and under her skirt. *She felt unclean.*

Haltingly—almost apologetically—she told Seth that she had quit her job.

"I hadn't meant to do it," she fabricated, "but both Jason and Dennis were giving me a rough time. Everybody in that office resents my being there. Jason was furious. He made it clear he'd never give me a good reference."

"So you'll go out on your own," Seth said and her eyes lighted. "You're terrific, Carol. You'll do well in no time at all."

"It'll be a drain on our savings," she reminded with fresh apprehension. "Rent isn't cheap in Atlanta office buildings—and we'll need Bonnie."

"We'll manage," Seth insisted, and she clung to this reassurance. "It's time you were on your own."

The next day Carol began the search for an inexpensive office. That evening she and Seth went with the children to have dinner with Seth's parents and grandmother. It was Leah's 84th birthday. It was impossible, Carol thought affectionately, to think of Grandmas as 84. Despite her arthritis—which caused some limitations— she was so active, regularly involved in local volunteer work.

Somewhat nervous about the family's reaction, Carol announced over dinner that she had left Arthur Gilbert and Son.

"So you'll manage," Hannah said encouragingly. "And it'll be good for the children to have their mother at home."

"Mom, the kids haven't suffered because she has a career," Seth said with a comforting glance at Carol. He knew that at intervals she felt guilty at not being home with Jonnie and Karen. "And the extra money has been great." His smile was meant to be reassuring.

"It's time to move out on my own." Carol tried to push aside unease. "I'm forty years old. It's time I moved ahead." Almost immediately she scolded herself for saying this. *Seth* was forty years old and still tied down to the shop. *When would the agent sell his book?*

"I think it's right for you to go out on your own," Leah said and Eli nodded in agreement. "Women today are making a place for themselves in the professions. That's the way it should be."

"Mama is one of the New Women," Eli said tenderly. "When no woman worked in Bellevue, she was there at the shop beside Papa. And he used to say she was the brains of the business."

"I worked, too," Hannah reminded. "It was necessary," she emphasized. "But why should Carol have to make that long *schlep* to Atlanta every day? All right, Seth doesn't make a big salary—but you can manage," she told Carol. "Have a woman in once a week instead of full-time. Watch for the grocery specials. Why should you have to work?"

"Mom, I love my work," Carol said softly. "It's important to me. Jonnie and Karen don't suffer because I'm not always home. Five days a week they're at school. In the summer they play with their friends. I don't have to be there to put their lunch on the table. We have breakfast together every morning." Not entirely true—she had to leave for Atlanta midway through their breakfast. "We have dinner together every evening." Some nights she was stuck at the office—but not often.

"Carol, you don't have to defend yourself." Leah was firm. "You're a good mother."

Long after Seth was sound asleep, Carol lay staring into the darkness of their bedroom. She wasn't depriving Jonnie and Karen of a mother because she wasn't at their beck and call twenty-four hours a day. When they were together, they had her full attention—nothing intruded. *She was there when they needed her.*

Sharon was having a rough time, she thought sympathetically. She needed her job to survive. When Michelle was home from school with a cold, *she* couldn't take time off from the job. *She* couldn't afford to pay for responsible child care. And her mother's health was uncertain these days. She couldn't ask her to rush into the city from the Island to look after Michelle. She had to park Michelle in front of the television set and call her every two or three hours to be sure Michelle was taking her medication, drinking her fruit juice—whatever was necessary. And five nights a week she had to rush home and make dinner for Michelle and herself.

Jonnie and Karen were *not* deprived because their mother was pursuing a career. Her work made her a better mother, Carol told herself defiantly, because she was a fulfilled woman. And her financial contributions helped provide a more comfortable life for them. Didn't Eleanor Roosevelt say—back in the Depression days—that we lived in a two-pocketbook society?

So why did she feel guilty because she was a working mother?

Chapter Forty-four

Carol focused on opening up "Carol Walden, Architect" as soon as possible. Her every waking moment seemed peppered with trepidations about Jason's efforts to sabotage her new firm. She rented a tiny office in a prestigious building—groaning at the monthly rent—because a good address was important. She sent out hand-written notes on lovely stationery to people with whom she'd worked during her years with Jason.

She kept reminding herself that the first commission on her own would be the hardest but grew impatient and anxious when her phone remained silent. She had to go out and rustle up business, she ordered herself, fighting against panic. She couldn't wait for it to walk in.

What was happening with Tom Brooks's proposed house? Had Jason and Dennis held on to him? She and Dennis had done just one night's work together—much more had been needed to design the house she visualized.

With sudden determination she reached for the phone and called Diane Wallace. From following the society pages of the Atlanta newspapers she knew Diane was in town despite the heat. Diane had said that she was free to show her home to a prospective client who might want to see a "Carol Walden house."

"Yes!" Carol told herself with soaring conviction. Talk to Diane—explain the kind of help she needed at this moment.

"Darling, I was so excited to see that you're moving out on your own," Diane greeted her warmly. "Is there anything I can do to help? Show my house any time you like," she urged again.

"I was wondering—do you know if Tom Brooks is staying with Jason?" Carol said, struggling to sound casual. "I knew they were not seeing eye to eye on the designs for Brooks's new house—"

"Well, let's find out," Diane purred. "Why don't I have Tom, you and your husband and another two couples for dinner on Thursday evening? Joe's out of town on business, and I've been so bored. I know it's short notice, but with so many people away for the summer, entertaining is very informal."

"Diane, that would be wonderful!" She'd have to go out and buy something smart, she pinpointed, but it would be a business investment. Seth still had one really good suit that he wore on special occasions. "If he isn't committed, I know I could design a house he'd love."

"I'll call around and get back to you," Diane promised. "Joe always says there's no better place to do business than at a good dinner party."

Carol was astonished that Seth felt uneasy about going with her to Diane's party.

"Do you really want me to go?" he asked.

"Of course I do. Diane took it for granted you'd come with me."

"I never know what to say to important people," Seth said wryly. "Especially when I know how much this means to you."

"Seth, people always like you. Even when you're getting passionate about some cause they don't like," she joshed.

"I won't talk about desegregation," he said, chuckling. "Cross my heart."

On Thursday evening she and Seth were the first guests to arrive. Taking advantage of this Diane gave Seth a guided tour of the house Carol had designed for her.

"Carol, that dress is exquisite," she approved, inspecting the line-for-line copy of an Yves St. Laurent bought at Rich's two days earlier. "And you didn't tell me," she scolded, turning to Seth, "that your husband was so good-looking."

Then all at once the other two couples were arriving and Diane was involved in introductions—making a point to stress that Carol was just opening her own architectural firm.

Tom Brooks arrived twenty minutes late and full of apologies. He'd flown down to Miami on business and had been delayed on his return because of motor trouble.

"I thought when I bought a plane for the company all these delays would be avoided—but today it was Murphy's Law all the way."

Diane had placed Seth at her left and Tom Brooks at her right, with Carol seated beside Brooks.

"I'm so excited that Carol has decided to move out on her own," Diane said enthusiastically to Tom as her houseman and a maid began to serve in the beautifully air-conditioned dining room.

"And what does that mean?" he asked Carol.

"I'm an architect," Carol explained. "I've just left Jason Gilbert." Her smile was disarming, deferential. "I don't mean to put down Jason, but we differed too much in our concept of the perfect house."

Tom grinned. "I've just left Jason Gilbert, too. He couldn't bring in anything that was right for me."

"Carol designed this house for me," Diane told Tom. "I threw a fit over the male architect he was trying to shove down my throat—and then, bless her, he sent Carol to me."

Before the dinner party was over, Carol knew she'd landed her first commission. Diane had conducted her guests through the Wallace house—none of whom had seen beyond the dramatic living room and the elegant dining room. Tom Brooks was convinced that Carol Walden, Architect, was the firm to design his house. One of the other couples asked to talk about an extension to their present home.

So easy, Carol thought in towering excitement, she was being launched as a serious architectural firm. Tonight she was opening a whole new room of her life. She would design a house for Tom Brooks that would be a showplace. And the publicity the house would evoke would lend luster to her name. She'd waited a long time for success—but now it lay within her fingertips.

Carol spent much of her waking moments on the design for Tom Brooks's house. In the midst of showering, of preparing a late evening snack for the family, of sewing a button on a pair of Jonnie's slacks, some small detail would leap into her mind and she'd rush to make a note. Now she understood what Seth meant when he said a writer was subconsciously at work twenty-four hours a day: *"I wake up in the morning, and all at once a problem in plotting or character development is solved for me."*

All three Walden households were involved in the coming presidential election. All were staunch Democrats but uneasy about the Kennedy Catholicism, which had done in Al Smith in 1928.

"If a Catholic makes it," Harvey said with the pompous air that set Carol's teeth on edge, "then he's paving the way for a Jew."

When Kennedy narrowly squeaked through, the country knew it was embarking on a new era. As of January 20th of next year the White House would be occupied by a young President and an even younger First Lady—both of whom exuded a glamour that had been much displayed by television. There was a fairy-tale quality with a touch of Hollywood in the new scene, Carol thought—not entirely impressed.

But she'd been pleased last month when candidate John Kennedy was reported to have arranged for Martin Luther King's release from jail on bail after being arrested for refusing to leave an "all white" restaurant in Atlanta.

"That'll buy a lot of Kennedy votes, particularly in the Northeast," Seth had predicted.

The mood in the country was that good times lay ahead. In addition to the Brooks house Carol had acquired commissions for two additions to houses in prestigious Buckhead, and by the approach of Thanksgiving another house seemed within her grasp. She would have to hire an assistant, she told Seth—simultaneously triumphant and wary. She would have been euphoric at this surge of success if they had not received word from Seth's literary agent that the publisher who'd held his manuscript for months had decided not to take it.

"A tough break," the agent wrote. "They loved the writing but were worried that the material was too controversial. But that's just one turndown. I'm sending it out again tomorrow."

In December Tom Brooks, about to leave for Rio on business, insisted she fly up to New York to bid on his behalf on a pair of chandeliers to be auctioned at Parke-Bernet.

"There's nobody else I'd trust to handle this for me," he said.

Carol knew Tom expected to be married shortly after New Year's, when his bride-to-be's divorce would become final. Tom him-

self had been divorced several years ago. While shopping chandeliers was hardly the kind of assignment an architect would be required to take on, Tom was making it worth her while.

"I'll only be gone three nights," she told Seth. "I'll fly out on
Monday morning and be back in time for dinner on Thursday."

"Stop fretting," Seth said. He was always able to read her mind,
she thought. "We'll be okay. And you'll have a chance to see Sharon
and Michelle."

Carol's face brightened. "I'm looking forward to that."

Tom's secretary arranged for her airline tickets, made reservations for her at the Plaza. On Monday morning his chauffeured limousine arrived at the house in Bellevue to drive her to the airport.
Settled on the plane, she remembered Jonnie and Karen's excitement about her trip to New York. Jonnie had hazy recall of the time
when he lived in Manhattan. Karen was too little to remember.

If business continued for her this well, she and Seth must take
the kids to New York on a vacation trip. They'd adore the zoos, the
dinosaurs at the Museum of Natural History, the Statue of Liberty,
the rides at Coney Island. For a few moments she was imprisoned
by nostalgia.

Perhaps, she dared to dream, she could persuade Seth to get out
of the store and concentrate on writing if her business continued to
thrive. His parents couldn't expect him to spend his whole life at the
shop. His father was there, his mother part-time now, along with
two clerks. They could hire someone to take Seth's place. But she
mustn't rush this, she warned herself. She must be sure of steady
earnings.

From LaGuardia she took a taxi to the Plaza. Sharon had been
shocked at the thought of her staying at a hotel until she explained
this was on her expense account.

"Yeah, you'll be a lot more comfortable at the Plaza than sleeping on the living room sofa," Sharon had conceded.

After checking in at the Plaza, Carol headed downtown for the
restaurant where she was to meet Sharon for lunch. It seemed to
her that New York was more hectic than she remembered—or was
she spoiled by the leisurely pace of life in Bellevue? Yet she found
an aura of excitement in walking the city streets, a sense of having
come home.

In addition to the auction at Parke-Bernet Carol was pursuing
the ultimate in plumbing fixtures for Tom Brooks's new house—

which would be a surprise for his bride. The new Mrs. Tom Brooks lived in Pasadena, had never visited Atlanta. She was a highly paid fashion photographer, Tom had said with pride, but was giving that up for domesticity.

On each of her three evenings in New York Carol met with Sharon and Michelle for dinner at a restaurant near their apartment. Afterward Carol and Sharon settled themselves in the living room of Sharon's apartment in the West Eighties while Michelle—angelically pretty at almost eleven—reluctantly retreated into the bedroom to do homework. The two women cherished these hours before Carol left for her hotel.

"God, I wish you were coming back to New York to live," Sharon said wistfully on their last night together.

"That's not likely," Carol admitted. "We don't know what kind of job Seth could land up here. He's getting a decent salary in Bellevue—and living down there is so much less expensive than up here. And I'd be starting out all over again; it could take a year for me to get a foothold."

"What about Seth and TV?" Sharon tried. "The blacklisting is gone forever."

"He wouldn't want to try TV again—and that's rough. Besides, he's sold on writing novels." She sighed. "I just wish he'd start on another while we're waiting for this one to sell. It's scary, the way the years go hurtling past."

"You're making real inroads careerwise," Sharon reminded. "I feel in such a rut with my lousy job."

"Have you considered going back for some courses in education?" Carol asked and then laughed. "I know, you used to say that was at the bottom of the list of what you'd like to do—but teaching is paying so much better these days."

"I'll stay with shitty Nat and his confession magazine and his 'tit' magazines," Sharon said after a moment. "I'm doing the work of three people—but that means Nat needs me. I feel secure." She sighed. "It ain't easy raising a kid on your own."

"You're doing a great job," Carol comforted.

"I just hope Michelle gets over this *shtick* about becoming a nun. Mom nearly *plotzed* when she discovered Michelle was in a parochial school. She'd die if she heard this bit about 'I wanna be a nun when I grow up.' "

"Michelle will decide on a dozen other things before she's eighteen," Carol comforted. "Right now Jonnie wants to be a newspaper reporter. I think his grandfather may have planted that in his head." She cherished the closeness between Jonnie and Karen and their grandparents—something she had not been privileged to enjoy. "And Karen's big ambition in life is to own a two-wheeler," she added with a chuckle. At this point Karen wanted to do whatever her brother did—and Jonnie rode his new two-wheeler at every opportunity.

As many Georgians had feared, the beginning of the new year created havoc at the University of Georgia in Athens, when two bright and determined Negro students arrived to enroll for the new quarter. Riots broke out in the town. Rabble-rousers gathered outside the dorm where Charlayne Hunter was to live and hurled ugly threats against the young student.

"What did they expect?" Harvey demanded. "They're trying to move too damn fast!"

While Harvey pretended to go along with the belief that since desegregation was the law, then the South must accept this, Carol suspected he was more in tune with the die-hard segregationists behind the riots. He was blatantly approving when Governor Vandiver had the two Negro students removed from the university "for their own safety" and ordered the school closed for a week. But before the governor could shove legislation through the General Assembly to thwart the enrollment of Charlayne Hunter and Hamilton Holmes, the Federal court ordered the university reopened and the two students reinstated. If necessary, the government would send in Federal marshals to insure their safety. The state government capitulated.

In Bellevue—as always—the residents took their cue from Atlanta. It was important that the public schools remain open—even if this meant desegregation. The first Negro students would be admitted in September of this year—1961. It would be a token enrollment, Eli pointed out, but it was a beginning.

With the Brooks house at last completed, Tom and his bride Gloria brought in a team of decorators, insisted on whirlwind furnishing. Finally in residence they gave a sumptuous party, with Carol as guest of honor. All Atlanta now knew that Carol Walden had become one of its top architects. Her office space had expanded to triple its original size. Before the party was over, Carol had scheduled half a dozen consultations.

Her career was soaring, Carol conceded, but Seth's couldn't get off the ground. They were impatient at his agent's failure to find a publisher for his book.

"Damn it, Seth, it's so timely," Carol railed, over and over again. "Why can't they see that?"

Still, she was relieved when Seth began to talk to her—as he always did when he was drawn into a new writing project—about a plot revolving around a family involved for generations in the munitions industry.

"The child of one son is killed in a hunting accident and all at once this son understands the havoc caused by the easy availability of guns. The family is split right down the middle with greed fighting reality. Look, we see right here what happens when just anybody can go out and buy a gun."

There was deep concern in the South that violence would erupt in the path of the newly formed so-called "freedom riders"—groups of Northern whites and Negroes traveling together to challenge segregation in interstate transportation. Ugly rumors circulated about the purchase of guns by outspoken enemies of desegregation.

"A strong story is the first necessity," he continued conscientiously. "A writer owes that to the reader—but at the same time I have this compulsion to zero in on critical issues."

"I've noticed," Carol teased.

"You're responsible for this, you know. The way you've always hated guns. The way you've talked about how in the United Kingdom guns are available only for sport—and that in the hands of only a few Britons." Seth chuckled reminiscently. "Jonnie was bowled over when you told him that in England the 'bobbies' don't even carry guns."

"Seth, write that novel. When the Second Amendment—giving people the right to buy and bear arms—was added to the Constitution, and was passed, the world was a very different place. The homicide statistics in this country are frightening. *Guns are too easily available.*"

"It seems crazy to start another book when the last one is going nowhere."

"It's not crazy," Carol said impassionedly. "You're going to make it, Seth. I know you will."

* * *

Late in August Carol and Seth—along with Jonnie and Karen—joined Elaine and toddler Timmy for a week at Sea Island. At the last moment Harvey had decided not to go to the rented cottage in order to work on his campaign for a seat on the Bellevue City Council.

"Harvey says he'll do whatever it takes to get on the Council," Elaine said somberly on their first evening on Sea Island. The three children were asleep and the three adults settled in cushioned chairs on the screened porch—a haven against pesky mosquitos. "He's determined to show my father he can do it."

"Knowing Harvey, I'll bet on his doing it," Seth said. "And your father's support will insure a lot of votes."

Carol knew Seth was sincere in hoping that Harvey won this first bid for political office, yet she sensed a hint of frustration in him that Harvey's future appeared so hopeful and his own uncertain. The competition between Harvey and Seth for their mother's approval never let up, she thought with simmering impatience.

"Harvey wants me to give a tea for women voters when we return to Bellevue," Elaine told them. "Will you help me, Carol? I'm so uncomfortable in these situations. So afraid I'll do something wrong."

"Of course, I'll help," Carol promised. Elaine was terrified of Harvey's anger, she guessed. What was there about him that kept Elaine in thralldom?

Carol had hoped that Seth would do some writing while they were at the cottage, but he never touched the portable typewriter they'd brought along. In some absurd way, she fretted, Harvey's race for the City Council seat was getting between him and the new book.

In October Harvey was elected to the City Council. It was generally agreed that his father-in-law's money and power had bought him that seat. Still, Harvey was triumphant and his mother ecstatic. Eli, too, was bursting with pride that Harvey had won. Only Leah seemed cynical about this success.

"He's getting too big for his breeches," she confided to Carol. "And that one will never be satisfied. He'll always be looking for something bigger. And it won't be Bellevue's good he'll be fighting for," she predicted. "It'll always be what's best for Harvey."

On the first night of Hanukkah, Carol and Seth went with the children to a dinner party at her in-laws. Hannah was self-conscious that Harvey had elected not to come.

"He has some conference with a client," she said. Carol guessed that Harvey didn't want to expose Timmy to his Jewish heritage—though he was surely too young to understand.

Tears of pleasure welled in Carol's eyes as she watched Jonnie and Karen solemnly flank their great-grandmother. They were absorbed in her lighting of the first candle of the Hanukkah season and saying the prayer that accompanied this. For the following seven nights they'd stand beside *her* as she lighted the number of candles appropriate for each night. And as happened on such occasions, she thought of her mother. Where was Mama these days?

Another year was almost gone, she thought, and felt a twinge of urgency that recognition still escaped Seth. It had been a year of explosive—and sometimes alarming—situations. There'd been civil war in Laos and in the Congo, Russian threats in Berlin, the ignominious "Bay of Pigs" misadventure.

This past October President Kennedy had declared that American families should build or have access to a shelter against fallout from a thermonuclear attack. He'd added that the U.S. Civil Defense should provide this for every resident of the country. Was this what their lives were to be like in the future? She gazed at the tableau of Jonnie and Karen hovering beside Grandma at the Hanukkah candelabra and was disturbed.

Seth and his family had brought her into the circle of her faith, she remembered with a surge of gratitude. Mama had been too engrossed in herself to observe her religion. Already Dad had taken on the task of arranging for Jonnie's instructions that would lead to his bar mitzvah at his thirteenth birthday. *Seth* had brought her the gift of family—and that was to be forever cherished.

Not until they were back in their own house and Jonnie and Karen asleep did Seth tell her he'd received a letter from his agent in New York this morning.

"I didn't want to spoil the evening for you," Seth said. "He's had another rejection. The usual shit about how the writing is fine but the subject matter uncommercial."

"But he's submitting it again?" Carol's heart was pounding. Each rejection was such a painful disappointment for Seth.

"He's still enthusiastic," Seth conceded and managed a weak smile. "Like you. But how much longer do you think he'll bother sending it out? It's time I was realistic. What I write publishers don't want to buy."

"Seth, that's not true!" she protested. "You just haven't found the right publisher."

"When will that happen?" he derided. "When I'm ninety?"

Chapter Forty-five

Carol knew that Seth disliked the society parties they often attended these days. He was impatient with small talk. She felt guilty that *she* found these stimulating. These were not parties given by "Old Georgia Families" but by the wealthy newcomers who lent Atlanta an exciting, cosmopolitan aura. Still, Seth realized these contacts were important to her, career-wise. Already she had extended her staff to include three additional employees.

She relished her success, worked hard and longed to build on this, yet it was ever unnerving that Seth was making no headway with his writing. He'd abandoned work on the new book. She retreated from efforts to encourage him to go on with it because each time he turned on her in anger.

"Stop trying to tell me how to run my life!" he finally yelled. "I'm not a puppet for you to push around!"

She wasn't a domineering wife—was she? She understood Seth was upset and frustrated, that he wasn't angry at her. Yet it seemed as though her success was an affront to him.

Seth took refuge in heated recriminations about the state of the country.

"Why are we spending billions of dollars to try to send a man to the moon?" he railed, "when there's such a need right here on earth? Every big city is desperate for low-cost housing. More money should be thrown into education. And what's this crap about our troops in Vietnam not being 'combat troops'? They've been told to fire if they're fired upon. In any language that's combat!"

At family dinners Seth and his father were apt to drag the conversation into politics. On the few occasions when Harvey was there he argued aggressively about the hazards brought on by the efforts to desegregate.

"Don't tell me about Martin Luther King," he said arrogantly. "Open your eyes to the damn young militants coming up! They want everything to happen yesterday! They'll throw this country into chaos before they're through."

In the late spring Tom Brooks's wife Gloria took Carol to lunch to talk about a new project she was considering. A professional woman for many years Gloria was bored, Carol interpreted—she needed something more demanding than a heavy social schedule.

"I don't want to talk to Tom about it until I'm sure the property up in Southampton will be right for the beach house I have in mind. I inherited it when an aunt died a few months ago. If you think it's right for a house where I can give rather large parties for Tom's business friends, then I'll spring the idea on him." Tom had the company plane at his disposal, Carol understood. Weekends at Southampton for Gloria and him were as simple as a weekend at Pine Mountain for most Atlantans.

With Gloria paying the tab, Carol took off for another brief trip—to New York and Southampton, on Long Island. While there was no way of knowing for sure that she'd be designing a house for Tom and Gloria at Southampton, Carol plotted to have herself registered as an architect in New York state. She must be ready to take on this possible assignment. It opened new professional avenues for her.

Carol arranged to be in New York over the weekend, so that Sharon could drive with her to the Southampton site. Again, at Gloria's expense, she stayed at the Plaza. It was easy to grow accustomed to the luxury life-style, she thought humorously. On a glorious May Saturday Carol and Sharon headed in a rented car for Southampton. Michelle was spending the day with a girlfriend from her new school.

"I hope Michelle understands that we don't have the kind of money the kids in that fancy school have," Sharon said, somber for the moment. "But when the parochial school insisted I move her out before the new term began, I didn't have much choice."

Carol recalled Sharon's anguish when Michelle faced one of two alternatives: withdraw from the school or face expulsion. She'd drawn outrage from the school when she'd organized a group declaring the rule that they wear uniforms was undemocratic and should be rescinded. Michelle's latest ambition was to be a rock star.

"How are you managing with that fancy tuition?" Carol asked solicitously. "I could help out a bit—" Seth would understand, she told herself. Her own income was climbing, despite the expenses of expanding the office and adding staff.

"I've used up my emergency money on this term's tuition," Sharon said. "But I have an angle that should see me through." She shook her head and chuckled. "Carol, you won't believe it. I just sold my first confession story. It's not much money, but if I keep it up it'll be enough to handle Michelle's tuition. I don't sell to myself," she said quickly. "That wouldn't be ethical. Not that Nat knows from ethical. Anyhow, I knocked out this little wonder and submitted it under Bev's name and used her address. I've been marinated in this stuff for years now—I just follow the formula."

"So you weren't an English major for nothing," Carol joshed.

"Seth will die laughing," Sharon predicted and paused. "He still hasn't gone back to the new novel?"

"I can't even talk to him about it."

"He feels isolated down there in the boondocks," Sharon sympathized. "He needs the stimulus of being with other writers. Maybe it's time for you to think again about moving back to New York."

Carol sighed. "I think about that often. I remember Seth's excitement about writing when we were in the city. But there's the financial problem. Seth is drawing a regular salary in Bellevue—and my income is really taking off. I don't know how either of us would do in New York."

"But you're registering as an architect in New York," Sharon pointed out. "You've got this possible commission out in Southampton. For you it might not be a tough leap." *But what about Seth?*

"I worry about moving the kids into a new area; they've got their lives down there all mapped out. I know," she hurried to anticipate Sharon. "The city is rich in advantages. But you'd be amazed at what Atlanta has to offer these days—and it's barely an hour away. And I worry about depriving Jonnie and Karen of family. Sharon, you know how important that is."

"I think you've come to like living in Bellevue," Sharon twitted. "You've succumbed to the easy life-style."

"I'm greedy," Carol confessed. "I'd love to be able to spend some time every year in New York—but yes, I'd miss Bellevue. I'd miss Mom and Dad and Grandma. But I wouldn't miss Harvey," she said wryly. "He makes Seth feel so low—and of course, in Mom's eyes Harvey is a *wunderkind.*"

Halfway to Southampton they stopped for coffee. Carol pulled out the map of the town that Gloria had given her and studied the locale of the property she was to inspect. It was right on the ocean, she recalled with approval—her mind already focused on a design that would fit Gloria and Tom's life-style.

Once in Southampton they sought directions to the property. Carol recognized that this project—if Tom could be persuaded to go along with it—could lead to other commissions in the resort town. With commercial planes making the trip between Atlanta and New York in around three hours, she could handle work in Southampton, she reassured herself. Seth had seemed rather taken aback by the whole situation, she remembered uneasily.

Stopping twice to ask directions, Carol finally located the property. She and Sharon left the car and walked the perimeter of the oceanfront area. It was an impressive piece of real estate, she thought, and reached into the pocket of her slacks for notebook and pen. Already ideas were flooding her mind. The house must blend with the magnificent view of the Atlantic, but at the same time it must provide for luxury entertainment.

"Oh God, it's gorgeous here!" Sharon said as they strolled along the pristine beach. "Wouldn't I love to be rich enough to have a house out here!"

"That's the one thing I miss down in Bellevue," Carol mused. "Access to the ocean. The Chattahoochee River just doesn't do it."

They drove into town again, paused for a late lunch before heading back to New York. Most of all, Carol thought, she'd enjoyed walking—shoes in hand because the sun had warmed the sand— along the stretch of deserted beach. Her mind shot back through the years to that weekend at Rockaway before the war when Leo and Greg had been alive—and she wondered about Jerry and Matt and how life had treated them. For a while the "group" had been her family. Hers and Sharon's.

Back in Bellevue Carol waited eagerly for word about the proposed Brooks house at Southampton. While she was busy with other commissions, she was impatient to know that the beach house—already taking shape in her mind—was hers. She sensed she was on the threshold of an astonishing advancement in her career. Remembering Gloria's connections in the magazine field from her days as a highly successful photographer, Carol suspected that the Southampton house would garner a spread in *Architectural Digest* or *Town & Country*. And Gloria would make sure the architect's name would be mentioned.

She'd sat down and discussed the situation with Seth. He realized that she would have to fly up to Southampton for a few days each month while the house was in construction. He said he could handle that.

"But don't build yourself all up on this deal until the word comes through that it's definite," Seth cautioned.

But it was Seth who told the family about the proposed beach house, Carol thought indulgently. He was always so proud of her. She suspected that Hannah disapproved. To her mother-in-law, this smacked of abandonment of husband and children. Hannah couldn't deal with the new demands women were making of their lives.

Not until late August did Tom Brooks finally agree to build in Southampton—a huge, expensive house that would be a masterpiece, he stipulated. And a gem for her portfolio, Carol exulted. It was important to move quickly in order to enclose the house before the winter weather set in. She was relieved that she had not waited for Tom's approval. On "spec" she'd gone ahead to work on the design—with Gloria's secret approval of each step.

"Seth, you have vacation time coming," Carol said on the evening she came home to report the "go ahead" had come through. "The kids don't start school until late next month. Why don't we rent a cottage for two weeks and go up there together?"

"Won't it be terribly expensive?" Seth seemed uneasy. Carol knew he was uncomfortable that her income so far surpassed his own. She tried to make him understand that their money went into one joint pool, that it didn't matter who was the major earner.

"It'll be off-season. And we won't rent in Southampton itself. We'll look for something in Wainscott." She remembered the weekend years ago when she'd gone with Sharon and Jerry to Wainscott to close up Vic Blair's cottage. "Seth, it'll be such fun."

As Carol anticipated, Jonnie and Karen were ecstatic at spending two weeks in the tiny house—right on the beach—that she'd rented. Sharon came up with Michelle each weekend. Carol enjoyed seeing the three children together. In some ways, she mused, Michelle was so much more sophisticated than Jonnie and Karen—but the three of them loved Bob Dylan and the Beatles, "Gunsmoke" and "Twilight Zone."

Seth seemed to relax here, Carol thought with pleasure, and she was able to work intensively each midweek day with the contractor and his quickly assembled crew, then spend lovely evenings with the children and Seth.

While the children slept each morning, she and Seth rose to watch the sun rise over the ocean in glorious splendor. They had breakfast together on the ocean-facing deck. Then she climbed into the car for the short drive to the construction site in Southampton.

Sun-kissed and relaxed, they returned to Bellevue to find a letter from Don Taylor—Seth's agent—waiting in the mailbox. Eagerly Carol read over Seth's shoulder.

"I still think it's a terrific book," the agent wrote, "but there just seems to be no takers. I feel it's a waste of time to submit it anywhere else. The consensus is that the subject is not commercial. I'll be happy to take a look at anything else you might have on the fire. Try, Seth, for a commercial subject."

Carol had expected Seth to be painfully depressed by his agent's reluctance to resubmit the book to other publishers. But she knew this was a crucial point in Seth's life. She geared herself for angry arguments with him—upset, though, when Jonnie and Karen happened to witness these unfamiliar flares between their parents.

"Seth, you've got to be practical," she said with new desperation. "Publishing is a business. Break through with one book, and they'll be lining up to buy this one. Seth, you're so good!"

"So good that nobody wants to publish me!" he shot back.

"You *can* be commercial," she insisted. "I'm not telling you to write formula fiction. But look around, find a subject that you can sink your teeth into but that will strike a responsive chord in the minds of editors." They'd both conceded the book he wanted to write about the munitions dynasty wouldn't be "commercial." "Seth, you can do it—*you have to go that extra mile.*"

Their eyes clung. Carol's heart was pounding. At this moment Seth wasn't fighting her.

"Let me think about it," he said warily.

She was making inroads, she told herself in relief. Please, God, let Seth be practical. He had to realize that publishing was a business. Later—once he'd made a breakthrough—he could write what he wanted.

She made no further efforts to prod Seth into launching another book, though she waited anxiously for word from him. She knew he would come to her when he was ready. But the weeks were hurtling past, and she prayed for Seth to find a subject—and a plot—that would excite him.

As always they went to her in-laws' house for Thanksgiving. At 86 and despite her arthritis, Leah insisted on preparing dinner herself. Hannah was allowed to make a pumpkin pie and Carol a pecan pie.

On this Thanksgiving—for the first since his marriage—Harvey was at the table with Elaine and Timmy. He exuded an almost overbearing smugness in his recent election to the Georgia General Assembly. Carol saw how Hannah's eyes kept dwelling on Harvey with a tumultuous blend of pride and love. Seth, too, noticed, she guessed unhappily.

As usual, the conversation had settled into a heated exchange on politics by the time Hannah and Carol were serving dessert. Seth and his father were contemptuous of reports that a weak attempt was being made to establish a chapter of the John Birch Society in Bellevue.

"Those people are off their rocker," Eli said. "For four years now they've been spreading their ugly message around the country."

"Even the Senate has expressed concern about the John Birchers," Leah contributed. "Look at the people they've labeled Communists. Harry Truman, FDR, Eisenhower—"

Carol knew when Seth didn't join the volatile conversation that followed—with Harvey defending the Birch Society as "concerned conservatives"—that he was remembering the horrific days when McCarthyism ruled. She wasn't surprised when later that evening—as they prepared for bed—he told her what he planned as his next book.

"Carol, I'm not going to write about the John Birch Society," he told her. "That would be almost like elevating their importance. But I'm going to take *Danger Signal* and rewrite it as a novel. The story line is strong—and God knows, the Birch Society makes it timely. It should be commercial."

Carol spent the next weeks wrapped in a new euphoria. Seth

was back on track. Every free moment he was at the typewriter. She toyed now with the thought of suggesting that he take time off from the shop—go in to work three days a week instead of six.

Dad could hire somebody to fill in for Seth those three days. Then Seth would have a stretch of unbroken time each week to work on the book. Right after New Year's she'd try to talk to Seth about that, she promised herself, exhilarated by this decision. It had been so long since she had seen Seth this absorbed in his writing. It was a new beginning for him.

On the first Sunday morning of the new year, Carol awoke to the sound of the phone ringing. Seth was still asleep. She pushed aside the blankets, slid her feet to the floor. It was barely 6 A.M. Probably a wrong number, she guessed as she reached for her robe at the foot of the bed. The morning was raw and cold, she thought while she hurried to respond to the insistent ringing.

"Hello—" She tried to clear her head, still fuzzy with sleep. They really should put an extension in their bedroom.

"Carol, something has happened." Leah's voice was shrill with alarm. "Eli woke up with a terrible pain in his chest. Hannah said he keeled over before she could even call me. I phoned for an ambulance—Hannah went with him. I stayed behind to call you and Harvey. Will you and Seth come over and take me to the hospital?"

"We'll be there in five minutes," Carol promised, her heart racing. "We'll dress and come right over. *He'll be all right, Grandma.*"

Chapter Forty-six

In anguished silence Carol and Seth rushed to pick up his grandmother, then drove through the early Sunday morning to the small Bellevue Hospital. Not waiting for the elevator they charged up the stairs to the second floor, where—a nurse had told them—Eli had been taken.

Hannah sat white-faced and numb in a chair in the reception area while a solicitous nurse hovered over her.

"He's gone—" Her voice was anguished and disbelieving. "He never opened his eyes again. How could it happen so fast? Why?"

The nurse whispered quietly to Carol that a doctor had given Hannah an injection. Seth was holding his ashen grandmother in his arms.

"How could Eli go before me?" Leah sobbed. "It's wrong that a mother should survive her child. Why wasn't it me? What did my baby do to deserve this? It should have been me—not Eli!"

The next forty-eight hours were chaotic, unnerving. Hannah and Leah were inconsolable, carried through the trauma of Eli's death by merciful medication. Friends moved in and out of the house in poignant sympathy. Everything was on Seth's shoulders, Carol thought in silent rage at Harvey—who made no effort to help with the myriad details involved in sudden death.

Remembering Gil's death and Sharon's debate about having Michelle attend the funeral, she told herself that Jonnie and Karen were old enough to understand what was happening. Let them have this final memory of their grandfather. With a twinge of pain she considered Jonnie's disappointment that his grandfather—who'd so looked forward to the event—would not be there at his bar mitzvah in July.

Later she was comforted by her decision to have the children attend both the services at the funeral home and at the cemetery. On this day it was clear to the family how loved Eli Walden had been by those he called "my colored friends." They came to the funeral home. Some came to the cemetery—all with grateful words about "Mr. Eli, who was such a fine man."

"I didn't know how important Dad was to the colored community," Seth confided to Carol as they lay sleepless in bed the night of the funeral. "Did you hear what they said about him? How he was never too busy to help them when they were in trouble—to advise them, comfort them. I knew he was respected by them—I didn't know how he was loved."

"It was a beautiful tribute, Seth," she said softly.

"That's how Dad was able to survive," Seth said. "He never had a chance to make it as a journalist—his Big Dream—but he gave of himself to people around him, and that made his life worthwhile."

Hannah struggled to pull her life together in the weeks ahead. Leah was stoic, clinging to family.

"Eli would want the family to go on with their lives," Leah said determinedly, arranging a family birthday party for Karen, now ten. Elaine and Timmy would be there, Carol remembered, though Harvey would be away from town at some political meeting. "And in July we'll celebrate Jonnie's bar mitzvah. Just family," she stipulated and tears welled in her eyes. "How Eli had looked forward to that day."

Carol forced herself to recognize that for now Seth had replaced his father in the business and in the family. His mother and his grandmother had become his responsibility. Neither he nor Carol had any illusions about Harvey's sharing this responsibility.

Now, too, Carol became aware of the family financial structure. Leah owned the house. At her husband's death the business became a partnership between herself and Eli. Now Hannah was a copartner of the business with her mother-in-law. Leah was outspoken.

"Seth, you make the business decisions," she said firmly. "Your mother and I put everything in your hands."

It appeared a death-knell to Seth's writing, yet Carol vowed this would not happen. For a while he'd be totally involved in keeping the business afloat, she recognized, but once he had this in control, Seth must go back to the new book.

Already the shop was causing the family some concern because of neighborhood changes. Three months ago there had been a holdup. Other shops in the area had since been robbed at gunpoint. Harvey had been outraged, blaming this on "fanatical young Negroes wanting to move too fast." He declared his mother should not be working in the shop even on a part-time basis.

"She won't be hurt in broad daylight," Seth protested. "Mom needs to be busy. What good will it do for her to sit at home and mope?"

Carol was flying up to New York twice a month to keep an eye on the Brooks's house. She confessed to Sharon that she welcomed these brief escapes. She was upset by Seth's grim determination to focus entirely on the shop for now.

"He hasn't touched the new book since Dad died," she told Sharon on one of their quiet evenings together while Michelle focused—somewhat belligerently these days—on homework. "He was excited about it before—"

"Is he worried about the business?" Sharon asked.

"He doesn't say as much, but I think he does worry. I mean, that's all Mom and Grandma have to live on—except for their tiny Social Security checks."

"Is business bad down there?"

"Seth doesn't talk about it," Carol said, fighting exasperation. "I know the neighborhood is getting rundown. In its way Bellevue is like Atlanta—whites are running to the suburbs. The shop always had a heavy colored trade—but that's all it has now."

"With the way Seth's tied down, I assume there's no chance of your moving back here."

"No chance," Carol said. "I could live with that if Seth was writing. I can't bear to see him push aside what's so important to him. I'd been hoping—before Dad died—to persuade him to work three days a week, focus on the book the other four. But, of course, that's out the window now."

With the Brooks house almost finished, Carol acquired another New York commission. If this continued, she thought with a surge of enthusiasm, she might have to open a branch office in the city. But she worried about Seth. How could she help to relieve the pressure on him at the shop?

She tried to involve Seth in some of Atlanta's admirable cultural life, but this he resisted. Then she concentrated on drawing him into the volatile desegregation struggle. Most of the Atlanta restaurants—in a deliberately quiet fashion—had desegregated. Many Atlanta businessmen realized that the city's future could be endangered if racial problems persisted, yet there was a core of Atlantans who vowed to resist desegregation. Nineteen sixty-three was shaping up as a troublesome year.

Ever sympathetic to minority problems, Seth allowed Carol to bring him into a local group that was trying to desegregate Bellevue's few restaurants. But on discovering this Harvey was furious.

"Look, it's tough enough to be a Jew in Georgia politics," he confronted Seth at a family dinner in the early summer. "I can't have our name mixed up in this 'Northern liberal' group. I'm running for reelection next year!"

"You're running for reelection—not me," Seth pointed out. "The group may have some Northern liberals," he admitted with a smile. Even Bellevue was becoming more cosmopolitan these days. "But we have a lot of liberal Georgians, too."

"I need every vote I can get," Harvey said through clenched teeth. "Damn it, back off!"

"Seth, don't help folks who're making things difficult for your brother," Hannah interceded. "The family should support him."

"It's good for you to have a brother who's in the Assembly," Harvey said with an air of superiority that flavored his relations with Seth and Carol. "You know how important the right contacts can be."

"Seth has a right to think for himself." Carol struggled to hide her anger. "We both believe it's time for Bellevue to respect the law."

"All you think about," Harvey shot back, "is where you'll pick up your next commission. What does family mean to you?"

"Harvey!" Elaine was embarrassed by his accusation.

"Enough of this," Leah ordered. "Times are changing—and we all have to accept that. Even your fancy friends, Harvey. If we don't accept changes peacefully, we'll see some ugly situations. None of us want that." Leah turned to Carol. "Tell the kids to come into the dining room." Jonnie and Karen had gone out to play ball with Timmy. "I'm putting dinner on the table."

In November the world was shocked by the assassination of President Kennedy in Dallas. For the fourth time in its brief history the United States had lost a president to an assassin's bullet. Vice-President Johnson was sworn in as President aboard *Air Force One* only two hours after Kennedy was pronounced dead.

The American public was vaguely aware that their government was committed to stopping the spread of communism in a country called Vietnam, its locale equally vague. President Truman had sent 35 military advisers to South Vietnam to stop a Communist take-over. Eisenhower had sent an additional 500. Kennedy sent 16,000, and recently approved their flying strafing missions. Now some Americans were becoming concerned with the country's involvement in the Vietnam conflict.

The arrival of New Year's, 1964, was a stark reminder to Carol that Seth had not worked on the new book since his father's death almost a year ago. The first book lay in a file drawer. How was she to motivate him again? she asked herself, feeling an agonizing helplessness.

The economy was supposed to be in great shape, she thought, though people constantly complained about rising costs.

"Costs aren't rising," Seth contradicted when they discussed this at the approach of Karen's eleventh birthday and the question of a birthday present arose. "People are just expecting so much more. I remember when I was eleven." He chuckled reminiscently. "I would have been happy to receive a good-looking sweater or a special new book for my birthday."

"When I was eleven," Carol recalled with rare bitterness, "my mother forgot my birthday. It wouldn't have mattered if she hadn't—it was the Depression and she was concerned about putting food on the table."

"Mom has never forgotten the Depression days," Seth said. "The family managed to hang on to the shop and stay off welfare—but I don't think Mom has ever felt really secure since the stock market crash. So don't be surprised," he joshed, "if she's shocked that for Karen's birthday you want to buy a whole bedroom suite—an expensive one—for her room."

"We can afford it," Carol began, and paused as she saw Seth's face tighten. They could afford it because of her earnings—but not on Seth's salary. Why did it upset him that she was contributing more than he to the family income? "And Karen will be so pleased," she added defensively.

"Yeah," Seth agreed after a moment. "She'll love it."

He was angry and depressed that he wasn't writing; she understood that. He spent six days a week in the shop; when did he have time to write? He was caught in a trap. He knew he must keep the shop running for his mother and his grandmother's sake.

Fifteen years ago Mom could have handled the shop on her own, Carol told herself—but she was sixty-seven now and had worked all her life. And when Dad died, something had gone out of her, Carol thought. For all the ideological differences between them they'd been poignantly close. But why must all the responsibility fall on Seth? Why was Harvey always home free?

Racial tensions were showing little improvement this year, Carol conceded with unease as the months sped past. She was particularly upset when the local Ku Klux Klan followed Atlanta's lead and demanded the right to hold mass rallies in Bellevue's beautiful Courthouse Square.

"I thought the KKK was forever dead," she said plaintively to

Seth as they watched a television newscast that reported on the KKK demand.

"There've always been a few rabble-rousers who'll drag out that dead horse," Seth predicted. "That handful of people who can't erase hate from their souls."

"The kind of people the John Birch Society is rounding up," Carol said, frowning in distaste. "They keep growing, year after year. I read somewhere that there are chapters in thirty-four states now, with over a hundred thousand members." She hesitated, her mind leaping into high gear. "It's a rerun of the Joe Mccarthy era—and not just rabble-rousers are joining," she reminded passionately. "You saw that article from the *New York Times* that Sharon sent us." Hoping, Carol interpreted, to help prod Seth back to the book. "So-called responsible businessmen, doctors, lawyers, teachers are joining—"

"It's scary," Seth said somberly.

"I know you don't want to write about the John Birch Society," Carol said, "but *Danger Signal* is a strong warning against those creeps. I wish you'd get back to writing it as a novel."

"Would anybody want to read it?" he countered.

"Many caring people would want to read it," she said softly. "Seth, it's so timely." Her heart began to pound. They both knew the Russian roulette aspect of getting a play produced—but hadn't his agent stressed he'd try again with another book that was "commercial"? This was commercial.

"I suppose I'm crazy," Seth said after some deliberation, "but I *might* just take a stab at the novel again. It'll take a hell of a long time," he warned. "If I get up an hour earlier each morning, write for that hour, I'll make some headway. Slow, but that's better than stagnating."

"You can do it, Seth." Her face was luminous.

"How many times have you said that before?" But she saw fresh hope in his eyes.

Each morning now the alarm went off in their bedroom at 5:30 A.M. Seth lingered in bed for another ten minutes, then arose to prepare for his morning's stint at the typewriter. It was a rerun of the stretch when he'd emerged from his writer's block to begin work on the first novel. But this time would be different, she promised herself. This book would find a publisher.

* * *

Carol came face to face with her own horror of guns when Karen witnessed the killing of a family of raccoons by an irate neighbor.

"Mom, Mr. Norman picked up this gun and shot them, one after another," Karen sobbed. "Just because they knocked over his garbage can. They were so cute. Jonnie and I have been putting food on the back steps for them every night. It was awful! I hate him! I hate him!"

"He shouldn't have done that," Carol soothed. She dreaded the hunting season each year, when Harvey boasted about the animals he put down. Jonnie had been shocked when his uncle had offered to take him deer hunting. Harvey had done that, Carol guessed, because he knew how she detested hunting—anything to do with guns. Thank God, Seth recoiled from hunting as much as she.

"Mom, can Mr. Norman do that?" Karen challenged. "Can't they arrest him?"

"He won't be arrested," Carol admitted. "I'm sorry, darling, but there's nothing we can do about it."

Was there some ordinance that would fine Bud Norman for killing those poor little raccoons? she asked herself while she cradled her sobbing daughter in her arms. She could think of none. She just wished there was a law that kept guns out of the hands of irresponsible people like Bud Norman. If guns were not so available, the crime rate—escalating in Atlanta and spilling over into Bellevue—would drop. Accidents—like the six-year-old who killed his three-year-old sister in Bellevue last month—wouldn't happen.

Then in May the devastation brought about by guns came into clear focus again. For the first time Americans were taking to the streets to protest the nation's involvement in the war in Vietnam.

"Are we doing wrong to be fighting in Vietnam?" Jonnie asked earnestly while they watched the television news report on the demonstration. "Aren't we supposed to be against communism?"

"Jonnie, anything that kills people is bad," Seth told him. "We have to learn to deal with these situations at a peace table. That's why the United Nations was formed."

But the United Nations seemed ineffectual, Carol thought, recoiling from the vision of Americans at war—of any nation at war. She glanced at her troubled young son and remembered that he was fourteen years old. The prospect of his ever having to fight a war was shattering.

With the end of the school year approaching Carol talked to Seth about sending the children to camp for a month. Don't let him start worrying about the money, she prayed.

"All their friends are going to camp for a month," Carol explained, striving to sound casual. "Jonnie wants to be with his friends and Karen with hers. It's right near home—it's not as though they were going hundreds of miles away." She knew her mother-in-law would be upset at the thought of the children at a sleep-away camp. She'd envision all kinds of accidents. Seth had never gone to camp, but who could afford it when he was their age?

"Camp will cost a lot of money," he hedged. It wasn't just the money, Carol guessed tenderly. It was the prospect of Jonnie and Karen being away for a whole month. Neither had been away for more than an overnight visit to a friend's house. "They might get homesick—"

"We'll visit every Sunday," Carol promised. "Mom and Grandma can go up with us. It'll be good for them. You know how hot it gets here in the summer. They'll be up in the mountains near a lake. Besides, it's time for them to grow up a bit. Michelle's been at camp for three years now."

"Summers do get bitchy—even with the two air conditioners. Okay, if they want to go to camp, set it up for them."

"Seth, I saw a piece of property for sale about a mile out of town," she began impulsively. "The people are anxious to unload it. We could probably buy it for a song."

"What would we do with it?" Seth was startled—and wary.

"Don't you think it's time we stopped paying rent, built a house for ourselves? I could cut the costs like crazy with what I know. And it'll be a good investment." In a new house Karen would stop having nightmares about Bud Norman's killing helpless little animals.

"You figure with your business you can get a mortgage," he said.

"Seth, *you* can get a GI mortgage," she emphasized. "That's no problem. We could break ground early in the fall, move into the house by New Year's. We have a chunk of money sitting in the bank—let's put it to use. Oh, Seth, won't it be wonderful to have an air-conditioned house next summer!"

"I feel so useless." He shook his head in frustration. "I can't start drawing more money from the shop until I can show more profits. Right now it's a rat race to keep the profits what they've been. We've lost too many of our white customers with the neighborhood running down the way it is."

"Seth, stop drawing a line between what each of us earns. It goes into one pot. And one of these days—when the books start selling—you'll make my earnings look like baby-sitting money. Anyhow," she said softly, "we agreed long ago that real riches are family—and we're very rich in that."

Jonnie and Karen went to camp for four weeks. On their return they would go with their parents to a rented cottage in Wainscott for two weeks.

"Business is slow in August," Seth said with a show of guilt at taking time off. "And Mom inists she'll come in full-time while I'm away—that it won't be too much for her."

Mom thought it was insane for them to go all the way up to Long Island, Carol guessed. Harvey was buying a place on Sea Island, and they could go there and stay with Elaine with no rent to pay, Mom had pointed out twice. Harvey would be out there only for a week in July and another week in August.

Harvey's growing influence in Bellevue—and his growing affluence, Carol thought—were a threat to Seth's image of himself. He was the older brother—eight years older—who was "making nothing of himself."

Carol knew that the children would be delighted to go to Wainscott. They loved flying. They loved the ocean the way she and Seth did. And for Seth, she told herself, it was a two-week escape from the Bellevue trap.

She was pleased that Seth was taking along the portable typewriter she'd bought for his birthday. He meant to work at the Wainscott cottage. She herself would be driving into New York twice a week on business. And Sharon would come out for the weekends.

The cottage she'd rented this year was larger than the one they'd rented on their earlier trip here—and considerably more expensive. She'd debated about telling Seth how much it was costing them, then decided against this. She'd pay the rent from her business account. Seth never looked at this. Besides, the prices on everything were rising.

On the Friday before their first weekend at the Wainscott house, Carol had a long business luncheon in New York with a prospective client. They lingered for over two hours at the Russian Tea Room while the client explained what he expected of a planned new wing to his Southampton beach house. The spread in a recent magazine of the Tom Brooks house had elicited much interest in her work. She'd have to start thinking about setting up a branch office in New York, she told herself. "Carol Walden Architects, New York."

After lunch Carol drove to Sharon's office. Despite the craziness of her boss Sharon was insisting on leaving at 3 o'clock on the two Fridays when she would be going out to the Hamptons.

This summer Michelle was a "mother's helper" on Fire Island.

"She really wanted to apply for a job as a Playboy Bunny—now that she has breasts—but I said, 'Mother's Helper at Fire Island or you spend the summer in the city listening to your Beatles records.' So I'm a swinging single," Sharon bubbled.

Even this early in the afternoon Carol and Sharon discovered the eastbound traffic to Long Island was murderous. Still, both women enjoyed the drive. It was a chance for them to exchange reports on their current lives with the thoroughness both enjoyed. At the first slowdown in traffic—where they moved a few feet, stopped, then moved another few feet, in the typical summer symphony—Sharon clued in Carol as to Jerry's latest activities.

"I couldn't believe it," Sharon admitted. "I'm reading the movie magazine—because Nat is making noises about adding one to our roster—and suddenly I'm reading about Jerry's marriage."

"To some Hollywood name?" Carol asked in astonishment. At their traumatic encounter in the hospital all those years ago, Jerry had talked about going out to California.

"The daughter of some hotshot producer. It appears that our Jerry is now a screenwriter," Sharon drawled.

"After all his talk about never 'selling out to Hollywood'?" Carol jeered. "Remember how he talked about what awful things Hollywood did to writers?"

"He's doing what he was convinced he'd never do. He's becoming rich. Of course, he had to marry the boss's daughter to swing this," Sharon surmised. "I never had a chance. I didn't have a rich Hollywood producer father."

"You were never in love with Jerry. Any more than I was in love with Matt." Carol hesitated. "Anything new in your love life?" Sharon had been frank about a series of brief affairs.

"At the moment nothing. When a guy realizes he's dating a widow with a fourteen-year-old daughter, he gets wary. But in the meantime," she said, "I've had some great sex."

"What about something serious?" Carol asked gently.

"I don't think I'd want it, even if the opportunity came," Sharon said, serious now. "I think I'd be afraid to love again."

As Carol warned, the trip took an hour longer than normal because of the weekend traffic. Carol and Sharon dissected Betty Friedan's *The Feminine Mystique*, the new best-seller. Sharon remembered an article in *Time* last November that said that "nobody is more noisily dissatisfied these days than that symbol of stability—the fortyish housewife with teenage children and a reasonably successful husband."

"Neither of us could qualify as housewives now," Sharon said, "but wow, was I dissatisfied at thirty at filling that post."

When they arrived at the Wainscott house, they were pleased that Seth had dinner waiting for them. He summoned Jonnie and Karen from the beach, and after a lively greeting between Sharon and the kids, he served dinner—with Karen's help—on the sprawling deck.

"Oh God, the air smells so sweet out here," Sharon said blissfully. "And it's so quiet. Remember that crazy weekend, Carol, when you and I came out here with Jerry?"

"It seems a million years ago," Carol told her. "We were so *young.*"

"Oh Seth, I didn't tell you about Jerry!" Sharon said. "You won't believe it. He's a screenwriter in Hollywood—and married to the daughter of some big producer. I'll bet he wouldn't even talk to us now. Of course, I never forgave him for what he did to you and Carol."

"Does it matter?" Seth's smile was ironic. "Jerry's a Hollywood screenwriter now—and I run a seedy store in a bad section of Bellevue, Georgia."

Chapter Forty-seven

In the months ahead Carol clung to the knowledge that Seth was keeping to a grueling schedule of working an hour each morning on the new book. He seemed happier than he had been in years. That brief hour each morning, Carol thought, helped sustain him through the day.

She drew him into the excitement of watching their new house go up. He was enthralled with the lot she had finally chosen—a wooded acre with a magnificent view of the river. Much of the woods was being preserved, with towering weeping willows surrounding three sides of the house—the fourth side providing an unobstructed view of the water. She had designed a California-style house that brought in the outdoors through great expanses of glass. One wing contained a huge master bedroom suite with a fireplace, a cozy office for Seth and another for herself, and a private patio.

The house was completed on schedule. They moved in right after New Year's—and instantly, Carol thought with pleasure, it was home. Now she was about to open a small office—Carol Walden Associates, Architecture—in New York. Her one New York employee—thus far—would be a young woman fresh out of architectural school. It was simultaneously exhilarating and intimidating, the way her client list was soaring. But she knew that each new success was a taunting reminder to Seth that at almost forty-five he'd achieved so little in the field important to him.

Again, she yearned to buy time for Seth to devote himself entirely to writing. He could hire a manager for the shop, she told herself at regular intervals—yet she knew that both his mother and grandmother would be upset that the shop was in the hands of strangers. Hannah was obsessive about "only family at the cash register."

It was unthinkable, of course, that Harvey come into the shop. He was the Assemblyman and busy attorney. The "successful Walden brother," Seth pointed out at painful intervals.

"Take two weeks off and let's go up to Wainscott again," Carol pleaded when sultry summer descended once more on Bellevue. So it was expensive, she thought defensively. They could afford it. "You need to get away from the shop."

"Not this year," Seth hedged. "And we're air-conditioned here in the house. It won't be that bad. Take the kids and go for a couple of weeks," he encouraged.

"They'll both be at camp," she reminded—Karen as a camper, Jonnie as a junior counselor. "Though Karen's got permission to leave camp on Wednesday, August 18th. The Beatles will be in Atlanta, and she can't miss that," Carol derided affectionately. "Maybe I'll run out for a week with Sharon when she gets her vacation." She'd work that out to tie in with the house she was designing in East Hampton. "But it'll seem so strange without you."

"Yeah—" His smile was wistful.

"I won't be going just for a vacation," she said quickly. "I'll be working on the East Hampton project. I'd have to be up there anyway."

"Honey, don't sound so apologetic," he scolded. "You work hard. If you can manage to do it out in the Hamptons—hey, that's great."

"Did I tell you Jonnie has worked out a deal with his camp to do a weekly newsletter? Our son, the journalist."

"That would have pleased Dad. Oh, did you talk to Bonnie about her sleeping in?" Seth asked. Carol had designed their new house to provide a private guest suite, which would be perfect for a cherished domestic. "Or would she rather not?"

"She'd love it. I told her she'll have her usual time off, plus extra time when she serves dinner and cleans up afterward."

Carol was pleased at this arrangement. Now Seth could invite Mom and Grandma for dinner those times when she was out of the city on business without worrying about cleaning up. It was enough that he spent ten hours a day in the shop. Mom and Grandma loved coming to the house for dinner, but without Bonnie here they insisted on helping to serve and do the dishes.

The following afternoon Carol made a point of coming home early enough to miss the insane Atlanta rush-hour traffic that seemed to grow worse each year. She would drive Bonnie to her house to collect her belongings, she plotted. Bonnie was ecstatic about moving into the house—with her own little suite, her own television set. No family battle about what program to watch.

"Mom—" Karen charged out into the porch when Carol turned

into the driveway. "Bonnie said I could come along and see her folk's cats. They have seven of them!" Karen adored anything with four legs. They had neither cats nor dogs because Seth was allergic to them.

"Don't rush like that in this awful heat," Carol scolded as Karen hurried to the car. "Where's Bonnie?"

"Right here, Miss Carol," Bonnie sang out from the doorway. "We can't be long," she warned. "I have to take that roast out of the oven in fifty minutes."

At Bonnie's direction they drove into the colored section of Bellevue. She had forgotten, Carol thought uncomfortably, how squalid the houses were here.

Carol saw Karen's face grow somber as she inspected the tiny frame houses, most needing paint and other exterior repairs. But Karen was enthralled at meeting Bonnie's mother and the three sisters still at home, and—especially—the seven cats.

Not until much later—when her father dozed before the TV while he waited for the evening news—did Karen express her concern about the shanties that made up the black section of Bellevue.

"Mom, I've decided what I want to be when I go to college," Karen added seriously. "I want to be an architect."

"Darling, that's wonderful!" Carol was astonished. Karen had given no inkling that she might want to follow in her mother's footsteps. Carol envisioned the new name—in time—on her Atlanta offices: Walden & Walden, Architects. No mother, she exulted, could wish for a higher tribute from her daughter.

"I know how rough it is for women," Karen conceded. She'd heard enough about *that,* Carol thought ruefully. "But it's what I want to be. I don't want to do big, gorgeous houses," she said intensely. "I want to do houses for poor people to live in. Nice houses that'll be comfortable and pretty. You're always saying how Atlanta—and Bellevue, too"—she added with a conscientious nod of her head—"has such a need for low-income housing. Somebody has to build them. I'd like it to be me someday."

"That's a fine ambition, Karen."

Carol felt tears fill her eyes. She thought regularly about the need for low-income housing, but she did nothing in that direction. It was time for her to give back a little. But how—and when?

* * *

"Don't faint when Michelle meets us," Sharon warned when they met on Carol's first evening in the city. "She came home three nights ago with her hair cut." Up till now Michelle's hair had hung to her waist, had been Sharon's admitted treasure. "She's got a shingle now—and bangs like an old English sheepdog. You know, that 'new look' from London that some hairdresser named Vidal Sassoon cooked up."

Carol tried to conceal her shock when Michelle joined them. After their customary warm greeting Carol made the required comment about Michelle's Mary Quant-inspired minidress that rose precariously above her knees.

"You look so grown up," Carol told her, and Michelle glowed.

"Mary Quant doesn't know women with breasts," Sharon said with a shrug. "On Michelle figure-skimming dresses look almost indecent."

Over dinner at the Russian Tea Room Michelle was very vocal about (1) her participation in peace demonstrations (2) her fascination for the new "folk rock" and Bob Dylan and (3) her ambition to become the first woman to walk in space.

"Karen wants to be an architect," Carol reported, "and Jonnie wants to be a journalist."

"That's this year," Sharon warned. "How do we survive the teens?"

The next morning Michelle left for Fire Island and her summer job as a "mother's helper." Carol and Sharon would drive out to Wainscott the following evening. As always Carol enjoyed the time spent with Sharon. Each night she phoned home to talk with Seth. Sharon explained there was no way to phone Michelle at Fire Island.

"When she feels the urge, she'll go down and call me from one of the public phones near the dock," Sharon said blithely. "This is my time—I refuse to worry about anything."

The fall of 1965 saw more protests about the war in Vietnam. Carol was unnerved that the military draft had been increased from 17,000 a month to 35,000. Jonnie was only fifteen, but she rebelled at the prospect of his being subject to the draft in three years.

President Johnson had announced that crime prevention was one of the country's most serious problems and would receive priority attention. Pope Paul VI came to New York and in an address before the UN General Assembly pleaded for peace. For two days in October demonstrations against the country's participation in the Vietnam War were held in cities across the country.

It upset Carol that Jonnie was so impressed when a student at a demonstration in Atlanta burnt his draft card. She didn't want him to have to worry about such things as fighting in Vietnam. Wasn't it enough that his father had fought in World War II? She had recurrent nightmares about Jonnie in military uniform and with a gun in his hands.

Early in the New Year Harvey told the family that he would, of course, run for another term in the Assembly, though he made it clear he was thinking ahead to a seat in Congress. He felt hemmed in by state politics.

"How much time does the Assembly require of me?" he said derisively. "We go into session the second Monday in January—and forty days later, it's over. Oh, pardon me—forty-five days in odd-numbered years and forty in even-numbered years." But the role was important to his career as attorney.

Harvey moved within Elaine's lofty social circle, yet he always felt himself an outsider. He resented the condescension always present in his in-laws. Gradually he was building a new circle for himself and Elaine. Atlanta was the focus of his major socializing now. He relished the cosmopolitan atmosphere of Atlanta, the company of very wealthy business executives who had moved their corporations into one of the most progressive and exciting cities in the country. He was acquiring important, top level CEOs as his law clients. His fees were soaring and—more importantly—he was building the power base he craved.

In early March Harvey arranged a small dinner party for the head of a corporation recently moved to Atlanta and whom he sought as a client. He was annoyed that his father-in-law had accepted an invitation with candid annoyance. Elaine had insisted her parents attend—because Harvey had made it clear he'd be furious if they didn't. Drawing two million a year from his corporation, Carter Holmes was eager for acceptance by "Old Georgia Families."

Holmes would never be accepted by the likes of Elaine's father, he thought realistically as he finished dressing for the dinner party—but the fact that *he* had introduced Holmes to "Georgia aristocracy" would put him in a good light. With all his money, why did Carter Holmes *care?*

"You asked your father and mother to come early, Elaine?" He wanted a few minutes alone with the old man to feel him out about a run for Congress in '68. You had to work ahead.

"They'll be early," Elaine promised with a conciliatory smile. "I told Mother I wanted to show her the dresses I bought in Paris last month."

"Talk about that with Carter Holmes's wife," Harvey ordered. "I hear she's a clotheshorse." He'd told Elaine to fly to Paris for a four-day shopping spree when he learned about Lila Holmes's passion for couture clothes. He planned every step in a campaign, he thought smugly. Like marrying Elaine. That had been smart. She'd been brought up to be the perfect hostess; she handled the role to perfection.

"Do the Holmeses have children?" Elaine intruded on his thoughts.

"Two in college," Harvey told her. "Ivy League. But I gather they grew up in boarding schools; she's not a doting mother." He knew his sarcasm was clear to Elaine. She made such a damnable fuss about the kid.

"Is this dress all right?" She was always a bit insecure—a trait he approved.

"You look great," he told her.

When he heard his in-laws arrive, Harvey hurried downstairs. Appearing moments after him, Elaine took her mother off to show her the Yves St. Laurent dresses she'd bought in Paris—at prices that would startle her mother.

"What about a drink before the others arrive?" Harvey suggested to his father-in-law with the expected deference. Pompous old bastard, Harvey thought as he walked with Eldridge into what he liked to call the library.

"I don't mind," the older man shrugged.

"I'll be starting the campaign for reelection soon," Harvey began casually, "but I'm getting some feelers about running for Congress from this district in '68."

"It'll be a waste of time and money," Eldridge said brusquely. "Voters in this state aren't ready to elect a Jew to Congress."

"I hear talk about Sam Massell—young as he is—running for Mayor of Atlanta in the next two or three years," Harvey shot back. His voice was calm though his face was flushed with rage.

"He may in the next year or two," Eldridge acknowledged, "but

Atlanta is a whole different ball game. Putting money in a congressional race for you from this district would be like throwing it down the toilet."

"I'll see how things develop." He wouldn't give the old bastard the satisfaction of knowing he was pissed, Harvey promised himself. "Oh, did Elaine tell you? We're thinking of putting this house on the market and building a larger one. I need to do a lot of entertaining." He hadn't discussed this with Elaine—he'd just decided it this moment. He felt a sudden, searing need to puncture his father-in-law's complacency. With real estate soaring like it was, he'd get a good price for the house. That would make a substantial down payment, and he didn't have to worry about getting a mortgage. With his contacts that would be a snap.

"What's wrong with this house?" Eldridge reared. *His wedding gift.*

"You know how it is when an attorney's moving up career-wise," Harvey said casually. He didn't need the old bastard—he'd make a run for Congress without him. He had clients who'd love to have their own man up in Washington. "You have to let the world know you're on the rise."

Elaine would be sore as hell when he made it clear that bitch Carol wasn't being hired to design their new house. Nothing he hated more than professional women who thought they knew it all. He'd tell Mom he had to give the job to an architect related to an important client. She'd believe him.

Carol was elated that—at last—Seth had finished the new book. Still, he showed some trepidation when he prepared to ship it off to his agent.

"I hope I'm right," he said. "That it's a subject that will grab readers."

"I loved it, Seth," she said enthusiastically.

"You're a biased reader." He smiled but his eyes were somber.

"A lot of people were hurt in the blacklisting—and a lot more have learned in the past few years what a plague it was. And the John Birch Society—here in the middle of 1966—is still running its hate-mongering newspaper, having its special phone line to spread its lies. Seth, this is your breakthrough book," she said passionately.

"Well, we're in for a lot more waiting," Seth warned.

"We've learned to wait," Carol reminded. "But don't just sit back while the book goes on its rounds. Start thinking about the next one."

"Did I ever tell you that you're a slave driver?" he teased while he attached the address label to the manuscript parcel. "At least, my wife is doing marvelously." he joshed.

"Grandma said that Elaine is very upset that Harvey's hiring somebody other than me to do their new house."

"Harvey looks on you as a personal threat. He can't forgive your success. A woman in a man's field." He reached to pull her close. "Where are the kids?"

"Karen's sleeping over at Irene's house." Irene was her long time "best friend." "And Jonnie's at a birthday party. I told him he has to be home by midnight, even though there's no school tomorrow."

"Then there's plenty of time," Seth murmured amorously. "Did I ever tell you, it's absolutely indecent for you to be so sexy at forty-six—"

This was one thing that the years hadn't dimmed for them, Carol thought with pride. Making love was still as wonderful for them as it was nineteen years ago. They had love, and they had family. They were rich.

Yet even as they made love, Carol thought how desperately important it was for Seth to fulfill himself as a writer. Had she pushed him too hard? What would happen to his tormented soul if this book didn't find a publisher? How many disappointments could Seth handle?

Chapter Forty-eight

Carol geared herself for a long wait on their hearing from Seth's agent. She remembered—unhappily—that one publisher had held the last book for five months—and then rejected it. Aware that Seth was on edge, she forced herself not to try to push him back to the typewriter.

Seth was upset—as she was—by the escalating war in Vietnam. They were both ever conscious that in two years Jonnie would be draft age, though as a college student by then he'd probably be exempt. They were unnerved by the dissension on college campuses. They were part of a generation that had enormous respect for prestigious seats of learning. This generation of college students were in rebellion.

At Amherst, 20 of the 270 graduating seniors—protesting U.S. involvement in the Vietnam War—stalked out of the commencement exercises when Secretary of Defense Robert McNamara was given an honorary degree. At Brandeis University and at New York University graduating seniors and faculty protested against the Vietnam War. At the University of Michigan last March there had been an all-night anti-Vietnam teach-in.

The subject evoked heated conversation at a July 4th dinner given for the adult family members by Harvey and Elaine. Carol was relieved that neither Jonnie nor Karen was present. Harvey was so arrogant, she thought with fresh distaste. He'd never fought in a war; he'd never even been drafted. Seth was honest in his feelings about Vietnam—feelings she shared. What was this country doing in a war halfway around the world? Why must Americans die there? To Harvey—in his safe little ivory tower—students who protested the war were traitors.

"Don't ever let Harvey drag you into a discussion about Vietnam again," Carol told Seth while they settled themselves in the car for the drive home after dinner. "He can't understand what's happening."

"It'll get worse before it gets better," Seth said grimly.

In September Jonnie was a high school junior. All at once it was imperative to start planning his college career. The choice would be Jonnie's, Carol and Seth had decided. He was bright, had earned top grades. His grandmother was blatant about prodding him toward Emory, where Seth had taken his junior and senior years. Carol knew Seth was eager for Jonnie to go to Columbia, though he was nervous about the price tag.

By the end of the year Jonnie had made up his mind. If his parents agreed, he wanted to go to Columbia.

"Fred's going there," he told them. Fred Wassermann was his

closest friend. "It'd be terrific if we could go to the same school, be roommates."

"It's so far away," Carol said wistfully. She would be up in the city at regular intervals, but Seth could see him only during long holidays. "But if that's what you want, then all right," she added quickly, exchanging a glance with Seth.

"It's a great school, Jonnie. If I hadn't gone to Columbia for two years, I'd never had known your mother," Seth added with a sentimental grin.

"I'll call Fred and tell him." Jonnie looked relieved, Carol thought, enveloped in love for her son. It was strange and wonderful how your whole world revolved around your kids—how a smile from a child could mean so much. "We'll both try for Columbia—but, of course, that doesn't mean we'll make it."

"You'll make it," Seth said, pleased with Jonnie's decision.

She was glad that Jonnie would be with Freddie. It would be good for them to have each other. Freddie's father had fled from Berlin in the late 1930s, had been brought to Bellevue by a cousin. He'd married a local girl, built up a substantial business, then four years ago—to everyone's astonishment—went to live in Israel. Freddie's mother—who had been Andrea Bernstein—had refused to leave Bellevue. She took over the business, and everybody said she was doing well.

Carol tried to be supportive when early in the new year the first rejection came on Seth's new novel. They'd held it so long, she thought in frustration.

"It was close," Seth's agent reported. "This one editor wanted to buy it. She put up a hard fight."

"Close means nothing," Seth said. "Either you have a contract— or you don't."

"That's just one publisher," Carol reminded. "The book's going out again."

Early in February Jonnie launched his campaign to join a school group that was to attend a camp in Switzerland for a month—where students would have daily French classes. The magic words were, "Fred's mother is letting him go."

"You're spoiling him rotten," Seth warned, yet Carol knew he was pleased that Jonnie could have these advantages. "At his age to spend a month in Europe!" For one somber moment she remembered the trip to London with her parents when she was nine—just weeks before her whole world fell apart.

"Seth, why don't we treat ourselves to a couple of weeks in Europe?" Carol said on impulse. They could afford it on a grand scale this time, she thought with a surge of anticipation. A suite at the Ritz, dinners at La Tour D'Argent with its view of Notre Dame and the finest pressed duck in France. "Wouldn't it be wonderful to see Paris again?"

"I can't get away from the shop for two weeks. Mom would insist on coming in every day. That's too much for her." But his eyes were nostalgic. Paris would forever be special to them. "And it'd be terribly expensive." Meaning, Carol interpreted, that they couldn't afford it on his salary.

Then all at once Carol and Seth were caught up in Jonnie's vacation plans. There were myriad details to handle—his passport, vaccination, clothes, camera and film, stationery so he'd be sure to write home. Without telling Seth, Carol took Jonnie to the bank to buy him an awesome amount of travelers checks. She'd feel less anxious, she told herself, in knowing that he had funds to handle any emergency that might arise.

Immediately after the close of school at the end of May Jonnie and Fred left with their group for New York. Carol knew Jonnie was pleased that she had to be in New York this week and had come to the newly renamed JFK Airport to be with him during their layover. Their flight to Geneva was scheduled for 8 P.M.

"Have you ever been in Switzerland, Mrs. Walden?" Fred asked her politely while they ate dinner in an airport restaurant—with the approval of the group's three teachers.

"No, but I hear it's beautiful." Carol was astonished that she felt anxious at having an ocean between Jonnie and herself. That was so silly—they'd checked out the organization that was sponsoring the teacher-led group and found them exemplary, she comforted herself. Jonnie was almost seventeen and so bright. He'd be fine. But anxiety came with the territory, she mused. Jonnie and Karen would always be her "babies"—even when they were forty.

"Mom's been in Paris and London," Jonnie told his friend. "She went to school in Paris for a while. At the Sorbonne."

"My father was born in Berlin. Now he's living in Israel." Fred paused. Carol, of course, knew this. "He keeps telling my mom we should come out there, too. Mom said she'd never live anywhere but

Bellevue. I was there for a month two years ago, when my dad was living in a kibbutz."

"Conditions in Israel are often rough," Carol reminded gently. She'd been amused when Jonnie had asked that his passport be valid for Israel, to match Fred's.

"Jews have lived in Israel for four thousand years," Fred said, his face alight with a messianic glow. "They have a right to be there." He was worried, Carol guessed, about the news reports that kept coming out of the Middle East—that Syrian terrorists were sneaking into Israel to lay mines, that Egypt was demanding the removal of the United Nations Emergency Force from the border between it and Israel, that tiny Israel was surrounded by belligerent Arab countries. And now Egypt had closed the Straits of Tiran—a blockade that isolated Israel from its trading partners.

"The rest of the world won't look on and see Israel attacked," Jonnie comforted his friend. "The United Nations won't let it happen."

"Israel's turned malarial swamps and deserts into farmland and beautiful cities. They took a wasteland and made it a home for over two and a half million people!" Carol knew Fred was quoting his father and was sympathetic. After the Holocaust, she remembered, Jews around the world had fresh respect for Zionism.

Jonnie was glad that he and Fred had adjoining seats on the plane—at the side rather than the intimidating clusters of four seats across. Long after many of the others dozed, they talked in soft whispers.

"I took most of the money out of my savings account," Fred whispered. "I've got that plus what Mom gave me in travelers checks."

"I feel rich, too," Jonnie bragged. "Mom gave me a lot of travelers checks, then my grandmother gave me a hundred dollars in cash and my great-grandmother gave me another hundred. Dad gave me a couple of twenties at the Atlanta airport." He giggled indulgently. "Each of them doing it kind of surreptitiously. You'd think we were going on a safari to Darkest Africa instead of a camp in Geneva."

"I'll bet Israel isn't more than three or four hours away from Switzerland," Fred said. "I'll phone my dad from Geneva. I haven't talked to him since my birthday. It costs a lot to call from Tel Aviv to Bellevue," he added conscientiously, "and Dad doesn't have much money."

Despite their conviction they wouldn't sleep at all, Jonnie and Fred had to be awakened when the jet approached the Geneva airport.

"Wow!" Jonnie gazed out the window as the plane prepared for descent. "We're in a foreign country."

"I hope they speak some English," Fred said, all at once self-conscious. "I don't know how far I can go on three years of high school French."

Then they were caught in the excitement of landing, of going through customs, of being taken by a waiting bus to the former monastery where they were to live for the month of June. The monastery sat a few kilometers beyond the airport, on a mountainside overlooking Lake Geneva. Grapevines covered every segment of earth.

"Do you suppose the monks used to make wine?" Fred whispered to Jonnie, and both suppressed giggles.

Jonnie and Fred were startled to discover that each student would be assigned a room—actually a cell once occupied by resident monks.

"We'll use one for our clothes and sleep in the other," Fred whispered. "We'll take turns sleeping on a mattress on the floor." To be dragged from the other room each night, Jonnie understood.

Classes and camp activities would not begin until Monday, June 5th, Mr. Coleman—the senior teacher—told the student group. From now through Sunday they would be tourists. This first day they were fighting jet lag, were content to nap in their rooms until they were summoned to dinner. Tomorrow—Friday—they would go on a guided tour of Geneva.

The following morning after breakfast the group gathered in the lounge. The atmosphere was convivial. They were about to leave for a day of sightseeing in the city. Then Fred approached Mr. Coleman and politely asked permission to remain at the monastery.

"I'm still bushed," he apologized. "I mean, this crazy switch in time—I couldn't get to sleep last night."

"Me, too," Jonnie chimed in. Fred was going to try to get a phone call through to his father, he surmised. That could take a long time. "We'd rather just hang around here and read."

"You'll have to eat at the snack bar," Mr. Coleman warned. "We didn't arrange for lunch to be served today. We plan to have lunch outside."

"The snack bar's great," Fred said happily. There was a small bar set up in the monastery entrance foyer that sold American-style franks, packaged cookies, popcorn, sodas. "We'll survive till dinner."

The three teachers consulted briefly, then agreed.

"There're copies of the *International Herald Tribune* for the past few days," Miss Griffith told the two boys and pointed to a nearby table. "And don't worry," she said, chuckling. "They're in English."

"What do you want to do?" Jonnie asked curiously when he and Fred were alone in the section of the monastery assigned to them. Another group of students—from somewhere in South Carolina—would arrive tomorrow to live in the adjoining section. "Why didn't you want to go sightseeing?" He'd kind of looked forward to that, he thought wistfully. "Are you going to try to call your father?"

"Jonnie, we can't be much more than three hours from Israel!" Fred leaned forward, his eyes holding Jonnie's with a mesmerizing intensity. "We've got enough money for plane tickets there and back. Let's fly to Tel Aviv and see my father!"

"You're nuts!" Jonnie was shocked by this suggestion. "They'll never let us do that!"

"They're going to be in Geneva all day," Fred pointed out. "I know where Mr. Coleman keeps our passports. We can get ours, hike to the airport, and be in Tel Aviv before they even get back."

"Our parents will kill us," Jonnie rejected. "I can't do that, Fred. My mom and dad have been so good to me."

"I'm scared of what's happening in Israel! Look what the news-papers are saying!" A vein throbbed in Fred's forehead. "Cairo radio said that the Arabs are out to wipe Israel off the map. Nasser said his country would not accept any possibility of coexistence with Israel. And look at this." He reached for a newspaper lying on the coffee table. "The president of Syria says: 'We want total war with no limits, a war that will destroy the Zionist base.' If I don't go to Israel and see my father now, I may never see him again."

Jonnie hesitated, fearful of his parents' reaction. But if it was Dad in Israel, he reasoned, he'd want to go.

"We'll have to leave notes to say where we've gone," he stipulated. "And we'll cable our folks that we're with your father and we're fine." Still Jonnie was anxious. "How do you know we'll be able to find your dad?"

"I write to him regularly. He has an apartment in Tel Aviv—he runs a little shop there. If he's not home yet, we'll wait for him."

In the stillness of their quarters they each packed a small knapsack, recounted their supply of money with fresh urgency, then left the monastery for the long hike to the Geneva airport.

The day was hot, the sun strong as they hiked toward their destination—too caught up in their adventure to observe the magnificent scenery of gleaming Lake Geneva, the towering French Alps across the lake. The windows of the low, mostly stucco houses along the route were closed against the heat, curtains drawn. At last—tired and thirsty—they reached the large, modern airport.

Both boys were relieved to discover that English was spoken here. They bought their round-trip tickets for the next flight to Tel Aviv. With almost two hours' wait until their departure they hungrily sought a restaurant. Though they knew their group was at this moment strolling around picturesque Geneva, they couldn't suppress a sense of anxiety about their truancy.

Late in the afternoon—tense yet exhilarated—they arrived at Lod Airport, took the bus into Tel Aviv. In the city they began to search for the apartment house where Fred's father, Erik Wassermann, lived. They hadn't expected Tel Aviv to be so large and noisy. At intervals tall, obviously new buildings rose among the spread of three-storied structures.

There weren't many tourists around, Jonnie thought. At intervals they saw a pair of Americans with cameras hanging about their necks. Because of all the trouble with the Arab nations, he surmised.

"Hey, there's the Tel Aviv Sheraton," Fred interrupted his musings. "That's where the Chess Olympics were held two years ago." Fred was a chess buff.

As they walked about the streets, asked directions to their destination, they became conscious of the absence of young men. They encountered only very young boys and middle-aged and old men.

"The younger guys have been called up." All at once Fred was somber. "For military service," he explained in response to Jonnie's blank stare. "Dad's in the reserves."

"You mean he might not be here?" *Where would they stay?*

"He wouldn't be called up now," Fred reassured Jonnie. "He's just getting over a broken ankle. He was on crutches the last time he wrote to me."

Finally they located the modest apartment where Fred's father lived. He wasn't home yet. They dropped their knapsacks on the floor and sat down to wait. When they were debating about leaving temporarily to look for a place to eat, Fred's father arrived. He greeted them with a blend of disbelief and jubilation, then pelted them with questions as he unlocked the door to his apartment. His eyes never seemed to leave Fred's face, Jonnie thought sympathetically.

"We'll have dinner, then find a place to cable your mother," he told Fred. He turned to Jonnie. "And your family. We must let them know you're all right. And first thing tomorrow morning we head for Jerusalem."

"Why?" Fred asked, exchanging an anxious glance with Jonnie.

"Because the way the situation looks, Tel Aviv could be dodging Arab bombs in another twenty-four to forty-eight hours. People are saying that Tel Aviv will get it first—I don't want you guys here," he said gently. "In Jerusalem we'll feel safe. We could get some sniping from Hussein—" He shrugged this off. "But nothing serious."

"Where will we stay in Jerusalem?" Fred asked.

"I have the keys to a friend's place. He's down in the south somewhere—with his unit. We'll be safe in Jerusalem. Nasser can't get to us there."

Jonnie tried to interpret these reassurances. Hussein would be King Hussein of Jordan. Nasser was President of Egypt. They were sitting on the edge of a war, Jonnie thought with a surge of excitement. Maybe he could write about it for the *Bellevue Enquirer* when he got home. *He might be an eyewitness.*

Early in the morning Jonnie and Fred were awakened by Erik Wassermann. Jonnie saw the packed duffel bag sitting by the door. It was weird, he thought—to be here in Israel with war hanging over their heads.

"All right, let's get cracking!" Fred's father said briskly. "The car's out front. We'll have breakfast in Jerusalem."

Chapter Forty-nine

Carol hurried to the front door when she heard Andrea's car pull into the driveway.

"Seth, Andrea's here," she called and pushed open the door.

"I can't believe this!" Breathless from exertion, Andrea Wassermann strode toward Carol. "Fred's always been so responsible. How could they do this to us?"

"Come inside and cool off," Carol urged. Thank God for air-conditioning on sultry days like this. "Seth's bringing us iced coffee."

"I feel so guilty about Fred's dragging Jonnie into this," Andrea apologized as they walked into the living room. "He'd wanted to visit his father again this summer. I was afraid—with all we've heard the last few months about the Arab nations mobilizing for a *jihad* to destroy Israel. His father tried to make him understand that, too."

"Do you have a phone number for Erik?" Carol asked while the two women settled themselves on the sofa.

"He's not there," Andrea told her. "I tried three times to get a call through."

"You mean there's no way we can contact the kids?" Seth asked, coming into the living room with tall, frosty glasses of iced coffee. "Where can they be?" His voice was sharp with anxiety.

"We know they're with Erik." Andrea was fighting for calm. "They're all right. He won't let anything happen to them."

"It's not as though Israel is at war." Carol ordered herself to be realistic. *Not yet.* "But they should let us know where they are."

"Erik ought to put them on the next plane home," Seth said brusquely. "Forget about Switzerland—" He paused, his face tensing. "Maybe he figures this isn't the time to be flying out of Israel. I don't like what I read in the *Atlanta Constitution* this morning."

"What's the latest word?" Andrea asked. "The Bellevue papers don't tell us much about what's going on over there."

"Israel is surrounded on every side by hostile Arab nations," Seth began.

"We know that!" Carol interrupted. *Jonnie could be shot—it happened to innocent bystanders in time of war.* She remembered—irrationally, she knew, but it was frightening—the old superstition that bad things happened in threes. Her father died by gunfire. *She* had been shot on the streets of Manhattan. Please, God, don't let it happen to Jonnie! "Seth, what is happening now?"

"You know about the massive buildup of the Egyptian armies in Sinai," Seth said. "Jordanian artillery and mortars are trained on Israel's heavily populated cities. Iraq, Kuwait, and Algeria have troops moving toward the Egyptian border. Arab forces are at both the southern and northern Negev."

"And Fred and Jonnie are there instead of in Geneva!" Andrea's voice was shrill. "Israel's a sitting duck for the Arabs!"

"There's nothing we can do but sit by and wait for news." His face taut, Seth lowered himself into a lounge chair. "When Jordan closed the Straits of Tiran by force, that was an automatic declaration of war."

"Shall I try again to get a call through to Erik?" Andrea gazed from Carol to Seth.

"Try," Seth ordered.

On the drive to Jerusalem Erik talked compulsively about the imminent war.

"For weeks we've felt it coming. When it will happen, nobody knows. In truth, we're at war this minute. We have our main supplies of fuel choked off by the blockade. We have enemy forces poised to attack on all sides. And the United Nations does nothing!" A vein throbbed at his temple.

"You said last night that every able-bodied member of the reserves had been called up," Jonnie remembered. "Can Israel fight off all the Arab armies?" Tiny Israel against all the Arab nations determined to wipe it out?

"We're in total mobilization," Erik told them. "Israel is at its greatest peril in its existence."

The apartment where they were to stay was far away from the border of Jerusalem, Fred's father pointed out.

"It's low, surrounded on three sides by somewhat taller buildings."

Jonnie understood he was determined to allay their fears. He would try to make this visit a festive occasion. But Jonnie was tormented by the realization that his family back in Bellevue must be distraught.

The weekend was quiet. They ate, talked, watched Israeli television. In much of the conversation Fred's father tried to make the two boys understand why he had come to live in Israel. At intervals they were aware that workers were cordoning off a field beyond with barbed wire and piling up boxes of ammunition. They knew that guns lay hidden in dugouts.

On Monday morning a member of *Haga*—the local civil defense organization—came to their apartment door.

"We're at war," he said briskly. "Tape and blackout your windows. When you hear the siren, go to the shelter."

"When did this happen?" Erik demanded. "We heard nothing on the news."

"Just now. I have to warn the others—"

Erik strode across the room to switch on the radio. Immediately the voice of an announcer reported that since 7 A.M. Egyptian ground and air forces had been moving against Israel.

"All right, we have to tape the windows. We'll use Scotch tape," Erik told the boys. "Fred, in that chest beneath the window you'll find tablecloths and bedspreads. Jonnie, go into the kitchen. In the drawer next to the sink you'll see a hammer and nails."

"Yes, sir!" Jonnie was enthralled at being part of this.

Erik began to tape the windowpanes. "We'll hammer cloth over all the windows," he told the boys.

Around noon Jonnie was startled to hear the sound of guns. Fred came to stand beside him. He went to pull back a stretch of window covering. They saw soldiers hurrying uphill with boxes of ammunition. It was exciting and scary, Jonnie thought—but he was glad he was here. He *wanted* to share this experience.

They watched until Erik warned them this was dangerous. Now they focused on listening to the radio, waiting impatiently for news bulletins until the radio went dead. Erik rejected their using the transistor radio; better to save the batteries for later.

"Let's go to the shelter," Erik ordered after a burst of gunfire. "Bring the transistor radio."

In the shelter Erik Wassermann took charge of the tenants gathered together. They closed off the cellar windows, piled sandbags on the outside. Discovering they had no candles, Erik hurried up to his borrowed apartment to bring down a few, along with a first-aid kit. Each of the tenants had arrived with a supply of unperishable food.

At brief intervals during the next two days the shelling stopped. Then appointed occupants of the shelter dashed out to find an open grocery to buy food and candles. Despite the shelling—knowing residents would be short of items—a small grocery stood by to serve them.

Jonnie fought against a feeling of claustrophobia. It was awful, he thought, to have to stay in this tiny shelter. He wanted to be outside, to know what was happening. And the reports from Cairo radio were unnerving.

"Our glorious Arab troops, our armies are marching on Tel Aviv." "Haifa is burning." "We are advancing everywhere." The nasty taunts came regularly.

"Don't believe a word they say," an elderly woman—exhibiting amazing serenity—told Jonnie and Fred. "They always lie. Wait till we get our own reports."

At noon on Wednesday word came on Israeli radio that all of Jerusalem was in Israeli hands, that it was safe to leave the shelters. But residents were exhorted to return to the shelters if the sirens were heard. General Rabin announced triumphantly, "All this the armed forces of Israel did alone and unaided." Tomorrow would be a holiday in Jerusalem—but the war was not yet over.

In six unbelievable days—one by one—Israeli forces destroyed those of Egypt, Jordan, and Syria. The Arabs ran. The Israelis held East Jerusalem, Gaza, and the West Bank. So much for Nasser's threat to wipe Israel off the face of the map, Jonnie thought in triumph—feeling himself an Israeli in this critical time.

"Forever these hard-won areas will belong to Israel," the old woman gloated. "Whoever returns land won in war?"

As soon as it was possible to make phone calls, Jonnie called home. He felt guilty when he heard the relief mixed with joy in the voices of his mother and father, yet he felt a sense of exhilaration that he had been here at this time.

"Mom, Fred and I want to stay another two weeks—to help with the clean up," he said hopefully. "Fred's father says it's okay with him."

"It's all right, Jonnie," his mother agreed after a brief consultation with his father. "Thank God, you're all right."

"Mom, I know now more than ever—I want to be a newspaper

correspondent. Maybe I can write about the Israeli War for the school newspaper next term!"

In her towering relief at hearing from Jonnie, knowing he was all right, Carol gave a family dinner party to celebrate the Israeli victory and Jonnie and Freddie's well-being. Andrea, too, was invited.

"I'm proud Jonnie was there," Leah told the others gathered about the dinner table. "It was the kind of thing Eli wanted to do. My great-grandson," she predicted, "will do what my son wanted to do with his life."

"When Fred finishes high school—if Erik still wishes to live in Israel," Andrea said softly, "then Fred and I will go there to be with him. I want my family to be together."

Carol relished being surrounded by family tonight. She was glad that Karen had chosen to stay home this summer, with the promise of accompanying her mother to New York and the Hamptons for brief intervals. Tonight even Harvey seemed less obnoxious, she thought with wry humor.

Israel had performed a miracle. Jonnie and Fred were safe. She felt a rush of love as she listened to Karen talk with pride about how Israel had emerged victorious in spite of such formidable odds.

"Maybe I'll go to Israel some day and help to build houses there," Karen said later as she lingered at the door of her parents' room.

"Meanwhile, go to sleep," Seth ordered, reaching to embrace his daughter. "You've got awhile before you can build houses."

Carol and Seth began to prepare for bed. This had been a beautiful evening, she thought. One of those pockets of serene happiness that followed a tumultuous time.

"Something good came of the boys' escapade," she told Seth as she sat at the edge of their bed and kicked off her slippers. "Andrea and Erik are reconciling."

"It's been a rough time for you," he said compassionately. "Worrying about Jonnie and Fred in the midst of a war—" He didn't say, "with your phobia about guns"—but she understood.

"You know me so well, Seth." Strangely, she felt the sting of tears. How would she have survived if Seth had not come back into her life?

"Something else may have come out of Jonnie's trip to Israel."

Seth sat down beside her, and she was conscious of an electric excitement in him.

"What would that be?" she asked softly. But her heart was pounding. She knew what generated that kind of excitement in him.

"I was thinking that I should be practical, get back to the munitions book. All at once it's exciting to me again. And it can be so long before word comes back from a publisher on the other."

"Right, Seth." She had a sense of *déjà vu*.

"I've turned out a book before despite the job," he said with an enthusiasm she relished. "I'll jump into the old routine. Up by five-thirty, work an hour at the typewriter each morning before I go in to the shop. Squeeze in some time on Sundays."

"You can do it." How many times had she said this?

"I look at the calendar, and it scares me. I know I've got one book in a file drawer and another making rounds—but I have to do this one and hope. I don't want to end up one of those bitter old men who spend their last years mourning about what they should have done with their lives—but didn't."

Chapter Fifty

For Karen the new school year started off inauspiciously. Always a model student, she was in rebellion. During her lunch period today she'd gone to the principal's office to register her protest and had been dismissed with a few impatient words. Why did she have to take cooking when her schedule would allow her to take mechanical drawing? *Why could only boys go to mechanical drawing?*

Too impatient to wait in the air-conditioned comfort of the house, she sat on the veranda in the still steamy September afternoon and waited for her mother to arrive from Atlanta. If she had a year of mechanical drawing behind her, she thought with a surge of high spirits, then maybe Mom would let her work in the office next summer.

She leapt to her feet as her mother swung into the driveway. Mom would understand, she told herself righteously. What was the matter with the school? Women were demanding their rights these days.

"Mom, you won't believe what happened at school today!" Karen burst out, incensed, while Carol emerged from the car.

"Tell me about it inside the house," Carol soothed. "This heat is unbelievable."

Bonnie brought them tall glasses of lemonade, though the house itself was deliciously cool. The words tumbling over one another in her haste, Karen reported her confrontation with the principal, waited for her mother to offer to go to school and fight in her behalf.

"Are you the only one who wants to take mechanical drawing?" Carol asked.

"No," Karen told her, then giggled. "Hillary and Jan want to go, too—but just because of all the boys in the class."

"Then why don't the three of you organize? Start a petition. You'll be fifteen in January," her mother reminded. "Old enough to handle this without me."

"Yeah." Karen's face lighted. "We'll organize!"

Carol watched with pleasure as Karen and her friends fought for the right to be part of the mechanical drawing class—and won. Mom was at first shocked, then wistful, Carol realized. Mom felt that her whole world was changing—yet with some reluctance she approved of this move toward "women's rights," as Karen labeled it.

She remembered her mother-in-law's reaction to the ugly riots this past June in Dixie Hills, an area of well-kept middle-class Negro homes edged by a large, low-rent development that was privately owned. On one of those times when the family gathered for dinner at Harvey and Elaine's ostentatiously expensive house, Mom had scolded Harvey for his scurrilous description of the riots.

"Harvey, that low-rent development is like an inferno during the day—and not much better at night. Not a blade of grass or a tree anywhere. Folks living there were just ready to explode."

At regular intervals Carol remembered Karen's reaction to the riots: *"Mom, why doesn't the city—or the Federal government— build decent houses for people who don't have much money? Did you know that the windows in that development are designed in a way that won't even allow the people to bring in air-conditioning?"*

Karen had paused for a moment. *"Not that they could afford air conditioners."*

Karen, Carol thought, was *her* conscience. All those years ago—when she first faced up to her ambition to become an architect—she'd envisioned herself building modest but comfortable houses for people who were forced to live in hovels because of lack of money. She'd wanted to build beautiful homes, too, that would give something special to the lives of their owners—but there was to be a time to contribute to the needs of people who couldn't afford these beautiful homes. In that respect, she acknowledged with painful guilt, she was a failure.

This was an era of volcanic changes, Carol told herself repeatedly in the coming months. A minor change, she reported whimsically to Sharon—the Margaret Mitchell buff—was renaming the intersection where Pryor, Forsyth, and Carnegie Way merged into Peachtree to Margaret Mitchell Square. Here stood Loew's Grand Theater, which showed the world movie premiere of *Gone With The Wind.*

Antiwar sentiment was mounting. Martin Luther King Jr. was vigorously rejecting Stokely Carmichael's Black Power movement, that had ordered blacks—as segments of the colored population preferred to call themselves now—to arm for "total revolution." The "hippie" movement was flourishing in Atlanta—its Atlanta colony the subject of a movie made in the city this past summer. Carol was mildly upset when she found a copy of *Rolling Stone* on the floor of Karen's room. But for Karen this was just a subject of curiosity. In New York, Sharon moaned about Michelle's fascination for this raging "counterculture".

Within her own household, Carol thought, this was a time of working and waiting. Her own career continued to soar. She'd enlarged her staff in both the Atlanta and New York offices. She commuted regularly between Bellevue and New York. Seth was doggedly working on the new book—and in that awareness she found a poignant sense of "all's right with the world'"—despite the chaos outside their home.

"The book's taking so damn long," Seth complained early in the new year while they were dressing for a dinner at Harvey and Elaine's house. "That hour in the morning—plus Sundays—gives me so little time." But there was no way, Carol knew, that Seth would break clear of the shop and concentrate on the book. Mom and

Grandma needed the income from the shop. And Don Taylor had stopped submitting the last book. This one was Seth's big hope.

"Good things are worth waiting for." She radiated serenity and confidence. "Your time is coming." *She had to believe that.*

"What do you think brought on this dinner?" Seth asked curiously. Usually, they both knew, Harvey had a motive. "I doubt we're celebrating Lincoln's birthday." He chuckled. "Is Harvey about to announce he's running for Congress?"

"That's a huge jump, even for him." Harvey was all excited, Carol interpreted, because Sam Massell was expected to run for mayor in October. If Atlanta could vote for a Jewish mayor, she gathered, he figured the time was ripe for a Jewish congressman from the district.

At his decorator-furnished house Harvey was leisurely dressing for dinner. In a chic new Yves St. Laurent, Elaine was preparing to go downstairs to see that activity in the kitchen was on schedule.

"Harvey, I don't know why you make such a fuss when your family comes to dinner." An array of silver suitable for a formal banquet, three wines to be served. "Carol told me your mother runs out to buy a new dress each time we ask them over."

"Mom loves it," Harvey drawled. "It's a long way from family meals in the kitchen when I was growing up. Did you tell Elvira to chill the champagne I left in the kitchen?"

"I told her." She paused, sighed. "I don't know why we can't have Karen and Jonnie over with the others."

"It's so unsophisticated to have kids at a grown-up dinner." He glanced warily at Elaine. She was pissed because he'd insisted they send Timmy off to boarding school this year. Hell, it was only fifty miles away. She was always driving over to see him. In their income bracket it was the thing to do. Didn't Elaine understand that was a helluva lot better than sending him to an integrated school? She boasted regularly that Atlanta was the first Deep South city to desegregate its schools—and Bellevue right behind. He loathed this distinction.

Harvey reached for his tie, then put it aside for a moment to sip at his martini. Wait till Mom hears he had a group willing to bankroll his run for Congress! He could hear her boasting about "my son, the congressman." They weren't doing it for him, he told himself frankly—they wanted "their man in Congress," somebody to fight for "their bills." They knew he could deliver for them.

The phone rang—his private line, that nobody else picked up. He frowned, put down his martini and reached for the phone.

"Hello—"

"Harvey, this is Chuck Williams." The just-appointed chairman of his newly arranged campaign committee.

"Yeah, Chuck," he said ebulliently. "What's up?"

"We have problems." Williams was terse. Harvey stiffened to attention. "The committee's had an emergency meeting. You can't run, Harvey."

"What do you mean I can't run?" He was startled, belligerent.

"We've got the word. The competition will massacre you if you run. They—"

"I have a good record on the City Council! Who's going to massacre me?" he challenged. *Chuck Williams was off his rocker.*

"We've got the inside info. They suspect we plan to back you, and they're out to smear you if you run. Hell, you leave a trail a mile wide. They've got photos of you coming out of three motels—with three different bimbos. The whole scene is dead. We can't back you."

Off the phone, Harvey stood motionless. Damn Chuck Williams! Okay, so he wouldn't run for Congress. He could make out like a bandit with his corporate clients—working in the Washington arena. He was having lunch tomorrow with Bruce Singleton of Singleton Industries. Singleton was anxious about a couple of bills coming up this session. He'd confide he was stepping out of the political ring to move backstage. To manipulate. He'd talk about setting up a lobbyist group in Washington—commuting between D.C. and Bellevue.

He didn't need to run for Congress. This new approach was surefire. No need to worry whether he'd make it or not in an election. This was a power scene that would pay off like a diamond mine in South Africa. He was whistling as he left the master bedroom suite to go downstairs.

This had been an insane year thus far, Carol told herself on a late August morning as she drove with Seth and Jonnie to the Atlanta airport. It would be forever etched on the memory of every living American. On March 31st President Johnson—in a dramatic television appearance—announced he would not seek another term. On April 4th, Martin Luther King, Jr. had been assassinated in Memphis, Tennessee—which brought on a week of rioting in urban ghettos.

On June 6th Senator Robert Kennedy was assassinated in Los Angeles, only minutes after delivering a victory speech following his win in the California primary. Within five years the nation had suffered three assassinations.

At the airport Carol and Seth waited with their eager-to-be-en route son in the reception area at the boarding gate.

"Be sure you call Sharon once you're settled in," Carol told Jonnie. "She'll want you to come down for dinner whenever you have time. She's just a few minutes from Columbia on the Broadway bus."

"Yeah, I will," Jonnie promised. Sharon was like a close aunt, Carol thought sentimentally. He and Karen hadn't seen much of Sharon, but they felt close.

Seth was reminiscing with Jonnie now about his years at Columbia. Seth was as upset as she about the campus demonstrations these past months, she thought. Between January and the middle of June, she'd read somewhere, there had been 221 major demonstrations on 101 American campuses. Student violence had broken out at Temple University, New York State at Buffalo, Princeton, Barnard, Colgate—the list seemed endless. White students demanded an end to ROTC on campus. Black students demanded more courses in black studies—and all called for an end to the Vietnam War.

But what worried Carol and Seth most was the Columbia uprising this past April. For days the news had been monopolized by the happenings. She and Seth understood what was taking place—they sympathized with the students—but she prayed the coming school year would be calmer.

They'd known, of course, that Columbia owned around $230,000,-000 of Manhattan real estate, including the land occupied by Rockefeller Center. They hadn't realized until Sharon told them that much of that real estate consisted of rundown Harlem tenements close to the Columbia campus. Then Columbia announced it planned to pull down stretches of those tenements to build an expensive gym—and as Jonnie expressed it, "all hell broke loose."

Karen had been drawn in immediately by the prospect of residents in the deteriorating tenements being thrown out on the streets.

"Instead of building a fancy student gym," she'd demanded in the same outrage expressed by the college's students, "why don't they build some decent apartments for those people?"

"They're posting my flight." Jonnie was instantly on his feet.

With a matching reluctance Carol and Seth saw Jonnie off, left the terminal and headed for the parking area. Despite her anxiety about the campus upheavals she felt a guilty relief that Jonnie was on his way to college; as a college student he would probably be exempt from the draft. Surely the war in Vietnam—now the longest war in U.S. history—would be over by the time he finished school.

Jonnie vowed to graduate in three years, then go on for a year at Columbia's School of Journalism. Ever since his trip to Israel, he talked about becoming a foreign correspondent. She didn't want to think about the dangers that could involve, she told herself grimly. Did you ever stop worrying about your children?

As they drove away from the airport, Carol sensed that Seth was recalling his own two years at Columbia and their special, private world those years. They'd had such wild, extravagant convictions about their futures!

For her, she acknowledged, the dreams had become a reality. But Leo and Greg had been cut down so young. In a way, she mused, Jerry had acquired some success—though not in the field he'd chosen and she suspected he was bitter about this. What had happened to Matt? Was he a working architect? He'd been so enthusiastic, so convinced he'd make it big.

She winced in pain, remembering Seth's fears that life was running out on him. He'd soon be forty-eight—"staring at fifty," he kept saying. The years sped by so fast. It was difficult to believe that Jonnie was in college and Karen—in such a rush to be there, too—would follow him in two years.

"It'll be weird to sit down to dinner tonight without Jonnie at the table," Seth broke into her thoughts. "And in another two years it'll be just the two of us." One hand left the wheel of the car to reach for hers. "Does that make you feel like an old lady?"

"Not at all," she said with deliberate casualness, meant to reassure him. "It's just another phase of our lives. And it'll give us a kind of freedom." She broke into tender laughter. "We won't have to worry about the kids popping into our room at inappropriate moments!"

"That's one part of our lives that will never change," he predicted. "What do you say I delay going into the shop for another hour this morning?" Carol had arranged to go into her Atlanta office in the afternoon. "I have a sudden hankering to make love to my wife."

"In broad daylight?" she joshed but she, too, was aware of arousal—brought on, she guessed, by the drama of Jonnie's departure.

"I suppose Bonnie will be home," he remembered. "Damn!"

"Why don't we go to a motel?" Carol's smile was impish. "I'll feel deliciously decadent."

Seth grinned. "What's the nearest motel between here and Bellevue?"

While she waited in the car for Seth to register at the office of the posh motel, Carol thought about Jonnie, dashing off to college with his wagon load of ideals. Let things go well for him. Let there be no uprising on campus this coming school year. They were living in such insane times.

Chapter Fifty-one

Just days before Jonnie came home for his spring "break," Seth told Carol that he'd finished the new book. He was elated, spilling over a new confidence.

"I have a good feeling about this one," he told Carol. "My time is coming."

But some of his enthusiasm ebbed away when he tried to contact Don Taylor, his old literary agent. Through Sharon he learned that Taylor had retired and was living on a farm in upstate New York. Too impatient to go through the arduous search for a new agent, Seth decided to submit the manuscript "over the transom"—direct to a publisher without an agent.

"Books do sell this way," he assured Carol. "You hear about it every now and then."

On Jonnie's second morning home the family was thrown into shock. Leah Walden had died in her sleep. At ninety-three she'd still been active, still involved in volunteer work. Just yesterday she'd been to a Hadassah meeting.

"I thought Mama was indestructible," Hannah sobbed. "I thought she'd go on forever."

Leah was laid to rest beside her son. Again, there was a large turnout for a Walden funeral. Leah, too, had been loved despite her sometimes unorthodox thinking. Carol was grateful that for their growing-up years she'd been part of Jonnie and Karen's lives.

Carol was shocked that Harvey had not brought Timmy home from his private school out of respect for the death of his great-grandmother. Timmy was such a sweet kid, she thought—so much like his mother. Why had Elaine allowed Harvey to ship Timmy off to boarding school when he was so young?

Carol suspected Harvey was annoyed that he had to come home from Washington—where he seemed to be spending so much time these days.

"It was a bad time to pull Harvey away from Washington," Hannah confided self-consciously to Carol when the family returned to the house after the burial, to a lavish buffet prepared by friends. Elaine came to the house with them; Harvey did not.

"He's in the middle of a very important case," Hannah alibied when a friend asked about Harvey's absence. "A corporate client wants him to fight against the passage of some bad bill before Congress." It was ever clear to Carol that Hannah was in awe of Harvey's "connections." "He wanted to be with us, but he had to fly right up to D.C." Harvey, Carol remembered, had an affection for referring to the nation's capital as "D.C." "He's flying up in the client's company jet."

But Harvey found time, Carol thought cynically eight days later, to return to Bellevue for the reading of Leah's will. Hannah had observed the Jewish ritual of *shivah*. Through the years she and her mother-in-law had become as close as daughter and mother.

Carol and Seth joined Harvey and Elaine in the living room of the family house for the reading of the will. Moments later Hannah came into the room with Bonnie to serve freshly baked cake and coffee.

"Judge Cohen will be here any moment," Hannah told them. "He called to say that he was finishing up a conference with a client that ran longer than he'd expected."

"I don't know why the hell Grandma didn't have me draw up her will," Harvey grumbled. "This is crazy."

"Your grandfather and the judge's father were close friends for years," Hannah pointed out. "When the judge took over his father's practice, it was only natural for Mama to go to him."

The quiet, dignified attorney arrived shortly and prepared for the reading of the will. This was just a formality, Carol realized. The family knew that Grandma—always so generous—left little cash. Just this house and her share of the business. Still, Grandma was always one to want everything to be handled properly, Carol thought in loving recall.

After disposing of a few items of jewelry—equally divided among Hannah, Carol, and Elaine—Leah had willed her share of the business to her daughter-in-law. That was what she and Seth had expected, Carol told herself—Grandma would want to provide security for Mom. She noticed a faint glow of triumph on Harvey's face. He'd been afraid Grandma's share of the business would go to Seth, she interpreted. To Harvey this was a small victory.

Then Judge Cohen delivered what to Harvey's thinking, Carol surmised, was a deadly bomb. She saw the ruddy flush that rose from his throat up to his forehead as Judge Cohen read:

"My house at 1032 Maple Avenue is to be held in trust during her lifetime by my beloved daughter-in-law, Hannah Walden. At her death the property is bequeathed to my grandchildren, Jonathan and Karen Walden."

"What about Timmy?" Harvey interrupted furiously. "How could Grandma overlook my son?"

"There's more," Judge Cohen said with a caustic smile. "To my grandson, Timothy Walden, I bequeath the ivory-covered bible, which I carried at my marriage to his great-grandfather." A reminder to Harvey that her third great-grandchild was being raised outside her faith, Carol understood.

"Grandma always hated me," Harvey said when Judge Cohen had left the house. "In her eyes I could never do anything right. All she ever thought about was Seth."

"Harvey, that's not true," Elaine chastised. Her eyes were eloquently apologetic as she turned to the others. "Grandma was a wonderful woman."

* * *

Carol and Seth waited with strained patience for some response from the publisher to whom he'd submitted the new book. In August—four months after he'd sent off the manuscript—Seth's latest book was returned.

"With a form rejection slip," he told Carol bitterly when she arrived home minutes after him. "They didn't even consider it worthy of a personal letter!"

"Because you submitted it without an agent," Carol quoted Sharon, who was closer than they to the publishing world. "It never got past some little assistant editor. Talk to Sharon. Let her dig up some leads for you."

"All right," he said tiredly. "I'll call Sharon and talk to her."

Sharon came up with names. Seth began the grueling search for a new agent. The first agent replied to his inquiry letter with a question about his age.

"I never take on a client who's over fifty," the agent wrote. "I don't want to invest time in an author who hasn't made substantial progress by that age."

"The lousy bastard!" Seth blazed, and Carol flinched at the defeat she saw in his eyes. Early next year he'd be fifty. "I won't bother answering."

Two months later he received a friendly letter from a second agent. Yes, the agent assured Seth, he'd like to see the manuscript. Seth sent it off again. A few weeks later he received a reply, assuring him that there was much admirable in the manuscript—"and the writing is fine"—but it wasn't right for the current market. He suggested Seth go out and look at "current genre paperback fiction."

"At the moment," he ended his letter, *"editors are hot for 'slave books.'"*

"I don't even know what he's talking about," Seth dismissed this. "I belong to another era."

Sharon kept insisting that Seth must find an agent—"somebody on your wavelength." She talked, too, about his trying to move into what was known in the trade as "genre fiction."

"Sure, paperback fiction doesn't pay much in the beginning, but a writer can move up into decent money, even make it a springboard to hardcover," Sharon confided privately to Carol after a persuasive phone conversation with Seth. "So it's not literary—I know one writer who turns out eight to ten gothic or romantic suspense novels a year. She's not Daphne DuMaurier," Sharon conceded, "but she's pleasing a lot of readers. And she's earning a living at writing."

Carol chuckled. Her eyes were tender.

"Can you see Seth writing gothic or romantic suspense novels?"

"Not really—" Sharon laughed good-humoredly. "But we're talking 'genre fiction.' I'm exposed to it because every six months Nat starts talking about our moving into the paperback field, so I have to know what's happening." Sharon's salary had escalated somewhat through the years, but she was still writing confessions on the side to help with the expenses of keeping Michelle in an up-state college. At rebellious moments she considered quitting her job to concentrate on writing for the confession market but admitted to Carol she was too accustomed to the security of a weekly paycheck. "Seth could turn out police procedurals with no sweat—and fast. He could write Vietnam novels. They're coming in strong now."

"What does he know about Vietnam?"

"Carol, these books aren't being written for posterity. He'll research—magazine articles, newspaper articles. With Seth's bent for research he could turn these out fast. What's he doing now? Waiting to hear from a publisher? A writer has to keep writing."

Now Carol made a serious effort to prod Seth into the thriving "paperback original" market. She feared she'd have no success—but she was desperate to lighten Seth's depression. When—as once before—Seth began to turn on her in rage, she abandoned this. He took refuge in the old cliché—"For God's sake, Carol, I can't do that shit. You can't teach an old dog new tricks."

But Seth wasn't old, she thought in frustration. Nor had his talent vaporized. He was as fine a writer—or better with the passing years—as when he was writing for network television. Before the damnable blacklisting.

In March of the new year Carol was astonished to be notified that she had been chosen "Woman Architect of the Year" by a national women's group. She would be presented with a plaque at a formal dinner in New York at the end of August.

While she was candidly elated at this honor—and realized it was great publicity career-wise—she confessed to Seth that she disliked being labeled a "woman architect."

"Damn it, Seth, I'm an architect! I can do anything a male architect can do." This honor was hers, she surmised, because the development she'd designed on Long Island was receiving high praise. "I hate the 'woman' label."

"I'm proud of you. Don't knock it, sugar." He pulled her close for a congratulatory hug. "Wait till the kids hear about this!"

Seth was disconcerted when he realized he was expected to be Carol's escort at the Awards Dinner in New York.

"I can't get away from the shop," he said uneasily. "At her age it's too much for Mom to put in full days."

"Seth, we'll fly up on Saturday morning and come home Sunday," she said as though talking to a small, rebellious but much-loved child. "You know Mom won't mind covering for you at the shop for one day."

"Okay," he capitulated after a painful moment. "You said formal dinner. Does that mean I have to wear a tux?" He grimaced in distaste.

"You've got one," Carol reminded. At intervals they attended formal affairs in Bellevue and Atlanta, though Seth claimed the typical male dislike for such events. "In fact, you look very handsome in a tux."

"Flattery will get you nowhere—except in bed."

"Oh, you look devastatingly handsome in a tux," she murmured.

"Okay, pay the penalty," he ordered.

"With pleasure," she agreed. It was Bonnie's night off, and Karen was at a friend's house. So they'd have dinner later. Thank God, they weren't locked into the Saturday night sex night scene.

At fifty, Carol mused later, Seth was more handsome than he'd been at thirty. For some men added years did that.

Carol reveled in having Jonnie home for a week in April. Again, he would be attending one of the two summer sessions at Columbia, so his summer at home would be brief. Each day he was home was precious to her.

"How's Dad doing with the writing?" he asked his mother in a private moment. "Is he sending out the book?"

Carol shook her head, sighed. "If I try to talk to him, he goes into a rage. But no, he's not sending it out again."

"And I suppose he's not working on something new," Jonnie said reluctantly. "I can understand that."

Carol spent much of the next two months commuting between New York and Bellevue. When school closed in Bellevue, she brought Karen into the office. Karen was like a sponge, she thought lovingly—she sopped up everything. At the dinner table each night the conversation was heavily interspersed with office activities.

"That young lady has a business head," Seth said. "In a year she'll be ready to take over the office."

"She'll be an architect," Carol said.

"I like the managing part, too," Karen admitted. "Wouldn't it be exciting," she said dreamily, "to do a whole low-income project—you know, a place that would be comfortable and efficient but could be built without the expensive frills?"

"I don't think we'll be seeing anything like that in Bellevue," Seth pointed out. "Atlanta, yes—but we're too small."

"The town's growing beyond everybody's expectations." Karen said, and Carol agreed. "Bellevue's ripe for a low-income project—if the funds can ever be raised. We're getting a tremendous population spillover from Atlanta."

Early in August Carol received a phone call from the *Bellevue Enquirer*. They asked for a photograph of her to run with an article about her award. In town and working for six weeks as an intern on the *Bellevue Enquirer*, Jonnie had handed in the story, she discovered—amused yet disconcerted about this splash of local publicity. Here in Bellevue she was Seth Walden's wife, Jonnie and Karen's mother. Of course, everybody knew she had an office in Atlanta, but she hadn't built one house in Bellevue—except her own. She liked that separation.

Hannah decided there must be a family dinner just before Carol and Seth left for New York.

"Of course, we have to celebrate!" Hannah declared.

Until her mother-in-law read about the award in the local newspaper, Carol realized, she had not considered it important. Hannah knew that Seth wanted to take that Saturday off to go up for a formal dinner in New York, but she had not understood that the award to Carol was of significance beyond her immediate business circle.

Sharon appreciated the value of the award to Carol.

"Also," she effervesced on one of their regular phone calls, "I'll have a chance to see Seth. It's been so damn long."

"I haven't talked about this yet with Seth," Carol confided. *Why was she so uneasy about discussing it with him?* "But I've decided it's time I rented a small apartment in Manhattan. It'll be less expensive—and more comfortable—than going to hotels every time I hit New York."

"I feel awful that you're not staying with me," Sharon apologized.

"I wouldn't dream of interfering with your love life," Carol laughed. Now that Michelle was away at school, Sharon admitted that she had a "male roommate except for those times Michelle comes home—then he goes to his own pad." "By the way, how's it coming?"

"As long as there're no strings attached, fine. And believe me, men are in no rush to marry a working woman who's putting a kid through college. Not that I want to marry again," she reminded. "But I worry about Michelle." All at once she was serious. "I mean, the way these kids sleep around."

"Sharon, they do it openly," Carol told her. "We did it, but we didn't talk about it."

"I keep telling her—be careful. I'm not ready to be a grandmother."

Carol shopped for a shockingly expensive dinner dress for the awards dinner, wore it as a sort of dress rehearsal for the dinner at her mother-in-law's house. Hannah insisted she would do all the cooking but agreed to have Bonnie make dessert and serve along with Della. Elaine, too, wore a formal dinner dress because she knew their mother-in-law would be pleased, Carol thought affectionately.

The table was set for seven. Only Timmy—at camp for the summer—was not present. Having taken the famous bartending course popular with Columbia students, Jonnie appointed himself the evening's bartender. He stood behind a card table doubling as a bar and served drinks before dinner. Thank God, Carol thought, she and Seth had finally persuaded Mom to put air conditioners on both floors. It was a typical August night—not a hint of breeze from the river.

Seth and Harvey stood off to one side with drinks in hand. Carol heard them discussing her award.

"Smart of her to hire only women in her two offices," Harvey drawled. "That's a great gimmick. How does it feel, Seth, to be the husband of a famous woman?"

Why did Harvey taunt him that way, Carol fumed. He knew how

insecure Seth was. *And she wasn't famous.* Just recognized in her profession.

"I love your dress." Elaine invaded her thoughts. "And you have the figure to wear it. Honestly, Carol, nobody would ever believe you have two grown kids if they didn't know you."

Their conversation focused now on Timmy—whom Elaine adored. It seemed so odd, Carol thought, that Timmy was rarely part of family gatherings. Grandma used to say—privately to Seth and herself—that Harvey didn't want their Jewishness to rub off on his Episcopalian-raised son. Sometimes it seemed as though Mom felt she had only two grandchildren. Mom was always sweet and loving to Timmy—who was such a likable child—but Jonnie and Karen held a warmer place in her heart.

"I'm not surprised Carol's flooded with work," she heard Harvey say as they were summoned to the dining table. "This area is going berserk with expansion. Not just Atlanta. Look at Bellevue. In the last ten years it's quadrupled in population."

Carol was relieved when table conversation was diverted from the upcoming awards dinner to be monopolized by Harvey with long-winded stories about his Washington activities. Tonight he confided that he was finally taking a step he'd talked about for over a year.

"I'm looking for a townhouse in D.C.," he told them. Carol saw Elaine's astonished stare. His mother glowed. "I need a place where I can entertain at regular intervals. Bellevue will be home, of course—" He smiled reassuringly at his mother. "But Elaine and I will spend more time in D.C. in the future."

Carol was annoyed by Harvey's flow of anecdotes about Washington bigwigs. He could be so charming if you didn't know him well, she thought bitterly, though he was acquiring a paunch and a bloated face from excessive drinking. At the moment he was mesmerizing Jonnie and Karen with his name-dropping—but Seth seemed enveloped in pain. Carol read his mind. His brother and his wife were successes—but he had accomplished nothing.

Seth was relieved that Jonnie and Karen talked nonstop on the drive home—about the student deaths at Kent State in May, which had shocked the nation. Nothing in the way of conversation was required of him. He felt suffocated by the heady atmosphere of the evening. *He felt such a damned failure.*

Not until he and Carol were alone in their bedroom and preparing for bed did he tell her what had been festering in his mind for the past hour and a half.

"Carol, I don't think I should go with you to that dinner in New York," he said, his voice betraying his tension. "I don't like the prospect of Mom's being in the shop all day Saturday."

"But she doesn't mind." Carol gazed at him in consternation. "Seth, you're supposed to be my escort."

"Jonnie has to leave for school in another three days. He'll go ahead with you and take you to the dinner. He'll probably love it." He couldn't face all those people at the dinner. All those successful people. *"And what do you do?"* they'd ask him. "The neighborhood around the store is getting too rough to have Mom there all day—especially on a Saturday. You don't need me; Jonnie will be your young and handsome escort. And he'll love it."

Why did Carol look so hurt? Jonnie would be with her. He couldn't go through that dinner—constantly embarrassed that all he'd done with his life was to manage a shop in a decaying neighborhood. Harvey's remark charged through his mind. *"How does it feel to be the husband of a famous woman?"*

Chapter Fifty-two

Frustrated by Seth's closing off his mind to his writing, Carol threw herself into work with an obsessive need for personal satisfaction. Involved in designing, she could escape her anxieties. She knew Seth hated managing the shop. But why couldn't he understand that in those hours he was writing he was happy? That was a precious gift.

The house seemed painfully empty with both Jonnie and Karen away at school. A poignant silence seemed to mock her. She even missed the battles between the kids, she thought wistfully. Jonnie was the typical brother intent on teasing his sister—and Karen was passionate in her reproaches. And their absence highlighted the rift she felt between Seth and herself. Karen was at Georgia Tech and euphoric at the prospect of a bachelor's degree in architecture. Carol was pleased that she made an effort to come home most weekends despite an active social life on campus—*"Mom, all those cute guys!"*

On her most recent weekend at home Karen talked with soaring enthusiasm about a local group that had come together to promote a housing project for low-income working families—the Bellevue Improvement Group, dubbed BIG. That Monday Carol approached the new organization and volunteered her services as an architect when the need arose.

"What kind of houses would you design, Mom?" Karen demanded when her mother reported on this at dinner the following Friday evening. "Not those tall, ugly monsters you showed me once in Atlanta?"

"We haven't actually got into that," Carol told her. "And they're not all ugly monsters in Atlanta. But there's a lot of work to be done first—including raising the money."

"What kind of houses?" Karen persisted.

"Garden apartments," Carol said after a moment. "With lots of open space and trees and flowers."

"What about government funding?" Seth asked.

"That can take forever," Carol pointed out. "If we can raise the funds locally and build, then we can turn the development over to the Bellevue Housing Authority. They're doing that in Atlanta with much success."

"Get on Harvey's tail," Seth suggested. His smile was cynical. "If he can see his name in print as a benefactor, he'll donate."

"This will take years," Carol warned and smiled indulgently as Karen grunted in youthful impatience.

In an effort to break through Seth's depression, Carol tried to bring him into BIG—the group working for the housing development. Though only an idea at this stage, it was already titled Woodland Acres. He brushed this aside.

"Carol, when do I have time for volunteer organizations?" he asked irritably. "You work with them."

In the coming months Carol acknowledged that the wall between Seth and her showed no signs of crumbling. She was terrified.

She'd always been so sure their marriage was solid. There were nights now when she reached out to Seth and he pretended to be asleep. He wasn't asleep, she told herself in anguish. She and Seth had always prided themselves on their never-failing ardor in bed. *Where was she failing him?*

On one of her trips to New York she discussed this with Sharon, over dinner in her new apartment a few blocks south of Sharon's.

"You come all the way up here to work and then cook dinner for me," Sharon said, smiling. "I never remember you being wild about cooking."

"I'm not," Carol admitted, "but these days it's kind of a tensional outlet. At home my cooking is minimal. Thank God for Bonnie. Maybe in a corner of my mind I worry that I haven't been a good wife and mother through the years. Maybe I was absent from the family kitchen too much."

"Bullshit," Sharon flared. "Sweetie, what's bugging you?"

"Something's happening with Seth and me. Or rather," she said wryly, "it's not happening. Something's gone out of our sex life."

"Look, you're not kids anymore—" But Sharon's eyes were sympathetic.

"People like us are supposed to enjoy their sex lives when they're ninety," Carol shot back. "What's happening to Seth and me?"

"You know," Sharon said compassionately. "Seth's eaten up by his failure to keep up with your success. The more women go out into careers, the more it happens."

"I don't know how to cope—" How *did* a wife cope in this kind of situation?

"He ought to get back to writing. And he's got three publishable manuscripts sitting in a file drawer. Make him send them out again. Somewhere there's an editor who'll see how good they are. Do you know how many best-sellers have been rejected fifteen or twenty times?"

"He won't send them out. He's convinced they're lousy."

"And he still won't try for the paperback field." Sharon sighed. "Honey, he's going to have to work this out for himself."

True to his plan Jonnie earned his degree after a final summer session this year. He came home to a jubilant reunion with Fred Wassermann—in Bellevue with his mother for ten days. Fred had chosen to study in Israel to become part of his father's world. His mother, too, had joined her family in Israel.

In September Jonnie headed back to Columbia for a year at Columbia's School of Journalism. Karen was a sophomore at Georgia Tech and determined to emulate Jonnie's speed in getting her degree. She was religiously following the efforts of the Bellevue group intent on building a housing development for low-income families. And Carol's anxieties over the state of her marriage intensified; Seth's failure in his chosen profession continued to carry over into their bed. He was shocked and humiliated. Her comforting words only deepened this.

Carol returned from a five-day trip to New York in October to discover a letter waiting for her from a new magazine devoted to women's interests. The editor was eager for her to write an article about her conception of the perfect vacation home, a growing factor in the housing industry.

"Seth, they're out of their minds," Carol said in astonishment, handing him the letter. "I'm not a writer."

"You sit down and you write it as though you were talking to a group of women," Seth told her gently. "We've heard you spout out tons of words at the dinner table. You can do it. It'll be terrific publicity for you."

"I don't know." Carol wavered. "Suppose I write what I think— then you polish it for me. Will you, Seth?"

"Sure," he agreed, yet Carol sensed he was self-conscious about being involved in this.

Utilizing flight time between Bellevue and New York, Carol quickly finished the article and handed it over to Seth. She was delighted with his revisions, sent it off immediately.

"You know, Carol, I think I'll talk to Sharon about this 'genre fiction' deal she keeps yakking about," Seth said with an unfamiliar self-consciousness the following evening. She gazed at him in joyous amazement. *Had editing her article put him back on track?* "I think it's time to be realistic."

"Great!" Carol glowed, yet an instant later doubts tugged at her. Was this a kind of fatalistic capitulation on Seth's part?

"I don't want to say anything to Mom yet," he said, suddenly serious, "but I don't know how long we're going to be able to hang on to the business. We're barely showing a profit. And the neighborhood's getting worse than ever. Maybe if I could find a black buyer—somebody the militants wouldn't try to intimidate—" He spread his hands in a gesture of futility. "Mom would have the income from the sale money, at least."

"The crime here in town frightens me." These days she was nervous about Seth's being in the shop. Such violence erupted in the area. "Not just the robberies—the murders. I wish you *could* sell the store."

"This is happening all over the country," Seth reminded. "And it won't stop while a part of a community lives in squalor. Remember what FDR said back in the Depression days about one-third of the nation being ill-housed, ill-clothed, and ill-fed? That's happening right now to a solid chunk of our black population."

"Seth, did you mean what you said?" Carol pursued. "That you'll talk to Sharon about trying for the paperback market?"

"I don't have much choice," Seth said tiredly. "If I can sell the shop for Mom, where does that leave me? I'm fifty-one years old. What chance do I have on the job market?"

"Call Sharon tonight," Carol urged. "She knows what's happening in the paperback field. Her boss is ready to launch a line." *And Sharon would be a position to buy from Seth.*

Carol forced herself to be casual about Seth's decision to try to sell to the paperback market. Sharon had persuaded him to write a "Vietnam novel"—currently "very hot," she told him. It wouldn't matter if the advance was low, Carol thought. To see a book in print would give him the confidence he needed to push ahead.

With Sharon as his mentor—"don't try to do a masterpiece—just a quick, easy read"—Seth was once again on his 5:30 A.M.-at-the-typewriter routine. After dinner each night he was back at the manuscript. Sundays he escaped from the typewriter only long enough for meals and to watch a half hour of TV news. By mid-January he'd finished the manuscript. Sharon had warned that with no track record in book publishing he shouldn't try to sell on the familiar "partial" deal—an outline and sample chapters.

"I've finished a first draft," he reported to Sharon while Carol made this a three-way phone conversation via an extension. "I need another two months for the final draft."

"Send it to me as is," Sharon told him. "I might be able to buy it for our first batch of releases. The money will be lousy," she warned. "Nat pays at the bottom of the barrel. He'll offer a thousand. I'll insist I can't buy it for less than fifteen hundred. Of course, you could try for a better house."

"Send it to Sharon," Carol broke in. "Once you have one sale behind you, then try a better market."

"Okay, I'll mail it out tomorrow," Seth said, yet Carol sensed doubt in him. He was unhappy with this rush deal. He knew this wasn't his best work. "You two can talk about the kids now," he said in gentle derision.

"It was so funny, the first time Jonnie was over for dinner when Michelle was home from school," Sharon told Carol. "I mean, Jonnie and Michelle haven't seen each other since they were tiny, but they've grown up with this kind of proxy closeness. In ten minutes they were battling like brother and sister. It felt good to see them both at the dinner table."

"Jonnie thinks Michelle is so smart and sophisticated. After all, she was at Woodstock and went up to Columbia during the riots."

"Did I tell you the latest? Now she wants to go for a master's in social work at Columbia after her B.A.—but she's switching her major. She's following dear Mom's tracks. An English major."

Three weeks after Seth mailed off the manuscript, he received a contract with an advance of fifteen hundred and a note from Sharon to start on another Vietnam novel. Two nights later Sharon phoned and talked to Carol.

"I hate doing this to Seth," she apologized. "I'm still shaking from what I did. Carol, I quit my job."

"Sharon, what happened?"

"That bastard Nat expected me to handle all the magazines *and* oversee the paperback line. He refused me a raise, then talked about firing one of my assistants to 'make the budget leaner because of all the money going into the new line,' " she seethed. "Only Nat would try that shit."

"With your experience you won't have any trouble finding another job," Carol told her with conviction. "And don't worry about Seth; with a book behind him he's lots more confident about submitting to another publisher."

"I'm not trying for another job," Sharon confessed. "I want to free-lance. I know all the problems—the awful insecurity—but I'm tired of the old grind. I've lined up a packaging deal—for Nat's competition. I can still do the confessions. And I want to take a crack at a paperback original myself."

"You know the market—" She was excited for Sharon, knew it was a scary situation for her.

"I'm not a writer in Seth's league. I know that, sweetie. But I see what's selling, and I figure if I'm sharp I can parlay a minuscule talent into something that'll pay me better than what Nat paid me— and in a hell of lot more comfort. It's hard work—though most people think writers sit at the typewriter two or three hours a day and party the rest of the time—but it sure beats the regular job scene."

"Now's the time to give it a try," Carol approved. "If you don't do it now, you never will."

"I'm hearing undercurrents about a new genre of women's novel that's coming out. Remember what Betty Friedan said about 'the mounting sex hunger of American women'? Well, these novels are beamed at those women. Lots of hot sex scenes," she drawled. "A fantasy life in a historical setting. My antenna tells me this new genre will mean big bucks."

"Go for it," Carol urged. "It's time for a change."

She and Seth, too, Carol thought, were entering a stimulating new period in their lives. He was doggedly working on a second Vietnam novel and putting out feelers for a possible buyer for the shop. Through a New York contact she had been approached to enter a competition with three other architectural firms to design a small but innovative development in Westchester—a tiny village in itself. The other firms were prestigious and all-male. It was up to her, she told herself, to show the developers that a project such as this required not only a superb architect but one who understood the needs and desires of contemporary women. And who could do that as well as a woman architect?

Carol focused all her efforts on this new challenge. She knew it would require her to spend much time in New York. Also, it would escalate Walden & Associates to new heights.

She would have been happy in this new venture if Jonnie hadn't told them that after receiving his master's in journalism at the end of May, he was going out on a magazine assignment to Israel—as ever the subject of hostility by its neighbors.

"It's a new magazine and they can't pay much, but it's a terrific opportunity for me. I got it because I was in Israel during the Sixty-seven War," he reported exuberantly. "I do an article on the Israeli Olympic team—following them from Israel to Munich."

Jonnie laughed off the thought of being part of the Columbia commencement exercises. He had no time for that—echoing Michelle who had told Sharon not to bother coming up for her graduation.

"What's the matter with these kids?" Sharon asked Carol. "Here I am, all prepared to play the doting mother scene—and she's rushing home to campaign for George McGovern."

Jonnie was coming home for a week before heading for Israel. Carol received a summons to the developers' New York office for a meeting the day after his arrival. She knew this was the moment of decision for the developers. The architect for this plum of an assignment was about to be chosen. She saw Jonnie for one night, then flew up to New York for the conference.

"I'll fly right back tomorrow," she promised, guilty at dashing off when he'd just come home. "Darling, it's so good to see you!"

In New York she learned that she had, indeed, been chosen to design the Westchester "village." When they assumed she'd be available for conferences the following few days, she geared herself to explain that she had to be in Bellevue.

"I can fly up next week. I have commitments for now." Her heart pounding, she contrived to sound calm. She saw the exchange of impatient glances. They were annoyed, she realized. "That will give me time to work out a couple of problems."

"Very well," the senior member of the group capitulated, and Carol felt encased in relief. "We'll schedule meetings for next week."

Carol had known this jewel of an assignment would be demanding. She hadn't realized the amount of time she'd have to spend in New York—and later on the Westchester site. Still, it was an exciting project. This was such an active period for all of them, she thought on one of her brief trips back to Bellevue. Seth had sold his second Vietnam book to Nat's new editor—with a grudging increase of two hundred fifty dollars. He vowed to try for a better market with the current one.

"If I have to sweat out this shit, let me see more money for it. Not that it'll ever be much."

Jonnie wrote brief but frequent letters from Israel. Karen was in summer school, but would come up to New York to be with Carol for the last two weeks in August, before starting her senior year at Georgia Tech.

Returning from her New York office on a sweltering day in July, Carol walked into the comfort of her air-conditioned apartment with a sigh of relief. She'd taken a cab from the office, but air-conditioned cabs were as rare in New York as they were in Bellevue. The phone rang. She picked it up.

"Hello."

"Don't tell me you have a business conference this evening," Sharon's voice came to her. "We're celebrating."

"What are we celebrating?"

"I finished the bloody book. I know—I should have been doing more confessions. They're surefire checks."

"If you need cash," Carol offered instantly, "I'm your banker."

"At the moment I'm okay. And thank God, Michelle's going for the master's at night school. I made it clear, I saw her through four years of college—now it's her turn to sweat. Oh, she's staying at a crash pad down in the East Village. I'm scared to ask who with. Anyhow, she's decided it's time to support herself. Of course, she knows Mommie is here if the going gets rough."

"I'll meet you for dinner at Tip Toe Inn in twenty minutes." She dreaded leaving the air-conditioned apartment for the hot city streets even briefly, but the restaurant was nearby.

Gulping tall, frosty glasses of ice coffee while they waited for their salads, they discussed Sharon's novel.

"When do I get to read it?" Carol asked.

"Oh God, never," Sharon shuddered.

"Sharon, I'm not expecting John Steinbeck." Carol chuckled indulgently.

"Not even Jackie Susann. Compared to this, *Valley of the Dolls* is a masterpiece. I told you—I'm playing a long shot."

"I'm betting on you to make it." Carol smiled confidently.

"This woman I know at a paperback house slipped me a copy of the galleys of that novel I told you about. Of course, they could be wrong and I've wasted months of blood and sweat on this thing. It's crazy." She squinted in thought for a moment. "I dissected those galleys, page by page, studying the format. I know how bad it is, yet I have this hunch that an awful lot of women are going to be enthralled. It's going to do for women what those sexy men's novels have been doing for men."

"What's the title?" Carol asked.

"The galleys or my book?"

"Yours. All at once you're shy?" Carol joshed.

"Hold your breath. My book is *Their Savage Lust*, by Janine Beauchamp. It's supposedly going in 'over the transom,' but my contact promises me a quick read. If their first one takes off, they'll be looking for more. Of course, the money at this point is shitty—but the house is talking big bucks if this genre takes off. And they're pushing it."

"If you run into a money shortage," Carol said seriously, then smiled, "while you're waiting for the 'big bucks,' let me know."

Seth saw the two clerks out of the shop, and closed the door behind them. Any minute now the New Yorker from Harlem was to meet him to discuss a possible sale of the shop. He left all the lights on, locked the door. A friend at the police station had told him if he ever saw anybody lurking around—saw anything suspicious—he was to call and they'd send over a police car.

A late model white Cadillac pulled up before the shop. A neatly dressed black man emerged, checked the number above the door of the shop and approached. Within fifteen minutes of conversation Seth knew he had a sale. The buyer would bring his attorney over the following day. Within a month the sale could be completed.

Mom would go along, of course. He knew she was anxious about the deteriorating neighborhood. Still, it would be traumatic for her to see the shop go into other hands. For over seventy years it had been in the Walden family—run by three generations of Waldens.

Where did *he* go from here? It was an agonizing—terrifying—question. So he'd sold two Vietnam books and had another in the hopper. Was this what he wanted to do the rest of his life?

In a sudden revolt against going into an empty house, he called Bonnie and told her to leave a cold dinner for him in the refrigerator.

"I think I'll take in a movie," he said. "I'll eat later."

Chapter Fifty-three

Seth's first Vietnam novel came out in July. Carol had hoped it would provide him with some satisfaction. Jonnie and Karen were candidly impressed. He never once considered showing it to Harvey—his brother was all wrapped up in high-level deals that swelled his income to astronomical figures. Harvey had acquired a reputation for being shrewd, manipulating, and dangerous to cross—a power in Bellevue, the state, and the nation.

His mother was ambivalent about the book, Carol realized while she and Seth waited for a comment.

"But that's not your name." Hannah stared at the cover of the slim paperback volume Seth had placed in her hands.

"Mom, I used a pseudonym," he explained. "A lot of writers do that."

"Why?" Hannah was puzzled.

"I'll use my name when I sell a book that satisfies me," he told her. "This was a 'quickie'—written for the check. Not that it was large," he conceded. "They paid me fifteen hundred dollars—and there won't be any royalties beyond that." His gaze swung to Carol. "They're on the shelves thirty to sixty days, then go off to be replaced by new titles. No chance to earn royalties."

"Wouldn't you do better to try for a job as a store manager? You have so much experience. And there are all the new shops opening up in that mall at the edge of town," Hannah reminded. Stores they all feared would be the death-knell for those on Main Street, where parking was so inadequate. "Everybody in town knows how well you managed the store since Dad died."

"Mom, these stores don't want me," Seth said tiredly. "They want twenty-eight or thirty-year-olds that they can hire for half the salary."

Still, Carol observed, Seth's mother was quick to look for his book in the local stores. She chuckled tenderly when she saw Hannah glance about in the local drugstore that carried a substantial selection of paperbacks and—certain that this action was unobserved—move the two copies of Seth's book to a more advantageous spot on the shelf.

"I don't know how much longer Vietnam books will be hot," Seth confided to Carol later. "By next month the last of our ground combat troops will be withdrawn from Vietnam. That might be the end of the genre."

"I doubt that."

"I'll hang in there as long as they're buying." But his bitterness was deep, Carol thought anxiously.

Jonnie was enjoying his visit with Fred—on vacation from medical school at Tel Aviv University—and with his father in their pleasant apartment in Tel Aviv. It was an all-male enclave for the moment—with Fred's mother visiting for a month in Bellevue. The family insisted Jonnie make their apartment his headquarters while he researched his article here in Tel Aviv. That helped his meager expense account go further, he told Fred.

They talked endlessly about the past and the future of Israel. Jonnie's optimism about the situation in regard to the country's Arab neighbors did not extend to Erik Wassermann.

"I don't trust this business between Sadat and the Soviets," he said bluntly. "Sadat said himself that this was just 'an interlude with our friend.' They pretend to be angry to put us off guard. The kind of hatred most of the Arab governments harbor for us won't disappear within a generation. From the fourth grade through high school Arab children are fed hatred for the Jews. Even their textbooks in geography and arithmetic and reading preach the theme that the Jews must be destroyed. This is done," Erik summed up with recurrent rage and frustration, *"by government decree.* Another generation is being raised to despise the Jews and to vow to destroy Israel."

From Erik—as he plotted the article for his magazine—Jonnie came to understand the trauma of the Israeli Olympic team that was to represent its nation in a city that had been the center of the Nazi regime. He felt humbled by the knowledge of how difficult their lives had been—when he'd had everything so easy.

He thought about Karen—always so intense, so vocal about what she thought was right and wrong. Maybe he wouldn't spend his life chasing around the globe in search of fascinating stories. A few years, he promised himself, and then he'd head for home and settle down to making a hands-on contribution.

He remembered Michelle, who was gung-ho for saving the earth. Two years ago—when he returned to campus from the spring break—she'd dragged him with her to march in the "Earth Day" parade. He was excited about journalism, but he needed something more in his life. Weird, how often he thought about Michelle when he didn't see her for a while. Kind of incestuous, he told himself self-consciously. She was like a sister—like Karen. Yet he couldn't quite bring himself to accept that designation.

On schedule Jonnie flew to Munich along with hordes of other newsmen representing the press from around the world. The atmosphere in Munich was high-spirited, gay. In the first days many were already declaring the Olympics a huge success. A host of records were being toppled. The political atmosphere was commendable. West Germans in attendance made a point of cheering each time East Germany was declared a victor.

Jonnie relished traveling about the Olympic Village at night making notes for his article. He was thrilled when he was able—through a youthful barter system—to acquire a U.S. track team jacket. He'd interviewed the members of the Israeli Olympic team in Israel, felt a special warmth toward them. The team included 28-year-old David Berger from Shaker Heights, Ohio. A graduate of Columbia Law and holder of dual U.S.—Israeli citizenship, he'd settled in Israel just last year. His parents still lived back in Shaker Heights. The Israeli team included emigrés from the Soviet Union, Rumania, Poland, and Libya.

Then on Tuesday, September 5th, the euphoria in Munich was blasted into horror. Shortly after 5 A.M., a thunderous knock on the door of the cheap hotel room Jonnie shared with two other young journalists prodded the occupants into instant wakefulness.

"All hell's broke loose," their caller reported tersely. "Get your asses over to the Olympic Village! Arabs have attacked the Israelis!"

Along with other alerted newsmen, Jonnie and his two companions arrived at the Olympic Village shortly after the Munich police, who had been summoned by escaping Israelis. They learned that the apartments occupied by the 22 male Israeli athletes and their coaches and officials had been under attack. The newsmen were frustrated at being kept away from Building 31, where the Israelis were being held by Arab terrorists. Over 600 men had been called up by the police chief—plus a stream of armored cars. The area of attack was being cordoned off.

"Let's head for the roof of the next building," Jonnie told his roommates. "We'll be able to see what's happening from there."

They watched from the roof as a *Krisenstab*—crisis center—was being set up in the administration building. They fretted at the lack of information that was coming through. Then they heard the shriek of an ambulance and saw it pull up before the Israeli compound.

"There's a body on the steps!" Jonnie was suddenly cold with shock.

They watched the ambulance crew take the motionless body— *was he dead?*—to the waiting ambulance.

"Hell, we're not learning anything here," one of the other two complained. "Let's go on down again."

Below they were told the first details of the attack. The 32-year-old Israeli wrestling coach Moshe Weinberg—whom Jonnie remembered passing around snapshots of his five-week-old son just yesterday—had opened a door to the attackers, tried to close it while yelling to his apartment sharers to run. He'd been killed in a burst of submachine-gun fire. That was the body they'd seen from the roof, Jonnie realized and felt sick. In another apartment, they learned, wrestler Joseph Romano fought off the Arab attackers with a knife but was mortally wounded.

Nine other Israelis had been taken hostage by the Arab terrorists. Word seeped through that the West German interior minister was trying to bargain personally with the terrorists. He made a frenzied offer of unlimited cash for the release of the Israelis being held inside Building 31. They turned him down.

"What the hell do they want?" someone close to Jonnie demanded in rage.

Now the newsmen learned that the interior minister had offered himself and other West Germans as replacement hostages. The terrorists were brusque in their rejection. Finally at 9 A.M. the Arabs threw a message out of a window. They demanded the release of 200 Arab prisoners held in Israeli jails—including terrorists who had killed policemen, who had taken part in the May massacre at Lod Airport in Tel Aviv, and who had bombed U.S. Army posts. Meanwhile, only 400 yards away the Olympic Games began for the day— most attendees unaware of the drama being enacted close by. Meet their demands by 3 P.M., the terrorists warned, or the Israelis would be shot.

Negotiations continued—although a decision had already been made not to release the Arab prisoners. Soon live TV and radio reports flooded the area and attracted crowds.

"Look at the nerve of the bastards!" Jonnie pointed to one of the terrorists, peering brazenly through a half-open door of Building 31.

The tension was almost unbearable, he thought as he hovered with others behind the police cordon. The sound of police sirens rent the air. Army helicopters circled overhead. A terrorist appeared on a balcony of Building 31, but no one dared fire on him.

"Take your guns and get out of here!" an athlete yelled from an adjacent building.

A group of at least 100 young Jews pushed against the police cordon and vigorously sang "Hatikvah"—Israel's national anthem. They followed this with "We Shall Overcome," the theme song of the civil rights movement.

Finally at 3:45 P.M.—with the Arab terrorists' deadline extended to 5 P.M.—the games were suspended at the insistence of Golda Meir. Negotiations continued, dragging into the evening with yet two more deadlines set. At 8:15 P.M. Munich time a frenzied call went out to President Anwar Sadat in Egypt. As had other Arab heads of state, Sadat bluntly said he didn't want to be involved.

With the terrorists becoming edgy negotiators agreed that the Arabs and their hostages would be taken to Munich's airport, to be flown out on a Lufthansa 727 jet to wherever they chose. They stipulated Cairo as their destination.

At 10 P.M. the eight terrorists prodded their hostages, tied together in chain fashion and blindfolded—into a waiting German army bus. Meanwhile, newsmen—including Jonnie—latched on to whatever transportation they could find to take them to the airport. The terrorists and their hostages, the newsmen learned, would be taken by bus, then helicopter to Furstenfeldbruck Airport.

Arriving at the airport the newsmen and TV and radio personnel discovered the area circled by 500 soldiers, with sharpshooters at strategic spots.

"What the hell do they expect five sharpshooters to do?" Jonnie whispered to his companions as they watched from behind the six-and-a-half-foot fence, manned by army guards and attack dogs.

In the melee that followed the German police captured three of the terrorists, then in a sporadic battle that lasted yet another hour five more terrorists—including their leader—were killed. Three more surrendered.

But in the interim, the police later discovered, four Israelis had burned to death when a terrorist threw a grenade that set fire to the helicopter where they sat. The Arab terrorists had gunned down the other bound-and-blindfolded Israelis.

The following morning 80,000 attendees filed somberly into the Olympic Stadium for a memorial service. The heavily guarded surviving members of the Israeli team sat in the center of the field, along with the other athletes. The stand was draped in black. The flags of the 122 competing nations—as well as the Olympic flag—flew at half-staff. Munich's Philharmonic Orchestra played the haunting strains of the funeral movement of Beethoven's Eroica.

The president of the International Olympic Committee insisted that the games must continue. To not do so, it was thought in some circles, would deny the Arab terrorists the satisfaction of stopping the games. The Israeli government protested. Some of the Dutch and Norwegian teams refused to continue, packed up and returned to their homes. Jonnie wrote an impassioned report, and shipped it off to his magazine.

Feeling a compulsion to be with Fred and his father at this tragic time, Jonnie decided to fly back to Tel Aviv. First, he phoned home—collect out of deference to his limited funds.

"Jonnie, we've been watching TV constantly. We can't believe what's happened! Are you all right?" Carol asked anxiously.

"I'm fine, Mom," he soothed. "It's been numbing—everybody here is in shock. I want to go back to Tel Aviv for a few days."

"I'll wire you funds. You're probably short. Shall I send it care of Fred in Tel Aviv?"

"That'll be wonderful, Mom. I'll be home as soon as I can."

"Hang on, Jonnie. Dad wants to talk to you, too. And we'll call Fred's mother and tell her you'll be going to Tel Aviv."

"I think they need me, Mom—"

"Go to them," she said, and her compassion reached out to include him. "Come home when you can."

Jonnie knew that what happened today in Munich would, somehow, affect the rest of his life. He had much thinking to do about his future. Being a foreign correspondent, chasing down exciting news stories, suddenly seemed of minor importance.

Chapter Fifty-four

Carol waited for weeks to tell Seth that Sharon had sold her romance novel and was hard at work on another. She knew he was unhappy at what he himself was writing—when Sharon was delighted just to be selling. Sharon was practical; she was determined to make money, cared not at all about what she wrote as long as it sold, Carol reasoned. Writing kept her off the office treadmill.

To Seth writing was kind of a religion. He was happy when he was writing what came from a special part of his mind and soul. He couldn't see it as a craft, though at defiant moments he quoted Samuel Johnson: "No man but a blockhead ever wrote except for money."

"Look, I know I can't live on what I'm making on this paperback original," Sharon told Carol at the approach of the new year. "But the idea is to keep them coming. With Michelle out of school and off on her own, I can afford to gamble a year of my life. And if I don't make it, I'll pick up a job on another shitty magazine. But I don't want to go back to that."

"When's the book coming out?" Carol asked.

"In March. They're in a mad rush to get on the bookshelves with this new title. My editor says they're really going to push. The climate is *right* for this genre. Women are liberated—and despite male thinking that this means less sex—women are expecting more and better sex."

"Nobody could say we're not liberated." Carol contrived a confident smile. But she wasn't getting more and better sex. "Oh, Seth said to tell you to keep your nose to the grindstone and make big bucks."

"From his mouth to God's ear," Sharon said fervently.

Carol worried about Jonnie, traipsing around the Middle East on yet another assignment. She'd hoped he'd be home soon after Munich. She was anxious about his reactions to the massacre of the Israeli athletes. He was *there* in all that horror—first the '67 War, now this. He was so young and sensitive. She'd wanted him to come home to be comforted.

Jonnie didn't physically fit into the stereotypical description of a Jew, nor would the Walden name—acquired at Covent Garden when his grandparents arrived in America—point him out to suspicious Arabs as a Jew. Seth regularly reminded her of this. Yet she knew that he, too, worried about Jonnie.

For his fledgling magazine—which he admitted paid him a minuscule salary and provided a matching expense account—Jonnie was writing a series of articles about the Kurds in Iraq. They had been struggling for a generation to obtain autonomy within Iraq but encountered successive Iraqi governments' intent to crush them by force. The Iraqis, Jonnie wrote home, vowed to eradicate the Kurds.

"When is he coming home?" Carol railed in recurrent anxiety—always in a corner of her mind the fear that he might want to settle in Israel.

"He needs to spread his wings a bit," Seth said gently. "He'll come home."

Carol breathed a sigh of relief when Jonnie returned to New York early in the new year. He stayed with her at her New York apartment for a week. Then they prepared to fly together to Bellevue. He'd acquired a new maturity after the traumatic months in the Middle East, she thought. The tragedy at Munich hadn't destroyed his beautiful zest for living; it had given him a deepening sense of the fragility of life.

"Mom, I'll never move to Israel," he told her gently while they waited to board their flight. "Bellevue's home to me. I want to be home with my family."

"That's what we want, too." Her eyes were suddenly blurred with tears. Bless Jonnie for putting her fears to rest.

On the flight home—while Jonnie dozed beside her in what seemed an endless need for sleep—she remembered their dinner with Sharon and Michelle at Sharon's favorite West Side restaurant the night before. She'd been caught up in a sense of *déjà vu*. She remembered Seth's impassioned denunciations of McCarthyism, his frustration at the slowness of school integration over other dinners with Sharon and herself. Now it was Jonnie who seethed at injustices. What children learned at home was what they carried into the outside world. That's why family was so important. Family values must be handed down from one generation to the next.

A smile touched her mouth as she envisioned her firebrand daughter at meetings of BIG. Members double and triple Karen's age were impressed by her eloquence—and her suggestions. Someone teasingly said that BIG ought to sponsor her for the City Council.

Children reflected what they saw in their parents, she thought. But too often these days, she remembered unhappily, families seemed to be abdicating their responsibilities. She had been haunted for years by the anxiety that she, too, was robbing Jonnie and Karen in her pursuit of career. But she was there when the kids needed her, she told herself with repetitious defensiveness. Jonnie and Karen had not suffered because she was an architect.

For three weeks Carol felt herself swathed in euphoria. Jonnie was home, Karen rushed home every weekend, Seth had finally convinced the new owner of the shop that his consulting time was over. Then Jonnie dashed back to New York to take on a local assignment for the magazine.

"They've got great ideas but shaky finances," he confided. "This could be my last assignment if we can believe the in-house gossip."

A few days later Carol was summoned to New York, though she'd expected to be in Bellevue at least another uninterrupted six weeks. The developers—intent on publicity for their "magnificent new village"—had hired publicists, who had booked Carol on the talk-show circuit.

On her first evening back in New York, Carol had dinner with Sharon.

"The book is already being shipped." Sharon was triumphant. "March release means 'shipping in February' usually. And the orders are sensational! I tell you, these books are going to be addictive. I got myself an agent. She's talking big money for the new one."

"When did you finish it?" Carol asked in astonishment.

"Last week. I've been working my butt off. I didn't do a partial—the whole shooting match. The agent's talking a four-book contract—with lots of money up front. I've had to wait almost fifty-three years," Sharon said ebulliently, "but the way it looks, I can ask for a charge account at Saks and Altman's and get it!"

"You deserve it." Carol was delighted. But Seth saw no future for himself in paperbacks, she remembered in a surge of anxiety. He hated churning out what he called "sixty-day wonders."

"What's with Seth?" Sharon asked, as though reading her mind.

"He's doing another Vietnam book—and hating it," she admitted. "Oh, he's finally out of the shop. Maybe now he'll settle down to working on the last novel. The munitions family book," she reminded Sharon. "I worry about him. He has a kind of resignation that scares me. You remember Seth—how passionate he got about his work. Like Karen with BIG."

"How's that coming?"

"We're making an impact. We've got promises of substantial funds. I was hoping for a time to bring Seth into it, but—" Her hands moved in a gesture of futility.

"He won't get involved in that," Sharon said bluntly. "That's your *schtick*—building houses."

"How can I help him?"

"He's going to have to work it out himself," Sharon told her. "Haven't I said that to you before?"

Seth had told himself that once the shop was off his back, he'd have a life again. But he was caught on the "paperback original" treadmill, he taunted himself. Let him at least be able to handle the mortgage payments and Bonnie's wages. He closed his mind to their swollen bank account. That was Carol's money. He self-consciously agreed to real estate investments Carol was carrying on these days. His name might be on the deeds along with hers, but he didn't feel himself part-owner.

Harvey was a bastard not to have had Carol design his house— not even the wing he added last year. But because she knew it would please Mom, she'd gone to Harvey's firm to handle the real estate closings for the property she'd bought. While Harvey turned these deals over to one of his junior associates, he'd seen enough to realize the kind of money Carol was earning. He'd mentioned it to Mom. She said he'd been quite impressed. He'd made some crack about Carol's "terrific luck." Not luck, he told himself—terrific talent and drive.

As customary in these last few weeks since he'd been out of the shop, Seth paused at the typewriter at 3 P.M., counted the day's output of pages, and decided it was time to go out for a walk. He needed to fight off the feeling of claustrophobia that attacked him each day at this time. The signs of spring were appearing everywhere—usually a spirit-lifter for him. But spring was not working its magic this year.

He left the house, strode toward town. He'd spend half an hour in the coffee shop that had become his afternoon rendezvous, then come back home and proofread his day's output. He kept himself on a stringent schedule. If he came up short one day, he made sure to make it up on the following day.

He dreaded the evenings alone in the house—when Carol and the kids were off on their separate lives. He felt shorn of family. He made sporadic efforts to get involved again in the munitions family novel, but he found it almost impossible to shift from his daytime Vietnam assignment to the novel that had tugged at him for years now. He needed to pour himself totally into that one, he conceded— live it every waking moment. The way he'd heard fine actors talk about pouring themselves totally into a role during the rehearsal period of a play.

One evening during each of those weeks when Carol was away, he went to his mother's house for dinner. Another evening he took his mother out for dinner. Bonnie designated those nights as her evenings off. Mom enjoyed having him to herself, he thought, yet he sensed she disapproved of Carol's absence from home.

He paused to chat briefly with a neighbor at the end of the block. Seeing him home now, she'd politely asked last week if he was retired. It wasn't normal, he conceded with wry humor, for the man of the family to be home all day unless he was retired. Didn't she know he was too young to be retired? If Dad was alive, he'd still be at the shop. He used to complain about all the "important man-power" lost to the retirement lists.

As he turned into Main Street, Seth quickened his pace. An unexpectedly cold wind had accompanied the sudden departure of the sun. He should have worn a sweater under his light jacket, he reproached himself. April was always a fickle month weather-wise.

He turned into the small, attractive coffee shop, felt a surge of physical pleasure as the indoor warmth engulfed him. There was something almost sensuous about walking into a warm, cozy area after having been chilled, he thought and headed for his customary table in a reclusive corner of the coffee shop. His regular waitress came over with the dazzling smile she reserved for regulars.

"The usual?" she asked and Seth nodded.

This was a comfortable retreat after six hours at the type-writer—broken only by Bonnie's appearance with his lunch tray. "The usual" was a toasted English muffin and black coffee. There were few patrons at this hour—midway between lunch and dinner. All that was required of him was a smile of approval for the kibitzing of the pair of waitresses who served the tables and the waiter on duty behind the counter.

Lottie, his waitress, immediately brought his coffee; she knew the English muffin was to justify his taking up a table. He relished the strong hot coffee that was the best in Bellevue. This was a brief but welcome period each afternoon.

The door of one of the two telephone booths at his right swung open. A tall, Twiggy-slim brunette with magnolia skin, astonishingly green eyes, and movie-star features emerged and walked to the table parallel with his own. Midthirties, he judged subconsciously, and well-heeled, considering her exquisitely tailored suit— something Carol had taught him to appreciate. A few moments later her conversation with Lottie told her she wasn't Southern born and bred.

Lottie left the table. Seth was conscious of his neighbor's scrutiny.

"Excuse me," she said after a moment, reaching into a crocodile purse. "Would you have a cigarette lighter or a match?" Her smile was appealingly apologetic.

"I'm sorry. I don't smoke."

"Don't be sorry," she said. "It's a rotten habit."

"Lottie can probably bring you matches," he offered and sensed her need to talk. He understood that need. Sometimes a day went by without his speaking to anybody but Bonnie. Catching Lottie's eyes he gestured his neighbor's requirement.

With her cigarette lighted the attractive brunette leaned back in her chair with a sigh of satisfaction.

"I thought when I moved here to Bellevue, I'd relax and stop smoking. You know, away from the madness and pressures of living in a big city."

"Where are you from?" Seth asked.

He learned that she was from New York, her name was Donna Raven, and she was recently divorced. She'd come to Bellevue, she said frankly, because she figured her alimony would go far in this kind of setting.

"And the real estate broker who sold me the house said that a great new private school had opened last year—and that it wasn't expensive. Andy's eight and sometimes he's a handful."

"I've heard good reports of the school," Seth reassured her. The one private school in town—and instantly popular with parents nervous about school integration. She wasn't worried about that, he assumed; she was the type who would automatically send her kid to a private school.

"It's taking Andy a time to adjust," she admitted. "We've just been here six weeks. And he's a little traumatized by the divorce. My husband got the 'hots' for this twenty-two-year-old sexpot. He and my lawyer worked out a good settlement—for me," she pinpointed, "and I went to Reno. Ten years of my life down the drain." Her eyes smoldered in retrospect.

Now she pelted him with questions about the social life in Bellevue.

"I have the feeling that you have to live here for three generations to be accepted," she said and laughed when she saw agreement in his eyes. "I don't give a shit about being part of the 'Old Families' scene. I just like to party now and then. Of course, a divorced woman—particularly if she's young—is considered a mortal enemy by the wives."

She drove a late-model white Cadillac, he noticed when they left the restaurant together.

"Can I drop you someplace?" she asked as they lingered a moment in further conversation. She'd seen all the Broadway plays of the season and reported on them to Seth's obvious delight.

"Thanks, but I'm just a few blocks away," he told her. "And I need the exercise."

"Do you come here often?"

"Almost every day," he said. Was she wondering why he was free in midafternoons this way? Did she take him for a retiree? "It's my runaway place."

"Then I'll be seeing you." Her smile was provocative as she slid behind the wheel. Why did he find that disturbing? he asked himself. " 'Bye now."

He walked home in the gray chill of the afternoon and dissected his brief encounter with Donna Raven. He felt self-conscious in her obvious approval. No, she *didn't* take him for a retiree. Her eyes told him she found him an interesting man. At fifty-three it was good for the ego to be judged an "interesting man" by an attractive woman probably twenty years younger than he.

When he turned into his block, Seth was whistling.

Chapter Fifty-five

Carol was delighted that Jonnie was coming home for Karen's graduation from Georgia Tech. Elaine planned a party at the country club, changed the locale when Karen candidly said she preferred not to go where Jews were not welcome. Harvey couldn't be at the party, Elaine reported apologetically. He had to be in Washington on business, Seth confided that local gossip suggested Harvey was playing house up there with his latest 23-year-old sexpot.

At the sumptuous dinner party in a private room at Bellevue's latest posh restaurant, Elaine whispered to Carol that she was arranging a surprise party for their mother-in-law's 76th birthday next month.

"I told Harvey he's got to be in town for that," Elaine said grimly. She knew about Harvey's trail of girls half his age, Carol thought. *Why did she stay with him?* "You know how Mom idolizes him."

Three days after the party for Karen, Jonnie returned to New York. He would stay at the New York apartment. Carol worried that he seemed restless. He wasn't trying for another Middle East assignment, was he?

Now Carol tried to persuade Seth to go up to New York with her. She had to be there for the final phase of the new "village."

"You can get away now," she pointed out cheerfully. "Let's spend a couple of weeks out at the Hamptons. I know it's late to look for a rental, but we'll find a little house somewhere. It doesn't have to be fancy—just on the water." Mom was going up to Hendersonville with a friend from the temple—they didn't have to worry about leaving her alone in Bellevue.

"I can't possibly take off for two weeks." All at once Seth appeared almost angry. "I've got a book to finish."

"Two weeks won't make that much difference," she cajoled. "Let's plan to go up next week."

"I know—you have to go up on business," he conceded, his eyes avoiding hers. "But I have a deadline; I can't just take off because I want to loll on the beach at the Hamptons."

She tensed at the hostility she felt in him.

"I'll leave on Monday," she decided after an ambivalent moment. Her heart was pounding. *Seth didn't want to spend two weeks alone with her.* When was the last time they made love? She knew there were some women who were relieved when their husbands relegated passion to rare moments. She wasn't one of those. "I'll try to finish up in a week."

She flew to New York on schedule. Despite their lovely air-conditioned office, she welcomed a respite from the turgid heat of their valley town. She found Sharon euphoric over the new contract she was waiting to sign.

"This agent is so sharp. The publishers know they're hopping aboard a gravy train and she pointed out she's got—via me—what'll keep that train running. I can't believe the advance on these four books," Sharon gloated. "I feel like I've won the Irish Sweepstakes. I know, I shouldn't get so excited until the contract has been signed—by me and the publisher," she emphasized. "But it's all happening so fast!"

Sharon decided to drive with Carol to the construction site the following day. As usual, Carol had rented a car for her current stay.

"Look, why don't we stay out there for two or three days?" Sharon suggested. "It'll be just as easy for you to drive from East Hampton or Wainscott to the 'Village' each day as it'll be to make the *schlep* on the LIE from Manhattan. And God, do I need a few days away from the typewriter. I just want to lie on a deck and stare at the ocean."

"Sharon, I can't just run off that way. Jonnie's at the apartment."

"Sweetie, at that age they just come home to sleep. We'll tell Jonnie and Michelle we're staying out at Montauk for two or three days. Believe me, they'll survive."

Carol hesitated. The prospect was appealing.

"This is June already. Do you think we'll find a vacancy?" She'd be at the site for a few hours each day, but the rest of the time would be hers.

"The rush doesn't start until the July Fourth weekend. We'll find something," Sharon said ebulliently. "Let's do it."

Leaving Jonnie fast asleep the following morning, Carol drove over to pick up Sharon. When they were together the years seemed to disappear, she thought. A friendship like theirs was a precious gift.

"I had to throw Michelle out of bed," Sharon said with a chuckle as she joined Carol on the front seat of the rented car. Michelle had abandoned the East Village crash pad for the comfort of her mother's apartment. "She's not particularly enamored of her job with that textbook publisher, but she likes the check. And they like her to be there at nine A.M. sharp."

"We'll stop for breakfast somewhere along the way," Carol said, reaching to switch on the air-conditioning. Even New York could be sultry in June.

"Instead of Wainscott, why don't we give Montauk a whirl? We've never been out there. It's the farthest point on the Island—and, I hear, heavenly quiet."

"Let's," Carol agreed, feeling adventurous.

"I've been thinking—maybe I'll buy a beach house with all that loot coming in. I hear prices are still decent out at Montauk. Isn't that a gas? Me, Sharon Randall, talking about buying a beach house!"

"You make sure I see that house before you buy it," Carol instructed. "All you'll care about is that it has a mile of decks and a fireplace."

Jonnie frowned in semisleep. He was trying to ignore the incessant ringing of the doorbell. Reluctantly he pried open his eyelids and inspected the clock on the night table. It was barely ten, but Mom was always out of the house by eight—whether in Bellevue or here in New York.

He sighed, threw off the sheet that covered him, and reached for a pajama jacket that lay across a chair—unworn as usual. Mom couldn't deal with his sleeping in jockey shorts, he thought with a flicker of humor; she casually always made sure there were pajamas in what had become "his bedroom" in the city apartment.

"Okay," he called as he strode down the hall past the living room and to the door—an unidentified finger never releasing the bell. "The marines are on the way."

He pulled the door wide and grinned down at Michelle in what she called a "Victorian granny dress."

"How did you ever manage to be awake for the massacre in Munich?" Michelle demanded. "Or hadn't you gone to bed?"

"Hey, I'm still trying to catch up on the sleep I missed in the Middle East." He clucked in disapproval. "You're not wearing a bra under that thing. That's like asking guys to throw you on your back."

"At least you've noticed I have boobs." Michelle stalked into the foyer with an air of impatience. "It's a gorgeous day out there. Let's head out for Jones Beach."

"You're supposed to be at work. What are you doing here?"

"I called in sick," she told him. All at once her gamine face wore a blissful smile. "Oh God, air-conditioning is the most wonderful invention of all time." She squinted in thought for a moment. "I don't suppose you could call sex an invention?"

"I'm starving." Jonnie strode toward the small but efficiently designed kitchen. "Did you have breakfast?"

"No, I figured you'd feed me." Michelle followed at his heels. "What's with the magazine?"

"Nothing's changed since we talked about it last night at the Chinese joint." He opened the refrigerator, inspected the contents—in the familiar pattern of homecoming children. "They're just hanging on. They're sending me up to Maine to do a story about some river being polluted by a paper mill." He grinned as he pulled out a carton of eggs and a butter dish. "Paying me damned good, too."

"Your mom has a coffee grinder, hasn't she?" Michelle opened a cabinet, peered inside.

"The question, do we have coffee beans? Ah, right here. You make the coffee, I'll do the omelets. And bagels," he murmured appreciatively. "God, do I love New York bagels. They've never got the hang of it down in Bellevue. I'll throw a couple in the oven to warm up."

They prepared breakfast with little conversation—content to be occupied with trivial activity in air-conditioned comfort. Then they sat down to eat with gusto in the small breakfast area off the kitchen."

"Okay," Michelle probed when they'd finished eating, "do we go to Jones beach or hop into the bed?"

"Michelle, that would be incestuous." He grinned self-consciously. Damn, she knew what she did to his hormones!

"Stop treating me like Karen! I'm not your sister." She shot him that provocative smile that always unnerved him. "I just want your body."

"You're crazy, you know—" But he was already pushing back his chair. At first he'd thought Michelle was acting like a show-offy kid. "Your mom and mine would have fits."

"So who's to tell them? Anyhow," she added, sliding to her feet in a slithering movement that sent heat surging through him, "they'd probably be thrilled. Of course, they'd prefer that we got married before we did it. But that was their generation—"

Carol and Sharon relaxed on chaises on their oceanfront deck at Gurney's Inn and watched the setting sun cast an orange glow over the glistening blue of the Atlantic. A last-minute cancellation had provided them with this oasis.

"Oh God, that was a great dinner," Sharon purred. "I shouldn't have had dessert, but I don't care. That peppermint mousse—with those luscious chocolate chips—was out of this world."

"This is heavenly. Every year I try to persuade Seth to come up here with me—you know he loves the ocean—but when was the last time he came out to the Hamptons? Ten years ago, I think."

"I figured once he was out of the shop he'd come up with you regularly," Sharon admitted.

"He keeps shutting me out." Carol's voice was sharp with frustration. "He feels himself such a failure." *Was that the real reason?* "Despite all the money in our checking and savings accounts he begrudges spending a cent on himself."

"Because he didn't earn it."

"He's been selling the paperbacks," Carol shot back defensively.

"That's piddling compared to what you earn," Sharon said.

"I thought he'd get over that, but it doesn't happen." She was tense again, remembering four nights ago, when she turned to him and he'd pretended to be asleep. "Each time I come to New York I run into Altman's or Lord and Taylor to pick him up shirts or socks or sweaters—pretending they're gifts. I had to force him to go out and buy a new suit to go to dinner parties with me back home. He knew he had to do that for my sake." But he didn't want to spend two weeks alone with her out here, she taunted herself again. She glanced at her watch. "Maybe I should call him—"

"Don't you move," Sharon ordered. "You can call Seth later.

Let's just soak up this glorious view. What time do you have to be at the Village tomorrow?"

"It's up to me. I figure on a late leisurely breakfast, then I'll drive down and spend three or four hours on the site."

"Let's get up early, have a quick breakfast, then call on a real estate broker in town," Sharon said breezily.

"You meant it about buying a house out here?" Carol was startled.

"Sure I meant it." Sharon exuded pleasure. "The way the loot is coming in, I want to invest it in something substantial—before I start pissing it away on designer clothes and jewelry. Real estate is substantial." Her face softened. "That's what Dad used to say. 'If you ever make money, cookie, invest in a house.' I want to buy out here before the prices go flying up to the sky. The Hamptons is a 'hot spot' now—and it's going to get hotter."

"I know your advance on the new contract is sensational, but are you sure you can handle a house?"

"I talked to my accountant. She said it would be a good tax shelter. And if I know I have to meet mortgage payments every month, I'll keep working—no goofing off. Besides, I need a runaway spot. I thought about building, but the way you've talked about overruns and all I feel safer knowing just what I'm getting into money-wise."

"Okay, early breakfast and we go house hunting." Carol was pleased by the spontaneity of their decision. "Why don't I go inside and make us some coffee? Isn't it great that they provide for in-room coffee?"

Sharon chuckled indulgently.

"I know. You want to call Seth. Go on—then we'll have coffee."

In the morning Carol and Sharon had a robust, early breakfast in Gurney's dining room, strolled on the beach for twenty minutes, then drove into town to talk to a broker. They discovered a charming woman broker who listened with respect to Sharon's requirements—three bedrooms, two baths, a fireplace, and a deck overlooking the ocean—and agreed to show them only houses within the price range Sharon stipulated.

"I don't want to get carried away beyond my budget," Sharon explained in high spirits.

They joined the broker in her car, listened while they drove to her explanation for the unexpectedly tall office building—seven floors, Carol counted—and the predominant Tudor-style architecture in the small stores and in what she called Shepherd's Neck.

"Before the stock crash," she explained, "Carl Fisher was out to make Montauk the 'Miami Beach of the North.' Thank God, the crash put an end to that."

In between showing them available properties the real estate broker told them about the Stanford White houses in Montauk, and Carol's eyes lighted. These she would love to see!

"There's an upside-down house that may be going on the market," the broker said after Sharon had rejected the four houses shown—none of which offered more than a distant view of a tiny bit of seascape. "That's where the living room, dining room, and kitchen are upstairs and—"

"We saw upside-down houses in Paris some years ago," Sharon said, her eyes meeting Carol's in recall. "The Le Corbusier design. But no, I don't see myself climbing a flight of stairs with groceries— though I imagine the views could be sensational." Sharon hesitated, a wistful glint in her eyes. "Maybe I could extend my price a bit—"

"I'll go over my list," the broker said eagerly. "I'm sure we have something you'll like. Would you want to see them this afternoon?"

"Tomorrow morning," Carol told her. She had working hours ahead.

"Same time?" Sharon asked.

"Fine," the broker agreed and rather hesitantly asked how much higher Sharon was prepared to go. Sharon gave her a figure that brought a cautionary glance from Carol. "Oh, that opens the door for me. We have three houses that are oceanfront property. I'm sure you'll find one of them right for you."

"I want a place out here," Sharon said determinedly as she joined Carol on the front seat of their rented car. "It's not like I mean to live out here altogether, but it'll always be here when I need to escape the city. And it's a great investment."

"Shall I drive you back to Gurney's or would you like to go down with me to the site?" Carol asked on impulse.

"I won't be in the way?" But it was clear she was avid to join Carol.

"No. I'll show you the place, then you can settle down in the office to read the papers or a magazine while I get down to work. I'll make it fast," she promised, "then we'll look around for a place to have a late lunch." This was a mini-vacation, she told herself.

Carol was pleased that Sharon was so impressed with the custom houses, the row of shops that made up the new village. Sharon asked intelligent questions, she approved—the kind of questions that told her where they might make some very minor changes. Then she pointed Sharon to a chair in the office and strolled off with the on-site contractor for further inspections.

It was almost two o'clock when Carol and Sharon returned to the car and went in search of a cozy restaurant.

"I'm starving." Sharon sighed. "Let's get off the main road and try the first decent place we see."

Carol swung onto a secondary road, searching for a local restaurant. She, too, was aware of intense hunger. They'd had breakfast so early.

"Carol, back up!" Sharon ordered, her voice shrill with excitement. "About fifteen feet. I want to check on a sign I saw."

Carol went into reverse, assuming Sharon had spied an out-of-the-way restaurant.

"Okay, left or right?" she asked.

"That sign there—" Sharon pointed.

The sign indicated an enclave of low-priced, drab houses that bore a strong similarity to the unimaginative suburban developments that Carol loathed. Beneath the arrow was the name of the developer: MATT HARRIS ENTERPRISES.

"It could be another Matt Harris," Carol said after a moment.

"Let's drive by." Sharon leaned forward, impatient to confirm that this was the Matt they had known. "We don't have to go in, Carol."

"I don't want to see Matt," Carol said flatly. "But could he have built houses as atrocious as these?"

"Drive," Sharon ordered. "We've always wondered what happened to him."

"All right—" Carol's mind shot back through the years. Would she even recognize Matt today?

They pulled up in a parking area beside the model house that was the sales office.

"Sharon, I don't want to see Matt." That was long ago—another life, Carol thought in rejection.

"He's not here," Sharon soothed. "He's the developer. Let's just go inside and ask for a brochure."

Her heart pounding, Carol followed Sharon into the sales office.

A plumpish woman of about their age—her hair tinted a strident auburn—rose from behind the desk. Her saleswoman smile seemed jaded.

"Welcome to Harris Woods," she greeted them effusively. "We're—"

"We'd like to pick up a brochure for my son and daughter-in-law," Sharon broke in. "They asked us to drop by."

Spewing a prepared sales pitch, the woman reached into a drawer to pull out a brochure, handed it to Sharon.

"While you're here, wouldn't you like to see the three models?"

"Thanks, no," Sharon told her, thrusting the brochure into her purse. "We're in a terrible rush. But you'll probably hear from my daughter-in-law."

"Just tell her to ask for Iris Harris," Carol heard the woman say—but her eyes were galvanized to a photograph on the desk. A photograph of Matt—heavy-jowled, dissipated, gray-haired. But unmistakably Matt.

Carol and Sharon were silent until they were inside the car again.

"He looks as though he's had a rough life," Sharon said dryly.

"I can't believe this is what Matt has done with his life." Carol reached for the ignition. "He was so talented, so aggressive. What happened that he's become a developer of garbage like those houses?"

"You're remembering Matt in his twenties," Sharon pointed out. "Aggressiveness can get lost with the years—and without a 'little bit of luck,' talent can drown."

"Seth's so talented," Carol whispered. "Why can't he find that 'little bit of luck'?"

Carol and Sharon both fell in love with the first house the broker showed them the next day.

"I know this is beyond your range," she apologized to Sharon, "but I just wanted you to see this house. I've been in love with it since the first time I laid eyes on it."

The house was in the Frank Lloyd Wright tradition and hung about forty feet back from the cliff—the ocean on view from every room.

"Oh, Carol," Sharon murmured when they'd explored every charming room, "isn't it gorgeous?"

"Perfect," Carol conceded.

"If I ever win a lottery, I'll buy it myself," the broker said.

"Could we postpone looking at the other houses for a while?" Carol asked in a sudden rush of inner excitement, ignoring the startled stares of the other two. "I just need to talk with Sharon for a few minutes," she told the broker. "If you could drop us off at some place where we can stop for coffee, we'll join you again at your office."

"Of course." The agent smiled politely. Sharon seemed bewildered, but Carol suspected the agent was reading her mind. "There's a pleasant little place right near the office."

Arriving there, Carol and Sharon left the car and hurried into the coffee shop.

"Carol, what's bothering you?" Sharon's eyes searched her face. "Were you scared I'd go berserk and buy that place?"

"Let's buy it together!" Carol's face was radiant. "People from New York fly to Florida regularly for vacations. Why can't people from Bellevue reverse the deal and fly up here?"

"You're sure?" But Sharon was radiant.

"If you want it, let's buy it," Carol repeated. "We love it. The kids will love it. Seth will love it."

"Do you think you'll ever get him up here?" Sharon was dubious.

"Either he comes or he doesn't," Carol said flatly. "If our marriage is dead, let me find out now."

Chapter Fifty-six

Bellevue was into the eighth day of a record-breaking heat wave. Lawns were turning brown from the relentless sun. Flowers drooped. The Chattahoochee River was sufficiently low at points for those so inclined to wade across into Alabama. In his air-conditioned home office Seth sat at his typewriter—relieved that he was about to complete the number of pages he demanded of himself each day.

He glanced at his watch with defiant satisfaction. He'd make the rat race today. If he hadn't, he would have stopped, anyway, to head for the coffee shop at his usual time and work again at night to make his quota. What else did he have to do with his evenings?

Carol had phoned yesterday morning to say she'd be delayed another day. She'd be home tomorrow evening. Mom was off to Hendersonville for two weeks. Jonnie was in Maine researching an article. Karen was in Carol's Atlanta office. Evening and weekends—ignoring Bellevue's punishing summer—she was involved in frenzied fundraising for BIG. Harvey was chasing off to Oregon on some business deal that, he bragged, would turn this town upside down—while Elaine had gone to Sea Island with Timmy as usual.

It amazed him how he looked forward to his swatch of time at the coffee shop each afternoon. For a little while he escaped into good-humored raillery with Donna Raven. Why did she stay in town in this bastardly heat? Anybody who could afford it—and God knows, she could—had taken off for cooler spots.

He straightened up his desk, dropped a cover over the typewriter, and prepared to leave the house.

"Mist' Seth, don't you go walking into town in this heat," Bonnie warned from the entrance to the kitchen. "You can fry eggs on the sidewalks. You drive, you hear?"

"I'll drive," he promised. "You keep the air conditioner running in the kitchen." Bonnie was prone to some economies that included rationing the air-conditioning.

Seth flinched as he walked out into the turgid heat of the afternoon. Bonnie was right. He'd take the car. Behind the wheel he rolled up the windows, reached to switch on the air conditioner, though he always warned the kids to drive a few minutes first—but this was a scorcher.

In four minutes he was pulling into a parking wedge before the coffee shop. Emerging from the car he saw Donna's white Caddy a few wedges down. Sometimes he felt uncomfortable at their daily encounters here. Six afternoons a week—like clockwork, he thought in momentary self-consciousness. But everybody in the shop knew they were just passing time.

Almost immediately he and Donna realized they were on the same wavelength. Donna had loved New York in earlier years—as he had. She'd been a television actress before her marriage—*"just bit parts but I could have gone places if I'd had the sense to hang in there.*" He talked about his TV and theater background—amazed that he did this. She'd seen most of the Broadway plays of the past ten years and talked intelligently about them. She read a lot—out of boredom, she said in candor.

"We're a lot alike," she'd told him on their third meeting. "We're two people who've never fulfilled their talents." How many more like them, he speculated. Millions.

Without knowing it, Donna made him feel like a man again, he thought in astonishment and gratitude. She looked at him with eyes that said she found him interesting. That was because she felt a lack in her life since her ugly divorce, he told himself, but she didn't see him as a man who was frightened about his sexual abilities.

He felt a fresh wave of anguish as he remembered the nights when Carol and he tried to make love—and he couldn't. Now he couldn't bear to touch her because he was terrified of more failures. He mourned for the wonderful relationship they'd enjoyed in earlier years.

Lottie and the others at the coffee shop knew he and Donna were just casual friends, killing time in the middle of the afternoon. More than casual, he conceded as he spied Donna at their usual table in the rear and waved in greeting. They talked about things they wouldn't discuss with anybody else in town. He'd even persuaded her to give up smoking. They were like exchange therapists, he told himself in momentary amusement—no fees to pay.

"What a bitch of a day," Donna complained at his approach. "If I had any sense at all, I'd be lying on the beach in the Hamptons."

Carol was in the Hamptons, he thought involuntarily. She was away from Bellevue more than she was here.

"Why aren't you up there?" he chided, dropping into the chair opposite Donna. It was relaxing to spend an hour or so with her after plowing through deadly hours of hack writing. "The planes are still flying."

"My 'ex' is at the house in East Hampton." She made a vicious stab at her whipped-cream-heaped chocolate sundae. This was her gift to herself on days when she was depressed. *"I tell myself chocolate is good for the soul."* "I don't know why he insisted on summer custody of the kid. How much does he see of Scott? He comes up for three-day weekends with that blond slut and spends most of the time running around with her. The rest of the time Scott's alone with the housekeeper. I'm his mother; he should be with me."

"Scott's father may get tired of the custody scene," Seth comforted. "This is the first year."

"Bellevue has become a ghost town. Except for you everybody I know has taken off. The rest of the people just sleep away the summer. There's nothing to do—and it's too hot to do anything, anyhow. But I get so damn lonely—"

"I keep telling you, Donna," he said gently. "You ought to join things. You've got too much time to brood."

"Oh, Seth—" She grunted in irritation. "You know how women in this town feel about a divorced woman." She said this at regular intervals. "They all look at me and figure I'm out to nab one of the husbands."

"What about that painting class you were going to join?" he asked. Poor kid—she felt like a fish out of water, he thought. He remembered that feeling, when he came home after the war. "You told me you used to love to paint. You said it helped you survive in rough times."

"I didn't know what was rough times until now." She exhaled a pain-laden breath. "Sometimes I wonder why I go on living. The good years were before I got married."

"You're young, Donna. Most of your life is ahead of you." His voice deepened with compassion. "This is just a temporary, rotten period."

"I keep asking myself. What did I do that was wrong? I got older," she pushed on. "I wasn't twenty-three anymore. And along came that slut in hot pants, wiggling her ass at him." She paused. "It's so bloody hot and nothing to do. Let's live it up and go to an air-conditioned movie. *A Touch of Class* is playing out at the Belmont. I love Glenda Jackson."

Seth hesitated. The Belmont was the new movie house at the edge of town. They wouldn't see anybody they knew on a midweek afternoon. Besides, they'd be driving out in their separate cars.

"Seth, come on. It'll cheer us up," she coaxed.

"Okay." He wasn't ready to go back to an empty house. Half the time Karen didn't even come home for dinner. She was all wrapped up in the low-income housing deal BIG was fighting to put across. "But only if you let me buy the giant-size bag of popcorn," he said with a fresh sense of levity.

They drove to the movie house in their individual cars. Both were pleased to arrive as the feature was beginning. The house was two-thirds empty. They settled themselves in an isolated area in the rear and made alternate dives into the popcorn. In the course of the film they made occasional whispered comments about the performances—both enjoying this respite from the outside world.

Afterward Seth walked Donna to her car, lingered in further conversation about the film.

"Seth, have an early dinner with me," Donna suggested impetuously. She knew Carol was out of town. "I hate going to the house when I know Scott's so far away. Fran's a great cook. Please?" She smiled with wistful charm.

Seth debated a moment.

"I'll have to call Bonnie and say I'm having dinner out," he said. A hundred to one, Karen was going straight from the office to a meeting at BIG, he reassured himself.

He'd never been in Donna's house, had never seen her except at the coffee shop. She'd told him she'd brought in a decorator. The results were what Carol would call "ostentatiously expensive."

"I'll go out to the kitchen and tell Fran we'll be two for dinner," she said, then stopped short with an air of consternation. "Damn, I forgot. This is her night off."

"No problem. I haven't called Bonnie yet—" If he took Donna to a restaurant, the word would fly around town in hours.

"I'll cook for us," she insisted. Her smile was dazzling. "I do the fast, simple deals. We have scallops in the fridge," she remembered. "I poach them in white wine in three or four minutes. Fran always leave a huge bowl of salad because I'm a salad freak. And there's cantaloupe chilling and half a strawberry shortcake. How does that sound for a hot night?"

"It sounds great," Seth said, yet he felt uneasy at being here.

"Call Bonnie," Donna ordered. "I'll go out and rustle up dinner. Let's have it in the breakfast room," she said gaily. "That's so much cozier than the big dining room."

Seth phoned to tell Bonnie he wouldn't be home for dinner, settled himself in a lounge chair in the overcooled living room. He picked up a magazine, flipped it open. He heard the sound of music from a radio in the kitchen. Should he offer to go out and help? No, he decided, still uncomfortable in this situation.

"Soup's on!" she called from somewhere down the hall in a few minutes. "Come and get it."

They sat in designed-for-comfort captain's chairs at a beautifully laid round table and ate the quickly prepared but delicious dinner. From the kitchen radio came the sensuous sounds of Gershwin's "Rhapsody in Blue." A vase of summer flowers lent fragrance to the air. With dessert the conversation turned to playful battle over the wisdom of the New York Drama Critics Circle awards for the past season.

Donna had pushed aside her depression, Seth thought as they finished up the superb strawberry shortcake. She was caught up now in vivacious recall of her one season in summer stock.

"Why don't we have my version of wine coolers in the living room?" she said when she'd finished a slightly risqué anecdote about the company's leading lady. "There's wine and club soda in the fridge."

"Sounds great," Seth approved. He was glad Donna had invited him for dinner. Solitary dinners at home were becoming torturous occasions.

"Look, you run out to the kitchen and bring out the wine—I always have trouble with the cork. While you're doing that, I'll phone Scott. I call him almost every night."

Seth went out to the kitchen, brought out the bottle of wine from the refrigerator. With the bottle uncorked, he found a pair of tall glasses, made two wine coolers and returned with them to the living room.

"Donna, I've made the coolers," he called tentatively, feeling guilty at interrupting her phone call to Scott. "Shall I bring yours to you before it goes flat?"

"Please, Seth," she said blithely. "The last bedroom on the right—"

Seth heard Donna humming behind the partially open door. She was off the phone. He pushed the door wide and stopped dead. Donna stood beside the bed in a sheer black chiffon negligée over what he assumed was a matching nightgown.

"You don't mind my getting comfortable, do you?" she murmured. Her face lighted by the provocative smile that had troubled him on earlier occasions.

"I think maybe we'd better—" he began cautiously.

"Seth, don't be stuffy," she interrupted, striding toward him with long, lithe steps. "We've been heading for this for weeks." She took the wine coolers from his hands and put them on the dresser that flanked the door, then slid her arms about his neck, moved in close.

"This wasn't meant to happen," he protested, startled by a sudden surge of passion. "Donna, I don't think—"

"Don't think," she admonished, lifting her parted mouth to his. "Just feel." A hand explored, found him, fondled.

"This is wrong—" His voice was harsh, but his arms moved—seemingly of their own volition—to close about her slender shoulders as she thrust her hips against his own. The room in darkness now as Donna fumbled with the light switches. "Oh God, Donna!"

Seth lay back against the satin pillows, spent and drowsy, conscious that one of Donna's endlessly long legs lay flung across his own. What the hell was the matter with him? In a corner of his mind, he'd known that Donna wanted this; why hadn't he admitted it? Then all at once the realization of what this encounter proved galloped across his brain. *He'd been okay. None of that craziness—that humiliating failure—with Carol. Why?*

"Donna," he said hoarsely, moving away from her, groping for the lamp on the night table. "We're out of our minds!"

"No," she murmured, "it was terrific. Wasn't it good for you?"

"It shouldn't have happened." He swung his legs over the side of the bed.

"What are you doing?" Her voice was a sensuous rebuke. "Seth, the night's young yet."

"I'm sorry, Donna." He was reaching for his clothes, lying on the floor beside the bed. "This shouldn't have happened." For the twenty-six years that he and Carol had been married he'd never touched another woman. *How could he have done this?*

"Seth, I want you to stay." Donna's eyes—wistful, hurt, implored him. "Come back to bed—" It was all at once an imperious command.

"I can't," he told her. Reproach blended with anguish in him while he dressed with desperate haste.

"Why not?" she demanded. "Carol's up in the Hamptons. You said she's not coming back until tomorrow evening."

"I can't stay here," he told her, "I'm sorry, Donna—" He tied his shoelaces, rose to his feet.

"You can't walk out on me this way!" she screeched. *She'd planned tonight, Seth realized in a hazy corner of his mind. She knew her housekeeper would be away.* "You bastard! You're as rotten as my husband!"

He fled, hearing her invectives follow him down the hall into the foyer. *How could he have let this happen?*

Donna paced restlessly about the master bedroom this afternoon. She still seethed at Seth's behavior last night. Damn it, it had been terrific for both of them! How could he run out on her that way? God, she was sick of men who ran away!

There was no use going back to the coffee shop today. Seth wouldn't be there. He was going to make damn sure they wouldn't meet again. But she'd make him pay for stringing her along this way. He wasn't getting off scot-free. Lying sleepless after he'd left her, she'd thought about that.

She left the Caddy in the garage and took Fran's car for her drive into town. She parked two-thirds down the block from Seth's house—in time to see a black woman emerge. That would be Bonnie, going to do her day's shopping for produce. Seth said she usually went out around the same time he did—what he called her "afternoon break from the house." Seth was a creature of habit, she told herself. He wouldn't go to the coffee shop, but he'd go somewhere for a break. He always said he needed to get away after his day's work.

There he was, heading into town, Donna thought triumphantly. What would be his new hangout? She watched while he walked in the opposite direction—toward town. He was gone now—he wouldn't be back, she told herself.

She drove down the street, parked across from the house. She left the car, watching to make sure she was unobserved—but who would leave their houses in this god-awful heat? As she expected, the kitchen door was left unlocked. Though people complained about the rise in crime, those in good neighborhoods were careless about locking their doors.

She walked with swift, impatient steps until she found the master bedroom. She pulled a black lace bra from her purse, slid it beneath the bed, with enough emerging to catch Carol's eyes. Bonnie had made up the room for the night; she wouldn't be back in again.

Her smile maliciously smug, she hurried from the house and

drove away. Later—when she knew Seth's wife was home—she'd make her phone call. If Seth answered, she'd hang up and call again. Bonnie wouldn't answer—this was the evening she went home to visit her family. Without living in Seth's house she'd come to know all the small details.

Oh, yes! Seth would be sorry he walked out on her that way.

Chapter Fifty-seven

Carol leaned back in the car with an air of relief. Her plane had been forty minutes late in taking off. She'd been seated beside a woman passenger who chattered incessantly. Later, she felt guilty at her annoyance. As they approached the Atlanta airport, the woman had admitted she was terrified of flying. *"You saved me from a panic attack."*

"Seth, you won't believe what's happening with Jonnie," Carol said tenderly as he pulled out of the airport parking area. "He's talking about coming back home to try to set up a weekly newspaper."

"Does he have any idea how much that could cost?" Seth asked, clearly startled. Yet Carol knew he'd be happy to have Jonnie back in Bellevue.

"He's working up some figures. He plans to keep it very small. And there's more." Her face glowed. "Both Sharon and I think Jonnie and Michelle may be getting serious. Remember how she and I used to kid about their growing up and getting married one day?"

"Did he say anything?" Seth cleared his throat—the way he did when he was nervous. "They're both young—"

"No, but we see the way they look at each other."

Seth seemed distracted, she thought. She'd told herself—with premature optimism—that once he was out of the shop, he'd forget about the paperbacks he'd hated doing and throw himself into the novel he'd been working on at intervals for years. He knew they could afford for him to take time off. Why was he so stubborn? But she knew the answer to that: his damnable male pride. She was doing so well financially and he was earning so little in comparison. *The same old problem.*

"Is Mom back from Hendersonville?" Carol broke the silence between them.

"Not yet. Elaine's insisting she come out to Sea Island to stay with her and Timmy until after Labor Day. I think Mom's going."

"Elaine's a good daughter-in-law," Carol said softly. It had taken Mom a long time to become close with Elaine, but it had finally happened. "And Harvey doesn't deserve a wife like her."

"Don't tell Mom that." Seth's smile was caustic.

Carol asked about Karen. "I haven't spoken to her in several days."

Seth filled her in on Karen's activities with BIG, which had become of major importance to both women.

"Funds are finally beginning to flow in," Carol said with satisfaction. "The last I talked to her, Karen said they had a lead on a possible site. It's part of an estate that's in probate, but she told me there was some verbal commitment in the works."

"Bonnie left dinner in the refrigerator," Seth said. "It just has to be reheated."

They heard the phone ringing as they pulled into the driveway.

"You get it, Carol," Seth said. "I'll bring in your luggage."

Carol hurried into the house, reached for the phone.

"Hello—"

"Bonnie, is Mr. Seth there?" a feminine voice—devoid of Southern accent—inquired sweetly.

"Yes, he is—"

"Oh, I'm sorry!" The voice sounded panicky now. "I'm afraid I've dialed the wrong number."

Carol stood immobile by the phone. Who was that woman? She hadn't dialed the wrong number—not when she called her Bonnie, then asked for Seth.

"Who was it?" Seth called from the hallway.

"A wrong number," Carol told him. Her heart was pounding. Never in a million years would she have thought that Seth was having an affair. "I'll change and then put up dinner." She was struggling to sound unconcerned. *Seth and another woman?*

She followed Seth into their bedroom. He dropped her valise and attaché case on the foot of the bed.

"I'll change and—" Carol stopped dead. Her eyes clung to a strip of black lace that lay on the soft gray carpeting. She bent to pick up the pungently perfumed bra that lay half submerged beneath the bed. *First that weird phone call and now this.* She dropped the bra—as though burnt by the touch—and turned to Seth. All at once her head was pounding. "Who did you have here in our bedroom?" Her voice was harsh with shock. "What's been going on behind my back?"

"Not here," Seth stammered. He recognized the perfume, she taunted herself. "Just once—last night—" He closed his eyes for a moment in pain. "She was furious when I told her it couldn't go on. She must have planted that here—"

"What was wrong with *me?*" Carol challenged. "Why did you have to go to another woman?"

"I don't know—" He spread his hands in a gesture of futility. The atmosphere was suddenly oppressive—like the aftermath of some horrible atomic explosion, Carol thought deep in her subconscious. "Do you want me to move out of the house?" The words seemed ripped from Seth's throat. "Do you want a divorce?"

"No," she said quickly. She couldn't envision a life without Seth. "We—we can't do that to the kids and Mom."

"I'll move into Jonnie's room," Seth said after a moment of leaden silence. "Carol, I—I didn't mean for it to happen. It was just last night—there was no other time." His eyes pleaded for compassion.

"I'll heat up dinner." The only way was to pretend it never happened, Carol told herself. "I'll call you when it's ready."

Carol went into the kitchen. She knew Seth was moving his things into Jonnie's room. They'd tell Karen that she was having insomnia problems, often read in the middle of the night and that was disturbing her father. Mom wouldn't have to know.

Was it true what he said, about last night being the only time? No! That woman knew about Bonnie. What else had Seth told her about their lives? *Did he tell her that he couldn't make love to his wife?* Seth had made love to her—and she hadn't wanted their affair to end.

In the weeks ahead Carol spent much time at BIG meetings—a welcome escape from the house in the evenings. Then on October

6th—Yom Kippur, the most sacred of Jewish holidays—the world was rocked by news that Egypt and Syria had again attacked Israel. For eighteen days the desperate fighting continued—until the intervention of the United Nations.

Carol was terrified that Jonnie would rush to Israel—not merely as a journalist but to join in the fighting. She knew that Seth, too, worried constantly about this possibility. Yet even this mutual anxiety couldn't draw them together. But Jonnie, she was relieved to learn, was on assignment in Oregon for his magazine.

Carol was increasingly engrossed in the BIG project, spent much time in designing the low-income housing they were determined to build. She gave more responsibility to her office staffs, both in the New York and Atlanta offices, to free herself for this. She knew that this kind of emotional involvement would be her salvation.

Shortly after the cease-fire in Israel Carol made her first trip to New York since August. She planned to work long hours with the staff each day, have a late dinner with Sharon each evening. Jonnie was up in Maine again, on a sequel to his earlier article about a Maine paper mill.

"Michelle's up there with Jonnie," Sharon confided on Carol's first night in town. "And they spent a long weekend together out at the Montauk house."

"Does she say anything?" Carol prodded eagerly.

"Does Jonnie?" Sharon asked and shrugged. "You know kids these days—when they're ready, they'll tell us."

Now they talked about Sharon's soaring success.

"I'm turning out books like spaghetti. I'm working my butt off," Sharon said complacently. "I went out and hired my own publicity gal. The number of books that are sold is phenomenal—and I want to be sure as hell a lot of them are mine. You know I make the rounds of book-sellers whenever I tour and they talk about regular customers who come in and buy five or six at a time—every week, sometimes twice a week." Sharon chuckled. "Writers like me are providing a service. We're giving millions of women pleasure—no matter that the literary establishment calls it erotic trash. And I'll bet we're improving the sex lives of a lot of husbands."

"Seth had to go to another woman to improve his," Carol said with unfamiliar bitterness.

"The situation hasn't changed?"

"It's getting worse." Carol sighed. "Sometimes I'm sure Karen and Mom suspect."

"What about a reconciliation? All it takes is a little move in that direction from one of you," Sharon cajoled.

"How do you make up with a man who can have a satisfactory sexual relationship with another woman but not with you?" Carol countered. "Do I have to give up my career, stay at home and play bridge and garden to make him feel he's a man? Maybe he's just tired of me!"

"In a lot of marriages sex is forgotten by the time the wives reach our age, but couples still have warm relationships without that. Like my next door neighbor. She's frank—she says sex meant nothing to her. She accommodated her husband because she loves him. Now they're pushing sixty and haven't slept together in a dozen years. She said if her husband gets a little something on the side, she doesn't want to know about it. Go figure." Sharon shrugged.

"It was always important to Seth and me." Carol felt swamped by frustration. "I don't know how to deal with what happened to us."

"It was important to Gil and me," Sharon said softly. "I've played on the side for years—but that's all it is. A game for a brief satisfaction. I knew when Gil died, part of me died, too."

While he and Elaine were dressing for a black-tie dinner at the Bellevue Country Club, Harvey told her he wanted her to come up to Washington to be hostess at a party on a Friday in mid-November.

"That's the weekend you told Mom you'd have her up to the Washington house," Elaine scolded. "You can't disappoint her again."

"She'll understand." Harvey brushed this aside. None of the family had ever been to the D.C. house, he remembered complacently. "So she'll come up in December. This is a not-to-be-missed opportunity."

"How many people?" Elaine asked. To her it was a job to be performed, Harvey understood.

"I haven't worked out the guest list just yet. Probably no more than ten." He'd met Peter Ransome three weeks ago at some diplomatic party. Right away he'd sensed big business there. Ransome owned a major paper mill in Oregon. He was considering a move to the South. Here labor was cheap, and Georgia pines that had been planted back in the Depression days by the CCC boys were coming into maturity. "I'm working on a deal that will be great for Bellevue. It'll bring in a lot of jobs, fat tax revenue. This town will be damn grateful to me," he boasted.

"What's in it for you?" Elaine asked, her smile impassive.

"Sugar, you wouldn't believe." His own smile was triumphant.

He'd offer Ransome not only cheap labor and the availability of Georgia pines. He'd make sure the City Council voted for a heavy tax abatement—and would approve a dam on the river to supply hydroelectric power. He'd offer Ransome so sweet a deal he couldn't refuse. And there would be more than a fat legal fee in this for him, Harvey plotted. He would just happen to own vast tracts of Georgia pine. At this point he could buy cheap—pine that was ripe and conveniently located for Ransome Paper Products.

If he played his hand smart, he'd earn millions on this deal. *Nothing was going to stand in his way.*

Seth dreaded Thanksgiving dinner. As usual Mom insisted on a big early afternoon family dinner at her house.

"I'm not an old lady yet," Hannah had chided when Seth protested that it was time she took things easier. "I'm not the type to sit in a rocker all day and knit, nor to run and play at 'glorious retirement' in Florida. For me that would be like being dead and not knowing it."

These days he felt uncomfortable at family gatherings—as though everybody could see past the front he and Carol put up about their marriage being the same as always. Sometimes he was sure Karen knew—and he suspected she might have talked about it with Jonnie.

Jonnie had come back to Bellevue last week with Michelle. They were living together in a small apartment in town. He liked Michelle but was having some difficulty in not being self-conscious in their "arrangement," as Jonnie called it.

"Look, we want to be sure we belong together before we get married," Michelle had said flippantly. "Call this a dress rehearsal."

He knew a lot of kids their age were living together, Seth scolded himself. Why did he feel so bloody uncomfortable about it? Michelle was terrific—and she and Jonnie appeared to be deeply in love. As Sharon said when she called last week to break the news to them in advance, they had to ride with the tide. This was the '70s scene.

As long ago arranged, Harvey came home for Thanksgiving dinner and Elaine went with Timmy—on school vacation—to her parents' house. Now Seth and Harvey sat before the TV set and watched football. Jonnie was engrossed in starting a fire in the fireplace grate. The women were out in the kitchen preparing to serve dinner. Their high-spirited voices drifted down the hall from the kitchen.

"Okay," Karen called ebulliently. "You guys come into the dining room."

Harvey ought to start watching his weight, Seth thought while he watched his brother pull himself to his feet. He should have started years ago. Little wonder he had that roll of fat around his stomach and hips; his most stringent exercise was lifting a martini glass to his lips. And not even that year-round tan Harvey cultivated could conceal the puffiness of his face. But Mom saw none of that—Harvey was her adored successful son, Seth taunted himself. *He* was successful at nothing. Not even his marriage.

Seth took his place at the festive table. Thanksgiving was always a warm, loving occasion in this house, but today he felt himself an outsider. He was relieved that the conversation was monopolized by the three young people. He was amused by the way they leapt with such enthusiasm from one subject to another. Still, they kept coming back to Jonnie's determination to start up a weekly newspaper here in town.

His eyes moved from Carol to his mother. Carol was enthralled at the prospect of Jonnie's being in Bellevue permanently. Mom, he surmised, was thinking how proud Dad would be to see his grandson fulfilling his own ambition. Carol had said nothing about it to him— she said *nothing* to him these days—but he suspected she and Sharon would be Jonnie's backer.

While his mother and Carol brought in the traditional pumpkin pie, Seth listened with paternal pride to Karen's zealous discussion about the latest BIG developments.

"We've got it set to buy that strip of land along the Chattahoochee that belongs to the Franklin estate. We can't sign papers, of course, until it comes out of probate, but the two elderly nieces gave us their word we could have it for the garden apartments." Karen refused to label it "the low-income housing project."

"Why would BIG want to buy that?" Harvey demanded, scowling in disapproval. "It would be a total waste to use riverfront property for cheap housing."

"Why?" Carol defied, sitting at the table again. "I suggested that site myself, as soon as I realized it would be going up for sale."

"That should be commercial property," he shot back. "It should be zoned for that—to bring in some real tax revenue to the town."

"There's other land available for commercial property," Karen broke in. "And like Mom says, low-income property doesn't have to be little more than ugly, sterile barracks. These will be garden apartments with a river view."

"They'd be crazy to sell it for residential use," Harvey scoffed. "The way this town is growing, that should be prime commercial property—bringing in commercial land taxes."

"You're always thinking of what's good for this town," Hannah said adoringly to Harvey. "I don't know why you've never gone back into politics."

"I am in politics, Mom," Harvey told her with a complacent grin. "Behind the scenes I throw around a lot of weight. More than I could do as a congressman from this district. Why do you think I had to buy myself a townhouse in Washington? To be there to protect my bills."

Harvey broke away from the family party at the earliest possible moment.

"I know it's a holiday," he said, "but my work never stops. I'm expecting an important phone call"—he glanced at his watch—"in about thirty minutes."

He rushed home, phoned one of "his men" on the City Council.

"I know it's Thanksgiving," he said impatiently when George Sexton remonstrated at being disturbed today, "but this is important. Remember who put you into office, George. I want the Franklin land rezoned for commercial use. And you go to the two old biddies—the Franklin nieces—and you tell them you've got a lead on a prospective buyer for that tract—and he'll double what they've been offered. I want that land, you hear? I'm dickering with this company about relocating in Bellevue; that's a prime spot for them.

It'll mean a lot of jobs coming into town. And that," he emphasized, "will look damn good for you."

Later he'd tell the City Council about the huge tax abatement Ransome would demand—plus approval to build a hydroelectric plant to run their machines. Out of seven City Council members three were in his pocket. Damn Mitchell for retiring, but then he'd see that Mitchell's replacement was beholden to him. And that fourth vote was all he needed to run this town.

The local banks were giving him loans to buy up enough pine forests to keep Ransome Paper Products operating for years. He'd sell high through his dummy corporation, bill Ransome to the sky for landing him this necessary rezoning law, huge tax abatements, and the right to build the hydroelectric plant.

He would become one of the richest men in the state, Harvey congratulated himself.

Chapter Fifty-eight

With the approach of Christmas Bellevue took on its usual festive appearance. The familiar red and green lights were strung across Main Street. Store windows were decorated for the holiday season. An avenue of holiday-garbed pines dotted the island that dissected the business street. Homes vied with one another to offer the most colorful exterior displays. Trees adorned with Christmas lights were set up on winter-drab lawns.

Holed up in his office—waiting for the nightly summons to the dinner table—Seth was assaulted by a growing need for escape. The convivial atmosphere that enveloped Bellevue highlighted his own despair. He lived in fear of Carol's asking him for a divorce—to order him out of her life—and the prospect was intolerable.

He heard a car drive up. That would be Jonnie and Michelle, he thought. They came over for dinner twice a week. Both so young and earnest and determined to do something useful with their lives. They'd be putting out the first edition of the *Bellevue Herald* at the beginning of the new year. Just the two of them, working by themselves, he told himself with tender pride.

"Dad—" Karen called from behind the closed door. "Dinner's ready."

As always these days dinner conversation focused on BIG's current activities.

"I don't understand why Miss Emily and Miss Margaret are suddenly hedging about making a written commitment on the property for Franklin Acres," Karen said, her gaze swinging from one to another as though in search of an answer. "They were both so thrilled when we told them the project would be named for their family." For generations the Franklin family had contributed to local philanthropies.

"Karen, get real," Jonnie admonished. "Somebody's come in and made them a better offer. They want to see how it'll develop."

"But they gave us their word," Karen said indignantly.

"I remember Harvey made a crack about it's being too valuable for residential use," Carol said. "Somebody else may have the same idea. Check with the City Council. They may be trying for a rezoning amendment."

"Find out, Karen," Michelle urged. "If it's true, we'll do a story on it in the *Herald.*"

Seth listened, made occasional contributions to the table talk, yet he felt himself an outsider now. An outsider, he thought in pain, surrounded by his own family. When Jonnie and Michelle began to reminisce about their weekend at Montauk—a place they called magical—Seth suddenly clutched at an avenue of escape.

Carol and Sharon owned the house out there—what both called the "family house." He'd go up there for a few weeks, try to sort things out—where he was going with his life. He couldn't continue living this way—never knowing where he stood, when Carol might decide she'd had enough of this phony marriage and demand a divorce.

He waited until Jonnie and Michelle left and he was alone in the living room with Carol and Karen to bring up the subject of Montauk.

"I'm running into a writer's block—with a damn deadline staring me in the face." He tried to sound matter-of-fact. "I thought I might spend a little time out at the Montauk place—if nobody's going to be using it," he added self-consciously. *The "family house," but he'd never even seen it.* "Does Sharon have plans?"

"She's holed up in her apartment finishing the new book," Carol told him. "She won't be able to get out until late spring." She was trying so hard to be casual, Seth tormented himself. *She'd be glad to see him out of Bellevue.*

"I'll fly up on Monday," Seth said, avoiding Carol's gaze. "I have to meet my deadline." Why was Karen staring at him in that weird way? She *knew* something was wrong between Carol and himself. She was thinking—why go all the way up to Montauk, he guessed—why not rent a cottage up at Pine Mountain, a short drive away.

"Sharon has a typewriter there; you won't have to drag up a portable." Carol's voice was strained. "And we bought a secondhand car to keep out there. I think she said the keys are in a vase on the foyer table. Call and ask her. And the house key in always under the doormat."

On Monday morning—his valise already packed for a trip of undetermined length and a down jacket draped across its bulk— Seth threw sundry office supplies into his briefcase. He hesitated a moment, then pulled the two-thirds completed rough draft of his munitions-family novel from a desk drawer and stuffed it into the case, also. His "security blanket," he mocked himself.

Karen drove him to the airport for an early flight. She was unfamiliarly somber. When she kissed him goodbye, Seth thought, she seemed to be fearful of when she would see him again. But she would be more cheerful this evening, he comforted himself. From her frequent chatter about the young attorney, new to Bellevue but now BIG's volunteer legal advisor, he was sure of a romantic involvement. Before the break in their marriage, he thought, Carol would be spilling over with tidbits of news about this.

At the Montauk railroad station—draped in late afternoon fog— Seth found it necessary to phone for a taxi. Few visitors arrived in Montauk in late December. On the brief ride to the house Seth remembered the earlier trips to Wainscott. Never a thought then in his mind that his life would take such an ominous turn. Carol was part-owner of a house he'd never seen, he derided. For a long time she'd lived a separate existence that didn't include him. Somewhere along the line they'd missed the warning signals that must have told of a marriage going awry.

Pulling into the circular driveway of the house, Seth understood instantly why Carol had talked about it with such affection. Sitting high on a cliff, the sprawling structure provided a dramatic view— today a mesmerizing gray seascape of fog hanging low over the water. As though driven by some inner force, he went into the house, dropped his luggage in the foyer, and hurried across the cathedral-ceilinged living room. He pushed aside a sliding glass door and walked onto the wraparound deck.

He stood there, washed by the dank fog, entrapped by a sense of towering solitude that simultaneously captivated and unnerved him. Was it quixotic of him to have run from Carol's world in Bellevue to the world she knew up here, that was strange and new to him? For another moment he stared down as the waves washed with frenzy against the beach, then charged into the house again. In irrational impatience he dug a warm sweater from his luggage and pulled it over his head. With down jacket in tow he headed out to the deck again and to the landing that led to a seemingly endless flight of rickety stairs. Feeling himself prodded by some unseen power, he moved recklessly down the stairs to the unmarked stretch of beach—deserted except for a lone Labrador retriever.

Arriving breathless and ten minutes late Carol apologized to the other members of BIG who were gathered around the conference table in their regularly borrowed meeting room. Empty coffee containers and the remains of sandwiches littered the table. Most members came directly from their offices or businesses. Carol sensed a collective air of disappointment at this first session of 1974—and Karen explained.

"Miss Emily and her sister promised us that land!" Karen was indignant. "What do they mean—they have to reconsider?"

"Karen, I told you before—that's prime commercial land," Jonnie said and the others nodded in agreement. "But there's plenty of other land up for sale in town."

"That had the perfect view! Mom's taken that into consideration in her designs." Karen turned to her mother for corroboration.

"All right, the Franklin sisters are playing games now. Nothing's sure until it's in writing—and they've probably gotten greedy." Carol refused to be ruffled. "Let's make a fast search for other property. A tract with the same physical aspects of the original one, where we've worked out all the construction costs. And with another piece of suitable property under consideration we'll have a bargaining chip with the Franklin sisters."

"Who else is after that tract?" Ed Nicholls, one of their major financial contributors, asked. "It has to be that for them to pull this. I heard just today that they're out of probate. We could close fast."

"They could just be horse-trading," their unpaid CPA suggested. "Maybe they're—" He paused as the door swung open.

Rob Lehman, the personable young newcomer in Bellevue who was BIG's unpaid attorney, walked into the room. The intensity of his expressive brown eyes was in sharp contrast to the easy manner in which he carried his slim, compact body.

"I picked up some news," he began without preliminaries. "Hanging around City Hall, attorneys do that." His grin was infectious, yet did nothing to erase the impression that he had urgent information to convey. "I know why the Franklin sisters have suddenly gone coy on us." Rob was the one who gave this word to Ed earlier in the day, Carol interpreted. "Some out-of-town corporation is angling to relocate here. Bellevue's 'great public benefactor'— that sterling attorney, Harvey Walden—is representing them," he drawled and suddenly stopped dead in confusion. "Wow, I really put my foot in my mouth!" he apologized to Carol and turned to include Jonnie and Karen in this.

"These three Waldens are not part of Harvey's fan club," Carol said searingly. It ever amazed her that Harvey could convince so many Bellevue citizens that his major concern in life was to improve the quality of life in this town. "Relax."

"What kind of corporation?" Karen demanded.

"Some manufacturing operation," Rob said. "I just know—from my private sources—that Harvey Walden is fighting to get them tax abatements 'to lure them here,' as he puts it. He's raving about the hundreds of jobs the corporation will bring into Bellevue. Of course, he's ignoring the tax revenue the town will lose."

"Why do they want that particular tract?" their accountant asked.

"Because," Jonnie pinpointed, "it's right on the river. I'll bet they're after cheap hydroelectric power. And that can cause big problems."

"Wasn't some act passed to safeguard water in these situations?" the civics teacher from Bellevue High inquired.

"Sure, Congress passed those Federal Water Pollution Control Act amendments last year—but it could be years before the Environmental Protection Agency can put them into force."

"We must find out what the corporation produces," Ed Nicholls pinpointed. "The City Council can't refuse to tell us that." His face tightened. "Even if Harvey Walden controls enough Council votes to run this town whichever way he likes."

"But Hank Mitchell is retiring this year," Carol reminded. "He has serious health problems. And Hank is the swing vote," she added meaningfully. "We'll have to be active in electing his replacement."

While the others argued about the two prospective candidates for the Mitchell seat on the City Council—neither of whom was in favor with BIG members—Carol allowed her attention to focus on Rob. If he had been in town longer, she thought, he'd be a prime candidate to back for the City Council. He was bright, charming, and dedicated to good government.

It was clear, she decided in a flurry of sentiment, that Rob and Karen were strongly drawn to each other. Oh, why wasn't Seth here to talk about it with her? Of course, it might come to nothing—but it could be serious. She'd known the time would come when both children would leave the family house—but she'd envisioned Seth as always at her side.

Harvey left his office and drove to the tavern at the edge of town for a hastily called meeting with George Sexton and Hank Mitchell. He had to move fast on this. Some town up in South Carolina— Peter Ransome wouldn't give it a name—was making a pitch to bring the corporation there. He couldn't afford to lose. He had too much money tied up in pine now. Hell, he shouldn't have jumped so fast! But he'd make this work. He couldn't afford to screw up.

He parked and hurried into the tavern, noisy with drinkers at this hour. George and Hank were already there, seated at their usual private booth at the rear.

"Okay," he said tersely as he slid into the seat opposite the other two, "what's this crap about the Council not yet making an offer to Ransome?"

"You're pushing too fast," George complained. "When Hank and

I talked at the Council about rezoning, they wanted to know why, of course."

"We expected that," Harvey dismissed this impatiently. "You told them you had a lead about a big corporate relocation, didn't you? How it could mean a shitload of jobs for the town?"

"Yeah, but—"

"So what's the damn problem?" Harvey broke in.

"They'll probably go along on the rezoning, but then we brought up the question of tax abatement and three of them stalled." George grimaced. "The usual three. They want a committee to check out this firm."

"Ransome Products is well financed and does a fabulous business. One of you is on the committee?" Harvey's eyes dared them to deny this.

"I am," George said. "But we won't meet again on it until next month. Look, I couldn't rush it through any faster."

"We didn't bring up approval for the hydroelectric plant," Hank said uneasily. "That'll have to wait until the tax abatement comes through."

"But I've got an option from the Franklin sisters," George cajoled. "A four-month option—for peanuts, like you offered. Ransome ought to be happy about that."

"I don't suppose you'll consider running again—" Harvey turned to Hank.

"No way, Harvey, the doc is giving me hell for staying on the Council for the rest of my term. The old ticker is in bad shape. My wife is mad as a wet hen because I won't retire right now."

"I want you to put out word that you're pushing Miles Judson to replace you," Harvey said, ignoring the reproachful stares this elicited. "Throw a lot of crap about needing new, young blood on the Council."

"What about the two already announced candidates?" Hank asked.

"You tell Evans he's out. Anybody can win against old Crenshaw; he was a damn fool to throw his hat into the ring. And don't worry about how you'll convince Evans," Harvey said smugly. "I've got enough on his skirt-chasing to make him back out." He reached into his jacket pocket, pulled out an envelope, slid a dozen snapshots onto the table. "If he gives you any trouble, show him these for starters."

In the low light of the tavern the other two men inspected the snapshots. George whistled in approval.

"No problem, Harvey. But why Miles Judson? He's a two-bit lawyer still wet behind the ears."

"I helped get him through college. He owes me." Harvey's smile was smug. "I intend to have the City Council voting my way—even with you off, Hank. We run a decent campaign against Crenshaw, and we've got our man in place. Anything you need to know about Ransome Products, George, you come to me. I'll dig up all the papers for you. That'll make you look good to the committee. And let's get that tax abatement through. My deal with Ransome depends on that."

Early in February Carol found it necessary to fly up to New York for three or four days to consult with her staff on a prestigious new commission.

"I hate to be leaving town right now," she admitted over breakfast with Karen on the morning of her flight. She'd become as emotionally involved with BIG as Karen—and now Jonnie and Michelle were also active. "I didn't think we'd have so much trouble tying up a new piece of land." The owners of the new tract they wanted were getting flack from property owners in the area who didn't want a "low-income garbage dump in our backyards."

"Rob's working hard to persuade them to sell," Karen encouraged. "And Jonnie and Michelle are running an article in next week's *Herald*. Rob's hoping we can shame them into selling."

"Nobody knows yet what this out-of-state corporation is manufacturing," Carol said in exasperation. "I don't understand how the City Council can consider granting them a tax abatement without announcing what they make."

"They have, Mom. They manufacture household products."

"Specifically what?" Carol challenged. Was she nitpicking out of annoyance at losing the Franklin land? she asked herself in a flurry of guilt.

"Rob said they throw out that general term—along with their financial statements and all kinds of official papers. They probably make dozens of items. Anyhow, the City Council is impressed." Karen sighed. "They're guaranteeing a lot of new jobs in town—and right now that's something this town needs desperately." The U.S.

d hours that seemed endless that
out the manuscript on which he'd
past seven years and had begun to
e he'd found himself working six-
in the lives of the family his mind

stairs with a sense of anticipation.
e saw the first rosy crescent of the
nd he remembered how Carol had
they'd stayed at the house in Wain-
til the complete ruddy circle lifted it-
ly moved upward into the sky.
ong the beach. This wasn't just any
lf. He'd finished the manuscript three
s in editing—all the while yearning to
he novel she had longed to see him fin-
voice now. *"Seth, I hate guns! Not just
t the death and pain they bring to inno-
it so easy for people to get guns? I re-
ause it had been so simple for him to buy
arty and I were shot down on the street. I
accidentally killed because somebody left
novel show readers how easy access brings*

ed a play or a book he waited anxiously for
y lived in separate worlds now. He wished
agent—but Don left publishing three years
c farmer.
*has become too much of a business. The bot-
deal. I was born too late,"* Don had mourned.
Max Perkins."
ack to the paperback originals, Seth warned
enses out here were amazingly low, his funds
d have to go into New York and talk to his old
imself, though he dreaded picking up that
ight as well do that today.
se he ate breakfast, changed from his casual
a business suit and dress shirt, debated about
pleted manuscript into Manhattan and having it
ht, he jeered at himself, he was starting the old

economy in general was sliding into what many were labeling the worst crisis since the Great Depression.

"I have a gut feeling something is wrong here. But that might be my reaction to their buying that tract right under our noses," Carol admitted.

"We'd better get moving if you're to make your flight," Karen said. "Even this early in the morning traffic into Atlanta is bitchy." She paused. "Mom, did Dad say anything to you about when he's coming home?"

"No." Carol forced a smile. "When he's ready, he'll tell us."

On the plane Carol stared out the window and saw nothing. How much longer could she and Seth expect the kids not to realize that their marriage was over? Even Mom seemed anxious at the way Seth remained up at Montauk. He'd been there almost seven weeks. What was he doing? *What was he thinking?*

From LaGuardia Carol went directly to the Manhattan apartment, left her luggage, headed for the office. She was pleased with her ambitious all-woman staff. They could handle this new commission without her constant presence here; a few days of heavy consultations and they'd be on top of the situation, she congratulated herself.

As usual when in New York she planned to have dinner with Sharon. They resorted to a long-ago routine when they were too tired to cook—and neither in the mood to go out for dinner. Sharon came to Carol's apartment and they sent out for "Chinese."

"You look different," Carol told Sharon while they settled down in the living room to wait for the delivery. "You've changed your hairstyle," she pinpointed approvingly.

"More than that," Sharon bubbled. "I got tired of the gray that kept showing up. I had it tinted. I've found this marvelous young colorist. She knew exactly what was right for me. She's sharp—and very ambitious," she added, knowing Carol would approve of this trait.

"My hair could stand some brightening up," Carol said after a moment. She took much care in selecting her clothes—but was she letting herself go physically? It was a disconcerting possibility. Did she have to tint her hair to make herself interesting to her husband?

"I didn't do it for anybody but myself," Sharon said—and Carol started. It was as though Sharon had read her mind. "When I know

I look my best, I *feel* better. Let me call and make an appointment for you while you're here."

"Sharon, I don't have time for that," Carol protested. She hadn't gained a pound in the last twenty-five years, she told herself self-consciously. She made a point of eating properly and exercising. Seth always teased her about looking 15 years younger than she was. *Why had he gone off into an affair? Where was she lacking?* "You know my schedule when I'm here."

"It won't take long. I'll set up an appointment for you with Margrith." Sharon smiled prophetically. "One of these years she'll have her own shop—Margrith of Switzerland."

"Oh, all right," Carol capitulated. "Now tell me how the book is doing."

Over lemon chicken and sautéed baby shrimp with cashew nuts—a tall teapot of Earl Grey in readiness for refills—Carol reported on Jonnie and Michelle's activities with their newspaper.

"They won't make a cent for the first year," Carol reminded, "but they're creating some interest, picking up a few small ads."

"Oh well, in our income brackets, we can afford that," Sharon said good-humoredly. She paused a moment. "When are you going to call Seth?"

Carol's fork froze in midair.

"Sharon, I can't call him."

"When he's just out in Montauk?" Sharon chided. "Are you going to let one little fling destroy all you two have built up through the years?"

"We don't have anything now," Carol said slowly. "That's why he had 'one little fling.'" Was there another fling—with someone he'd met at Montauk? she tormented herself. She hesitated. "Have you talked to him?"

"A couple of times. He said he's working hard."

"Did he make his deadline? That was his excuse for running to Montauk," Carol reminded.

"Both times I called he just said he was working hard. I had the feeling he's waiting for some word from you."

"That's crazy! He ran to Montauk to get away from me. He was using his writer's block to get out of the house." He'd asked if she wanted him out of the house, if she wanted a divorce, she remembered in anguish. *He'd expected her to say "yes."*

"At least call him," Sharon coaxed. "Just to report on the kids."

To fill the lonely, pain-wracke
first week out here, he'd brought
worked at intervals through the
plot years before that. All at on
teen hours a day, finding solace
was creating.

He paused at the foot of the
He felt a surge of pleasure as
sun rise above the horizon. A
loved this special moment whe
scott. He remained in place ur
self above the horizon and slo
Now he began to walk a
morning, he reminded himse
days ago, spent endless hou
lay it at Carol's feet. It was
ish. In his mind he heard he
for what they do in wars b
cent human beings. Why i
member my dad, dying be
a gun. I remember when M
remember all the children
a gun around. Make this
on crime."

Always when he finis
Carol's approval. But th
Don Taylor was still an
ago to become an organ
"For me publishing
tom line the important
"I belong in the era of
He'd have to go b
himself. While his exp
were running out. He
editor, he ordered
deadly routine. He
Back at the hou
Montauk attire int
taking the just com
photocopied. All ri

Forti
seemi
beach.
ization
the sun
needed to
the morni

Every
beach for h
routine. Rig
After the firs
ters of the pa
he'd written t
and returned th

To preserve
present was a me
lives would be ma
to acknowledge th

crazy routine again. Carol always said, "Don't leave manuscripts in a drawer—send them out." While he was in the city, he'd drop in the public library and search through the LMP—*Literary Market Place*—for a list of prospective agents. It wouldn't be easy to find an agent, he surmised—the only real success he'd had was almost twenty years ago—in television.

He pulled out the new manuscript, slid it into the fine leather briefcase Carol had given him for his birthday four years ago—and which he rarely used because it was so expensive. He left the house, took the car out of the garage. He was elated at finishing the new book—only now realizing that he was exhausted, running on nervous energy. And the high that usually accompanied his finishing a play or novel was diluted by his distaste for the need to try for another contract for a paperback original that would support his current, very modest life-style.

He harbored no illusions about the possibility of the "genre fiction" he wrote taking off and making impressive money. It had happened—and with incredible speed—to Sharon. She was at the right place at the right time with the right material, he rationalized, and Sharon was bright, shrewd, and knew how to play the game.

Traffic was light until he arrived on the LIE. Now he encountered the last of the commuter rush into Manhattan. How did people go through this five times a week? he asked himself, impatient at the delay. He chafed at the long wait at getting into the tunnel. Should he phone Sharon while he was in the city? No time, he told himself, though he nurtured a faint hope that she might have some word of Carol.

Surely Carol must have been in the city at least once since he'd been out at Montauk—but he'd had no word from her. There was still that ominous wall between them. Jonnie and Karen wrote—about Jonnie's struggling newspaper and Karen's anxieties about the BIG project. Always the plaintive inquiry about when he was coming home.

He'd find a photocopy place, have the manuscript run off, go to the library to check on the LMP, find a cheap Chinese restaurant for lunch. After lunch call his editor at the paperback house and try to mend fences. Then he'd drive back to Montauk. Hell, he had to earn some money, he thought apprehensively. He wasn't going to sponge off Carol.

At the midtown copy center he located via the Classified, he learned there'd be a two-hour wait before he could pick up a copy of the manuscript. He left it there and headed for the library. God, it had been a long time since he'd set foot in a Manhattan library! Long ago he'd done his intensive research for the new book in the Atlanta Central Library. He located the current LMP, sat down and turned to the listing for literary agents.

He felt a rush of excitement as Don Taylor's name leapt out at him from the page. Don was back in business! He sought out a public phone on the floor, dialed Taylor's office. Would Don want to be bothered with him now, Seth asked himself, after all the efforts that had come to nothing?

"Taylor Associates," a vivacious feminine voice greeted him.

"May I speak to Mr. Taylor, please. This is Seth Walden—a former client," he added self-consciously and waited.

"Seth!" Don sounded astonished and pleased. "How are you? What's been happening? You know I was out of the picture for almost three years—"

"You gave up on organic farming, I gather." The years since their last encounter seemed to evaporate. "It's great to know you're back in publishing." He hesitated. "It's been a long time between books. I've done a few paperback originals—the genre stuff—but I've just finished the novel we talked about a couple of times."

"The one about three generations in a munitions dynasty," Don pinpointed, astonishing Seth with this recall. "I've wondered every now and then if you'd gone ahead with it. Look, if you're not tied up, why don't we have lunch? About one o'clock? I'd like to hear about the new book."

."Great!" Seth felt enveloped in relief. Don had always been so encouraging. "Where?"

Over lunch at the same restaurant he had favored years ago, Don explained that not only did he discover he wasn't suited to farming—organic or otherwise—but that he missed Manhattan and the publishing world.

"I cut all bridges when I left Manhattan. Even my old address books went out the window. I ran a few ads in some of the writers magazines, hoping to spread the word that I was back, but I don't imagine you were reading them. Now, tell me about the new book."

Don's interest generated fresh enthusiasm in Seth. He talked eloquently about the newly finished manuscript.

"When do I see a copy?" Don asked.

"I'm picking up a photocopy as soon as we leave here," Seth told him. "I'll drop it off at your office."

"I'll read it fast," Don promised. "You know, your timing was always just off. I've got a gut feeling that's about to change. But don't expect overnight miracles," he warned.

"I'll put it out of my mind. Right now I need to pick up a contract for a 'quickie.' I may have screwed up with my paperback publisher," Seth admitted. "I turned back an advance and a contract because of what I told them was a writer's block."

"Give me all the dope," Don said. "I'll work on that, too."

Seth felt at loose ends, though he was grateful at renewing his ties with Don. He should be searching around for an idea for another paperback, settling down to do an outline and sample chapters, he told himself as he walked along the beach the following morning. His money was shockingly low.

He had been on such a disciplined schedule since he'd arrived out here, he thought. Now he was suffering from a kind of postpartum blues.

Restless this morning, he walked into town for breakfast and to pick up a copy of the *New York Times*. The day ahead seemed ominously empty. Settle down, he exhorted himself. He worked fast on the paperback originals—get something ready to give to Don. *He needed money.*

Arriving at the house again, he heard the phone ringing. His calls were rare. He rushed inside and picked up the phone.

"Hello—"

"Seth, you've cost me a night's sleep," Don chided. "I've been up all night reading the manuscript. I think we've got a winner."

"Great!" He clung to Don's words of approval, but an inner voice taunted him. Twice before Don had said that—and the books had gone nowhere.

"I'm going to sleep as soon as I call the office and tell Barbara I won't be in today. Tomorrow I'm going out and start hawking this one," he promised.

"But for now don't forget about paving the way for a paperback assignment." Seth ordered himself to be realistic. "I'll knock out an outline and two sample chapters within the next couple of weeks."

Seth knew he'd sweat out the coming weeks—probably months—ahead. Again, work would be his salvation. He'd sit down this morning and search his mind for a plot, push away the empty hours of each day at the typewriter.

Could Don be right? Was this his time? But what would it mean, he taunted himself, when he was separated from his family?

Chapter Sixty

Carol was relieved that by early March BIG was able to tie up a new tract for what had been renamed Bellevue Acres despite some resistance from neighbors in the area. The terrain would require only a minor change in the original plans. She was amazed at the pleasure she was deriving from working on this. She had accomplished her goal of becoming a successful architect—but involving herself in the urgent problem of housing for low-income families was providing a new and more potent satisfaction. It was something Seth would understand, she thought with painful nostalgia.

This would have been such a wonderful time in her life, she taunted herself, except for the breakdown of her marriage. Karen and Jonnie were both working in fields they loved. They were dedicated to the efforts of BIG. At least, Bellevue Acres was going ahead as scheduled. She was grateful to be so involved in its progress.

Then quite suddenly fresh chaos threatened. She and Karen were at a BIG meeting that focused on raising additional funds. Nationwide spiraling inflation presented serious budgetary problems for Bellevue Acres. In the midst of a heated, anxious discussion Jonnie and Rob stalked into the crowded meeting room with wrath etched on their faces.

"The City Council has just rezoned the Franklin estate for commercial use," Jonnie interrupted the discussion. "Now they're taking up Ransome's request for a tax abatement. And we—"

"Don't get so hot under the collar, young man," Ed Nicholls

broke in good-humoredly. "So they beat us to the draw on the Franklin land. We have a replacement. And in this bad recession we should welcome any new business that'll provide jobs. I don't like tax abatements, but the job shortage is critical."

"Mr. Nicholls, we *know* what Ransome Products make." Jonnie's voice was ominous. "They manufacture paper."

"Is that bad?" Their CPA seemed puzzled by this announcement, along with other BIG members present.

"What a paper mill will do to the river and to our water supply is bad!" Rob shot back.

"I've seen firsthand what happens to a paper mill town," Jonnie picked up. "Peter Ransome doesn't care about that. He knows this state has a rich supply of mature pines, which he's probably trying to tie up now with options. And he knows the Chattahoochee is a terrific source for hydroelectric power. He and his company figure they'll run into no fights here. After all, look at all the jobs they're already talking about creating." His voice was scathingly contemptuous.

"In manufacturing paper, substances other than the needed fibers are eliminated by strong chemicals," Rob explained. "And those chemicals—along with wastes—will go right into the river. Unless Bellevue wakes up and puts a stop to this deal."

"It's not just the chemicals that go into the river that we have to worry about. You know how the Chattahoochee overflows regularly. That water—loaded with dangerous chemicals," Jonnie emphasized, "will overflow into fields where food is being grown. When I was researching for a magazine article, I went to a paper mill town. I discovered that the chemicals remain so strong even in the air that the jewelry store in this town had to polish their silver every day or two to keep it from getting black. The street signs turned black. And the stench from the mill—" He grimaced eloquently.

"Forget about fishing," one of the men commented. "There won't be any fish if that mill goes into operation on the river."

"Won't that new Water Pollution Act make them take precautions not to pollute?" the high school civics teacher asked hopefully. Carol remembered that her twenty-year-old son who'd dropped out of college had been looking for a job for many months. "There must be some way of cleaning the water. The town desperately needs these jobs."

"That water pollution act won't go into effect for years," Rob predicted, and Carol recalled their discussing this at an earlier meeting. "Within less than a year that paper mill can be in operation and destroying Bellevue."

"All right," Carol said, reaching for outward calm. "We know the job that lies ahead of us. We've got to get the word around that we don't want Ransome Products in this town. People have to understand why—"

"We'll scrap the front page of this week's *Bellevue Herald,*" Jonnie picked up. "We'll run a strong article on what a paper mill would do to Bellevue."

"Let's send out warning circulars," Ed Nicholls said, glancing about the table for nods of approval—quick to come. "Jonnie, you handle the printing—we'll pay the costs." He chuckled. "No profits, but I'm sure you'll go along."

"We have to set up committees." Karen reached for a sheet of paper. "This must be a major campaign."

Harvey awoke on this gray, drizzling morning with an instant reminder that he'd drunk too much last night. But Peter Ransome had been bitching about the slowness in getting the tax abatement. Damn, he had the rezoning deal. Was he going to wait for the tax abatement to come through before signing the contract for the pine forests? Let him sign it, Harvey thought viciously, before he found out who owned Bellevue Timber Company.

He left his bed, went into the bathroom to prepare for a day that promised to be hectic. He'd just emerged from the shower when the phone rang. That was his private line, used only for business. Who was on his back now? His eyes sought for the clock. It was just past eight.

"Hello—"

"Harvey, have you seen the morning *Herald?*" George asked.

"What?"

"That new weekly your nephew puts out. The *Bellevue Herald,*" George said urgently.

"Who reads that piece of shit?" Harvey scoffed in annoyance.

"All of Bellevue this morning," George said grimly. "They've papered the town. The whole front page and half of the inside was trashing Ransome Products. Peter's going to flip out. We've got to do something fast!"

"Get over with a copy—" Harvey paused. "Are you telling me I'll find one at my front door?"

"You can count on it."

Harvey dressed with top speed, hurried downstairs and out of the house without waiting for coffee. The weekly edition of the *Bellevue Herald* lay on the veranda steps. He picked it up, read the headline, and groaned. Driving to the office, he managed to sneak glances at the newspaper. What did that fucking young bastard think he was doing?

At the office—deserted this early in the morning—he called out for breakfast, then settled down to consider how to handle the situation. Where the hell did Jonnie live? He was shacked up with some slut he'd met in New York. Call Mom, get Jonnie's phone number.

On the phone with his mother he vented his rage at Jonnie's treachery.

"What's the matter with that stupid kid? This town needs that mill! I've been working like a dog to sell them on moving here!" He forced himself to calm down. "Mom, what's his phone number?"

Nobody answered the phone at the number his mother had given him. They'd been up all night getting out that rag, he interpreted. Okay, where did he go from here? Call the *Bellevue Enquirer*. Give them a story about how he personally was fighting to bring desperately needed jobs into the town. Well-paying jobs that would save the local economy. Then talk about "his men" on the Council, Harvey plotted. How they were fighting—along with him—to rescue Bellevue from this terrible recession. The worst since the Great Depression, economists were saying.

In days, it seemed to Carol, the town was bitterly divided into two camps: those who recognized the dangers to the health and comfort of Bellevue residents versus those who recognized only the economic values—hundreds of new jobs—that Ransome Products would bring to the town. The City Council was besieged by letters. At least for now, Carol thought, the question of tax abatement was on hold.

Carol was convinced the new "Save Bellevue Campaign"—demanding that Ransome Products be given their requested tax abatement—had been organized by Harvey. The *Enquirer* quoted him at great length, labeled him a town savior for having gone out and brought new industry to their depressed economy. Harvey talked to hastily called meetings of local groups, spoke on local television and radio about "the crackpots who don't care if our unemployment rate is soaring, who want to deny jobs to those who'll soon be reduced to applying for welfare."

"We need new ammunition," Jonnie said bluntly over dinner at his mother's house after a week of soaring tensions. "How many times can we tell them about what's happening in other paper mill towns?"

"Where is Ransome Products located now?" Karen asked, her voice suddenly electric.

"Some small town in Oregon," Jonnie told her, all at once attentive. "Are you thinking what just hit me?"

"You need to go out there, get photographs, get quotes from local people. Find out why Ransome Products is so anxious to relocate," Karen said.

"The City Council will have to vote on the tax abatement at the next meeting," Carol pointed out. "They've delayed this long because they want to see which way public opinion is going. Remember, three of them are up for reelection in October. Ransome has an option on the Franklin land; once they have the tax abatement, they'll move ahead fast."

"Mom, it's important for us to find out about Ransome's operation in Oregon," Jonnie said. "Can BIG afford to send me out there?"

"I'll send you out," Carol told him. "Leave tomorrow morning. All you'll need is a couple of days there."

"I can help Michelle with the next edition of the *Bellevue Herald*," Karen said. "Mom, it'll be okay if I take a couple of days off from the office?" Carol nodded approval.

"Jonnie, phone in what you see out at the Ransome Mill," Michelle picked up. "Dictate a story to me—I'll get it set up." She hesitated. "Unless there is no story."

"I have a gut feeling that they're trying to relocate here for more reasons than cheap labor and tax abatement. Jonnie, you dig," Karen urged. "Michelle and I will hold the fort here."

"Mom, you talk to Jonnie," Harvey said grimly while his mother brought him coffee and a wedge of his favorite pecan pie.

"Are you sure you've had dinner?" she asked solicitously. "I can warm up some roast beef in just a few minutes—"

"Mom, listen to me." Harvey was straining to hide his impatience with her. "I want you to talk to Jonnie and make him understand he's got to stop those lying stories about Ransome Products. It's important to me—" he paused, then tried another approach. "It's important to this town that we let Ransome have anything they want to relocate here. I broke my back to persuade them to come here instead of going up to South Carolina. I'm their attorney. How do you think it looks for me to have my own nephew fighting against them?"

"I don't understand," Hannah said, troubled. "Jonnie and Karen—and Carol, too—are sure the company will cause all kinds of environmental problems here."

"Who do you believe, Mom—those two crazy kids and Carol—who's too busy with her own work to know what's going on in this town—or me?"

"I'll try to talk to Jonnie," Hannah said uneasily. "But he's sure he's right. I was in the bakery this morning, and I heard people talking about drafting Karen to run for the City Council." Her face lighted. "Can you imagine—running for the City Council at her age? A second generation of the Waldens might be sitting on the Council."

Harvey gaped at her in shock, then disbelief.

"What kind of crap is that? Karen's a kid! How old is she? Twenty? Twenty-one?"

"Twenty-one, but she's got the head of somebody twenty years older," Hannah said with pride. "I heard her talk Tuesday night at the Women's Democratic Club. She was wonderful. 'A firebrand' somebody called her."

"It's urgent for me that Ransome Products relocates here," Harvey emphasized. "Jonnie adores you; make him understand he has to stop trying to divide up this town. He's a terrible embarrassment to me!"

Leaving a half-eaten piece of pecan pie behind, he stalked out of the house and to his car. What was this shit about drafting Karen to run for a seat on the Council? He'd have to scuttle that right now. He'd worked too long and too hard to let anybody upset the balance he wanted on the City Council.

All at once his mind grasped at a way to handle this situation. Hell, yes, he gloated. When he got through, neither Karen nor Jonnie would ever get elected to any office in this town.

* * *

Seth crouched before the living room fireplace at the Montauk house and fed chunks of logs into an already healthy blaze. Unrelenting rain had fallen for the last three days—adding to his ever-present depression. The glow from the fireplace was, somehow, comforting. He tensed at the sound of the phone ringing. He glanced at the clock—it was past eleven. That wouldn't be Don this late; probably a wrong number. He reached for the phone.

"Hello—"

"Dad, am I calling too late?" Jonnie was apologetic. "I forgot about the time difference—"

"No time's too late for you," Seth said softly. "But where are you?"

"Out in Oregon," Jonnie told him and began to explain his project. "I just wanted to read some copy to you before I call Michelle and dictate it to her. I figure we shouldn't wait for the next edition of the paper; we ought to get out flyers."

Seth listened while Jonnie read an impassioned report of the terrible conditions in the town where Ransome Products was located. Jonnie knew about his own earlier personal crusades, Seth thought—knew he was sympathetic to what was happening in Bellevue. God, what a novel that could make, he thought involuntarily while he listened to Jonnie.

"Is it okay?" Jonnie asked when he'd finished reading.

"It's great," Seth told him. "You've got photos, too?"

"The works," Jonnie said, sounding exhausted but relieved. "People here just spilled out their guts to me. They hate what Ransome has done to their town. They've been fighting to get them out. Even with the loss of all those jobs, they can't wait for the company to close up and leave town." He hesitated now. "We miss you, Dad—"

"I miss you all, too," he said quietly. He knew the question Jonnie longed to ask. But what answer could he give?

They talked another few moments, then Jonnie said goodbye. Seth sat before the fireplace until dawn—feeding chunks of logs into the grate until the bin was empty. His yearning for family almost suffocating him, he finally went to bed.

Seth came awake with a hazy realization that the rain had stopped. Sunlight poured through the skylight above his bed. His inclination was to turn on his side and go back to sleep, but at the same time he became aware of the jarring sound of the phone ringing beside the bed. As he reached for it, he checked the clock. It was past 9 A.M. When had he slept so late out here?

"Hello—"

"Did I wake you?" Don's voice came to him.

"No," he lied. "What's doing?"

"Look, it's not a lot of money," Don said cautiously, "but I've had an offer for the book. It's just three thousand, but I think we ought to go with it. They're promising to do some real promotion and—"

"If it isn't in writing, it doesn't mean a damn," Seth said cynically. "But yes, if you think we should accept, go ahead."

"Great." Don's enthusiasm was obvious. "I can see a really big paperback sale for this. And I won't wait for them to get off their asses," he promised. "I'm going to work on that from my side, too. I think this is the beginning of a new deal for both of us. I'll give them the okay, then ship the contracts out to you as soon as I receive them."

"Thanks, Don."

"If you need a small advance to see you through, I can handle that," Don said.

"No, I'm fine. I can manage."

He wasn't fine. How could he be fine when he was cut off from Carol and the kids? Dad used to say that timing was everything. What did it matter if the new book earned a great paperback sale? The timing was all wrong.

Carol glanced at her watch as she headed for the car in the driveway. The sun was dazzling, the sky a cloudless blue. This was a perfect afternoon for the BIG public meeting in Bellevue Park. She mustn't be late, she exhorted herself. She must be there for Karen's speech.

Jonnie and Michelle would be there by now with the circulars they'd been printing up all morning. A bunch of teenagers would distribute them at the meeting, then make door-to-door delivery to every house in town. Mom had been so upset, she thought compassionately, when Harvey insisted Jonnie lied about Ransome Products' reputation out at their Oregon mill town. But Jonnie had quotes from the townspeople and their mayor—all determined to stop the mill's operation.

Driving past the Village Green en route to the park, Carol saw the crowd gathered before a speakers' platform. Most of them were men, she noted, rough types in an ugly mood because the recession *had* hurt workers in this town. That would be the "Save Bellevue Campaign" people. They'd scheduled their meeting an hour ahead of BIG's. Her hands tightened on the wheel as Harvey's sonorous voice filled the air.

"We have to bring new jobs into this town! We can't allow this opportunity to be lost! We're hurting in Bellevue—"

The crowd erupted into noisy agreement.

"You tell 'em!" one voice yelled above the others. "We ain't sittin' back and taking this crap! We need jobs! Ransome will give 'em to us!"

She stepped on the accelerator in a painful need to put this scene behind her. Knowing Harvey, she was sure he'd planted agitators in the crowd. Nothing was going to happen between the two groups on this beautiful Sunday afternoon, she reassured herself. Yet she was uneasy.

Carol left the car on a side street and headed for the park, already jammed with people. BIG was doing a good job of alerting them to what was hanging over their heads, she told herself—happy that she and her children were part of this effort.

Ed Nicholls was in the midst of introducing Karen as Carol made her way through the crowd. She was amazed at the soaring determination of a widening group of townspeople to draft Karen to run for the City Council. Of course, it was a part-time job, as Karen had conscientiously reminded; she'd still be working in the Atlanta office. *"If I do run, I won't be giving up on architecture."*

Carol felt herself fighting tears as Karen came forward and began to talk about what Bellevue must do to save the town. Her precious baby. Her very young firebrand.

"Shut up with that shit!" a raucous voice yelled, startling onlookers. "We need jobs in this town—not talk!"

Frozen in place onlookers saw the heckler raise a gun in one hand and fire—she saw Karen gasp, stumble, and fall.

"Oh, no!" Carol moaned as she fought her way through the stunned crowd to the stand where Karen lay unconscious, blood staining her beige jacket. Remembering her father lying in a pool of blood. Remembering herself, shot down on the street. "Not again! Not again!"

Chapter Sixty-one

Assaulted by persistent restlessness, Seth searched for a television program to alleviate this, admitted defeat and switched off the set. Time to scrounge for an early dinner, he told himself. The phone rang, disturbing the late afternoon quiet. Out here each call was an occasion, he thought as he reached to pick up the phone.

"Hello—" An involuntary expectancy in his voice as he responded.

"Seth, Karen's been shot! She's in surgery now—" Carol was close to hysteria. "I keep telling myself this is some awful nightmare—but it isn't. It's real!"

"I'll be on the next plane out," Seth told her. *Karen—his little girl—shot?* "She's going to be all right, Carol. You just hold on to that thought."

"Why can just anybody get a gun?" Her voice was unfamiliarly shrill. "It was some hothead, enraged because Karen was fighting for what is right!"

"I'll come directly to the hospital from the airport," Seth soothed. "It'll take me about an hour and forty minutes to get to LaGuardia. Another two and a half hours to Atlanta once I have a flight. Karen's going to be all right," he reiterated.

"Seth, I need you," Carol whispered. "I love you."

"I love you, Carol." In the midst of pain, tenderness surged in him.

Not knowing when he would be back, Seth called for a taxi to drive him to LaGuardia. In five minutes he was in the taxi and relieved that the driver was intent on making record time in reaching the airport.

"I got a hot date," the youthful driver had said good-humoredly when he mentioned his need to catch a flight. "And this time of day—on a March Sunday—we won't hit much traffic."

Seth had barely a ten-minute wait before boarding his flight. From his window seat he gazed out into the night and battled with apprehension. He knew that what happened this afternoon had thrust Carol back into excruciating recall. First there had been her father, who'd shot himself amidst the horrors of the stock crash—then she had been shot down herself only a few years later—and now their precious daughter.

Every word she had spoken to him over the phone ricocheted in his mind now. *"Seth, I need you. I love you."*

Please God, let Karen be all right. Let him have his family together again.

The flight seemed endless in his impatience to be at Bellevue Hospital. When the plane landed at the Atlanta airport, he pushed his way through departing passengers, sought for a taxi.

At the hospital he was directed to the surgery floor. Emerging from the elevator he spied Carol, huddled in the corner of a sofa in the reception area. Jonnie and Michelle—and a strange young man—stood at a window in somber conversation.

"Seth—" Carol rose to her feet. "Thank God, you're here."

Jonnie and Michelle rushed forward to greet him. When Jonnie introduced Rob Lehman, Seth understood this was someone close to Karen.

"She's been in surgery so long—" Carol searched Seth's eyes for reassurance. "They won't tell us anything," she said plaintively.

"It won't be long now," Seth soothed, drawing her into his arms.

They stood, traumatized by fear, and talked in low voices about the afternoon's happenings.

"There's Dr. Feldman!" Jonnie said a few minutes later, his face mirroring the anxiety of the waiting group.

"Karen's going to be all right," Dr. Feldman called out as he approached. "She's had a close call, but she'll be out of here in a few days."

They were allowed to see Karen briefly. She had not yet emerged from the anesthesia. With communal relief they lingered beside her bed until a nurse gently shooed them out.

"Nobody's eaten since lunch," Michelle said cheerfully. "Let's go over to our place and I'll make hamburgers and coffee for us."

"First, let me call Mom," Carol said. "She was exhausted from waiting around; I insisted she let Jonnie drive her home. But I know she's waiting for word from me. She won't sleep until she knows Karen's going to be all right."

Seth felt as though his life had been renewed, as the family—and Rob—gathered around the dining table in Jonnie and Michelle's furnished apartment. At moments it seemed as though he'd never been away. After their very late dinner—everyone drained from the day's experience—Jonnie drove Rob to his apartment and then his parents to the family house.

"It's great to have you home, Dad," Jonnie said softly. "We all missed you."

Walking into the house with Carol, Seth was conscious of a disconcerting uncertainty. Was her relief in having him here a temporary situation? he agonized.

"Welcome home, Seth." Her voice was tremulous. Her eyes searched his. "I haven't been the best of wives—"

"You've been the best," He insisted. *Everything was going to be all right for them.* "For a little while we lost communication. And there was just that one time—" His eyes pleaded for her belief. "I don't know how it happened."

"We lost communication," she whispered and reached for his hand. "We won't ever let that happen again."

Hand in hand they walked into the night darkness of the master bedroom. Seth reached to draw Carol into his arms with a deep hunger that he knew she shared. Each knowing this would be a glorious reunion.

Each day Carol and Seth visited with Karen in the hospital—her room a fragrant, colorful arbor of flowers. Dr. Feldman was delighted with Karen's progress. On Wednesday afternoon he agreed to allow her to go home the following morning.

"But you take it easy for a couple of weeks, you hear?" he told her with an indulgent smile.

"Yes, sir," Karen promised.

"I'll make sure she does," Carol told Dr. Feldman. She felt herself garbed in serenity. Karen was all right. Seth was home. And she knew that a segment of her life from this time forward must be dedicated to fighting for national gun control.

Ever since the attempt on Karen's life this town had been ricocheting with recriminations. *"How could one of our young people be shot in broad day light in a public park?" "How can we let an outsider come stalking into our town and ruin it forever?"* And the other side—supporting Ransome Products—screamed that smug, comfortably set locals were trying to rob workers of desperately needed jobs. *"They don't want to see progress come to this town. They don't care about workers and their families."*

Late Thursday morning Carol and Seth drove Karen home from the hospital. A small welcoming committee—Jonnie and Michelle, Hannah, Rob, and Elaine—were there for a celebratory luncheon. A beaming Bonnie emerged from the kitchen for a minute—"to welcome our precious baby home."

"Karen, you look just beautiful," her grandmother told her. "And we're so proud of you."

"We've got this week's *Herald* out on the streets," Jonnie told Karen. "With what we're showing people, they'll know they have to make sure Ransome Products doesn't do here what they did in Oregon."

"What about the *Enquirer?*" Karen asked. Carol had made a point of keeping the Bellevue newspapers out of Karen's sight, but she'd known this was only a delaying move.

"This morning's *Enquirer* ran a letter from Peter Ransome on the front page," Michelle said indignantly. "Can you believe he has the nerve to say *we're* lying? That the stories and photos Jonnie brought back from Oregon have nothing to do with his mill?"

"Peter Ransome is a powerful man. He's convinced he can take over any town he likes." Elaine seemed caught up in some painful inner debate, then she forged ahead. "I overheard Harvey say this morning that Ransome is flying in this afternoon for a conference tomorrow with the City Council. He's giving them an ultimatum: vote him the tax abatement immediately or Ransome Products will relocate in South Carolina."

"That mill won't open in this town!" Karen vowed. "We'll make people understand what it'll do to us."

"When the City Council convenes for that meeting tomorrow," Rob promised, reaching for Karen's hand, "we'll have hundreds of demonstrators waiting at City Hall."

But could earnest demonstrators win against the money and power of Peter Ransome—backed by Harvey Walden, who had ruled this town for years? Carol was uneasy.

"You'll have dinner on a tray in your room," Harvey told Elaine. "This is an important dinner meeting with Peter Ransome and a few of the boys. I want no interruptions. Stay in your room until I tell you otherwise," he ordered.

"It'll be a pleasure," Elaine said coldly. This had been a policy for years—ever since Harvey had moved into his own room and abandoned any pretense of a real marriage. "Or I could go to a movie."

"No," Harvey rejected. "I don't want you to wander around town alone in the evening. I don't want people to talk. You know how they gossip."

"You're worried about my reputation?" she drawled, knowing he wasn't.

"I care about mine," he said bluntly. "No movie."

"Yes, Your Highness." To the residents of Bellevue she was Harvey's elegant, somewhat remote wife, active in local philanthropies. This bitter woman was a stranger to them.

Reading in the sitting room of the master bedroom suite—which she'd had redecorated to her liking when it was clear she would be occupying this alone—Elaine heard cars pull up into the circular driveway below. Harvey's guests—four, she gathered from the place setting in the ornate dining room—were arriving. They'd go into the study for a predinner drink, she surmised. While they were drinking, Consuelo would bring up her dinner tray. Twenty minutes later Harvey would summon Consuelo and tell her to have Maddie send in dinner. It was a familiar routine to the servants and to her. And she found a kind of stygian humor in listening to the voices that drifted up to her—as though part of a bad movie.

Downstairs in the study Harvey was struggling to appear confident about the outcome of the City Council meeting tomorrow morning.

"Of course, those bastards from BIG are trying to twist arms—but who does that better than me?" Harvey said with a show of tenuous good humor.

"This is it, Harvey," Peter Ransome reminded grimly. "Either I get the tax abatement, or I move on. I don't like the way this is playing."

"Peter, we've got everything under control," George boasted. "We'll—"

"Have you shut up that young shit and his rotten newspaper?" Ransome challenged. "I want this deal—but I'm not waiting around beyond the Council meeting."

"They won't vote tomorrow," Harvey told him. "A member will be taken ill suddenly." Harvey allowed himself a smug smile. "I can guarantee a two-week delay."

"You have to shut up the opposition," Ransome warned. "Do something to discredit the BIG leaders. A major smear, Harvey."

"That's in the works," Harvey assured him, turning to the other men for confirmation. "With one slam we get three of them. My sister-in-law, my nephew, and my niece. A private investigator has been on it for days. I don't think this town will take well to the news that one of their highly respected citizens—now known as Carol Walden—was shot down with her gangster husband on the streets of New York. I can see the headline now," he said with savage satisfaction. " 'Local Woman Civic Leader A 1920s Gun Moll.' That will finish her and her precious children—and that crummy 'do-good' organization they manipulate."

Upstairs in her suite Elaine sat frozen in shock. What did Harvey mean—Carol a '1920s gun moll'? *How did he dare slash his own family that way?* But she knew Harvey, Elaine taunted herself while heated—but now smug—voices drifted up the stairway from the study. Early on she'd discovered his corrupt manipulations, his determination to do anything that would achieve his goals.

Mom would be distraught if Harvey was allowed to slander the family this way, Elaine thought in anguish. Her mother-in-law had seemed reserved—almost cool—toward her in the early years of her marriage, but that had long ago given way to a genuine affection that was mutual. She was closer to Mom than to her own parents. Mother and Dad withheld their love from their only grandson because his father was Jewish—and that was contemptible.

But what could the family do to stop Harvey? At least, let her warn Mom. In sudden resolution she tossed aside the novel she'd been reading, hurried to the closet for a coat. She reached for her purse and strode out into the carpeted hall and down the stairs— walking with calculated quietness, though she doubted that the five men in the study were aware that she was leaving the house.

If Harvey heard her driving away, he would be annoyed. He'd given her specific orders not to leave the house. But she was not taking orders from Harvey any longer.

In the comfortable, pleasant living room of her home, Hannah listened—her mind in chaos—while Elaine told her about Harvey's latest maneuvering.

"I couldn't understand what he was talking about," Elaine said, "but it sounded ominous—and I thought you ought to know."

"Harvey's my son—my baby—and I've always tried to see only the good in him. He's so bright, so ambitious. Such a charmer—everybody said he was. He was the son who was fulfilling my own dreams." Hannah paused, pale and trembling. Visions of Harvey as a toddler, starting school, graduating, darted across her mind. Her baby, who in her eyes could do no wrong. "But I can't allow him to do this. It's wrong, not only for the family but for this town."

"Mom, what is this all about?"

"Carol was married at sixteen—pushed into marriage by her mother in the heart of the Depression. She didn't know she was marrying a small-time hood. He was murdered, and she was shot at the same time. Carol and Seth told Eli and me of this when they'd been married for a few years. It meant nothing to us, of course." Her voice broke now. "Once—when Harvey was being terribly sarcastic about Carol's work—I told him what she had been through. I never dreamt he would try to use this against her. I just wanted him to understand what a wonderful woman she was."

"But how do we stop him from spreading this all over town? Mom, we can't let him do this!"

"I don't think he will." All at once Hannah was conscious of an unexpected strength. "We'll just have to play his game. Harvey couldn't bear having this town know that his only son is not, in truth, his child."

"What are you saying?" Elaine's face was etched with shock. "How do you know that Timmy isn't his child?"

"Harvey can't have children. He had a bad case of the mumps when he was little. Doctor Rollins—our pediatrician—told me Harvey was sterile as a result. I didn't want to believe it. I ran with him to specialists; they all said the same thing." Hannah's eyes searched Elaine's. "Surely he told you? He led me to understand he had—"

"He never said a word. He made me believe it was my fault I wasn't getting pregnant. That time we went to Monaco—he'd been cold and unresponsive for a long time. He pushed me into an affair with a warm, sweet young man there. In truth, I didn't know if Timmy was his child or Harvey's." Her voice erupted in rage. *"He didn't want me to know.* He wanted me to feel guilty, to be grateful to him for giving Timmy respectability."

"I knew for years that your marriage was on shaky ground," Hannah confessed. "But I came to love you and Timmy and prayed Harvey and you would work things out."

"I'm going home now to pack a bag. For the present I'll stay with my parents. Harvey won't want an ugly divorce. We'll arrange something quiet—through my attorney." Elaine hesitated. "Mom— do you believe you can stop Harvey from this insanity?"

"We're stopping him," Hannah said compassionately. "Thank you for coming to me this way, Elaine."

But Hannah sensed that Elaine was dubious about her ability to abort Harvey's diabolical plan. *She must do this.*

Chapter Sixty-two

Hannah stood immobile for a few moments—fighting a wave of giddiness as she geared herself for what must be said. For all of his life she had spoiled Harvey, reared in anger at any word said against him. She had blinded herself to his faults because this was her perfect, adored child. Now he threatened to tear down this whole family. So confident, she thought in pain, that he would be excluded.

She reached for the phone, dialed Harvey's private number.

"Walden residence." Consuelo's gentle voice came to her.

"Consuelo, this is Mr. Walden's mother. I must speak to him, please."

Struggling for composure, Hannah waited for Harvey. Instead, Consuelo picked up the phone again.

"Miz Walden, he said he'll call you back. He's having dinner now," Consuelo reported.

"Tell Mr. Walden to get on the phone," Hannah said sharply. "I have to talk with him."

Moments later Harvey was on the line.

"Mom, I'm in an important business meeting," he said brusquely. "Didn't Consuelo tell you I'd call you later?"

"I want to see you within the next hour," she told him. "You be here, Harvey." Without waiting for a reply, she put down the phone.

Hannah returned to her chair and mentally debated about calling Seth and Carol. No, she ordered herself. Talk to Harvey first. Phone them later. But Carol and Seth and the children must know. They must have this protection against Harvey's manipulations when she was gone. For a while Harvey would be cowed—careful—but he would fight to pull himself up again. Let the others have ammunition to keep him in control. But it would be a family secret. Pride dictated that.

In barely forty minutes she saw Harvey's white Cadillac turn into the driveway. He was angry, she was sure, but he was also uneasy.

"Mom, what is this all about?" Harvey demanded as he stalked into the house. "I was in the middle of an important business deal!"

"You're preparing to disgrace this family." She saw his gape of astonishment. "I won't have that."

"Mom, what kind of craziness is this?" His voice was guarded now.

"I know what you're plotting to do to Carol—and that concerns all of us." Later he'd figure out who provided her with this information. "You planted those agitators at the public meeting in Bellevue Park. That makes you responsible for Karen's being shot."

"I had nothing to do with that!" He turned white with shock.

"You didn't order the shooting," she conceded, "but you triggered it, Harvey. You drop all thoughts of smearing Carol and the kids—and you make sure Ransome Products moves on to some other hapless town. We don't want that paper mill here—and we want Karen on the City Council."

"Mom, you're out of your mind!" His usual charm was in eclipse. "Who's after you to start up this way? Those bastards at BIG?"

"You drop this whole thing—and don't fight Karen's campaign for a seat on the City Council—or everybody in Bellevue will know Timmy isn't your son. They'll know you can never have a child." How could she be doing this to Harvey? Yet she knew she must.

"Nobody's going to believe that crap," he defied. "They'll think you're a senile old woman!"

"They'll believe Doctor Rollins. I still have the report he sent me after your attack of mumps. God knows why I hung on to it—but I did. It's in the safe-deposit box with my will and my marriage license and Dad's death certificate. I'm not grandstanding, Harvey. I'll do this."

"You'd do that to Timmy?" he blustered. "That innocent little kid? You'll do that to Elaine?"

"I'll do it to protect Carol and my grandchildren." Her heart was pounding, but she was determined to see this through. "And they will know about this, so if you start making wrong moves in Bellevue after I'm gone, they'll have the ammunition to fight you. I would hate to do this to Timmy," she conceded, "but I must put Carol and my real grandchildren first."

"You're doing it for Seth!" His face was taut with resentment. "You've always put Seth first—since we were little kids. He was the oldest; Seth knew everything."

"That's not true." Hannah was shaken. She'd never showed favoritism. Seth and Harvey were her two wonderful sons. If anything, she admitted now—remembering her mother-in-law's pithy remarks on occasion—she'd favored Harvey. "But you do what I say, Harvey, or this whole town will know Timmy isn't your son."

She watched Harvey's usually impassive face—aware of the bitter inner struggle he fought.

"You win," he said at last, aware that he had been dethroned. "But people in town don't have to know we're not—not—" He sought futilely for words.

"To people in Bellevue we'll still be the happy Walden family," she promised. But they'd soon know that Elaine was divorcing him. Still, divorce was common enough these days. Harvey could live with that. "You'll come to dinner one Sunday every month, as always. You're still my son, Harvey, and I love you." But not to the point where she would allow him to wreck havoc on the family—or help to ruin this town.

"I could have been the richest man in the state," Harvey said vindictively. "You ruined that for me." Without another word he strode from the house.

The phone rang sharply in the midst of a jubilant announcement by Jonnie. Carol hurried to answer.

"Hello—"

"Carol, I know it's late but—"

"Mom, I was just about to call you. Jonnie and Michelle are here. They're getting married in June!" Now her voice dropped to a whisper. "And I suspect Karen and Rob will be giving us the same news any day now. Seth and I are so excited."

"I'm so pleased," Hannah told her. "Like Mama, I can't wait to be a great-grandmother. But there's something important we must discuss. I'd like you all to come right over to the house."

"Are you all right?" All at once Carol was anxious.

"I'm fine," Hannah reassured her. "But I want all of you over here as soon as you can. I gather Jonnie and Michelle are there, too."

"And Karen and Rob. Shall we *all* come over?" Curiosity surged in Carol.

"Yes. This concerns us all."

At Carol's orders they left the house and piled into the waiting cars.

"Grandma found out something about the Ransome deal," Karen guessed as they settled themselves in the car. "What else could it be?"

"Grandma?" Jonnie was dubious.

"Harvey must have dropped some word," Karen said. "And she figures it's important for us to know."

"Mom has always been so proud of this town." Carol searched her mind for an explanation for this summons. "She's terribly unhappy that Harvey's representing the Ransome people." And the attack on Karen unnerved her. Everybody in town knew Harvey had been inciting the group that wanted the mill to relocate here.

Hannah was waiting for them with a pot of freshly perked coffee and a coffee cake defrosting in the oven. She prodded them into the living room and in a halting voice reported on her confrontation with Harvey. Jonnie and Karen knew about their mother's brief and disastrous first marriage. She saw Michelle and Rob's astonishment—but it was all in the family, she told herself. They had to know.

"King Harvey's rule in this town is over," Carol said softly. "He'll tread with care from this point on."

"And Ransome Products will move on to other grounds." Seth raised two fingers in the familiar victory sign. "Hallelujah!"

"We'll be busy campaigning with Karen for that City Council seat," Jonnie pointed out, "and working on Bellevue Acres. But the *Herald* will have to get behind a drive to bring new jobs into Bellevue. Maybe more construction jobs. More housing for low-income families. What do you think, Rob?"

"This is our town. My town, too," Rob said with a sentimental smile as he dropped an arm about Karen's shoulder. "We want to work for what's best for Bellevue."

"You've given me such riches, Seth." Hannah's face was luminous. "A wonderful daughter-in-law, two wonderful grandchildren—and I'm expecting a lot from you two kids," she told Jonnie and Karen. "Now let's all go out into the kitchen for cake and coffee."

"Karen, you go straight up to bed," Rob ordered before heading back to his car. "Dr. Feldman wouldn't approve of all this running around when you're fresh out of the hospital."

"We'll make sure she does," Carol promised. "Good night, Rob."

Carol lingered briefly in conversation with Karen while her daughter prepared for bed.

"Sleep well, darling. And sleep late," she told Karen.

Arriving at the door to the master bedroom, she heard the phone ringing inside.

"Carol, will you get that?" Seth called from the bathroom. "I'm brushing my teeth."

"Okay—" She reached for the phone, dropped to a corner of the bed. "Hello—"

"Where have you been all evening?" Don's voice came to her. "I tried you half a dozen times."

"The kids took Seth and me out to dinner, and then we went over to his mother's house."

"Are you sitting?" he asked exuberantly.

"Yes!" What was up? The book wasn't due out for months. "Seth, it's Don!"

"I've got great news for you two," Don continued while Carol held the phone so that Seth, too, could hear. "There was a paperback auction today. The book went for three hundred thousand. Of course, you split that with the hardcover house," he reminded.

Seth grabbed the phone.

"Hey, that's enough for all of us!"

"The publisher wants to work out a three-book contract," Don told them. "We'll be talking big numbers."

Carol relinquished the phone while Seth and Don talked a few moments longer. She leaned her head against Seth's shoulder. It had happened. At last Seth had proved himself.

"What do you know?" Seth put down the phone. "I finally made it. Mom won't have to worry anymore about my finding myself a decent job."

"In my eyes you made it a long time ago. With that first play at Leo's little theater. I've believed in you every minute of every day of every year."

"As I've believed in you," Seth said tenderly. "We lost our way for a while—but the memory of that will bind us together forever."

"I wish I were a poet—" Carol's face was luminous. "So I could write an ode to us."

"One writer in this marriage," Seth joshed. "And one architect. It's greedy to be overly ambitious."